Tears Over Tower Bridge

– HELEN RUSSEL –

An environmentally friendly book printed and bound in England by
www.printondemand-worldwide.com

This book is made entirely of chain-of-custody materials

www.fast-print.net/store.php

Tears Over Tower Bridge

ISBN 978-178035-065-3

First published 2011 by
FASTPRINT PUBLISHING
Peterborough, England.

Thanks to Maggie, for being a good friend to me,
and for the hours she spent going through
chapter by chapter, and offering much needed advise,
also to Nigel for his continued support and
encouragement during this project. HR.

Chapter One

Tears Over Tower Bridge

As the plane banked towards the east on the descent into Heathrow Airport I could see the Thames and Tower Bridge. I felt my eyes moisten and then tears slowly trickled down my cheek. Wrestling with the seat belt, I found a tissue in my jeans pocket and dabbed at my face. My tears were partly through relief and partly through fear. Relief that it actually was London that I could see; it was truly the UK that I was due to land in. I could hardly believe that I was here and would soon be leaving the plane at Heathrow. Here, I would be safe, here I could say what I liked about the government, here I could trust the police and here I would have to face the unknown. What would I do? Where would I live? I was alone, jobless and homeless and very nearly money-less. None of that mattered at the moment I was simply relived to be out of Shendi in one piece. Waiting to meet me at the airport would be Euan. We had been good friends for several years and he and his wife had offered me a safe haven and time to get my thoughts into perspective, before embarking on a new life. As the plane continued on its way to Heathrow, my mind travelled back to the start of what could be termed my own African adventure.

Nine years prior to this tearful landing, Simon, my husband and I had been starting our annual holiday in Shendi on the west coast of Africa. Married in the late sixties, we had long dreamed of visiting far away places and once the children had grown up we had been able to put our dreams into action. So far we had been to Mexico, India, Nepal and Kenya. But this was to be our first visit to West Africa and we were eager to see the contrasts between West and East Africa. It was November; the weather had turned decidedly cold on our small island home in the English Channel, so a fortnight's break in the heat of Africa was extremely appealing. The holiday was coming at the end of a busy year for both of us, and I could only just contain my excitement at the thought of two weeks relaxing in the sun, away from life on the island that had been home to us for nearly half a century. As the plane came to a halt outside of the airport terminal building, my adrenaline was flowing with the anticipation of the fourteen days that lay ahead.

The terminal was truly amazing; it looked ultra modern, not at all what I had expected. I nudged Simon who was busy looking for our landing documentation. "Look at the terminal" I said, "I wasn't expecting such a building, after reading of all the poverty here. It is supposed to be a third world country and that terminal could put many in Europe to shame."

"Yeah, it is rather grand," replied Simon, "But remember many of these countries get their priorities wrong, look at Kenya. We will have to see how basic our hotel is. If the brochures say basic, it usually means pretty poor!" (I was later to learn that the Americans had built the modern terminal building, and excessively long runway, as part of the escape plan for the space shuttle. The airport was in direct line with Houston and if there were problems during take off, there were possibilities of a successful landing in Shendi.)

We passed through immigration and customs without too much trouble having hired a porter to take our bags to the coach. Both Simon and I had noticed that those tourists who insisted on "doing it themselves" seemed to be the ones whose bags were opened by customs. No matter. We made our way past the welcoming dancers, to our coach where the bags were loaded on ready for the journey to the hotel. The bus was full and many people seemed to know what the guide was going to say. Nevertheless, I listened attentively to his briefing, eager to learn about this new country. Among the advice to take anti malaria medication, to avoid the free lance guides otherwise known as "bumsters" who were keen to try out the latest scam on tourists, and to change money only at recognised money changers came information about the country. We were told that many children would call out "Taubab" when they saw us. Many explanations were given for this, some people said it derived from "Two bob", the old coins that visitors used to give, others said it came from one of the local languages. Wherever it came from, most children would call it when they saw a white person. It was not an insult and we were told simply to smile. The country had six main tribes speaking many different languages and so it was no wonder that English was widely spoken especially in the tourist belt, although as we found out, it was not always fully understood.

The journey took us through the country's largest town, Malaville and I looked out of the coach windows in astonishment. The edges of the road were uneven and there was no pavement simply a dry, dusty strip full of pedestrians, cyclists, carts, litter and parked cars. Jammed in between were small road-side stalls selling vegetables, fruit or cigarettes. Behind these stalls were the shops. These were single storey buildings crammed to bursting with sacks of produce, cartons and tins and soft drink crates. Each shop had its name written either on a board and fastened above it or on the side, detailing its owner, address and what it sold. What amazed me was that these signs were in English, it indicated that English was much wider spoken, read and understood than I had imagined. As the coach passed through the town a wider variety of shops appeared, tailors making "the best in the west", hairdressers whose specialty was hair straightening, shops selling beds and car repair shops. Everywhere I looked there were people, standing waiting, shopping, walking, crouching down by the side of the road, signalling to buses and taxis and when ever the bus slowed down, children ran alongside, waving and shouting at us. It amazed me how clean everybody looked. Whether they were dressed, as most of the men were, in European clothes or in traditional costumes as many of the women were, the clothes were clean. Some children passed us dressed in school uniforms and even after a day at school the blue and white dresses and the white shirts were clean. Eventually we left the town behind and made our way past the local rubbish tip which late in the day though it was, had a fair complement of scavengers on it until finally we reached the hotel. Now we would see if Simon's qualms about the standard of the hotel had been right.

Despite Simon's fears of a basic hotel it more than lived up to our expectations. This was no run of the mill holiday. We were in Utopia soaking up the sun, sand and surf all of which were in abundance. The food and drink were cheap; taxis easily available and everyone was so friendly, willing to talk and even to invite us to their compounds. We had never encountered the number of repeat tourists as we did on this holiday. There were so many, including a couple of fellow islanders, that in fact we felt that we were the only first time visitors in our hotel and very soon with the help of visitors and locals we were being carried along on the unexplainable carousel of life in Shendi. (Even now, after living there for many years I do not understand the feelings that this small African country provokes in all who visit her. In latter years I've joked with many Europeans that going through immigration involved depositing all common sense for collection on the return flight. In fact the only explanation I can think of for the illogical attitudes that so many holiday makers and residents take lies in an article I read over twenty years ago. One of the mega Hollywood corporations was making a bid to purchase a country in West Africa with a view to converting into a giant African theme park. They found a suitable site, a small English speaking country, with a river running through it and no one tribe taking precedence over the others. However, the idea fell through – or did it? Just imagine all the unsuspecting Western tourists visiting a country sized theme park. It would explain such a lot.)

Thanks to our fellow islanders, who were on their sixth visit, we were introduced to Kebba who became our personal guide. As with many visitors, our compatriots trusted "their boy" Kebba implicitly. (Kebba like many of the locals could not find a job and was of course a "bumster", a member of the street wise group we had been warned to avoid.) However, he came highly recommended and took us many places that the tour bus missed. With him we visited compounds, clinics where I held newborn babies which was a sure way to a woman's heart and even schools out in the bush. Everywhere we went we were warmly greeted and made to feel that our visit was special. Of course we left donations after our visits. It seemed to us that the locals had so little and we had so much that it was only fair to leave something. It seemed just as fair to pay for Kebba and his friend who often accompanied us, for their services and to include them in some of our meals. It was all so different from our previous impressions of Africa. The only things that life in Shendi seemed to have in common with that of Kenya was the erratic water supply, (the day we came back covered in red dust from a trip 'up country' was of course the day that the water supply failed for a few hours) and the similarly erratic electricity supply. Here, however, the hotels quickly switched over to their generators and the candles we had become used to in Kenya were not needed. There seemed no racial or tribal animosity in Shendi and apart from the pictures of the President which every building seemed to have, politics had no impact on our holiday.

I remember sitting outside one of the local cafes one lunchtime near the start of our stay and simply watching the life on the street. Simon and Kebba were busy discussing their plans for the next day but I was content to sip my fruit juice and 'people watch'. The street was lined with cafes, supermarkets, bars, shops and money-changing kiosks. Like the road through Malaville there was no pavement, just a wide dusty strip on either side of the road full of pedestrians, parked cars, dogs and billboards for the cafes whose waiters all tried to entice the passing tourists to come in for lunch. Failed attempts were greeted with a grin and a "Perhaps tomorrow?" a seller of sunglasses walked slowly passed each café, hawking his wares as did a newspaper seller. (These papers had been gathered from passengers arriving the previous day and were straightened before reselling to the tourists.) Intermingled with the hawkers were deliveries to the shops and bars. I watched in astonishment as one young boy pushed a sack truck full of soft drink crates down the slope of a nearby bar and up the road to disappear into the distance. Shortly afterwards he came back with what I assumed to be full crates as his pace was much slower and he found it hard to negotiate the ramp up into the bar. Two school girls walked down the road carrying a lunch pail wrapped in a yellow cloth. Ten minutes later they returned without the lunch pail but sucking a lollipop each. A smart policeman, who was obviously an inspector or similar as he had a swagger stick, marched up the road towards the tourist police check point at the top. Close behind him came two more policemen who were in no hurry as they strolled on up the road and stopped to chat to a couple of taxi drivers. A cyclist with a heavy load of cigarette boxes came along weaving in between the pedestrians who in turn were trying to wend their way between the traffic. Admittedly there was not much of that and what there was tended to be delivery lorries, tourist coaches or taxis. There were very few private cars, but those that there were, seemed to think that they had right of way over everything. I was quite content to sit there in the sun, sipping my drink and reflecting on how different it was to life at home, how peaceful it was and how friendly everyone seemed.

The year prior to this holiday had seen Simon offered a job in Kenya. Although we had had a thoroughly enjoyable holiday on the beaches and visiting the safari parks, we had seen violence on the streets and had dismissed out of hand the idea of living there. This time Africa seemed so different and we were quite happy to stroll around the streets either by ourselves or with one of our friends. One night, towards the end of the holiday, we were walking back after another round of African culture with Kebba and his friend Esau, calling "No thank you" and "Goodnight" to the taxi touts cries of "Taxi please?", when Simon stopped in the middle of the street. He turned to me, grabbed my arm and said, "Helen, this is so unlike Kenya, isn't it?" You don't seem afraid to walk down the streets here". I agreed with him, it felt perfectly safe to be out at night even if the only lights came from the bars and cafes. After a brief pause, he continued, "We've been here less than two weeks and we've made friends already. There seems no reason why we couldn't live here. We have no family to consider in the UK and we could have a better life than at home. Perhaps put something back into the community; get involved in a charity or something, do something for the clinic and the new born children. Then just think of the weather, wall to wall sunshine most of the year. And palm trees, plenty of palm trees, you could even have some in the garden. We both know how much you love palm trees. I can just see it, you out in the garden in December, sitting under a palm tree, instead of huddled round the fire back on the island!" As he spoke, the enthusiasm in his voice grew stronger and stronger and his speech faster and faster as he listed the many benefits of life away from the UK. When he finally ran out of breath I said nothing, stunned by his fervour but simply nodded and remained non-committal. Although I have to admit, even now, it was an idyllic picture, my native caution made me wary, but I knew better than to disagree with an enthusiastic Simon. It could simply be another great idea that came to nothing, we would see.

Our holiday passed all too quickly, and with me suppressing a few tears, as were our new found friends (though I am sure that these crocodile tears quickly turned to beaming smiles when the new intake of tourists arrived), we boarded the coach for the airport terminal. Once again we were struck by how modern it was, but at the end of our holiday the contrast between the terminal and the poverty we had encountered was immense. Perhaps it was this contrast that had made the holiday so memorable but it had to be the people and the place that made its effect so enduring.

We settled back into our everyday lives, with hefty workloads following our fortnight's break. Soon the holiday was pushed to the back of our minds. Christmas came and went, and then the dreary cold winter months stretched endlessly ahead. After our holiday in the sun, the thought of a cold, sunless January and February seemed more forbidding than ever. We had spoken briefly, while in the grip of Christmas fever of the possibility of returning to Africa during the New Year, but otherwise neither of us really mentioned our holiday, we were both wrapped up in our hectic lives. I was working regular hours but Simon's job involved shift work including overnight duties and some week-end work. Consequently there were times when we rarely saw each other for days on end and communication was by note or phone. However, sometimes Simon was home in the evenings and it was on one such occasion in January that he made the remark that changed our lives.

It was a cold, dark night and we sat lingering over a cup of coffee in the kitchen, after our evening meal when quite out of the blue he said, "Helen, I want to go and live in Shendi. We have found the perfect place, Kenya without the problems. What possible objection can you have?"

I hesitated, put down my coffee cup, and replied "Well, I don't know. This is a surprise. Yes I know we talked about it but I didn't think … I just don't know what to say. Give me a minute to think. Yes it is a great idea but we must look into this properly first, I mean, have you thought about the family, what will their reaction be? Where would we live and what about health? There's malaria, how would we cope with that? How could we earn money, what about pensions? I don't know this is so out of the blue". I paused, it was an attractive idea especially in theory but the practicalities seemed immense. I just did not know. I continued, "I suppose we could find out. There would be no harm in doing that."

Simon was not deterred by my hesitation. "Other people from Europe live and work out there, malaria is just an illness, they manage we will manage. And as for family; what family? Neither of us have our parents. Kevin is in the U.K and so is your brother. You've no family left on the island anyway. I have but I'm not very close to them and besides it's our lives we must do as we please. We did our best for both sets of parents when they were alive. Now it is our turn. We are free of responsibilities now."

Simon was right. Kevin our 29 year old son had lived in the UK since he was 18, and although he was and still is proud of his roots, no longer considered the island his home. Simon had a brother and a sister still living on the island but there was a huge age difference between them and they had never been close.

"Well, yes, I suppose, if you look at it like that, and as you say Kevin isn't here, so we would still only be a plane journey away. And yes, there are lots of expats out there. They cope with the health and the job issues, it certainly bears thinking about."

That response changed my future more than any other decision I've ever made. Why did I not consider it more? We decided to return for a week in June, but rather than it being a holiday, we would make it a fact finding mission. In the meantime we phoned the Shendian embassy in London to make a few enquiries. As British passport holders, we were entitled to live there and be employed there. This was essential, as we would need a source of income. There was a zero crime rate and of course, the previously mentioned wall-to-wall sunshine. It just seemed like Utopia. But, in the middle of a bitterly cold island winter, June seemed a lifetime away. I felt we were wasting six months, neither of us was getting any younger, Simon was 51, and I was 48 and here we were freezing on a tiny island when we could be in the sun. Simon still had two weeks leave, that he had to take before the end of March. We talked it over and at my suggestion, he returned to Shendi to survey the scene. I equipped him with a list of questions I wanted answering before we embarked on our adventure of a lifetime.

I was blissfully happy while Simon was away, anticipating the future that lay ahead. This would be a new start for both of us. After 31 years of tumultuous marriage, that had included the sudden death of our 18-year-old daughter, furious arguments that lasted days and the care of elderly parents, we could begin again – on our own. Things would be as they were in the 1960s. We would be on our own, working together, far from reminders of the past, away from the island which, much as I loved it, was very claustrophobic. We could be ourselves. I had no concerns about our 'rushing into things' as one of my friends suggested. Yes my suggestion, that we no longer wait until June for a fact finding mission but that Simon go out in March and find a home and job, was out of character for me. Usually I like to plan things out and to know exactly what is happening, but suddenly I had had enough. I wanted, in fact needed, to get away from everything I had known for all my life. Moving to the UK would not do, I needed a completely fresh start. I think Simon felt the same. Certainly he was quite happy to hand in his notice and go job seeking in Shendi. It would do us and our marriage good to be on our own, as we had at the start. On his first night away, I went to sleep feeling a deep inner peace, and woke in the morning eager to get on with our lives, our marriage and our future.

The two important items on Simon's agenda were somewhere to live and a source of income for both of us. Although we were going to sell our island home to fund the move we would need a source of steady income, though what the employment prospects were I had no idea. When Simon rang up and announced he was interested in purchasing a bar cum restaurant I was initially apprehensive. However, on reflection I changed my mind. We had visited the bar, called The Dominion, on our holiday and I remembered it as being a pleasant place with the added attraction of a garden. It was situated in a good tourist area, near three hotels one of which was Shendi's only 5 star establishment; so it should have good business potential, and as Simon described it, I began to warm to the idea. Not only would it provide both of us with a job but there was also living accommodation attached. Besides the bar, the compound consisted of a three bed roomed house, the master bedroom had a balcony with a sea view, the large beer garden, an even larger private garden, and out buildings. Simon had suggested we could rent out some of the rooms, and mentioned the possibility of building a couple of self catering apartments in our garden, so this would provide us with adequate income, besides a home. According to Simon, the present owners, a Dutch couple, wanted to sell quickly and therefore we might be able to get a bargain.

Over the next few days I started to think what running a bar could involve and my initial trepidation grew into definite misgivings. Whilst both of us had middle management experience that had been enough for me. I had always been adamant that I simply did not want to run my own business - And catering!!!!! The sum total of our joint experience of catering was Simon working a couple of evenings a week in the local bar, many years ago when our children were small. Somehow or other I did not think this qualified us to run a tourist restaurant or self catering accommodation. How would we know the amount of food to order, the prices to charge, which drinks to stock and how did you mix cocktails for instance. I started to voice some of these doubts to Simon, during one of our nightly phone calls.

"I'm concerned, really concerned," I told him.

"What about now?"

"I'm afraid we will be out of our depths, we really don't know much about the catering trade. I mean, how will we know what to order and what to charge? What happens about cooking, who will do it, and I've absolutely no idea about running a bar. How do you pull pints? You at least have worked in a pub before, I haven't"

"You worry too much," was his response "You always have to see problems before they exist. The staff are very good. They will basically run things; we will only have to supervise. We both have experience of that, and you will keep the books, you are well able to do that."

I was clearly worrying about nothing. Supervision I could manage, so that was alright. It all seemed so easy when I was wearing rose tinted glasses, and was three thousand miles away.

Towards the end of Simon's stay, I found a fax waiting for me when I arrived home one night. It was from Esau, whom we had met, and made a friend of, whilst on holiday. This fax was in broken English. Esau was explaining to me that there could be a problem with the car park of the neighbouring hotel. The Dominion's main entrance was into this car park, and if the hotel expanded, as it was rumoured to be planning to do, then this was likely to cause problems for us if we became the proprietors of The Dominion.

I could hardly contain myself as I waited for Simon to phone that evening. When he did, he was full of excitement telling me of the plans he was making for the bar. "Helen, I can see it all now, the barbecue really isn't up to much. We will knock it down and build a much-improved version. I was also thinking we could erect another outbuilding, where the shaded thatched area is now, I find that a bit tatty also, and we could make this building a games room. You know what I mean, snooker, darts that sort of thing, there is a lot of Lebanese here, they would love that."

There was no mention Esau, nor did he mention anything about possible problems with the hotel car park. In fact it was all his plans for the bar and nothing else. Finally I could contain myself no longer and broke into a long description of possible improvements to the beer garden. "Wait a minute Simon. Yes it all sounds fine, fine but I've had this fax from Esau, telling me there maybe problems in the future over the bar's entrance."

"Just forget it", he replied. "I've had a fall out with Esau, I caught him trying to swindle me over a deal I was making with a taxi driver, and he is causing problems and anyway he has told me all this."

"Fine, but are you looking into this? It is something that we need to clear up. Perhaps Esau is exaggerating but I would like to know if there is any foundation in what he says. Is this the reason that the Dutch couple want to sell?"

"No Helen, stop worrying. They want to sell because the husband is ill. In fact he has already gone back to Holland. There is no problem. I keep saying that. I have a lawyer working for us; he would advise me against going ahead, if there were any real problems. Helen, you always worry too much."

"As long as you are sure, we are putting our life savings into this."

"Helen, they are my life savings as well. I wouldn't put them into something that wasn't safe."

As I put the phone down, a small doubt crossed my mind, I soon banished it.

We decided to go ahead with the sale, and Simon arrived home a few days later, very pleased with himself. I immediately caught his enthusiasm, and we both threw ourselves wholeheartedly into selling our house, and preparing for our new life, in a new country. What could possibly cloud our horizons? We had had many problems during our lives together, but now we were going to enjoy an idyllic life style, enjoying the sun, the golden sands, and I could see as many palm trees as I wanted, even in my own garden. My only official duties in the bar were going to be responsibility for the book-keeping and such matters as staff rotas so I intended to get involved with charity work during the day, maybe going to the beach for a swim, in the latter part of the afternoon. During the evening I would play 'mine host' in the bar. What a lifestyle, after years of a hectic working life, I deserved this. So did Simon.

Therefore, less than a year after visiting, and weeks before our planned reconnoitre visit we moved. First our 20-foot container, part filled with our personal belongings, and part filled with second hand items, we had collected as charity for the locals, went off on a boat. This was closely followed by Simon who flew out on his own as I had to remain on the island to complete the sale of our house. Finally a few weeks later, after living in a home that only boasted an inflatable mattress as its furniture, I followed.

As my flight took off from my island home, and I headed for Utopia, I looked out of the window, and said good-bye, not only to the cliffs, that I knew and loved so well, but also to my need to take 'St. John's Wort' to keep me on an even keel during my hectic and often demanding life. I did mean good-bye not au revoir. Although I had just said tearful good-byes to some very dear friends and Simon's family, I sincerely felt I would never return.

My last night in the U.K. passed all too slowly; I could not sleep for excitement. The next morning I had an early wake-up call to ensure I was well in time for my check-in, as I was somewhat over my weight allowance. I also had a rather large painting in tow, which Simon had managed to forget to collect from the framers, in time to take with him. I disliked the picture; it had been given to Simon as a parting gift from his work colleagues and we could not leave it behind. They had meant it as a reminder of the island, but it was badly painted, I felt and also of what I considered one of the less favourable views of the island. Nevertheless I had it with me.

When I arrived at the check-in desk there was already a long queue. Many tourists were starting to get irritated about the length of time they had been waiting. Directly ahead of me were two, larger than life Shendian ladies, absolutely laden down with luggage. They were returning home and seemed to have half of London with them. I simply took my place in the line, and prepared myself for a long wait. I had my whole life ahead of me, why get uptight about queuing for the journey of my lifetime?

By the time I got to the front of the queue, the clerk was looking rather harassed; this was nothing to how she looked when she had completed my check-in.

"You're over the weight allowance. That will be £54 excess baggage please."

"I don't think that's fair" I replied, "I'm emigrating to Africa, and your airline insisted they couldn't sell me a one way ticket. I would like to claim my homeward bound allowance on the way out."

"No, you can't do that, but I will speak to someone about how you feel. Please wait here" (I distinctly heard the tourist behind me sigh as the girl walked away to consult someone.)

She returned saying that the airline had agreed I could pay £20.

"O.K. that's fine" I said "but I'm leaving the country, I don't have any sterling. I will have to give you my credit card."

"Sorry we don't accept credit cards."

"Fine, I will give you a cheque, to whom do I make it payable?"

"Oh, I don't know," she replied, "I will have to go and find out." (Another sigh from behind me and a muttered "I don't believe it!")

Whilst the clerk went to make yet another enquiry on my behalf, I wrote out the cheque and as she returned I handed it to her. She took it from me saying, "We don't accept cheques either."

I stared at her as she tore the cheque into pieces, and threw it into the air, telling me to just go away. As I picked up the picture and started to leave the check-in desk, I considered that maybe the clerk would benefit from a course of 'St. John's Wort' to relieve her stress, but thought best not to suggest this. Then I was halted by a cry of, "What is that? And where do you think you are taking it?"

"Oh this------It's my picture, a well loved family picture, which will remind us of home, I'm taking it to Africa with me." I didn't think that she needed to know that I hated it.

"You can't take that on the plane with you. It will have to go in the hold."

"But it's glass. It will be smashed to smithereens before I collect it from the carousel."

"Oh, - just go!" I was instructed, which reaffirmed my opinion that a little 'St. John's Wort' wouldn't go amiss, but rather than suggest this, I left swiftly before she changed her mind. I had got away without excess baggage charges and the picture, without any undue fuss.

Waiting in the departure lounge, I took out the package of photos Simon had taken on his trip, and re-examined them. They were basically of people; I knew what the people looked like. And views of the beach, I had already seen the beach. I had expected to see the bar, the garden and my new home. However I had faith in Simon's judgement. He had assured me I would love it, of course I would. It was our new start.

I boarded the flight and settled into my seat after much to-ing and fro-ing of the picture, which as the flight was half empty, was eventually allotted its own seat. Suddenly I wasn't so sure anymore. I felt overcome by nervousness, and it was completely unexplainable. Shortly after take-off the flight crew announced that we were flying directly over my old island home and my thoughts of the day before returned. I'd never go back! Was this what I wanted? Was this all a horrendous mistake? Could we make a fresh start? Back home there had always been family and friends to lean on, and offer support. How would we get on just the two of us? I gave myself a shake; of course things would be fine. Our marriage was fine, I was fine, and Simon was fine. How could I be thinking this was a huge mistake? These thoughts passed fleetingly. We were lucky, at an age that our parents had been thinking their lives were over; here we were making a fresh start.

I then settled into an uneventful, but pleasant six-hour flight. Once again I was feeling happy about the situation, until we started the descent into Shendi. Shock! Horror! I had boarded the wrong flight! We were landing in an arid, in fact nearly desert country. I was going to a green, lush country. Then reality dawned. This was the end of May; rains were due in a few weeks. I looked out the window of the aircraft, and was expecting to see the 'green and pleasant land' I'd left behind in November. In later years we were instructed to refer to wet season as 'The Green Season'. True, but it certainly is wet! Like most of Africa, the countryside varies greatly depending on the season, of which there are only two, wet season and dry season.

We taxied up to the now familiar terminal building, and I knew there had been no mistake; I was in my new homeland. As I stepped off the plane, I could smell the strange evocative smell of Africa. It seemed to welcome me back and I was glad to be back. On entering the arrivals hall, complete with the picture, I was greeted by a more than familiar voice calling "Helen." Simon was there, accompanied by a local that I hadn't met; somehow he had managed to be in the arrivals hall. He gave me a quick peck on the cheek, glanced at the picture and introduced his companion—the local M.P. The mere fact of being met by an M.P. caused Simon's less than enthusiastic welcome to fade from my mind. After all it would never happen back home. I gave Simon his picture, and shook hands with the M.P. who took my passport from me, and told us to collect my luggage.

Modou, the M.P. was soon by our sides again with my passport duly stamped, and we were whisked through the airport, driven at breakneck speeds through the, soon to become familiar narrow pot holed streets of Malaville and on to The Dominion. During the journey I said very little to Simon. I was too busy looking at my new homeland and wondering just what awaited me. Simon left me to my thoughts, perhaps he sensed that I needed some quiet after the journey or perhaps he simply wanted to talk to Modou about his plans for the bar.

The car pulled to a halt outside The Dominion, our new home. I felt a huge rush of excitement, a new home a fresh start and a new way of life. My memory from our holiday had served me well; The Dominion was just as I had pictured it. Maria, the Dutch lady we had purchased from, was still here, she was leaving the country in three days time, to be reunited with her husband, who had left a few months earlier. She was at the entrance to greet us, so were the members of staff that were on duty. Their welcome was polite, but reserved. Obviously they were as nervous as I was, as they met their new 'Boss Lady.'

I had a tour of my new home. Pleasant yes, but like the welcome, something was missing in this case namely two rooms from upstairs. Also the sea view from the balcony was not as I had imagined it. If you looked carefully you could see a very small area of sea on the horizon, between the rooftops of The Peace Haven. The Dominion had been built a few years prior to The Peace Haven, I'm quite sure the sea view from our upstairs would have been absolutely magnificent in those days. But all would be fine, what were two missing rooms and a sea view to someone who was making a fresh start in life? Nothing, absolutely nothing.

We spent a pleasant evening dining in our own restaurant with Maria; she had been running the business single-handedly since her husband had had to return to Holland. She was friendly towards us, but appeared very abrupt with the staff. She also seemed to be continually on her nerves. Another one that might benefit from 'St. John's Wort' I thought. She was helpful explaining things, such as how to react to the authorities, which would make their presence felt, and warning us to be cautious of the staff. She even told us that each morning she counted out the matches she considered should be needed in the course of the day. I took note of her warnings – but did consider counting matches as being slightly over vigilant! There seemed to be caution in all her words. We took on board what she had said, and decided to leave her in charge until she left. We would then sit back for a few days before making decisions on what changes we would implement.

When we retired to our bedroom in a nearby hotel that evening Simon dropped rather a large bombshell on me. "There's something you should know, Helen."

"Yes, well there are lots of things but what in particular. Is there a problem about the bar?"

"Well no, not exactly a problem, but something I don't think you will be very happy about"

"Yeah, well go on."

"I decided to put The Dominion in my name only."

"What!" He was right! To say I wouldn't be happy was a definite understatement!

"Well the thing is, you weren't here when the purchase went through. Also, you must remember, this is an African and Muslim country, where women are considered second- class citizens. Ousman, our lawyer, who you will meet shortly, thought this would be easier for us."

"Easier for you or easier for us?"

"Come on, don't be difficult over this. It was a decision I made."

"Without consulting me, without even telling me over the phone. You waited until I get here and then tell me. Simon, I am not happy."

"Yeah, but it's been done now."

Yes, the deed was done. I decided not to make an issue over this at this point. I knew that I could trust Simon financially, but in other ways, I was not so certain, after the turbulence of our marriage over the past few years. I was completely shattered by this. Here I was three thousand miles from home, we had just sold a jointly owned property, and now I had nothing, or that's how it seemed to me.

Before she left Maria promised to introduce me to all her suppliers but as she was leaving three days after my arrival that did not leave much time.

Consequently the morning after my arrival was marked for a visit to the local open air market at Bankou where she purchased most of her fresh food. After an early breakfast and leaving Simon to his own devices I made my way from the hotel to The Dominion. In my mind was a list of questions that I wanted to ask. Did she have a regular supplier or did she check prices every time, how did she barter if in fact she did, where did she get her fresh food from, did she have deliveries of goods. There were so many questions churning over in my mind that I was at The Dominion before I knew it. Outside was a local taxi. Who was it picking up I wondered. It was for us. Maria did not own a car but like most of the expats used the local taxis, which explained the battered old yellow and green vehicle waiting outside. It was to be our transport to Bankou.

Ours was a typical taxi; it had seen better days and was seemingly held together by the will of the driver. I was very surprised when he suddenly pulled up on the side of the road. Where was the market? I could only see a few children playing in the sand, there were no signs of any market stalls. I need not have worried; he had only stopped to top up the radiator with water from a jerry can he carried in the boot. This happened twice more before we arrived at Bankou but as Maria made no comment on the stops, neither did I.

The road, which was part sand, part tarmac and part pothole , was busy with all kinds of four wheeled traffic, lorries, tourist coaches, pick-up trucks, a few private cars and white vans. These latter were packed with people, and, Maria informed me, were called bush taxis which the locals used to travel around the country. They went when they were full and stopped when asked, therefore their progress along the road was erratic. There was other traffic too, cyclists weaving their way between the potholes and trying to stay off the sand, two wheeled carts pulled by donkeys and laden with everything from coconuts to firewood and meandering along the road sheep (or it could have been goats , I never did learn to tell the difference) being driven to market. As we neared the market, I saw more and more women, often with babies on their backs, carrying fresh fruit, vegetables and ground nuts in bowls on their heads.

Maria explained that this produce was all grown by the local women in their communal gardens. These gardens were the main source of income for many villages and the women often walked miles along sandy tracks and paths to reach the market. As we neared Bankou our progress grew slower and slower. Apparently the market was held either side of the main road through the town and customers at the stalls spilled over into the already busy road, therefore any one in a hurry was advised to avoid Bankou on market day. Afterwards I was to learn that the market spread back a long way from the main road. There was a network of tiny alleyways crammed full of stalls selling everything anyone could want. Not all compounds had cooking facilities and a roaring trade was being done by sellers of 'cow's foot stew' and 'bunga fish pies' – fast food local style.

I was looking forward to seeing just how Maria worked in the market. It was the real Africa, not the tourist Africa that I had seen on holiday. The stalls stretched along the road and were piled high with local produce, every kind of fruit, vegetable, spice and herb that could be grown was for sale. The colours were amazing and in complete contrast to the dusty brown road and countryside that we had driven through. The shouts and cries of traders mingled with the blare of horns and the bleating of the sheep/goats filtered in over the engine noise as did the smells. These were a pungent mix of petrol and diesel fumes, unwashed human with hint of sewage and an added amount of animal effluent.

The taxi stopped at a command from Maria and we were immediately surrounded by a mob of stallholders eager to sell us the 'best buys' of the day. Maria stayed in the car, bought a small amount of fruit and then the taxi drove on. Once more we stopped and once more we were surrounded by a throng of eager traders. I was very surprised that she made no attempt to barter with the stall holders. "I thought bartering was common practice in the markets and yet you just gave what they suggested", I commented.

"Oh I don't bother", she told me. "They all know me and give me a good price. You will be OK too, now that they know you are my friend."

I was not so sure. The market, which initially had looked vibrant and alive, a true picture of African life, was now looking very scary. The stall holders were pushing and shoving each other in an attempt to reach our taxi, hands were being thrust in the windows and all I could hear were shouts and yells. How on earth was I going to cope with shopping if this was the usual experience?

We moved on, still in the taxi, to the seafood area of the market. This time I was glad to stay in the taxi. The smells were even worse than in the food market. Bankou has its own fishing village, just below the market and so the produce was fresh but in the heat of the African sun, it soon started to reek. This was added to the malodorous brew drifting down from above and it was so awful that I had serious doubts about the wisdom of visiting the market after eating. I was very relieved to see that the fishmongers conducted their trade with Maria in the same way as the fruit and vegetable traders. That is, they surrounded the car shouting and calling to her and encouraging her to buy from them. At least they did not thrust their produce in through the windows as one enterprising fruit seller had tried earlier on. She bought a few prawns and then we turned for home. I was very surprised at the limited amount of shopping she had done. It hardly seemed worth making the trip. (Had I been less naïve I would have realised that she was purchasing just enough to last out her ownership of The Dominion, just two days.)

I was very pleased when we slowly made our way back from the fishing market through the main market and out of Bankou. At one point I had thought that Maria might take me to the butchers' area. I vividly remembered visiting this area at Malaville market when we had visited last November. I had never seen so many flies in one place at one time. All local meat dishes are simmered at boiling point for a long period which presumably kills off bacteria and germs left by the flies but I wanted to be able to tell my customers that I purchased meat from a much more hygienic source than the local market which they had just visited.

Eager as I was to return to Simon and discuss my market experiences with him, we had one more visit to make. We stopped at a supermarket on the main highway just outside Malaville. This was similar in size to supermarkets back home on the island but much smaller than those in the UK. We were greeted by the Lebanese manager. (Simon had told me that many successful businesses in the country were run by either Lebanese or Indian managers.)

"We don't want anything today", Maria told me. "I simply thought that you would like to see where we do the remainder of the shopping."

"Don't you use wholesalers?" I asked.

"Well, no there is little point. This is where I shop. The Dominion doesn't get too busy. I've never considered it necessary to buy in bulk".

(There went another illusion on my part; it was not a thriving business we had bought.)

"What about things like paper napkins and toilet rolls? Surely you don't buy them by the packet. You must keep a stock."

"Sometimes, but there is a smaller branch of this supermarket up the strip only a few minutes from the bar. It is fine if you run out of anything, although it is not as well stocked as this one but it is alright in emergencies."

"Fine, thanks. Now where do you buy your wine and spirits? I suppose the brewery delivers the beer and soft drinks."

"Yes they do. I get wine and spirits from here. And any meat that I want. It all comes from here"

I looked at the prices. The supermarket was well stocked but it seemed expensive. Was Maria being unhelpful or did she really just buy everything from here? I would have to make some enquiries. After Maria had left I found out that there was a wholesaler on the main Jambula highway but that afternoon when I returned to Simon and I were discussing my morning, I was very down hearted.

We decided that as Maria was leaving in two days we would let her run the business and we would simply relax and try to find our feet. Simon took me down to the beach, and introduced me to some of his newfound friends that ran some of the beach bars. We had a good time and I was introduced to Sidi, a friend of Kebba's, who was to become invaluable as we endeavoured to learn the local customs and how to run a bar. I tried some of the local dishes including bunga fish pies and cows feet stew. The former was lovely, the latter, I cannot and will not recommend to my worst enemy. Gradually I grew calmer. So things weren't quite as I had been led to believe, but I was determined to make a go of things. This was my new life and I was going to make the most of it. In due course we said our good-byes to Maria, and thanked her for her advice. She seemed very relieved to be flying back to Holland to be reunited with her husband. Here we were, with our own business in a strange country and eager to get started. Now it was ours things would be different.

Next morning we were sat out in the garden, underneath the trees, about to start breakfast, which had been served to us by one of our own waiters. I was thinking, what more could I want, than to be having breakfast alfresco in our own garden surrounded by palm trees, many fascinating varieties of coloured birds, and lizards. This was the life. Then Simon, once again threw my mind into turmoil. "Helen, you won't understand this", he started to explain, "but later you will, so just trust me, and go along with all I tell you."

"Pardon, what are you saying? Oh, go on tell me, what now?"

"Kebba and I have found lots of bad jujus in the bar and garden. We have to destroy them and replace them with good ones."

"What have you found?"

"Jujus."

"Ju what's? What are you on about?"

"Jujus- Spells, good or bad charms. They can protect you or they can be harmful. There are lots of bad ones here. You must have noticed the small leather pouches most of the locals wear on their upper arms, well basically those are for protection. If you have one of those jujus, and anyone does anything bad towards you, it is reflected back at them. That comes originally from the crusades; the Muslims wore passages from the Koran in leather pouches, when they went into battle."

"OK. I understand that and yes I have noticed the leather pouches. What has that to do with you finding some in the garden?"

"But there are harmful ones, and these are what we have here. Kebba had one read by the Imam. It was against Maria's eldest daughter."

"So how does that affect us, she has gone."

"The daughter was involved with one of the staff. This juju was to make the two of them be in a road accident, Eileen, the daughter was to die. The staff had been hoping Maria would return to Holland, leaving Eileen here. The staff would have taken over The Dominion before anyone could arrive from Holland to sort things out. In other words the staff were hoping to take over the business. They tried to do this to the Dutch folk, so why would they not try it on us?"

"Oh, come on I find this all a bit far fetched", and I sliced the top off my breakfast egg as Simon grabbed my hand.

"Just listen a minute. I know more of the history of the bar now. First there was the Welshman Tom who built it; his wife left him, and he couldn't handle things alone. Rumour has it the staff came between them; I think she may have left with one of the barmen. Then an English couple that rented from Tom, both died of malaria in the same year. Apparently they both had a drink problem, which is a disadvantage if you get malaria as it attacks the liver, or could this be a juju at work. Maria and her husband then bought the business from Tom, three years ago. Now the husband has had to return to Holland due to ill health. Maybe The Dominion is just an unlucky place, but I'm not prepared to take that chance."

"I'm not convinced. Let go of my hand and let me get my breakfast"

"O.K., but remember what Kebba said to us yesterday? He said be careful the staff will be trying to split us up; they would rather have one boss to contend with than two! Please just go along with things."

"Are you telling me you believe all this?" I looked at him aghast. Where was the rational man I had married, the man who had poured scorn on my herbal remedies like St John's Wort? He had only been out in Shendi a few weeks and already the heat seemed to have affected him.

"I'm not sure what to think, but just go along with me on this. At three o'clock, tonight, we have to send the night security away, so he doesn't see what we are doing. Kebba is going to bring the Imam of Famara, who is very well respected; we are going to take all the jujus down. He will say some prayers and will bury some good ones for us. The Dominion will prosper, and all will be well for us in this country."

"Three o'clock tonight or rather tomorrow morning are you sure? What a time to pick."

Simon simply looked at me. I thought, yes I was expecting a new way of life; but I had only been here for four days, and here I was confronted with a husband, I really thought I knew, telling me he had faith in what sounded to me like witchcraft.

"Ok if you are sure", I added and ate my breakfast in a much more thoughtful frame of mind than I had anticipated.

Once the staff had left at the end of the evening, Simon and I set about looking for these jujus. Simon had had clear instructions from Kebba about what we were to look for. The more common ones being paper wrapped in cloth, or knotted string, sometimes knotted strips of material. Usually they would be hung somewhere. They could be tied to trees, hanging from rafters, or maybe hidden in concealed corners. I couldn't believe how many we found. There was a ceramic dog near the entrance of the bar, which actually looked like a wood carving, of which there were many in the bar. We had been told this was a gift to a waitress, who couldn't take it home, as locals don't like china in their houses. The dog had many jujus concealed in a hole in the bottom. In the grounds guarding a small bridge that led to the beer garden was a three-foot high plastic gnome; which had an arm missing. Yes, this contained jujus, so maybe it wasn't completely 'armless'

Prior to our night visitor arriving, we had instructed our night security to go and drink attiya with The Peace Haven night security. Attiya is a local form of green tea; it is a ritual to brew, and is very time consuming. As true Muslims abstain from drinking alcohol this ritual, preformed mostly by men in small groups, generally under the trees, in the evening, is similar to Western men drinking in a bar. I did think that surely they would see Kebba and the Imam arriving, so must be aware of what we are doing-but apparently that would not be a problem.

Kebba and the Imam arrived at the allotted time. The Imam made a very awesome sight in his lilac Muslim robes, including a matching lilac Muslim 'pill-box' hat. These robes were very ornate, highly embroidered with gold thread; the hat was similarly embroidered. He was not particularly tall, but what he lacked in stature, was compensated for by his ample girth. In most of Africa it is a status symbol to be overweight; it is considered a sign of wealth. I was later to learn that the Imam was well respected, as he was an adviser to the president. I was also later to learn, that services such as these that he was about to perform for us; are only carried out for substantial financial rewards.

The Imam walked around the compound, praying and drifting into a semi-trance at times. Then we all sat cross-legged, on the concrete garden slabs, just inside the main entrance of The Dominion. Here we all prayed, part of me thinking this is the real Africa, part of me querying, is this really happening? The Imam produced a juju, in the form of many beads, all of which we were told were significant; they all had a meaning. He also bought out writings in Arabic, these along with the beads were placed in a jar, which Kebba buried under a tree, near the entrance, so that everyone that entered The Dominion would walk passed them and be influenced by them. The Imam also gave Kebba three small passages written in Arabic, these he was to have covered in leather, and give them to us later in the day. These were one each for Simon, me and our son, Kevin for when he visited; these were to be worn on our wrists, rather than on our upper arms, to make them more conspicuous. These were to protect us, anyone seeing them would be afraid to take a juju out against us, for fear that it would reflect back on them.

Finally the Imam announced that the jujus we had found, including the dog and the gnome must be thrown into the sea. Simon and I were to go with him and Kebba to do this. Kebba drove us all to the closest beach, only a short distance from The Dominion. Here the Imam threw the ceramic dog into the sea. The offending animal would not drift out to sea, despite Kebba wadding waist high into the water in an attempt to submerge it. The three men were inclined to put this down to the strength of the jujus, until I commented how unfortunate it was that with the tide coming in and the prevailing wind also coming in, it was unlikely that the dog would drift out.

It was therefore decided we would throw the jujus off the road bridge leading into the capital, Jambula, The capital had been built on an island with the only road access over this bridge and it seemed to me a very public place to be disposing of jujus. However, I was tired now, and keen to bring what I regarded as a charade to a close. Nonetheless we had to finish what we had set out to do and so we set out for the bridge.

The drive to the bridge took about 20 minutes and by this time it was 4.30 am. Because of its importance the bridge always has check points near it, manned either by the police or army. We were stopped at an army checkpoint. The soldiers pointed their AK47s into the vehicle, and demanded to know where we were going at that time of the morning. I was terror struck. I was, and always would be, scared of guns. How would we explain this? Kebba, at the wheel, the Imam sat next to him, with Simon and I sat in the back seat, with the armless gnome sat between us. Taking our armless gnome for a drive at 4.30am really did not sound very feasible!

Luckily one of the military recognised the Imam, who explained that, Simon and I had a very sick friend, who we were all visiting in the hospital. Surprisingly no one queried the early visiting hours, and we were allowed to proceed. We stopped at the far side of the bridge, and threw our offending cargo into the ocean. As we stood on the shore and watched them float away, I felt that not only were we throwing the jujus that had affected The Dominion away, but also because we had done this together, we were throwing away the juju that had tried to ruin our marriage. I actually felt a strong unexplainable sense of relief.

We then had to wait an hour before we dared return to the checkpoint, as that was how long it would have taken to visit the hospital and return. There was nowhere to go at that time of day and so we sat in the car each with our own thoughts until we could make our way back through the check point. "Yes, yes our friend is fine, fine" we told the soldiers.

It was approaching 7am before we finally retired for the night. I was opening the bar at 9.

I certainly had a lot to learn about Africa!

Chapter Two

Settling In

Tired after our early morning trip to Port Albert, we still opened the bar promptly at 9 and by 9.30 we were serving breakfasts to a couple of expats. It was a thrill serving customers in our own bar but we could not simply soak in the satisfaction. We had an 11 o'clock appointment with our lawyer, Ousman, to complete the many details and pay the many fees that taking over a business in Shendi involved. True to our UK origins we had ordered a taxi for 10.30, not realising that it would be simpler to walk up to where all the taxis waited and take the first one in line. However, the taxi arrived, we collected the papers we needed and along with Kebba set out for the capital city and our lawyer.

On the way there, Kebba looked at us and asked if we had the money.

"Of course," said Simon, "I have my bank account details here"

(My bank account, I thought, what happened to our bank account? I would pursue this latter.)

"Bank account details no good. You have to pay in proper money, in cash"

We looked at each other, the amount we wanted was huge and neither of us had enough cash.

Fortunately the bank was near to the lawyer's office and after asking the taxi driver to wait for us we went in to draw out the money. When Simon told the girl how much we wanted, she looked at him, took his slip, closed her desk and disappeared into the depths of the bank. We waited and waited and realising that we would be late, sent Kebba to tell the lawyer we were on our way. He returned before the cashier and we all stood around waiting. Finally she reappeared carrying a huge carrier bag stacked with notes. Shendian money did not have large denomination notes and the amount we had requested would have filled a small suitcase. The bank would not let us borrow the carrier bag and so while the girl counted out the money which, at 50 shillings a time took a while, Kebba went on a shopping expedition for bags. Quickly stuffing the money into the bags, Simon, Kebba and I made our way along the narrow streets to the lawyer's office. As we hurried along grasping the bags of money, it crossed my mind how easy it would be for someone to rob us. A quick push and grab and our hard earned savings could vanish into the crowd. It didn't bear thinking about. Fortunately, we made it to Ousman's office building safely and panting in the heat climbed the stairs to his office.

This was my first visit and although my experience of lawyer's offices was extremely limited, I thought that it was untidy, dusty and very very shabby. It was also very small and the four of us and the money bags seemed to fill the space. Ousman showed no surprise at our arrival with bags of money; it appeared that he had expected to be paid in cash. He quickly found chairs for us all and took us, or rather Simon, through the paperwork for the various licences. He then dealt with our residence permits which again had to be paid for. All of these had to be renewed in January every year and our residence permits were to be carried at all times. Eventually all the paper work was finished and we left the office with empty bags but a great deal of paper. Our first meeting with Shendian bureaucracy was over.

The next morning I was trying to come to terms with the need to go shopping, when Sidi turned up. Simon and I had spent time with him over the past few days and both liked what we saw. We had asked him to come to the bar that morning to discuss an idea we had about transport. Leaving me behind the bar, still thinking about shopping, Simon took Sidi into the office where he put forward the suggestion that Sidi become our main form of transport. Although he did not have a car of his own, he had access to his uncle's small four wheel drive vehicle. He agreed and the deal was done. It suited both sides, we would not have the expense of taxis and Sidi would have a guaranteed income.

His first duty was to take me shopping and we drove to the wholesalers I had been told about. On the way there I explained that I did not intend to buy anything this morning, this visit was in the nature of a fact finding mission. I needed to find out what stock the wholesaler held, what his prices were and how to go about paying for it. After yesterday's visit to the lawyer I was not surprised to find that we had to pay in cash. (This in fact made it easier for me as Simon had set up one bank account in his name but none for the business. Whenever we needed cash to pay bills – and all bills in Shendi were settled in cash, Simon would go and draw some money out or it would come out of the takings which we kept in a safe in the house prior to banking them.) However, our strategies for coping with a cash economy were in the future and that morning were no concern of Sidi's. As we drove to the store we talked generally about life in Shendi and I found out a little about his family. I also watched his driving. If he was to be employed as our driver, it was essential that I felt safe with him. I was accustomed to driving on the island and had, occasionally driven on our visits to the UK but it soon became apparent that driving in Shendi was in a different league to our narrow and hilly island roads. Shendians drove on the other side of the road, and there was much more traffic, few traffic lights, no roundabouts, and seemingly no speed limit. In its favour, Shendian roads were wider than I was used to, parking looked easier because of the wide 'pavements' on either side of the road and the roads were flat. Clearly the Shendian driving test could not include a hill start as there were no hills. When we arrived at the wholesalers I was quite content with his driving, the near miss with the cyclist had been the cyclist's fault for turning left without warning and the donkey cart driver had simply pulled out into the traffic.

"Are you sure this is the place?" I asked as we pulled into the car park of a small building on the side of the road.

"Yes, this is it. I can be trusted you know."

"Yes Sidi, I know, it just seems smaller than I expected."

Once again, my UK perceptions were colouring my expectations. It was an African wholesalers not a UK one. I spent an hour there, squeezing along narrow, cluttered aisles, climbing over boxes and rubbish and getting filthy from the dust laden wares. I was pleased to see that their prices were cheaper than the supermarket's but concerned that their stock was very limited. Feeling, hot, thirsty and in dire needed of a shower I asked Sidi to take me back home.

The next day he suggested that we head for the fishing village at Bankou. He had listened to my story of the visit with Maria and knew that I was worried about the cost and the freshness of the fish. He was sure that we could talk to some of the fishermen and buy directly from them. This would be cheaper than the market. As we turned off the main road to start the small descent into the village, I was able to take in some of the details that I had missed on my previous visit. There was a long wooden pier with brightly painted fishing boats tied up along side and additional boats were moored in the bay. The shore was a hive of activity with both men and women wading out to the boats and returning with baskets overflowing with fish balanced on their heads. On the shore were rows of old rusted chest freezers packed with ice collected earlier in the day from the ice factory. With no electricity here, this was the only way that the fishermen and traders could keep the fish fresh.

"I'm very impressed by this", I told Sidi.

"Good, I thought you would be".

"I'm much happier buying our fish here than from the market where it will have been exposed to the sun. Do you think we will be able to do it?"

"I'll talk to some of the fishermen and explain who you are and that you need to buy fish for your restaurant. They will be eager to supply you."

"Fine fine", I said as he went off. (Had I really said "Fine, fine"? The local habit of repeating words was catching. I hadn't been there a week yet and already I was doing it! What other things were catching I wondered, hopefully not malaria.)

I climbed out of the car and watched as Sidi talked to the fishermen. Soon he called me over to see some their catches. There was barracuda, ladyfish and captain fish, Spanish mackerel and shrimps. All were much bigger than fish I was accustomed to buying in the UK. Back home the shrimps would be classed as king prawns by some fishmongers. The only disappointments were the lobsters and the oysters. The lobster had no claws and would have to called crayfish whilst the oysters which were cheap and in abundance were, in reality, mussels which local women collected by paddling through the mangrove swamps. I was satisfied; this was the way to purchase our seafood. I agreed what we would purchase that day and left Sidi to barter with the fishermen whilst I went for a leisurely walk on the beach. Because it was a working village, I was not bothered by people wanting to 'be my friend' or wanting 'just to talk, no problem' nor were there any children around shouting the ubiquitous "Taubab", I presumed that they were all in school. It was good to stroll along the sand observing life in the sunshine. Last time I had been near here with Maria I had felt depressed and unable to cope but this was very different perhaps because I was on my own. The swing between high and low moods worried me but then I decided that it was normal with so many changes in such a short time. I really would have to appreciate the huge transformation in our life style that we had made and expect to have moments of doubt and even despair. For the moment I felt happy and for whatever reason I was certainly enjoying this walk amidst the bustle of Bankou's fish market.

When I returned to Sidi, he was in the midst of what seemed to me to be a heated argument with the fishermen. I thought about intervening and then stopped myself. I could interrupt negotiations at a delicate point. Sidi was the expert, we had hired him for his local knowledge and remembering bartering I had seen in other countries it could all be part of the process. Sidi had seen my return and would call me over if he felt it necessary. It seemed to take for ever but finally a deal was struck, Sidi shook hands with the fishermen and we loaded three large fish into the back of the jeep. I was very pleased with the price but I would certainly have to get used to the time it all took. There was no sense of urgency about settling one deal and moving onto the next as there would have been in the UK. This attitude was fine when on holiday and probably added to the ambience of the place but I was not certain how it would work when running a business.

Nevertheless I returned to The Dominion feeling pleased with our purchases. I had a few moments of worrying because the fish market was only one of our sources. There were still other suppliers to meet such as the baker and whoever supplied vegetables. I was aware that all the restaurants sourced their meat from those suppliers who imported their stocks, (local sources of meat were not recommended) but we had to come to terms with how all the different suppliers operated. The supermarket/cash and carry was easy, the prices were marked and I soon came to terms with paying in shillings rather than pounds. However, in many cases we had to barter with suppliers to obtain the best price, which we found difficult. We also realised that because our skin was white the original price was often inflated. As in most third world countries there was a belief that all Europeans were wealthy and could afford prices well above those offered to locals. That may be true of tourists but we were part of the local economy, subject, like our supplies to all its up and down turns. Bartering in a business environment seemed alien to me, it belonged to holidays and tourist purchases. I could manage the fixed prices in the local currency but when it came to bartering it was very different. It took a long time for me to get out of the habit of converting my offers and their counter offers into sterling. I was grateful that it was low season and therefore there were few customers. I was confident that we would be on top of things by the time November came and the high season. Simon left all the sourcing of goods to me; he was fully occupied with his plans for developing the site and getting to know the staff. With so much to deal with, my mind was fully occupied from waking till bedtime to dwell on the disappointments I encountered when I first arrived at The Dominion. Life was new and exciting I would wake in the morning and not have a clue what would happen before returning to bed at night. Life did have a 'buzz'. On reflection, life on the island had become boring, this was the 'new beginning' I had hoped it would be.

Slowly we managed to find suppliers for meat and fresh vegetables and over a working lunch in the garden we were deciding our next step when Jed, the chief barman approached us.

"Sorry, Simon to interrupt your lunch but I want to introduce Mohamed," and he turned to a local standing behind him. As it was Friday, I was not surprised to see Mohamed in the traditional Muslim jalaba, a long-sleeved, ankle length tunic. His elaborate outfit was pale blue with a neckline heavily embroidered with purple silks to match his hat, but the effect was somewhat spoiled by the black and dusty push bike he was wheeling into the garden. I realised that I had seen him arrive just before we sat down for lunch and I thought then that riding a bike wearing those robes could prove difficult. Simon stood up and shook Mohamed's hand. I held out mine but it was ignored and our visitor glanced at Jed. I realized that I had offended against Muslim etiquette. Mohamed was obviously a strict Muslim who would not touch another man's woman especially on a Friday. Hastily I sat down before I could commit another faux pas.

"I have asked Mohamed to come because he is a friend of the staff", went on Jed, "We buy things from him. He can get you anything you want."

"What kind of things can you supply?" asked Simon.

"Anything, anything you want. I will go and get it for you. No problem."

"How much would you charge us for a case of paper napkins?" I asked, forgetting for a moment that he might prefer not to talk to me.

"So sorry, I don't know what you mean", he replied.

I went into the bar and returned with a packet of napkins.

"These", I said, putting the napkins on the table so that he could take them without touching me. "We use them in the restaurant but I don't want just a packet like this. I need a big box, full of packets like this."

Mohamed studied the packet, turning it over and examining it. It was obvious that he had never seen them before and was unsure of what they were.

"OK no problem. I will go and look for this. Can I take this with me? I will be back soon."

Simon and I went to the gate and watched as Mohamed left on his bike. He seemed to have no difficultly riding a bike while wearing long robes.

"What do you make of him?" Simon asked as we resumed our lunch.

"I have seen him before, talking to the staff and what Jed said is right. They tell him what they want and off he goes on his bike and gets it. They seem to buy quite a lot from him. At least he is trying to do something enterprising and not just sit under the mango tree like many of the men seem to do. He has no overheads so anything he makes is pure profit. He probably makes a fair living."

"Yeah, but he must charge more than the shops do or he wouldn't make anything."

"Obviously, that is why I asked for something I have already priced. The wholesaler's is the only place he will be able to buy a case. If he is going to collect and deliver a case of napkins on a push bike, I don't mind paying him a little to do it. If he asks too much I will tell him he is too dear. I don't mind getting a few things from him if he is not too greedy. At least he is doing something."

Mohamed returned later in the afternoon, gave me back my packet of napkins and quoted a price for a case that was only slightly higher than I would pay at the wholesalers. We agreed to let him supply us and I gave him the money to go and buy a case. Simon and I eagerly awaited his return. We were very keen to see how he managed a large cardboard box on the back of his bike. As he had said, it was 'no problem'. The box was securely tied to his back wheel with a thick rope. I knew that I would not have found it easy to cycle carrying such a heavy weight and on sandy roads, but Mohamed rode up the slight incline of the car park without showing any signs of breathlessness.

He became our regular supplier of napkins and toilet rolls. Although it was slightly more expensive than getting them directly from the wholesaler it was a great deal cheaper than buying by the packet from the local supermarket as Maria had done and we were directly helping the local economy. Simon and I christened him "Mohamed on a bike", following the local custom of giving everyone nicknames. This was essential as there were only about twenty first names in use in the whole country and with all first born boys called Lamin and first born girls called Fatou, some kind of differentiation had to be made. Thus we had Jed Bar (our barman) Latif Garden (the gardener) and Latif Night (our night security man). In later years I became known as Helen Dominion.

On our way back from a shopping expedition I asked Sidi to take me to where I could buy a copy of the Koran but in English.

"That won't be easy to find", he told me. "Most editions are in Arabic. Why do you want one anyway? Are you thinking of being a Muslim?"

"An Arabic copy will be no good for me. I would like to read it in English and try to understand a little more about your beliefs. After all we are living in your country now and most of you are Muslims. I need to find out what you believe in and the rules that govern your lives. I don't want to insult people or do the wrong thing like trying to shake hands with devout Muslims."

"That sounds like a good idea. You are trying to understand us. We will have to go to Malaville to look for what you want. I don't think we will find it in the market but I know a street where most of the traders sell Muslim books. We might find it there."

We drove deep into the heart of the town, past the market and into the narrow back streets. Once off the main roads the surface became strips of sand, deeply marked by tyre tracks and Sidi steered carefully between ruts and pot holes trying to avoid wayward pedestrians. Eventually we came to the market which was full of people and corrugated iron stalls, very different from the ones on the tourist trail. This was definitely a local market not one for the tourists. There appeared to be hundreds of such stalls on view selling everything from fast food Shendian style, through soft drinks, bags and buckets to a store whose rolls of elaborate and brightly coloured material seemed out of place on that dusty, drab lane. Opposite this stall was a 'tele centre' where the locals went to use the phone or the fax machines. Although mobiles were becoming more common, they were still a rich person's accessory and these centres provided a very necessary service. Outside many of the shops were tyres sunk into the earth whose function as a crash barrier would become clearer in the wet season. Also outside the shops and encroaching onto the road, making driving even more difficult, were seats ranging from broken plastic garden chairs to battered armchairs. The shop keepers provided these for their customers and most of them were occupied by people who seemed in no hurry to buy anything. We crawled past a hardware and plumber's shop whose armchair had certainly seen better days with its springs on view and the back coming off; still it provided a resting place for a local sheep/goat.

Sidi turned a corner and stopped the car. This lane, very reminiscent in size, if nothing else of the market in Old Delhi, was crammed with stalls, all of them selling books and was far too narrow to drive through.

"Stay in the car", Sidi instructed. "I will go further up the road and see if I can find an English Koran. You know that if they see you the price will go up. You will be OK here, just stay inside."

I realised that what he was saying was correct. I sat in the car watching Sidi go from stall to stall picking up a book here, putting it down, haggling and moving on. Why was it, I wondered that when I had bartered and haggled on holiday, it always seemed such a quick thing to do? Here it always took ages. The car was parked on the side of the lane but in the full sun and I began to feel hot and bothered. I felt very isolated in the car, the hustle and bustle was much worse than any I had encountered before and very reminiscent of the market visit with Maria. It was no good, I would have to get out, but Sidi had told me to stay in the car. I needed some air; I would have to open a window if nothing else. Carefully I wound the window down and gasped as the hot African air came into the car. This was not a good idea but before I could close it, children's hands were thrust through and childish voices called "Taubab, Taubab, you give minties, you give money". I ignored the voices and the hands but soon the children climbed onto the bonnet of the car and started bouncing on it. What could I do? I had to do something but what? If I climbed out, it would only attract more children and I dare not shout at them. Suddenly I heard Sidi's voice shouting out. I have no idea what he said, but it was effective. The children scattered like leaves in a gale and Sidi climbed back into the car.

"Are you alright? You look hot and bothered"

"I am now. I am pleased to see you. Are the children always like this in this country?"

"Most of them won't have seen many white people and certainly not here. If they have seen them it will be at school when the tourists visit and give out exercise books, pencils and sweets. They expect all white people to give them something, you can't blame them."

"I hated it when they called me Taubab"

"I keep telling you, it isn't disrespectful. Look it is no problem to be called that.

Anyway forget them. I have your English Koran and I got it for a good price."

"I should hope so, it took a long time." I said peevishly.

"Helen, you will have to understand how long it takes to get a good price, if you are to succeed. Now, do you want to go back to The Dominion?"

"Yes please, I need a coffee and I expect you want something to eat."

As we drove back I reflected that even though I had not enjoyed the visit to the back streets of Malaville, it had been a good learning experience. It had given me an insight into the lives of the ordinary people of the country, lives like those of my staff. Everyday I was learning something new about my new homeland and now with the Koran I should be able to learn about their religion. With over 85% of the population being Muslims, I felt I needed to have a greater understanding of their faith. I resolved to read a passage of the book everyday to try and gain that understanding. I did eventually read the entire Koran and it did help me understand certain aspects of the people's lives. (Although I never did find the passage on jujus which the staff had assured me was there and if I would only read the relevant chapter all would be explained. Obviously that chapter was missing from the English translation.)

Over the next few weeks we gradually settled into our new life. It was a very different life to the one I had imagined back in the winter on our cold island. Neither of us had thought through the practicalities of moving to another country with different customs and languages. There was the bureaucracy to come to terms with, residence permits, a bank account, licences, insurances etc etc. Fortunately we did have Sidi to help us work our way through all the paper work, he was also a great help when dealing with suppliers and traders as I had quickly found out. Our decision to employ Sidi turned out to be one of the best decisions we had made. We saw a great deal of him and much less of Kebba, in fact Kebba seemed to have disappeared from the scene a few months after introducing us to Sidi. When I asked Sidi one day where Kebba was, he muttered something about visiting friends up country. Simon too seemed to have no idea and never mentioned him. I took the hint and said no more on the subject.

Together Simon and I zealously undertook our various duties in the bar and restaurant. Catering being alien to us, we were both determined to make a success of this. Even though we were in official low season, the business was prospering. We were both in the bar each evening, conversing with the customers and soon came to know our 'regulars'. It seemed that Maria and her husband had worked behind the scenes and our presence behind the bar was commented on and seemed to be appreciated. We were slowly coming to terms with the practicalities of running a bar and restaurant. This was one area where Sidi lacked expertise. Like us he had very little idea when it came to the mechanics of running the bar, how to pull a pint, how much to order, when to order, how to change barrels and similar matters. The bar and kitchen staff were not much help either, they obviously thought that as 'Boss Man and Boss Lady' we should know how to do these things. It was a steep learning curve. The first few times I pulled a pint the customer got more froth than beer and I got a swift lesson in bar repartee and how bar staff are always wrong. As for Simon's first attempt at changing a barrel this produced more beer over the floor than I had managed to get in the glasses and a queue of thirsty customers all shouting their advice. Practise makes perfect and we had plenty of that. Soon we could both pull pints and change barrels with the best of them. At least Simon could, I was not allowed to change barrels but in the interests of learning all about bar management I watched both Simon and the bar staff and was sure that provided someone moved the full barrel for me, I could carry out the operation if I had to.

We also had to learn how to manage without electricity. Neither of us had been prepared for the frequency of power cuts, these happened two or three times a day sometimes and rarely a day passed without at least one. Clearly during our holiday we had not been aware of power cuts during the day because we were out and during any evening power cut the hotel generators kicked in almost without our knowledge. It was very different when we were running a business.

Marie had left us a generator but the power went off during our first evening, the whole place was plunged into darkness and confusion reigned. Neither Simon nor I knew how to work the geni and the staff also appeared clueless. Fortunately Kebba was there and quickly started it. With the lights back on and more importantly power to the kitchen, fridge and pumps everything was back to normal. However, there was very little fuel left, so Kebba sent a member of staff out to get some, and the next day arranged a lesson for Simon in generator repair, maintenance and use.

All of this was hard work but we were both used to it, having worked hard back in the UK. Having had to work shifts back home, Simon was used to late nights and long hours and I had never needed too much sleep so the long working day did not bother us. Simon and I made an effort to have two fixed points in each day when we would be together. The first was at breakfast when we would outline the programme each of us had for the day. Initially we had tried to have lunch together but this was often interrupted by staff with queries or deliveries or customers. Because it was the low season we were very reliant on the expat community and we could not ignore this customer base simply because it was our lunchtime. We learnt to take our lunchtime meal on the go; if we felt hungry we ate. The same rule applied for our evening meal and it was in those early days that my grazing habit developed. As a result of having no fixed meal times when we could talk we started to go out for a walk in the afternoons with Sally the dog. Sally was one of the (many) things that Simon had forgotten to tell me. She was an old golden Shendian bred dog, and was included in the purchase of The Dominion. Maria and family had inherited her when they had bought the bar and in turn they passed her on to us. I like dogs and Sally was very amenable. All she asked was food, a place to sleep and regular walks. Most afternoons when the bar was quiet, Simon and I would take her for a walk along the beach. These walks gave us time together, time when we could talk about the bar and its problems and time when we could simply get away from it all.

During our first weeks there we found these walks and the break it gave us from the restaurant essential. Back on the island, with us both working very different hours we often became like 'ships that pass in the night' seeing each other only when Simon's shifts coincided with my more traditional Monday to Friday job. Although I had found it hard at the time, I had come to like it and to appreciate my time on my own. This was the complete opposite, we were always together and I, for one, was finding it very difficult to be with Simon all day and every day. Even though we had been married for a long time, we had never spent that much time on our own, jobs and then family commitments in the form of children and elderly parents had always intervened. Even in recent years when we were back to living by ourselves we had had the different working patterns and had rarely been together for long, perhaps just for our annual two week holiday. Now we were together all day and every day, in a new country and with new jobs and responsibilities. If either of us had realised what a difference this would make to our relationship perhaps we would have been better prepared. But we didn't and we weren't.

Not only was the constant presence of Simon disconcerting - and no doubt he found my constant presence equally, but I found life at The Dominion like living in a goldfish bowl. There was a complete lack of privacy and I was finding this almost impossible to come to terms with. We were living and working on the job. Not only was the bar attached to our house but Simon was using our private garden to grow vegetables for the kitchen and as a seed bed for flowers for the beer garden. He was proud of this and would often show customers round "his patch". This meant that if I sat in the garden, I was often disturbed by Simon and his customers, by Latif Garden doing some of the many tasks that he had been set or by Aysha who did the laundry for the bar, hanging out washing on the line which had to be in our garden. Even if I was alone out there, I could hear conversations from both the bar and the beer garden. It was useful to know what was happening when I was off duty but it was no way to relax. I found it very difficult to read or knit, I simply could not concentrate with the noise and bustle from over the wall.

Giving up on the garden, I next tried sitting out on the balcony attached to our bedroom. This was worse than sitting in our garden. The balcony overlooked the beer garden I felt like a prison supervisor watching the inmates at recreation time. Moreover if customers saw me there, they expected me to acknowledge them and I am sure that they wondered if I had nothing better to do than to watch them. I had to find somewhere else and so I retreated downstairs to the lounge with its French doors leading into our garden. This was slightly better. I could not hear what went on in the bar and I could not be seen from the beer garden. But and it was a big but, anyone who went into our garden could see straight into the lounge and that meant no privacy when anyone was in the garden. I found this out quite early on, when Aysha reported back to the staff that she had seen me sweeping up in the lounge. It was not the 'done thing' for Taubabs to clean, most expats had maids and our staff found it very amusing that I should spend time cleaning my home (They found it even more amusing when I had to clean the bar whenever the domestic staff let us down.) Even at night, after the bar shut we were not alone because the night watchman, Latif Night or his partner, Lamin Night were around. This lack of privacy annoyed me but it did not bother Simon who seemed to thrive on it and could not understand my feelings. Even when Simon eventually stopped coming on our daily walk, I kept up the routine. Not only did it give Sally much needed exercise but it gave me a chance to be on my own. So much so, that I was always quite glad when Simon refused to come and would set off gaily on my own.

Not only were Simon and I finding it hard to be together all day but it soon became clear that we had different opinions about staff management.

Back in the UK I had managed a number of staff and had had no difficulty in running a business. Simon, too, had held managerial roles but it appeared that we had vastly different styles. Whilst I felt that Simon was too rigid and inflexible with The Dominion staff, he felt that I was too much of a 'pushover' as he succinctly remarked on one of our walks. Perhaps I was but regardless I did try to be firm and to deal with any matters as I thought Simon might. It was hard, they did not like taking instructions from women and I sometimes was telling them things that I disagreed with. Nevertheless I knew it was important for Simon and I to present a united front to the staff and I did try. We had only been there just over a month when the issue of staff management came to a head and I realised that Simon would not always support me.

Musa, one of our waiters, sent a message to say that his brother had died. He would not be coming to work that day as he had to attend the funeral. (I had not realised how quickly funerals follow deaths out in Shendi and was very surprised at the speed of it all.) As good employers should, Simon and I sent our condolences and thought no more about it. A few days later I was walking through the streets of Port Albert when I saw and spoke to the 'dead' brother. I said nothing to Sidi who was waiting for me back in the car but waited until Simon and I went out for our daily walk.

"You will never guess who I saw in Port Albert", I started.

"Come off it, Helen, I haven't got time for guessing games. If you have something to say, just say it."

"I saw Musa's brother, the one he said had died and whose funeral he went to the other day."

"Oh, have you said anything to anyone about it?"

"No, I didn't even mention it to Sidi. I wanted to talk to you first."

"That was sensible – for a change. Right, I don't want to sack him, he is popular with the customers and the staff. Just don't pay him for that day when you do his wages. Don't say anything to him either. We will see what he says"

I duly did as Simon told me and gave Musa a pay packet with one day's less wages in. When he queried it, I told him we were not paying him for the day he had been absent. To my fury, he then went to Simon and I saw Simon pay him the difference out of his pocket. I asked Simon why he had gone back on what he had decided.

"Musa told me he wouldn't be able to feed his family if he didn't get a full pay packet," he said.

"But he should have thought of that before he took a day off. Besides it was your idea to stop him his wages and not really explain why."

"I don't think so. And if it was, I changed my mind it is as simple as that."

"Simon, do you realise you have overruled me with a member of staff? It is hard enough for me to get respect from them without you doing that."

"You are making a mountain out of a mole hill again. Just tell Musa I changed my mind if you want an excuse but I think you are being stupid about it all. Now shut up about it, I've heard enough."

After that incident the staff started to play us off one against the other whenever they could. I could sense them watching us with amusement as we bickered over situations that they had caused.

The staff understood and spoke English with varying degrees of success which seemed to alter depending on who was saying and what they were saying. They seemed to understand Simon much better than they understood me. He rarely had any trouble getting requests or orders across; I often had to repeat myself several times, especially at the beginning. None of the expats misunderstood me neither did any of the locals I met outside, so I can only put it down to one of two things. Either my staff were the only people in Shendi who found an island accent hard or they simply did not like taking orders from a woman. Over the years, this became less of a problem at The Dominion but it was something I was to encounter throughout my stay in Shendi. The locals, the men especially, simply regarded women as second class citizens and resented having to take orders from them. (Taking orders from tourist women was different, not only were they a source of money but they would soon leave the country and therefore no loss of face was involved.) As the staff usually spoke amongst themselves in one of the many local languages, I decided to try and learn to speak at least one. I knew I would find it hard, nevertheless I would try. Most of the staff were Mandinka, which is the majority tribe in Shendi and this was the one I would start with. When I mentioned my plan to Simon, he laughed and told me I would be wasting my time.

"Why bother, you know you find languages hard and I should think you have enough to do learning about the bar without worrying about languages. They all speak English, don't waste your time. You've never been good at languages. At school you always came bottom in French and I don't think being able to order two coffees in German, Italian and Spanish counts as mastery of languages"

"It is something I want to do "

"Ok, it's up to you", he shrugged, "but don't expect to use language learning as an excuse for not pulling your weight. Why don't you get Sidi or someone to help?"

"I'll pull my weight; I have no intention of not doing so. And no, I don't want Sidi to help. May be later but not now, so don't say anything to him or to anyone else. This is something I want to do on my own."

Simon said no more about my plans and he did respect my wish not to tell anyone. Initially I did not want anyone to know because I thought they might laugh at me and pour scorn on the idea, just as Simon had. Perhaps when or if I became fluent in Mandinka I would ask for help but not at the start. I bought two books from the local supermarket written to give tourists an insight into the local languages. At my first attempt I was totally bewildered; they gave different meanings for the same words and phrases. It took some time for me to realise that Mandinka, as with all the local languages, had no written script and therefore the written word simply reflected the individual compiler's idea of how it should be spelt. Once I realised that it was a spoken not written language I started to make progress. Many of the words were simple sounds such as 'ta'. 'ba', 'ma' and 'la' . I was surprised how quickly I could pick out some of the words that the staff were saying.

This early success was pleasing but I ran into a brick wall and my own inability to learn languages when it came to learning how to count. I spent days trying and trying to remember the numbers which seemed to follow no logical pattern. I was near to despair and about to seek help when I listened to Jed Bar talking to one of the staff one night. In the middle of a stream of Mandinka came the words "two" and then a little later "four hundred". It seemed, and indeed, was the case that English words for numbers were very widely used. In fact there were many English words interspersed in their conversations, not only words for modern technology, such as computer or phone but other descriptive words. With the little I learnt along with the number of English words used and using clues such as body language and tone of voice, it became easier to understand what was being said. Although, like native speakers of any country, the staff appreciated the effort that visitors made to speak their language, I never let anyone know just how much I understood. At the start it was shyness that stopped me intruding into their conversations but later on it became a matter of caution. If they realised just how much I did understand, and my understanding was always far ahead of my speaking, they could simply switch to another of the six local languages. I had had enough trouble coming to terms with Mandinka; I simply could not fact trying to learn another one.

Unlike me and many British people, the Shendians appeared to have no difficulty learning to speak a whole range of languages. Not only were most of them proficient in three or four local languages but those who worked around the tourist areas could carry on conversations in a range of

European languages. They may not have been able to read or write but their language ability far outstripped mine.

Much against our expectations, our expat trade increased. There was already a well established British expat bar just further along the coast and we did not expect people to change their 'local'. However, we did succeed in sharing their business from the resident expat community, which consisted mainly of single men working out in Shendi or middle-aged couples taking early retirement. Once this group heard that a British couple had taken over The Dominion they came to inspect us. We must have been doing something right as many of them stayed and became our 'regulars'. Tourists were few in the low season but we considered that we were attracting more than our fair share and many of those who came once, returned again and again during their stay. We were able to answer some of their questions about Shendi and if we could not, then the expats were only too eager to help out with suggestions and explanations.

One of the ideas we had had back in the UK was to become involved some kind of charitable work and we had, in fact brought out some goods to donate to worthy causes. These, however, were still in the container at the docks but we both felt that we could donate some of our time to a local charity, preferably an educational one. Some of our expat customers poured scorn on the idea when we mentioned it, but we were determined to try and put something back into the community. One evening, Joe and Sarah, a couple who had lived out in Shendi for several years spoke to Simon.

"Couldn't help hearing you last night talking to Tom about wanting to help with a charity. What kind of help are you thinking of? Is it just donating goods or do you want more involvement?"

"Well, we've brought some stuff over, if we can ever get it out of the docks, but we would like more of a hands on involvement if possible. Why? Do you know of something we can do?"

"Sarah and I work with an educational charity – "Schools for Shendi" and have done for many years. There are lots of places in the country where there are no schools and SFS works with the local community to build schools."

At that point I came over and Simon introduced me to Joe and Sarah. Building a school seemed well beyond my competence but Joe explained that it was schools in Shendi were much simpler than UK schools and I recalled the ones I had seen on holiday last year. They were simply large huts with a blackboard and desks in with the luckier schools having concrete floors and tin roofs. We agreed that one of us would go with Joe on his next visit to a school and make a decision about becoming involved with SFS then. It was Simon who went with Joe and he came back full of enthusiasm.

"It is just what we wanted to do, Helen," he said. "You should see the conditions the teachers are trying to work in. The rainy season has destroyed the palm roof and the mud walls are crumbling. Those kids are so keen to learn and they have to put up with conditions I wouldn't keep a dog in. I've told Joe that we will help."

That was fine with me and when I went out with Joe on his next visit I could see why Simon was so keen to help. We quickly became very involved in SFS and when Joe and Sarah had to return to the UK, Simon and I were voted in as Chairman and Secretary. Although it was hard work running the charity as well as the bar, it was an opportunity to do something for our new home and it gave both of us a chance to see the country and meet people away from The Dominion.

On one of our afternoon walks Simon came up with what at the time seemed an excellent suggestion. As we were in such close proximity to The Peace Haven, we should introduce ourselves to Paul Smithers their M.D. Some of the staff had told us that prior to the Dutch couple, there had been a good relationship between the two establishments. Apparently The Peace Haven even hired The Dominion for their staff Christmas party. We were hoping to rebuild this relationship with them. Maria and her husband kept themselves very much to themselves other than mixing with a small circle of Dutch friends. Whilst not being completely unfriendly, Maria had come across as being unapproachable, and we wondered if this was partly the cause of the breakdown between The Dominion and The Peace Haven.

Simon made arrangements for us to meet Mr. Smithers. At the appointed time we took the short stroll out of The Dominion main entrance, to the entrance of The Peace Haven, a distance of only a few metres. We entered the hotel, walked passed their small fish restaurant and along the tree lined pathway, with its bedrooms on the right until we were level with the banqueting hall. I had hoped that we would be able to see inside this as we had been told of the many times it had entertained The President and his visiting dignitaries. However, the doors were firmly closed and we were nearly late. Another time perhaps. As we entered the main reception area, I was feeling optimistic that this interview would have positive results. I was remembering that the Imam had buried 'good jujus' at The Dominion; Simon had put a lot of faith in these jujus.

We were ushered through the reception area, into an equally plush office where Mr. Smithers was awaiting our arrival. Simon led the way; greeting the managing director he introduced us and extended his hand for the customary handshake. (Newcomers though we were to the country, we had noticed how common handshakes were as greetings, even more so than back home.)

Mr. Smithers, ignored his hand and without saying a word, turned round, opened the filing cabinet behind him, and produced plans that he spread out on the desk in front of him.

"These are the plans for phase two of our redevelopment," he announced. "You will see we are constructing an arch here at the entrance to our car park." He pointed to an area which, without local knowledge, anyone would assume was common ground. Certainly there was no indication that it belonged to the hotel. "This arch will become our main entrance. Furthermore we are building a new bar here," and he pointed to the existing fish restaurant. "Opposite it we are building shops and a coffee bar. Really you could say our arch is the second Berlin Wall. I'm afraid that you have invested in a 'white elephant'. It will be impossible for you to operate. I predict that your establishment will be closed before Christmas." With that, he sat back in his chair and folded his arms as if he was defying us to comment.

A quick glance at the plan showed that if the arch was built, not only would it define the entrance to The Peace Haven but also enclose the entrance to our bar. In addition if the proposed extension to their fish restaurant went ahead, it would completely mask our entrance from the main road.

"I think we need to discuss this," answered Simon.

"There is nothing to discuss" came the reply. "We already have both planning permission and Government approval, including a letter from Physical Planning giving us permission to erect a wall that bridges the gap in the perimeter of our car park. Unfortunately for you this gap happens to be your entrance. All that remains is for us to implement this. We intend to start this phase of our development during the next few weeks."

There seemed little point to me in continuing with this conversation. Knowing Simon and his temper all too well I half expected him to throw a punch at Mr. Smithers. Any form of angry outburst would only add to our problems so I was very pleased when he muttered something along the lines of, "Well maybe we will have to wait and see if you succeed in closing The Dominion. We won't give up without a fight." With that, we turned and left.

We strolled along their tree-lined pathway, acknowledging the greetings of their security at the entrance, and back the few metres to our own entrance in silence. We were both collecting our thoughts. In contrast to the last few weeks, when I had thrown myself whole-heartedly into my new African life, and convinced myself things really were good. I was now plunged into uncertainty once more. We could not possibly allow them to close our business, we had sold our home on the island and our life savings were now invested in The Dominion.

Chapter Three

War or Peace Haven?

We opened at 9.00am every morning and often our customers would be waiting for the gate to be unlocked. I was amazed at how popular our English breakfast was. Fried egg, bacon and sausages have never been a favourite of mine and out in the heat of Shendi I liked it even less. Early one morning, soon after our talk with Mr. Smithers, I was stood in the bar watching Modu serving two of our regulars with their "Full English". I decided that the early morning was my favourite part of the day, it was quiet, the air seemed fresh and not tired as it did in the afternoons and there was a sense that any worries from yesterday had vanished. Even the threat of Mr.Smithers and his wall seemed less powerful in the morning. True to his word, Mr. Smithers had had the builders move in, and the construction of the arch, or as he called it 'The Berlin Wall' had begun and it was by now about four feet high.

Suddenly my musings were disturbed by loud engine noises from outside. The roar of racing engines was quickly replaced by loud shouts accompanied by clattering and two enormous crashes. Simon rushed out from the garden to see what was happening. Two empty twenty-foot containers, which, we were later to learn, were intended to be 'workman's huts' for the construction workers, had been strategically placed in front of our entrance at 90 degree angles; completely blocking our entrance.

The handful of customers who were all enjoying their breakfasts ignored the noise: "Maybe they wouldn't be so happy when they realized that they are unable to leave." I thought. Simon phoned Ousman, our lawyer for advice. He suggested we arrange to have the containers moved, not very far, as he thought that would probably antagonise the situation, just sufficiently for our customers and staff to have access to our premises.

With the help of Sidi, Simon arranged for a lorry to come from Malville, to move the containers. As we had come to expect, the negotiations for this task took a long while, with much haggling over the price. It was a couple of hours before the lorry arrived and by this time our customers were getting irate. As one of them said, "I came to The Dominion for breakfast not for morning coffee. Come on Simon, get it sorted I have work to do."

"I'm doing my best", snapped Simon, "the lorry driver should be here soon."

Once at The Dominion, the driver completed the manoeuvre in only a few minutes. He simply moved one of the containers along and placed it still at a 90-degree angle to the other but clearing our entrance. This allowed us free access to our premises once again, and our bemused customers to leave. Simon went out to the driver and paid him. As the lorry driver pulled away from The Dominion, The Peace Haven's Operational Manager, a Mr. Stairs, drove out from the hotel, and skidded to a halt across the arch blocking the lorry's exit. Quickly, the lorry and car were surrounded by a crowd which included members of our staff and staff from the hotel all of whom where shouting and gesticulating. Whilst tourists watched in amazement, Simon and I coerced our staff and the lorry driver back into The Dominion, hoping this would prompt Mr. Stairs to move his vehicle, logic told us he couldn't leave it where it was indefinitely. Five hours later Mr. Stairs ultimately decided to move his vehicle. The fact that this followed the arrival on the scene of a press reporter and cameraman may just have been coincidence. The frustrated lorry driver was soothed by the large payment of 'overtime' from Simon and roared away up towards the main road. The report in the local paper the following week was more favourable to our cause than it was to The Peace Haven's. Our fight was only just beginning, but we felt we had won the first round.

This small victory was short-lived. A whole succession of incidents then occurred. Our maintenance lads lit a small bonfire to burn dried weeds. Mr. Stairs shouted over the garden wall to our lads, "What are you doing? You stupid black bastards, you are polluting our tourists' air!"

Simon was in the house; he heard this and immediately went out, rightfully, in my opinion, being angrier with Mr. Stairs for his terminology than his reaction to our bonfire.

"You may call your own staff what you wish", Simon told Mr. Stairs, "but I will not let you speak to my staff like that."

Neither Simon nor the lads could understand what the fuss was about. It was a small bonfire, with very little smoke, the lads were watching it carefully and no-one from the hotel could see it. Half an hour later, we heard sirens. My first reaction was to think that The President was arriving at one of the neighbouring hotels. I was wrong, two fire engines, supplied to the Shendian Fire Service from the Avon fire brigade, were heading down the main tourist strip. One came to a halt outside our main entrance the other pulled up at our rear gate. Watched in open mouthed astonishment by Simon, myself, staff and guests, firemen wearing their full fire fighting kit, poured from each machine and like the perfectly trained teams they were, coupled up their hoses and attacked the bonfire in our garden. The whole effect was only spoilt by the fact that by now the bonfire was nearly out and only emitting the occasional puff of smoke. In fact the fire-fighters enthusiastic efforts at dowsing what was obviously a threat to all Shendian life resulted in more smoke than the fire had emitted in the first place. Once convinced the fire was out, the two teams rolled up their hoses and left.

We thought no more about it, except as an example of Shendian efficiency in fire fighting and tourist entertainment. However, a month later we received a letter from the fire chief, threatening us with closure, if we continued having bonfires, as we were creating our own hole in the ozone layer, directly over the main tourist area, putting the tourists at risk.

Just after the fire fighting incident a main water pipe burst in Malville. Accordingly, when the taps ran dry, we assumed this was the reason and organised the collection of water from stand pipes in local villages. Three days later, when we knew that other properties that had been affected by the burst pipe had been reconnected, we contacted the water company. They were reluctant to do anything, telling us the burst pipe had resulted in many premises being left without water. We finally sent Sidi to collect someone from the water company to come and investigate. He found that our water pipe had been cut and capped, near the arch. A representative of the water board questioned some of the construction workers, who informed them that they had been instructed to do this as our water pipe ran through the hotel's property. The Water Board told the hotel it was unlawful to do this. We were finally reconnected four days later.

Although the arch was still under construction, The Peace Haven security guards were moved from their existing main entrance, to their new entrance at the arch. This meant that they could, should they so wish monitor everyone who came and left The Dominion. One evening, at the start of the tourist season when business was good, it seemed strange that as the early diners left, our trade seemed to be dropping off considerably. One of our 'flyer boys', who distributed advertising leaflets for us on the main strip came into the bar, and said to me,

"Helen, do you know they are stopping our customers coming through the arch?"

"What do you mean, how can they do that?"

"They are asking everyone, where they are going. If they say they are coming here, they tell them they can't walk through Peace Haven property."

"No wonder trade is poor tonight. O.K. O.K. Thanks for letting me know, I will be down in a minute."

Simon had gone with Sidi to visit the Imam, at his home in Famara, and it obvious that Peace Haven management had seized on his absence to try this new tactic. I went down to try and reason with their security and found four guards there instead of the usual two. I was not looking forward to a confrontation but I had to deal with this attempt on our business. As I strode down to the gate I reminded myself to stay calm at all costs. "What do you think you are doing? You can't stop our customers entering." I asked in what I thought was a reasonable voice, but judging by their expressions was anything but reasonable.

"Sorry Helen, we are carrying out instructions." was the reply from one of them. "You can't do this!" I shouted, forgetting my intentions to remain calm.

"We have been instructed to allow you and Simon through, and your staff, but no-one else."

"But that isn't only our business. That is our compound, we live there."

"Yes, we know that, but that is our instructions."

I thought quickly and replied, "You can't stop us inviting friends to our compound."

"Er, well, I suppose not."

"Fine, fine". With that response, I had my solution to their tactics

Without another word I stood near the arch close to the security guards. On seeing some of our regular tourists approaching, I waited to see what they would do.

"Good evening, can I ask you where you are going this evening?" one of their guards asked politely.

"Yes," my potential customers replied "we are going to The Dominion for our evening meal."

"Sorry, we are unable to let you enter Peace Haven property."

I stepped out of the shadows trying to sound much braver than I felt "Nice to see you. If you wish to come to The Dominion, I will invite you to visit us."

"Helen, you can't do this", cried the guard.

"Watch me." I said firmly, and taking a deep breath walked across the car park with my guests. I asked Jed to show them to a table and immediately went back to the arch to 'collect' some more customers.

As the evening progressed these confrontations became more hostile. The guards, whether fearful for their jobs or enjoying the chance to deal aggressively with a Taubab resorted to pushing or pulling me out of the way, as I continued to interrupt their attempts to forestall visitors to The Dominion. When Simon and Sidi finally arrived back which according to me was about four hours later but by any other measurement of time was less than half that, they were shocked to see me, in the midst of yet another angry confrontation. "Go back to the bar Helen," Simon told me, for once much calmer about the situation than I was. "You aren't helping things; we will just leave this for this evening. I will contact Ousman in the morning and see what his advice is."

Early the following morning, even before Simon had had the opportunity to speak to Ousman about the events of the previous evening, came our first experience of the S.S.G. (Shendian Security Guard.) the country's equivalent of the MI 5. Several of them descended on us, accompanied by senior management of The Peace Haven, and representatives of the hotel's security team. Simon phoned Ousman, when the S.S.G. agreed we needed him to represent us and they gave him time to arrive from Port Albert before commencing a meeting of all parties in our beer garden.

The meeting quickly grew in size and volume as members of our staff became involved and some of The Peace Haven staff wandered over to hear what was being said. Everyone present felt that they had to right to speak and took every opportunity to do so. Later on, I became accustomed to the fact that meetings between more than a few people involved raised voices, gesticulations and many conversations being carried on at the same time all in a variety of languages. In short, it appeared to be total chaos. However, at the time, I could only sit back and wonder where it would all end. It became a complete fiasco. The S.S.G. officer in charge of the proceedings ruled that as the hotel had already been given planning permission, and had government approval, they were at liberty to continue with their redevelopment. It was also made clear to us, as Paul Smithers, had already pointed out, they had received planning permission the previous year to 'bridge a gap in their perimeter wall' this gap as well we knew was our main entrance, and the only access for our customers. I produced a letter I had found among Maria's business papers, written on Peace Haven headed paper, giving The Dominion permanent access through the car park. This letter was declared by the S.S.G. to be a forgery. So much for the Imam and his jujus, I thought.

Later that evening, Jatou who was our lunchtime waitress, came into the bar with her husband and asked to speak to both Simon and myself. In our office she told us that they said that they had someone they would like us to meet but did not want to bring him into the bar. Eventually we arranged that their friend, Omar, would call in early the next day when Jatou came on duty. When we talked to Omar the following morning, it turned out that he was a member of the NIA and was willing to help us, if he could, in our dealings with that organisation. We thanked him and Jatou but we both hoped that we would never need his help.

Once Omar had gone, we contacted our lawyer again who advised us that our only course of action would be to obtain a court injunction to stop the hotel continuing with their construction work that would impair our business. Ousman explained all that this would entail to Simon in detail. Unfortunately he did not pass all this information on to me. I was naïve enough to think that this injunction would simply leave us in a position to be able to run our business in peace, and would be an end to the matter. I was not aware that this could be the beginning of a very long and very complicated case in the Shendian courts.

We knew that Ousman would be in court the following Wednesday morning trying to persuade the judge to award us this court injunction. Ironically, we had received inside information from hotel employees that this was the very day that they intended erecting the wall to block our access. It was essential that we took action. If we were awarded the court injunction the work would have to stop and be left as it was, at the time that the injunction was served on the hotel. We had to stop them building this wall.

As we partly expected on Tuesday afternoon we heard a heavy vehicle stop outside our entrance. When we went out we saw that the builders were unloading concrete blocks outside our premises. The information we had of our entrance being blocked on the Wednesday seemed to be correct. Our staff, who were obviously concerned about their jobs, some of them had been employed at The Dominion since it was built in 1985, were being very supportive, and agreed to take an active part in preventing the construction of the wall. It was essential that we achieve our aim but we wanted this to be done in a peaceful and orderly manner. We decided that we would ask our staff to assemble early next morning. This they did, which in itself gave our morale a boost. When they arrived we explained that we were taking our inspiration from the peace protestors of the past, (I think Ghandi's name was mentioned). That being so, we would all stand across our gateway in an attempt to keep the builders at bay until a court official arrived on the scene with the injunction. One of our regular customers also came along to support us - Terry from Yorkshire who was over building a retirement home for himself and his wife -he was impressed not only with the turn out from the staff, as the locals are not renowned for supporting the taubabs but also with our idea of a peaceful protest. "That should stir something up; they will be expecting shouting and arm waving," he commented.

I wish now that I had been able to see what the workmen saw as they came towards our gate. Sitting in splendid isolation under a gaily covered garden umbrella (to protect him from the sun), was Simon. Artistically arranged behind him, but sitting on the garden slabs were the staff and myself and behind us, drinking a breakfast cup of tea and puffing on his pipe sat Terry. What the workmen thought, I do not know. They must have known that we would not take the blocking of our entrance lightly, but we were up against some very important people, so perhaps they thought we would accept it. (They failed to take into account our island temperament!)

A workman loaded a wheelbarrow with blocks while his partner walked directly towards Simon, stopped within a few feet of him and asked him to move.

"Sorry, I don't intend moving." Simon told the workman.

"You have to, you are in our way."

"We aren't going to let you block our entrance."

"You can't stop us going about our work."

Unfortunately, at that point, our staff started raising their voices and gesticulating in a manner very reminiscent of the earlier garden meeting. I did my utmost to calm them down; we had asked them not to react like this, as we knew this could only hinder our cause. Two of the workmen went into the hotel, obviously to report what was happening to their management.

Within a few minutes a police vehicle entered the car park. Three officers got out and walked in our direction.

"You can't sit there, you will have to move." one of them said to Simon.

"Why?" replied Simon, "I'm sat sunning myself, on my own property. What's the problem?"

"You are preventing these men doing their job."

"They wish to build a wall on my property. You must understand that I can't allow this."

Without replying, the three officers strolled back to their vehicle and drove off.

By now the workmen had all gone to the top of the car park and were doing what all workmen do. They were making tea – only in this case it was not British tea but Attiya, the local green tea. It had exactly the same effect as British tea does. The group of workmen simply sat there, waiting for instructions. We were left sitting in our gateway, wondering what would happen next.

We didn't have to wait long to find out. Within half an hour the same police vehicle returned, inside were the same officers.

"We have come to arrest you", one of them told Simon.

"On what charge?" he enquired.

"You are preventing these men from working."

"I have already told you, I'm sat relaxing on my own property. What am I doing wrong?"

"Yes, but be reasonable these men have a job to do, they can't do their job, you are obstructing them."

"As I said, I'm sat on my own property, I haven't asked them to do a job for me, so how can I be preventing them from doing their work."

The police officer looked rather bewildered "Yeah. O.K. we do see what you are saying, but we do have our instructions to carry out. We will return to the station and report what is going on here. I'm sure we will be back again, so think about what you are doing."

The police returned to their vehicle, and once more left the scene. I was not happy about the situation, Simon appeared to be thriving on it, but I was apprehensive, I felt we were not strong enough to be fighting the country's only five star hotel.

Within ten minutes of the police leaving, three black vehicles, without number plates pulled into the car park. These were very high standard vehicles for Shendi. We were well aware by now, that these belonged to the S.S.G.

"This is where the fun will start." Simon said to me, "Have the camera ready."

Several S.S.G. officers approached us, most of whom had been present at the meeting in our garden. Much shouting ensued, both by the officers and our staff, in one or more of the local languages, making it impossible to understand what was being said. I became totally confused as to what was going on and with all the noise I couldn't hear what was being said to Simon, or what he was saying to them. I stood in the background, and as Simon had instructed I took photographic evidence of the proceedings.

"She's got a camera." I heard one of the S.S.G. officers shout. "Get it from here."

An officer pushed some of the staff out of the way to come towards me. I was man handled, as another officer grabbed the camera from me. He opened it, exposing the film to the light, ruining the shots that I had taken. He then dashed the camera against the wall. I still had hold of the straps, and pulled it back towards me. Latif, one of our maintenance lads, being tall managed to reach over all those around me, seized the camera, and ran off into our garden with it. Two S.S.G. officers chased after him. I followed to witness what they did to him, if he was caught.

By the time I had followed, through the beer garden, through our garden, and on beyond the house. Latif was coming out of the garage which was still full of boxes we had not had time to unpack. I noted that he didn't have the camera with him. I was confident it wouldn't easily be found if he had hidden it in the garage, but as the photos had been spoilt it really wasn't of much use.

Latif was handled roughly by the officers, as I suspected he would be, which is why I had followed.

"Leave him alone. He is only trying to help me." I shouted at them.

"If you are going to survive for long in this country, you will have to learn how to conduct yourself better." I was told. "You are only a taubab woman and must learn to behave like one!"

Momodou, one of our waiters called me, saying Simon wanted me. When I returned to the gateway Simon was still sat fast on his chair, obviously not intending to leave it. There was still much shouting going on, by both staff and S.S.G. officers. Terry was still sat at the rear, puffing on his pipe, and looking as confused as I was, but never the less seemed to be enjoying his morning's entertainment.

"If you look in my wallet, in my bedside cabinet," Simon instructed me, "you will find Ousman's card with his mobile number on it, see if you can get hold of him, and tell him what is going on here."

I went inside to our bedroom. As I was looking for Simon's wallet, Sidi called me. I went out onto our bedroom balcony to see what he wanted.

"Come quick, Helen, they are taking Simon," he told me. Forgetting about phoning Ousman, forgetting about Latif, forgetting about everything, I rushed down the stairs calling Simon's name. There was no sign of him. I pushed aside the staff and NIA agents who were all trying to tell me something and dashed to the entrance just in time to see Simon being hustled into the back of one of the NIA vehicles.

What could I do? Here we were in what we had thought of as paradise, only a few short weeks into our new life, still with the unpacking to complete, still learning how to run the business but aiming to be free from the troubles and stresses of life on the island and my husband had been arrested. Not only had he been arrested but he was being driven away without anyone telling me anything. Taking a deep breath, this was definitely not the time to panic, I told Sidi to take Momodou with him, and to follow, so at least we would know where they had taken Simon.

Not all of the S.S.G. went; some of them stayed behind at The Dominion, and proceeded to bully the staff and me. They insisted I close the business down; I refused telling them I didn't believe they had the authority to make such demands.

At that instant the phone rang, I was very relieved to hear Ousman's voice.

"I've just come out from court Helen," he explained. "I have managed to obtain the court injunction; I will explain it all to Simon when I get there. A despatch rider from the court is on his way to the hotel now. He should be there in half an hour. Work will have to stop then; they dare not go against the injunction. How are things your end, did you manage to keep the workmen at bay?"

Trying to stay calm and focused, I explained the morning's events to him: the sudden arrest of Simon, his subsequent disappearance in an NIA car and the demand by the remaining NIA agents that we close the bar at once.

"Don't do that, play for time; the dispatch rider won't be long getting there. I think I know where they will have taken Simon. I will go and see what I can do for him. I will see you later."

"Come on, come on." shouted the leading NIA officer, "Stop chatting on the phone, I've told you to close the bar. You say we have no authority; I'm a representative of the government. Will you disobey an order from the government?"

"That was our lawyer on the phone. He has obtained a court injunction preventing the closure of our entrance. Do you want me to act against your High Court?"

"What authority do you think the courts have against a government instruction? You had better think carefully before you act against our government."

As I put the phone down, I turned to see Aisha, our cleaning lady come into the bar from the kitchen. This was the first time I had seen her since the workmen had arrived, obviously she had just been getting on with her work during the excitement. She was saying something as she came towards me but there were still several raised voices and it took me a moment to realise that she was not speaking to me, but calling to Allah. The thought passed through my mind divine intervention on our side was definitely needed. Suddenly, with one last call to Allah for help, Aisha simply crumpled to the ground completely blocking the main walkway between the tables. Some of the staff hurried to her side, the NIA ignored the interruption and I just stood there for a moment. Taking another deep breath (oh for some St. John's Wort now) I told two of the kitchen staff to attend to Aisha and turned to the NIA. They started haranguing me again, telling me I had to close. All the staff joined in; including those I had asked to see to Aisha, all trying to put their case. The noise was tremendous and between the waving arms, I could see Terry still sitting there, puffing on his pipe. One NIA man came towards me and in an attempt to intimidate me, loomed over me from his 6ft plus height. I backed away and bumped into something. It was Aisha who was still in her trance on the floor. I stepped over her to put her body between me and the NIA man. To no effect, he simply stepped over her and continued berating me. I knew that I had to stay on my feet and not let anyone back me into the corner. As a result, every few moments I would move, backwards, sideways, any way in an effort to make the NIA come to me. It was like some insane ballroom dance, but it would not be the last tango in The Dominion if I could help it.

Suddenly, everything stopped as one of the NIA personnel who had been posted at our gateway came in and spoke to the officer in charge. He in turn summoned all his staff into a corner of the bar and spoke to them. I had no idea what he said but as they finished their discussion they filed out of the bar so I can only assume that the dispatch rider had delivered the court injunction. As they went out, he turned to me and hissed, "We are leaving I'm sure we will be back. Listen to what I say, you are in our country now, you are not in the U.K. You can't just do as you wish here."

I was just so relieved to see them leave. Now for the first time since Simon had been taken into custody, I had time to think of him. The thought of him on his own with the S.S.G. was frightening. I had been scared stiff though I tried hard not to let it show. Thank goodness I had had the support of the staff, faced alone the S.S.G. were formidable.

Aisha was still lying on the floor and as I turned to her, feeling very guilty because I had simply forgotten her, she started groaning. In a few moments she was on her feet, sobbing. She had been on the floor for about three quarters of an hour. It took me, a farther half an hour sat in the kitchen; attempting to console her before I could convince her that everything would be all right.

The phone rang again, this time it was Sidi. "Simon has just left the S.S.G. headquarters with Omar, you know who I mean, the friend of Jatou's husband." "The S.S.G. have all left here now." I told Sidi, "So I assume Omar is bringing Simon back here, but follow them in case they are just moving him elsewhere."

Terry, still puffing on his pipe, said "Well that looks like the fun is over for this morning, I assume you will be open for business later. I will see you this evening."

Omar did bring Simon back to The Dominion. Simon put on a brave face, but I could tell that he had had a bad experience, of which he spoke little. All he did say was that had Omar not been there to help, he dreaded to think what might have happened to him. Ousman arrived shortly afterwards, and explained the terms of the court injunction to us. The Peace Haven were entitled to continue with their redevelopment as long as they did not obstruct or conceal our entrance, or hinder any customers coming to The Dominion. This injunction was only in force for as long as we were trading; which meant we must remain open even during low season, when most tourist related businesses close. Rather than being the end to our problems with The Peace Haven as Simon had led me to believe, this heralded the start of the court proceedings to resolve our differences.

"How long would you expect the court case to last?" Simon asked Ousman.

"Difficult to say for sure. It depends how regularly we get court hearings. This is an important hotel; they won't want this hanging over them for long. I can't imagine it will be longer than say six months."

All this unsettled the staff. Their initial support for us when Simon was arrested was very different to supporting us in the long term against the powers arrayed against us. Not only were we fighting a hotel which was the President's favourite but there was the involvement of the security services. At best they are scared of the NIA officers, no-one became involved with them willingly, and they had a formidable reputation in Shendi, no doubt because people who disagreed with them tended to disappear. The staff also felt that with the threat of closure hanging over us their jobs were in jeopardy and many were the sole wage earners in their family. They sent Jed, the barman, as their representative to come and discuss matters with Simon and myself.

"We would like all these problems with The Peace Haven finished," explained Jed. "We know a very good marabout, she is expensive, but if you allow us to bring her here, all these problems will be over in no time. This will be much quicker than any court case." (A marabout, I knew was similar to a witch doctor and could be male or female. They could arrange jujus and similar matters. Most Imams were also marabouts.)

"O.K." replied Simon. "Bring this lady here, we will speak with her, and then decide what we will do."

I was not too happy about this. Yes, I was unsettled and uneasy just like the staff. Although I was trying to put a brave face on in front of customers and staff, I was feeling very troubled. This was all very different from my island home, but was it the new beginning I had hoped for? We had already had one experience of local magic and that had included the military and AK47s. We were still wearing the jujus from the Imam on our wrists and even with their 'help' Simon had been detained by the NIA. What would this experience lead to? Would this intervention by a marabout be any more effective than that of the Imam? I just did not know.

Simon, whilst we were discussing this alone said, "We have to let them call this marabout in, they are pretty restless at the moment. We had the

Imam to protect the place for us, but remember they don't know this. Anyway, it can do no harm, we will be double protected." Simon's logic did nothing to settle me. I felt very ill at ease and it seemed to becoming a permanent state of mind. I was starting to question whether or not this really was the new beginning I had hoped for. Yes it was different from the island and I had enjoyed most of the settling in process but did I want to live where magic seemed to walk alongside religion and where organisations such as the NIA appeared to be very powerful. I was not sure.

Two days later, at the appointed time, the lady marabout arrived. She was as formidable a character, as the Imam had been. My gaze was drawn towards her large bulbous eyes that seemed to dominate her face. She wore a very ornate, loose Shendian robe. This attire would be to demonstrate her wealth, thus giving the impression that she was a successful marabout. She appeared to be excessively tall, but this may have been due to built up shoes that I had noted were the fashion, as her robe was long; I was unable to determine if this was the case, but her height did add to her startling appearance. She carried a wicker basket that contained a collection of jars and bottles, which I looked upon with suspicion. Jed, who had used this lady's services in the past, and had great faith in her, had made her familiar with The Dominion's problems.

"This is a simple matter to remedy." She told us, "I will need your cooperation, and the help of your staff. I will make some juju juice, which will need to be sprinkled around the compound. As time goes on, we may need to do other things. Initially I will need you to give money to this man, (she pointed to Botu, one of our gardeners.) to go and buy a pure white sheep. At high tide this evening he must take this sheep to the beach. He and some of your other staff will sacrifice it and let its blood flow into the sea; they know how they must do this. The sheep must then be given as charity. I will instruct your boys were they must take it."

"This is fine" Simon agreed, "I have an appointment this afternoon, is it necessary for me to be here whilst you are working?"

"No, you need not be here but she stays" and her long, bony finger pointed to me as she stared at me with her bulbous eyes. "I need her here." I had been uneasy before but now I felt fear creeping in. Why did she want me? What influence could I have on the proceedings? If I had known that my presence was a necessary part of the arrangements, I do not think that I would have agreed to let it go ahead. Looking back now, with all that happened later, I wonder how much Simon knew before she came. It seemed strange that he would absent himself during an important ceremony and certainly I had not known about his appointment, but before I could voice my reservations, Simon went off with Sidi. I was left at the mercy of the marabout alone.

The marabout went into the middle of the garden with some of the staff. Following her commands they brought a range of items and laid them at her feet. First a bucket then various liquid substances which she mixed all together in the bucket. She gradually added the contents of the jars and bottles, which she had bought with her. She and the staff were muttering over this concoction. I was told this was prayers. I was not convinced, to me it sounded like spells and the witches' scene from Macbeth sprang to mind. Her eyes seemed to glaze over, and even appeared larger and more bulbous than before. I thought she was going into a trance, when suddenly she stopped, and pointing at me said.

"You--- Bring me two bottles of your perfume. Different ones."

This certainly unnerved me. Why did she want my perfume?

I was very relieved to see Simon and Sidi walk into the garden. I hadn't expected them back for another couple of hours yet. Fortunately, Simon had forgotten some papers he needed for his meeting, and had returned to collect them.

I rushed over to them, "I'm not happy about this, she's asking for two bottles of my perfume."! I said, grabbing hold of Simon as I spoke.

Simon didn't reply, he simply glanced at Sidi and shook my arm off. Although Sidi had seemed apprehensive when the staff first mentioned this particular marabout he had seemed to warm to the idea of using her. Sidi simply nodded and said, "O.K., Helen, do all she says." Glancing at me he added, "What do you think she will do to you? She is here to help us."

I was not convinced nor did I understand Sidi's change of mind towards this woman, but as Simon collected his papers I collected my perfumes. Simon and Sidi once again left, leaving me at the mercy of this strange woman. I was very scared and my hand shook as I handed over the perfume. It brought to mind a novel I had read about Marie Leveaux, the last Voodoo Queen of New Orleans. The marabout requesting personal belongings of mine was reminiscent of things I had read in this book. Although I was sceptical about jujus, I was uneasy about my present circumstances, and felt things were out of my control.

Amid voices that rose to a crescendo, my perfume was added to the mixture in the bucket, which was destined to become juju juice. The concoction, in spite of its importance was stirred with a very ordinary looking stick. It was not only stirred by the marabout, but also by each member of staff in turn. I was offered the stick, but declined saying I preferred just to watch. It was now apparently perfected.

In a seemingly uncontrollable trance the marabout commenced flinging both herself and her juju juice around our garden. The staff, following her lead also worked themselves into a frenzy. I stood in the background watching in complete bewilderment. To my utter horror she flung a substantial amount of the foul smelling concoction directly at me. I was drenched, the smell was vile and I was certain that I was going to vomit. Heedless of any offence I might give and in desperation to escape from this woman and her magic, I hurried into the house, tearing off my clothes as I went. I almost ran into the shower and scrubbed my skin and my hair in a desperate attempt to remove the liquid and its smell that seemed to surround me. Half a bottle of shower gel and shampoo later, I dried myself, dressed and went downstairs to find that the woman had left. Jed came to speak to me. "You upset our marabout," he explained to me. "You shouldn't have walked away when she was trying to help us. That was an insult to her."

"She upset me flinging her foul smelling liquid all over me."

"You mustn't say these things, you are insulting her again! This is juju juice. Sometimes it has to smell bad to do good things. This juice was made especially to deal with our problems, you will see how it will work, and then you won't insult her anymore. She wanted to scatter her juice in the bar and the beer garden, but decided it may be better if we do it to-night after the customers have left."

I felt great relief on hearing this. What would the customers have thought of this cultural entertainment?

"She has also given me this stick." Jed continued as he showed me a stick, which to me looked as if was a stick that had been picked up in our garden. "At 8 o'clock tomorrow morning the staff must beat the sacred tree with it. Is that O.K. with you?"

"Yeah, fine."

The 'sacred tree' was an exceptionally large coconut tree in our garden. We had been told that when it was only bush land where The Dominion now stood, a 'holy man' from the neighbouring country visited, and preached under this tree. He chose it as it was the tallest tree in the area, and provided the most shade, for his congregation. The story goes that when The Dominion was built, this tree was the only one that wasn't cut down, as it would offend the locals to do so. Legend has it that when this tree dies, The Dominion will also die. It is a fact that the tree bears fruit continually which is very unusual but as to its link with the life of The Dominion only time will tell.

That evening after we had closed, Jed stayed behind to douse the bar, and the beer garden with the marabout's juju juice. Observed by Simon, our two security boys, and myself, Jed set about his task, which he took very seriously. I was relieved to see that he preformed this duty in an orderly manner. I had been afraid he was going to go into a trance like state, similar to that of the marabout during the afternoon. On completion of his task, a very smug looking Jed went home obviously satisfied that he had done his chore to the marabout's specifications.

Early the following morning the staff assembled for the ceremonial 'tree beating'. Simon and I were surprised to see the number of staff that had arrived. We had only expected the staff on duty to take part in this. The eagerness of so many of them wishing to be involved, bought home to us the importance of this to our staff, and made us realize that we had made the right decision, allowing them to involve a marabout of their choice. The 'tree beating' began at 8 o'clock prompt. The staff formed an orderly queue, all striking the tree several times before passing the stick to the next in line. The poor tree was hit with great force. I was very confused as to what was being achieved by this beating. Surely a 'sacred tree' is good, so why beat it?

Sidi stood behind Jed, and despite the fact that we had noticed they were not often on friendly terms they were chatting whilst waiting their turn to beat the tree. Jed took the stick from Momodou, who was in line before him. He struck the tree twice with great force, on his third strike, as he swung the stick backwards he hit Sidi in the face with it. After completing his strike he gave the stick to Sidi and apologised.

"Sorry, sorry, I didn't know you were so close to me. Are you alright?"

"O.K., O.K., it stung at first, but is O.K. now."

Over the next few weeks, Sidi's face and left eye were swollen, the result of an infection, according to the local medical centre. This whole incident played on my mind. First my perfume was used in the juju juice that was thrown over me, and now Sidi was hit with the 'blessed stick'. This was probably of no significance, but over the coming years, I wondered many times about this episode.

The staff were more settled now that they were confident that their marabout's intervention had secured their jobs. Meanwhile, Simon and I sat back patently waiting for the court case to start. We were hoping this would once and for all solve all our problems in Shendi.

As Simon was returning to The Dominion, early one evening, after walking Sally, he was stopped by a Peace Haven a security guard, as he entered the car park.

"Excuse me, sorry sir but we believe you have been having problems with Mr. Stairs."

"Well, yes, you know we have. You have seen some of the problems we've had." Simon replied.

"He has been causing big problems for us also. But there is no need for you to worry about him anymore; we have taken care of him!"

"What do you mean?" Simon asked.

"We have taken out a strong juju against him. He won't be around much longer."

"What do you mean by, won't be around?"

"This is a very strong juju; he will die, probably within the next two weeks."

Back at The Dominion Simon repeated his conversation with the security guard to me.

"I don't know how I feel about this." I said.

"Well one thing is for certain, it will certainly put jujus to the test."

"Yeah, it will, but Simon, I really don't like all this witchcraft stuff, and I can't understand your interest in it all. Can't you just leave the locals to get on with it, and make out we don't want to know about it?"

"You don't believe in it, so why does it bother you?"

"I may not believe in it, but all this is making me very uneasy."

It was true, I didn't believe in jujus, but I was also very wary of them. Did Africans have powers that Europeans know nothing of, or was it supposition that sometimes appeared to make them happen. If the latter was the case, jujus may work against other Africans, but not on westerners like Mr. Stairs.

The following week, when I returned from taking Sally for her walk, I also was stopped by the Peace Haven security.

"Did your husband tell you we have taken care of Mr. Stairs?" I was asked.

"Oh, yes. Simon has told me this."

"Well it has worked. We told your husband it would. You taubabs don't always believe what we say; you know nothing of juju's powers. Anyway Stairs won't be causing any of us any problems now."

"What do you mean? He hasn't died has he?"

"Not exactly. Not yet anyway, but he is very ill, and he has left the country, we won't be seeing him back here again."

"Oh right---I'll tell Simon." I really didn't know what else to say, and didn't even think to ask him anymore about what had happened to Mr. Stairs.

I hurried the short distance back to The Dominion. I was eager to recount the conversation I had just had to Simon. He was as astounded as I was by the news I had just heard.

"I wish you had asked more questions of the security guard, Helen. I would have quizzed him on exactly what had happened."

"I know I should have done. I was so taken aback when he told me I just didn't think, but we are bound to hear the full story from someone soon."

Very shortly news of Mr. Stairs' health reached us. Apparently he had been smitten by a mystery illness during the night about five days earlier. In the morning he had been admitted to a nearby private clinic, where perplexed by his symptoms, they had him transferred to the general hospital in Port Albert. Two days later, with his undiagnosed illness getting progressively worse, he boarded a U.K. flight by stretcher. Whether he survived his illness or not, we never did learn but he never returned to Shendi. At the time, we experienced a mixture of amazement and disbelief of this whole incident. Looking back from an older and wiser perspective, I can say with almost 100% certainty that Mr. Stairs was poisoned. I was soon to learn that the administration of poisons, whether quick or slow acting, was a preferred local method of dealing with troublesome adversaries.

Chapter Four

Goodbye and Gallstones

I was no stranger to severe headaches having been a migraine sufferer since my early twenties and so when I started with a brutal headache that refused to respond to treatment I was not really surprised. I simply put it down to a reaction to all that had happened in the past few weeks. Nor was I alarmed when after two days I started vomiting. The accompanying fever I just took as part and parcel of all the anxieties and stress of starting our new life in the middle of the rainy season with its associated humidity. It took my husband, not normally the most observant of men, to make me aware that this was no ordinary migraine and that I was, in fact, rather ill.

"You really don't look good, Helen," he remarked, "I think we should get you to a doctor."

"Nonsense," I replied, "It is only a severe migraine brought on by the stress of settling in. I am taking my tablets, I will be fine. Anyway where could we go? We haven't yet found ourselves a doctor, there has been so much else to do."

"A doctor will be no problem. The staff tell me that Maria always used a private clinic, not far from here. How about me taking you up there? You really don't look well."

"Not now, "I snapped, "I'm fine, fine, OK. But if you really want to help, you could sort out some of the stock." Then, realising how rare it was for Simon to comment on how I might be feeling and to offer to do something about it, I added in a more conciliatory tone, "If I am no better tomorrow I will go."

As the evening went on, I knew that I had made the wrong decision. I was getting progressively worse. My headache, while similar to migraine, lacked some of its blinding characteristics. Although Simon was becoming more and more troubled by my worsening condition, he was also less and less sympathetic as I had not taken up his offer of a visit to the clinic. The next morning my fever was worse and Simon firmly said,"Now, there will be no arguing. As soon as Sidi arrives he will drive us to the clinic"

This must have happened, although due to my condition, my memories of the journey and the consultation are very vague. As Simon had suspected, but had not mentioned, I had malaria which as we were both to learn is an occupational hazard of living and working in Africa. Although we had considered it a potential risk when discussing the decision to move here, it had only been a possibility. Now, as I lay in my dingy room in the clinic only a few weeks after my arrival, feeling ill and depressed it was no longer just a possibility but a reality. Each time that I drifted off to sleep, I hoped that I would wake up in my own bed, in my own house back on the island and that the malaria along with all the other problems that we had experienced was only part of a nightmarish dream.

It was not to be. Instead I woke up to an African nurse who had obviously not been sufficiently trained in the art of inserting needles into patients' posteriors. Malaria injections have to be given directly into muscles and need to be massaged afterwards to allow the solution to circulate round the body. This is not a pleasant experience. In fact it is a very painful one. At the time of my first bout of malaria, large needles were commonly used but nowadays the needles are smaller. Having been on the receiving end of these malaria injections I later had enormous sympathy with members of my staff who were scared stiff of injections and would run away rather than have one.

As I started to drift off into a delirious, fever ridden sleep, my dreams were haunted by the image of a nurse with a face like that of a 'Spitting Image' puppet, hair tied in braids that clunked and clanged as she moved and holding a three foot long syringe in one of her hands. This was replaced by my own pale white posterior being injected and the injection site rising up and erupting like a volcano. The fact that I was sharing my room with a large community of mosquitoes and a lizard plus the fear of these visions prevented the sound sleep that I needed. The staff of the clinic took great delight in telling me that this lizard which was pale grey and very ugly was the most dangerous African lizard that existed. "He will not bite and only comes out at night. He is attracted to any form of moisture. If you leave your toothbrush out at night he will try and drink from it and leave behind poisonous venom in his saliva," my needle wielding nurse told me. Normally, the mere fact of a lizard in the room would not have worried me, but in my feverish state I was terrified. The fever and my naivety left me vulnerable to the local folk lore. Now my dreams included a monster lizard gorging itself on my toothbrush. It was only later, as I recovered that I learnt that my room mate was in fact a gecko and to be encouraged into any house as they fed mainly on a diet of mosquitoes.

Fortunately, once on the correct medication and in spite of the pain of its administration, my health soon started improving. I was very relieved when the doctor told me that I could be discharged. Even though I had wished to wake up back on the island, the thought of returning to The Dominion seemed so much more favourable than my 'home' of the last few days. If this was the clinic used by Maria and her family, I was not impressed. I had had a fairly large room to myself but it had been dingy and dirty. The bed was never changed even though with my high temperature I was sweating profusely and no-one on the staff even asked if I had washed or showered. In fact the only time I saw the staff was when I was due to have an injection. The toilet and shower private but not en – suite. They were down the corridor a few yards away. I have never run a marathon but after crossing this distance in a fevered state, I know how the runners must feel. Every foot felt like a mile and once there I had to negotiate the water jump. Between the toilet and the sink was a pool of water but it was not clear which one was leaking. Given my shaky condition and the unappealing look of the shower, I decided to give showering a miss. Instead I freshened up at the sink, taking care to stand astride the pool of water, which was not an easy thing to do when quivering with fever.

As I left, my nurse with the coloured braids advised me to go home, place plenty of ice between two tea towels and sit on the resulting 'cushion'. She assured me it would help my bruises and soreness and I thanked her for her advice. Back at The Dominion I simply sank into a chair too relived to worry about cushions of ice. Although I was tired for quite a time after this first bout of malaria, slowly my health improved. (When Simon went down with his first bout of the dreaded malaria, he was determined not to return to the clinic and instead consulted Pedro, a doctor from Cuba, who with many of his compatriots, was stationed out here. As a result, although Simon did suffer very badly, he suffered it in the much more comfortable surroundings of The Dominion.)

Shortly after I returned to perfect health – or what passed for perfect health in my case – Ousman, our lawyer, gave us the date of our first court appearance. We were pleased, hoping that soon everything would be resolved as even after the marabout's visit, the staff were on edge. They were adamant that The Peace Haven had a rival marabout staying in one of the Avenue Rooms (which were adjacent to our garden) and insisted that he was spying on us. An incident with a large hornet-like insect, soon after my return from the clinic, only confirmed their opinions. One evening a large flying insect flew over the wall from the direction of The Peace

Haven. The staff came running to inform us that it had been sent by the rival marabout.

"Helen, Helen, that insect. If it touches us we will die" gasped Jed.

"Nonsense," I retorted. "It is only a hornet."

"Oh no, Helen. You must listen. Make her listen, Simon. It has been sent by a very important marabout from The Peace Haven. It is spying on us and will report back to him. It must not touch anyone at all", added another of the waiters.

I shrugged and walked away. We had a bar full of customers to look after and the antics of an insect were unimportant. The hornet flew into the crowded bar and customers looked on with amusement as the staff tried to serve them, all the while ducking and diving to avoid the attentions of the hornet. The noise level rose quickly as yells and screams from the waiters were added to the usual evening hubbub. Eventually, the inevitable happened and one of the waiters dropped a tray of drinks in his attempt to avoid certain death. "This has gone on for long enough," I told Simon. "I will get rid of this hornet and perhaps we can carry on working normally."

"Be careful," he said anxiously,

"Surely, you don't believe in all that nonsense"

"No, well not really. It is just that I don't want you to upset the staff otherwise we will get no work done at all."

Seizing a newspaper and rolling it up as I went, I marched out from behind the bar to face the flying hornet. After a few failed attempts, I managed to administer a fatal blow and swept it up, expecting everyone to be relieved that I had halted the marabout's attack on us. This was another example of my naivety in the face of African beliefs. Anything sent by a marabout could be resisted or avoided but on no account could it be destroyed. Jed was most concerned. "You must be very careful. First you insult the lady marabout when she was trying to help and now you have killed the insect belonging to The Peace Haven's marabout. Do you not know that he will be waiting for it to return and will be very angry when it does not come back?"

"But you said it would kill anyone it touched. I thought it would be best to kill it before it could kill anyone."

"It is better to let the insect kill you than you make a marabout angry", was his reply.

"Oh really?" was all I managed to say as I returned to the bar and continued to serve our customers.

Eventually the court date arrived and dressed in smart clothes we made our way to the court house, hoping that all would go our way. In the event, all our anticipation, all our hopes were wasted. Nothing happened we were simply granted an adjournment very early in the proceedings. As we left the court wondering what the adjournment meant, fortunately we were not aware that this was only the first step on what would be a marathon court battle. I now know that this granting of an adjournment is quite normal in the judicial system of this and perhaps other, African countries but at the time I found it very unsettling.

I was uncertain about our next step but Simon argued vociferously for continuing with planned renovations. He felt that it was important we show The Peace Haven that we were unperturbed by their threats of closure. Whilst I agreed with him, I argued that his plans were too adventurous for the stage we were at but despite my reservations we went ahead with an extensive and expensive redesign of the beer garden with its old, unfriendly concrete surface. The existing lighting, which consisted of a few lights with their flex wound round tree branches, was changed to street type lamps with flex in conduits under our new slabs. I had to agree that this was an essential repair as not only was the existing flex an eye sore, it was incredibly dangerous. Most of the plastic covering the wire was cracked with the heat of the sun and as we were now well into the rainy season anyone switching the lights on took their life in their hands.

The other major alterations in the garden were more cosmetic. We - or rather our staff working alongside Simon – enlarged the pond, built a water feature using small rocks from the beach, installed a pump and replaced the bridge. We added new plants and enlarged the seating area near to the fountain. In time this became one of the most popular spots in the garden with its sound of trickling water and shaded as it was by a huge tree which we were told was a candelabra tree, although no one could confirm this. Although the customers liked the tree for its shade and beautiful yellow flowers, it was not popular with the locals. The staff who would use roots, leaves, flowers and seeds from most plants in the garden for medicinal reasons, stayed well clear of this one and could not or would not explain why. Simon then constructed a stage at the far end of the garden. We intended to have cultural entertainment during the high season. This was to be in addition to Jele, the kora player who came every night to entertain our customers. The kora is a traditional Mandinka stringed instrument and is played in many parts of West Africa. Our customers enjoyed listening as Jele sat plucking the three strings singing both traditional local and popular songs and he was always well rewarded with schilling notes stuffed into the body of the kora. One of his sure fire money earning techniques involved simply talking to the tourists and then saying farewell by incorporating their names into a song. It never failed to earn him extra money and I was very impressed with the way he always found words to rhyme with strange European names.

Once all the alterations were completed, Simon was eager to embark on Stage 2. He planned to construct several additional buildings including two shops for use by the jeweller and the dressmaker who already sold their wares in The Dominion. He was also very keen to build a house at the side of the garden for the staff to use as a room in which they would be able to shower, eat and rest. Included in this part of the plans was a mosque. The provision of the mosque pleased the staff who were overjoyed when its presence was graced by a visit from the local imams. After many years of rebelling against religion (probably in response to a deeply religious childhood) Simon was showing a keen interest in Islam and he felt that by providing his staff with a mosque he could show his commitment to his new-found faith. They were even more pleased when Simon, once a professed atheist, began to wear Muslim robes on a Friday and fast with them during Ramadan.

Simon and the staff were full of glee as our empire grew and attributed it to the intervention of the lady marabout. As Jed said, "These good fortunes and the way the business in prospering are due to the lady marabout. You must give thanks for what she has done." I remained sceptical but said nothing. In the end, watching how our savings fell as quickly as the walls rose, I had to say something. I managed to persuade Simon to call a halt to the building work until the following low season. As all the blockwork was up and all that remained to add were doors, windows and a roof he reluctantly agreed.

There was a very positive atmosphere during these changes. Everybody, staff, Simon and I felt that we were making headway and that our initial difficult start was behind us. Even the fact that Simon was called to court as a witness in our fight with The Peace Haven failed to put much of a dent in the air of optimism. Once more we made our way to the courthouse but this time there was no quick adjournment. Instead it was a very long drawn out experience as all evidence was written in long hand by the judge and many witnesses had forgotten the question before they were asked to answer. The whole atmosphere of the room was threatening; it was hot and stuffy despite all the fans whirring away and the open windows high up in the wall. In fact the fans simply served to stir up the dust which covered every surface and the open windows simply served to let in the noise of the city centre traffic. In addition to the blaring of horns and squeal of brakes there were the shouts and yells from heated discussions both from outside and inside the court building. This tumult was added to by frequent arguments within the body of the court so, all in all, it was very difficult to hear what was being said. Although the court proceedings were carried out in English, the mere fact that the lawyers were facing the judge, not the public, coupled to the strong accents of some of the participants made it very difficult to hear what was happening especially when, as sometimes happened, the discussions would drift into one of the local languages.

I found the courtroom very frightening but Simon seemed to have no fears. He assured me that he had a very strong juju in his pocket, provided for just this occasion. Sidi had given him this, which was a knotted piece of string, that morning, so I was not to worry, all would be well. Simon took the stand and faced the lawyer representing The Peace Haven. Ousman, who was fighting our corner, had told us that the opposition lawyer was a lady who had a reputation for ruthlessness, so despite Simon's juju, I was understandably nervous. Many of the questions asked seemed to bear little, if any, relation to what we were trying to establish – our right to continue using our entrance. Even now, I cannot see how some of the questions he was asked ,such as how many times our dog walked through the car park or where our driver parked our car, had to do with the problem. As time went on, I noticed his hand straying more and more often to the pocket containing the juju as if he needed the reassurance it provided. Finally, after three or more hours of this, Simon was allowed to step down. I was more than grateful that it was he and not I that had gone through this ordeal. For once I was grateful for the secondary position held by women in this society and for the fact that The Dominion was in Simon's name not mine. The next witness to be called was Mr. Smithers and we waited with bated breath to hear his evidence. Unfortunately, the court was adjourned before he could take the stand. He was due to be out of the country on the date suggested for the next sitting and so we would have to wait until a convenient day could be decided upon. At that point, I really did not care if I never saw the court room again. The heat, the noise, the many distractions and very long winded nature of the whole process had taken it out of me. I simply wanted to return to The Dominion and a long, cool orange drink, and Simon was in need of a beer.

It was now the beginning of November and the business, mainly from the ex-pats, had grown satisfactorily over the last few weeks and so as we moved into the dry season and the start of the tourist season we were optimistic for the months ahead. We were also determined to present ourselves to The Peace Haven as a thriving and successful concern despite their attempts to thwart us. This was even more important when we remembered Mr. Smithers forecast of closure by Christmas. Nothing could have prepared us for the opening of the tourist season. We were accustomed to the weekly flight from the UK and then the flood gates opened. Suddenly there were seven flights on a Friday and more on Tuesdays and Thursdays and the quiet area outside the hotels was alive with pale skinned Europeans eager to find some winter sun. We were determined to have a share of this market and as such made plans to attract them to the new Dominion. Although when we had first visited the country the previous year we had been amazed at the number of repeat visitors, we had not realised what this might mean for our business. As the flights from the UK and other parts of northern Europe swamped the airport, their passengers made their way to their regular haunts. To our delight our own Dominion was one of these and attempts by the security staff at Peace Haven's arch to deter our visitors were a complete failure. These regulars were determined to support us in our fight with Peace Haven and many have remained friends until this day.

However, we could not rely solely on regulars, we had to attract new custom and so, using the newly built stage in the beer garden and like many of the bars and hotels, including The Peace Haven, we instituted regular concerts. The customers liked it and it did attract new trade. Perhaps, Simon had been right and this would be a fresh start, not only for The Dominion, but also and more importantly, for us. I was not fully convinced but it was certainly easy to project a confident face to the customers and staff. In fact I felt secure enough to agree to his absence the day before we were due in court for another hearing despite the fact that that evening we were having one of our weekly entertainment shows. It was to be a complete African cultural experience with dancers, musicians, fire-eaters, snake swallowers and stilt-walkers, but we had held such evenings before and I was certain of my ability to manage the bar on my own. The evening was a success. All of the acts had been well received and the bar was full both inside and out with many diners staying to watch the show and ordering extra drinks. In the middle of the busy bar a tourist came up to me. He thrust his face towards me and barked, "You are the owner, aren't you? I need to talk to you. My wallet has been stolen with all my money. It was the fire-eater. He was hanging around our table for ages. What are you going to do about it? You will have to call the police. What sort of entertainers are you employing anyway? You will have to call the police before they leave. What are you waiting for, go and call them now!"

Calling the police was not easy. There were only two police cars, one always with the president and one kept in the capital. I had to send a taxi to fetch the police who were not pleased at being called out to investigate a theft from a tourist. While waiting for them to arrive we had kept the entertainers on and also searched the area around where the tourist had been sitting for the wallet to no avail. When the police arrived they started to question the entertainers and I sent the staff to search the garden once again. Momodou, one of the waiters, came rushing in, clutching a wallet in his hand. It was the missing item complete with contents. "It must have fallen out of his pocket," he said, "it was on the ground near the table he was sitting at." It did cross my mind to wonder how the first search had missed the wallet but I was too relieved at its discovery to ask difficult questions. Three disgruntled groups of people then left: the police; irritated with being called out on a wild goose chase, the tourist party, annoyed at the losing of the wallet, and the entertainers; bitter about being suspected of theft.

Fortunately the bar was still full of customers but they too were becoming disgruntled. Many were complaining of overdue meals and as I struggled to serve drinks, I realised that I was the only person working. Where on earth were the bar staff and waiters? Asking customers to wait for a moment (I did not like to mention that I had lost all my staff, it would seem a very careless thing to do especially in view of the 'lost' wallet) I went in search of them. Stepping through the gates I saw a sight worthy of a scene in a Western. The car park, which was lit only by a light near the entrance to the hotel and the glow from surrounding buildings, seemed to be a mass of struggling figures, some of whom bore more than a passing resemblance to my staff. It was my staff. They were fighting with the entertainers. I was just in time to see one of the dancers hit one of my waiters around the head with her handbag. It was a mighty blow and as he reeled back in surprise straight into my arms, I understood the meaning of the term 'handbagging'. I grabbed him, turned him round and while he was still reeling from the blow, demanded an explanation of the scene. It appeared that the entertainers had taken exception to a remark made by one of the staff regarding the missing wallet and the entertainers. The resulting scuffles were the result of each side trying to uphold their honour. With my appearance on the scene, the scuffles ended and my staff made their way back into the bar and the hungry and thirsty customers. With our court appearance early next day, a disturbance of that magnitude in the hotel's car park was something we could have done without. Realizing that staff from The Peace Haven would have been avid witnesses of the fight and would also know all the details of the missing wallet was a huge concern. We did not want The Peace Haven claiming that our presence was detrimental to their business. As it happened the court hearing was simply another adjournment and was over in less time than the time taken to sort out the missing wallet.

Around this time there were two other incidents in the country which really brought it home to us that we were living in another culture. In one week a 15 year old girl was raped whilst in police custody and in a separate incident a boy who was being held in a fire station (because there was no room in police cells) was made to eat cement and subsequently died. In both cases no action was taken against the guilty parties. Although very little information about either case was reported in the press, the news spread quickly. As a result of these two incidents there was much unrest amongst the students. They organised what was advertised as a peaceful protest march in the capital for a few days later.

On the day of the march, Sidi was out shopping with Tani the chef. He phoned us in somewhat of a panic. I answered the phone in the office where I was doing some of the never-ending paper work whilst Simon was out working in the garden. "Helen," yelled Sidi, "there are big problems by the police station. You know the students were marching; well it has got really bad. They've broken into the police station, released all the prisoners and have set the police station on fire. I don't believe it, how could they? Now they are pulling people out of their cars and telling them to go. They've turned cars over and set them on fire. The place is a mass of flames and smoke and we can't get to the market. What shall we do?"

I called Simon saying I needed him quickly and asked Sidi where exactly he was.

"Near the market. I can see the flames from the police station and I can hear the students, they are getting closer. What shall we do, Helen we can't stay here?" I quickly filled Simon in with what was happening. I could hear Tani in the background telling Sidi that the students were getting closer and in fact, I could hear shouts and screams over the phone.

"Both of you, come back here at once, your safety is much more important than the shopping," I ordered. Simon nodded in agreement and made a grab for the phone to add his support. However, Sidi had already rung off; he was so desperate to get away from the riots.

When they returned they were greeted as returning warriors by the staff, who already knew what was happening despite the fact that neither Simon nor I had said anything to them. Several of us went out into the car park to try and find out what we could. As we stood near the entrance to The Peace Haven, we heard what, at first, I thought was a series of car back fires but I quickly realized was gun fire. It seemed very close, almost at the top of the road.

"Surely that can't be all gun fire", I observed, more for something to say than anything.

"It is. They are shooting at the children outside the police station," replied Sidi.

"Shooting? Not with real ammunition? Surely not at children? They will use rubber bullets won't they?"

"Rubber bullets – what are they?"

"They are bullets made of rubber. They stun whoever they hit. So they will stun the students and the riot will stop. They must be rubber bullets; they wouldn't shoot children with live ammunition."

"We don't know about rubber bullets. They are shooting the children. This will teach them a lesson because they are out of control. It will be proper ammunition. We cannot have unruly children here. "

I gasped and walked slowly back to the safety of the bar. It was certainly a different way of life to that of the island I had left only a few months before.

The events of the Student Riots were the hottest topic of conversation for a few days but were very quickly relegated to history, especially when fresh plane loads of tourists came in. Nothing could be allowed to interfere with the tourism industry and although we too had a vested interest in this, we were amazed at how quickly the locals seem to forget and dismiss any attempt to discuss the trouble. Over the coming months, we found out a little more about what became known as the Student Riots but most of our information came through the unofficial grapevine as there was little in the official press for us to read. Although the official death toll was 26, with the youngest victim being aged 3, it was generally agreed that this was a gross underestimation. We knew of a Red Cross worker who was caught in cross fire and died almost immediately. The official verdict of the inquest, which the Red Cross had insisted on, was death by natural causes.

The low season was fast approaching and it was time to take stock of what we had achieved. Our concerns over our ability to attract new customers now seemed unfounded. Not only had we managed to retain the regular tourist costumers but we were also attracting new customers both expat and tourist. We were particularly pleased with the way some of the Cuban doctors had become regulars and we valued both their professional advice and their views on life in Africa. However, running a bar was hard work and my dream of being almost a lady of leisure with time for long swims and charity work had proved to be just that – a dream. There was no time for swimming and we regretted becoming involved with the charity. There was too much for us to do, running our business without taking on the roles of Chairman and Secretary. Added to this were the difficulties of communication between the UK and Africa (this was in the days before mobiles and e-mail became common place), plus the UK Committee did not always fully understand the complexities of working in a different culture. Reluctantly, early in the New Year we had tended our resignations and although we continued to let them store goods in our garage, had no more involvement in its day-to-day affairs.

Simon was still keen to carry on with the renovations although he had unwillingly called a halt on major building projects until we had more money behind us; I was still concerned that we were spending too much. Every time I voiced my concerns, he accused me of pessimism and inventing things to worry about. I was apprehensive both for us and for the staff. Many businesses in the tourist industry laid off their staff in the low season. I was determined not to do this as the local Social Security system did not allow such staff to claim benefits and I knew that many of our staff were the sole breadwinners for their families. Finally, shortly after the Student Riots and after a great deal of insisting on my part, Simon and I sat down and started to discuss the next few months.

I explained all my concerns, the court case, my wish to keep the staff on, the cost of the renovations and the drop in income that would soon be upon us with the low season.

Simon's grew more and more impatient as my list of concerns lengthened. Tapping his fingers on the table he snapped, "You are over reacting again Helen. For goodness sake start looking on the bright side. Yes, sure we are short of money but we have been short of money before and we have always pulled through."

I looked at him; yes we had been short of money before but never 3000 miles from home in a strange country. Before I could say anything else he added, "If things get really bad, I will go back home and work. It is Dale's wedding next month and I've been thinking that I will probably go back for that anyway."

My mouth fell open. To say that I was astonished is an understatement. This was the first time in all our months there that Simon had even mentioned going back. We couldn't go back and then I realised he had not talked about us going back only himself. What was he thinking?

"What are you talking about? Going back? Are you suggesting that I stay here and keep the bar going? Simon that's just horrible. I can't do it. I'm sorry but I don't fancy being here alone. It's impractical anyway if you do go back to work, you will not be able to save that much money as you will need some to live on." (Knowing my husband as I did, I thought it more than likely he would need all of it to live on.)

Simon stood and short temperedly pushed his chair back. "Don't get hysterical. There's no problem. You know you can cope with running the bar, especially in low season and anyway," he said, walking out of the door, "I haven't made up my mind yet. I might not go, so I am not prepared to discuss it." The door shut firmly behind him and I was left wondering what on earth my husband meant to do.

Before I could get another chance to talk it over with him, we both had to go to see our lawyer and discuss the progress of the court case. This was the first time I had been to Ousman's office since our initial meeting to pay for licenses and as he and Simon discussed tactics, I noticed that the office was even more dingy looking than last time. My eyes wandered from the grimy window, past the tattered grey curtains hanging from a rough wooden pole to the filing cabinet whose top was covered in papers and files. Were the drawers empty or did they too contain bulging files? I wondered. Just as my eyes came to rest on Ousman's feet which were propped up on his cluttered and battered desk, I heard Simon ask, "If I was out of the country, would Helen have any problems running the business, being as it is entirely in my name?"

I sat bolt upright in my chair as Ousman replied, "Well legally no. You could be an absentee landlord and Helen could be appointed manageress. But, I have to warn you Simon, that Helen would find it hard. It is not easy for women running businesses here, she would have many problems."

"Hmm, well it is just an idea at the moment. I just wondered if it was possible," my husband replied. The conversation then returned to the court case but it was clear to me that Simon was serious about going home and leaving me here to run the business. I wondered if this was why Simon had decided to take me along to Ousman's office. In Africa, women were expected to be seen and not heard especially in business and I certainly had not been included in any earlier discussions.

Despite my concerns I did not raise it on the way home. Sidi, as usual, was driving us and it was not the sort of thing I wanted to discuss in front of a third party. On our return, it was lunchtime and we were both thrust straight into dealing with our lunchtime trade. In between serving customers and making out bills I had time to think and decided not to say anything until later. It was no good saving for the afternoon walk, Simon very rarely accompanied me now, so the first chance I would have would be in the evening. Hopefully then we would find time when we could both sit down and discuss the matter without interruptions. However, the chance to be on our own came sooner than I thought.

Early that afternoon I was in the office preparing the staff wages for the following day when Simon came in. I stood up and shut the door. Despite my intention of not discussing the mater until the evening, I found myself asking, "This morning, you asked Ousman, if I could run the business on my own, how serious are you about going back?"

"Serious. My plane leaves in an hour. Sidi is waiting to run me to the airport. I've just come in to see if you want to come along and see me off".

"What, but but but you can't," I stammered, not really believing that this was happening. "You can't leave me here alone. We haven't discussed it. I thought it was just an idea."

"You knew I was going."

"I didn't, Simon you simply can't go"

"I can and I am. This is the last week of the season, so I can get a cheap ticket at the airport from one of the holiday reps. If I wait until next week when low season starts the price of tickets will go up. The season is over, you will cope."

I was speechless, as he walked out of the office. However, I pulled myself together and watched as he collected some things and took them to Sidi's car. I climbed into the back seat and the three of us drove to the airport. Simon and Sidi chatted as if this was a normal journey but I found my self unable to say anything. I wanted to scream at him, I wanted to stop the car and talk over the problem, I wanted to cry, I wanted to go home but I simply sat there and said nothing. At the airport Simon was able to buy a ticket as he had predicted. With no more than a casual wave and a few parting words he walked through to check in and so out of my sight.

"Shall we go and see the plane off?" suggested Sidi.

I looked at him blankly. My husband of over 30 years had gone without so much as a goodbye kiss, what was I going to do? "Yes, yes that will be fine." I muttered.

Sidi and I went to the viewing point and watched Simon's plane take-off. That was it, he was gone and I was still here. What was I to do?

Slowly I made my way back to the car, still struggling to believe that in the space of a few hours I had been abandoned in Shendi. I climbed into the front seat and tried to make conversation with Sidi. His casual mention that Simon had told him the day before that he would need him to drive to the airport for the afternoon flight, left me speechless. Why hadn't Simon said something to me? Didn't I count anymore? What was going on? By the time we pulled up at The Dominion, I was numb.

Back at the bar, I had customers to attend to and staff to keep occupied. They all of course knew that Simon had gone back home and were wondering what difference it would make to their working lives. In bed that night, listening to the sound of the sea beyond Peace Haven, I felt really alone. Simon had gone, out of the country not simply on an up country trip, and the whole weight of the business was now on my shoulders. I decided that his leaving had been inevitable. Life in our new homeland was very different and difficult. Simon had had malaria twice, the first time very badly and I think the affair of the student riots had shaken him more than I had realised. Furthermore we had had many disagreements concerning the running of the business and the treatment of the locals. After each incident or set back it appeared that his eagerness for life in Africa diminished. Instead of cementing our marriage it appeared that Africa had dissolved it.

Next morning, before any of the bar staff were around, I threw on a dress and went down stairs into the garden. There was no sign of the night watchman, as it was daylight, he was probably asleep. I walked over to the stage and looked around. With the garden empty of staff and customers, I could see that the alterations had been worth all the money spent on them. The water feature looked good, the terrace was smooth and easy to walk on, the plants were an array of colours and the stage was fantastic. I turned around to see the wall of The Peace Haven. My good mood dissolved. We hadn't been here a year and Simon was gone. How had things turned so sour? Was it my fault? Had my disenchantment on arrival made me exaggerate the faults? Was it Simon's fault? In his enthusiasm to adopt local culture had he left me behind? Was it our problems with The Peace Haven and the mounting pressures of a court case that was heading nowhere? Was it the continual problem of working alongside locals who, I felt, resented working for expats? Perhaps we had been slow to appreciate the difficulty of running a business in an alien culture.

Undoubtedly it was a combination of all these things that had caused Simon to go. My mind travelled back to our parting at the airport. Simon stood there, ticket in one hand, passport in the other anxious to go through to check in.

"Just carry on as best you can. Don't let those bastards next door get the better of you", were his parting words of advice.

"How long are you going to be away?" I asked.

"Don't know"

"You are coming back though aren't you?"

"What do you think?"

"I don't know. That is why I am asking", I said as with a final shrug of his shoulders, he went through the door to check in. Now, in our garden that he had worked so hard to improve, I realized that I was truly on my own. Simon had left me with no indication of when or even if he would be back. I was firmly convinced that he would not come back, but had lacked the courage to tell me so. He had simply gone, without showing any interest in how I would cope without him.

I had to face facts. I was on my own, three thousand miles away from home. I had nothing in my name, no property, no bank account. I had a court case against the neighbouring hotel. I did have customers that I was on friendly terms with, but we had not been there long enough to make real friends and there was no-one I felt I could rely on. I was also sure, having listened to ex-pats in the bar and having experienced some small problems as a woman boss, that I would not find it as easy as Simon had to manage the staff. Despite all this I was determined to make a go of The Dominion. It would mean more work for me, much more and I would have to find staff to do some of the heavy work that Simon had done, but I would do it. I would show Simon and everyone else that I, Helen, could cope and what is more, not only cope but make a success of it on my own. With that thought, I finished my analysis of the past and future, got off the stage and walked into the bar showing much more authority than I felt. With a clear and steady voice, I gave the staff their instructions for the day. I knew the odds were stacked against me but I was determined that they would learn who was "Boss Lady".

It was not easy. On reflection I did not cope nearly as well as I considered I was doing at the time. Sidi's guidance was invaluable in those early days. With his help I struggled through. I was still very unaware of how the country worked. It is a long and gradual process for any outsider to come to terms with the structures in a foreign country, especially one with a completely different cultural system to the one familiar from childhood. One thing was extremely urgent. We had recently received notice of closure for failure to file applications for our licenses. Sidi and I had only a few days to complete and return these forms which were essential if we were to stay open. Simon had taken a very belligerent attitude towards their completion, refusing to allow me to fill them in. "If they want my money they will have to come at get it", was his comment the first time I mentioned it to him. After that he refused to discuss it with me. Between us, Sidi and I filled in the forms and we were granted our licenses, due in no small part to the intervention of some of Sidi's family and friends. In such a small country it was inevitable that everyone knew someone in a position of authority and the use of such connections to obtain favours was the norm.

Over the next few weeks I came to the conclusion that in many ways it was easier on my own and I realized, to my shame, that the feelings I had felt as his plane took off had included one of relief. It became easier to run the business, doing the necessary paper work, taking decisions and talking with suppliers without the constant private battles that had become so much of our lives. It certainly became easier with Sidi's help to manage the staff who, in the short time we had been there, had become masters at playing Simon and I off against each other. Now, there was only one person in authority and that was me. Despite being a woman and a foreigner at that, I felt that I was succeeding although the opposite was probably more accurate.

Sidi and I were spending more and more time together and it was almost inevitable that our casual friendship developed into something that for a brief interval had a greater meaning. However, I become conscious of the fact that I was putting myself in a very vulnerable position. Sidi came from a very influential family who had close links with the president, the very president who had recently acquired huge financial interests in The Peace Haven. The mere thought of being up in court against presidential interests was scary enough. However, should Sidi's family turn against me then the Dominion's closure was a foregone conclusion. Very carefully, I returned to the casual friendship that Sidi and I had had and he seemed happy to accept this. He knew that I still needed him to guide me through the legal system and that the staff regarded him as someone of importance. He also knew that as The Dominion prospered, so would he. The staff looked upon him as a mediator, I looked upon him as a friend and we all settled down to work together.

However, it was not long before I started to feel really ill. The symptoms I had displayed on one of my beach walk with Simon a few months before became much more severe and I eventually took the step of discussing them with Pedro when he came into the bar one evening. "Hmm, I think you need to go for an x-ray. I will arrange it and ask Lanso, my brother to look after you. I would do it, but I think you will be better off with someone you know but who is not a friend."

"OK, OK, you do that," I replied, wondering how pains that I had always assumed were caused by nerves and stress and anxiety and all the other components of modern living could show up on x-ray. Must be some new African X-ray machine. Nevertheless Pedro was a doctor and he had after all treated Simon for malaria. He must know what he was talking about. I was reassured to think that Lanso, who was not only Pedro's brother but the top surgeon in the country and often travelled with the president, would be dealing with my case.

Unfortunately, the results of my x-rays showed that I had two large gall stones positioned in such a way as to possibly cause a blockage to my gall bladder. Lanso was insistent that I come into hospital immediately so that he could operate before it became an emergency. I insisted that I needed time to make arrangements for my business. We finally agreed that I would have the operation in a fortnight but if the pain worsened there was to be no arguing, no delay and no prevaricating. I was to go straight in.

During that fortnight's grace I made what arrangements I could for the running of The Dominion. I was due to go into hospital on a Thursday and be discharged on the following Monday. Luckily the Tuesday was a holiday. It was the Muslim festival of Tabaski and I decided to close and allow all my staff to spend the day with their families. This would give me one day of recuperation. However, what to do for the five days of my stay was a much more burning issue. We could not close; I could not afford it especially as I would still have to pay the staff. After discussing matters with Sidi and with some of the ex-pats, I spoke to the staff the day before I was due to go in.

"I am going into hospital tomorrow and will be back on Monday. There should be no problems but if there are ask Sidi if he is here or phone Adam and Jane for advice. They have said that they are only too willing to help, so do not hesitate to phone them. I will leave their number at the back of the bar."

The staff nodded their agreement. I was very grateful to Adam and Jane who had had years of experience in running a bar for their offer of help, but I thought it unlikely that my staff would seek their advice.

Just as I was sorting out the final details, Ousman called and dropped a bombshell that threatened to disrupt all my carefully laid plans. I had to appear in court on Thursday morning at 9.00am, two hours before my hospital appointment. I had no choice, I had to appear in court but I also had no choice about my surgery. The pains by now were very bad and I wondered how close I was to Lanso's threatened emergency. Sidi drove me to the court and I climbed out of the car, clutching papers and an overnight bag. "Helen..." Ousman started.

I interrupted him, "Look, Ousman, I cannot stay long today. I have to be at hospital for an operation at eleven. I cannot afford to be late. The hearing must be over by then."

"No problem," he replied, "the way things have been going recently, I expect another adjournment without much taking place. We will be in and out in no time and you will be able to make it to the hospital on time. Why didn't you say you had an operation? We could have applied for an adjournment."

The thought had simply not occurred to me and even if it had, I think I would have still gone ahead. It was important not to show any weakness in the fight with The Peace Haven.

Ousman was correct. The case, which he had initially predicted would be over in six months and was, now well into its second year, was adjourned again. Luckily for me the hospital and the court were very close together and by eleven o'clock I was booked into the private room that I had arranged on Pedro's advice. "The general wards are noisy and crowded. You will feel ill for a few days after your operation and will benefit from the peace and quiet of a private room", he told me. "They are not too expensive either," he added when he saw the look on my face. I was not sure, private hospital rooms back home were only for the wealthy, which I certainly was not, but when I found out the price for my five day stay, I was pleasantly surprised and decided it would be a good investment.

The room was cluttered but clean and the bed linen, though tattered was also dirt-free. This was a much better room than the one I had endured in the private clinic. And, joy of joys I had my own, spotless en-suite complete with shower. The final icing on the cake was the provision of a balcony which overlooked a crowded street scene. Before I could settle down though, there was the difficult question of blood to overcome, specifically the pint of blood that all patients attending for an operation were supposed to provide. Pedro who was the same blood group as myself, told me not to worry. He would, he assured me, be at the hospital during the operation and stay with me for the first twenty four hours. Therefore if I needed any blood, Pedro could provide it via an arm-to-arm transfusion. However, he had not yet arrived and the admitting doctor insisted that Sidi, who was still with me, donate a pint of blood for the blood bank. Sidi who was terrified of needles and, after my experiences with needles, I could not blame him, turned very pale at the thought of giving blood. As I was left alone in my room, I could hear Sidi and the doctor arguing outside. Their voices were becoming louder and louder and I began to worry. Suddenly the door opened and Sidi came in, grinning from ear to ear.

"I take it from the look on your face that you haven't given blood," I remarked

"No I haven't"

"Coward"

"No problem," he told me. "That stupid doctor. He didn't listen. I told him it was all sorted. He rang Lanso who informed him that if blood was needed, Pedro would provide it. Stupid man. Now, come on and unpack. Everything will be fine, fine. You get yourself well and back at The Dominion. Come on Helen, unpack and settle down."

I unpacked and spent the rest of the day being entertained by the view outside of my window. Across the street from my room was the main entrance to the children's hospital, outside its gates was a small shop, constructed from corrugated iron. Despite the hostial's small size, it was very busy and there was a great deal of pedestrian traffic through its doors. Although this was a back street, the road was busy with people and traffic. The foot traffic was a cosmopolitan mix of locals and tourists. Many of this latter group were probably staying a short distance away at the capital's only hotel and using this street to reach the shops rather than risk the busy main thoroughfare. The traffic was more local, cyclists making their way to and from the market and 'gilly-gillys' the twelve seater mini buses used by the locals for moving around the country. Sitting on my balcony I had a bird's-eye view of the contents of their roof racks. Huge pink and white checked bags bulging with goods from the market were there, as were the expected sacks of rice. What I had not expected to see was that the roof racks appeared to be the main form of animal transport. It seemed that every gilly-gilly that passed beneath me also had at least one sheep or goat tied to the roof rack. (I always found it difficult to tell the difference even at ground level and from above it was nearly impossible. Though with Tabaski only a few days away they were probably sheep.)

I awoke next morning feeling rather poorly and glad that I was finally getting my health sorted it. Once this operation was over and I had recovered from it, I promised myself that I would go from strength to strength and continue building up The Dominion into a thriving business.

My door was thrust open and a large nurse appeared. As she advanced towards me, pulling a drip behind her, I realised that her bedside manner was not going to win her any prizes, a view that was only confirmed as she inserted a catheter into me and put me on a drip. Before I could recover from the aches left behind from her first appearance, she reappeared. "What now?" I muttered to myself, "Has she come back to see if I have survived her first treatment?" But no, there was to be no treatment now. She simply left an operating gown on my bed, and told me to put it on "That's all very well for you to say," I said "but you are not fastened to a drip. How on earth am I going to manage without help?" But she had gone and I was left alone. "Right, come on girl," I said, "this had to be done. First we have to get ourselves out of this nightdress - no problem!" With a series of twists and turns worthy of any contortionist I managed to get the nightdress over my head, pass it up my right arm and over the drip stand where I could let it drop onto the ground. I left it there for later retrieval. Stage one was complete but it was no time to rest on my laurels or even my hospital bed. There was still the very tricky problem of donning my operating gown. I twisted and turned, shrugged and shuffled and at one point seemed to have the best dressed drip stand in the country, but all to no avail. I could not get the operating gown on in the approved style. Finally I wrapped it round myself, just in time as the door opened to reveal a nurse, two porters and a hospital trolley.

I expected them to wheel the trolley to my bed, where with some semblance of dignity I could transfer myself from bed to trolley. It was not my lucky day. The trolley was too wide for the door and displaying the bedside manner that I had come to expect, the nurse and porters watched as I transferred myself complete with flapping operating gown and drip stand from the bed, across the room and onto the trolley, which must have been one of the highest ones available. To me, at the time, it looked like Mount Everest. I was wheeled down slopes, through corridors and wards. When I saw the grim general wards, I was so glad that I had a room to myself. Not only were the beds full but there were patients lying on mattresses on the floor and there was pervading smell of urine. The porters pushed open another door and wheeled me, not into the operating theatre but into an overcrowded children's ward. The trolley stopped by a bed and I was told to get into it. The surgeon was not ready for me yet and the one hospital trolley was in great demand. Although I was only in that ward for less than half an hour, it seemed like a life time. Not only was the bed uncomfortable with its grey, stained sheets which stank of stale perspiration but I was the focus of all eyes. For many of the children on that ward, I was probably the first white woman they had seen, certainly the first one they had seen wearing a gown and fastened to a drip. I was very relieved to hear and see the trolley return, even though my unaided efforts to climb onto it again proved to many of the children that more than my face and hands were white.

The next stop was the theatre which looked clean and seemed fairly well equipped. I lowered myself from the trolley and climbed onto the operating table. A male nurse came in and silently wired me up to a range of machines. The door to the theatre opened again and in came Lanso. I was relieved to see him. Not only was he a friendly face but it meant that my operation should start soon and I was feeling very ill by now.

"Hi, Helen, how are you?" he asked

"Fine, fine", I replied. There was no point in telling him how ill I felt now that he was going to operate.

"Good. I am going to scrub up now for your op. I will be starting in about 5 minutes, OK?"

"OK", I replied at the same time as wondering whether or not I should have had that conversation. I felt sure that I should have been unconscious by now. The door swung back again and another figure came into the room. This one was fully robed, wearing what all television programmes had led me to believe was the correct gear for a doctor going into an operating theatre. "Good morning," said the figure, "I am Mario, your anaesthetist". I had never been so glad to see someone in my life as I was to see him and surrendered myself willingly to his needle and mask.

The next thing that I knew was when I awoke back in my room. Both Sidi and Pedro were there and assured me that the operation had been a success. Pedro's blood had not been needed and, all being well, I was still on course to be discharged in three days time. Things did go well and the following Monday saw me back at The Dominion.

Everyone assured me that they were glad to see me back. I was not to worry, there had been no problems but a quick glance at the figures made me thankful that I had not been away any longer. There appeared to have been a substantial drop in takings during my absence so that evening, despite the urgings of my staff, I went into the bar.

"I am fine," I assured them "I promise you that I won't work. I will just sit here, at the till end of the bar, out of the way. All our customers will then know that I am back. This will be much better for me than sitting in my room on my own." Strangely enough, it was much better for the takings as well.

Chapter Five

Medical Matters

"Hi, nice to see you back again so soon," I said as Reggie Preston strolled into the bar one Friday evening. "I suppose you came on this afternoon's flight from Birmingham"

Reggie nodded. "Yes, we've only just arrived."

"Where's Reg, your Dad? Hasn't he come out this time?" I asked. Reg and Reggie (called that to distinguish him from his father) were building a home in nearby Kerr Shomme. Reg had been a keen radio ham for many years and now he was retired he wanted somewhere where he could pursue his hobby. Apparently West Africa has excellent conditions for receiving and transmitting radio signals and the fact that English was widely spoken and the cost of living was cheaper than the UK, led Reg to decide on Shendi. Reggie decided to help him and the two of them came out to Shendi on regular visits to supervise the building and to enjoy the sunshine. On one of their visits they came into The Dominion and over time they became some of my regular tourist visitors.

Reggie sat down, shook his head in answer to my question about his father and turned to introduce his companion. "This is Paul, my brother. He has come out instead. Dad has had a slight stroke and even though he's out of hospital, the doctor won't let him travel. We talked about it and decided not to waste his ticket but to give it to Paul. Paul, this is Helen. She owns The Dominion and you will be seeing plenty of her this week. Dad and I come here a lot. The food is great and so is the company. What's more the beer is cheap."

Paul nodded a hello to me, sat down at the bar, ordered a pint and in answer to my inquiry about the flight, proceeded to give me his impressions of the country so far. The airport had been chaotic and hot, porters had tried to insist on carrying his case, customs had searched his luggage, the bus had been uncomfortable and the hotel was hot and humid. It was his first visit; he had only landed a few hours ago but was already disenchanted. Africa, I have discovered, either gets a grip on its visitors who keep yearning to return or it totally depresses them. This group hate it and cannot wait to leave. From his comments, it was obvious that Paul fell into this latter category. "We've popped over to see how the house is going," he said. "I think my Dad and Reggie are crazy. Who on earth would want to build a house in this God forsaken country? They can't even run a decent electrical supply", he said as the lights flicked off and the generator kicked in. There was really no reply to this and I watched with interest as the two brothers went their separate ways over the next few days.

After that first evening, all Paul saw of the country was the hotel and the interior of The Dominion. Meanwhile, Reggie struggled to monitor the building work. He was becoming more and more frustrated with some of the problems that had arisen. Much of his time was spent talking to Datu, the local friend who was living at the compound and helping with the construction work. Reggie was finding it very hard. On previous visits he had simply supported his father in the discussions but now the full weight of overseeing the project fell on his shoulders. As with any project, let alone one managed at long distance, there were difficulties and I sympathised with Reggie in his efforts to keep the building work on track. It was not as if he was getting any support from his brother. The few comments that I did hear Paul make to Reggie were either downright rude or derogatory. As the week progressed I became concerned with Reggie's behaviour in The Dominion. He was more and more agitated and seemed to be taking everything personally. He looked and behaved like a very different person to the one who had walked into the bar only a few days ago. He spent a great deal of time going over and over the list of supplies and was often seen pacing up and down the bar. Usually very polite, he started snapping at the waiters and then over apologising. I mentioned my concerns to Paul who dismissed them with a shrug. "Don't worry about him. He's just getting himself worked up. He gets like that at times. We're going home in a couple of day. The family will sort him out. This is nothing. You should have seen him when Princess Diana died ....He takes everything to heart. He'll be alright."

I was not so sure. Reggie's behaviour reminded me of a friend I had known back in the UK who had been diagnosed schizophrenic, but surely Reggie was not that bad. He was just upset and worried about having all the responsibility for the house on his shoulders. At that point, I gave myself a severe talking to. With all my worries, I had too much to do to start worrying about customers. I really would have to stop letting my imagination run away with me and get down to some work. I was running a bar not a mental health service.

I did not see the boys on the Friday morning before they left but that was not unusual. The next day, I received a phone call from the UK. It was from Maria, a regular visitor who occasionally phoned me to keep up to date. I was surprised to hear from her, as I had spoken to her only a fortnight earlier. "Hi, lovely to hear from you. I wasn't expecting you to ring for a couple of weeks but I'm not complaining. Far from it, it is lovely to speak to someone other than the staff and customers who all want something from me that I can't give usually. How are things in the UK?"

"I'm sorry, Helen, I want something too, that's why I'm ringing," she said. "I am hoping that you will be able to help. I have a friend, Reg Preston, who is building a house in Kerr Shomme."

"Never mind that you want something. It is good to hear you. I know Reg," I interrupted her. "Fancy you knowing him. I guess you know his sons, Reggie and Paul. They've just been out here and went home yesterday. They've been out for a week checking on the house. Well, Reggie has, Paul just doesn't seem to like Africa. In fact, I am relieved that they have gone home. I was getting really concerned about Reggie. There are problems with the building work and Paul was no help at all. Reggie was getting more and more agitated as the week went on." I stopped, should I tell her my thoughts. After all she had said she wanted something and it was obviously about the Preston family. I decided I should at least mention my concerns. I continued, "I know you will think it was stupid of me but I began to wonder if Reggie had some sort of problems."

I heard a sigh of relief over the phone. "Yes well. Thank goodness you know them; that makes it easier for me. You were right about Reggie having problems, he is schizophrenic. Helen, I don't quite know how to say this except, last night Paul came home but not Reggie. He's been arrested and the family are desperately worried. They've been in touch with the British authorities in Shendi obviously, but it is the weekend and you know what that means. When they phoned me for advice, I said I knew someone who might be able to help and so I've rung you. I do hope that you will be able to do something. They are at their wits end."

"Good gracious! Reggie is schizophrenic and hasn't come home? He has been arrested? Why, what happened? Is he OK? What did Paul do? Never mind. Tell me what you know and I will see what I can do. I saw them Thursday night and just assumed they left for home on Friday. Of course I will help if I can but you know how things work out here, I might not be able to do anything."

"This is what I have been told," Maria went on. "Apparently, the boys fell out big time on Thursday evening when they got back to the hotel. I don't know what it was about but Paul left the room, planning to go out again. Reggie followed him out of the room and then threw the coffee table off the balcony at him. It missed him but someone, presumably another guest, called the hotel staff. They managed to calm Reggie down and, I think, they separated the boys. I don't know what happened over night but yesterday Paul took a taxi to the airport and Reggie went by coach. According to what I have been told, he was quite aggressive on the coach and at the airport. Somewhere between getting to the airport and boarding the plane he caused enough of a problem for him to be arrested. Paul got on the flight and came back home."

"Where is Reggie now?" I gasped. I had heard descriptions of the local jails and the thought of Reggie being incarcerated in one was not a pleasant thought.

"I don't know exactly. I believe he was taken to three different police stations and then to a psychiatric clinic in Port Albert. Look, Helen, I don't want to bother you but do you still have contact with that Cuban doctor, Pedro. You know, I talked to him during my last visit. I was hoping he would be able to help."

"Yes I do. But he is flying home tomorrow so he won't be able to do anything himself. Maria, listen I'll ring him and get back to you. He might know the name of someone who could help. You were quite right to ring me. The thought of Reggie in a clinic is frightening. I will do what I can. Leave it with me."

Pedro was only too willing to help. He put me in touch with a fellow Cuban doctor who might be able to help after the week-end and also gave me the contact details for Rita, the Cuban psychiatrist. I rang Maria back with the news and she passed it on to the family. She also gave me the name and phone number of Reggie's sister, Sharon so that I could contact the family direct without going through her. This was to make life a great deal easier in the days to come.

When I came off duty at 4pm I asked Sidi to drive me to the clinic. Not knowing what we might find or what Reggie might need, we took with us a few sandwiches and drinks which would come in useful wherever he was. It was very fortunate that Sidi knew exactly where the clinic was as without his local knowledge I would never have found it. It was situated in a tiny back street deep in an insalubrious part of Port Albert far from the tourist areas. Leaving the car in a tiny car park, we walked towards the high walls which were topped with broken glass and knocked on the small unnamed metal door that seemed to be the only entrance. At the sound of our knocking shouts and yells erupted on the other side of the wall, presumably from the patients. Eventually the door was opened a little way and a shabbily dressed male nurse glared at us and snapped, "What do you want?"

"We want to visit Reggie Preston. We have been told that he is here." Sidi replied. "You know the taubab who was brought in yesterday, from the airport."

The nurse nodded reluctantly. "Is she coming too?" he asked, pointing at me.

"Of course she is, she is a friend of the taubab" answered Sidi.

"You had both better come in," muttered the nurse

The door opened onto a courtyard which was completely bare except for three large trees providing some shade in the middle. I was mobbed by patients shouting; "Taubab, Taubab". It was obvious that they did not have many Taubab visitors and to have a taubab patient was unheard of. I stuck very closely to Sidi as they all insisted on showing me the way to the Taubab's room. In a shouting and seething mass we crossed the courtyard and turned a corner to where the rooms and offices were situated. Here we were left by our guides and followed the nurse across another smaller concrete courtyard which had an open sewer running its entire length. Stepping over it, we came to the room where Reggie was being kept.

The first thing that struck me was Reggie. He lay on top of the thin mattress on one of the two beds and was covered in what looked like mosquito bites. This was not surprising as not only did the bed not have mosquito netting but the slatted window overlooked the sewer (which accounted for the smell in the room) and lacked both curtains and netting. The only other furniture in the room was a small metal bedside cabinet which was empty.

Reggie, although groggy whether from lack of sleep or medication that someone had administered, I do not know, did recognise me. He got off the bed and started walking around the room. He was convinced that he was on an island and that there had been a coup. "Helen, thank goodness you are alright. I am worried about you. With this coup, you are stuck on the island. I was in a fight at the airport. Paul got on the last plane. You should have got on it as well. It isn't safe. I heard gunshots last night. We are going to be killed. Helen, you should have got on the plane. It isn't safe. They were firing guns last night. I was in a fight, Helen you are not safe."

I tried to calm him down and promised to return the next day with toiletries, a proper meal, a mosquito net and something to treat his bites. As I gave him the sandwiches and drinks we had brought, he grabbed my hand and said forcefully, "Thank you Helen, but don't bother if you are putting yourself in danger. The gun shots last night were close."

"Don't worry about me, Reggie. All is OK; maybe you only thought you heard gunshots. "

"No, no, no. I know I heard them. I heard real gunshots."

"OK, we will take care I promise but we will come back tomorrow."

With that, we left him to another miserable night in the clinic. On my return to The Dominion, I rang the UK and spoke to Sharon, his sister.

The next day, Sunday, was my day off. I had a long standing arrangement to go to the airport to wave goodbye to Pedro who with other Cuban doctors including his brother Lanso my surgeon, was returning home for good. I knew I would miss him and his support and it was with tears in my eyes that I waved farewell to the group, many of whom had become regulars at The Dominion. Their plane took off and I asked Sidi to take me back home. I had to get ready for my next visit to the clinic.

Now I knew what to expect, I was able to ignore the shouting and the smells. Reggie was no better, still speaking of the coup and gunshots and very concerned that neither of us would be able to leave the island. I spoke to the nursing staff. As with nursing staff the world over, they could not, or would not, give me much information. However, they did arrange an appointment for me to see Rita, the psychiatrist recommended by Pedro, the next afternoon.

Sidi and I returned to the clinic at the appointed time on Monday. I explained my connection with the family to Rita and told her that I was in contact with them in the UK. Furthermore, Sharon was intending to fly out on Thursday and take Reggie back to the UK with her. I told Rita that Sharon would be staying with me at The Dominion as I had plenty of spare rooms and I suggested the possibility of Reggie being discharged to my care until his sister arrived.

At first, Rita was very unsure. She felt that the atmosphere of a bar would be too upsetting for Reggie and despite my assurances that he could stay in my private quarters and use my own garden; she was reluctant to release him to me. "I will need to come and see your arrangements before I make a decision," she said. "Now, pardon me, but your face is familiar, I seem to have seen you before and your companion. Have we met?"

"No, I don't think so but I do have some friends who are Cuban doctors."

"Now, I know where I have seen you. It was at the airport yesterday."

"Yes, I was saying good bye to Pedro who was a close friend of mine. In fact his brother took out my gall bladder."

Before we went through to see Reggie, Rita invited both Sidi and I to visit her in her compound for coffee before we went home. It would allow us to discuss what arrangements we could make for Reggie and for Sharon in more relaxed surroundings. (It appeared that my friendship with Pedro and Lanso had provided me with an entrée to the usually close-knit group of Cuban medical staff.) Reggie was a little better but I was still glad to get away and drink coffee in more civilised surroundings. Once Rita learnt that I had more than enough spare rooms at The Dominion, she agreed to discharge Reggie the next day providing that she could stay overnight until Sharon arrived. I was only too happy to agree to this as it would take the responsibility of Reggie away from me.

The next problem was meeting Sharon at the airport. I did not know what she looked like and what if her reactions to Africa were similar to Paul's. What would I do? At least with Reggie at The Dominion, I was saved the necessity of escorting her to the clinic but how would I know who she was and could I spend time away from The Dominion. The problem was solved by Datu. He had obviously seen photos of her from her father and Sidi told me, would meet her at the airport and bring her to The Dominion. Reggie was much more relaxed when he met his sister and I need not have concerned about her reactions to Africa. As a member of a police murder squad back in the UK, she had seen too much of the darker side of life to worry about African treatment of psychiatric patients.

Everything was fine. Reggie was more settled in Sharon's company and seemed to be making progress. Datu came to visit them regularly, presumably to give them updates on the building. One morning I was having a coffee break in the house and Sharon and Reggie were talking to Datu in the garden when I saw Reggie get up and come towards me. "Do you mind if I join you," said Reggie, coming into the house." I don't know why but I don't feel comfortable around Datu anymore."

I simply took this as a symptom of Reggie's illness, offered him a chair and did not delve anymore into his reactions to Datu. Sharon was pleased with her brother and convinced that he was fit to travel so made arrangements to get them both back to the UK. Datu offered to drive them to the airport and this seemed to upset Reggie. The evening before their flight, we were sitting in the garden when he suddenly remarked,"Could Sidi take us, Helen? I would like you to come as well."

Sharon gave me a quizzical look, we were both puzzled by Reggie's apparent dislike of Datu but neither of us wanted to upset him this close to departure. Sharon was already concerned about going through the airport with Reggie. She thought that being returned to the place of his arrest would cause further agitation and so we agreed that Sidi would take us all to the airport the next day.

Reggie gave no cause for concern as he went through check-in and boarded the flight to the UK. Sharon rang me when she arrived home to thank me for my help and that was the start of a long correspondence that continued via emails. When Reg was finally allowed to return to Africa, I introduced him to Rita, who with her house-mate Yvette, an eye doctor, had become regular visitors to The Dominion along with my new doctor, Miles. Reg also gave me news of his family. Unfortunately, Paul had died shortly after his return to the UK but Reggie was making good progress and his medication was controlling his behaviour. Reg was delighted to be able to thank Rita personally for her help and offered us all an open invitation to visit his compound. As it was far from complete Rita and I simply nodded noncommittally and said our goodbyes.

One quiet afternoon, soon after Sharon had returned with Reggie, I stood behind the bar listening as a few of the regular expats talked amongst themselves. Life was generally so hectic that I was always glad when the afternoon trade slowed down; it gave me chance to catch my breath and contemplate my success – or otherwise - at running a bar. On the downside, I now had two not one cases in progress. The Peace Haven had taken out a court injunction against The Dominion which prohibited any form of music or entertainment except for a CD behind the bar. I had no idea whether this was a tit-for-tat gesture on their part or if it was another move in the battle to close us down. On the plus side I was so busy with the general day-to-day running of the business that I had very little time to dwell on my own problems.

More importantly, the success with the expat trade that Simon and I had seen increase over our first season continued. Perhaps it was because I was British as were many of the expats but The Dominion certainly attracted a fair number. Never having worked in the catering industry before I was amazed initially at how open customers were with me and how keen they were to discuss their problems. Bar staff all over the world act as sounding posts for their clients and I should not have been surprised at how eager many of my regulars were to talk to me about their problems. Their problems were manifold. Many of them were single, albeit with local partners, and I often heard far more than I wanted to about the difficulties of living with someone from another culture. Perhaps this should count on the down side!

“Oi, service!, Come on Helen, wake up there, you are neglecting your customers. Here I am, gasping for another pint and there is no-one to serve me. The staff are at lunch and the landlady in a dream!”

The call came from Terry, the outspoken Yorkshire man who had been a witness on the day that the NIA had arrested Simon. I stopped my day dreaming and quickly served Terry his pint. A rapid look around showed no-one else needing service and I returned to my thoughts. Terry was a case in point. After a nervous breakdown in the UK he had taken early retirement and with Sally, his wife, had decided to move out to Shendi. When we had first met him he had been over with his daughter building a compound for himself and Sally, who was still back home. When the house was finished, Sally came over and they held a great housewarming party. However, Sally had only lasted two months out in Shendi. Like many Europeans including Simon and myself, Sally had hoped to use her skills for the benefit of her new homeland. She was a very experienced health visitor and had wanted to open a family planning clinic supplying free contraception in her compound. However, even though she was working as a volunteer, she would have had to pay taxes as a European worker. She became very disenchanted and when her mother suffered a heart attack back in the UK, Sally returned home leaving Terry behind.

Terry's relationship was not the only one that had fallen apart after a move to Africa; I had only to look at the ways things were between Simon and me if I needed more evidence. I remembered that Kebba had warned us very early on that 'they' would try to split us up and would very likely succeed. Perhaps it was the local jujus or perhaps it was just the locals. It was certainly easier for the locals to handle a single person rather than a partnership. Would Simon and I still have been together if we had not come out, I did not know, anymore than I knew if Terry and Sally would still have been together in the UK. Enough of the contemplation, I had a bar to run and customers to serve.

The men were talking about Lena, Terry's new girlfriend. After Sally's return to the UK, Terry had soon settled into his new role of a single man. Before long, he was behaving like many unattached expat men – drinking heavily and looking for a young local girl to look after him. This followed what I recognised as the traditional local pattern, a short term affair which ended suddenly to the detriment of the expat's finances. Lena appeared to be a more successful find. She was in her early forties and despite not dressing in a way that showed her figure off to its best, was still attractive. I had met her once or twice when Terry brought her to the bar and she had seemed pleasant. Any oddities in her behaviour I had put down to her unease at the situation. It cannot have been easy for her to meet a crowd of expats who knew what she was and why she was on Terry's arm. However, as I cleared away the glasses I remembered a conversation I had had with Sidi only the other day on the very subject of Lena.

Sidi had been on his way out with Ebou the chef to do some shopping but, as was often the case, stopped to bring me up to date on the local gossip.

"Good morning, Helen", he said "I have some news for you. The Peace Haven security staff stopped me on my in this morning. No, no problem" he added as he saw my face. "They only wanted to tell me about Lena – Terry's Lena. They say she is crazy, crazy mad. She is dangerous very dangerous. They say you have to warn Terry about her. "

"Sidi, I can't do that. I can't say she is dangerous. I don't know her. The only times I have met her is when Terry brought her into the bar. I can't tell Terry anything. I do think she is a bit odd, but it can't be easy for her coming into The Dominion with all the other expats about. Remember she is Ghanian, she is far from home and her behaviour could be to do with different customs."

"Well they are saying really bad things about her," responded Sidi, but he did not elaborate on what the 'really bad things' were, so I was none the wiser.

Just as I started to wipe the bar down, Adam asked Terry how Lena was.

"I told you, she's fine. Taking into account she's only been here a few months she's doing really well." Terry said.

"Oh," replied Adam and glanced at me.

It seemed that Adam too had heard the rumours about Lena.

Over the next few days several people added to my store of information about Lena. One or two mentioned how strange her behaviour was but the locals spoke of her long residence in the country. Despite Terry's statements that she was a new comer to the country, it appeared that she had been settled long before she met him. I decided to say nothing. All I had heard was local gossip and it could have sheer envy on the part of the local girls. A Ghanaian managing to find a Taubab boyfriend where several of them had failed would not go down well and this could be their revenge. Terry looked happy and Lena was looking after him.

One of my regulars was Musa, a Senegalese builder, who had been head of maintenance at The Peace Haven for several years. Despite the fact that he worked for 'the opposition' I was quite happy to have his custom and he got on well with many of the expats who were builders themselves. Musa's work load had increased with the extensive redevelopment of Peace Haven and the local grapevine had it that they had now employed a French engineer to work with him during their building programme. I wondered how he felt about it, perhaps he was grateful. However, it seemed that he was glad of the help because calling in for his regular morning coffee one day he told me about his new colleague, Pierre, and promised to bring him in the next time he came. My French at its best ranged from non-existent to inadequate, and Pierre's English was even worse, so we were only able to converse through Musa, or by using sign language. With Senegal being a French speaking country, Musa was quite at home with Pierre, and he also spoke English fluently.

Pierre made little effort to join in our conversation, he seemed quite content to let Musa and I chat away during their coffee breaks. Even though Musa worked for The Peace Haven, he had some sympathy for my plight, and he kept me well informed as to what the next part of their building plans were likely to entail.

One morning while we were all sat around the bar, Pierre suddenly stood up and without a word went out into my beer garden, and taking his large retractable builder's measuring tape out of his pocket, started measuring my garden, moving the tables and chairs that were in his way.

"What does he think he is doing?" I asked Musa, who like myself was looking on in amazement.

"I don't know, ignore him, he is a bit strange at times."

"No, I can't just allow him to carry on. I have customers out there. What will they think if they see the garden being measured out by the hotel's staff. There will be all sorts of rumours, and it will unnerve my employees. I don't know what he thinks he is doing."

I went out into the garden, closely followed by Musa. As I crossed the small wooden bridge, into the garden I could see the bewilderment on the faces of some of my customers. Latif, my maintenance man, who was working in the garden, downed tools and came to watch the proceedings with interest. I didn't want my staff to think that The Peace Haven was intending to build on our property.

"What are you doing? Why are you measuring my garden?" I angrily asked Pierre.

I'm sure that he didn't understand what I had actually said, but he could tell from my tone of voice that I was cross. I understood part of what he said, but not all. I was under the impression that he thought they were going to extend the fish restaurant, which was an outdoor extension of La Parisian, into my beer garden. The restaurant was situated the other side of our adjoining wall, so had they owned my property this would have been a possibility.

"Don't worry." Musa told me. "This is a misunderstanding,"

"I did understand some of what he said. Does he think The Peace Haven own my property; he is talking about having seen the plans for an extension here." I told him, trying unsuccessfully to conceal my concern.

"It's O.K., it's O.K. calm down, maybe there are plans to extend, but he doesn't understand that we cannot do this now."

I could feel my cheeks redden; I was getting really worked up. "I should think you can't do this now. This is my property not yours. I don't care if he has seen plans that include my garden. He will not be building on my land."

Musa was trying his best to keep the peace; he patted my forearm in an effort to calm me down. He had seen me in a temper before, and knew if I lost control I was a force to be reckoned with. He spoke quietly to Pierre, who was by now, ranting and raving in French. Pierre, ignoring me took out his chalk and started marking out part of my garden, as if no one had spoken. I went behind him, rubbing these out with my flip-flops. This fuelled his anger, in true French style, his arms were waving everywhere, and he was pointing in my direction and yelling at Musa. I couldn't understand all that he was shouting, but I was aware that he was telling Musa, I was a difficult woman, he was only doing his job, and I was interfering with his work, and being a nuisance to him. He would come back, and mark out his measurements when I was not around.

"Keep calm." Musa told me. "He is saying, he may have read the plans wrong. He thought the extension was coming this way, but I think they are going in the other direction."

"Don't tell me bull shit Musa." I retorted, trying to keep my voice on an even keel. "I may not speak French, but I can understand a little. I know that is not what he said. Besides you are telling me they are extending the fish restaurant in the other direction?"

"Yes, that's what I think."

"Don't talk daft. In the other direction is the only access to the hotel, how could any of your guests get in or out of the hotel if you build across the access roadway? Pierre is an engineer; I don't think it very likely that he would read a building plan upside down. I'm not completely stupid."

In the meantime Pierre continued to pace out and measure sections of my garden, with Latif at his side shouting at him and being ignored. The rest of my staff, including the kitchen lads, that should have been preparing lunches, gathered around to see what was happening. It might have been good entertainment – an angry man, an angry woman and a tape measure – but it wasn't very good for their morale, or mine either. They would start to think that we were going to become part of The Peace Haven, which in turn would cause me problems.

"Make him stop." I ordered Musa.

"Fine, fine, I will get him out."

After a lot of coaxing from Musa, and much jeering from my staff, Pierre finally abandoned his work and left my premises, giving me a thunderous look as he stormed past me. This did upset my staff; they had not really understood what was going on. I was bombarded with questions.

"Have you sold The Dominion to The Peace Haven?" they asked.

"Will we be keeping our jobs?"

"When is this going to happen?"

"Why have we not been told?"

I did my best to calm the situation, but like me they were confused by the whole incident. I kept trying to reassure them, but in reality I was unsure myself about what had happened. Simon and I had been shown plans by Mr. Smithers, with bedrooms and apartments being built over our property. If plans existed for an extension of the fish restaurant on my land, I was unaware of this, and this meant that new plans had been drawn up, so their intention of taking over The Dominion was still a very real threat. The hotel knew I had no intention of selling to them, but I knew that they were much more influential that I was, and that they were likely to be in a better position to know the eventual outcome of our court case than I was. They did always seem to hold the trump card. Maybe this was a pure misunderstanding on Pierre's part, but I doubted this. To me this was yet another incident that niggled away at the back of my mind, and it caused me to have several weeks of unrest amongst my staff, who suspected that I knew what this had been about.

I never saw Pierre again, other than if I glanced over my wall and saw him working, he disappeared all together a couple of months later, I never learnt where he had gone, or why he didn't remain to finish the job that he had started. It was several days before I saw Musa again, then he came in one evening and ordered his beer as usual. He offered no explanation as to what had happened on our last meeting and I decided not to ask him anything, he was only doing his job after all. Generally I got on well with him, and it might be useful for me to have an ally that worked at the hotel.

I had enough to think about without worrying about possible plans of extensions. I was suffering from diarrhoea and vomiting which I put down to another bout of malaria. If Miles, one of the Cuban doctors had been available, I would have gone to see him, but he was away in Cuba on his annual leave. I was relieved when the sickness went.

"Just shows you", I told myself, "if Miles had been here you would have worried him about nothing. Now stop malingering and get back to work."

Unfortunately my health still remained poor. I felt dizzy, suffered stomach cramps at fairly short intervals, my hair became dull and lifeless and I had lost a great deal of weight. I told myself it was some sort of physical reaction to my current life: the mounting pressure from The Peace Haven, the long hours I worked, the irregular meals that I took, well snacks more than meals, and the regular attacks of malaria. Of more immediate concern than all these strange symptoms was the fact that I was having problems with my staff. There was a general atmosphere of uneasiness whenever I appeared in the bar, the till rarely tallied with receipts and food and equipment was going missing from the kitchen. Perhaps it was related to the incident with Pierre but I felt there was more to it than that. I chose not to talk to Sidi about these problems, thinking perhaps that he would side with the staff. Certainly in some of our recent discussions, he had appeared to take their side and not to listen to mine, but perhaps that was simply paranoia on my part.

One day, whilst we were talking about the general running of the place, he noticed that I was not looking too well and offered to take me to a local doctor.

"No. I'll wait for Miles to come back. He knows me. If I go to a local doctor and say I am tired, he will simply say that I am wasting his time. Miles is due back at the weekend and I will ring for an appointment on Monday."

On entering Miles's clinic I slipped into the examination chair and just looked at him. I felt far too tired to explain. He took in my weight loss and general appearance: ashen skin, limp hair and nails which had once been my pride and joy, brittle and chipped and gave me a full examination. He looked into my eyes, took my blood pressure, felt my stomach and sent blood and urine samples for examination. Then he sat and talked to me.

"You are not well, how much weight have you lost?"

"Oh I don't know about two stone. Please sort me out Miles. I have too many problems at The Dominion to be ill. I've been getting impatient waiting for you to come back. I didn't want to go to any one else, you have to sort me out" As I finished speaking, I realised that my voice had risen higher and higher as I spoke. It was then that I realised just how low I had been feeling.

"Don't worry, Helen. The blood tests will give me the cause of all this. I don't want to alarm you but I think there are only two possibilities. You may have some form of cancer and we will not know for a while since that blood test takes longer than others. The other possibility will be proved or disproved by this evening since that is a quicker blood test."

"Well, come on don't keep me in suspense. What do you think is the matter with me?"

Miles leant over and took my hand, "Well, I believe that you are in the advanced stages of slow poisoning but we must wait for the blood test to prove it."

I sat there, shocked, my hand still in Miles's hand.

"I've been poisoned?" I gasped, "But, who? Why? I don't understand, how can I have been? Who would do it? There has to be another explanation. No Miles, I can't have been. And if I have, what can I do? I have to go back there and live and eat."

"I really do think so. Go home and eat nothing until I come to see you this evening with the result. If you need a drink take an unopened bottle straight from a fridge and drink out of the bottle. If you don't drink it all, throw it away and get a fresh one. You do understand what I am saying don't you?"

"Yes, Miles, this is Africa" and I stood up and walked out of his office very shakily.

Despite my comment to Miles about it being Africa, I was still shocked. Sidi took my silence on the drive back to mean that I had received some bad news – if only he knew! I realised that all my symptoms could be explained by slow poisoning and the more I thought about it the more sense it made. The symptoms had appeared just after the Cubans had left for their six week annual leave. Who ever was doing it would know that I would have problems receiving good medical assistance. Back at The Dominion, I took a bottle from the fridge and went to my private rooms. There I waited for Miles and while I waited I continued the line of thought started on the journey back. Given that I was being poisoned there remained the motive and one or two other matters to clear up. Who was doing it and how? The how was the easier matter to solve. Obviously the kitchen staff or at least one of them had to be in on the scheme. It would be a simple matter to dose my food and drink with the poison of choice. But who was paying them to do it?

Was it an inside job? Were all the staff in on it? Or was it just one or two of them? Was it Sidi? All or any of them would benefit if I died. By the time Simon heard of my death and managed to come out, there would be little if anything of value left at The Dominion. Was it someone from outside? The only suspect there was The Peace Haven. They had some very powerful influences behind them and they would definitely benefit from my death. They would have difficulties administering the poison in small doses over the long period necessary but any of my kitchen staff would be prepared to take on the task for financial gain.

I favoured an inside job but could not decide the likely culprits. When Miles called that evening he told me that although the exact cause was uncertain, I was definitely suffering from slow poisoning. We abandoned fruitless speculation into both poison and poisoner in favour of planning a survival strategy. Consequently, it was given out that I was suffering from an ulcer. This meant that I would need a special diet and so as not to overburden the kitchen staff, I would prepare all my food myself. During my stay in Shendi, so far I had learnt to be very cautious about trusting people and now I trusted even fewer, especially those close to me. I became very proficient at smelling and tasting food before I ate. The maintenance men could not understand why the plants outside my living room kept dying. They thought there was a problem with the soil. I was more inclined to think it was the bitter tasting coffee I tipped on them some evenings.

Chapter Six
Love in a Hot Climate

Even when I was feeling ill I could not afford to miss any sessions in the bar. The till receipts bore even more resemblance to a work of fiction than usual if I was not there and I was not in the mood for fairy stories so I had to go down. However, life went on and with Miles's help I slowly recovered from my 'ulcer'. Once I was able to take an interest in my surroundings again, I was a little surprised to see that Terry's friendship with Lena was still very strong. She had moved out from her lodgings and was now living at his compound which like most European built compounds was luxurious by local standards. He looked happy and well cared and initially it seemed her presence was doing him some good. But then over the next few months there seemed to be a slow deterioration in his health, however because we saw him every day, none of the regulars or myself noticed it for a while. It took a comment from a regular tourist "Terry's starting to look his age" for us to pay attention to his health. When I talked to him one night, it turned out that he was starting to display similar symptoms to those I had exhibited with my 'ulcer'.

I instituted a 'Terry watch'.

"How are you Terry?" I would ask when he came in for his regular evening drinks. "Lena looking after you OK is she?"

"You're looking a bit under the weather. Are you Ok?"

"Remember Terry, look after yourself. You don't want to get an ulcer like I did. Take care what you eat"

It was all to no avail. My comments fell on deaf ears. According to Terry, he was fine and I was an old woman for going on at him. Lena was fine, too and knew how to look after him. In fact everything in the garden was rosy and he'd have another pint please.

One evening, Adam came into the bar with the shocking news that Terry had been admitted to hospital and Miles was looking after him in the Intensive Care Unit. Adam had no idea what was wrong but the general consensus around the bar was malaria. "I don't know about that," said Jane, Adam's wife. "Terry has been ill for weeks and the incubation of malaria is only 12- 14 days. Perhaps it is malaria but on top of something else."

"Yes", I thought, "and I can guess what the something else is."

Adam and Jane visited Terry regularly in hospital and reported on his progress back at The Dominion. Lena was bringing him his food as is the norm in most parts of Africa and it appeared that one of their visits had coincided with her lunch time call. "You know," Jane remarked over an afternoon beer in the garden, "I was so relieved when Lena ate the left-over food. I was beginning to wonder about his illness, it just doesn't seem like malaria. I was getting a bit concerned that she was still feeding him. I know it sounds strange but I began to doubt what she was putting in the food. I was wondering if we should suggest bringing him his food but I didn't know how to mention it without Terry taking it amiss."

I looked around the garden before I answered. None of my staff were in earshot. "Yes, well OK you obviously had the same thoughts as I had. At least now he's on the road to recovery."

Adam looked at us both, "Women and their imaginations" he snorted.

Terry was well on the road to recovery, though from what no-one was certain. Lena visited daily and told Adam and Jane that she had everything ready in the compound for his discharge from hospital. She told them she would be very glad to get him back and that she missed him. It was very lonely without him. Therefore I was very surprised when the phone went in the bar one evening and it was Lena sounding very anxious.

"Helen, its Lena. Is Adam there yet? I need to see him"

"No but I expect he will be in later, he comes in most nights. Can I give him a message? How's Terry by the way?"

"He's fine, fine. Look, it is really important that I see Adam. Tell him that I need to see him and am coming down. Don't let him leave till I've been. Helen you must tell him I need to see him. It really is very important."

Adam came in and I gave him the message but by the time Lena arrived it was well after midnight and Adam was the only customer left. So much for the urgency of the matter, I thought. If he had not been waiting for Lena, he would have gone home and I would have closed up. Both of us were quite irate at the lateness of the hour and just as we were deciding not to wait any longer, however much we were concerned about Terry there was the sound of running feet and a flustered looking Lena appeared. She dashed up to the bar carrying a plastic shopping bag and without any apologies or thanks, launched straight into a speech that she had obviously prepared.

"I have to travel. I have no choice. I have to go to Datrina. You know I went there to order a new passport because I cannot get one here. Now I have a message from my embassy that my passport is ready. I have to go and collect it. I will leave early in the morning and I will be back as soon as I can. I haven't told Terry I am going. I thought it might upset him. I will be back before he comes out. Miles told me he will be discharged in a few days. I will be back by then. I am not happy to leave all Terry's money in the safe while the compound is empty so I have brought it for you, Adam, to lock in your safe. Here are the car keys. Could you go and get it and park it at your compound? Here is the key to the compound as well."

After the longest speech I had ever heard Lena make, she passed Adam the plastic bag and a bunch of keys, turned round and walked out of The Dominion.

Adam stood there, clutching the bag of money and the keys and we both looked at each other in total amazement. "I can't believe that she has access to Terry's safe," I said.

"No, neither can I. Umm, look Helen, I don't feel very happy about this. How is she funding her trip? Terry paid for the first one. Will you count this with me so that you can witness what she gave me."

Adam and I tipped the bag out onto the bar top and amidst the debris of a night at The Dominion counted out what was a considerable sum of local currency.

Adam stopped and looked at the money. "There is no sterling here, where is it? Terry must have some sterling, we all do: I wonder if it is somewhere else," he said, scratching his head and pushing his glasses onto his head.

"No it would be in his safe. Lena told us this is from his safe and I can't imagine Terry keeping cash anywhere else. He's lived here long enough to know not to leave cash around. I bet that is what Lena is using to finance her trip – but surely he would have had more than that will cost," I answered.

"Umm, yeah, well it is not our problem really. I am glad that I asked you to count it with me. I'll go around in the morning, check the compound and collect his car to be on the safe side."

When Adam and Jane next visited Terry, they told him that Lena had gone to Datrina to collect her passport but expected to be back before Terry was discharged. Terry was quite happy with this and looked forward to seeing Lena and leaving hospital. Adam, Jane and I expected Lena to return within a couple of days but when Terry was discharged five days later there was still no sign of her. Terry was quietly confident that she would return. "She will be back today or tomorrow. She will have gone by bush taxi and that takes longer than you expect", he said as they drove him home. "You are all making a fuss about nothing."

Back at the compound there were a few friends waiting to greet Terry. He climbed out of the car with a huge sigh of relief. "It's good to be back, that hospital is not the place to spend too much time. Come on in and we will have a drink." Adam took Terry's things into his room and stopped. The room looked empty. Quietly he called to Terry who stood in the doorway and stared. The only things left in the room were his. There was nothing that had belonged to Lena – no clothes, shoes, ornaments, nothing. She had gone and taken all her things with her. "It really doesn't look as if she is coming back Terry", Adam tried to tell him as Terry sat on the bed with his head in his hands looking a broken man.

The friends who had come to welcome him home quickly drifted away and Jane and Adam spent the rest of the day trying to help Terry come to terms with Lena's desertion. They were able to find out using the usual channels – i.e. through the relative of a friend of a friend - that Lena had flown to her native Ghana the morning after she had seen Adam and I at The Dominion. When Adam returned the contents of Terry's safe to him, he realised how the flight had been funded. £2,000 in sterling was missing.

Terry slowly took up the reins of his pre-hospital life and returned to his habit of nightly drinks in The Dominion. He had his favourite seat at the bar where he could talk to the regulars, ignore tourists and side with the bar staff against me. Like most of his friends I assumed that Lena had been consigned to history and therefore was amazed to hear him say one night, "Lena rang me the other night. She went back to her family because she was afraid I would die. If I had died, she said that Sally would have come back and blamed her for my death."

"Afraid you would die? She knew you were due out in a few days", I thought but did not say. It was not worth upsetting Terry. It was just as well I said nothing for after an absence lasting over six months, Terry welcomed back Lena with open arms. He had found it difficult to cope on his own and was completely besotted by the woman and never mentioned the missing money. The mere fact that she had returned was enough.

However, he continued his nightly visits to The Dominion, usually leaving about midnight to go to The King's Arms another expat bar near his compound. He would stay there until the early hours and then drive home. With the police having neither transport or breathalyzers, the drink-drive laws were disregard. One Saturday night, when the only other customer left in the bar was a fellow Yorkshire man, Nick, Terry tottered very unsteadily to the door and slurred a good bye. He staggered out of the gate and made his way to his car, a very expensive silver and grey 4 wheeled drive. It was a very distinctive car and there was only one other like it in the country. It was Terry's pride and joy and he took enormous pleasure in driving it on the country's roads knowing how rare it was.

"Surely, the silly old so and so isn't going to drive home like that?" Nick said.

I looked at him. "Not yet, he'll be going to The King's Arms for a few more and anyway that remark is a bit rich coming from you. I've known you drive back under the influence."

"I hope you're not suggesting I drink too much. I have to replace all the fluid I've lost doing building work in the hot African sun. I do drive when I shouldn't but never in that state. Anyway if you are going to accuse me of drinking too much, I think it is time I went as well. Goodnight Helen" and with that, Nick made his way out of The Dominion, saying farewell to the night watchman on his way.

I too, said my goodnights to the watchman and tucking the takings under my arm, made my way to my room. I thought no more of Terry or of Nick or of how many expats did things out here that they would not do at home. I simply counted the money, locked it away in the safe and climbed wearily into bed. Early next morning, I was awoken by a phone call from an agitated Lena. "Helen oh Helen, something awful has happened, I am so worried. You must come over, you must talk to him, and he won't listen to me. We need help. Terry has had an accident. He got out to open the gate. You must come."

(In fact, I found out later that Terry had not had an accident. His car had been stolen. He had arrived home, got out of his car to open the compound gate and had been hit on the back of the head.)

"Look Lena, I don't understand. Why did Terry have to get out of the car? Why didn't the night watchman open the gate?

"The watchman isn't here. I gave him time off. He will be back in about a week and the lad that does his work when he is off is ill."

"Lena, that shouldn't be. I can't come over but I'll send one of my security lads over to your compound until you can sort something out. I'll also fax the insurance company and report Terry's car as stolen."

When Adam came in later that day, he told me that Lena had phoned him during the night when she had found Terry laying outside the gate in a pool of blood.

"I reckon Terry is lucky to be alive," Adam reported to an audience of expats eager to hear the details. "I took him to the only place I could think of that would be open at that hour, the local clinic."

We all groaned but Adam had been right, there would be nowhere else at that time of night.

"They cleaned up the back of his head where he had been hit and put stitches in. That seemed to be where most of the blood came from. They also cleaned up a gash in his forehead from where he fell to the ground and stitched that. I tell you, it was like a scene from a horror movie. Terry sat with his head over a bucket to collect the blood which seemed to pour out. And the needle they used for stitching ... well, it was a good job he couldn't see it. It was a large, very old looking needle. It looked as if it would be better used stitching shoes than stitching heads. Poor Terry, he was in awful pain. They gave him no pain killers at all. Just put his head over the bucket and stitched him up. I'd have to be at death's door before I'd let them treat me."

After a round of drinks to recover from the tale of Terry and the bucket of blood, the talk turned to the likely recovery of the car. It was very distinctive and ran on diesel unlike the only other 4 x 4 which looked like it and ran on petrol. Despite police assurances that the car would soon be returned, the general opinion was that it was very unlikely. With the border less than an hour's drive away, it could have been out of the country before it was reported stolen. If it was still inside the country then it could be hidden in a remote village or even locked in a compound in the vicinity of Terry's house.

Over the next few days, Adam, Jane and I helped Terry as much as we could with the practicalities of the attack and car theft. Whilst I helped sort out paper work and statements, Adam and Jane chauffeured Terry and Lena to and from the police stations. Terry could give the police very little information, he had no memory of what had happened and it was inevitable that they focused much of their attention on Lena. Their lines of enquiry mirrored many of the conversations around the bar.

"Why did she open the compound gate at that time in the morning? Wasn't it gone two? It isn't safe to open the gate at that time. That is why we all have high walls and dogs and night watchmen. Don't tell me she was looking for Terry" was one comment.

"Didn't she think to ring his mobile? Why on earth did she think he was outside the gate? She couldn't have heard the car"

"I want to know why she sent the night watchman on leave" someone muttered.

"I tell you what," added one of the wives, eager to give a woman's viewpoint on the matter, "I tell you most women whose man habitually comes home tanked up to the eyeballs in the middle of the night if they woke up and found him not at home would curse him, roll over and go back to sleep. They wouldn't get up and go and look for him. They certainly wouldn't open the compound gates not if the security man was away."

"I still think it funny that the night watchman was away" said an elderly expat.

The whole situation coupled with Lena's earlier desertion of Terry made for exciting conversations in the bar and many were only too willing to think the worst of Lena. One rumour that kept reoccurring was that two young men had been seen by someone, no-one knew who, loitering around the compound. They were believed to be Lena's brothers. Now that degree of kinship is not as tightly defined in Africa as in the UK but they were certainly believed to be related to her in some way. What made it more suspicious was the fact that no-one had seen them since the attack.

Just as we were all rehashing everything we knew Terry came into the bar. He looked pale and the line of stitches on his head looked angry. He sat down on his favourite bar stool and gave us the news. "I've just got back from Kudo Police Station. They took Lena and me there and then after going over it all again told me I could go but Lena would have to stay. I refused to go without her. How could I leave her there, you would not believe what I've seen at Kudo. I'd heard how brutal the police could be, but hearing is different to seeing. Now I've seen it and heard it. We've been sat outside on the veranda listening to them torturing people inside. The screams were awful. One lad was being whipped with a length of garden hose. I don't know what they were doing to others. I can't think. I love Lena, how could I leave her there to face that. It was terrible. And anyway, I don't understand why they are asking the questions they are asking. Anyone with any sense would know that she couldn't be involved in this. She loves me."

"Loves the size of his wallet more like", Nick muttered to me.

"Love is blind", I said smugly.

Terry continued. "I sat there and insisted that I wouldn't go and leave her there. In the end, they said she could go as well. She is so scared. She went to bed as soon as we got home, she petrified poor bairn."

Anyone less like a bairn I had to see.

A week after the attack there was a change in the investigation. The British High Commission had been following the investigation and were not content with the way the locals were handling it. They intervened and the case was handed over to the Police Headquarters in Port Albert. Lena was questioned intensively by the police in the capital and they decided to hold her in custody for three days to give them time to pursue their inquiries. Terry would have none of it. Although the building in the capital was brighter and cleaner than the one in Kudo, the police methods were the same. He knew that the moment he left Lena there, there was a huge chance that the investigation would turn physical. The only way he could prevent Lena being detained was for him to drop all charges.

Although he realised that this meant he could no longer claim for his car on his insurance and that it would anger the British High Commission, he insisted that he no longer wanted the police to follow any leads that they had and that he wanted the case closed. He signed papers to that effect and took Lena back home. The High Commission was furious. Cases of muggings and burglary against British citizens were common but were not usually as brutal as the attack on Terry. They took the unusual step of inviting both Terry and Lena to the High Commission for an interview. Adam drove them there and although he did not know what was said, he did know that in attendance was the High Commissioner, the chief police prosecutor and a representative of the NIA. All in all a very high powered interview for a mugging victim and his girl friend to attend.

As far as I know, Terry never told anyone what was said in the interview and to this day many expats are left wondering what was said. However, one of the staff at the High Commission told me, when it was all over, that Lena had confessed. "She paid two boys to steal his car. Goodness knows what she paid them or where the car went, but pay them she did. It was amazing, they were all in HC's office and suddenly she burst into tears. 'I did it' she said, 'I paid two boys to take your car, Oh Terry I am so sorry.' Well you should have seen his face, he was thunderstruck. The HC and the other bigwigs looked grimly delighted, they had known that she was behind it all but then Terry stood up and went over to her. 'It's all rubbish, you didn't have anything to do with it. I know you wouldn't hurt me. Darling. Shh it will be alright. You are only saying it because they have made you' and so it went on. No matter what HC or anyone else said, he would not admit that she had taken it. He kept saying she had only confessed because she was scared. He flatly refused to allow the police to prosecute and walked out of the office with his arm around her. What will it take to convince him that she is a piece of no good? I reckon the sun has fried his brain."

"You know my theory, every taubab who comes here, parks their brain at the airport and collects it on the way home. That means I'm in trouble. I've been here so long; my brain has probably been stolen. But I don't know what will convince Terry. Lots of us talked to him, I know you did, about Lena when she went away with his money, but it was no good. He loves her, or says he does, which amounts to the same thing so there is nothing we can do."

There was nothing any of us could do. Terry and Lena continued to live at the compound, though how Terry felt going back to the place where he had been so brutally attacked we could only guess. He came into the bar one night looking tired and depressed.

"What's the matter?" asked Nick, "You look worried."

Terry replied with a shrug, "I am worried. Lena has said that she doesn't feel safe in the compound any more. Whoever stole the car has got the keys to the gate and the house and although I've changed the locks she thinks they will try again."

Glances were exchanged behind Terry's back. What was Lena up to now seemed to be the main thought. Fortunately he was busy drinking his pint and failed to see them.

"You know I've told her we've new locks and a new watchman but she won't calm down. She's said she is going to move out. What do I do? She has already rented a room in the compound she used to live in. Her idea is that we both sleep there and come back to our compound during the day. I know she is doing what she thinks is best for us, but I don't want to leave my house. I planned it and built it and I want to stay there. She should have asked me first before renting a room."

Despite Terry's protestations, we all knew what would happen and we were right. A few days later, Terry moved with Lena, to a room in her old compound. It was close to Terry's home but in a predominantly native area and a rough area at that. Certainly not one where a Taubab could live happily, especially one of Terry's temperament. He settled into a routine. Adam collected him every evening and brought him to The Dominion for a few drinks. He seemed to enjoy the break from Lena and the local way of life. One evening when it was quiet at the bar, he talked to me about his new way of life.

"You know our space is so small, I can't get away from Lena. She is always, always chatting either to me or to someone else. All I seem to hear is her voice. Then at night I can't sleep. They sit outside our window all night smoking wacky-baccy. I tell you, Helen, I could get high just breathing deeply in our bedroom. And another thing, I'm sure half the girls are 'ladies of the night'. If not, I'm not sure what they get up to at night. I just don't know what Lena was thinking of when she moved us back there."

"She thought you would feel safer than at your own compound", I suggested.

"Safer than at my own compound" he spluttered. "When she moved in with me, she said that she couldn't cope with living there any longer. She said then that they were all prostitutes; she said she was afraid of being classed as the same. Sleep, I haven't had a wink of sleep since we moved in. I've made up my mind. I will tell her tomorrow that I am going back home again and she can come or not!"

This was fighting talk from Terry and I mentioned the proposed ultimatum to Adam. "I'm not surprised. I've lived in different parts of Shendi over the years but I feel uncomfortable and unsafe around Terry's new home. When I go there, I pull up as close to the compound door as I can. I let Terry out and check and double check that all the doors are locked before I drive off. I don't like going there and would hate to live there."

To everybody's surprise, Lena readily agreed with Terry's ultimatum and they moved back to his compound, but not to the main house which they felt was too big for them but to a small house that Terry had built for the staff. Just as things seemed to be settling down again, Terry suffered another shock. Lena announced that she was returning to Ghana. He sat in the bar and gave us her reasons. "She is scared. She thinks that the police are going to charge her with the theft of my car. She thinks that you all blame her for that," he added glaring at everyone in sight including the bar staff. "Locals and expats you all blame her she thinks. So she wants to go home to her family, she wants their support. I don't want her to go but I know how you all feel about her," and again he glared at everyone. "She will be safer back home and the police won't be able to charge her. I wouldn't put it past them to rake up the car theft again so perhaps it is a good thing that she is going."

We all agreed that it was a good thing that Lena was going. However, it did leave Terry, an elderly man of a nervous disposition living alone with only a night watchman at night in a compound that he had been told was not safe. Over the next couple of weeks we watched as Terry became more and more agitated. He was spending more time at The Dominion, coming in for morning and evening beers and for occasional meals. Uncharacteristically he picked at his food and snapped at the staff, his clothes were no longer smart and well pressed but shabby and faded. I began to wonder if he would benefit from talking to Rita, the Cuban psychiatrist but when I suggested this to Terry, he flatly refused.

"No I don't want to talk to her or anyone else. Of course, I know who you mean. She's the one who helped with Reggie. I'm not mad, I'm just old. I don't want to talk to her either here or at her office. Stop sticking your nose in where it isn't wanted. It is none of your business how I look after myself. Haven't you got enough problems? Now leave me alone."

So, I had to leave him alone. I did have the UK phone numbers of his daughter and his ex wife but although I was tempted to ring them, Terry was right in a way, it wasn't my business and I did have my own problems. Time went by until early one morning the phone went. It was Terry.

"Helen, Helen please help me. I'm in a terrible state I've not been to bed. I've walked the living room floor all night. Maybe I do need to talk to Rita."

"OK Terry, I think that is a good idea that's why I suggested it. It will help to talk to someone outside about your problems. Good. I'll phone her straight away and get back to you but it may be this afternoon before she can come."

"Would you do that? Oh Helen that would be wonderful. It will be fine to know that help is on the way."

Rita, like all of her compatriots was willing to help and I phoned Terry with the news. "Now listen Terry, Rita has to work this morning as I thought. She will come to your compound but she doesn't know where it is so what she suggests is this. After work she will come here and then Sidi will drive both her and me to your compound. She thought you might feel more comfortable if I was around, is that OK? It won't be right away though; will you be alright on your own?"

A small, timid thanks came down the phone line from Terry.

Unfortunately it was early evening before we could get to Terry. Our only access to the main road was cordoned off from lunchtime because the President was due to open the new craft market, at the top of road that afternoon. This meant that Rita was late getting down to us and we then had to wait for the President to leave before we could get out. Sidi was finally able to drive us to Terry's using the back roads and avoiding some of the hold-ups from the Presidential visit. During the long wait I had filled Rita in with some of the background and, not wanting Terry to feel abandoned, had kept him informed of our progress.

At the compound, we found Terry sat in the lounge of the staff house, wearing the same clothes as he had had on the previous day. He did not come to the door to let us in but simply called and told us where he was.

"I've been sat here all night", he told us. "I've got up several times to go to the bedroom but I get scared when I get to the door and can go no further. I can't go into the kitchen either. I get so far and have to come back to my chair. Please help me, I've never felt like this and I am scared."

I went into the kitchen to make us all a coffee and find something for Terry to eat. When I returned with drinks and a plate of sandwiches he was sat calmly talking to Rita. He told her how much he missed Lena and how the attack had shaken him up. Now he was really scared when he was alone. Rita asked him very few questions, she simply let him talk and when he had finished, sat back in her chair and looked at him.

"You might not like what I am going to suggest. I think it is time that your wife Sally isn't it, and your daughter in the UK knew of your present circumstances. "

Terry shook his head.

"If you don't want to phone them will you let Helen phone them?"

"No, I don't want to worry them. What can they do anyway? Vanessa knows about the car being stolen. It happened soon after she went back and I told her. No, I don't want them to know."

"I do think it will be for the best though Terry, and I know that Helen has their phone numbers."

I interrupted another refusal from Terry to tell him that both Sally and Vanessa had given me their phone numbers and told me to ring them if it was necessary.

"We know Dad", Vanessa had said, "he's a stubborn old man and would rather suffer out here than admit that he was in trouble or that he was wrong about anything." I didn't tell Terry what Vanessa had said, just that they did expect me to ring if he was in trouble.

After a great deal of persuasion, Terry agreed to come back to The Dominion while I rang his family. Sidi took the two of us back to the bar and then drove Rita back to Port Albert. I sat Terry in his favourite stool at the bar with some of the regulars that he could talk to, arranged a meal for him from the kitchen and then went inside to phone the UK. I decided to phone Vanessa first. I knew her better than I knew Sally as she had lived in Shendi for a time with her father and had been a regular at The Dominion. She did not seem surprised when I spoke to her.

"Helen from The Dominion? Of course I remember you. In fact, Mum and I have been expecting a phone call from you or someone else. What is happening, we have been so worried."

"I know that you have spoken to your father since the car theft but how much do you really know?"

"Just about the attack really, we've had very little news since. It was the Wicked Witch that arranged the attack wasn't it?"

"I don't know if Lena arranged the attack but that does seem to be what a lot of folk are thinking."

"We are 3,000 miles away but we have drawn the same conclusion, although I suppose Mum and I are a bit biased against her. I didn't think much of her when I stayed with Dad and I think the feeling was mutual. So what has gone wrong now?"

"Lena has gone – back to Ghana – but she has put the fear of God into your father. He is in a terrible state and a Cuban psychiatrist friend of mine suggested that I call you. He is living on his own, he can't cope and he is very scared. Rita, the Cuban friend, is worried that with only security at the compound at night, he might meet with another 'accident' if the locals realize how vulnerable he is. I didn't want to burden you with this, but although Rita didn't say so, I think he is heading for another breakdown. I'll help if I can but I'm tied to The Dominion. Adam and Jane have been very good but there is a limit to what we can all do."

"I'll phone Mum, Helen. She has your number and she'll ring you back. We've both been very concerned but now they are not together we both felt that we couldn't do anything until we were asked to. Don't worry, Mum will ring you as soon as she can", and with that Vanessa rang off.

Sally phoned me about ten minutes later. We discussed Rita's opinions and I described how Terry had been behaving lately. Finally she told me, "It's lucky for us all that you and Adam and Jane are there to help. Can you cope with him for a couple of weeks? I will come out as soon as I can but I will have to sort out a few things here. I think you are right. If he stays where he is, he is heading for another nervous breakdown, he could even be exhibiting signs of senile dementia but I don't know about that until I see him. I'll be over as soon as possible and will bring him back with me. Thanks Helen, are you sure you will all be able to cope. Give me a ring if things get worse."

I put the phone down and made my way to the bar. Terry was looking a little happier, surrounded as he was by people he knew and it took me a little while to find the space to tell him that Sally was coming out to see him as soon as she could. I made no mention of the fact she intended taking him home with her, I knew he would simply refuse to go.

Five of us banded together to look after Terry until Sally could arrive. Adam, Jane and I were joined on the "Terry Watch" by Paul and Diane who kept a guest house near his compound. Sally arrived as promised two weeks later. I had only known her for a short time during her stay in Africa but she had impressed me as someone who was well organised. Even so we were all amazed at the speed with which she moved. She moved Terry out of his compound and they both stayed with Paul and Diane. Sally sold most of the contents of the house and arranged for the compound to be put on the market, giving Adam power of attorney to sell it in their absence. It was clear that she had no intention of either of them ever returning.

The Terry that left on the Friday plane was only a shadow of the man I had met soon after our arrival in Shendi. In a few short years he had become an old man. His weight loss was considerable, his face lined with hollow cheeks, his eyes faded and dull, his shoulders were stooped and his eyes downcast. He gave me a hug as he left but it was limp and I felt done more out of duty than sincerity. Gone was the proud, self assured upright man who had watched with us the day that the NIA had arrested Simon.

Chapter Seven

Such is Life

I was very glad when Terry went home. Not only was it the best thing for him but, as he had pointed out a few weeks earlier, I had my own problems. The management at Peace Haven were persisting with their construction work despite the continuing court case, and it seemed to me – although I may have been biased here – that every effort was being made to obscure The Dominion and its entrance. For two seasons I had watched unconcerned as flats and shops were built on the opposite side of the car park, but the construction of the fish restaurant at the front of their property was very worrying. It was not as bad as the one that Pierre had measured out on the day that he had stormed out of my garden over a year ago but it was still bad. The back wall of the restaurant ran at right angles to our gate and hid both it and the signboard from the street. I had to extend my signboard so that it was visible above the wall. I did this with caution, leaving the original poles intact but simply extending them. (Caution was necessary as it had been debated at length in one of the interminable court sessions I had attended as to whether or not the signboard was trespassing on Peace Haven property. Can inanimate objects trespass? I didn't know but the lawyers seemed to think they could.)

Once the bar "La Parisienne" was completed, its sign board was erected on the back wall, which coincidently was directly in front of my board once again obscuring it from view. This left me with two options. I could extend my poles even further and given that in the high winds of the last rainy season they had swayed dramatically over The Dominion, the car park and Peace Haven this was one option I was very reluctant to take. My second option was to do nothing for a while. This was the better policy I decided. They would be waiting for me to take action, well let them wait I thought. My regulars knew where I was and word of mouth was attracting new customers. Peace Haven and its tactics would not succeed. Even the fact that their toilet block was situated next to my entrance and seemed to requiring emptying often, usually at lunchtimes could not deter me. I would succeed.

It was all very well being upbeat and most of the time I could be, but there were times when I felt it was all too much. One of these occasions was shortly after Terry had gone. I went down with a really bad bout of malaria and it left me feeling weak, feverish and with aching joints. Early one morning, when all I wanted to do was to roll over and go to sleep again, the phone went. It was Ousman reminding me that I was due in court the next day.

"Really Ousman, I can't see the point in going. I feel so ill and it is all a waste of time. I've heard of the never-ending story, this is the never-ending court case."

"Helen, you have to attend otherwise they will reach a decision in your absence against you."

"Very, well, somehow and with great reluctance, I will be there."

The next morning, as Sidi drove me to court, I wondered again what I was doing there. The whole court case was ludicrous, simply a way for lawyers to spend a day earning a great deal of money for doing very little. It would never be settled, I would never be able to sell The Dominion and was doomed to spend the rest of my days in this forsaken, mosquito ridden, pestilential hole where they couldn't even organise the parking at the court properly. At that point, I sat up and looked out. The traffic outside of the court house was always chaotic but today it was worse. The whole area was cordoned off and Sidi was being directed by a pompous policeman away from the car park.

"What on earth is going on?" I asked him.

"It is the trial of Mr X today. Had you forgotten?"

"Oh no," I groaned. Mr X, as he was reported in the press, had for many years been the President's right hand man. Somehow, I was not clear how; he had fallen from grace and was now on trial for treason. This explained the police cordon, the army cordon and the huge numbers of men with guns walking around the court house.

Sidi dropped me as close as he could; he was concerned that in my feverish state I would have to walk much further than usual and I might collapse in the heat.

"Wait and I'll come with you," he said

"Thank you, that is a kind offer, I know how you dislike the court house. I'll be fine. Don't worry. I need you to go and pay the taxes. Do that and park up. But please park up as close to the court house as you can. I'll find you as soon as this comedy of errors is over."

I made my way to the court house. In my post malarial condition, I felt each stone under my foot and each degree centigrade of the sun's rays. Although it was still quite early morning, the sun was powerful enough to suck every last ounce of energy out me and replace it with something that caused my joints to complain and ache. If I had had sufficient energy I would have set down on the kerbstones and cried. The only reason I didn't was that the kerbstones were so high that once I had climbed them, it seemed like a complete waste of precious energy to sit down. Staggering slightly across the courtyard I made my way to the door longing to get inside into the shade. Not this morning. With the treason trial due to start any minute the military were taking no chances. Before I could go into the building I was searched and cross questioned by a high ranking army officer. I was obviously a suspicious character because the cross questioning went on for a long time as his tone of voice became more and more hectoring. Finally he let me go and I crossed the inner courtyard between two rows of soldiers, all with their guns at the ready waiting for their guest. Ousman was waiting for me and hurried me into court as if the delay had been my fault.

As I had suspected the court case was a waste of time. It was adjourned again to a date to be fixed later when everyone had consulted their diaries. Everyone, except me that is. What ever date they fixed, I knew I would have to put in an appearance. I made my way out of the courthouse to try and find Sidi. Either the trial had started or I was no longer considered a threat, but my slow journey across the courtyard and out of the building was unhindered by any interference from the military. In fact, I was surprised to see how few soldiers there were in the courtyard and those that were there were talking, not guarding.

Outside the street seemed noisier than ever. Everywhere I looked I could see small groups of people huddled together, some crying, some shaking, some yelling into mobile phones, some simply standing looking dazed. The noise pierced my head like a drill. What was the matter with this benighted country? Did every conversation have to be carried out at full volume? How could anyone understand what was being said when all everyone did was shout at each other. Where was Sidi? All I wanted to do was find him and go home. At last I saw him and I made my way, looking neither left nor right towards him. It was with a huge sigh of relief that I sank into the car, told him to go home and not to talk and closed my eyes.

Back at The Dominion I went straight to my room, unplugged the phone, turned off my mobile and stayed there in peace and quiet until it was time for my evening stint behind the bar. Consequently it was not until I went down at just after 7.00pm that I found out why Port Albert had been so disturbed at the end of my court case. It appeared that one of the small vessels that the locals use to cross the river had struck a sandbank in bad visibility. Close behind it had been the official car ferry which, as I knew from my journey upcountry during the time Simon and I had worked for the charity, was always overcrowded. The ferry had been able to take on board many survivors from the smaller vessel but was now so over laden that it capsized itself. The official death toll was 70 but there was no way of telling how accurate this was.

As Pete was relaying this news to me, my evening chef, Babu, came hurrying up. "Helen, I need to go home. My sister has been drowned and I must go home for the burial." I sent him off immediately and he made his way to a remote village on the North Bank. When he got there he was amazed to be greeted by the very sister he had thought drowned. It was a case of mistake identity which in a country which has only about twenty common family names and a similar number of forenames is not surprising. It was not uncommon for several people in one village to have the same name, which taubabs like me found very confusing. Babu returned to The Dominion in great delight. The following day he learned that his uncle had died on the ferry.

I was surprised at the attitude of many of the locals to what would have been classed in the UK as a disaster. I found it hard to accept that life is so cheap in Africa, certainly cheaper than in Europe. After a great deal of thought I decided that there were possibly two main reasons for this. Africans encountered death at an earlier age than most people in Europe. Young children were accustomed to watching family and friends die and die quickly especially if they had malaria. Also there was their firm religious conviction that after death they would move onto a better life in Allah's garden. I found that most of the locals, whether strict Muslims or not, firmly believed in this aspect of their faith. In addition, it is part of the Muslim way of life that funerals follow death very quickly, usually within a few hours. This perhaps gives outsiders the impression that the dead are soon forgotten and even national catastrophes seem to have little impact on the national psyche.

I was to have another example of this a few months later when a large ferry travelling from the south to the north of our neighbouring country capsized off our coast with a huge loss of lives. It was early September, during the wet season and whilst there had been some terrible storms on land that year, the night of the disaster had been wet and windy but not excessively so. However, out at sea it was a different story and the storm generated some huge waves. One of these freak waves hit the ferry and it turned turtle. The death toll was believed to be in the region of two thousand, many more than died when the Titanic sank. No-one could provide an accurate count of the numbers on board. Twelve hundred tickets had been sold for a vessel with a capacity of eight hundred and twenty but there would have been many additional passengers on the ship. Students returning to college travel for free (it was the start of the school year) as do children under 8. An amateur video taken as it left its anchorage for the last time showed it listing badly to port in the calm waters of the port; what chance would such a vessel have in the stormy waters of the Atlantic Ocean?

There are little or no rescue services in that part of the world and no-one was rescued from the wreck. I knew one local lady whose father phoned her to say that he was trapped in the hold and there was no way of getting out and no chance of rescue. When I heard this I thought of those passengers on the plane on 9/11 who had called their families and I wondered whether mobile phones in that situation were a blessing or a curse.

The weather was much calmer next day and all the available boats were out attempting to retrieve as many bodies as possible. Many were pulled from the water but many more were washed up on one of the tourist beaches further along the coast. This beach was a popular lunch spot and was often used by the tour companies during the season but was quickly dropped from their itineraries for the coming months. The bodies which were recovered were swiftly buried in mass graves near to the beach by volunteers. As they buried the bodies they could see the upturned keel of the ferry less than a hundred yards from the shore. It was visible from many of the beaches along the coast, like an obscene memorial to the disaster.

A few days later the tragedy took another turn. Officials in the neighbouring country decided that their fellow countrymen should be buried in their own native soil, not in the mass graves provided. Consequently the bodies were exhumed for transportation to their homeland. However, because of the way the bodies had been buried initially, there had been a build up of gases. Thus when exposed to the African sun during the exhumation, many of the bodies simply exploded. I heard some of the eyewitness accounts of the exhumation and had no desire to hear anymore. The smell and sights were enough to turn the strongest stomachs according to someone who was working at the scene.

For a few weeks we thought that was the end of the tragedy. There was still no definitive list of passengers and there probably never would be. With the tourist season only a few weeks away, the disaster faded from the national memory until someone in the government decided that the sight of the upturned ferry was not conducive to good tourism. It was decided to sink her and make it an official grave site for the many bodies still on board. Our neighbours objected. They insisted that the ferry belonged in their waters and they announced that they would tow it back home and sink it there.

The actual date for towing the ferry back coincided with the first week of the tourist season. As they attempted to move the vessel many of the remaining bodies were dislodged and drifted into the sea. The prevailing winds and currents had changed since the storm and these bodies were washed up onto the main tourist beach near The Dominion. What made it even more horrific was that many bodies were very fragile after being immersed in water for weeks. With the disturbance caused by the towing operation, plus buffeting by winds and sea many bodies fell apart. The Peace Haven and neighbouring hotels closed their beaches early in the mornings and sent teams of workers to collect the bodies before the tourists could see them. The collecting teams had to retrieve severed arms, legs and torsos as well as whole bodies. The final touch in this horror story was provided by the packs of wild dogs who roam the coastline. They were in their element as they ran into the waves to gather this fresh harvest from the sea. The snarling and fighting of the local packs were a background accompaniment when I sat cashing up in the office after closing. The noise would continue sporadically through the night and then be replaced by shouts of The Peace Haven staff driving the dogs off in the morning. This was one occasion when I was very glad that I did not have the promised sea view.

The ferry disaster was given only a few paragraphs in the local paper, after all it belonged to the neighbouring country with whom they were not on good terms. In contrast the news broadcasts seem to show endless footage of the wild dogs enjoying the situation. Whilst this appalled the ex pats, it seemed to amuse the locals who were also collecting their own harvest. Rubber flip flops were being washed ashore, so many that for weeks after the high water mark was a row of multi coloured shoes and two years later shoes from the victims were still being found on some of the beaches.

A few days after the ferry sank, but before the start of the tourist season proper and attempts to move the ferry, my phone went one afternoon just as I was about to go off duty. It was Sharon, Reggie's sister who I had kept in touch with by email since she had taken her brother back to the UK. I was very surprised to hear her voice as I knew her father was out trying to complete the house. She was trying to find out where he was.

"Hi Sharon", I said, "Yes, I have seen Reg, but only very briefly. He came into the bar the evening he arrived, I passed him a message from a fellow radio ham enthusiast and he said he would come back one afternoon when I wasn't so busy and have a chat. I haven't seen him yet so I suppose he has been very busy."

"You haven't seen him for just over a week?"

"Yeah, that's about right. Why, is something wrong?" My heart sank. I liked Reg and I hoped that he was alright.

"Well yes there is. I am getting really concerned about him. As far as I can tell he hasn't been in contact with anyone for a week now. I usually hear from him every three or four days but I wasn't too worried because I thought he'd be busy. He is desperate to get the house finished you know."

"Mmm yes"

"Well", she went on," what has really upset me is a phone call I had from another radio ham who Dad contacts every day. He told me that he hadn't heard from Dad since last Friday and there is no answer from his call sign."

"I don't know but we've had lots of storms recently which have affected the phones; perhaps they have affected the radios as well. Maybe there is a problem with the frequencies"

"Perhaps but what is really strange is this. My cousin Steve flew out to you on yesterday's flight. Dad knew all about it and before he left, arranged to meet Steve at the airport. He wasn't there. Now Dad wouldn't have forgotten. He was really excited about Steve coming over and was dead keen to show him the house."

"Yes, well OK that is odd. Look Sharon, I'm sure that there is nothing to worry about. Perhaps your Dad is ill. I tell you what I'll do. Sidi is coming in, he is going to take the chef shopping. Your Dad's compound is almost on the way. I'll get him to go and check for you. I'll ring you back as soon as he gets here with any news.

"That would be fantastic, thanks Helen. I hope you don't mind but I've told Steve where you are and to call in to see you. He is staying at The Soma Hotel. Thanks again – you do seem to get mixed up in sorting out our problems but I had no body else I could ask."

When Sidi returned from his visit to Reg's compound, I rang Sharon with the news. "Hi, Sharon, it's Helen. Sidi has been to the compound. The only people there were Datu and his family who say not to worry. Apparently, according to Datu, your father has crossed the border to visit an old army friend. He will be back in a few days"

Sharon did not seem too convinced about this reply and neither was I. It raised more questions than it answered. Why did Sharon not know about his visit, why was Steve left at the airport and how come an old army friend had settled in an ex Portuguese colony when there was an ex English colony next door. I wondered what had happened to Reg and if I would once again be drawn into the family's problems.

The next morning, I was in the bar talking to Karen, a friend of mine who had married a local. We were discussing the prospects for the coming tourist season when Datu came storming into the bar shouting and waving his arms around accusing me of being an 'interfering taubab', an officious white woman who didn't know her place' and many similar phrases.

I sat him down and asked what the problem was.

"Why you send Sidi around to my compound? What you think you doing?" In his anger his English had deteriorated.

"Actually I sent Sidi around to Reg's compound. His family are worried about him."

"Reg, he is not there. It is not your business. You are interfering."

"I agree it is not my business but his daughter is concerned about her father. She phoned me and asked me to check for her."

"You need to learn to mind your own business. It is not your concern. I not tell you anything if I not want to. This is my country not yours."

"You are right Datu, none of this is my business but as I told you, Sharon is worried about Reg and you know Sharon is my friend. She asked me to help. I don't understand why you are so aggressive. But if I am honest, I'm not very happy with what you told Sidi. I think you need to talk to Sharon. She has a right to ask you questions about her father. Will you talk to her on my phone if I ring her now?"

Datu looked at me, looked around the bar where Karen was trying hard not to listen, shrugged his shoulders, stood up and said. "OK no problem. Let's go."

He phoned Sharon on the landline in my room. According to what he told her, he had left Reg at the ferry. After the crossing, Reg would get a coach to cross the border. Reg had given him the phone number of his army friend which was back at the compound. Datu promised to bring it down to The Dominion as soon as he went home. He also apologised for leaving Steve at the airport. Apparently Reg had asked him to collect Steve, but Datu had been ill and had forgotten. With a quick good-bye, he put the phone down and walked out.

Sharon rang me back almost immediately. I told her how aggressive Datu had been when he had first arrived. We agreed that this coupled with Datu's explanation left us both very worried. We felt it unlikely that he would ever willingly return to The Dominion with or without the phone number of the friend and I suggested sending Sidi round for it when he came back from his daily task of taking the chef shopping. Sidi agreed to call round on his way home and to ring me with the number; I would then pass it on to Sharon.

"Datu hasn't got any phone number. You got it wrong", he told me. "He says he told Sharon that he had seen Reg with a phone number, not that he had it."

"No, he did say he had a phone number. I was in the room. I heard him say it."

"OK OK. Perhaps he said that. But you know, you and Sharon have frightened this boy very much. He is very confused. You know he isn't well educated. He can't read and write. Maybe he thought he saw this number written down and he didn't."

"Sidi, you are talking rubbish. You know he can read and write. Don't you remember the last time Reg was over, I gave him some money to get the generator sorted and I made him sign for it? His signature is fine, not like someone who can't write. What's more I've seen him texting, so have you the last time when Sharon and Reggie were staying here. It seems like you are sticking together just because he is a local and Sharon isn't. I get very angry when you make excuses for people you hardly know."

"Well I can't understand why you people are making such a fuss. So Reg has gone travelling, what is that to you?"

"It is nothing to me, I told Datu that, but it is to Sharon. She doesn't know where her Dad is. Nobody has heard from him in over a week. I would be worried if it was my father missing like that."

Sidi sniffed and put the phone down, leaving me no wiser about Reg's whereabouts and annoyed with his habit of defending the locals against any criticism.

Over the next few days I recalled what I knew about Reg. According to one of the radio enthusiasts, Reg had a local girl friend. I had no idea whether or not this was true, he had certainly never been to The Dominion with anyone but as he had been a widower for several years it was a possibility. However, that certainly wasn't my business although the tale of visiting an army friend may well have been a cover for a visit to a girl friend. When I met Steve, he seemed more concerned with enjoying his week in the sun than with a missing uncle. However, Sharon kept in constant contact with me and her original concerns became almost an obsession. She even suggested that her father had been murdered.

I hastened to refute this. "Oh no, Sharon. You know what the locals are like; they will do anything to con you out of money. But murder – no. I think you are over reacting because of your job."

"Maybe but I'm not so sure. I will be talking to Steve shortly. If he agrees would you go to the compound with him and look for anything that may be a clue to Dad's whereabouts?"

I thought quickly. I really did not want to go to Reg's compound and face Datu again. "Sorry Sharon but I'm not too happy about that. Datu's reactions could be quite unpredictable. Talk to Steve and see what his opinion is and ask him to come and talk to me. I think you should contact the High Commission and see what they say." I do not know what Sharon said to Steve as I never saw him again, simply heard that he had caught his flight back to the UK safely, however in the light of a phone call I received a few hours later from the High Commission, I assume that he preferred not to become involved. The High Commission had listened to Sharon's worries and then they suggested that as I was the family's only contact in the country, I should go to the police and report Reg missing.

Much to the anger of the High Commission I refused to comply with their request. I argued very strongly that as they were now involved it was their responsibility to report him missing. (I still held on to the girl friend theory, although I kept this to myself. The last thing I needed was to go to the police and tell them Reg was missing, only to have him walk into the bar later on in the week, alive and well. Not only would he not thank me, but the police would be furious.)

"So are you saying that you won't help the police with any enquiries," came an angry voice down the phone.

"No, I didn't say that. I said I will not report him missing. Now that the family has involved you, I consider it your responsibility. If the police contact me I will help them all I can. I just feel it is your place to decide if this is a police matter or not."

The person on the other end of the line reluctantly agreed to report Reg missing and warned me to expect a phone call from the police. Later in the day the expected phone call came with a request for Sidi and me to go to Bankou police station at 6.00pm. They wanted written statements from both of us and asked that we take them in already written out so I assumed that we were going simply to hand over the documents. I wrote both our statements at Sidi's request as he felt that whilst his spoken English was good, his command of written English left something to be desired.

On our arrival we were ushered through the outer office, down a narrow dark corridor and into one of the several small interview rooms that led off it. Like many offices I had seen, notably my lawyer's, it was in complete disarray. Light filtered into the room from a small window high up in the wall and served only to emphasise the dustiness and general disorder of the surrounding. In one corner was a small filing cabinet with papers spilling out of every drawer. In the opposite corner were the coffee-making arrangements: an electric kettle, a tray with three coffee mugs with only a passing acquaintance with water, a lidless jar of instant coffee and a spoon covered in congealed coffee powder. I made a quick mental note to turn down any offers of coffee. Behind the desk, which dominated the room and was cluttered with books, papers, pens and blotters, sat an overweight police inspector in a very impressive chair. He simply waved Sidi and I to the two plastic garden chairs which sat in front of his desk, took our statements and started reading them. Outside in the corridor, shouting and scuffling had erupted which we all ignored until it reached such a volume that I could not make out what the inspector was saying.

Suddenly the door was flung open and Datu stood there with two military officers. Several policemen were trying to stop them entering the room. I realised that they had been the cause of the shouting we had heard.

"That's her, that's her" shouted Datu pointing at me as he and his companions forced their way into the room. "That's the taubab woman I'm telling you about."

The room which had just been large enough for the inspector, Sidi and myself, was now seriously overcrowded with Datu, his two allies and numerous police officers. I was uncertain whether my breathlessness and fainting feeling came from lack of air or nervousness.

Datu continued with his tirade and pointed at Sidi, "She sent that boy to my compound to harass me. I go to her bar to complain which is my right, it is my country not hers and she insults me. She called me wicked names. She even accused me of murdering her friend."

I interrupted his stream of accusations, "What!" I retorted, "I thought Reg was visiting a friend. Is he dead? I don't know this? Why would I say you murdered him?"

"You've come here to cause problems. You cause problems wherever you go. You are a wicked, wicked taubab woman. Why you come to our country when all you wanted was to treat Africans bad? We shouldn't allow your sort here. You should be sent out of our country."

At that point, being sent out of the country did have its attractions.

Sidi jumped to his feet, very annoyed by Datu's accusation and started shouting at him. Datu's army friends and then the police joined in. I remained seated, worried in case they all came to blows and watched the police inspector seemingly unconcerned fiddling with his pen. Suddenly, he jumped up and shouted "Quiet!" The mayhem stopped instantly and when everyone was calm we were able to start discussing the reason we were there – the disappearance of Reg.

Datu's statement, which he had given to the police earlier in the day, was read out. It differed in several places from what he had told me originally and from what he had told Sharon on the phone. When I tried to point this out to the inspector, Datu started shouting again. "See – see what I say. She is here to cause problems for me. She is a bad woman. We should not allow taubab women to behave like this in our country. I want her charged. She is harassing me and preventing you from doing your duty."

The inspector turned to Sidi, "Take her back to her bar. Give her a good talking to. Stress that women should only speak when they are spoken to"

I was speechless. I got up out of my chair and walked out of the room, not saying anything to anyone. I was shaken by the whole episode, the different versions of events from Datu, the number of people who seemed to be involved and the inspector's final comments to Sidi.

As we climbed in the car, Sidi turned to me and said, "Helen, I've told you before, your behaviour is not good. It upsets people. Look how you upset the inspector."

"Don't say a word, not one single word. Just get me home", I retorted, too angry to say anything else. When I thought about the whole scene later one thing did stick in my mind – the whole scene with Datu had been played out in English, almost as if it was for my benefit. In later dealings with the police I often had to ask for an interpreter. That and Sidi's continuing defence of Datu seemed very strange but I never did get to the bottom of it.

Answering the phone the following day, I found myself talking to a metropolitan police officer called Peter. He explained that he was Sharon's boss and asked me questions about Reg, Datu and the compound as well as more general questions about the country and its people. He explained that much as he would like to bring a team of officers out to investigate Reg's disappearance they could only come as invited guests when and if Reg was declared missing. Reg was booked out on tomorrow's flight so until the plane took off without him, there was very little that Peter could do.

However, in the meantime, he wanted me to go to Reg's compound and speak to Datu. Peter wanted me to tell Datu that Sharon had asked me to look through Reg's belongings for any clues as to his whereabouts. Reluctantly I agreed to go to the compound but told Peter that, in view of what had happened at the police station the day before, I was not going to put myself in any danger. At the first sign of resistance to my presence from Datu, I would leave.

I felt far too vulnerable and scared to go alone and so told Sidi to drive me to the compound and to stay with me. The gate was unlocked and Reg's jeep was missing. I assumed that Datu was out in it somewhere. We walked through the garden to the front door and I saw a teenage girl sitting cross legged preparing vegetables on the veranda. When she saw us, she jumped up, knocked over the bowl of vegetables and ran indoors. Sidi started to follow her but I held his arm and told him that we would wait in the garden for someone to come to us. The girl returned with a young, pregnant woman, who turned out to be Datu's wife. I decided to let Sidi do the talking.

"Is Datu here?"

"No, he's gone out. He took the jeep"

"Reg's daughter has sent us to look for something in her dad's things."

"You are not coming in."

"This is Reg's compound. His daughter has sent us."

"Datu told me not to let anyone in."

"But the family have sent us. We just want to go to Reg's room."

"No. Datu told me not to let anyone in."

I pulled Sidi away by the arm. "Come on", I said as he was starting to get angry at being defied by a woman, "I don't want anymore trouble with this family." We turned tail and walked back to the car. Back at The Dominion I phoned Peter and reported on our abortive attempt. I again stressed that I was not prepared to put myself in any unnecessary uncomfortable situations.

Sharon phoned me later that day and told me that she had found a current bank statement for her father. It showed that cash had been withdrawn since he had gone missing. The withdrawals had been in large amounts and two had been from a bank very near to The Dominion. Obviously this money had been drawn out by someone who knew Reg's PIN number, which in a way pointed to Reg still being alive. Sharon was not so sure. She seemed convinced that the flight the next day would take off without Reg on board. If that did happen, Peter apparently was determined to insist that he and a team of officers would come over to investigate. Toward the end of the phone call she put forward one possible solution to his disappearance.

"Helen, the last time Dad spoke to anyone was the evening that the boat sank. If he did cross the border, would he have done it by sea? Perhaps he went down with the boat. Do you think that is possible?"

Although I felt that it would probably be better for Reg's family if he had drowned on the ferry, I had to tell her that it was very unlikely.

"I'm very sorry Sharon; he couldn't have been on the ferry. He would have had to have gone miles out of his way to catch it. No I'm sorry; he is not one of the missing people from that disaster."

The next morning the High Commission's office rang and told me that they would have someone at the airport accompanied by local police monitoring whether or not Reg caught the flight home. If the plane took off without Reg on board then he would officially become a missing person. Also during the afternoon Karl, a representative of the High Commission, would come to The Dominion with the local police to talk to me. Karl came at the end of the lunch time rush in what would have been my off duty time. I heard a car pull up and door slam but Karl came in on his own. "Sorry about this, Helen. We heard about the scene at the police station the other evening and that is why I've come along. I thought that only one or two locals would turn up but there are six of them. Is it OK to bring them in?"

I nodded weakly. It made me nervous but I also found it amusing that they felt they needed six police officers to talk to one woman.

Acting on Karl's suggestion we went inside to talk away from the customers. The police officers who were from Bankou police station asked me some routine questions, covering the same ground as in my statement. They then asked me if I would accompany them to Reg's compound. They were going to do a preliminary search and had no-one else who had been to the house. I pointed out that I had only been once, sometime ago, but they still felt that I might notice something out of place or something missing. Unenthusiastically I agreed to face Datu again on condition that Karl drove me and came in with me. I had no desire at all to travel with the police or be left alone with them at the compound.

When we arrived at the compound it appeared deserted at first but then Datu appeared from behind the house. He seemed alarmed to see such a large party of police walking down the path and demanding entrance to the house. When he queried their presence the police simply told him that Reg had not arrived for his flight and he was therefore a missing person. That being the case they needed to search his house. Should Datu refuse they would return with a search warrant.

Datu unlocked the door and led us in. He went into the lounge cum dining room and stood looking out of the window. The room was simply furnished with table chairs, settee and a gaudy glass shelved unit to house the TV and music system. It was all locally made and looked as if Datu had had a huge input into its selection. In the kitchen there was evidence that Reg had not finished the work he had come over to do. Units still need installing, painting and tiling were incomplete and there were still doors to hang. There was nothing in either room that aroused my suspicions.

Next we went into Reg's bedroom which like the lounge was basically furnished. It held a simple wooden bed, small bedside table, wardrobe and a chest of drawers with three drawers. The only modern item in the room was Reg's radio. I looked around and froze. Hanging on the outside of the wardrobe was a lightweight beige, sleeveless safari style jacket. It was Reg's. I pointed it out to the police.

"That jacket, I have never seen Reg when he wasn't wearing that."

"Are you sure, maybe he had two the same."

"Well that is possible but I am just saying he always wore that jacket or one like it."

The police spent some time searching the room looking for anything including his passport that would prove he had not left the country but they found nothing out of the ordinary. I sat on the bed and wondered what had happened to Reg and how much Datu really knew. Next we all trooped into Datu's room which was furnished in a similar style to Reg's, i.e. very sparsely. Again we found nothing until the police opened a door at the back of the room. It seemed to be a walk-in cupboard which was acting as a rubbish dump for debris from the construction work. The police looked through it quickly and were about to shut the door when Karl stopped them.

"Wait a moment, please. What is that box there?"

"What is it, what have you seen?" asked the officer in charge.

"That box there. I think it is some of Reg's radio equipment."

One of the officers picked up the box which had been underneath some of the building debris, blew the dust off the top and brought it into the bedroom. The senior man opened the box. It contained a small travelling radio and headphones.

"No radio enthusiast like Reg would travel anywhere without taking a small radio with him."

"Maybe he has another one."

"Maybe, but this is expensive equipment. Why would it be cast aside in that cupboard? Everything else in there is rubbish. If he had another one, surely he would have left this by the main radio in his bedroom."

There was no answer to this from the police and we all left the house having found nothing other than the jacket and the radio to arouse suspicion. Datu showed us out looking strained but explaining this by saying that he was ill and hadn't been sleeping. People like us were upsetting him, coming round and asking questions. The police said nothing to him neither did Karl or I.

Back in the car, out of earshot of the police Karl and I discussed the visit.

"What did you make of that? There was the jacket and the radio and that boy, Datu looked very ill at ease."

"He was certainly nervous", I replied, "but you know how brutal the police can be with the local lads. They are scared stiff as soon as they see a police officer. For Datu to have to show a group of them around the house would worry him."

The next morning, as I was walking the few hundred metres to the local supermarket with the owner's breakfast, Datu came driving down the road in Reg's jeep. He tooted and waved at me as he went past. He seemed in high spirits, gone was his subdued mood of yesterday. Surely, I thought as I waved back, if he knew anything about Reg's disappearance, he would avoid me. If he hadn't drawn attention to himself I wouldn't have seen him. Perhaps my suspicions were misplaced.

I was still wondering about the complete change in Datu's behaviour towards me two days later when a group of four men came into the bar. I was sure I knew the voice of the one who appeared to be the leader and I was right. It was Peter, Sharon's boss, who I had spoken to on the phone a few days earlier. Peter and his team had come out to investigate Reg's disappearance. Peter introduced his team and I led them to a table in the garden where we would not be overheard. Once they had been served with their drinks, I joined them to discuss the events of the previous couple of weeks.

"Sharon suggested that maybe Reg was on the boat that sank," I informed them. "Now I know that the last time Reg spoke to anyone was a few hours before the boat went down and I know that there is no way it can be checked as there is no passenger list but it is so improbable that he was on the boat that you can dismiss that theory,"

Peter glanced at the others, lent his arms on the table and looked straight at me. "You do realize, don't you Helen, that Reg has been murdered?"

To hear someone come out with my worst fear just over a glass of beer in my own beer garden, made my blood run cold. "Surely not," I protested, "surely not. I know it is Sharon's alternative theory but how can you be so sure. You've only just got here, you can't be certain." My voice died away. They were certain and after all what other explanation could there be for Reg's absence. I sounded so naïve.

"Believe me, we know. It is our job, remember. Men like Reg don't go off visiting friends without telling someone where they are going. If he did go visiting, he would not go anywhere without the travelling radio equipment that the police here found thrown at the bottom of a cupboard. Reg, if for some reason, he decided not to take the equipment would not throw it with the rubbish but treat it with respect. Remember, as well, that money has been taken out of his account since he disappeared. Some of it went from a bank near here. You can't tell me that he would have withdrawn the money himself and not called in here or spoken to other people that he knew. He has gone. We had the local boys take the lad from the house into custody this morning."

"Datu is in custody? What would he have to gain from it?"

"Plenty for a local. The compound may be basic but it is a palace compared with many homes. Don't forget the money from the bank as well. He has had access to untold wealth."

"But Datu already had the compound. Reg was only coming out twice a year for a month at a time. For ten months the compound was Datu's. I know that Reg was generous towards Datu, if he had looked after him, he would have been set up for life."

"Maybe he was too generous and the boy realized he could have it all. Anyway the boy is now in the hands of the NIA. I'm sure you are aware of their methods of interrogation. He'll talk soon."

"It will be torture and he may confess to something he hasn't done."

"Sure, but we need to know where the body is. I have promised Sharon that we will bring her dad back with us and we will."

With that, I left them to finish their drinks and returned to the bar shaking my head and wondering what on earth I had become involved with.

Peter's hopes of a quick break in the murder were dashed. Datu did not talk, but neither was any more money taken out of Reg's bank account after his arrest. I saw little of Peter and his team over the next few days. They called in briefly if they wanted confirmation of anything and to give me an update on their investigation. As they days passed they seemed to be following leads that lead nowhere. Their main theory seemed to be that Datu had been taking Reg to Janika his home and had murdered him on the way. Janika was the hard-to-reach island famous for its cannabis fields that I had visited with Simon whilst working for the charity. The UK team thought that the journey through the bush provided an ideal place for leaving a body especially as that area was heavily populated with hyenas the natural scavengers of the bush.

The bar was rife with rumours from expats and locals. The most common one was that Reg's body had been found with his eyes gouged out. This related to the local superstition that the image of a murderer can be found on the victim's eyes. Other rumours suggested that Reg had been killed in a ritual killing with any variety of atrocities committed before and after the murder. Every evening seemed to give rise to another and more far fetched tale. I was tired of listening to them and thought sadly of Sharon back in the UK waiting for news of her missing father.

One evening Peter and his group called in to tell me that they were booked on a flight back to the UK the following week-end. "We promised Sharon that we would bring her father back with us and we are still confident that we will do that. It is getting really intense down at NIA headquarters, we walked out this morning. People complain in the UK about police brutality, they should come out here and see what goes on. At least we don't stick live wires up the genitals or anus."

I blanched. No wonder they were confident of getting a confession and no wonder the UK policemen gave the impression that they were eager to go home.

A day or two later Lamin, who had been helping the police, came running into the bar.

"Helen, Helen! Datu has confessed he gabbled, pulling me into the garden. "Come and sit down, I've so much to tell you. I've got friends in the police they tell me. I've been helping them you know. I told them about the other boy."

"What other boy? Calm down Lamin and tell me slowly otherwise we will all get muddled up."

"Listen Helen I am telling you. Datu went to Brikokunda a few weeks ago. He met a boy in the night club there. He gave this boy lots of money."

"Eh, what? Gave what boy, lots of money, why? What boy are you talking about?"

"This boy, I am telling you. This boy he met, he gives him lots of money. He is in a rebel gang over the border, so he has lots of guns and weapons of all kinds, this boy I am telling you will be arrested, he did the killing."

"Lamin are you sure of all of this?"

"Yes, yes. You will see soon. I told you I have important friends in the police. They told me. The men from the UK, the NIA and the local police are crossing the border this morning to go and get the body. Helen it is really bad. Listen let me tell you all about it. Datu drove Reg up country and crossed over where there is no border point so the other boy was on his own territory. Datu stopped the jeep in the bush and told Reg he was going for a pee. Datu went into the bush. Reg, he got out as well. He had been sitting for a long time. Kresba, the other boy, came from behind a tree with a gun and shot Reg. Reg fell down but he is a big strong man and he didn't die. He got up holding where he had been shot."

"Lamin, are you sure? This is awful I don't understand. Why would Reg go with Datu into the bush?"

"Yes, yes Helen. The boy tell him that he is taking him to see some land. Reg wants to buy some more. Listen it gets worse. Datu come back from pretending to take a pee and Reg, he asks him what he is doing. Why does he try to kill him? He will give him anything he wants. Then he lean against a tree and Datu and Kresba start shouting at each other. Datu is angry that the boy didn't kill Reg because they only had one bullet. Kresba says it isn't his fault, Reg moved. They have to kill Reg now and so they beat him with the butt of the gun. He falls down and they bury him alive."

"Oh no Lamin, don't say that!"

"Helen this is true, I not lying to you. You will see. Anyway I am going now. I have lots of things to do. You will know soon that I don't lie, that I tell you the truth. Lamin does not tell you what is not true", and with that he stood up and strode out into the car park, full of self importance at his news. I sat for a few minutes trying to come to terms with Lamin's news. Reg was dead, I was almost convinced about this but how he had died was another matter. I had heard so many stories about Reg and his possible death that I was able to convince myself that Lamin's was just another exaggeration.

Late in the afternoon, after the post lunch rush had gone and just before I went off duty, Frank and Dave, two of Peter's colleagues came to see me. I ordered drinks for them and we went to sit in the garden. Gone were the smart slacks and neat shirts that I was accustomed to seeing them in. Instead they were wearing filthy cut-down jeans and old Tee shirts caked in mud, dirt and perspiration.

"Excuse the state of us, we wanted to come and tell you before you heard it from someone else. Datu confessed last night", Frank told me draining his coke and ice.

"I have never worked so hard in my life as I have this morning," he went on. I had to admit that Frank, who was somewhat overweight, looked drained and exhausted. Then he continued. "After what Datu told us we had to go up country this morning to cross the border where there is no border post."

I interrupted him and told them both what Lamin had told me earlier in the day.

"I can't believe it," Dave said shaking his head in dismay, "Yes, what he said is basically right but I don't know how he could possibly know all this. We were there and some NIA people, that is all. No one should have mentioned this to any one."

"This is a very small country", I explained," Everyone is related to someone in the know. It is amazing how news travels"

"Yea, I appreciate that but Lamin should not have known. Helen, before I go on, how well do you know him. Peter is viewing him with suspicion, not in connection with Reg's death but we think he is a dodgy character."

"I knew him through a charity we were involved with when we first came out here but that is all. He is not a friend. In fact I agree with your assessment of him. Lots of things he says don't add up. I didn't really believe him this morning. As you said, how could he know? But when you both walked in looking as you do, it was obvious to me what you had been doing".

"We're glad to hear that you are not involved with Lamin. He has been saying down at the police station that he is a close friend of yours."

"Well he is not." I stood up; I was annoyed with Lamin for claiming to be a close friend and needed to move around for a moment. "Let me get you both a pint of beer before you go on. I think you need it and I need to just pop back into the bar."

I put two ice cold beers down in front of them and sat down. I knew now that what Lamin had told me had been near enough the truth but dreaded hearing the actual details.

Frank continued with his tale. "Apparently when we crossed the border, we were going into rebel held territory. We had to seek permission from the rebel leader to enter. He gave us just four hours to enter, do what we had to do and return back across the border." He broke off to take a well earned swig of his pint. Then he carried on. "We had driven a fair way over the border with Datu desperately trying to find the place where the murder took place and yes it did happen as Lamin described. I think that Datu genuinely didn't recognise where it had happened, one place looked just like another. We drove back and forth over the same area for ages. Anyway eventually he found it, but time was getting tight. It was mid-day and the sun was blazing down and if we were to get back over the border within the four hours we definitely had to get a move on. I will not tell you the gory details but we did exhume poor old Reg. It has been the hardest day of my life and not simply because I am not at the peak of physical fitness. Sharon is a colleague and I have often heard her talk about Reg. That is what has made it so much harder."

"Never mind mate", said Dave. "We promised Sharon that we would bring Reg back and we will. I know it is not the outcome she wanted but at least we will be taking him home. At least the family will know what happened to him. They will be able to have a proper funeral and say their own goodbyes. Much better than him lying in a shallow grave in the bush, so far from home."

Peter called in later to say goodbye and we discussed possible motives for the murder. Peter still maintained that Datu's only motive had been to obtain the compound. I was unconvinced. My theory was that Datu was involved with the rebels over the border, certainly Kresba the actual murderer was. I argued that Reg may have stumbled across something and he was killed for what he knew rather than for gain. Peter disagreed even when I told him about the reaction of Debra, a friend of Reg's who had come over with him but had stayed at a hotel. Over afternoon cups of coffee she told me that she neither liked nor trusted Datu and if she came over again, she would still not stay at the compound. I also told Peter of Reggie's reaction to Datu. How he had suddenly spoken of his distrust of the African, to the extent that he asked if Sidi rather than Datu could drive him to the airport. Peter stuck to his opinion but I wondered. Schizophrenics, being hyper sensitive are often better judges of character than most of us. He also told me that in addition to searching for Reg, they had been able to show the local police some different techniques, for example how to trace mobile phone calls. This had been invaluable in solving Reg's murder but Peter hoped that it would also help in combating the growth of paedophile rings which were now targeting West Africa.

The UK police flew home at the week end, sadly taking Reg's body with them. Reg's remains were laid to rest in his home town on November 11th, a fitting date for an elderly military gentleman.

Peter told me that I would see them all again when they came out for the trial. As I said my farewell to the team, I wondered what would have happened if Sharon had worked in a different job. Would there have been such a thorough investigation and would a team from the UK have come out to search. People go missing all the time especially in Africa, in fact some people come here specifically to disappear. I remembered back in the early days listening to two old hands discussing locals and expats who had disappeared. At the time I had put it down to scaremongering but now I wondered how many had chosen to disappear. I remembered Pete, the boy we had met trying to set up a garage. He too had vanished, maybe for good reasons and maybe not. After Reg's case, I was more inclined to think not.

Chapter Eight

The Scales of Justice

In addition to my regular expats and tourists I had a steady stream of locals who came in either with tourists or on their own. A few of these were undercover agents for the S.S.G. It was easy to spot the regular S.S.G. officers as they often wore the unofficial uniform of a long evening length jacket and matching trousers. Identifying the undercover men was harder, but all of us became expert over time. Any local who sat nursing a soft drink, listening but not joining in conversations was regarded as suspect until proved otherwise. Although I took care not to express any controversial opinions in the hearing of anyone who I did not know and trust, some of my regulars were not so careful. I grew skilled at quashing conversations that could turn contentious and turning the topic to something more anodyne.

Seeing a low ranking S.S.G. officer enter the bar one night, I gave a warning glance to my regulars and with my heart pounding, approached him. He showed me his S.S.G. card and said, "Good evening, will you step outside. I want a private word with you."

I followed him out into the garden, my heart pounding faster than ever. This was obviously an official visit which as I well knew, spelt trouble. He halted just outside the bar door. That was good, by speaking to me here we could be seen from inside the bar. My regulars would keep an eye on the situation.

Nervously I asked him what he wanted.

"You know the boy Datu Bota, who we have in custody?"

"Yes, you know I do."

"He has asked me to come and see you. He has a request for you."

"What do you mean? I want nothing to do with this boy."

"Datu is hungry. Do you know that food is not given to anyone in custody? Food must be sent into them."

"OK, OK, but what has that to do with me?"

"You have a restaurant, you have plenty of food, this boy has nothing. He thought you would help him as you are a friend of his English family."

"What! Is he crazy? Doesn't he realize that any friendship he had with Reg Friend's family ended when he murdered Reg?"

The officer looked sternly at me.

"Are you saying that you won't send him anything?"

"Yes, that is exactly what I am saying. I can't understand you coming here and expecting me to do this. He murdered someone I knew."

"But you must understand. This boy holds you responsible for him being where he is. If you had left things as they were and not caused all this trouble, everything would have been fine."

I could not believe what I was hearing. It was my fault that Datu was in prison?

Taking a firm grip on my temper, I replied, "I can't believe that you are blaming me for Datu being in prison. Anyway he has a wife and mother besides numerous brothers. Let them feed him."

"You know the wife is pregnant. She needs looking after. Datu cannot look after her now because of what you did. He is very angry about all of this".

He was very angry. What about Sharon and Reggie, wouldn't they be angry too?

"I am not responsible for the position Datu is in. All I did was send someone to ask about Reg as his family were worried. I wasn't the one who shot him."

I could not believe that I was having this conversation with an officer of the law. I knew that there were different cultural values at work over here to those I had grown up with but surely they were not so twisted as to make the perpetrator of the crime into the victim.

The officer turned to leave firing one final shot in the conversation as he did so.

"It was not your business to ask about the man. You must learn to keep out of matters that don't concern you. Now this boy and his family are suffering whilst you refuse to help. You taubabs come here to make money in our country and you cause all sorts of problems for the local people who are just trying to survive. You need to learn how to behave in this country."

He left empty handed but on the other hand he had unnerved me. In his book that was probably a partial success.

Apart from my feelings of natural justice, I was disinclined to become involved with Datu and the S.S.G. The less I had to do with the S.S.G. and the police the better. Regrettably, I would need to be on good terms with police for the coming months as Sharon had asked me to supervise the compound until it could be sold. Reg's death meant that the compound became the sole property of Reggie. In view of both Reggie's earlier experiences and her father's death, Sharon was understandably eager that the family have nothing more to do with it and persuaded Reggie to sell it even though it was not finished. She also persuaded him not to come out to Shendi again and instead had asked me to take responsibility for the compound until it was sold. Reluctantly I had agreed and was more than pleased when Sidi volunteered to help. The compound lay between his home village and The Dominion so it would be easy for him to call in on his way to or from work.

The police, who had been taking care of the compound since Datu's arrest were informed by the High Commission that I would be taking over responsibility for looking after it. I had told Sharon that I would request a complete inventory before I took over, so that I knew exactly what I was responsible for. The High Commission thought this an excellent idea and the police agreed to provide one. However, during a phone call to discuss the hand-over the local police inspector asked me why I felt I needed a list.

"That is the correct way to do things. You have been looking after the compound since Datu was arrested but now the family of Mr. Preston have asked me to take over. I should sign for what you are passing on to me. This is to safe guard not only me but you as well."

"You know that the family told us we could take the radio equipment including the aerials on the roof and the generator."

"Yes, I know that but there is all the furniture, there are tools there are all sorts of things. It is proper that everything is accounted for."

"Are you saying you don't trust me? I am the police you know. You can trust me."

"I did not say that I didn't trust you. I know I can trust you. This is just the proper way to do things."

"Very well, you will get your list, but we are very busy you know. This list will take a long while to complete. You could have this property sold whilst you are waiting for a list. Are you sure you need one?"

"I'm sure. Thank you for doing it. Please let the High Commission know when I can take the property over."

Several months past and I had no contact with either the High Commission or the police. Twice a week, Sidi would take a detour on the way home and drive past the property to see if things seemed to be in order, but we had no access to the compound. On one of this visits, Sallyman the owner of a small shop which was opposite the compound called to Sidi, "You came to this compound with a white lady didn't you?"

"Yes", answered Sidi, "she is going to look after it after the police have finished with it. I drive past now and then to check that it is OK"

"Oh, yeah. Well I tell you, she will not be getting this place for a long while."

"Why?"

"Too much goes on there; they won't want to give it up".

"What do you mean? What goes on there?"

"I can't be sure what they do when they are there but there is people in and out all day long. I'm surprised you never see no cars there. At night, I often see the inspector himself arriving with different girls; they are always there for a while before I see them drive away."

Sidi related this conversation to me next morning and asked me what I intended to do.

"Well there isn't much we can do about it" I said, "I've had enough problems over this case and have been told enough times to mind my own business. I don't really want to know all this. All I hope is that everything is in order when the property is finally handed over, Sharon and Reggie have been through enough."

Sidi looked at me and I could swear he nodded approvingly. Perhaps he thought that I was really beginning to see what life was like in his country.

Almost eight months went by with Sidi still making regular checks and still not seeing any cars at the compound. Then I received a phone call from the High Commission to collect the keys from the police. The High Commission advised me to sign the inventory and salvage what I could. That did not bode well. At the police station, Sidi and I were ushered straight into the inspector's office where I was immediately handed a list of contents and told to sign it. Now I understood the advice I had received. The list was short with just one item on it - a bed frame. All the furniture that I had seen on my last visit with the police was missing from the inventory. My hand hovered nervously over the page. Sidi looked over my shoulder, nudged me and hissed in my ear, "Sign it".

Feeling a complete coward and with great reluctance I did so. In two months time I would need to renew the police liquor license for The Dominion. I would have to apply to this same police inspector who was staring hard at me as if daring me to question the list. I knew that if I gave any hint of my concerns, any suggestion that things were missing I would not get my license. I signed and dated it and only then did I look straight at the inspector. Not letting my gaze drop, I reached for the keys, turned and walked out without saying a word.

Back in the car, Sidi looked at me with disgust. "Helen, I am tired of telling you. You do not know how to behave. You must not behave like that, the inspector is a very important man, and you didn't even say good-bye to him. We have the keys, what more do you want?"

"A bit of furniture in the house might have been nice. How can I explain this to Sharon?"

"There is nothing to explain. You didn't take the furniture. It is OK there is no problem."

"It is not OK by me, there is a problem. He is a high ranking officer. If he hasn't emptied the house, then he knows who did."

"You make a fuss over everything. As you say he is a high ranking officer and you walked out of his office without speaking to him. You cannot be rude to people like this."

"Well I can be rude to you. Just drive me home and don't speak to me. I don't feel like talking."

Peter and his team came out shortly after for the start of Datu's trial. They were horrified by the state of the house. Not only was there no furniture but when the police had removed the radio aerials from the roof, they had left holes in its concrete surface. During the rainy season, water had poured in through these holes causing an immense amount of damage. Sharon and I dissuaded Peter from raising these issues with the police. Sharon felt that beside the loss of her father, the loss of a few pieces of furniture was negligible and living in the country I knew that only bad repercussions could come from questioning the police about their care of the compound.

Reg's murder and my involvement with it had brought some harsh facts about living in Shendi home to me. The decision to start a new life out there was made after a visit of a fortnight, not perhaps the wisest thing Simon and I had ever done. I had often heard gossip in the bar about people dying or disappearing in bizarre circumstances and had usually ignored it. People do exaggerate and tales become twisted in the telling and some of the things I had heard were beyond belief. Now putting Reg's murder alongside the attempt to poison me, made me more cautious about dismissing the bar tales as simple exaggerations and I began to worry about what kind of country I was living in.

Conversation in the bar one night recalled one such incident. The previous year I had been approached by Tim on holiday from the UK with his girlfriend Liz. A mutual acquaintance, Harry, who was involved with charity work in Shendi, had suggested that they call in and see me. When it became obvious that they wanted to talk in private, I took them out into the garden and asked Jed to bring us all drinks.

"My mother died last year from cancer. I know this will sound silly to you," said Tim, "and feel free to tell me that both Ben my brother who is in the UK and I have over active imaginations but I just know that something was wrong about her death."

(At that point, I must admit that I thought, "Oh no not again. I don't want to get involved in other people's problems.)

"I'm sorry to hear about your mother but why do you think something is wrong. Tell me what the problem is and then I will tell you if I think you are imagining things," I replied.

"OK well, Mum lived here for three years, she had a local husband. Now, Harry said that you know lots of expats and thought you might have known her. But that's not the reason I have come out. I've come out to try and find her husband – I suppose you could call him my step-dad."

"OK, so far, what was your Mum's name and where did she live?"

"Oh yes, I haven't told you sorry. Her name was Gwen and she lived in a village not far from the coast. She didn't work here but did bits of unofficial charity work – helped out at a couple of schools that sort of thing. Whenever she went back to the UK she would collect discarded things from schools like desks and blackboards and ship them out for her schools."

"Gwen, Gwen, living near the coast….. no, sorry I didn't know your mum but I had heard about her. The expat community is too big to know everyone but small enough to have heard about almost everyone. Someone did tell me that your mum wasn't here now but no one has told me she died. So I assume she died back in the UK"

"Yes, she had been ill over here for a few months and the doctor had diagnosed cancer. She was being treated for it here until we persuaded her to come home. As soon as she arrived she was admitted to hospital but died two days later. It seems that whilst she had symptoms of cancer no-one in the UK could pinpoint its source. All their tests were inconclusive and that's what is so strange"

"Oh, that does sound odd but I suppose it is possible. Look before I say any more I need to ask you a question? It may seem silly and as if it has nothing to do with things. Is this your first visit?"

"Yes. Ben and I had planned to come and visit Mum this year and meet her new husband; he is called Lamin by the way. I was hoping to find him and talk about my mother's house. She had paid for it and had it built for them. I know she paid for it because he had no money. That was OK by us but I do think that Ben and I are entitled to half of the house. She was our Mum. Don't you agree?"

"It doesn't matter if I agree or not, you will have a hard time trying to claim anything I think. If your mum built a house for Lamin it will most likely be in his name. That is the norm here. Locals can sort out legal things much more easily and cheaply without a European name appearing on the documents – or at least that is what they tell their partners. From what I remember being told about your mum she lived in a village called Bakumpa about ten minutes or less by car from here. If you get a taxi outside your hotel, it will take you there. Talk to the locals there aren't many Europeans living there so they will remember your mum and I am sure that Lamin and his family will be living in the compound that she had built. However I will warn you, Lamin is a very common name here"

"That's great we will do that in the morning. Now I have another problem to solve. Before Mum died she was collecting a container of things to bring over and Ben and I have finished it. In fact it has arrived over here now. We want to donate it to her schools in her memory. Harry told me that it is not always easy to get clearance from customs and gave me the phone number of another Lamin who he says will help. Do you think we should ask him to help with the container?"

"You do need a local to help or it will be very costly. Harry's Lamin is a taxi driver and he is OK. In fact if I were you I would phone him and ask him to take you to Bakumpa. Tell him you are friends of Harry and he will take care of you. Which schools do you want to take the things to?"

Tim handed me a piece of paper. "These two are the ones where Mum worked"

"I know where they are. They aren't far away. Harry's Lamin should be able to arrange for the contents of your container to be transported there"

Tim and Liz stayed in the garden and I went back to the bar. As I was drifting off to sleep that night, it crossed my mind to wonder if they would find Lamin the stepfather. It must all seem terribly strange to them especially to Tim who was still recovering from the loss of his mother. Still Harry's Lamin would help them. And with that cosy thought I turned over and went to sleep and thought no more about them.

Two days later they both came into The Dominion, looking very haggard and in need of a good night's sleep. Liz, who on our previous meeting had been somewhat of a fashion plate, had bags under her eyes and her hair needed a wash and comb. They came over to me at the bar and asked if we could all go into the garden and talk. I collected some drinks for all of us and led them to the table we had used on their first visit.

"Did you get Lamin to take you to Bakumpa?" I asked.

"Yes we did and you were right. It was where my mum lived. I phoned Ben and as soon as I mentioned the name he said that was where she had lived."

"Good, good, how did you get on?"

"Harry's Lamin took us but we didn't get on at all. We can't understand it. We didn't see any white people there. It was all locals."

"No, that doesn't surprise me, it's not far away from here but it's not an area where ex-pats live."

"OK, so if Mum was the only white person there then someone should have known her shouldn't they? They must have known the only white person in the village. But they all said that no white woman ever lived there. It was so odd. Some people we spoke to didn't even answer us, they turned and walked into their compounds. Lamin spoke to some of them in their own language but he got nowhere either"

"That is odd. I would have expected them to remember the only white woman in the village."

"Yes but there is something I didn't tell you the other day. Ben was supposed to come out with me, not Liz. We had told a few people we were coming out, you know how you do, just talking with friends. Well late one night Ben and I were in our flat watching some TV when there was a loud knocking on the door. We didn't usually get callers that late, so I opened the door a fraction to see who it was. The door was pushed wide open and I was knocked out of the way by this big black guy who came in followed by three of his friends. Honestly, Helen, I was scared stiff. They barged into the lounge where Ben was standing wondering what the noise was. They pushed us both into chairs and stood there. 'Right boy', said the first guy,' I understand that you are going to Shendi to find your Shendi Daddy. Is that right?' I told him that we were going to see where our mother had lived and to meet Lamin our step father. He laughed and then said, 'One word and one word only, boys. Don't. Don't go to Shendi or any other part of Africa. Africa is for the Africans not for you. What happens over there is none of your bloody business.' Then he picked up a framed photo of Mum and simply dropped it on the floor. 'You remember your Mummy how she was in that photo. Don't try to cause problems now she has gone.' I was shaking but I asked him who he was and what right he had to treat us like that. 'Me, I am Lamin's brother and so are these three men here. We have every right to do what we want to you. Remember Lamin is your stepfather. You are just two little white shits trying to make problems. We are going now, but remember we can come back any time' and with that all four of them left us. I don't know what frightened me more, what he said or the three silent men who stood there."

Tim sat back in his chair as he finished his tale and took a long drink of beer. It had obviously been a strain telling me the story but I was glad that he had.

"Oh Tim," I said, "I can see why Ben didn't want to come. I think it is very brave of you and Liz to come out after that."

"I didn't want to come out at all," said Liz, "but Tim was hell bent on coming, he said he owed it to his Mum. I don't think we should be here.

Helen it was awful in that village, like Tim said some of the people went into their houses when we asked about his mum but some were really hostile. They crowded round us and almost tried to push us. I'm scared."

"I can understand that, but how do you feel?" I asked turning to Tim.

"I don't know really. Those men back home were awful and, Liz is right. Some of the villagers were very hostile towards us. It was obvious they knew Mum, but why would no-one say where her compound was or that they knew her. I am starting to agree with Liz. We shouldn't have come."

"Hmm, well I will say that from my experience the locals do all stick together if there is something that they don't want you to know. If that is the case you will never find it out."

Tim looked down at the table and started playing with a beer mat. It was obvious he wanted to say something but didn't quite know how to.

"Do you think," he started, "do you think that Lamin killed my mum?"

"I don't know," I answered slowly. "What I will say is this. Sure Lamin has the compound now; it was more than likely in his name only anyway. What you have to think about is, if he did arrange your mum's death, would it help you to know?"

Tim looked at the beer mat again which he was busy shredding with his fingers. "I suppose not. Mum is dead and nothing will bring her back. What I don't understand is that she always seemed so happy here. She even told us that that village felt like home, she felt she was a Shendian not someone who lived in the UK. I just can't imagine her living in that village and being happy there. It was so creepy, so eerie so … not right."

"Will you go back?" I asked.

"No. Lamin the taxi driver has arranged for us to get the container out of the docks tomorrow and then we will visit the schools. I want to do that for Mum. After that we will stay in the hotel until we go home. I don't want to go out into Shendi again and I know Liz doesn't." Liz nodded in full agreement and with that they stood up and left.

That was the last time I saw Tim and Liz, but when his friend Harry arrived, he told me that he had seen them in the hotel and that they could not wait to fly home.

"What do you reckon to Tim's story?" Harry asked me.

"I don't know. Who can tell? Tim and Ben would be upset, loosing their mum like that, perhaps it helps having someone to blame. I find the episode in the UK very strange. I wonder why Tim and Ben didn't go to the police. Don't suppose I will ever know", I replied.

Had I heard this story after Reg's murder, perhaps I would not have dismissed it so lightly. Now I was wiser, or so I thought. What could I do? I could go home or I could stay. In the dark hours of the night, lying in bed worrying about how safe I was, going home seemed like the perfect option. However, in the cold light of day I knew that I could not return to the UK. The court case dragged on and until that was resolved I had to stay. If I left, I would leave with nothing. Simon and I had sunk our life savings into The Dominion and I could not return to the island empty handed. There was no other option, I would have to stay and fight it out alone.

Alone, that was the key word. Who could I trust? Simon would not come back, I was not even sure where he was, and who was there in Shendi that I could trust. There were no locals that I felt I could depend on to support me. As I had said to Tim the previous year, the locals tended to stick together against the Taubab community. Our presence in Shendi, although vital to the economy was only tolerated and that tolerance was wearing thin. Even in the time that I had been there I had noted a greater antagonism to Taubabs from those I came into contact with on a business basis. My staff, who I considered were well treated in comparison to others employed in the tourist trade, were outwardly friendly but on many occasions I found them to be disloyal and dishonest. Tourists, even the repeat visitors still thought of Shendi as "Smiley Shendi" but those of us who lived there were learning to call it "Slyly Shendi".

If I could not trust a local then perhaps I could trust an expat. When I considered the expats that I knew, I realised that they were a very mixed bunch of people. Some were on the run whether from a situation in the UK or from the law or from ex partners whilst some had chosen to take early retirement in the sun and were financially unable to settle anywhere more luxurious. I realised that I was in the running away category. If we had not lost our daughter, I was sure that I would never have agreed to leave the island. But an island of less than 30 square miles is too small to escape memories and so I had chosen to leave them behind and escape to the sun. I had achieved my desire to some extent. In Shendi, I was too busy and had too much on my mind to dwell on the past. Nevertheless, could I trust anyone? They were more likely to be sympathetic to my case than the locals but I was not certain. There were two people; a British man and a British woman who I was certain were informers for the S.S.G.. Whether they did it for financial gain or to ensure that they were allowed to run their businesses in peace, I did not know. But I was sure that if not informers, they were far too friendly with the S.S.G. for my peace of mind.

Running my mind over my regulars I thought of Adam and Jane. They had been more than helpful when Terry had been here and having his problems with Linda. Adam also helped me in practical ways, printing my menus on his computer and being paid in the local manner, with cigarettes and beer, rather than cash. Nick, a builder from Yorkshire who had started out as a tourist and decided to settle here, he was a potential ally. Now he was here permanently, he was building a holiday complex along the coast and had a steady local girlfriend with family in the military and other useful high connections. This link had already proved its worth as Nick had, on occasions brought some of the off duty soldiers in for a drink if he thought that there would be problems in the bar. So there were three people, was there any one else?

There was Jack, another builder who often did work for the High Commission and therefore was always a source of information about potential problems. Unfortunately, he had recently lost his wife with malaria and her loss had hit him very hard. It would not be fair to burden him with my problems if I could help it. Jack had lived in many parts of Africa for many years, unlike 'Danish Dave', an Englishman who had been brought up in Denmark was a new comer to Africa and Shendi, but his feet had led him to The Dominion, very shortly after his arrival. Was he a possible source of help?

How could I forget Rick? Rick, (sometimes known as Nightclub Rick, a name which was guaranteed to infuriate him) was always my first customer of the day. He would call in for his breakfast whilst out on his early morning cycle ride. He had moved to Shendi for a less stressful life and had opened a very successful nightclub, spending a small fortune on renovating the premises that he was renting from some locals. When it became apparent that his nightclub was making a profit, his landlords decided that they wanted to run the business themselves. Nine months after opening, he was closed down, illegally he always argued by the tourist board. He did consider taking the tourist authority to court but seeing the length of time my case was taking, he decided against it. Nevertheless the nickname Nightclub Rick stuck to him for many years. I knew that I could rely on him for a sympathetic ear and sound advice as he would understand some of the difficulties I was encountering in a tourist related business. What about Kevin, I wondered. He was a larger than life lad from Liverpool who was also a friend. Unfortunately, like many expats he had a drink problem and it was getting worse. When he was sober, which was becoming less and less often, he was only too willing to help, but I knew that I could not rely on someone like that.

That was the men, was there a woman who would help? That is apart from Jane Adam's wife of course. There was Di who, with her husband, ran a guest house and had been a nurse in the UK. She was a friend and of course there was Karen. I had known Karen almost from the start and our friendship had grown. She was married to a Shendian and lived only a short distance from The Dominion. Every morning she called in for a coffee and a chat to the others around the lunchtime bar. She became my verbal punch bag as I did for her, and together we would try to sort out each other's problems. Karen had come out intending to work but found that the system discouraged expats from working by levying a punitive tax rate on all expats. As a result she had to return to the UK every few months to earn the money to fund her life in Shendi. I knew I could trust Karen and I missed her support and her view on Shendian life whenever she was in the UK.

So, these were the people I could trust, who I counted as my friends. It was only a small group and consisted solely of customers, but tied to the bar as I was, there was no opportunity for me to meet anyone else. I knew that I could depend on them if I was in trouble but they all had their own lives to lead and came to the bar to relax, not to listen to my problems. They were after all customers first and I tried very hard not to burden them with my troubles but to listen to their stories.

Many of their stories were about the things that made daily life so different to life in the UK. It may have been dangerous, it may have been frustrating, it may have been frightening but one thing it never was and that was humdrum. Every morning when I woke up, I knew that by the time I went to bed, I would have learnt something knew about life in Shendi and that I would have experienced at least one thing that I would never have experienced if I had stayed on the island. Take the incident with the dog for example.

I have never been too keen on unknown dogs and stayed out of the path of the wild dogs which roamed the beach and the streets. Fortunately they seemed to keep away from The Dominion and so when early one morning when Tami, the chef and I were alone and Black Cat (another animal left by the previous owners) streaked past me straight up into the rafters, I simply thought that Buster, my larger than life feline friend was exercising his male prerogative to dominate her. I went out into the garden to chastise Buster but instead came face to face with a large black and tan rottweiller. I froze, there is no other word for it, I simply froze. Rottweillers have always scared me and this one was huge.

"Attacha – go away," I shouted, holding out an arm that I was amazed to see was shaking and pointing to our entrance. "Attacha!"

To my relief and amazement he obediently turned but then made his way, not to the entrance but through the beer garden and behind the outbuildings into my garden.

What a time to have sent Latif to fetch petrol for the generator. He was very good with animals but he had only just gone. It would take him quite some time to fill the jerry cans and then bring them back in the push-push (which was the local name for a wheel barrow.) I was on my own.

"Hannie attacha!" I shouted again.

The dog turned back and walked right past me, crossed the bridge and headed for the entrance, which was presumably the way he had come in. That was fine by me; he could go and bother someone else. Who needed Latif, I thought. This Boss Lady can handle dogs and I turned to go back into the bar.

I heard a scrabbling noise behind me, but before I could turn to see what it was, an incredibly sharp pain tore through my ankle. The rottweiller had attacked me. I screamed and that seemed to make it worse. Again and again he tore at my ankle and then inexplicably let go, turned and left The Dominion.

I hobbled into the bar leaving a considerable trail of blood behind me and collapsed onto a chair. Tami, who had come out of the kitchen in response to my screams asked, "Do you have a problem?"

Before I could summon up the energy to give him the sort of answer that deserved or even simply to explain what had happened, Karen and Robert, a long term 'tourist' friend of mine who made many visits to Shendi and had been having breakfast when The Peace Haven had the empty containers placed outside our entrance, came in. They had been outside and, hearing my screams had rushed in, passing a large black and tan rottweiller on the way.

"Here", said Robert, "let me have a look at that foot."

"You need to get that looked at straight away", said Karen. "Have you anything at all that will stop the bleeding."

Liverpool Kevin came, attracted by the noise, "Oh my God, what have you done?"

I managed to tell him and the others what had happened.

"You never turn your back on a dog. You will remember that another time won't you? ", he said. "Good job you were wearing a long skirt and leather sandals. The only bit of flesh he could see would be your feet and your sandals would give you some protection. I have some antiseptic in my truck; I'll go and get it."

"Oh no, Kevin, not antiseptic. My foot stings enough without you pouring that neat stuff all over it."

"Are you sure, I think you ought to have some on immediately. Well, OK then, at least let me take you to a clinic."

"No, I'll go with Sidi. Tami," I called, "phone Sidi and tell him what has happened. I need him to come straight away, straight away mind and take me to a clinic."

"Let me take you. I am here and Sidi isn't. It is important that you get there quickly", urged Kevin.

"Helen is right, Kevin," Karen looked up from where she was helping Robert who was trying to wipe some of the blood from my foot. "It is much better for her to go with a local. Sidi will get her seen as soon as they reach the clinic.

"OK, OK if you both agree, then Sidi it is. Are you sure you don't want some antiseptic?"

"I'll be fine and thanks Kevin. Sidi will sort me out."

Karen and Robert carried on trying to clean my foot. They wrapped it in a towel to absorb some of the blood which was still pouring from my foot. It was impossible to see just how much damage the dog had caused as every time the blood was mopped away, some more oozed out.

Sidi came in, took one look at the bloody foot resting on a chair and said, "Helen, I had no idea. When Tami spoke on the phone, I thought it was only a little bite. I think I had better take you to the general hospital in Port Albert."

"No Sidi that will take too long. Take my to Aunt Sammy's"

"Helen, you don't like Aunt Sammy. You say she is a fraud."

"She may be but today I need her, in fact today I like her, so take me there."

Sidi was right; I did not trust Aunt Sammy. She was the nurse in charge of the clinic in Sidi's home village of Famara and was a formidable lady. Medically she was excellent and I did have faith in her nursing skills but otherwise I did not trust her. However, unlike tourists who donated drugs and equipment to the hospital which she later sold, I simply needed her nursing skills. There was nowhere else for me to go, all the Cuban doctors had returned home and the hospital in the capital was too far away. Aunt Sammy's it would have to be.

By the time we had driven the 7Km to Famara an hour had elapsed since the dog bite and the reaction was beginning to set in. Sidi pulled into the clinic's compound and we were faced with queues of women. All of them were accompanied by toddlers or babies and many of them were in the advanced stages of pregnancy. It was Tuesday, the day for Sammy's mother and baby clinic.

Aunt Sammy heard the car and pushed her way through the queues towards us. She reminded me very much of an old fashioned UK hospital matron and although she was not very tall, she was large and had a commanding presence. I could understand why her nurses jumped when she gave orders. Neither of us was particularly fond of the other; back in the early days of our stay in Shendi, I had found out that Kebba would take tourists to visit the clinic and share the proceeds of their donations with Aunt Sammy. Also, Pedro had found out that she was in the habit of selling drugs that had been donated to the clinic and using the money to fund the building of a new compound. Keen though Aunt Sammy was to welcome taubabs to the clinic she was always wary of me, perhaps she wondered just how much I knew about her goings on. As I sat in the car and watched her approach us, I decided that I would have to learn to accept the way things were done in Shendi and give up my one woman crusade to put the country to rights. Certainly sitting in Sidi's car with a foot covered in a blood stained towel was no time to stand up and fight for justice, if I could even stand up.

"Well good morning, Mrs Dominion and hello Sidi," she said. "What brings you to old Sammy's clinic this morning? You have malaria, Madam?"

"No, Sammy, no malaria this time", I told her, "neither am I pregnant so I haven't come to join your mother and baby clinic. I've been bitten by a dog on my foot."

"Oh my, yes a lot of blood", she said peering in through the open door. "Are you going to be able to come inside?"

"I'll manage," I said.

Sammy led the way as Sidi came around and helped me out of the car. Using him as a prop, we slowly followed Sammy into the clinic. After the blazing light of the sun, the clinic was dark, dull and dreary and a quick glance assured me that hygiene standards were very different to those in the UK. We followed Sammy down a narrow corridor lined with new mothers waiting to see a nurse. The corridor was so narrow that Sidi had to walk in front of me and let me lean on him that way rather than help me from the side. The corridor opened up into what had once been a reception area but now served as an office. This small space already held a man in a white coat carrying out malaria tests, the nurse who was providing him with blood samples from the patients queuing in the corridor and two rickety chairs.

I sat on one of the chairs and Sammy bent down to unwrap my foot. She looked horrified when she saw what was under the towel.

"Oh my, you sure must have upset that dog," she said. "When did you last have a tetanus jab, was it more than five years ago?"

"Yes, I think, er yes it must have been."

"Well that is the first thing I have to do. I have to give you a tetanus jab, but I can't deal with your foot here, you will have to go to Port Albert"

"Aunt Sammy, that is what I told her," said Sidi, "Why don't you ever listen to me, Helen," he went on.

"Hmm well there is a white doctor, a Hollandaise here for the morning, helping with the clinic. She works at the Medical Research Centre near the High Commission. I will ask her what she suggests."

(For a moment, I wondered how sauce would help my foot and then remembered the local name for Dutch people was Hollandaise.)

The Dutch doctor looked at my foot and then asked the one question which, looking back, is the obvious one to ask but which had quite escaped all of us at the time.

"When did you last have a rabies jab?"

"Let me think, it was a ten year jab and I had it when we went to Kenya which was - oh no – eleven years ago." It was perfectly clear to all of us that my answer was not the she wanted to hear or that I wanted to give.

"You know there is rabies here, you should not have let it lapse. A boy from Malaville died last week from rabies. The MRC is the only place with the treatment and it must be given within four hours of the bite. When were you bitten?"

"Over an hour ago, maybe two"

"Right, no time to waste then, do you have a car?"

"Yes, this is Sidi, he is driving me."

"Sidi, I am in an official vehicle, you can follow me. I will get you to the MRC in time", and without further ado she left the room, leaving Sidi, Aunt Sammy and me looking totally bemused.

Quickly or as quickly as I could manage, Sidi and I went back to the car and followed the doctor out of the compound. Most of the roads around the clinic were of sand and our progress was slow at first but when we reached the tarmac, the doctor put her foot down, switched on her siren and we raced down the highway towards the capital and the MRC clinic. I was not in any frame of mind to appreciate the speed with which we cut through the traffic. All I could recall was the vivid memories of my last visit to the clinic to have a blood sample taken before my gall stone operation. That simple task had involved me sitting on a wooden bench for six hours waiting my turn in the long queue. I had no reason to suppose that the system had improved, but could only hope that my emergency transfer would get me emergency treatment.

Sirens blaring and brakes screeching, we pulled into the MRC compound. The Dutch doctor parked her car and came over to us. She leant into the car window and said, "I am unable to treat you. You must join the queue to see Dr Abuka from Nigeria. He is very good and will look after you. The waiting area is over there", and she pointed to a waiting area at the side of the compound. This area was out in the open and consisted of six narrow wooden forms, each holding about ten people. It seemed that things had not changed since my previous visit and the emergency transfer had simply resulted in my joining the queue earlier than otherwise.

Sidi helped me to the end of the queue and told me to wait whilst he parked the car. Where he thought I was going to, I did not know. I simply sat there, the focus of many curious glances not only because I was a

Taubab and a rare sight in the MRC compound but also because of the blood stained foot.

The queue moved very slowly and I began to be concerned about the four hour time limit for the rabies injection mentioned by the doctor. I did not like to "queue jump" but I was in agony, the sun was beating down as it was now mid-day and I felt that if something did not happen soon, I would pass out.

"I think you had better go and speak to someone, Sidi", I suggested. "That doctor said that I must start the treatment within four hours of the bite and it must be nearly that now. This queue is hardly moving. I am amazed that she got us here at high speed, and then just abandoned us. She must have known how long these queues are. Maybe she just likes her siren or maybe she just needed an excuse to get away from Sammy's clinic. Whatever, please go and see if you can get me seen."

Under protest, Sidi went towards the nurse. I could see his point, I would look like a typical taubab if I was seen out of turn, but at that point, I really did not care if it set back taubab/local relationships, I just wanted to see a doctor. Up near the door to the clinic, Sidi was fighting my corner with a nurse and two men in white coats and after a great deal of arm waving from them all, he came back with his mission successfully accomplished. Doctor Abuka would see me next.

Slowly and painfully with Sidi's help, I hobbled into the cramped office. Between the desk, two chairs and a filing cabinet there was hardly any room for the doctor, let alone the nurse or patient.

"Oh my, oh my, that is bad," he said as he lent over and looked a few small marks on the top where my sandals had protected the skin from the dog's teeth. "This is a normal dog bite, but this, this at the side I have never seen as much damage done by a dog before. This is very deep and torn. Where is the dog now?"

"It ran off", I replied.

"Oh my, oh my, you should definitely not have let it do that!"

"What, I don't understand, what would you expect me to do? It bit my foot and did all this", I answered, waving my hand towards my foot.

"You should know that you have to catch the dog and put it in a cage. That way we can see if it has rabies. It is very important; you must remember that next time"

"This was done by a rottweiller that was probably heavier than I am. How am I expected to catch a dog like that?"

"It doesn't matter. Next time you must bring the dog with you. Remember to put it in a cage."

Next time! There was not going to be a next time if I had any say in the matter.

The doctor's next words took my breath away.

"I can't do anything for your foot, you just leave it and in time it will heal itself".

"Doesn't it need a bandage or something to keep it clean?" I asked.

"Oh no, oh no. Just take a look at what I have written in your notes."

He showed me my notes, where after he had detailed the damage to my foot, he had written in capital letter – NOT TO BE COVERED UNDER ANY CIRCUMSTANCES.

"I don't understand, won't dirt and germs get in."

"You do not have to understand. I have to understand, I am the doctor. It has stopped bleeding now and as I said it will heal in time. A bite is different to other wounds, it has to heal from the inside out not the other way around."

"But what about infection? I am worried that it will become infected. I thought it should have antiseptic on it as the dog could have had all sorts of infections in its teeth."

"Oh no, oh no, you are still thinking like a European. I know best about Africa and its infections believe me. I have written you a note. Take this to the ward sister and she will arrange for you to have rabies injections", and he handed me a scrap of paper folded in half.

As Sidi walked, and I hobbled across to the main hospital building I said, "Well that was a complete waste of time. We sat in the queue for ages and when we get to see the doctor, he does nothing to my foot. We could have come straight over here for the rabies treatment."

"You always complain about it here" Sidi retorted. "Anyway the ward sister would not treat you without the doctor's letter, you should know that."

Sidi was right but I was too upset by all the events of the day to acknowledge this.

I had never been into the hospital part of the MRC before and I was astonished. My first impression was that I had stumbled into a hospital back in the UK. The reception desk was manned by a nurse in a neat, clean uniform who took my note and asked me to wait in the nearby reception area. Before long a sister came through who read my note and came over to speak to me.

"Just wait here and I will get one of my housemen to start your treatment. He won't be long; you should have had your first treatment by now."

I settled down on the chair to a long wait but before I could get comfortable an efficient looking houseman arrived, introduced himself and ushered me into a small but clean and tidy consulting room.

"Now, I am sure that you know why you are having to have this treatment but had you had it explained to you exactly what form the treatment takes?"

"All I know is that it is injections, other than that I know nothing."

"Right, well this treatment takes four months. Yes four months. The good news is that today is the worst. As the treatment goes on you have fewer and fewer injections. Today I am going to give you eight."

Eight injections, four months, I was so astonished that I only just grasped how the treatment would continue. Apparently, the next week I would have four, followed by two the week after that and then one every fortnight.

"That's fine" I mumbled, thinking to myself, I know how painful Shendian injections are at the best of times and according to what I had heard, rabies injections were renowned for the agony that accompanied them.

"Are you clear about the treatment?" asked the houseman. "Today's injections need to be spread around your body. I will give you one in each thigh, one in each arm, two in your back and two in your stomach."

"OK" Just get it over with I thought, gritting my teeth at the thought of one injection in my stomach, let alone two.

Compared with my earlier experiences of Shendian injections, these were not too bad; the anticipation was the worst part. They were not pleasant by any means but not as horrific as I had expected. The side effects later that day were not pleasant either but then rabies would have been much worse. I returned over subsequent weeks for my follow-up injections and finished them to find that the whole course had cost me £300, which in Shendian terms was a small fortune.

Back at The Dominion with the potential of rabies taken care of, I received an update on the fate of the dog. According to Robert who had come rushing in with Karen when he had heard my screams, he had seen the same dog on the beach in the afternoon. It had bitten a local lad and was being stoned by onlookers. He did not know its fate but was pretty certain that it was my assailant. Someone else had heard from a friend who had heard from someone else, the usual way stories were relayed in Shendi, that the army had been given instructions to shoot a rottweiller on sight after it had bitten a German tourist on the arm and rear shortly after my attack. It seemed that the tourist agency was taking the threat seriously. Rottweillers and other European breeds were scare in Shendi being brought over by expats who did not want the bother of training a local dog. These were sometimes released and made to fend for themselves when their owners returned to Europe. It always amazed me that people would go to the trouble and expense of bringing a dog out to Shendi only to abandon it when they went back home. Local dogs could be trained to be pets and made excellent guard dogs but I suppose it was a touch of 'one-upmanship' to have an expensive European dog. However my attacker had got out to Shendi, it was never seen again for which I was more than thankful.

I tried to follow Dr. Abuka's instructions and leave my foot to heal from the inside out, but after a couple of days of continually cleaning sand and dust away from it, I decided to cover it during the day and leave it uncovered at night. Every time Di came to The Dominion she would dress my foot but she was not at all happy with the lack of progress. About a fortnight after the bite I woke one morning feeling incredibly ill. I had a high fever complete with headache and every time that I put my foot to the ground a terrific bolt of pain shot right through me. Somehow I had to struggle through the day until evening when Di and her husband would come. I knew that they would call in because they had a small farewell party planned as they were returning to the UK the next day for a break from the pressures of running a business in Shendi. Although I did not want to spoil their party, I seized Di's arm the moment she came it.

She unwrapped the bandages from my foot and gave a gasp. "Oh Helen, this is not good. I don't even want to touch it. You must get to the clinic as soon as possible. The wound is very badly inflamed and full of infection. It must be lanced."

"That's what I was afraid you would say. I can't leave this place now. I will go in the morning to see Aunt Sammy. There is no way I am going back to the MRC, so much as I don't particularly like the woman, I'll go and see her tomorrow."

"Helen, you must go. Promise me that you will. I won't rest easy unless you promise."

"Don't worry, I will go. Now come and have a farewell drink. It is on the house for all your help and support especially over the last two weeks."

The next morning Sidi took me to see Aunt Sammy. I was feeling very unwell but her astonishment at the lack of treatment by the Nigerian doctor managed to penetrate my cocoon of fever and pain.

"Your foot is very infected; you will need lots of treatment. An infection like that can make you feel very ill. It can give you a fever but your fever is very high and you look awful. I will give you a malaria test before I lance your foot" and with that she rolled up her sleeves and set to work.

The malaria test proved positive which I have to admit was no surprise. I was at such a low ebb with the dog bite that I was obviously easy prey for any mosquito that fancied a quick bite. In what I had come to realise was the Shendian tradition of using the largest needle around, Sammy proceeded to lance my foot. Of course she did not apply any local anaesthetic she simply carried out the procedure. Somehow or other I managed not to make a sound. She may have enjoyed having one of her severest critics at her mercy but I was not going to add to that enjoyment by yelling with pain.

Over the next few weeks I visited Sammy every other day to have my wound dressed and she was able to practise her lancing techniques on two of those occasions. I was interested to note that she seemed to gain a great deal of kudos from treating a taubab and my sessions with her were often watched by her staff. One day towards the end of my treatment, she sent Sidi to the pharmacist to buy some drugs for me and held a teaching class over my foot for the benefit of her student nurses, cleaners, patients in fact anyone who wanted to watch. Speaking in Mandinka evidently she was unaware that by now I had a working knowledge of the language, she turned to her audience and pointed at me. "This woman was bitten by a dog a few weeks ago. Just look at her foot. I have lanced it three times and removed all the infection. It has been cleaned and dressed regularly but still it does not heal. Does anyone know why?"

They all inspected my foot and then turned to Sammy with blank faces.

"No-one knows! Hmm. I will help you", she said. "Take a good look at her. She has a problem, no one know what sort of problem?"

The thought flashed through my mind that my main problem at this precise moment was sitting there being used as a teaching dummy by a good nurse but an even bigger con woman. What was taking Sidi so long?

Sammy looked at the blank faces surrounding her. They looked back at her, at each other, at my foot and then back at her. Again there was no response and I was starting to worry. Dog bite, malaria, now what, surely not another health problem.

Sammy was starting to get annoyed with her students. "Come on have a good look at her skin, what's wrong with it. This is so simple."

Still the silence and the wondering looks continued.

"Oh it is so easy. Her skin is very pale. This skin is much too thin, it looks like tissue paper. If she had a good black skin like us, she would have healed in a week. I can do no more for her now but keep dressing it and pray to Allah." With that she dismissed her class.

Now I understood the problem. When Sidi returned, the receptionist called him over and I heard her telling him about the class. He seemed to find it hilarious. Back in the car I turned to him and said, "Your friend the receptionist seemed to find my skin problem very funny."

He looked at me as he started to drive out of the gate. "Helen, she is not my friend as you put it. She lives in Famara like me; you know how we all know each other. Anyway I didn't know that you understood that much Mandinka"

"You would be surprised at what I know". I retorted.

A mistake of course. I should have kept quiet. It would have been much better not to let Sidi know how much Mandinka I understood.

Chapter Nine

Trials for Little People

Whilst I was making regular visits to see Aunt Sammy, the President of Mali visited Shendi. The Peach Haven, in which the Shendian President had business interests, always housed important visitors and also often hosted regular high level functions. Such visits as these were no good for my business. Security was always high and very visible. On these occasions the tourists passing under The Peace Haven arch to enter their car park, would be faced by a large military truck with a machine gun on it, just what a tourist needed to see when going for a drink. (On reflection though, some of them may have found it more disturbing when leaving the bar.)

On the morning that the Malian President was due to leave, I had an appointment to have my foot dressed at Aunt Sammy's. I spoke to the hotel's security guards who advised me of the best time to go, to avoid too many delays from the presidential traffic. When the President travelled around the country, his vehicle was part of a large convoy of about 20-30 vehicles all travelling at an extremely high speed. Usually one or two S.S.G. vehicles led the way, followed by the military truck with the machine gun, then a two or three more trucks with soldiers with their AK47s at the ready and finally a string of more cars and trucks one of which was carrying the President. Somewhere in the convoy would be a military ambulance. The whole spectacle was frightening to anyone seeing it for the first time and no allowance was made for any other traffic on the road, pedestrian or vehicular. I knew that the guards would not be able to give me an exact time because for security reasons this would be kept secret, but I did hope that they would have some vague idea of when the roads would be free of presidential traffic.

Sidi and I left for the clinic, hoping we would have time to get there and back before the convoy left The Peace Haven. We would be travelling along the Coastal Highway which was newly opened and linked the resort area where The Dominion was with the airport. We were expecting many more checkpoints because the President was on the road and we were not disappointed. The first checkpoint came near the turntable, (the local's name for our only roundabout). Very often we would be waved through checkpoints but not today. The soldiers carried out a thorough check. First they asked to see our papers. Sidi, being a local, had to show either his I.D. card or driving licence, and I had to show my alien I.D. card. (Ex-pats always had to carry a current alien card with them; they were renewable, at great expense every January.) Once they had checked these, Sidi had to show them the insurance and tax papers for the car. When they were satisfied with these, we were told to get out the car while they searched it. They carried out a thorough search of the inside of the car and examined the contents of the boot. We were then let through to proceed to the clinic.

About half an hour later, after Sammy had treated my foot and we were on our return journey, we were stopped again, on the approach road the opposite side of the turntable. The soldiers repeated the same procedure we had been through earlier, but this time we were questioned about where we had been. They had seen us pass through in the other direction not long before.

"I've been to have my foot dressed at Aunt Sammy's clinic in Famara." I explained showing them my bandaged foot.

"What you? A taubab using Aunt Sammy's?" came a giggled reply.

"Yes, me a taubab, I use Aunt Sammy's. Is that funny?"

"Don't upset them." Sidi nudged me.

I knew he was right so said no more. We were then allowed to go through. There was no other vehicle in sight, travelling in either direction. Being the only vehicle on a wide, newly tarmaced road, and aware that I wanted to be back at The Dominion as soon as possible, and out of the way of the convoy, Sidi was driving fairly fast. As we approached the only sharp bend on this stretch of road, a car with its headlights blazing suddenly confronted us on our side of the road. It was heading straight for us at high speed. What struck me later was the absence of noise, there were no sirens, no horns blaring, nothing. Only this very large black car with its headlights full on heading straight for us. My fears had been realised. It was the Presidential convoy on the way to the airport. There was only one thing for us to do and Sidi, who for all his faults was a good driver, did it.

I let out a small, petrified scream, Sidi swore, pulled off the road and despite the back of the car sliding and skidding on the sand managed to bring us to a safe halt. I looked out of the passenger window. There was an eight-foot deep storm drain at that part of the road, designed to take the monsoons in rainy season. We stopped so near the drain that I could not have got out of my door without falling down it. By the time we stopped several of the convoy vehicles had already passed us.

"Shit! That was close. Are you alright?" he asked.

"Yeah, but look at me I'm shaking. I thought we were going to roll over down the storm drain."

"You know I can drive, I wouldn't let that happen."

"I know you are a good driver. I couldn't have done what you did, but we might still have rolled over, especially if the earth had given way. Why do they do that? If he had had his siren going we would have heard him and could have got out of the way in plenty of time. Why was he not on his side of the road? Even in the middle would have been alright, but on our side that is just ridiculous! If we had been a couple of seconds nearer the bend, we would have hit him full on." Reaction to the near miss was making me angry and garrulous.

"Yeah, but they don't care. You know this!"

"But it wouldn't only have been us; they would have killed themselves also."

"Their job is to protect the President, not themselves" Sidi replied.

"You are as crazy as they are. We aren't a threat to the President, so why drive us off the road like that?"

"They didn't drive us off the road; they simply cleared the way for the President. You still don't understand things here do you?"

"You're right there! I don't even understand why the soldiers let us through they must have been radioed as the President left The Peace Haven, they should have kept us at the turntable till the convoy had gone through."

By this time all the convoy had passed us. "Are you O.K. now," Sidi asked, "if so, we will carry on."

We drove to The Dominion without any further incidents. I still felt shaken, but was very relieved to be home. Sidi was right; I did not understand things in Shendi and never would. When you see or hear the Presidential convoy coming, you have to pull off the road quickly, if not the military will shoot your tyres, so we were lucky to be just driven off the road. A couple of months after our incident with the convoy, a local driver failed to move over quickly enough. The escort did not shoot the tyres instead they shot the driver. Luckily, he recovered after the bullet was surgically removed. Not everyone involved in incidents with the convoy was as lucky as Sidi and I had been. Life is cheap in Shendi.

I wasn't the only person with leg troubles. One of my regulars, Ken, had a huge ulcer on his leg and it did not appear to be responding to treatment. Ken had been a used car salesman in the UK but came out to Shendi during the aftermath of his divorce a few months earlier. I had met him through one of my other regulars, Jim otherwise known as Gypsy Jim. He had persuaded Ken to come out to Africa and make a fresh start. It may have been a fresh start for Ken, but to the experienced expats in The Dominion it was nothing new. Ken's fresh start followed the usual pattern of a new country, a new love. In this instance Ken met a Freetonian girl and opened a small local bar with her. The regulars at The Dominion did not have long to wait for the inevitable collapse of both relationship and bar because before long both had disintegrated to the detriment of Ken's pride and his bank balance.

Ken disappeared from the scene for a while and the next thing I heard was that he had moved in with Liverpool Kevin. This surprised me because as far as I knew Kevin was building a house for himself and living in a small caravan on his land until it was finished. From descriptions from Kevin and other expats the caravan was minute, scarcely large enough for one let alone two. However Ken was penniless and homeless so Kevin's caravan did at least provide a roof over his head. Although I knew Ken was penniless I let him run up a tab in the bar, on the reassurance of Jim, who had told me that Ken would have plenty of money when his divorce was finalized and the marital home was sold. Both Kevin and I were hoping this would happen sooner rather than later.

Things took a turn for the worse when Kevin went back to the U.K. for a short period. It became obvious that Ken, who on his own in the caravan, wasn't coping too well. Nobody said anything for a short while but when we noticed an ulcer on his leg that was failing to heal, I was deputised to say something to him. Whether this was because I had leg troubles of my own with the dog bite or because I was a woman I was not sure but the opinion around the bar was that I was the best person to talk to Ken about his ulcer.

"You need to go to a clinic about your leg." I told Ken one afternoon.

"Don't worry about me," he answered as he sipped his usual double vodka, "when I leave here I will go up to the little pharmacy, up the back street at the top of the road here. You know the one I mean?"

"Yeah, I do, but I think a clinic would be better, that looks nasty."

"Don't fuss woman, I'll sort it. Worry about your own leg not mine."

"Fine, fine."

It was obvious he did not want to talk to me about it or have me nagging him so there I left it for the time being.

The following morning I was surprised to see Ken come in at breakfast time with Euan. Both Euan and his wife, Pamela, who had a holiday home in Shendi, were close friends of mine and although Pam would come out perhaps once a year, Euan was a much more regular visitor. When he was out on his own he often came to The Dominion for his breakfast but I had never seen Ken at this hour of the morning.

"Morning lads." I greeted them.

"Morning Helen," said Euan, as he winked at me. "Meet my new lodger, I found him wondering the streets last night when I left here."

"Oh come on!" piped up Ken, "It wasn't quite like that, and you said I could stay at your place."

"She knows I'm only joking, but Helen, you've seen Ken's leg, haven't you? Don't you agree we should get him to a clinic?"

"Quite, quite. See Ken I told you this yesterday."

"Just get us some breakfast Helen. We will see how I feel later." Ken replied. "It's worse than being married around here."

I took the hint and said no more to him about his leg.

Ken stayed at Euan's compound for a few days. His leg was no better in fact it was festering more each day. Euan did his best to persuade him to go to a clinic, but Ken simply would not hear of it, saying that he was responding to the pharmacist's treatment. Maybe he was, but consuming a high volume of vodka, combined with his medication probably delayed or even hindered the healing process.

After a few days, Euan came into The Dominion alone one evening looking worried. He collapsed onto his usual seat at the bar and demanded a large beer. Without saying a word he drank half of it, put it down and said. "I needed that."

"What's the matter?" asked Nick, "trouble with your lodger?"

"Trouble, that's putting it mildly. Yes Helen, I will have another one please, I need it. What a day I have had and it is all Ken's doing."

"Ken's doing? Where is he? I thought he was staying with you?"

"Not any more", he said, "I've just dropped him back at the caravan. He insisted he went back. I'm concerned about him but what can I do if he insisted on going and anyway in a way I'm glad that he has gone. You will never believe what happened last night. There we were, a couple of old men having a quiet night in watching a DVD – nothing violent or horrific, no Nightmare on Shendian Boulevard or anything like that. Anyway there we were, feet up, beer in hand and suddenly Ken yells 'Bloody hell! Look at that" "What? " I said, sitting up so quickly I nearly spilt my beer. I looked round expecting to see a lizard or even a snake. 'There look at that spider' says Ken pointing to the corner of the room behind the TV. I stood up and peered in to the corner. 'What spider' I said. He looked at me in disgust. 'You blind or what? There, look it's coming down from the ceiling, it's massive! I've never seen such a bloody big one!' I looked around" continued Euan, "I didn't see a spider, but thought it best not to tell him I couldn't see it!"

"What happened then?" I asked.

"Well he swore at me for needing glasses and went off to bed reminding me to get rid of it before morning."

There were peals of laughter from around the bar.

Euan went on, "Wait a minute it gets worse. This morning, not a word about spiders but right out of the blue, he tells me I should chop down the banana plant near the window, or in the winds it would damage my house. I asked him which banana plant he was talking about; I don't have any bananas near that side of the house. He went over to the window and points, and says 'that one'. I told him there weren't any bananas there, and he said I was an argumentative sod, shook his head and walked off. So you can see why I am concerned about him and didn't like taking him back to the caravan, but on the other hand I am pleased to have my home to myself with or without spiders and banana plants."

Amidst the laughter that greeted this comment, I heard Rod, from Rotherham, a friend of Kevin's, say "Don't worry; you've done what you can. I will pop around tomorrow and check that he is alright. I can use the excuse of checking up on Kevin's van."

As I walked away to deal with another customer I heaved a sigh of relief. From the sound of it Ken needed help but I really did not want to get involved in another expat mess. I had other things on my mind. Not only was I still making visits to Aunt Sammy's I was having trouble with the staff and my relationship with The Peace Haven was deteriorating. On top of this Sharon was due out today to attend the last week of Datu's trial and I knew that she would want to see me. I just did not have time to sort out Ken's mess.

Sharon, and a friend, Sandra, were here unofficially to sit in on the trial of Datu, and his accomplice. It was expected to finish shortly and Sharon was determined to be in court to hear the conclusion and hopefully the sentences given to the two accused so that she could close that chapter of her life. Peter and his team had also arrived on another flight earlier in the day as they were due to give evidence in the trial.

I had kept in touch with Sharon but had not seen her since she stayed with me, when Reggie was taken ill, and she had flown out to take him home. Whilst listening to the tales of Ken I was keeping one eye on the entrance, not wanting to miss her arrival. When she walked in, I was astonished at the change in her. If I had not known that she was coming, I don't think I would have recognised her. She had lost weight; her face was gaunt, with expressionless eyes. She had been through a lot. Not only did she have her father's murder, and Reggie's illness to contend with. Her brother Paul, who had visited here with Reggie, had died a few months before their father. This all amounted to a lot of emotions to handle, when she also had a husband and two sons to look after, besides coping with a highly pressured career.

I came out from behind the bar and went to greet her and Sandra. I could see the tears in Sharon's eyes as I gave her a hug.

"You look well," she said to me, "I'm so pleased to see you. This is Sandra my friend I told you was coming out with me."

"You're looking good too." I lied; I could hardly tell her she look awful.

"Have you time to sit and chat, or do you need to be behind the bar?" Sharon asked.

"The boys can cope for awhile, we aren't very busy." Then I called across to Jed. "I'm going to sit and talk to Sharon, call me if you need help, and send one of the waiters over, so we can order some drinks please."

I sat and chatted with Sharon and Sandra. Sharon did brighten up as we spoke, she asked about some of the ex-pats she had met on her previous visit, and some of the tourists, we shared several laughs, but I knew that Sharon's heart was not in it. The laughter never reached her eyes which were full of an underlying sadness.

"Would you have time to come to court with us tomorrow, or must you be here?" Sharon asked, "We are only expecting the trial to be in the morning and then adjourned again till the next day."

I was uneasy about leaving the business for too long, but I could see she would like me to go with them, and it was the start of low season, so trade was slow. "Yeah, I can do that; the lads can cope for a morning."

Peter and his colleagues came in and we all sat and chatted together and then Sharon and Sandra left saying they wanted an early night to be fit for court in the morning.

"How do you find Sharon?" Peter asked after they had left.

"To be honest, if I hadn't known that she was arriving today I may not have recognised her."

"I know what you mean I'm concerned about her. I just hope the court case finishes this week, as they have promised us it will. Then hopefully she can put all this behind her and start afresh. It's not easy to close a chapter of your life until there has been a conclusion."

The trial had been going on for a long time, about two years at this point. It had been moved from one court to another. First it was in a magistrate's court, and then transferred to the High Court, then to another magistrate's court. Now it was being heard in the main magistrate's court in Port Albert. I was under the impression that the magistrates and judges that had been given the case had done their best to off load it onto another court as soon as possible. It almost seemed that they were afraid to give a verdict, in what to me was an open and shut case. I wondered if the problem lay with his accomplice, Kresba, who was allegedly a high up member of a rebel group, which had hold of the area where Reg's body was found, rather than with Datu. If this was the case this could be the key to the courts' reluctance to pass a verdict. I was also aware from my own experience that court cases here simply did not end.

Datu had not been in custody the entire time, as the U.K. police had been lead to believe, he had been released several times that I knew of, maybe many more times that I was unaware of. The first occasion I knew of him being free was when his wife had her baby, a few months after Datu's arrest. Sidi phoned me one evening and said, "Datu is free, he has been seen walking around Kerr Sohma."

"That can't be." I said.

"I'm telling you, I've just had a friend phone me to tell me he has seen him. He said they had let him out to see his baby."

"Come on. I can't believe that surely they wouldn't let a murderer out to see his new baby."

"But of course, why not? He's not likely to murder anyone again! But I want you to be careful, just in case, remember he has it in for you, he blames you for getting him arrested. Go and tell the security lads, so that they know not to let him in if he comes to The Dominion, I will phone again later to check you are alright."

Datu stayed away from The Dominion this time, in fact he never came near the bar again but he did make threatening phone calls to both Sidi and I on several occasions.

Being busy with the bar I had never been to any of the previous hearings of the trial, but had read the sketchy reports of the case in the local paper. Sharon had also e-mailed me the reports of the trial that the family had received from The High Commission. Datu's confession had been dismissed, as his lawyer had been able to prove it had been given while he was being tortured. I believe this to be right, but he did lead them to the body, to me this was proof of guilt.

"I'm confused as to why it is only in the magistrate's court," I said to Peter.

"Well yeah. They can't be sentenced there. The magistrate's court can only give up to two years. A verdict will be given and the sentencing will be in the High Court"

"Sharon seems to think she will hear the sentencing, but surely if it is being given by the High Court that won't all happen this week."

"No, it won't, you're right. Courts finish on Friday for the summer recess. The magistrate will finish hearing the case, it's a lady magistrate you know, it's amazing how many women hold high positions, more than in most of Africa, I'm sure. She has a U.K. visa; she will leave for her holiday next week, and will submit a postal verdict from the U.K."

"Oh, I see."

This confirmed my theory to me. I felt no one was willing, or maybe they were actually afraid to give a verdict. Obviously Peter was unable to tell me all that the U.K. police knew.

"Are you coming to court tomorrow?" Peter asked me.

"Yes, Sharon has asked me to come, and to be honest, I am curious to hear some of the case, all the previous hearings I have only read what has been reported in the local press. Some of it, had it not been so serious, would have been amusing! Did you know that Datu had been to a marabout, to get a juju to kill Reg and that the marabout refused to make one for him."

"Yeah, we have heard all that, you do have to grin all the same. Then after they had murdered Reg, they both went back to the marabout to get a juju to stop them from getting caught. I think that was just after you first asked Datu about Reg."

"All that has been in the paper here, the marabout gave evidence you know."

"Yeah, unfortunately this week will be of a more serious nature, we have bought over the video we made, we aren't sure yet if they will allow it to be shown in court. It is quite graphic, it includes the exhuming of the body, but does prove their guilt, and so it should be over soon."

"Good. Now, if you'll excuse me I've got to go back to the bar. I'll see you in the morning."

When I returned to bar, the main topic of conversation was still Ken, everyone was wondering how he was going to manage in the caravan by himself, especially now that he was starting to imagine things. Ken wasn't entirely alone at the compound, Kevin's watchman/gardener, Mr. Babu, lived in a small house by the entrance that Kevin had built for him. Although Mr. Babu was a conscientious worker, he would probably be oblivious to the fact that Ken was behaving strangely.

The topic of Ken was finally exhausted and with Rod repeating his promise to look in on him, the expats slowly made their way home. For once I was able to shut the bar at midnight and I was glad of the early night. I wondered what was the matter with Ken, but his problems did not surprise me. Whether it is the climate, the atmosphere, African jujus or whatever, I have seen many Europeans change in time: often a very short time. Some get depressed, some behave completely out of character, we say they have gone bush! Many ex-pat girls myself included, experience vast mood swings, I can only explain this similar to having permanent P.M.T. I have wondered if maybe we suffer from the reverse of S.A.D. that some people experience in Europe during the long, dark winter months. We are in wall-to-wall sunshine, even in the rainy season, there are hours of sunshine, and it is very hot and humid. Our bodies were not built for this climate. In the time that I had been in Shendi I had seen several cases of folk becoming unhinged, and imagining all sorts of things. Besides the possible causes I have mentioned, many do consume large amounts of alcohol, and often taking some form of medication; even if it is only anti-malarial tablets. Not to mention that smoking wacky-baccy is almost the norm in Africa, a combination of which may account for the susceptibility of some.

I had arranged to meet Sharon and Sandra at the magistrates' court the next morning, as I had a few things to sort out in the bar before I could leave. I had asked Sidi to come with me; I knew he would like to come, as he was initially involved also. The girls were being collected from their hotel by the High Commission's driver, who was going to look after them, so I had no concerns about their safety. I had never been to the magistrates' court before; in fact I didn't even know exactly where it was. I will admit to being impressed as we approached it. It was situated next to the main police headquarters in Port Albert. It was not nearly as grand as the High Court, where my court case was being heard, but it was none the less impressive. It had large windows that were all wide open, so it would be airier than the High Court, which was very stuffy. There was a large semi-circular turret like construction, in the middle of the building, which, I later saw housed a rather grand staircase. Unlike many buildings in Port Albert, this one looked freshly painted; many buildings have several different coloured layers of peeled paint on display.

"So this is the magistrates' court," I remarked to Sidi as we pulled up outside, "I'm impressed, I was expecting a dilapidated building."

"No, this is new, it hasn't long been built."

That would explain the good quality paintwork, I thought. Sharon and Sandra were stood in the small forecourt, Sharon was looking distressed and in fact she was so upset she ignored our greetings and whispered in a voice fighting to hold back the tears, "You will never believe what's just happened."

"Tell me, what's happened?" I said as Sidi shook hands with Sandra and tried not to notice Sharon's misery.

"Datu is up there," she replied pointing to an open window on the first floor next to the staircase. "He leant out the window, and shouted to me, 'Hi Sharon, good to see you, long time.' How dare he? How could he, how could any one let him do that? Does he not understand what he has done? Doesn't anyone care? "

"Well that sums things up eh? Shendians have different emotions to us; he probably doesn't understand the full implications of what he has done."

"Maybe, maybe but it's not right. He shouldn't be allowed to do that. What is worse is that he did seem to expect me to be pleased to see him."

"Best we wait out here for a while, till they have taken them into the court room." I replied.

We stayed outside and went in just before the case was due to start. Like the High Court, the interior failed to do justice to the exterior. The downstairs was a maze of small offices, all looking dusty and generally uncared for. The staircase that led to the upstairs courtroom, where Datu's case was being heard, was wide and quite spectacular and was much too grand for its surroundings. It was too large to be described as spiral, but curved around the circular part of the building with a large window on the small landing, half way up, making it very light and giving a birds-eye view of the bustling Port Albert street below.

We entered the courtroom, which, as I expected, was smaller than the rooms in the High Court. The rows of wooden benches that the public sat on were closer together, which made the room claustrophobic. To my disgust Datu and Kresba, were sat in the back row of benches, near to the entrance. They were sat by warders from the prison, but were not handcuffed. The court was crowded; this had become a high profile case, besides the two boys' families, members of the public had come to hear the proceedings out of curiosity. Sharon and Sandra were ushered in, by a court official and shown to seats directly in front of Datu and Kresba. I was horrified. Sidi and I were shown to seats the other side of the small aisle, to where Sharon and Sandra were sat. I saw Datu tap Sharon on the shoulder and start talking to her. How could the warders allow this? I watched with disbelief and waited for someone to intervene. No-one did and Sharon was becoming more and more upset but still determined to ignore Datu. Fortunately the case soon began and Datu and Kresba were escorted to the dock.

As soon as the case was announced the boys' lawyer stood up and asked permission to address the court. "Yesterday evening I was permitted to watch the video the U.K. police have bought over with them." began their lawyer, "Having viewed this video, filmed at the time of their investigation, I now realize that I have been somewhat misinformed by my clients. After much soul searching last night, I have spoken to my clients at the prison this morning and advised them to change their plea of not guilty to one of guilty. This advice they have decided not to take. With this new information I now have, and my clients' refusal to change their plea, I feel I can no longer represent them in this case. I wish to ask permission of your honour to leave the courtroom."

As he finished his remarks the room fell silent. This coming from the defence lawyer, must have told all present that the U.K. police video held conclusive evidence of the boys guilt. In my ignorance I considered the case to be over.

"You have my permission to leave the court", said the magistrate.

There was still complete silence in the court as their lawyer collected together his papers, and put them in his briefcase. All eyes were on him as he walked up the short, narrow aisle and out of the court. "Do you understand the position you are now in?" the magistrate address Datu and Kresba. "Your lawyer is no longer representing you. I advise you to get a new lawyer, would you like the court to assign one to you?"

Datu responded in a loud clear voice, "I wish to speak with my mother; I would like an adjournment so I can do this. I will not take another lawyer without her advice."

I knew that mothers were considered very important in Shendian culture, but I considered an adjournment to speak to her while on a murder charge, was taking this a bit too far. The magistrate did agree, and adjourned the proceedings until the next morning, advising Datu and Kresba that if they failed to find a new lawyer they would have to accept the counsel offered to them by the court. All the time this short hearing was in progress, a young woman, whom I recognised as Datu's wife, was visible through the internal windows, pacing up and down the corridor with a crying baby in her arms. I assumed that she was hoping for a sympathy vote.

As we filed out of the courtroom we passed her and an elderly lady, who I later to learn was his mother. She gave me a long, despising stare; she had obviously recognised me from my visit to the house but said nothing. Datu's ex lawyer approached Sharon, while we were stood in a small group discussing the morning's events in court. He shook Sharon's hand and said, "I'm so sorry for what has happened to you and your family. I would not have taken on this case in the first place, had I known all of the facts. The boys had convinced me of their innocence."

This restored a bit of my faith in human nature; I really though by now that Shendians had no conscience.

We left the court going our own separate ways but all arranged to meet up at The Dominion for lunch. Sharon and Sandra went with Karl back to the High Commission. Peter and his colleagues went off into the town and Sidi and I went back to The Dominion where we had agreed to meet at lunch time. I was pleased with how the court case was proceeding. Surely after the defence lawyer refusing to carry on representing his clients, the case would soon be over. The others all arrived for their lunch, and their apparent light heartedness convinced me that they were also happy with the morning's proceedings.

Peter asked me to go outside with him. "Assuming they find a lawyer before tomorrow and the case proceeds, I will be in the witness box first, and then Frank will give his evidence, so we will expect to get you in the stand about tenish. Is that O.K. with you?"

"Hang on Peter, I wasn't expecting this! Why do I need to give evidence?"

"Well, maybe Frank can give your evidence from your statement, but it would be better coming from you."

"If I really have to I will, but please remember you are all getting on a plane next Friday. I'm left here. Datu is blaming me for his arrest anyway."

"When we convict him, he will be no threat to you."

"He has brothers, cousins, friends, you know how things work here, and they hold grudges for a long while; but yeah, if I'm needed but only if I'm really needed I will go in the witness box."

"Good girl. I will do my best not to call you. I'm sorry, none of us thought about the position this could leave you in."

As Peter and I entered the bar by the garden door, Rotherham Rod and Nightclub Rick strolled in the other doorway. Rod called out to me, "Ken has really flipped now. He is seeing little people all around the compound, when the only person that is there is Kevin's watchman, Mr. Babu." He shook his head in dismay.

Grinning I replied. "What do you mean little people, like fairies Do they have wings do you know? It seems very strange that Ken should see fairies. Perhaps there is a softer side to him that we don't know about."

"You can laugh; He is busy at the moment putting the little people, who are only a foot tall into the back of Kevin's jeep. Mr Babu is scared to death to be left alone with him. You can't blame him really."

"Yeah," interrupted Rick, "and guess why he is putting them into the jeep? He says he is going to bring them to The Dominion, as Helen will know what to do with them. Still find this funny?"

"Well you have to laugh eh? Tell me more about these little people, if I'm going to look after them I will need to know about them."

"Most of them are Rastas not fairies," Rod began, "they had a party at the compound yesterday, and kept Ken awake all night with their noise."

Rick continued the story "They were all dirty little so and sos, but not anymore. Ken has washed them and hung them on the line to dry."

"What!" I exclaimed.

"Well what would you do if they were all dirty?" Rick picked up the story. "Problem is, now some of them are missing, some fell apart in the wash, and poor old Ken has been trying to put them back together again."

"Well that's good." I said. "At least he is taking care of them."

"Not all of them," Rod informed me, "apparently he has put a white head unto a black body and is scared stiff about what will happen when this guy realizes what he has done."

"You're having me on!"

"No, honest Helen," Rick confirms, "He has well and truly lost the plot. Anyway get us a drink, we need one, we will go back later and see how he is."

The boys enjoyed themselves, telling their tales of Ken and his little people to the other ex-pats around the bar, while I carried on serving them. Karl came over to me. "Helen, what's going on?" he asked. "Is an ex-pat in trouble, do we need to be involved?"

"I don't know if this is a High Commission matter, but we will have to sort something out for Ken. Perhaps you can help."

I went on to explain to Karl that Ken was living alone in Kevin's caravan, and what was happening to him. Karl told me he would go with Rod and Rick after he had finished his lunch, and assess the situation. This he did. Rod and Rick returned to the bar, in need of another drink and to keep us all up to date with things.

"Well, we arrived at the caravan with that guy from the commission, and we couldn't believe it." Rod began, "Ken was as right as rain, chatting to him, showing him his leg explaining everything. Karl asked him did he have anyone in the U.K. that he would like informed that he wasn't well. Straight away he tells him maybe Gypsy Jim should know, and gives him his address and phone number without even looking them up. He was absolutely fine; he made us look a right couple of idiots."

"Yeah, but the crunch came when Karl told him he wanted to take him to the clinic, to get his leg sorted out. When he agreed to go, Karl tells him to get a few things together, in case they admit him." said Rick. "Then Ken says, 'I can't go now' 'Why not?' Karl asked him, 'who would look after all these little people?' he replied'"

This bought on hoots of laughter from around the bar, and Nick nearly choked on his beer.

"What is going to happen now?" I asked.

"Karl has gone back to the High Commission to seek advice. He is going to ring you to let you know what is going on. He thinks they will send the commission nurse down with some of the staff to take Ken to the clinic."

Karl phoned me a short while afterwards and told me that the High Commission had contacted Kombi Clinic and arranged to have Ken admitted. He continued, "I would like the boys to go back to the caravan, and try and persuade Ken to go in willingly. If not we will go later and uplift him from the compound. He's not safe to be there alone. I will give you the number of the clinic, they must phone them to let them know when they are on the way."

"Thanks, Karl, I will keep you informed as to how he is, and if we need any further help."

I spoke to Rod and Rick; they suggested that I go with them. They thought I might have more success than them in persuading Ken to leave his little people.

Although I had already been out once that day, to the court in Port Albert in the morning and because of all my problems rarely went out at all, I had no hesitation in agreeing to go to see Ken.

"You know, this is the second time I've been out to-day, this is the most outings I have had this summer." I remarked as Rod was driving us to Kevin's compound.

"See how us lads spoil you?" said Rod. "Now we are even taking you on your summer holidays."

At this Rick, always the clown, burst into song. "We're all going on a summer holiday." He sang. Rod and I were quick to join in. All three of us were singing heartily, and waving our arms in the air. Rod had an open topped vehicle; we were making quite a din. People stopped and watched us in amazement as we drove past. Was it really Ken that was crazy, or had the Shendi sunshine affected us all? In my case, I think it was any welcome diversion from my own stresses.

On arrival, we knocked on the compound gate. A bewildered looking Mr. Babu let us in. "Glad to see you, Mrs. Dominion." He said, "Ken's in the caravan, I'm scared of him he's not normal."

"Don't worry, Mr. Babu, we are here to take him with us, he is sick, all will be O.K." I tried to reassure him. Mick, Kevin's faithful rottweiller came bounding up to greet us, as we entered the compound. I froze on the spot. This was my first encounter with a rottweiller since I had been bitten. I felt sick and almost burst into tears. Rick, realising why I had not moved from the side of the car encouraged me to pat Mick, put his arm round my shoulders and walked with me through Kevin's garden towards the caravan.

I was pleasantly surprised by the garden, Kevin had often sat in the bar talking about what he and Mr. Babu had been doing. I had thought this was all in his mind. But this was a floral extravaganza. Flowers were cascading everywhere I looked, until on closer examination, I saw Kevin's inflatable boat, once his pride and joy, now laying, looking the worse for wear, in the undergrowth. Nevertheless I was impressed, both Kevin and Mr Babu had obviously put in a great deal of work. There was one blot on the landscape though, the small, dilapidated, rusting caravan in one corner of the plot.

The tiny door was open. "You in there Ken?" I called out.

"Helen, fancy you coming to visit me, come in."

"The lads have bought me down to see you. They say you are not too well."

"Me? I'm fine, only my leg is giving me a bit of jip. In you all come."

There was hardly room for the three of us all to join him. I could not believe my eyes. How the two of them could live in here I didn't know. This caravan was more squalid than most local compounds I had been to, and this belonged to someone, that continually criticized the Shendians. Kevin had a double bed that dominated the interior, this was unmade, and didn't look as if it had been made up or had its sheets changed in months. Ken slept on a small bed at the foot of the other one. A small fridge and tiny gas cooker stood in a corner, neither of which I would want used in any food I was to eat. Kevin always had an unkempt appearance, but how he spoke of his caravan with pride, and he often talked about the girl that came in and cleaned for him. What did she clean? There wasn't room to clean properly without emptying it out, besides the bedding hadn't been washed for ages, I was aghast.

Ken was stood by his bed slowly and painstakingly folding a pillowcase. "Careful where you tread, there is a hole in the floor there, we don't want you falling down it," he said, pointing to an area near the door

"What are you doing?" I asked.

"Isn't it obvious? I'm just sorting out this little bugger here. He keeps running off, you see, and causing me all sorts of problems. I'm packing him up in this, and putting him in that box under Kevin's bed. Just let's see him try and escape from there. I'll be with you in a minute when I've got him sorted. "

I looked round at Rod and Ron. They were no help, they had smirks on their faces and I had to step outside before Ken could see that I was laughing. I left all the lads chatting together, while I composed myself. When I was in control again, I popped my head inside the caravan and said, "Come outside lads, there really isn't room for all four of us in there." I could not bear going back inside the caravan, with us all in there it had become claustrophobic, and the smell of stale perspiration, and stale cooking smells was unbearable.

Once they were all outside I said to Ken, "We are all going out for a drive in Rod's car, we thought you might like to come with us."

"Can't do that." he replied.

"Why not Ken? Do you good to go out. You haven't been out for ages."

"I tried to explain to that fella that came here before. I'm having all sorts of problems with these little people. I can't leave them here; Kevin will go spare when he comes back."

"Look Ken, we are worried about your leg."

"Me, too now, it is painful, but I have my responsibilities here."

Somehow I had to persuade him to go to the clinic even if it meant acknowledging the existence of his little people. "How about if you come with us, we will take you to Kombi clinic, if they keep you in, we will come back here, and look after the little people for you."

"Would you Helen, you are a good girl, maybe you could take them back to The Dominion."

"Umm maybe!"

"That sounds a good idea to me; they look as if they could do with a couple of pints." chipped in Rick.

"Careful Rod, you nearly trod on that one, you don't realize how they dart about." Ken informed Rod.

Mr. Babu was hovering in the background bemused at what was going on. Rod and Rick left to get Ken into the jeep, while I stayed and explained to Mr Babu, that we were taking Ken to Kombi Clinic, and that he should not worry as Ken would not be coming back to the compound while Kevin was away. By the time I joined them, the lads had Ken sat in the front with Rod. I opened the back door, to sit next to Rick.

Ken turned round to me and said, "Before you get in Helen, go and talk to that bastard over there, he's been giving me hell."

"Who Ken? I don't see anyone. Where is he?"

"Him sat on the ground over there. For goodness sake can't you see him? I've had problems with him for ages. Listen, don't you hear the abuse he is giving me now?"

"I can't see anyone Ken and I can't hear anyone either." I answered.

"You're as daft as these two silly buggers; they wouldn't speak to him either. I think you are all scared of these bastards."

"Best to ignore them Ken," I told him as I climbed into the jeep. "We'll just get on our way now."

With a wave to Mr Babu Rod pulled away heading for the clinic and Rick dialled he number that Karl had given us for the clinic. "I think you should speak to them." He said handing me the phone. "Try not to let him hear what you are telling them."

That was easier said than done in the small jeep but in an effort to muffle my voice so that Ken would not realise what we were doing I ducked down between the front and back seats. I heard Ken say to Rod. "Hey, look at them, what are they doing? The silly bitch is on the floor now. We need to keep an eye on them, Rod." Fortunately I managed to get through and warn them of our impending arrival. The rest of the journey proceeded without any scares, sightings of little people or songs from the back. Although when we arrived at the clinic they were surprised to see us so soon and it seemed as if my contortions in the back of the jeep had been a waste of time.

I was by now, used to local clinics, so Kombi held no surprises for me, in fact I had seen worse. There was a power cut so the ceiling fans, in the room that we were shown into to wait for the doctor did not work and it was very stuffy. Rod, Rick and I stood around, a nurse waited with us and Ken lay on the examination couch, continually watching the fan.

"Cut that out! Stop it! I've got my eye on you." he said loudly.

"What's up Ken?" asked Rick.

"That bloody fan, look at it. It should be going around, but no it's going back and forth across the ceiling, it's bloody dangerous, can't something be done about it, before it hits one of us? Nothing ever works right in this bloody country."

I took the nurse that was with us outside. Africans are not always quick to recognise mental illness and she had looked very confused when Ken was saying this. I tried to explain Ken's condition to her, that he appeared to be having hallucinations which we all found upsetting. I told her about the little people, and all the other things Ken was imagining and added that the High Commission had spoken to the doctor, so he was aware of Ken's problems. "This is serious." is all that she said over and over again, at everything that I said. The doctor eventually arrived. He didn't examine Ken's leg; he simply informed us that he was admitting Ken, and that we could visit him that evening, reminding us to bring food with us, as the clinic didn't supply it.

Rod, Rick and myself, returned to The Dominion, by which time, Sharon, Sandra and the police lads had finished their lunch and left. The regulars were still sat at the bar, waiting for our return so that they could hear the latest news on Ken.

"We've got him safely admitted to Kombi." I told them.

"Yeah, but a fat lot of use she was." Said Rick, "She started wetting herself as soon as Ken started packing his little people up, to put in boxes!"

Judging by the laughter around the bar I wasn't the only one amused by this. Maybe life in Shendi gives us all a warped sense of humour.

"What is going to happen now?" asked Adam, who had popped in with Jane, to get an update on Ken, whose plight was grabbing every-ones attention.

"I'm going back to the clinic this evening." Rick informed them. "I will see what I make of him, once he has had a chance to settle in at the clinic."

Rick collected a take-away for Ken before he left on an early evening visit. Many of the expats hung around for his return and the expected medical bulletin.

"He seems happy enough in there," he started, "he didn't mention the little people at all. They are going to do tests on his leg in the morning. I think I can smell his leg. I first smelt this in the caravan, and thought it was something in there, but now I'm sure it's his leg."

"I hope you are not implying that Kevin's caravan smells, Rick," asked a small voice from around the bar. More titters from the ex-pats.

Rick went on, "I do really think this is serious. Remember what happened to Jack last year?"

"Which Jack?" Rick was asked.

"Jack that had the little boat, he moored it down by the bridge, he sometimes took Terry out fishing, you remember him. His leg was very similar to Ken's; he was advised to go back to U.K. but wouldn't go. He was dead within a week with blood poisoning."

"Yeah I remember him, I didn't know him well, but he did come in the bar sometimes. We need to know exactly what the doctor has to say. It's good that his mind is alright though." I said.

"I didn't say his mind was aright." went on Rick, "I said he didn't mention the little people. He kept stabbing at his bedding with his fork. When I asked him what he was doing, I was told that he was trying to catch the bloody chips that were running all over his bed." Ken was certainly keeping my regulars amused around the bar, but like Rick, I did consider his condition serious. Ken's health and Datu's trial dominated the conversation around the bar.

Sidi arrived early next morning to take me to court.

"Peter mentioned that I may have to give evidence." I told him as we drove into Port Albert. "I really don't want to."

"No, you mustn't do that, Peter doesn't understand, this is Shendi not U.K. This would be dangerous for you."

When we arrived at court Peter explained, to my relief that I would only be called if it were absolutely necessary, He and Frank would take the stand first, and then they were hoping that the magistrate would give permission for their video to be shown in court. Datu and Kresba had a new lawyer representing them, so this caused no further hindrance to the case. Peter and Frank were both in the witness box for fairly lengthy periods, answering questions in detail about all aspects of their investigation. I didn't see what evidence I could give that hadn't already been covered. The magistrate granted permission to them to show parts of their video in open court. I was sat several rows back, and the video was only being shown on a small television screen, so I didn't have a very clear view.

The beginning of the video was basically a detailed walk around Reg's compound. Initially it was thought that he maybe buried somewhere within his own walls. Datu is later shown, he is asked his name, which he gives, and it is explained to him that he is bring filmed, and that the video may be used in evidence against him. With a commentary explaining at all times what is happening, the video arrived at the spot where Reg was killed. Datu's voice is heard telling the interviewer, what happened when they arrived there. He pointed out where Kresba had been hiding, waiting for Datu to arrive with Reg. He explained that he stopped the jeep, telling Reg he needed to go to the toilet.

At this point Sharon and Sandra left the court, the video was clearly too much for Sharon who was understandably in tears as she left. Datu pointed out where Reg was buried, and the video went on to show his body being exhumed. I remained in the courtroom, but looked away from the screen; the commentary was sufficent for me. The magistrate switched off the video, as soon as she felt that the court had seen enough. I was relieved when she did this. This must be the end of the trial. Datu on film, leading the police and the S.S.G. to the body, this had to be conclusive evidence.

The magistrate adjourned the case for two days, until Friday, which was the last day of hearings, before the summer recess, and also the day that Sharon and Sandra flew out, hopefully this would see the end of Datu and Kresba's trial. Datu had still seemed very full of himself in the courtroom but surely by now, he realized there could be no other result to their trial, than them being found guilty.

Late that same afternoon, Rick and I had an appointment to see the doctor at Kombi clinic, to discuss Ken's health with him. Rod came with us and went in to see Ken, while Rick and I went in search of the doctor. When we did eventually track him down, he showed us into his office, which was reminiscent of most offices I had visited in Shendi, small, cluttered and in general disarray.

"What is your opinion of Ken?" we asked.

"Well, as for his mind, which seemed to be concerning you, I really don't see a problem, he hasn't said anything to me that would suggest that he has mental health problems."

Rick and I looked at each other. Surely the nurse or someone had seen or heard something.

"That's a matter of opinion." Rick whispered to me as the doctor looked at his notes and continued, "As for his leg, this is gangrene."

"That's what I thought, I could smell it when we saw him in the caravan," said Rick.

"What will happen now?" I asked.

"It will be fine we are treating it."

"How?" I wanted to know, because as far as I knew the treatment for gangrene was amputation.

"It is being dressed regularly by my very experienced nurses. They are putting on a very powerful, effective cream on it."

"I thought you had to amputate for gangrene?" I said anxiously.

"Come, come," laughed the doctor, "You can't go around cutting peoples legs off. If you get gangrene in a finger, well yes, remove it, that's for the best. But a leg- no." He shook his head; he seemed to be amazed at my suggestion.

"Please, I don't understand. Can you explain what will happen to his leg with your treatment," I asked him.

"The affected area will gradually dry and change colour, it will eventually turn into black powder, then it will just come away, and the leg will heal. You see he will be fine, you must have faith in black man's medicine, white man's medicine is not always the best."

Rick and I glanced at each other; I could see by Rick's expression that he was waiting for me to comment. Taking a deep breath and continuing to look at Rick for reassurance and support I said, "I'm not very happy about this, how would you feel, if we suggested that he returned to the U.K. for a second opinion."

The doctor looked at his notes, fiddled with his pen and said, "Umm yeah, I would think maybe in this man's case that might be a good idea."

"Good. Now there is a problem. We know he doesn't want to return to the U.K. so if we suggest it to him, and he refuses we will need you to back us up. Will you do that?"

"Yeah, I'll do that, I can see you don't like my treatment, and I don't want you to blame me if my medication doesn't work."

"Fine, fine, we'll go and speak with Ken, then come back and tell you what has been decided."

Thanking the doctor for his time, Ron and I walked out of the office to find that Ken was sat outside with Rod.

"We came out here for some air," Ken told us, "they don't seem keen to switch their gennie on, so they can't use the fans, and it's so stuffy in there."

"It's better out here anyway; we need to have a chat with you." I said as I took his hand and held it.

"I like that." Ken said.

"Behave now. Rick and I have been to see your doctor."

"Right, he is ever so pleased, how I'm getting on."

"Yeah, but we are not quite so happy. Rick and I would feel happier if you would agree to go back home and get a second opinion." Ken's expression changed instantly. "It really would be for the best Ken." I continued, as put a bit of pressure on the hand that I was holding. "Once your leg is sorted out, you can come back. We could try and get you on Friday's flight. Bob, the builder, is here, and goes home on Friday. We will ask Bob to sit with you, would you like that?"

(Bob worked with Nick in the U.K. and came out regularly to visit him. He was well known by all my ex-pats and for obvious reasons became affectionately known as 'Bob, the builder'.)

Rick butted in "If the promise of Bob the builder isn't enough to tempt you we will try and arrange Thomas the tank engine, or anyone else you fancy sitting with."

This even bought a smile to Ken's face. "Bob, the builder, will do fine, I haven't seen Bob for a while, that will give us six hours to catch up on each other's news, how is Bob getting on with his girl?"

"They seem fine; you will have plenty of time to ask him yourself."

We were all relieved and surprised that Ken had agreed so readily to return home, we suspected that maybe he realised his leg was more serious than the doctor was telling him. Before we left the clinic we went back to speak with the doctor, who agreed to keep Ken at the clinic, until Friday. At a price, of course!

On the way home, Rick said to me. "Right we have agreed to try and get Ken on Friday's flight, but aren't you forgetting something?"

"Like what?"

"Plane tickets need to be paid for, and the bill at the clinic must be building up nicely."

"That has gone through my mind. We all know Ken's got no money; he wouldn't have been in that darn caravan if he had any cash. Gypsy Jim has assured me that Ken will have money when his house is sold, that is why I've let him have a large tab at The Dominion. In fact Gypsy has told me if Ken doesn't pay me he will; we all know Gypsy isn't without a bob or two. I will pay it all, and hope they don't let me down, we have to get him home."

"You sure Helen, the low season is coming up and you will need your cash."

"It'll be O.K. let's just hope the housing market in the U.K. doesn't fall. Come on, back to The Dominion to get some cash, and straight down to get the ticket, before Ken changes his mind."

Rick and I gave each other a sideways glance as we walked out of the booking office, considering ourselves lucky to have obtained a ticket for Ken. Jenny, the manageress of Shendi Tours, the only company with flights to Shendi, during low season, was also the High Commission's warden for our area. In her official capacity, she had been informed of Ken's condition. At first she wasn't too keen to allow Ken to travel on one of her flights. Rick and I can be quite persuasive when needs be, and we were both eager to get Ken back to the U.K. It took time but after both of us gave her our assurance that his mind was now all right and there was no danger of him causing any disruption on the plane, she agreed to sell us a ticket.

I decided not to accompany Sharon and Sandra to the court on Friday. I felt nothing much was likely to happen, and having spent quite a bit of time away from the bar that week, both with the court case, and with Ken, I was aware that I was neglecting the bar. Several of my regulars, both ex-pats and tourists, were travelling, back on the afternoon's flight, and I wanted to be there to say my good-byes to them all.

The girls came to say good-bye, when they returned from court, so did Peter and his team. As I suspected the court hearing was a bit of a non-event, but they were still expecting the magistrate to submit a postal verdict from the U.K. All of them seemed pleased with how the trial had progressed that week, but would obviously liked to have seen a result. Rick bought Ken to The Dominion for a drink and to see me, before driving him to the airport. Ken was cheerful and seemed quite pleased to be going. Nick came in for a drink with Bob, before taking him to the airport, so together with my tourists that were flying home we had quite a party atmosphere in The Dominion that lunchtime.

Sharon's horror was not over however. I found out afterwards that when they had all gone through to the departure lounge, Sandra went off to the ladies leaving Sharon sat alone looking after their hand luggage. An S.S.G. officer, who she did not recognise but who obviously recognised her, approached her and started speaking to her.

"You do realise that they buried your father alive, don't you?" he informed her.

Sharon was unaware of this; there had been no need to tell the family all the gory details of Reg's death. Sharon was mortified; it took her a long time to come to terms with that revelation. I did not understand why that officer felt it was essential to tell Sharon this, and to do it while she was alone. I felt I was living among a nation that thrived on cruelty to all other nations.

On their arrival back to Gatwick, they all went their own separate ways. Sharon and Sandra back to their families. Sharon was eager to report the week's events to her brother Reggie, and her husband. Bob the builder who had had an uneventful flight with Ken travelled up to his home in Yorkshire, to pass on news of Nick to all their mates in their local bar, many of who, were customers of mine when they came out to Shendi on their visits. Ken was met by Gypsy Jim and Kevin who had travelled down from Liverpool to meet him and take over from Bob. Jim and Kevin took Ken to the A & E at their local hospital, where he was admitted and operated on early the next morning. Fortunately he didn't need an amputation, but a large portion of his leg, which was infected, had to be cut away. Ken needed several further skin graft operations to repair the damage. If we hadn't got him back to the U.K. when we did Ken's story may have ended very differently.

Chapter Ten
Family and S.S.G.

One Friday night, a few months after the safe return of Ken, I was on duty in an empty bar wondering who would come in. Friday was exodus day when up to five flights returned to the UK and this particular afternoon's flights had taken away many of my regulars. It was early evening, too early for the expats and too early for the new tourists to find us. They would still be busy unpacking, changing money and trying to work their safes and air conditioning. This was my quiet time and I was surprised to see Nick walk in, but when he told me that he had just come from the airport, I realised why. With his friend and fellow builder, Bob – otherwise known as Bob the Builder - having been one of the UK bound passengers that afternoon after another of his regular visits, Nick had obviously feeling in need of a little friendly conversation. It was no good looking for it from his girl friend, Maria.

Soon after coming out to Shendi, Nick had started a relationship with a local girl called Maria. Like all the expats who developed a relationship with a Shendian, Nick had been full of high expectations, convinced that their relationship would work. Unfortunately, like so many other expats, he soon realized that he had made a mistake; the relationship did not provide the companionship he wanted. Things went from bad to worse when he found that she had blatantly stolen a substantial sum of money from him. He had never expected her to be totally honest with him; no relationship with a Shendian is ever on the same level as a U.K. partnership and he accepted from the start that she would tell him little white lies to acquire money. Nevertheless, the theft of a large amount of money was in a different league and Nick decided to end the association. However, once in a relationship with a Shendian, it is often difficult to get out of it and Maria had been and still was an asset to him, as several of her uncles held high positions in Shendian bureaucracy. These had proved invaluable to Nick and the smooth running of his building project and on Maria's side, her connection with a European was an advantage and so a compromise was reached. By now Nick and Maria's personal relationship was now over, but it had become a convenience for both of them. Although they continued to live in the same compound, Nick spent most of his evenings in The Dominion, and enjoyed the many visits he received from friends back home, like Bob.

That day, as on many similar occasions, we cheered each other up with light conversation. "This place is like a giant Meccano set." I said looking around the bar at the framework of large iron girders and wrought iron work all held together by huge nuts and bolts.

Nick turned in his seat and looked around the bar. "Yeah, you're right. I'd never thought of it like that but it is. I bet it was easy to put up"

"If my darn court case goes on much longer, I'll take it down and build it elsewhere. That should be easy enough."

"It could be done, I'll help. All we will need is the right tools. Where will we rebuild it?

"I don't know, further along the coast, anywhere as long as it is well away from those sods next door."

"We need to think bigger than that. Let's get away from Shendi altogether. I know we will put it into a container and ship it to Thailand," joked Nick.

"I don't know about that. Thailand is a bit too far away and I bet it is no better than here."

"No, it'll be alright. In fact it'll be great. I can see myself in a couple of years from now, laying on a sun lounger, with you pulling a pint for me at The Dominion in Phuket."

We were fantasising about this and finding wilder and wackier places to move to when the phone rang. It was Kevin, my son, he had chosen the right night to phone me. I was always cheered up by a call from him. Part way through the conversation he suddenly said, "I may come out and see you soon Mum."

"That would be fantastic". It was three years since I had last seen Kevin, and a visit from him would be most welcome.

"That's not a promise though, but I would like to see you. It has been a long time since I last came out to Shendi. I will come as long as I can get a cheap flight, when I can get a break from work. Steph would like to come also, but again it depends on getting a good deal and us being able to get time off together."

"I would like that. I would love to meet Steph." Kevin and Steph had been together for a couple of years, but we had yet to meet, although I felt

I knew her quite well as Kevin had told me so much about her and of course he had sent me photos. Still I was very keen to meet her.

The phone call lifted my spirits and its effect lasted for days. Two weeks later, I was even more pleased when Kevin phoned and told me that he and Steph were arriving on the following Friday. Due to pressures of work they were only coming for a week, but I knew that week would be very precious to me. I was determined not to let Kevin know that 'Life in Shendi', was starting to prove too much for me. Kevin had only been out once before, our first Christmas when Simon was still here. In spite of our efforts to hide it from him, he must have realized that Simon and I had problems with our marriage but neither he nor Simon and I said anything. This was to be the first time I had seen Kevin since our split and although I was keen to see him, I felt a little uncomfortable and even a little shy about seeing him again.

Finally Friday came and Sidi drove me to the airport. I waited anxiously at the arrivals gate to meet my V.I.P. guests. This was only the second time I had been to the airport since Simon had left. Possibly the memory of this may have been haunting me, perhaps it was the shyness of seeing my son after three years, perhaps it was the anxiety of meeting his girlfriend for the first time, I do not know what it was, but I was in a state of high anxiety waiting for them. There was the usual crowd of 'meeters and greeters' outside the Arrivals Hall, locals and tour reps holding welcoming signs and calling out as passengers from Kevin and Steph's flight started to filter through from the customs check. After what seemed like hours but in reality could only have been minutes I caught sight of Kevin amongst a crowd of tourists. Waving frantically and calling out his name I pushed my way through to the front of the crowd. As my eyes filled with tears, I forgot my shyness but simply focused on my son. I was so pleased to see him that I missed seeing the other person behind him.

He dropped his case, hugged me and said. "Hi, Mum, good to see you, this is Steph." He turned to the person behind him. Steph put down her case and just as Kevin had done, put her arms around me and gave me a huge hug. Immediately all the worries I had felt on the way to the airport, all the ghosts of that last visit to see Simon off, all left me. I knew all three of us would have a great time and that by the warmth of her greeting that Steph and I were going to get on well together. After Simon had left I had had moments of dark despair when I had thought that I would never have a family again. As we walked out of the airport to the car and the waiting Sidi I banished those irrational thoughts for ever. I simply knew that whatever happened I would always have Kevin and most probably Steph.

It was only to be expected but the week passed all too quickly. Steph and I bonded well, and I was thrilled to see Kevin so relaxed and happy.

The three of us sat in the garden the following Friday lunchtime having a final drink before we headed back to the airport. We were talking about the places they had been to and the things they had done during the week. Because I had been tied to The Dominion, Kevin and Steph had had to do 'the tourist bit' on their own. They went to places I had never been to and saw sights that I had never seen. We were laughing about this when Kevin turned to me and said. "I can't believe that it is three years since I last came out. We've had a really good week. It won't be so long before I come back again. In fact we were chatting last night and have decided to come back next year."

"That's brilliant, you don't know how much better I feel now that you've been to see me, and another visit will give me something to look forward to."

I have never known the journey to the airport go so quickly and before I knew it we had said our good byes, they had boarded their plane and it had taken off for Gatwick. I shed a few tears as Sidi drove me home from the airport. It had been a fantastic week and although I had had to work, I had managed to spend some time each day with them, usually in the mornings. Their visit to Shendi had given my morale a huge boost and my sadness at their departure was tempered with the hope of another visit in the next year.

When I returned to the bar, Adam and Jane were sat in the garden. I went out to greet them. "We are waiting for Oliver Stewart. I don't think you know him do you?" Adam asked.

"No, no, but I have heard the name."

"He's been here several years, but he told us that he hadn't been to The Dominion. In fact he didn't know you were tucked away here."

"Then he doesn't know what he's been missing." I replied.

"He has put in a bid for Terry's compound." Jane told me. "We are hoping the sale goes through this time."

I hoped they could find a buyer for Terry's compound also. Sally was eager to get the property sold, to ensure that it did not tempt Terry to return. Adam and Jane had thought that they had buyers on two previous occasions, but these offers had unfortunately fallen through. I was sure they would be relieved when they no longer had the responsibility of the compound. Adam went on. "Oliver has made a fair offer, we just need to iron out a few details with him, we are quietly confident of a sale this time. Ah, there's Oliver now. I will introduce him to you."

After the introductions, Oliver glanced around the garden, "I like this, your garden is lovely, and I can't believe I didn't know you were here. This might be my first visit, but it won't be my last." True to his word, that was not Oliver's last visit to The Dominion. He became a regular lunchtime customer, and in time a valued friend. He did buy Terry's compound, and Adam was pleased to have completed his duty as attorney over Terry and Sally's property. It was a weight off both his and Jane's shoulders.

I was still on a high from Kevin and Steph's visit when a few days later I was due to attend a tourist meeting at The Soma Hotel, near to The Dominion. I had Momadou working during the day instead of his usual evening duty, to assist Jatou, my daytime waitress, in case the meeting went on longer than expected. There were a few customers in when I left including a family of four, two teenage boys and their parents who were all enjoying a late breakfast at a table by the door. I stopped and talked to them on the way out, asking them how they were enjoying Shendi and their breakfast.

It was well into the lunchtime rush when I returned to The Dominion. The garden was full of tourists and the bar was surrounded by regulars including Oliver who was with Adam and Jane finalising the sale of Terry's compound. After greeting some of my tourists, I went straight behind the bar to get back to work. Not until the lunchtime trade died down did I have the time to check my receipts from the morning. When I did check them there was no sign of one from the family I had spoken to earlier in the day.

"I can't find the bill for table two." I said to Jatou.

"What do you mean?"

"Table two by the door. There was a family having breakfast at that table when I left for my meeting. I can't find their bill."

"I don't understand what you mean."

"I know there were people at that table; I spoke to them before I left. I don't have the bill for them. Do you know where it is?"

"You weren't here then."

"I know I wasn't here when they paid their bill. I was at my meeting, but I want to know what had happened to their bill."

"It is not your business what happens when you are not here."

It was not 'not my business', it very much was my business. I knew that when I was off duty, some of my bills went astray, especially things that were hard to account for during stocktaking. For example draught beer was much more difficult to keep a check on than bottled beer. My staff would sell the odd pint of beer, and not put the sale through the invoice books. However, a missing receipt for a breakfast for four, a family that I had seen and spoken to was taking things a little far.

"It is my business that is the problem. I will speak to Momodou when he is free, but between you, you had better remember what has happened to that bill."

She walked away from me without saying anything. Momodou was eating his lunch; there was only Jatou and myself serving. I was busy with customers around the bar, and it was a few minutes before I became aware that there was no one serving the customers in the garden.

I went in search of Jatou. She was easy to find, in fact I heard her voice before I saw her. She was in the small back yard, outside the kitchen door, speaking on her mobile phone. This was against staff regulations. Because I had had problems in the past with waiters using their mobiles out at the back and ignoring the customers, staff were forbidden to use their mobile during working hours. Finding Jatou on her phone, coupled with my anxiety over the missing bill, I was furious. Without stopping to think I shouted at her, "Get off that phone and start serving. I'm busy inside, and people in the garden are not being served." I hurried back to the bar without waiting for an answer. She followed shortly afterwards, and glared at me as she passed the table I was serving on. I was too busy to cash the till until after the change of shift, but when I did, the cash tallied with the invoices that I had. With table two's invoice still missing the cash must also be missing.

The next day Jatou failed to turn up for work. This was no surprise to me. She had a habit of not coming to work for a few days, if she had been reprimanded as she had been the day before over the missing bill, and using her mobile phone. I fully expected her to return to work a few days later, when she would think I had calmed down. She would come in armed with an excuse for the missing bill and saying that either she or one of her children had been ill. I had no thoughts of sacking her; I simply wanted the money back. In Shendi it was difficult to fire staff. Many of them were likely to have relatives that in a position to be detrimental to a business and if that failed, staff could also create problems for their European employers by complaining about them to labour and welfare organisations. Jatou did not however return to work. I saw this as admission of guilt over the missing invoice. In many ways, I was glad to be free of her; she was prone to stir up problems with the staff, and this certainly was not the first or second instance of missing bills. I was hoping this might serve as a warning to other members of staff.

The following Monday, about mid afternoon, when the lunchtime trade was easing off, I was stood behind the bar, having a much needed cup of coffee, and enjoying a chat with to a few ex-pats including Liverpool Kevin, who had recently returned from the U.K. Rod had joined Kevin, and together we were telling him about Ken, and his little people. Kevin in turn was explaining to us, what had happened, when he and Gypsy Jim had picked Ken up from Gatwick airport. We were chatting light heartedly, then Rod said to me, "I thought I saw Lydia, from the supermarket in earlier ordering her take-away. Don't tell me your phone line has been mysteriously cut again."

"Indeed it has! I realised mid morning that it had been cut, as usual, just outside my back gate, on the road leading down to The Peace Haven's tradesman's entrance."

"How many times is that now?" Kevin asked.

"I don't know I've lost count. Telecoms are getting annoyed, but what can I do? It is obviously a deliberate act. If it is not the hotel, their security at their back entrance knows who it is, it is impossible for them not to see it being done. Besides I don't think I've upset anyone else enough for them to bear a grudge for so long. It has to be the hotel, but I don't see what they aim to achieve by it."

"For a start Lydia had had to come and order her food, instead of ringing. Maybe they think you do more business over the phone than you do."

"Yes, yes, you are probably right. I think it is just another ploy to try and wear me down. I should get a mobile; they would have difficulty to cut that off"

We were continuing our conversation when we heard the slamming of several car doors, and there was a commotion in the car park. About fourteen Shendians, some of whom I recognised as being S.S.G. officers, entered my premises. Without looking into the bar, without acknowledging anyone or anything they walked straight into the garden, spread out and sat at all of the vacant tables. I stayed where I was and instructed Momodou to go out and ask what they wanted.

"What are they up to?" asked Kevin.

"Don't ask me! But I think I'm about to find out." I replied.

I nervously watched from behind the bar, as Momodou went out, menu in hand, as if he expected them to place an order. He approached the table which, both he and I knew, was occupied by the officer in charge of the tourist area. Momodou offered him the menu, which was refused, listened to the officer and then returned to speak to me.

"They want you to go out," Momodou told me and then walked away into the kitchen.

I looked at my expat customers but before I could or do anything, Rod asked, "Do you want me to come with you?"

"No, no that's alright, they've sent for me. It might make matters worse if you come with me, but both of you stay here please. I may need you. I have no idea what they want but I had better go and find out." Even as I spoke, I was moving towards the garden. I knew better than to keep S.S.G. officers waiting.

I went out and went to meet the senior officer. I still had a few lunchtime tourists in the garden, who were giving both the S.S.G. men and me curious looks. So many Shendians arriving together, making so much noise and sitting at separate tables, must have seemed strange to them.

"You want to see me?" I asked.

He leaned back in his chair. "Indeed we do Madam, we have been hearing bad reports about you, and how you treat your staff. We want you to come to our headquarters at The Lakeside Hotel. Meet me there in half an hour with all your business papers."

With a nod from him all the other officers left their various tables and filed out of the garden. The tourists looked on in total amazement and I went back into the bar, to report to Kevin and Rod.

"Humm Jatou, I bet, "said Kevin.

"Yeah, she has to be behind this. I know her husband has a S.S.G. officer friend, which is in a much higher position than any of these. Whoever is behind it, this looks like hassle for me."

"Don't go alone, get Sidi here." Rod advised.

"I can't contact him; the phone is out of action, remember. Maybe that is why it isn't working. It could be deliberate so that I can't contact anyone."

"I bet you are right. No matter, you can't go alone; you need a Shendian with you. Phone Sidi." said Kevin as he handed me his mobile.

I phoned Sidi, and while I was waiting for him to arrive, I went into the office to collect my business papers. I was trying to convince myself that this was all going to be O.K. I knew my papers were all in order, if they were hoping to find fault with them, they were going to be unlucky. Sidi arrived very quickly and we made our way to The Lakeside Hotel in silence. I knew the power of the S.S.G. and my mind was too occupied to be making conversation. I was also concerned with what the tourists in the garden had made of this. An incident like this was not good for trade.

I had never been inside The Lakeside Hotel before. We approached the main gate and were beckoned in by their security guard. He seemed to be expecting us. It seemed strange to me that the S.S.G. had their tourist area headquarters in the grounds of a prominent hotel. "Do you know where we have to go?" I asked Sidi as he parked in the almost empty hotel car park.

"Yes, it's around the back, not in through the hotel. Don't worry this is going to be O.K. This is only Jatou's doing."

"That's what I think."

Sidi led the way and I followed, we walked around the side of the hotel, in the opposite direction to the pool area. The further we went around the hotel the less well-kept the gardens became. They took on a wild appearance, and in some places were completely overgrown. I suspected this may have been to deter too many tourists from wandering around this part of the hotel. As we turned another bend in the path, we were confronted by an open door, which led straight into an office. We could hear voices from inside but these fell silent as we approached.

As I had come to expect of Shendian offices, this one was a mess, there was hardly room for us to enter. In fact there was so much clutter over the floor that it was difficult to find somewhere to stand. A shabby looking couch in the corner was being laid on by an equally shabby looking officer, who sat up as we entered. A desk in the opposite corner had a tattered old swivel chair on either side of it. These were both occupied, but neither of these officers looked up from the board game, they were playing, as we came in. Another officer was sat on a child sized wooden chair; he stood up and indicated for me to sit on it.

"What kept you?" demanded one of the men at the desk, without looking up from his board game. "Have you bought your papers with you?"

"Yes I've got them." I said.

He held out his hand to take them from me, yet again he didn't look up or even glance in my direction.

He looked at my papers disinterestedly and said, "Why do you think we have bought you here?"

"I really don't know." I replied.

"We are concerned about what is happening at The Dominion."

"Can you explain what you mean please?"

"Don't try and act innocent with us!" he raised his voice. "We are not happy with the way your staff are treated."

"What!" exclaimed Sidi, in an equally loud voice, "I would like to know who has complained about The Dominion. This woman treats her staff very well."

"No-one asked you to speak." he was told.

"I won't stand here and listen to you saying things about this women and The Dominion. She is good to her people."

I was surprised at Sidi's vehemence. I had been in many conversations and similar situations before with Sidi at my side and he had never intervened in such a manner. It was most unusual.

"Some of us don't agree with that. One of her staff has reported that she doesn't have all of her business papers, but they do appear to be in order."

"I know they are all correct, I go and pay all her taxes for her, and sort her business papers at the start of every year. No other members of staff have any dealings with this, so no one else would know, if her licenses had been paid for or not." Sidi told them.

Another S.S.G. officer came in, who I recognised as one of the men that had been sat in my garden, only a short while ago. Pointing at Sidi he said. "Your car is parked in the way, come with me and move it."

"It's in the main hotel car park, which is nearly empty, it can't be in the way." Sidi informed him. Again I was surprised at his attitude. It was not usual to contradict S.S.G. officers.

"You have been told to go with him and move it." Sidi was told by the officer at the desk, who had been doing most of the talking. Sidi followed the officer out of the office. I became aware of my heart beating, and my breathing coming in rapid, short pants, I was feeling hot and clammy, and fear was taking a grip of me. I knew they had taken Sidi away on false pretences to get me alone. The room suddenly seemed smaller, and overcrowded. I felt cornered; they seemed to be closing in on me. Now the man slumped on the couch spoke, "There didn't used to be problems at The Dominion."

I turned to look at him directly. "There aren't problems there now." I told him.

"We think there is. There were no problems there when your husband was here. He respected your workers, you don't."

"That's not true." I could feel my hands trembling now; I hoped none of them would notice.

"Who is that boy to you?" asked the other man who sat at the desk, and who had, up until that point, seemed to have been preoccupied with his board game.

"He is my driver, he takes the chef out shopping every morning, and runs errands for me. He pays all my taxes and sorts my paper work as he has told you himself."

"Some say you are married."

I laughed weakly, "Whoever has told you that has a good imagination."

"Why have you bought him here with you, if he is not your husband? He wasn't at The Dominion when we came and invited you here. We didn't ask for him to come only you, so why did you bring him?"

"I didn't want to come alone, I didn't even know where these offices were. I take him most places with me, in case I have any problems."

"You do have problems Madam, and will get more unless you learn to treat your staff correctly."

"I still do not know what I have done."

"You don't trust your Shendian staff. Who has told you not to trust them? Is it this boy, who you bring to our offices?"

"He is hardly at The Dominion, only in the mornings, and then he goes out with the chef. He has a small shop of his own in his village. He is there for the rest of the day. I have learnt for myself, which staff I can trust and which staff I cannot."

"You had better start trusting all of your staff, most of them have been at The Dominion longer than you have. They are good hard working people, and deserve to be treated with respect. If this is not done you are going to be in trouble. We will be keeping a close eye on you and your business. We don't like it when Europeans come to our country and treat Shendians badly."

It was with great relief that I saw Sidi return again. As he stepped back into the office, he asked if I was alright, and turning to the officer, sat at the desk, who was obviously in charge of these proceedings, said "You have seen that Helen's papers are in order. Have you bought her here for any other reason? If not is there any need for her to stay here any longer?"

"No, you can both go, but I'm warning you, advise this woman wisely. We don't believe she knows how to behave towards her Shendian staff."

"O.K." was all Sidi replied.

Somehow I managed to turn and walk out without my legs giving way. Sidi and I went back along the overgrown paths, pushing aside overhanging branches that were in our way, towards the cared for gardens and open spaces of the front of the hotel in total silence.

It was not until we were back at the car that I felt I could speak. As we got in I said, "They asked why I had bought you with me. I wouldn't even have found their office if I had come alone. Who would imagine that there was an office tucked away around the back of the hotel. If I came across those paths alone, I would have turned back thinking I had come the wrong way."

"Yeah well they like it like that. They don't want tourists wandering around there, do they?"

"Humm, what do you make of all this? It is Jatou eh?"

"Has to be. Remember her husband is a friend of Omar's. He has probably told them to frighten you, so they make out there is a problem with your papers. Don't worry they can't do anything, all is in order."

"They asked if you were my husband."

"Again that would be Jatou trying to cause problems. She did everything for Maria's husband before Maria arrived. He was here for six months by himself. That is why all the staff looked up to her, they were scared of her. She was afraid of losing that power. She is jealous of me because she knows I advise you. You know what people are like here."

"That explains a lot. I wish I had known before about Jatou and Maria's husband. Ah well, do you think this will be an end to this, or will they be back?"

"Hopefully not. You didn't accuse Jatou of stealing did you?"

"No. I only asked where the missing bill was."

"That's O.K. The guy who took me outside, who I know, he used to live in my village. He told me you had accused her."

"Definitely not, but if he told you that, that proves this has come from Jatou."

Rod and Kevin were still sat at the bar, when I returned, waiting to hear the outcome, and to know that I was safe. I explained to them what had happened, making sure that I could not be heard by any of my staff. I was sure that Jatou would be keeping them informed as to what was going on. I was determined not to let any of the staff know that this had unnerved me. Sidi's information about the relationship between the previous owners and Jatou really did explain a great deal. It was understandable that she would resent her loss of influence and power and thinking about it all, it seemed strange that she had done nothing earlier.

It was now my afternoon break time. I went into my house and flopped onto the bed. I was still trembling inside. I knew it would be impossible for me to drift off for my customary afternoon nap. I just lay there reflecting on the events of the afternoon. Life was certainly different from back home, on the island. I had never had any dealings with anyone, with the sort of authority that these officers had. I imagined what Simon must have been feeling when he was taken into the S.S.G. offices, when we were first here. He was alone; I had had Sidi with me. I had been scared, but I would have been much more so, by myself. I had lived on the island for 49 years, and only used a lawyer for buying and selling property. In contrast I had only been here 4 years, and regularly had to seek advise from Ousman, my lawyer. Everything came flooding through my mind. The court case was going nowhere, and seemed unlikely to. Until there was some sort of solution with The Peace Haven I was stuck here. I would have liked to sell the business, I needed to get out of here, but this was impossible at the moment. Who would buy a business that was in the midst of a court case that was unlikely to end in The Dominion's favour?

My thoughts turned to Ousman. Esau had introduced Simon to him; in fact like so many people here they were related. Simon had fallen out with Esau, but had continued to use Ousman's services. I was not convinced that Simon had really pursued the possible problems over our entrance, before we purchased the bar. He had told me he had, and that Ousman had advised him that everything would be all right. As far as I could see, the only real winners in this court case were Ousman, who had advised Simon to take court action, and The Peace Haven's lawyer. Were the two of them deliberately using delaying tactics? Ousman's regular bills were becoming a heavy burden to me. Had he advised Simon against buying The Dominion, he would not have had this source of income. I often wondered where his allegiance lay. Was I being too sceptical?

Then I thought of the staff. I knew that Jatou knew what had happened to the money from table two, but would I have been wiser to turn a blind eye? That would have saved me this afternoon's stress. I knew I wouldn't have done that at home; I would have simply sacked the staff concerned. Things were different here, Europeans were rarely the winners in any situation; but was this all the more reason to stand up for my rights? I decided it was. If I failed to stand up to the staff they would walk all over me. In many ways I was trapped, but I would not behave like a trapped animal. I would keep my dignity, and not show the fear I was starting to feel. If I did the staff would use this to their advantage. I would go back out into the bar for my evening duty putting on a brave face, and the events of this afternoon behind me.

I returned to the bar, feeling more positive than I did before my break. Kevin was back and was sit with Nick. Both seemed to be in good spirits.

"You O.K. now darling?" asked Kevin.

"Yeah, I'm fine, fine now."

"Kevin was telling me what happened." Nick said, "Thieving bastards, and then they turn things on you, when you catch them. Remember Maria has family that maybe able to help, if you get any more problems."

"Thanks, Sidi is going to have a word with some friends of his, I think it will be O.K."

"Well listen to what I've got to say. It may make you chuckle. At least it will take your mind off your problems," Kevin said. "Terry has phoned me, he is talking of coming back."

"You must be joking! Sally won't be happy about that. He hasn't even got a house to come back to, Adam and Jane have just sold it."

"He is only thinking about it at the moment, surely he won't come back? But he does sound O.K. again."

"How long will that last if Lena comes back too? Do you know if he is in contact with her?"

Nick said, "She will come back as soon as she knows that he is back. She's madly in love with his wallet."

"That's a bit unfair." replied Kevin.

"I don't think that's unfair." I told him, "What about the £2,000 she took the first time she went to Ghana? Terry didn't see that again."

The tourists started to arrive for their evening meals, after a day soaking up the sun, all of them oblivious to what had been happening to me that afternoon, or of our concerns for Terry if he did return. Like Simon and I when we were on holiday, they all thought they had found Utopia, neither I or my ex-pats were about to disillusion them. The rest of the week passed uneventfully. I became lulled into a false sense of security. If the S.S.G. had intended to come back; they would have done so by now. The telephone company had been and repaired my line, yet again. If I did get any problems while Sidi wasn't here at least I knew that I could contact him. This made me feel more secure.

The following Monday morning, Nightclub Rick was in for his usual breakfast, Rod was in having a coffee, so was Robert, who was here again on one of his many visits. He enjoyed chatting to the ex-pat lads whilst having his 'morning cuppa', and would refer to them as 'The Breakfast Club.' They were all sat at a large table in the garden. Kevin arrived at the same time as Sidi, and joined the others. I ordered coffee for Sidi and myself and we went to sit in my garden, on the other side of the wall to discuss some errands I wanted him to do while he was out with the chef. No sooner had we sat down, than Momodou came to me.

"There are some men here to see you; they said they have come from the State House."

"What now?" I said to Sidi.

"Don't panic, I will come with you to see them."

We went back into the bar to be faced by Omar, Jatou's husband's S.S.G. friend, and four other Shendians that I assumed were also S.S.G. officers.

"Ah, there you are, it is harder to get to see you at The Dominion, than it is to get into Fort Knox," was Omar's greeting.

"I'm always here. You didn't have much trouble getting to speak to me. I was only having a coffee in my garden." I was trying to sound full of confidence, although that is not how I was feeling.

"We need you to come to our headquarters in Port Albert." he said to me, and turning to Sidi he added, "Do you know where that is?"

"Yes." Sidi replied.

"Then meet me there in half an hour, with all your business and immigration papers."

"Some of your colleagues checked my papers last week, and they found them to be in order." I told him.

"As I said fetch your papers and bring them to me in my office in Port Albert in half an hour."

All five of them left. We heard them slamming their car doors and then drive off.

"Keep calm" Sidi instructed me. "Your papers are fine, so what can they do?"

I went to my office to collect my papers. Before I left The Dominion, I went out into the garden to speak to the Breakfast Club.

"What was that all about?" asked Kevin. "We saw them come but didn't want to interfere unless it was needed. Was it needed?"

"No, but thanks for watching. It was the S.S.G. again; they want me to take my papers into Port Albert this time."

"Port Albert, not Lakeside, that doesn't sound too good." remarked Kevin.

"Shouldn't you let The High Commission know where you are going?" asked Robert.

"No, best not. They get annoyed if you do that, but mind you, if I'm not back by six this evening, will one of you inform them, please."

"You sure you will be O.K. till then?" asked Rick.

"Yeah, I'll be fine, Sidi is coming with me, but please check later and see if I'm back."

We set off. My stomach was in turmoil. I had heard horror stories from people that had been taken to the Port Albert offices. I kept telling myself that folk do like to exaggerate, and for me all would be well. Sidi took a turning I didn't expect him to take.

"Where are you going?" I asked him. "We are meant to be going to Port Albert."

"I've told you to keep calm. We are going to the water board."

"What! We don't have a problem with the water board; I have a problem with the S.S.G. I'll have an even bigger problem if we are late. What are you doing?"

"The secretary to the director of the water board is also a high ranking S.S.G. officer. She was once the Imam of Famara's wife. They are divorced now, but she knows me well, I want to speak to her before we go to see Omar."

"Omar will be angry if we are late getting there."

"Don't panic. Why do you always get yourself in such a state?"

"Because, because. Oh forget it, just please get me there as soon as possible"

Sidi was not long at the water board though every minute he was inside seemed like an eternity. It was a wasted side trip as far as I was concerned; the lady he wanted to speak to was absent. We proceeded to Port Albert in silence. My nerves where getting progressively worse with each minute that passed. We finally pulled up outside large green painted double gates. There was a brightly coloured notice board above the gates, which read 'Milk Marketing Board.'

"Is this it?" I asked.

"Yes, they are hardly likely to put S.S.G. Offices, above the gate are they? They don't want everyone to know where their offices are."

The gates were opened for us by a man in a shabby uniform, who showed Sidi where he had to park. At least he would not be called out to move the car this time. We were shown into a tiny bare waiting room, with only a small desk and chair that was occupied by a security guard. There were wooden benches by two of the walls, the small windows, that were too high to see out off, but did let in a bit of light, had bars to them. There was an interior doorway with no door. This led into an equally bare large room, its only furniture was several rows of wooden benches, and the windows of this room also had iron bars to them. There were many people sat on the benches in this room. Sidi approached the desk and told the security guard whom we had come to see.

"Do you have a mobile?" asked the stern voice of the security guard.

"Yes" replied Sidi.

The security guard without speaking held out his hand. Sidi gave him his phone.

"And her's."

"I don't have one," I told him.

Again without speaking the security man pointed to the wooden bench in his office. We both went to sit down.

"No, she sits there, you go in there," yelled the security man sharply, as he pointed to the interior doorway.

"I'm staying with her." Sidi told him.

"I have been ordered to keep you here in security, while she visits the offices."

"I go everywhere with her."

"Not to-day you don't."

I was gutted. I had come to rely on Sidi to support me in difficult situations. Alone I might crumble. Not only was he not going to be with me, but also he had had his mobile taken away, so I knew he would not be able to inform anyone what was happening. Each minute I sat there seemed like an hour. Omar had only given me a short time to collect my papers, and get here, so why was he keeping me waiting now. I assumed his intention was to make me nervous before the interview started, if so, he was succeeding. I glanced at the clock on the wall, the hands hadn't seemed to move, maybe it had stopped. I looked at my watch. They both gave the same time Time was passing very slowly.

I watched the many comings and goings in the car park. Were these staff, or others like myself that had been 'invited' here? I began to wonder why the two other people sat in the same office as myself were here. They were African, but not Shendian. I had started to distinguish the different nationalities. Did Shendians ever get bought here or just outsiders? My mind was wondering again. Did it matter why the others were here? I didn't seem to want to concentrate on my own problems. What could Jatou have possibly told Omar? What was he going to accuse me of? I would soon find out. I was getting hot, I was perspiring. I was feeling faint; no please don't let me pass out. The windows had no glass, and the door was wide open, it shouldn't be this hot in here. Sweat began to trickle down my face, a pain was starting in my right temple; a tension headache was setting in. I didn't need this I needed to be able to concentrate. Come on Helen get a grip.

A shadow came over the doorway. It was a suited man that I recognised as one of the officers that had accompanied Omar to The Dominion earlier that day.

"Come" was all he said as he beckoned to me to follow him. He turned and walked out of the door, clutching my folder containing all my papers I followed him across the car park. Opposite the large double gates that seemed like the gateway to the outside world was a large two storey building. He pushed open the door and I trailed behind him. It was unexpectedly dirt and dust free. The corridors were narrow, but generally brighter, and much cleaner, than most office blocks I had been in over the last few years. I was shown into a downstairs office which was large, smart, bright and airy. Omar sat at a large and surprisingly uncluttered desk, whose only ornaments were an elaborate blotting pad and an ink well, (which I doubted had ever been used) and a standing calendar. There were plenty of comfortable seats. Two office chairs either side of the desk and in one of these sat a lady officer. Near by were two leather armchairs; officers that had also been with Omar earlier occupied both these. Omar indicated that I was to sit on a matching leather settee. The lady officer got up and came to sit beside me. If this was to put me at my ease it failed. The man that had come to collect me from the outer office filled the seat vacated by the lady.

Omar asked for my papers. I handed him my folder. I hoped he wouldn't notice that my hands were trembling. He took them out, and started examining them, slowly he read each one, and placed it on the table, in front of him. When he had looked at them all he stretched out his hand towards me and said. "The others?"

"What others?" I asked.

"The rest of your papers, I asked you to come here and bring all your papers, and all you have given me are these."

"That is all my papers, my business papers and my personal papers, what others do you want?"

"You arrived here in May '99. You have only bought me 2004's papers, where are the rest?"

"You didn't explain that you wanted all my papers from when I first arrived. You must know that to obtain my 2004's licenses, I've had to produce 2003's and so on back through the years. I therefore assumed to bring you 2004's papers was sufficient."

"You are not to assume anything."

"Sorry, sorry, that was my mistake."

"Now tell me about the other problems that there are at The Dominion."

"What problems?" I asked.

"I hear that you don't treat your staff with respect."

"That isn't true!"

"Remember I knew your husband, he was a gentleman, there were no problems when he was here. Things were done correctly then. I would like to bring your husband back now, running The Dominion, then I would send you back to your own people."

"Simon won't be coming back."

"I want to contact him, I need his address or telephone number."

"I don't have it. I'm not in contact with him." That was a white lie. It had been a long while since I had heard from Simon, but I was able to contact him, if I needed to.

"What!" yelled Omar,"The Dominion is Simon's business, not yours; you only work there, the same as the staff. Do you not send Simon the money that you are making from his business?"

"What money is this? You know that a clause in my court injunction with The Peace Haven, states that I must trade at all times. Most businesses in the tourist area close in low season. I keep all my staff employed all year. I spend most of my profit during high season, to run the business in low season, and to pay my lawyer to fight our court case."

There was much tutting from all in the room. One officer shouted at me. "Your husband sets you up in business, a very good business, with good, loyal staff to run it for you, and make plenty of money, and you steal all that money from him. You are a wicked, wicked woman. No Shendian woman would be so wicked to her husband. You steal from him, and then you accuse your good Shendian staff of stealing from you. You get these ideas about your staff because that is how you behave yourself.

I looked at Omar and said. "I thought that was what this was all about. It's Jatou, isn't it?"

"Never mind what this is all about, we will get to that later. I want to get hold of Simon. I want him back in Shendi and then I know that The Dominion and its staff will be looked after properly. Then he will get all the money he makes from his business, nobody will be able to steal it from him."

"I've told you I don't know where he is."

"You have a son?"

"Yes."

"Where is he?"

"Birmingham."

"I remember Simon telling me your son lived in London."

"He did, now he is in Birmingham."

"He will know where his father is. Give me his address?"

"I don't have it." again I lied.

"You aren't in contact with your own son! You come to our country and you abandon your child? You really are a very wicked women, no Shendian woman would even think of behaving like you do."

"No, no I can't believe this." said the woman sat next to me, in a slow and exaggerated voice. "So wicked to your own child this is bad."

If these comments were designed to completely unnerve me, they had succeeded. I felt a lump in my throat, I thought I was going to cry, but knew I must do all in my power not to. Remarks like that would hit home to any caring mother, especially when I had witnessed and been appalled by, some of the local mother's lack of natural maternal instincts. In my defence I said." My son is 35, and hasn't lived at home since he was 18. How can I have abandoned him?"

"You are here, enjoying a good life. Your poor son is in the U.K. and you don't even know what is happening to him. Of course you have abandoned him. So selfish! I cannot believe that you don't even contact him."

"I e-mail him, I don't have his address." As soon as I said this I knew it was a mistake. It just came out instinctively in my attempt to defend myself.

"Give us his e-mail address then, that will do, we can e-mail him for his father's address."

"I don't know it. It is on the computer."

"We will talk about this later. Back to Jatou." continued Omar. "She has gone to social security to claim her dues, since you sacked her."

"I didn't sack her, she didn't return to her duties."

"After you sacked her," he shouted back at me, "she went to social security to claim her dues, and has been told that she is unable to claim all her entitlements, as no payments were made for her before 1999. She has worked at The Dominion since 1991. Why has this not been paid."?

"When we arrived in 1999, several of the staff approached us and told us that no social security was being paid for them. I knew this was correct as I had the books from the previous owners. We agreed to put all the staff on social security; our social security officer, who wanted us to pay back payments on our staff that had not been included, visited us. We explained that we were not even here so this was not our responsibility."

"You have to pay this, all employers have to pay on all their staff, this is law."

"The social security should have picked up that The Dominion had staff that were not on their books, they do visit my premises regularly and look through the books. They must have known there were more staff there than they were being paid for."

"That is not your business, but it is your business to put it right now."

"Then I will rediscuss it with my social security officer. When we arrived he suggested that we terminate all our staff, and reemploy them, then we would not be responsible for the non payment before we arrived."

"So you benefit from non payment and your staff suffer. O.K. but she was also told that the earnings that social was paid on, is actually less than her salary.

"That is not true. I have told you my social security officer visits regularly and examines my books. Social is paid on basic pay, maybe Jatou has told them her full take home pay, this also includes travel expenses that social is not paid on."

"Mmmm so once again the staff lose out because you fiddle the system. The fact remains Jatou is not satisfied with what they are going to pay her."

"Has Jatou also told you that I pay all of the staff's social security, not just the employer's contribution. I also pay their income tax. They receive all of their salary with no deductions, so I fail to see how you can tell me that I treat my staff badly."

"You will go now." instructed Omar, "but I want you back here in one and a half hours, with all of your papers from 1999, when you arrived."

I stood up to leave, as I reached the door, Omar said. "Don't forget to bring me your son's e-mail address."

"I don't have a computer at The Dominion, so I can't look it up."

"You think you are clever Madam, you are not, when I bring Simon back, he will make you sorry for how you behave."

The same officer that had shown me in escorted me out. As we approached the building where Sidi had been told to wait, my escort signalled to the security to release Sidi, then he followed the two of us to Sidi's car.

"You O.K?" Sidi asked as he started the engine.

"Just get me out of here. Omar has given me one and a half hours to get back to The Dominion, and return with all of my papers from 1999."

"Have you kept them all?"

"Yeah, but finding them is a different matter. I think they are in one of the boxes in the office, but remember we're still my immigration papers missing the year Simon left, it was so late by the time we sorted the rest, and it couldn't be done."

"Don't worry about that I did talk to immigration remember and it was them that said it was alright, as it was nearly time to pay the next year's."

He didn't say another word as we drove out of the gates, and around the corner heading back towards The Dominion, but as soon as we were around the bend, Sidi suddenly pulled over. Without turning off the engine, he jumped out and hailed a taxi.

"What are you doing?" I asked.

"I'm staying in Port Albert, you get in this taxi, and go back and collect your papers."

"Why are you staying in Port Albert?"

"I told you I will sort this out, and I will. I know people that are higher than Omar; they will call him off of you. Don't worry, Omar is nothing."

"He is not exactly nothing! Do I get a taxi back too?"

"Maybe he's not nothing, but he is nobody that you need to worry about. I will phone you. If you don't hear from me, you come back in a taxi."

I was not as confident as Sidi that he would be able to find a solution for this, but I had no one else to rely on. On the journey back to The Dominion my head was in turmoil, over things that Omar had said. Would he really try and get Simon to come back? I was sure that he wouldn't come, but did Omar have the power to close me down if he didn't, or was Omar just bluffing to frighten me. Reflecting more, I could not understand Omar's attitude towards me. It is essential to the smooth running of your business to have some Shendian 'friends' in high places to help you. In order to ensure these 'friendships', you are expected to show favour towards them, for example, to entertain them in your establishment. Simon had supplied Omar with many free meals, a tradition I had continued. Omar had been to The Dominion every New Year's Eve, since I had been there, bringing a large party of his family, to enjoy our festive entertainment, all free of charge. On numerous occasions, he had phoned me and asked for a secluded table in my garden, as he wanted to bring a girl friend for a meal. He would also ask that my waiters were told that Jatou was not to be informed that he had been there, as she was a friend of his wife. Surely in view of these 'favours' I had shown him, I deserved more respect than he had given me that morning. I knew he was aware of the thieving that seemed endemic especially in the catering trade and that employers had a constant battle to protect their own interests.

Then I wondered where Sidi was, whom was he going to see? Did he really know someone who would sort this out for me? And at what price? I was used by now, to the fact that all Shendians think they could sort anything out. Admittedly Sidi was usually able to help me. Although our early friendship had waned and by now often we fell out frequently especially when I realised that he also, was trying to obtain money from me under false pretences, he was still always there for me when I had problems, and could usually find a reasonable solution for me. I did consider he was well worth what I paid him to do this, but these were powerful people. Could he really solve this for me? At that moment I needed to have faith in him. I wasn't feeling as confident as I felt I should.

When I arrived back at the bar, the lunchtime regulars were already there. Among these were Nigel and Alana, who lived in the same village as Adam and Jane, farther along the coast. They came in for lunch, every week, while they were in this area doing their shopping. Nigel was the High Commission's warder for this area, and having heard from 'The Breakfast Club' where I had been taken, came and offered his assistance.

"I think it maybe alright." I told him, "I have to go back with all my papers since '99. I do have them, but I mustn't stop chatting. I need to find them."

"Where is Sidi? He should be with you."

"He stayed in Port Albert, to see someone he says will sort this out. I don't know if he can, you know how things work here."

"That's fine as long as he is with you." He slipped a piece of paper into my hand. "That's my mobile number, phone if you need help."

I thanked him, and went in search of my papers, which were actually easier to find than I thought they might be. I didn't go back into the bar; I couldn't face answering lots of questions from well meaning folk. I went into the house, and paced up and down the lounge, anxiously waiting for news from Sidi. My impatience got the better of me, I dialled his mobile number.

"Don't panic." He said as he answered. "I'm on my way to get you, have you got your papers?"

"Yes."

"Then relax Helen. Order us some coffee, I will be there before it's ready."

He arrived, just as Momodou bought our coffee into the house. "All is going to be fine. Just take Omar your papers, and I will be going into the office with you this afternoon."

This made me feel better, but I was still sceptical. Had Sidi managed to arrange something to help me, or was he trying to make me more confident about my present situation? His mobile rang. I could only hear one side of the conversation, and it was in one of the local languages but I did understand some of what Sidi was saying.

"See I told you." Sidi said as he came off the phone. "Would you believe that was Omar? He has obviously had my boys who are more important than he is get on to him and tell him what he must do. He has told me to tell you not to worry, just come back with the papers you have, if any are missing it doesn't matter."

"I do have them all, but I feel better for that phone call. Come on drink your coffee, I'm eager to go back and get this behind me. ......But how did Omar know your mobile number?"

"I don't know, my boys must have given it to him."

My mind questioned everything that happened to me now. I did wonder how Omar got Sidi's number. Had he just been given it, or were he and Sidi closer than I realised? Sometimes my mind did work overtime. The part of the phone conversation that I had understood, was as Sidi had related it to me, so why did I doubt the situation? I also remembered the start of the questioning this morning. Even when the S.S.G. and Sidi had been speaking, they had used English not one of the local languages. The S.S.G. did nothing accidentally so why had English been used?

I still felt nervous on the drive back to Port Albert. Sidi and I hardly spoke. I knew he was feeling smug. I was not convinced that he could solve things as well as he kept telling me he could. I was still not sure that Omar's phone call had been genuine, or was it a ploy to get my confidence. My feeling of being trapped was nearly becoming an obsession. I liked to be in control, this control was fast slipping away.

The gates were opened as soon as we pulled up outside 'The Milk Marketing Board.' The same suited gent that had escorted me into Omar's office, only a few hours earlier, warmly greeted us. He shook Sidi's hand and led the two of us back to the same office. I was invited to sit on the settee as in the morning. Sidi was made very welcome by Omar, and told to sit at the desk opposite him. All the same officers were present except the lady. This time the officer that had escorted us in sat by me. They were all, Sidi included, chatting and laughing cheerfully; I could only understand part of their conversation.

"Can we please speak in English? I want to know what is being discussed."

"O.K. Madam Dominion, I forgot you couldn't speak our language. Don't worry all is well. I was greeting Sidi, and explaining to him that there is no problem that we cannot sort out between us. He knows that I know what a good woman you are and that many Shendians hold you in high esteem." answered Omar.

That is a complete contrast to the wicked woman I was not so very long ago. Omar took my papers from me and quickly glanced through them. I could have handed him any documents for all the notice he took of them.

"All this is in order, I knew they would be." he told me, "but I would like you to be reasonable about Jatou's problem. They will only pay her benefits on the social security that has been paid for her."

"I know that, but like I told you this morning, we started payments for all of our staff, when we took over the business in 1999. We were asked to do this by the staff, and considered it only right that we should. All of the staff that had not had payments made for them previously, including Jatou, was aware of this. They should have taken it up with the Dutch couple as they did with us. The social security officer must also have been aware of this. I have paid on their basic pay since I have been here, so I don't know what you expect of me."

"I know you have done this, you are a good woman, but you know that the transport money that is paid to your staff, they spend on other thing and it is not used for transport, so they consider it part of their salaries."

"It is law that social is not paid on extra allowances like transport money or bonuses. Whatever the staff spend their transport money on is nothing to do with me."

Sidi spoke to Omar in Mandinka, they had a long discussion, and again I only understood part of this. Omar then asked me if he sent my social security officer to see me, would I discuss with him how we could make arrangements for my long term staff to receive higher benefits, should they need to claim.

I agreed to speak with social security, but once again pointed out to Omar that I paid both the employer and the employee's contributions for my staff, and that I also paid their income tax for them. I pointed out that I might not be able to continue to do this, if I had to pay higher contributions. Sidi glared at me, to warn me that I had said enough. Omar said, "I knew if we all spoke about this properly we would sort this out. I know you are a reasonable woman, and will do what is the right thing. I'm sorry if your staff give you problems they don't know when they are well off."

Omar showed us out of his office. As we stepped outside he gave me a friendly slap on the back. My nerves still working overtime, I visibly jumped. "Madam, you are so nervous. You must learn to relax; you have nothing to worry about. You have a good business, good Shendian friends, you will get no problems in Shendi."

As we walked across the car park, Omar and two of his companions came with us and were chatting cheerfully to Sidi in their local language when an exceptionally large, dark suited gentleman, stepped out from an adjacent building. It soon became obvious that this person commanded respect from Omar, who walked ahead of us, and taking him by the hand, nodded his head, in respect. Sidi then shook his hand and introduced me to this elderly gentleman. "Meet a friend of my father's, Tamsir Fantana, he is an S.S.G. officer, who understands the importance of our tourist industry, and likes to see the smooth running of business like The Dominion."

"Pleased to meet you Mr. Fantana." I said, wondering how expensive this handshake would be.

Turning to Sidi, Tamsir said, "Remember to speak to this lady about my daughter Mami, I'm sure she would be an asset to her kitchen."

So that is to be my payment for this favour, I was to have an S.S.G. officer's daughter planted in my kitchen. I wondered had Sidi already agreed to this? I would speak to him later, now I just wanted to get out of here. I smiled sweetly at Tamsir, as I got back into the car. As we were waiting by the gates for them to be opened to allow us to leave, one of the security guards stepped forward and bending towards my open window, he said "If they even bring you here again, you must refuse to go into these offices without this man with you."

"They wouldn't allow Sidi to come in with this morning, they held him in security."

"It is not safe for a lady like you, to go with them alone. You must tell them he is your husband, then they can't refuse if you ask for him to be with you."

"But he is NOT my husband", I replied.

"Doesn't matter, they don't know that. You must tell them, he is your husband, then they are not allowed to take you into the offices without him."

With that advice, he opened the gates, and we headed back towards home. I told Sidi to take me to The Samba Bar. This was a small bar, restaurant situated on the beach, at the next resort to The Dominion. I was in desperate need of a quiet cup of coffee, in pleasant surroundings. I wanted to relax, where I could see the sand, the sea and the palm trees, to calm myself down before facing the busy evening ahead of me, in the bar. I needed to be in high spirits to entertain my tourists and regulars who would be sat in my bar to relax, and get away from their own problems.

Chapter Eleven

In Court and Powerless

The following morning after a good night's sleep, I felt calmer and able to tackle Sidi about Tamsir Fantana's daughter. Whatever he said I was determined to remain unruffled and put my opinions across calmly, something that I seemed unable to do with Sidi. However, as usual, my good intentions vanished the moment I saw him come into the bar with a grin on his face. How dare he be smiling after all that I had been through yesterday, who did he think he was? His cheery "Good morning" to the cleaner inflamed my temper and his conversation with the bar staff added fuel to the flames. By the time we had sat down at our usual table I had forgotten all my good intentions and before he could say anything I greeted him with, "Now explain to me what deal you made with that friend of your father's."

"Good morning to you too, Helen. Come on, calm down. It is too early to shout at me. Let me get a cup of coffee and before you say anything else I didn't exactly make a deal with him. I told him I would speak to you about Mami. She is a good girl; I have known her since she was a child."

"That's not necessarily a recommendation," I snorted.

"Hey Helen, come on now, don't get nasty with me. It's not my fault you were with the S.S.G. yesterday."

"No and it's not my fault. I'm not getting nasty, I'm being honest. I have done nothing wrong. I didn't accuse Jatou of anything, I only asked her to explain where a receipt had gone and now you expect me to agree to have an S.S.G. officer's daughter planted in my kitchen to spy on me." My voice rose and I could see the cleaner looking at me. I took a deep breath and added, "Besides it's obvious that when this social security guy calls it is going to cost me money."

"OK O.K. but if Tamsir hadn't helped you out, they could have done anything to you. Have you thought about that? Maybe they would have got Simon back. Maybe they would have closed The Dominion, who knows? They may have kept you in custody. You know they have the power to do these things. Anything could have happened."

He was right, anything could have happened yesterday and it was unfair to take it out on Sidi, but he was there, the S.S.G. wasn't and I was angry. "It's so unfair. As I say I've done nothing wrong. More than half the staff weren't even on the social security before we came. How did the Dutch folk get away with that?"

"You know what Hollandaise people are like. They are all up to trickery. They must have had some very important friends."

Again he was right. I would have to accept the inevitable. "This Mami, will she work?"

"Of course she will work, you see she will be good, and you have been looking for someone for in the kitchen."

"Ok, OK I hear what you are saying. Get her to come and see me. I really don't suppose I have much choice. This darn country is so unfair. I work all the hours God sends, for what! There is always someone wanting to relieve of the money I earn."

"Stop complaining and face it. As I said before Tamsir helped you out, now you must help him, or next time, no-one will help us, they will just leave you there."

We finished our coffee in silence, it was impossible to win an argument with a Shendian, and in reality I knew he was right. If I wanted to survive in this country, I had to be prepared to do little favours for people that were willing to help, when they were needed.

My social security officer was a unremarkable person and I would have failed to recognise him except for his clothes. These, like his face were ordinary – he wore the Shendian lower official uniform of smart brown trousers (made shiny by being pressed with a charcoal iron) and white shirt but what distinguished him from the rest was his taste in Disney ties. The following week when he walked into The Dominion he was sporting Minnie Mouse, looking bashful and holding a bunch of flowers. I hoped, somewhat forlornly that this was the indication of a peace offering.

"Good morning, nice to see you again. Would you like a coffee?" I gave him a warm welcome, even though I was aware that this would not be a friendly meeting.

"I'd rather have a bottle of coke."

"Fine, fine, you go and sit in the garden, I'll fetch my staff wages book and my waiter will bring you your coke."

I placed my staff salary records in front of him and said, "Well, I'm sure you know why you have been sent here, but you come every year to inspect my books, so you know everything is in order here, and that I pay my dues to the social security."

"Yes, but I've been in trouble with my boss, because of you. You put too much of their salary down as transport money so that you don't have to pay social security on it."

"I pay my staff 200 Shendian shillings transport allowance a month, that's less than 10 shillings for every day that they work, how can that be too much?" I asked innocently.

"I've been told 2 shillings a day is plenty, so it should be 40 shillings a month."

"Each trip on a gilly-gilly is 5 shillings that's 10 shillings for a return trip."

"Yes, but most of your staff walk or ride bikes, I've seen them arriving."

"They are still entitled to transport allowance. If they choose to make their own way into work then that is their choice, surely?"

"Leave me look through your books, and see what I can make of this."

He sat in my garden for over an hour going through all my salary books back to 1999, when Simon and I first arrived. I saw him making plenty of notes; I could tell this was going to spell trouble, and expensive trouble at that. He finally came into the bar bringing my books back to me, and said, "I have made notes of all of your staff's payments. I must take my findings back to my boss. I will be back next week to tell you what you must pay us in back payments. Can you give me transport money back to Port Albert?"

I took a 2-shilling piece out of the till and handed it to him. He looked at the coin I had given him, and turned it over in the palm of his hand, staring at it in disbelief.

"This is only 2 shillings, but you know I must get a gilly-gilly from here to Malaville, that's 5 shillings, and then another one to Port Albert, that's also 5 shillings."

Grinning I gave him a 10 shilling note. "Now you see my point. You need 10 shillings to get to Port Albert, but you only give my staff 2 shillings a day transport allowance."

He just looked at me dumbfounded and walked out of the bar, shaking his head and muttering.

"Who was that joker with the Minnie Mouse tie?" asked Kevin, who was sat at the bar.

"That was my social security officer; he always wears ties like that. I can see this problem over Jatou is going to cost me. It would have been better, if I'd kept my mouth shut in the first place."

"It's bound to cost you; everything here is at a price. You've probably got some strong jujus against you."

"Yeah," I said, wiping some glasses and putting them back, "I reckon you're right about the jujus, I don't seem to get much luck."

"Never mind love, there isn't much you can do, the S.S.G. have your hands tied. Forget about that, think on this. Terry phoned me again last night, I think he will be back soon."

"That would be another worry. Not so bad if he is by himself, but if he's with Lena, I will not be happy." It just did not seem right, after all the trouble that Terry's family and the expats had had with him, for Terry to be coming out to Shendi again. It was none of my business really but I felt that I was entitled to an opinion.

Kevin looked at me and shook his head, "Oh, she's coming too, in fact he said she maybe here next week looking for a compound for them to rent. They have nowhere to live now, do they?"

"No they don't, but you know I don't really care anymore. I feel sorry for Sally, she came out here and took him back to the U.K., she sorted everything out for him, set him up in a flat, and she and Vanessa have looked after him. What for, so that he can come back here to Lena? At the moment, I've got too much on my mind to concern myself with Terry."

"That's true, don't worry love, if he comes back, us lads will keep an eye on him."

"Humm that will be interesting, we will all be eager to see what will happen next."

The following morning over coffee I explained to Sidi the social security officer's visit.

"You shouldn't have tried to give him only 2 shillings for his transport, you know these people always need money for transport when they call on you, of course he was annoyed, and what's more, I don't understand why you always try to upset everyone that is why you keep getting problems."

"I wasn't trying to upset him. I was trying to make him understand that to let me give the staff a 2 shilling a day transport allowance was unrealistic."

"Don't worry about this, just wait and see what happens when he comes back, they aren't going to ask for much."

"I don't know about that, he went through all the books, right back to '99, but no I'm not going to worry too much about this for now, I'm more concerned about the court tomorrow. You have remembered I need you here early in the morning to take me into Port Albert, haven't you?"

"I've remembered, but why are you so concerned about it. You go to court every month, what's so special about tomorrow?"

"Smithers is on the stand. I'm eager to hear what he is going to say."

It had taken a long time to get Smithers into the witness box. He was supposed to have given evidence straight after Simon, right at the start of the case. It was now three years since Simon had left the country and nearly four since the case had started. The whole business was taking a toll on me. It was quite simply going nowhere. After most hearings, I would sit in the car on the way home, pondering at exactly what had happened. There never seemed to be any progress, it appeared to be going around in circles. The Peace Haven knew that until there was a conclusion, I was unable to sell The Dominion. I considered that maybe they were content for me to sit there until they wanted the land. I did realize that if they wanted my property they would have no problems obtaining it, they had the highest connections possible in Shendi, the president himself. My business was not a threat to theirs, our cliental was different, but my land did encroach on theirs, and I knew they wanted it. I was looking forward to Smithers being in the witness box. If nothing else, I could imagine Ousman making him squirm under cross-examination. This at least would give me satisfaction. Simon's ordeal in the court although long ago, was still fresh in my mind.

Sidi did remember to arrive early the next morning to take me to court. He dropped me off at The High Court, and arranged to come back after he had been to pay my sales tax for the month, and the staff's social security. I wondered if he would see my officer whilst he was at the social security office. Sometimes my officer was on duty in the cash office. I wondered what they would say to each other.

Ousman came to speak to me as he entered the courtroom. I had been sat there keeping a keen eye on the clock. Like most Shendians, even though he was a lawyer, Ousman was a poor timekeeper. On several occasions the hearing had been adjourned because either Ousman or The Peace Haven's lawyer had failed to arrive on time. When it had been Ousman's fault I had always made my displeasure known but there was nothing I could do about The Peace Haven's lawyer's lack of respect for the court. Court was scheduled to start at 9am, but due to the judge also having a lack of respect for time, the sittings seldom started before 9.45. As he approached me Ousman said, "You know Smithers is due to give evidence this morning don't you Helen?"

"Yes, I've been waiting for this for ages."

"Don't get too excited, he may not even show, I haven't seen him yet. Also remember he is well used to giving evidence. This man goes to court cases, like most men go to football matches."

"You are joking?" I said. No wonder the man was not bothered about a simple court case. It seemed the only person who was bothered was me.

"I'm not. He has been in Shendi for 13 years, in that time he has been involved in 22 court cases. And what is more, he has lost many of these cases, but nothing ever happens to him."

"What sort of cases?"

"Different ones, mostly involving past employees of his. The most recent case was for sexual harassment."

"And he gets away with it?"

"As I've told you many times, these are powerful people, with friends in high places. The very highest places, you understand what I'm saying."

"O.K. I know what you are saying; just put plenty of pressure on him."

Sidi arrived at the court having paid the taxes before the case had even started. He whispered to me, "The staff at the social know about their guy coming to The Dominion, they were all chatting about it, it is all going to be fine, you will see."

The case at long last was called. Mrs. Sullais, The Peace Haven lawyer questioned Mr. Smithers first. This was obviously very gentle questioning, mostly concerning the second phase of the hotel's development. In my opinion this, like so much of the case was leading nowhere. Then came Ousman's chance to cross-examine, while Smithers was obviously still under oath.

"I would like to ask you about The Parisian Club, that you have built obscuring The Dominion. It is going against my client's court injunction to either obstruct or obscure their entrance."

"The Parisian isn't a new building, it was constructed on the site of our existing fish restaurant."

That was a lie. Despite being in court, despite knowing that it was against all the rules, I shouted out "That's a lie!"

"Sssh" Sidi grabbed my arm and Ousman turned to glare at me.

"I put it to you that this is a new development, not a construction on an existing one."

"No, there has always been a building there."

"No!" I called out again, this was awful. How could he say this under oath? I could feel my face redden as my tension rose. I simply had to speak.

"Please refrain from speaking." The judge told me.

"Helen, be quite, you will get into trouble." Sidi warned me in a whisper.

Ousman continued, "We will go back to that building later. Now tell me about the building at the rear of The Dominion that has been built as a lean-to onto my client's garden wall."

"What building?"

"There is a toilet and shower block built outside of your premises in the roadway leading to your tradesman's entrance."

"There is no building there, or if there is I am unaware of it."

"I don't believe this!" I meant to whisper to Sidi but my comments were much too loud, they echoed round the room. I even took myself by surprise.

"Keep that woman quiet." The judge said firmly, pointing at me, whilst I was wishing the ground would open up and swallow me. "If you say another word, I will have you removed from this room, and charged with contempt of court."

"Told you." Sidi whispered to me, "Now be quiet."

Ousman went on, "If you are unaware of these buildings, may I suggest you take a stroll around the back of your hotel and then you will see this for yourself. I know it is there as I have seen it with my own eyes. It is illegal to build in such close proximity to your neighbour, especially as a lean-to. It is also illegal to build on a public roadway that does not belong to you."

"As I have already said I am unaware of this."

"You are the Managing Director of your hotel, how can buildings be constructed that you are unaware of?"

"I don't know I will look into it."

"I am concerned about this." The judge interrupted. "I attended a function at The Peace Haven last year, and I saw what I shall describe as a screen to the side of The Dominion's entrance, making it difficult to see, I don't believe this was there before this case started. I am wondering if this screen is the wall that the opposing lawyer has mentioned in this court before, and maybe the back wall of this Parisian Club. I would like to investigate this matter further."

Facing the judge, Ousman continued. "May I suggest to your honour, that we all pay a site visit to the area, then we may all be clear in our minds of the layout of these new buildings, as it seems that even Mr. Smithers is unsure of his new developments, and I believe that some of these buildings contravene my client's court injunction." The judge agreed that this was a good suggestion, and adjourned the proceedings saying that the next hearing would take place after she had visited The Dominion, at a date yet to be decided. I was thrilled by this. I felt my heart give a small leap; maybe at long, long last, there was a small glimmer of hope on the horizon, of my epic court case. I would have been happier yet, if we had been given a date for the site visit, it could lie a long way in the future. As we drove back to The Dominion, I was feeling in great spirits, in complete contrast to my usual feelings on leaving court. Maybe I was pinning too much hope on this visit, but it made a pleasant distraction from my daily routine for a while. I sat back and enjoyed the journey home, looking at the landscape through fresh eyes once more, and appreciating the country, rather than looking at it in a derogatory manner.

"You seem chirpy tonight, what have you got to be so happy about?" Nick asked as I came on duty that evening. He was sat in his usual bar stool, deep in conversation with Rick and Kevin.

"I've been to court this morning. Smithers was on the stand, and he lied through his teeth, while he was under oath. He said La Parisian has always been there, and denied that he knew anything about the buildings down the back lane. The judge is going to come here to see for herself."

"Yeah, that's fine for now, but you know as well as we do, that you don't have a hope in hell of winning in the end, so don't get too excited." Kevin told me.

"Fine, fine, I know, but let me dream."

"Dream on this, Rod has seen Lena in Malaville this morning."

"No!"

"Straight up, she told him she is looking for a compound to rent, Terry has told her he will be back when she has sorted somewhere for them to live."

"Oh well, time will tell. I would have thought he would have let one of us know he was coming back, especially Adam."

"No, he won't bother with things like that, you see, he will walk in here, one evening and sit at the bar, expecting you to produce his own glass as if he had never been away."

"You are probably right. I do still have his glass, waiting for him so that's alright."

We didn't have long to wait. As Kevin had predicted Terry strolled in half way through the next week .He sat down at the bar, saying good evening to everyone, as if he had never been away. He told us that Lena had been unable to find a compound for them, so they had booked into a holiday apartment, until they could find somewhere more permanent to live. Terry once again looked the proud man he had been when I first knew him. He stood upright again, and having put on weight during his absence, he appeared younger, as his face was no longer drawn and haggard. His clothes were freshly laundered, his trousers well cut and a good fit. He was a striking contrast to the man Sally had taken back to the U.K. not so very long ago. We were all pleased to see him looking so well, but the eye contact and unspoken words around the bar, suggested to me, that I was not the only one concerned about his welfare.

I was stood behind the bar, during the latter part of the following Monday morning, talking with Terry, who was having a late breakfast of a bacon sandwich as he usually did when he was in Shendi. Rick was sat with him having a cup of coffee. My only customers, other than them, were a family in the garden, tucking into our All Day English Breakfast. I heard a car screech to a halt in the gateway, and then there was much slamming of car doors. Four well-dressed Shendians lazily strolled in. They were all dressed in dark suits, with brightly coloured shirts, and matching ties. One was carrying a clipboard. He looked around then walked up to my notice board, and started making notes. The notice board had adverts for local excursions, fishing trips, and taxi rates for the tourists, and a few adverts for painters, plumbers etc for the ex-pats. Also a few charity appeals, there was nothing that could be construed as being controversial. My heart missed a beat. I was not certain as I did not recognise any of them, but they looked like, and their behaviour suggested that they were S.S.G. Officers.

One of them approached the bar. "Can I help you gents?" I asked.

Without answering me, he got out his I.D. and showed it to me. They were S.S.G. My heart was now beating rapidly.

"I see who you are, but what can I do for you?"

"We will have four cokes. Bring them out into the garden; we will have them after we have looked around."

A second man went to the notice board, they were pointing out different adverts to each other. Another picked up a menu and glanced through it. They then all strolled out into the garden, and sat out there drinking their cokes and chatting.

"What's all that about?" Rick asked.

"God knows! I've been brought to their attention again; maybe they are trying to frighten me. Maybe they are looking for a good plumber! Or maybe they were just around this way and fancied a free coke, who knows?"

I always tried to put on a brave face, but events like this did unnerve me. I had Mami working in the kitchen now. To be fair on her she had settled in well, and was working hard. I may have misread the situation, maybe her father did just want a job for her, but I was always aware of her presence, and was watchful of what I said when she was in earshot. These S.S.G. visitors sat in the garden for about half an hour. Then they left, all of them waving at me and shouting out "Thanks," as they passed the bar. I sighed with relief when I heard their car drive off.

Very shortly afterwards, Sidi and the chef arrived back from the mornings shopping. Sidi usually just waved, and left again as he was always in a hurry to get back to his little shop in his village. It was unusual for him to bother me, if he saw that I was busy behind the bar. This morning he beckoned to me to go out into the garden to speak to him.

"The S.S.G. have just been here." he told me.

"I know that, I was here, but how do you know?"

"They stopped me as I was driving down the strip and told me they had been here."

"Do you know what that was all about? They had a look around, I gave them cokes, and they sat in the garden and drank them, then just left."

"Don't worry all is O.K. but they said you have an advert for Ryan Pike's holiday apartments."

"Yeah, so what?"

"Apparently Ryan owes a small fortune in income tax. He has sold several of his apartments, and not paid any tax on his profits. They asked me to tell you to take his advert down."

"What if I don't?"

"Come on Helen, what is it to you is Ryan sells his places or not? And you know it is best not to upset the S.S.G."

"I know, but it does make me angry that they can come in here and dictate to me what I will do, on my own property. It also annoys me that they will tell you this, after walking out of here and saying nothing to me."

"You know how things work here."

"Yeah, that's what I'm complaining about."

That was the first, of what was to become a weekly visit from the S.S.G. I would joke with my regulars that I was on their Monday morning calling list, but in reality I didn't find the situation funny.

True to his word, a week after his first visit, my social security officer returned. On this occasion he wore a Donald Duck tie, which made him easily recognisable, not only by me, but by my regulars sat around the bar. Donald was wagging his index finger at Hughie, Duie, and Louis. Maybe I was in for a ticking off also. I ordered him a coke and went in the garden with him. We sat at a secluded table, as I didn't want my customers or staff to overhear our conversation.

"Well madam, as I told you last week, I have had big problems with my boss allowing you to declare so much of your staff's salary as transport money, and this makes me angry." he told me.

"I thought I demonstrated to you last week as you were leaving that my staff do need that much transport money."

"That is not for you to decide Madam. That is for my boss to decide, and he says you have to pay extra social security on all your employees from when you arrived in 1999."

I could feel my anger rising, but did my up most to remain calm. "That's ridiculous." I said.

"No, it's very simple to understand, we have it all here on this paper, for you to see." He handed me a computer read out. "Look there at the bottom is what you must pay 32,000 shillings."

That was a small fortune, considering the average monthly salary at that time was 1,000 – 1,500 shillings.

"What?" I was shaking with disbelief, "You can't do that; that is much too much to expect me to pay. I'm prepared to pay you a reasonable amount, but I don't even have that much."

"This is what my boss says you have to pay, and as I said he is very angry. I will leave you this paper for you to study. Good afternoon Madam."

He finished his drink and left without asking me for transport money this time.

"You been upsetting the locals again?" asked Terry as I returned to the bar looking subdued.

"That was the social security; the joker wants 32,000 in back pay."

"I keep telling you not to upset them."

"Get Sidi to go and see them, they will bargain with him they won't with you." advised Kevin.

"Yeah, you are right. I will speak to him in the morning."

When Sidi arrived the next day, I discussed the visit with him.

"This is a ridiculous amount to have to pay, all because of Jatou. I wouldn't mind if I hadn't been paying my dues, I know plenty of folk that put down more transport money than I do and get away with it."

"If the S.S.G. told them to find a problem with your social payments, they will and you know that."

"What if I refuse to pay"?

"You can't do that, they will close you down. Send Ebou out shopping in a taxi, and I will go into Port Albert and see if I can talk to them."

"Do you reckon you can get them to bring it down?"

"Maybe, at least I can try."

Sidi did manage to see the director at the social security, and also managed to get him to reduce the payment. After what he assured me was hard bargaining, he was in Port Albert for four hours, so maybe it was, he negotiated it down to 18,000 shillings payable in six monthly instalments. I was happy to agree to this but knew it would cost me a few free meals.

Weeks passed and nothing happened. It seemed to me that Jatou's malice had run its course. My life was settling into something that resembled normality, business was going from strength to strength, the staff weren't causing me too many problems and the sun was shining. The S.S.G. visits were a pain, but even they had stopped coming every week and when they did come I made certain that there was nothing for them to find. I stood behind the bar pondering, on my life in my paradise home, and thinking that maybe it wasn't as bad as I sometimes imagined it to be.

Suddenly six large Shendian workmen wearing overalls marched purposefully into the bar. Two of them walked into my kitchen. My sense of calm and satisfaction vanished.

"Excuse me," I shouted, "you can't go in there, that's my kitchen."

"Yes, Madam, we know that, we have come to remove your electric meter."

"What? Why? Come on quickly explain, I'm busy."

"As I said we are taking away your electric meter."

"You can't. Who says?"

"Our boss says you have been tapering with your meter. We are taking it away to examine it."

"I wouldn't know how to tamper with my meter. You can't do this I have a business to run." I stood between the kitchen, where the meter was just inside, fixed on the wall, and the burly Shendian that was trying to force his way through.

"Out of the way, we have business to do also." he said as he pushed me aside.

They set about removing the meter, which took only a few minutes. I watched helplessly, my face turning redder and redder with anger, as the men worked and the kitchen and bar staff looked on. At least I wouldn't have to worry about power cuts for a while. I knew I wouldn't be having any power.

"Come on." I said turning to my kitchen staff as the electricians left with my meter. "You have meals to prepare and I have a business to run."

I returned to the bar and as I pulled him a pint, an ever-reassuring Oliver said, "You're in the shit there. If it wasn't tampered with before, it will be by the time they get it back to their office. Who have you upset now?"

"God knows. Yet another little problem to sort out!"

I knew he was right, anything could happen between here and the electric company, but there was a genuine worry niggling at the back of my mind. In the early days Simon had been approached by an employee of the electric company, who offered to 'fix' as he put it our electric meter. I knew nothing of this at first and when I did find out I was dumbfounded. Simon would not have entertained anything like this at home so why was he doing so in Shendi. I was very apprehensive about it and there had been several heated exchanges between Simon and myself about the matter. This electric company man would come to the bar, early in the morning, a few days before our meter was due to be read each month. He would inform Simon when he was going to come. Simon would get up early, and send the night security home. The electric man would then come after he had seen our security leave, and before the day staff arrived, and wind our meter back to give a false reading. When Simon left, I quickly stopped this arrangement and much to my amusement my electric bills did not go up. This was yet another Shendian scam. This man was taking a bribe from Simon and doing nothing in return.

All this had happened a few years ago now and unlikely to show on my meter but the knowledge of this was causing me some concern. Was it possible that this man had been caught doing this illegal scam, and given names of other meters that had been tampered with? Or maybe I had upset someone else, which I was unaware of?

I phoned Sidi, and explained to him what had happened, and told him that I had to report to the director of the electric company at 3:30 that same afternoon. He agreed to come with me.

We arrived at 3:15, although Shendians have no sense of timekeeping, I always made it my policy not to be late for appointments, I was a good timekeeper in the U.K., and was determined to keep to my standards not Shendian standards. We were ushered into a large airy office, which was full of the usual clutter that could be found in most Shendian offices. There was hardly a space on the grand, elaborate office desk. Files were spilling over onto the floor; I was amazed how they ever found any files they needed. Time lost looking for things in Shendian offices must be extensive. In the corner propped up against a threadbare armchair, with its door open was my meter.

After what seemed an excessively long wait, one of the directors entered the office. Even before he sat down, he pointed towards my meter and said. "Madam, without a doubt you have been tampering with this meter, just look at it."

I tried to explain to him that I didn't know what I was looking for, as I didn't know what a tampered meter looked like, nor would I have a clue as to where to start tampering with a meter.

"See this little lever?" He said pointing to a small lever inside the meter, near to the dial that turns when the meter is recording electrical consumption. "It is broken. You have done this to try and swindle my company."

"I haven't done anything to it. Can I ask why did you suddenly come and remove my meter to-day?"

"This is nothing to do with you, but if you feel you must know, our meter reader has seen this, and correctly reported it to us."

Trying to keep calm I said. "I'm not clear on two points. First the meter was last read three weeks ago, why has it taken so long to act on his information? Secondly this lever is inside of the meter. I'm not even aware that damaging it would affect my reading. If I was aware of this, how could I get into the interior of the meter without damaging the lock of the meter, you need a special key to open the door. Surely only one of your employees would have the means to be able to do this?"

"You are a very rude woman; you should not speak to me like this. You will sit here and think over how wicked you have been, while I go and talk to my bosses and we decide what we are going to do about this."

He left the room, slamming the door behind him, leaving Sidi and I alone.

Sidi angrily told me I had upset him, and this could only make matters worse. "Why do you always have to say things that upset people? I keep telling you to be quite and let me do the talking. I know you like to handle your own affairs, but you must know by now that a woman cannot act like you do here, you are not in the U.K. now. You must let me handle things my way; I won't upset folk, like you do."

I glanced long and hard at him, he knew it was best not to say anymore for now. When I was calmer he continued. "We must decide what we are going to say when he comes back."

I replied. "There is nothing to decide. I will simply tell him, if you don't reinstate my meter, I will have no electricity, so I won't be able to run my business. I will have to close the bar. This will mean making 22 Shendians redundant. I will ask him if he wants to make himself responsible for that."

"Oh Helen. If you say that to him, you know you are going to make him ever angrier than he is now. See what I mean you never listen. Why won't you let me deal with it. I can't see the point of me coming if you don't let me sort it out."

When he returned, I ignored Sidi's muttering and told the director exactly what I had said I would. Sidi was right it did make him angry.

"I can't believe how wicked you white woman are." I was told which in turn made me pretty angry also. "Now listen carefully to what I am telling you. You must first write a letter to the commissioner of the electric company, begging his forgiveness for tampering with your meter. You will be fined for this tampering, and must pay for a new meter. Then we will assess how much you owe us for electric we have supplied and that you haven't paid for. Until all this is paid, we will not replace your meter. Expect to see two of our employees at The Dominion in the morning to assess how much electric you use each month."

Without waiting for a reply he left. I was shaking with temper; goodness knows how much this would cost me. I was struggling to pay the social security, and now this. I felt impending doom. We left, Sidi's face gave away his feelings, and I decided it was best not to say anything just yet. We walked out to the car in silence, both with thunderous expressions on our faces. We hadn't driven very far, when we skidded to a halt on the sandy road. We had a puncture.

"I don't have a spare." Sidi told me. "You wait here. I will go to the garage up the road and get it repaired."

"That will take ages. I'm not sitting here, in the car in this heat I will walk."

"Let me call a taxi, if you don't want to wait."

"No, no, no. I told you I will walk; it doesn't seem I have any money to waste on taxis."

"Helen, come on, don't be stupid, you know how far it is. You can't walk."

"Can't I? Watch me!"

Without another word, I got out of the car, and strode off in a temper, taking long rapid strides. A long walk would do me good. I needed to get this out of my system before I returned to The Dominion. Much went through my mind, as I headed home. I knew that Sidi was right, I did not know how to speak to Shendians, I did upset them, but their ways of doing business was so foreign to anything that I had ever met that I could not help myself. Take for example my behaviour in court. I knew that it was totally wrong to call out, but I had been unable to help myself. Smithers had lied and I had just had to have my say. It had been the same in the manager's office just now. I could not bottle up my feelings, I had just had to speak my mind, however much trouble it caused. Why couldn't officialdom be reasonable? Look what had happened last time with the social. Their extra 3,000 shillings a month, was becoming a burden, and for now the amount that the electric company would demand was an unknown quantity.

How had I got into this mess? I did not deserve all these extra worries. Would I ever be free of this continual stress? Life never ran smoothly here. As soon as I sorted one problem out, another always reared its ugly head from an unexpected source. I paced on, near to tears. I had no one I could really confide in. Nor was there anywhere to go and have a good cry, there was little privacy in The Dominion and I could not get away even for a day. According to the court injunction I had to open every day and I did not trust my staff to do that for me. I had to be behind the bar every evening, and I could not let my frustrations show. My problems were of no concern to my customers, especially the tourists who were in the bar enjoying their holiday. I felt so very, very isolated. I knew numerous people, expats and tourists but there was no one to talk to. I thought about my Kevin and Steph, and how I would love to see them, I couldn't go to the UK I was stuck in this foul country. They would have to come to see me that would be enough, just seeing people I cared for, people who did not see me as a source of money, people who were not trying to cheat me. I could never tell Kevin the problems that I had here just trying to survive; I would never cause them that much worry. But if only I could see them. As I walked along the coastal highway, I could hear the Atlantic Ocean beating against the shore. I could see the palm trees gently waving with the prevailing wind blowing off the sea. A sight fit for paradise but the mid afternoon sun was striking down and making my journey resemble the hell that Shendi had become for me.

I walked into The Dominion two and a half hours later, with aching legs, knowing deep down that I had been stupid to walk so far in the full heat of the day. I did feel calmer now, but only waved at customers sat around the bar, and in the garden. I didn't feel ready yet to be engaged in conversation. I was due back behind the bar in a little over an hour. By the time I had had a shower and a relaxing cup of coffee, I would be ready to cope with the busy evening that was ahead of me, and all that it would involve. I knew I had a business to run, and my determination would not let me down.

I causally strolled into the bar that evening with aching leg muscles and a slight headache from the relentless sun beating down on me that afternoon. Terry greeted me with a grin and said. "Do I hear your genie? We had power when I left home."

"Anymore remarks like that and you can go home and enjoy your power." I retorted.

"Get your life together." Nick told me. "If you wanted your meter fixed, you should have got me to do it. At least I would have done a proper job."

"Too late, I'm powerless." I thought I might as well join in with the lads' banter, if not it would get me down, and they were only trying to cheer me up.

"What do I keep telling you?" Nigel chimed in, "You need some testosterone. A woman can't survive here without."

Nick nudged him. "I could help her there too, but she doesn't take the hint."

"Did they give you give you a hard time?" Kevin asked.

"It's going to cost me, never mind eh? Easy come easy go."

"Stop moaning woman, look at your garden, it's full of tourists paying exaggerated prices for your beer. You must be the wealthiest woman in Shendi, they all realise this, that's why they keep relieving you of some of it." Terry told me.

"Shut up you silly old bastard! You don't want her to start charging us tourist prices do you?" Kevin told him.

The lads banter was relentless all evening, electric jokes, or the lack of it went on until the early hours. I climbed exhausted into bed at around 2.30am. Alone again panic took a hold of me once more. Why, oh why, did I have all these problems in this country? If it wasn't for the court case and all the uncertainty that, that bought, and the other problems that seemed to crop up all too often, I would have a good life here. Not the life that I envisaged when Simon and I left the island, but I had built myself a satisfactory life style if it had not been for the continuous hassle that Africa brought. I knew what Nigel meant; he had told me on numerous occasions that I needed some testosterone. A European woman alone has an up hill battle in Shendi. If I was a man, or had a man beside me the authorities would treat me better. Simon must have realised this when he left. I tried to push all these thoughts from my mind. It was getting late, I had to try and sleep. With all these things going around in my head sleep eluded me. I would have another busy day ahead of me tomorrow. Kevin and Steph crossed my mind as I lay there, thoughts again whizzing around my poor tired brain. It had been 14 months since their last visit. They had said they would come out again this year, but the year was progressing, rainy season would be here in another three months, and I knew if they were to come, that it would be before the rains. Kevin had hinted in phone calls about visiting soon, but no more than a hint. I was aware that they both had busy lives and I never pursued this with him.

The next morning I awoke to the relentless noise of my generator, its loud, monotonous, rasping sound was a form of Chinese torture to me. We rested the generator for two hours during the afternoon and for two hours at night; this respite was sheer bliss to my ears. The generator was as far as possible away from the bar, so that the noise caused the least disruption possible for the customers, but this meant that it was situated near the house, in close proximity to my bedroom. I originally thought it was a noise I would grow accustomed to, I knew now that I never would. Considering my current circumstances, I was in fairly high spirits the next morning as I showered and prepared to face the day ahead. Rick cycled in shortly after I opened, for his breakfast. I made myself a coffee and sat with him, we were soon joined by Nick, in for his morning coffee.

"Can I hear your genie?" he asked as he sat down.

"Don't you start this early in the morning, and you had better get used to it, I think it will be working overtime for a while."

By this time Nick had collected his workers, and taken them to his building site. He was now on what he called his 'water run'. He was in the process of having a borehole sunk on his site, but in the meantime his first job every morning was to return to his compound with several bright yellow, plastic containers, in the back of his pick-up truck. He would fill these with water, to take back to his site to mix the concrete to make his building blocks. Whilst he was on his water run, he usually popped in to for his breakfast of a cup of coffee and a couple of cigarettes with the lads, before starting his working day in earnest. Liverpool Kevin would soon arrive also. The lads, even at that time of the morning would soon slip into a round of friendly banter. I, being the only woman was usually the butt of their jokes, but light-hearted patter was just the tonic I needed to help me through the day.

As I was cleaning the bar, soon after Nick and Kevin had left, I heard a truck parking in my gateway. As I suspected it was the men from the electric company, come to assess my electrical appliances. Latif, my maintenance man, was working in the garden and realising who the men were, he followed them into the bar, and asked if I wanted him to stay with me. I trusted Latif more than most of my staff, and knew he would stand my ground for me, so I welcomed his assistance.

Two electric company employees had come to make their assessment, one smartly dressed in a suit, the other in overalls and carrying a clipboard. The suited gent called out my appliances, whilst the other man listed them for him. They first made note of the drinks fridges that I had in the bar then they moved into the kitchen and listed the fridges and freezers I had there.

I asked them. "How do you intend estimating how much electric I use?"

"That's simple, Madam, we are listing all the appliances that you have here. We are experienced electrical personnel you know. We know how much power each uses. We will then calculate how much power you have used."

"Fine, fine, but what about the power cuts?" I asked.

"What do you mean?"

"I understand what you are saying, and if we had continuous power, that would be fine, but how are you going to account for power cuts?"

"I don't understand what you are saying."

"We get power cuts everyday. Sometimes two hours, sometimes four hours, sometimes we get no power at all. On these days I use no electric, I use my genie, so how are you going to calculate that?"

"Madam, you are a very difficult woman, my boss warned me of you. You must just stand aside and let us get on with our business here."

Oh Helen, I thought, you've done it again. Just keep your mouth shut.

I considered it was best to do as he said, and see the outcome, before I protested too much. They asked to see around my house, I led the way followed by Latif.

As the foreman, telling his workmate what to put on their list, stepped into my lounge, he said. "TV, video, two light fittings, a large A.C. unit."

"Excuse me," I interrupted. "The TV doesn't work. Where is the video? And I don't use the air conditioning."

"Of course the TV works, and everyone who has a TV has a video, you will have hidden it, because you knew we were coming, and all taubabs use their A.C."

"Why don't you switch the TV on?" I invited him.

"I have no time to watch T.V. now."

Latif told them. "I have never heard the air conditioning on since she has been here, the last owners put it in and they used it."

They went into my bedroom, and again listed the A.C. unit, and once again my spirits sank. I knew I was at their boss's mercy.

As we were making our way back towards the bar, the foreman stopped and said. "What is up these stairs?" pointing to the outside stairway to the bedrooms above, which I hadn't used since my gall bladder operation, when I had to move to the downstairs bedroom, and continued to use it as I found it more convenient.

"There are two bedrooms and a wash room, up there, but I never use them, I live alone. I don't need all the bedrooms I have here. I don't even go up there, it is always kept locked."

"We only have your word for that. I can see A.C. units from here; we need to go upstairs too."

"She tells you the truth." Latif told them. "No-one goes up there now."

"We will decide that."

I once again led the way, and unlocked the door.

"If you don't come up here, why do you have the key on you?" He asked

I could see what he meant, but I kept all of the keys for The Dominion, even them that I didn't use often, on a flexi key ring clipped to the inside of the side pocket in my uniform, so that I always knew where they were. They listed the A.C. units in those upstairs bedrooms, and noted the number of mains sockets in each room, even though I had no electrical appliances upstairs.

After I had locked the upstairs door, and we were making our way back downstairs the foreman was honest enough to say. "I must admit those rooms don't appear to be in use, I will mention this to my boss. Calculations will be done from our findings, and my boss will be in touch with you. Can we have a drink Madam? This is thirsty work."

I instructed Momodou to give them each a coke, I knew this was expected of me, and if it appeased them I didn't mind.

"I saw that." Rick, who was now on his third cup of coffee said, as I went back into the bar. "Taking strange men into the upstairs bedrooms. Wait till I tell Nick and Kevin about this, they won't be happy."

"I did have Latif as a chaperone, don't worry."

"They'll still be jealous none of us gets invites like that."

"Yeah, well those so and so are going to charge me for the pleasure, not the other way round."

"See what I mean, Nick and Kevin would gladly pay you! Or at least they would tell you to put it on their bar bills."

"Just drink your coffee up will you, I've got my work cut out without supplying any extra services."

The commissioner of the electric company was obviously a mathematical genius. When Sidi came back from the morning's shopping, barely an hour later he told me, he had received a call on his mobile from him, and that we had an appointment to see the director we had seen the previous day at 2 o'clock, the same afternoon.

I was relieved that I was not going to be kept on tender hooks for too long, awaiting the outcome of this. A break from The Dominion and the incessant groaning of the generator would also be most welcome.

After reporting to the reception desk at the electrical board, Sidi and I were shown into the same office as the previous day. My electric meter, with its offending little lever, was still propped in the same position as the day before. We were not kept waiting long. A brief muttered "Good afternoon," came from the director, as he entered and walked towards the desk. As he sat down he took a scrap of paper from his pocket, and placed it on the desk, pushing it towards me.

He muttered, hardly audibly, "On calculating, it is possible that you have been paying too much for the electric, for the appliances that you are using, but obviously this can't be so. We have to assume that you don't have many power cuts in your area. This is what you must pay to get your meter reinstated."

My trembling hands unfolded the paper and glanced at it. On the tatty scrap of paper, that had been roughly torn from a sheet that had computer figures on the reverse side, written in child like script was: -

Fine for tampering with meter 14,000

Cost of new meter 9,000

Estimated cost of unpaid electric 5,000

TOTAL 28,000 Shendian Shillings

"We will come and fix your new meter, as soon as you pay this bill," he told me.

Having seen the total, I slid the paper along the desk to Sidi. After he had looked at it, he said. "This is a lot of money; we need to talk about this."

"No. There is nothing to talk about, we have been very reasonable. Look at the small charge for used electricity. If I charged for all the appliances the lady has in her house the bill could be much more than double this. There will be no bartering. The bill gets paid, and then the electric will be put back on."

I stood up, and with a nod in the direction of the desk, walked out of the office. On the journey home Sidi said, "I was amazed that you left like that, I expected you to make a fuss."

"No point. I know when I'm beaten, I'm not happy about all this, but I know I have to pay or I will have no electric, and I can't run the business without it."

"Have you got the money?"

"In the bank, not at the bar, but it is money that I'm likely to need in low season to pay the wages, but this has to be paid. I will go and get the money when I go off duty this afternoon, and you can go and pay it for me in the morning. If they don't put the meter in soon after it is paid, then I will make a fuss. The noise of the genie is driving me crazy."

"I hear you've had men in your bedroom." Nick told me as I started my evening shift.

"Yeah, but don't get excited there won't be any others it cost me too much."

"How much have they done you for?"

"28,000"

"Bastards! But you don't have a lot of choice, do you?"

"Nope. But it's made a big hole in my bank balance. What with this and the bloody social, it's going to be touch and go this low season, I can tell you."

"Yeah, I expect it will, but stop waffling woman. You are only trying to take my mind off you taking those guys into your bedroom. Just pour me another beer; that will help your finances."

I gave Sidi the money to pay the electric company, as he went shopping with the chef the following morning. Before they had returned, so only a short while after Sidi had paid the bill; I was sat in the garden, having a mid-morning coffee and a chat, with my friend Karen when I heard a commotion in the bar.

"I don't believe this." I told her, "I think it is the electric company delivering my new meter. Excuse me, I must go and check on this."

It was indeed the electric workman about to reinstate, what was without a doubt my original meter.

"What are you doing?" I asked.

"Putting your meter back, of course Madam."

"I don't want that meter back. I've paid for a new meter, and that is what I want."

"Why don't you want this one? This is yours. We took it out only a few days ago."

"Exactly. That meter has been tampered with. I don't want that one; I want a new one,"

"We don't have any new ones at the moment Madam, but this one is fine; it's not been tampered with. If you don't take this meter, it could be at least nine months before you get another one."

Again, I had no choice, I let them install it. Ironically when they switched it on, we were in the midst of a power cut, so I was still not released from the continual rasping noise of my generator.

When Sidi returned and I told him, I had the same meter back, I was informed that I always found something to complain about. Maybe I do, especially when I know that I've lost a substantial amount of cash, in what amounts to a scam. Life in Africa was so very different to my cosseted existence on my now far, far away island.

When Oliver came in for his lunch, he said he would like a chat with me, when I had a few minutes to spare, he said he wanted to put some business my way. I ordered his usual pot of tea, and a coffee for myself, and we sat at a table away from the bar, so that we could chat undisturbed. Extra business, in my present economic crisis was more than welcome. As he poured himself some tea he said, "I intend making an honest woman of Fatima. Will you do the reception for me?"

I was astonished. I knew that Fatima was Oliver's Freetonian girlfriend and they had been living together for several months now. Everything had seemed fine but I hadn't expected him to marry her.

"Well, of course Yes. I would love to. In fact I'm flattered that you have asked me, but I must tell you that I have never hosted a wedding before. I'm sure the kitchen will cope fine as long as I plan things for them. How many guests do you have in mind? And when are you thinking of?"

"About 45 guests. There is no date fixed yet, but I'm looking at mid September."

"No problem. That's still low season; we will be able to cope fine."

We continued to discuss the menu, and other arrangements that would need to be finalised later. I was thrilled about this. As I had told Oliver, this was to be my first wedding, but I knew that if I made a success of it, maybe others would follow. It would be good P.R. for The Dominion. A function like this in low season, when I didn't get much custom was just the sort of boost that I needed; especially with the two financial problems I had had to face recently, leaving me short of funds. I knew things were going to be tough this year. The prospect of this wedding was a morale boaster for me, and gave me something to focus my mind on, other than dismal thoughts.

"Ah, no sound effects tonight." Terry exclaimed as he arrived for his evening meal, and a few beers, which he used to tell me, were essential, or he would have a sleepless night.

"No. I have power that's the wonders of Shendian science, albeit I have the same meter back again."

"You've been had!"

"I know. I could have done without paying them so much. I probably need the money more than the sods that are sharing out the spoils. But never mind Terry, if you drink a few more beers every night this low season, I will be fine."

"You are a heartless bitch, I keep telling you that."

"And you know that I need to be heartless to survive."

For the rest of evening I was a barrage of teasing about the electricity. Most of the ex-pat lads came out with some quip or other. It was harmless banter, it gave them something different to talk about and at least I could rely on them to make me laugh and raise my spirits when I was feeling down. When I went to bed that night I was in a much lighter mood than the previous evening. I had less in my bank account, and I knew that money was going to be tight, but surviving was more important than money. I had Oliver's wedding to look forward to towards the end of low season. The profit from that would tide me over, till the tourists arrived in November. I had a good nights sleep.

Two days later was Liverpool Kevin's birthday, and I was laying on a buffet for him. It was a Friday, a night that many of the ex-pats came in, so I was expecting a good party atmosphere. It was also the fifth anniversary of my arrival in Shendi. I did not feel like celebrating this; but a causal remark to Kevin a few weeks before, that I arrived on his birthday, soon made this public knowledge. Everyone else seemed to think that I did have something to celebrate. I was in high spirits as I worked with the kitchen staff in the afternoon, making preparations for the evening's buffet. I knew we would have a good evening the ex-pats knew how to enjoy themselves; there would be dancing in the bar before the night was over. It would also be a profitable evening, so maybe I did have something to celebrate. I worked through, what should have been my afternoon break, decorating the bar, with balloons and banners in honour of Kevin's birthday, whilst keeping an eye on the preparations in the kitchen. Events like this were hard work, but I did thrive on them, I was enjoying every minute of the preparations.

I made myself a coffee and took it into the house to relax for a while before facing the festivities of the evening. As I sank into my armchair, with my feet up on a foot stool, enjoying my coffee, and lost in my thoughts, the phone rang.

"Hello, The Dominion." I answered it.

"Hi Mum, you O.K.?"

"Kevin, hi, good to hear your voice, yeah, I'm fine. I was just grabbing a quick coffee, we are having a birthday party this evening, and they have also decided to celebrate for me, as it is five years to-day that I arrived here."

"Gosh, is it that long. Well. I'm glad things are going O.K."

If only you knew, I thought; but I would never tell him how hard things really were.

Kevin went on, "I will give you something else to celebrate."

"You're coming out both you and Steph?"

"Emm, no Mum. We can't. But for a very good reason. Steph is having a baby."

Before he had the words out, my eyes were stinging, and large emotional tears were burning my cheeks. I had difficulty answering him.

"Oh Kevin, that's marvellous." I hope he picked up the joy in my voice and not the tears.

"You're crying, I knew you would."

"You know what my emotions are like, a bit screwed up. I'm thrilled, you will never know what this means to me. Is Steph alright?"

"Yeah, she's fine; we waited till we knew things were alright before telling anyone. That's why I was being evasive about us coming to see you."

I was still having difficulty speaking. "I'll ring off and phone you in a few days. Love you."

As I replaced the receiver my tears really flowed in earnest. Kevin had always said he didn't want a family, and had reaffirmed this when he lost his sister. I can remember him saying to me once. "Do you want to shed tears over your grandchildren, as you have over your children? No, I won't go through what you have been through." Here he was 35 and giving me my first grandchild. Had I known that this would happen, I would not have allowed Simon to bring me so far away. I was going to be a grandmother, and in the foreseeable future I would not be able to go back to the U.K. to see my grandchild. I slumped onto the footstool unable to return to the bar.

Chapter Twelve

Ceremony and Matrimony

I was desperately trying to compose myself before returning to the bar for Liverpool Kevin's birthday party. Making my way towards the bathroom I bumped into Sidi. He was the last person I wanted to see. Sidi, like most Shendians had little patience when it came to tears, possible because they were regarded as a "woman" thing. I wasn't expecting him at this time of day and I knew I couldn't cope with his lack of sympathy for my emotions.

"What's happened, why are you crying?" Sidi asked me some what aggressively I thought, given my state of mind. Wiping my tears away, I turned to him, sniffed and said in as firm a voice as I could manage, "I'm fine, please leave me."

"You don't look fine to me. I came back to check that the staff weren't making any problems for you, being you are having the party this evening, but it seems there is a problem. I came into the bar looking for you when someone told me you were taking a phone call. So I ordered a coffee and came back here. What is it, what has happened?"

"Nothing, all is fine, fine, everything is ready for the party. It's just that phone call. Steph is having a baby."

"What? Kevin's Steph?"

"Yes."

"Then why are you like this? Why are you crying? You should be happy for them."

"I am happy for them. I cry because I'm happy and I cry because I'm sad that I won't be able to go and see my grandchild."

"I always knew that white women were crazy! How can you cry when you are happy, that is ridiculous? I come here and I find you like this. I think there is a big problem and you tell me good news."

"I know you don't understand, just leave me alone and I will be fine. Go, go and have your coffee with the lads and let me deal with this my own way."

"It doesn't matter how you want to deal with it, you must stop crying please. There are a lot of people in the bar. Kevin is here and lots of the ex-pats. You should be out there."

"I know, I know. Look, O.K. I'll be out soon, now PLEASE leave me alone."

Sidi left me and went to have his coffee in the kitchen with the staff, and I went into the bathroom and put a cold flannel over my face in an attempt to calm the redness around my eyes that the crying had caused. I knew I must pull myself together, and get on with the business at hand. I soon realized that it wasn't hard to put on a brave face and a smile to return to work. After all I was happy, I was absolutely elated. I was going to be a grandmother, long after I had considered the possibility of this only a pipe dream. I stood outside the bar for a moment and glanced at everyone enjoying themselves, before I entered.

"Happy birthday, Kev." I gaily said as I gave Kevin a peck on the cheek.

"Thanks luv, you O.K.? You don't seem too good, they been playing you up?"

"I'm fine, Kev, really fine. My Kevin's going to make me a gran." I was so angry with myself as I felt a tear dampen my cheek.

Kevin wiped the tear away and said. "That's brilliant darling," and in a louder voice announced to everyone in the near vicinity. "Our Helen is going to be a gran."

"Shh." I told him. "Give me a chance to cope with this before telling everyone. I'm a bit tearful."

The evening was a roaring success. As I thought would happen, we did have dancing in the bar before the evening was over, there was lots of laughing and joviality around the bar, which was a good tonic for me. I was in high spirits again. The kitchen had worked well with me to produce a good, tasty, well-appreciated buffet. This boasted my confidence for Oliver's wedding, if we can do this for a birthday party, why not for a wedding?

Kevin, Nick and Terry were still sat at the bar long after everyone else had gone. I was pleased when they decided, with a slight hint from me, to call a halt to their late night celebrations. I still had a lot of glasses to wash, and the till to cash up before I could retire for the night, and I was feeling the need to sleep. I was physically and mentally exhausted, it had been a tiring day, in more ways than one, but as I reflected on the day, as was becoming a habit, when I slipped into the solitude of my bedroom, I considered it the best day that I had, had in a very long while.

I know that Sidi was bewildered over my reaction to Kevin's good news, but now I was bewildered by it myself. In a few short months I would be a grandmother. This was something most mothers assumed would happen to them in the course of time. I did not. I was completely overwhelmed. Besides the news of the baby, it had been a good day. To watch lots of people enjoying themselves in your own bar is very satisfying. When I was down and depressed, I didn't always think so, but I had made a success of some aspects of life in Shendi. Many repeat tourists used The Dominion as their 'local' while they were on holiday, many of these would come and see me on their return as soon as they got off their coach from the airport, before they had even booked into their hotel. Some of my regular U.K. charity workers used my beer garden to hold committee meetings while they were here, or to interview sponsored children. I was providing a good service to these people, who did appreciate it, and to The Tourist Board, who did not always appreciate it.

The next morning I woke up still feeling very positive and received another surprise with an unexpected phone call from Ousman.

"The judge has decided on a date for the site visit."

My heart skipped a beat. Was my life starting to move forward at last?

"That's brilliant; I didn't expect to hear any news of this so close to summer recess."

"Ah well, it is good that she has given a date, but it isn't for a long while yet. As you say, summer recess will soon be upon us, which lasts for three months, and she knows that the courts will busy after that, with the build up of cases over the summer; they always are. The date that she has given is December the fifth."

My heart did sink slightly when Ousman gave me a date that was in six months time. It seemed a long way off, but in reality it wasn't that far away, and at least I did have something positive to set my sights on.

"You built up my hopes then, but as you say we do have a date. That at least is something positive."

The visit was a little way in the future, but this was a step in the right direction. I maybe mistaken, but I was confident that this site visit would be more to my advantage, that to The Peace Haven's.

Later in the day, I was further surprised to see some unexpected visitors. Peter and Frank from the U.K. police walked into the bar, they were accompanied by two others, that looked as if they could also be police officers, neither of whom I had met before. One was a lady in her early thirties. She was tall, over six foot, and her height was farther exaggerated by her stylish, navy, three inched heeled, sling-backed sandals. She was slender, her snug fitting, classic straight pin stripped, french navy, skirt, and simple light blue cotton blouse, showed off her figure to perfection

From the heads turning, and the comments I overheard around the bar, I was not the only one to consider her an impressive looking lady. A smartly dressed elderly gentleman, possibly in his mid sixties, made up their party. Unfortunately, even though he was distinguished with his well-groomed white hair, and gold rimmed glasses, he sank into insignificance besides the lady. Peter and Frank waved to me, and all four of them went and sat at their usual table, by the door leading into the garden. I went over to greet them and offer them drinks.

"Hi lads, I didn't know you were coming out. Is Datu's case continuing?"

"Yeah, we always seem to get a hearing as summer recess approaches, not that I would suggest that, that was deliberate." Peter told me. "Let me introduce you to Tony he is a forensic expert, and this is Jenny she is our dental expert." Turning to them he said. "This is Helen, who owns this bar. You have heard us speak of her. Sharon always refers to her as, 'Our lady in Africa'."

"Hi, pleased to met you both, but may I ask why you are needing a forensic expert and a dental expert?"

"You obviously haven't heard the latest in the case."

"No. I haven't seen any reports in the paper, for a long time, if there has been any I have missed them, and I don't get a lot of news from Sharon. She e-mails me occasionally, when she does I always answer, but in between times I don't contact her. I would hate to be a further reminder of Shendi, when she is having a bad day."

"Yes, I know what you mean, poor Sharon, does get more than her fair share of down days. I just wish we could get this bloody trial over with, and then she could put a closure on all this, and start rebuilding her life again. Not only that, it is costing the U.K. government a small fortune, to keep sending us out here for the trial. Anyway the reason that we have bought Tony and Jen with us this time is that, it has been suggested in court that the body we exhumed and took back to the U.K. was not Reg at all."

"Never. That can't be right can it?"

"Certainly not." Tony intervened. "Extensive tests were done, before we gave leave for burial in the U.K. Without a doubt, from our tests it was Reg the lads bought back, and Jenny here is going to back this up from Reg's dental records."

I thought of Sharon and her family. They must be going through hell. I simply could not imagine what it must have been like for them to live through the experiences of the past few years. The death of a parent is always upsetting but for your father to be murdered in a foreign country must be horrendous. Then to take his body home for burial, to cope with sorting out his affairs thousands of miles away and all the while waiting for a trial must be unbearable. But surely the final straw must be this. To have it suggested in a court of law that it may not have been his body that you buried, whose grave that you visit and place your flowers of remembrance must be one of the tortures from hell.

"How long will you be here?" I asked.

"Only until Friday, a short visit this time. Just long enough for us to go over our evidence again, and for Tony and Jen to take the stand." Peter told me.

"Will this be the end of the trial for you, or do you expect to have to come back again?"

"Hopefully this will be our last visit, I don't want to have to come out again, and we have done all that we can. We can't understand what is going on here, and why there is all these delaying tactics."

As I expected when I went back behind the bar, the boys bombarded me with questions.

"Come on you nosy bitch, you've found out, now spill the beans. Who's that gorgeous looking wench that is with the police guys, and how long is she staying?" Kevin eagerly asked.

"They are only here till Friday, she is a dental expert."

"Wish my dentist looked like that, I might be tempted to go more often." piped up Nick.

Rick said. "That will come in handy; we don't have a decent dentist here. A new bit of talent wouldn't go amiss either, shame she's not staying longer."

Terry reprimanded them. "All you lads are women crazy. You should get yourselves decent girls like my Lena and then you wouldn't worry about eyeing up every new woman that enters the bar."

"Yeah, we all need girls like your Lena, like a hole in the head." Nick told him. "I've got Maria, and look where that has got me. Sure she has influential family, that have been an asset to me, but she's a stealing bitch, just like Lena, and now I'm stuck with her, because in some ways I need her darn family. But I'm not so bloody stupid, as to be blind to it all."

Terry relit his pipe and took two deep puffs, and ignored Nick's remark as he always did. Every night he would sit at the bar, and tell us tales of things that had happened to Lena, and what it had cost him to put it right. We were all exasperated at trying to explain to him that she was relieving him of his money a little at a time. He believed that she was a good honest girl, so why shatter an old man's dreams. The incident with his car, and her subsequent return to Ghana, should have registered in his mind, but it didn't, and none of us ever spoke about that now. Lena did appear to make him happy, or at least she did at the moment. I shot Nick a warning glace across the bar, to tell him to leave well alone, which he did.

The police lads and their experts returned to the U.K. at the end of the week, after giving evidence in the Shendian court that the body that they had exhumed and taken back to the U.K. was without a doubt that of Reg Preston. Other than that they had told me no significant advance had been made in the trial, and they were not in the least pleased as to how things were progressing.

The next few months of low season, ticked along without too much happening. Things were getting tough financially as they did every low season, and the added burden of the extra social security and the electric bill, I had had to face, were making this year extremely difficult; but I was keeping my head above water, even if only just.

Oliver's wedding, even though he had never given me a definite date, had been pushed back several times; he was now mentioning the possibility of late November. This was later than I had hoped. I had been relying on the profits from this tiding me over until the beginning of the tourist season. November was traditionally our busiest month, but I was confident that we could cope with the wedding besides our regular tourists. There was the added bonus that in November you can rely on it not to rain. If the wedding had been at the originally suggested time in September, rains would have been a major threat. What did concern me was the number of guests. Oliver had mentioned approximately 45 at the onset. With more of his family flying out from the U.K. than he expected, and with an ever-increasing number of Fatima's family and friends travelling up from Freetown, this number had now grown to 75. Among these guests were a handful influential Shendians, Oliver had told me that at least one of these would have his personal bodyguard in attendance.

The Dominion had not during my time here, hosted an event of such magnitude, or with such important guests. Whenever Oliver spoke to me regarding various arrangements for the reception, I did my best to keep a cool and calm exterior, while inside I was feeling quite panic struck. As I have mentioned before, I had no previous experience in catering, I was entirely self- taught during my time at The Dominion. I was now proficient behind the bar, my waiteressing skills were much better than I ever imagined that they would become; but what I lacked in finesse, I managed to compensate for with friendly chatter to my customers. This wedding was really going to put my catering skills to the test. In one way I was looking forward to it, it would give me the chance to see what I was capable of doing. In another way the thought of it was daunting. Not only was this a chance to possibly generate further business with the ex-pat community, but I was also conscious of the importance of making the influential Shendian guests welcome. If the latter enjoyed themselves, it could only be to my advantage.

The wedding date was finally fixed for December the sixth, the day after the judge's site visit. Whilst I was glad to have at last been given a definite date, it's falling the day after the judge's visit wasn't ideal, but on the other hand, preparations for Oliver and Fatima's big day would stop me from unduly dwelling on thoughts of the court. The first task to be tackled was the wedding cake. I would use my Christmas cake recipe, that had always been well appreciated, but first I had to decide what to cook it in. The cake tin that was used for birthday cakes would have been too small. Cake tins are not readily available in Shendi. Some locals possess a bottled gas hob, but seldom an oven, but the majority cook over charcoal burners or an open wood fire; so an assortment of cake tins is not a priority to a tradesman running a hardware stall in Malaville market. Eventually I decided that the tin the kitchen staff generally used to cook the steak and kidney pie would be ideal. The size was fine, and it was oblong with rounded corners, which would make it easier to apply the icing.

I knew purchasing all the ingredience maybe a problem. I managed to get all the dried fruit I required, but I couldn't get any ground almonds, ground cloves or candid peel. I was able to get flaked almonds and whole cloves. The day before I made the cake I spent a long while pounding these with the steak tenderising hammer, I actually found this quite therapeutic! I had managed to buy one packet of mixed fruit, which contained a small amount of mixed peel, but this wouldn't be sufficient to give the required taste. My citrus trees in the garden, had produced a lot of fruit that year due to the heavy rains the previous season, so I decided to improvise and make use of my own home grown, orange, lemon and lime peel.

As I smelt the cake when I took it out of the oven, I was content that I had produced an acceptable Shendian substitute for a traditional British wedding cake. Each week until the big day I would add a little of the very best Napoleon brandy that Shendi could offer at £1 a bottle. Satisfied with the cake, I felt that I had taken care of an important part of the preparations.

I was always relieved as the first tourist flights started at the beginning of November. Each year I worried that the profits from the previous high season would prove insufficient to run the bar during low season, but I always seemed to manage to eke the money out, until the next round of tourists arrived. However, this year was different; there was the added tension as November progressed, of both the site visit and the wedding. My mind was so full of plans for the wedding that I hardly had time to spare the judge's visit a thought. My regulars most of whom had been invited, were also getting gripped by wedding fever. I hoped I wouldn't disappoint them. I had initially told the regulars about the forthcoming site visit, but I hadn't told any of them the actual date. It was scheduled for 10am, a part of the day, when I'm not usually very busy. I was afraid if too many knew when it was to take place, that they would come into the bar, to offer their support and to watch the proceedings. I didn't want too many spectators.

The day before the site visit, I iced the wedding cake. The day before, when I removed it from the tinfoil that it had been wrapped in since I had baked it a pleasant aroma of brandy, fruit and spices filled the air. I assured myself that if it smelt good, it would taste fine. I allowed myself ample time to ice it, as I obviously wanted the cake to look as good as possible, and I knew from past experiences with birthday cakes, that the heat and humidity makes the icing behaves quite differently here, to how it reacts in the U.K. climate. I had started using butter icing or a frosting on birthday cakes, as this was easier to apply, but this would not be acceptable for a wedding cake. In later years, having had much practice, I did become more proficient in decorating wedding cakes, but this first one took me a long while to get the top as flat I wanted; any imperfections on the sides could be hidden with a ribbon. By the time that I was satisfied with it, it was lunchtime, and I had customers to attend to, so after taking one last look at my creation I left the cake in the pantry to set. I would go back and decorate it after my lunchtime customers had left.

When I returned to my masterpiece, my heart sank. Rather than setting as I had expected, most of the icing had melted in the heat, and was running off the sides of the cake onto the tray I had placed it on. There was nothing else I could do but set to work again. This time on completion, I put it in the fridge, where by evening it had set. I decided I would leave it there until it was due to be cut. I would put the ribbon and decorations on just before I presented it to Oliver and Fatima. I was taking no more chances with the Shendian heat.

Wedding day minus one. I didn't sit and drink my morning coffee as my regular morning lads drank theirs and eat their breakfasts, instead I stood behind the bar with a pile of papers related to the wedding and worried about the site visit.

"We not good enough to sit with this morning?" Nick asked.

"Not to-day, I'm too busy checking the chef has everything on his shopping list that we need for tomorrow, and going over the menu with him. Can't risk the kitchen not getting things right. This wedding is going to be 'The Dominion Showcase', you know."

To escape further questions I disappeared into the kitchen. In reality I checked the shopping list yesterday evening, and had gone through the menu repeatedly with the kitchen staff. I was keeping an eye on the clock, the judge was due to arrive at 10 o'clock, and I wanted to be ready for her arrival.

Soon after 9.30, I went out into the car park; I was determined to be outside to welcome my guests to The Dominion. All was normal in the car park for that time of the day. I had expected to see a welcoming committee from The Peace Haven also. There were tourists coming out of the hotel and walking the short distance across the car park to the small supermarket, which had been built near the arch, to purchase their bottled water and other provisions for the day. A few cars were driving under the arch and entering the hotel, but no more than I would have expected on any other day. The hotel's security guards waved to me as they saw me standing at the top of the car park. I seemed to be the only one that realized that this wasn't just an ordinary day.

I didn't have to wait long for my lawyer, Ousman's car to pull under the arch. I looked at my watch, it was just before 9.45. Ousman was a notoriously bad timekeeper, so I took his early arrival as a sign, that like me, he understood the significance of this occasion. As he parked next to my entrance, I was surprised to see that he was dressed in his court robes. Before getting out of the car, he took his ceremonial wig out of his glove compartment, and looking in his rear view mirror, he put it on.

As he got out of his car and shook hands with me, he said "Morning, Helen. Are you alright?"

"Morning Ousman, I'm fine, but why are you in your court robes? I expected to see you in a suit."

"This is court business. This visit will be conducted exactly as if we are in the court house."

I wasn't sure what he meant by that. Ousman and I stood near my entrance waiting for the others to arrive; we were getting curious looks from the steady stream of tourists going to and from the hotel.

Mrs. Sullais, The Peace Haven's lawyer was the next to arrive, she drove under the arch and straight into the hotel's main entrance. I could see as she passed through the car park, that she was already wearing one of the many wigs that I had seen her wearing in court. Soon afterwards she walked out from the hotel accompanied by Mr. Smither's, two other directors, the hotel manager, and several other suited gents, whom I didn't know, but I thought these were possibly departmental heads.

They acknowledged Ousman and myself, but stood a fair distance away from us. Many tourists and local passers-by were gathering to see what entertainment was to follow. Lawyers complete with their wigs and gowns, must have seemed a curious sight, in the middle of the tourist area. Most of the locals looking on probably had never seen a lawyer dressed like this before, as this was a rarity outside of the High Court.

The tension rose, as we all stood in silence waiting for the judge's arrival. In the distance I heard sirens, as Shendi only has two police cars; this in itself was a rare occurrence. I assumed that the President's cavalcade was in our area. The sirens grew louder; they were getting quite close; I realized that they were coming down the main tourist strip. They were not coming from a police car, as I had at first thought, but from two police motorbike outriders, who came under the arch at brake neck speed, closely followed by a small military vehicle. The motorbikes and the military vehicle pulled into the parking spaces allotted to the shops, opposite both my, and the hotels entrances. Next followed two black unmarked S.S.G. vehicles, at the rear were two more police officers on motorbikes. The first black car drove up the car park and jerked to a halt near to where Ousman and I were standing. An S.S.G. officer, whom I recognised, agilely jumped out of the car, almost before it had stopped and quickly opened one of the rear doors. Out stepped the judge, as by now I expected in her full court robes and ceremonial wig. Travelling in the second S.S.G. vehicle were the clerk of the court, who by now knew me, and nodded me a greeting as he got out of the car, with him were three other court officials.

The small crowd that had gathered to watch the proceedings were not disappointed, such a spectacle was almost unheard of except in Port Albert, but their entertainment was short lived. The judge followed by the court officials glanced over towards the shops, she pointed in that direction and told the clerk some points she wanted him to take note of, he was writing down her every word as if in court.

Next the judge walked towards La Parisian and looked inside, without entering the building, and then came back in our direction. She strolled into the main entrance of The Dominion, and she was then out of view of the onlookers. She paused by the door of the bar and looked inside; she glanced around taking notice of the entire interior. She gave a friendly wave to my customers that were inside and continued with her tour. She crossed the small wooden bridge into the beer garden, flanked by the lawyers, of whom she was asking questions, this was still all being written down by the clerk.

After saying a few friendly words to my customers sat in the garden, she went up onto the stage, and peered over the wall to look down on The Peace Haven, as I have done so many times. My stage gave a perfect bird's eye view of all the comings and goings in the hotel. I had watched our President and many visiting Presidents arriving at functions on numerous occasions. I felt that this was one of my few privileges in Shendi. Customers sat outside, enjoying a late breakfast or a mid morning drink looked aghast to see such a procession pass through my normally peaceful garden. I had thought this was going to be a low-key visit. I had been much mistaken. We all went on into my own garden, the two opposing lawyers still closest to the judge familiarizing her with her surroundings, they were closely followed by the clerk, who seemed to be having difficulty writing everything down as he walked along, I felt sympathy for him, this couldn't have been an easy task. As they passed my house I heard Ousman say, "This is my client's apartment, she is the caretaker/manager so therefore needs to live on the premises."

Mrs. Sullias had previously bought it up in court, that it was illegal to have a dwelling in the tourist area. At one time she suggested that I move out of my house, and incorporate the building into the business. Ousman had argued that I was the caretaker as well as the manageress, so must be allowed to remain on the premises.

We all proceeded out through The Dominion back gate, which The Peace Haven had claimed we should be using as our main entrance. This would not be a viable solution to my problems, as it was over 500 meters down a narrow unlit road. No tourist would walk down this in the dark; it would not be safe. There were two containers in this lane, one was empty, the other housed the generator for one of the other neighbouring hotels, and anyone could be lurking behind these. There was also a six-foot deep storm drain at one side of the lane; this would also be hazardous in the dark. We were all stood in this narrow sandy lane, which beyond The Dominion's back gate, led only to The Peace Havens tradesman's entrance.

The judge looked down the lane towards the building, that I knew to be a toilet and shower block, which had been built as a lean-to against my garden wall. This and the small construction the other side of the lane, which I believed was a storeroom, are the buildings that Smithers had denied any knowledge of in court. I could not hear what the judge said to the clerk, as I was too far away, but I could tell from her body language, and her tone of voice that she was not impressed.

In reality I heard very little of what she had said during her tour, as she only spoke to the clerk and the lawyers, I was following a short distance behind, but I did again feel her displeasure as she walked around and closely examined the two permanent diesel tankers, serving the hotel's generators. These tankers were situated just opposite my rear entrance, and only a few yards from my bedroom.

Ousman remarked to me. "I know you have mentioned these tankers to me, but I didn't realize that they were so close to your house. I would rather you sleep here than me."

"Thanks, but where they are also makes the use of my back entrance for customers unrealistic, there isn't enough room in the lane with them there to swing a car around and drive into my gate"

"I agree."

The judge indicated that she wanted to go back inside my garden. In the small slabbed area between my generator room and my garage, which I used as a storeroom, in the full heat of the sun; with all of us standing, instead of being seated, she proceeded to hold court. I looked on in disbelief as the two lawyers conducted themselves in exactly the same manner, as they would have done in the courtroom.

An hour later, when I was feeling drained by the midday sun; the case was once again adjourned, but was not really any further ahead. Nothing concerning the visit was discussed; they were covering no new ground at all, simply going over and over again, many points that had been bought up previously in court. Mrs. Sullais did raise again that I should not be living here, that the building was registered only as a bar and restaurant not as a dwelling. This was correct, but totally irrelevant to the case, that was only to establish our rights to use our main entrance that led into the hotel's car park, and to gain a permanent right of way through that car park. I had discussed this with Ousman when this point was first raised. He had ensured me that this was not a problem. Once the court case was over, he said we would return to court and apply for change of use to include a dwelling for the caretaker.

Other points that were also raised again, included which entrance was used for deliveries, which entrance was used by my staff, and did I personally ever use the back gate. Under Ousman's instructions I used the back gate only when it was absolutely necessary. This gate was kept locked most of the time. Ousman had told me, that if we used that entrance too often, it would give their lawyer a stronger argument that we could use it all the time. We did use the back entrance for our refuse collection, this we had collected once a week, by a donkey and cart. I didn't think The Peace Haven would appreciate a donkey and cart coming under their arch, and the donkey being tethered in their car park, each week, while my rubbish was loaded onto the cart.

After declaring the hearing closed, the judge, court officials and lawyers, strolled back through my beer garden, and returned to their vehicles, and with sirens blaring from their police escort they headed back to Port Albert. Even if no other progress had been made, I was hoping that now that the judge was aware of the layout of both properties that she would have some sympathy for my plight.

"Who were that lot? Did you hire them for the morning's entertainment?" asked Kevin as I went back into the bar.

"That was the judge's site visit. I couldn't believe it they held a court sitting outside by my genie room."

"Just as well the genie wasn't on, no-one would have heard anything with the row your genie makes." said Terry, "How did it go?"

"Hard to tell, she wasn't very impressed with their buildings in the back lane, she didn't say a lot, I'm only going by her facial expressions."

Oliver, who was sat at the bar, having his lunch said, "You shouldn't be unduly worrying yourself over things that you have no control over. You should be concentrating on serious matters, like my wedding, it is tomorrow you know. I hope the cake has been iced."

"Stop fretting Oliver, all is under control. The cake is iced." I said sounding confident, but suddenly remembering the cake. With other things on my mind, I had forgotten to check it this morning. As soon as most of my lunchtime customers had left, I headed straight to the fridge to check on the cake; I breathed a deep sigh of relief, when I saw that it was in exactly the same condition as it had been when I placed it in the fridge the previous day.

Later that evening I was approached by Colin who had turned up during the judges visit. He was in his early forties, from the south of England, who had come to live in Shendi about four months earlier. He had a long history of working in hotel maintenance; he had worked in many parts of the world. After a spell back in the U.K. he looked once again for work abroad, he missed being in warm climates. He applied for many positions, and had several interviews, before he finally agreed to take up the appointment of head of the maintenance department at The Peace Haven. He lived in an apartment on the hotel's premises and used The Dominion as his local, usually popping in for a sandwich at lunchtime, and joining my ex-pat lads around the bar, for a few drinks during the evening. He had become popular among the ex-pat community.

During a quiet spell Colin called me aside. "What was that charade going on at lunch time? All the lads seemed to know what was happening, I didn't like to show my ignorance and ask you in front of everyone."

"That was the judge in our court case on a site visit to accustom herself with the lay of the land between here and The Peace Haven."

"What court case? I'm afraid I'm in the dark here."

I had assumed that Colin was aware of all the problems between Peace Haven and The Dominion. I briefly explained to him, the events that had originally led to the court case, explaining that it was basically over the entrance leading into their car park, but in reality that they wanted my land, and if possible they didn't intend paying for it.

"I'm absolutely amazed. I was given the impression that this belonged to the hotel, so I assumed that you were renting it off of them."

"Oh no, this is our land and I will fight for it as long as I have to. We were initially told by our lawyer that the case should be over in six months, it is now in its fifth year."

"But I've seen the plans of the next stage of the redevelopment. The Dominion is coming down, and several blocks of bedrooms and apartments are being built here."

"Not if I can help it. I know the plans you mean. I have seen them too. Smithers showed them to us, when my husband was still here, but being the case has gone on for so long, I thought maybe they had changed their minds."

"No, they haven't, I've seen the plans. I know where they keep them, when I get a chance, I will take a copy of them, and give them to you, they might help your cause."

"That would be great, but don't do anything that is likely to land you in trouble."

"You already know what I think of their management. Smithers is bad, but this new manager of his, Claus, is even worse yet. I knew they were ruthless, but I had no idea that they were doing this to you. No wonder the lads keep telling me I will get the sack when they find out I drink in here."

Colin had had disagreements with Mr. Smithers ever since he first arrived, I knew Colin had a low opinion of him, and now with Claus' arrival, and the problems that he was causing him also, Colin was seriously thinking that he had made the wrong decision when he decided to come to Shendi and work for The Peace Haven.

"Quite a way back in the court case," I went on to explain, "their lawyer bought up the possibility of their claiming damages from me for the difference in the cost of building those bedrooms in '99 and when they are eventually built. That would be me more than bankrupt. They priced everything out, and came up with the staggering amount of 7,500,000 Shillings, and they said this amount was rising daily! Frightening tactics yeah?"

"I reckon, the bastards! I will keep my ear to the ground, and let you know anything I hear, and when I can I will get you a copy of those plans."

Until then I hadn't realized that Colin was unaware of my situation. As for the damages I had tried to push that possibility to the back of my mind. I knew my court case hung precariously, and that in reality the chance of me being the final victor was slim, but in the meantime I was a thorn in the side of The Peace Haven, in the light of the various problems that they had caused me, this gave me a certain amount of satisfaction. If I eventually lost The Dominion for no financial reward it would be devastating for me, but I could return to the U.K. and hopefully get a job, I would survive. Alternatively if I lost The Dominion and they were awarded these astronomical damages, I would have debts I could never hope to repay. I had never been money orientated, but I have always found having debts hard to live with. Discussing this with Colin, had bought this possibility to the fore of my mind, once again. My head was in a complete whirl, when I retired to bed that evening.

The judge's visit ticked over and over in my thoughts as I twisted and turned in an attempt to drift off to sleep. I needed a good night's rest, tomorrow was Oliver and Fatima's wedding, and it was to be an important day for The Dominion. I had checked every detail several times; I had repeatedly gone through the menu with Ebou, my head chef. Although he wasn't always reliable, it was seldom that he, or his staff let me down over important matters. I had made several lists for him, and pinned them to the kitchen wall, not only what needed to be done, but the times when the preparations for everything need to be started. These lists were flicking before my eyes as sleep eluded me. If only I had been able to relax more, I wouldn't have felt as continually exhausted as I did.

The big day arrived. I was unnecessarily gripped by sheer panic. Preparations were going well in the kitchen. With the help of Momodou I had rearranged the tables in the bar, so that the two long ones, which we would use for serving the buffet, were put together at the far end of the room near the kitchen, and well out of the way of the bar area. As it was December there was no fear of rain, the reception was being held in the garden. Where we had positioned the serving table would allow the guests to enter through the main door, to collect their buffet, and go out through the garden door, so that there would be no congestion inside. Never having held a buffet for so many people before, I realized that all these things needed to be taken into consideration.

Karen, who had volunteered to help me decorate The Dominion for the occasion, arrived bright and early, and we set about our task. The beer garden was large with many nooks and crannies; we knew it would take a long while to decorate. Latif was put to work, blowing up balloons for us, while Karen and I hung them absolutely everywhere. We pinned them to the trunks of the trees, tied them on the lamp- posts, pinned them to the wooden bridge, we even hung them over the water feature, and floated them in the pond. We were festooned in balloons. It was amazing how long this took, especially with me, flip-flopping at full speed in and out of the kitchen keeping a watchful eye on the proceedings in there.

Next we sent Latif out into the back lane, to collect as much overhanging bougainvillea as he could gather. Meanwhile Karen and I arranged the tables in the garden, I had had to hire extra plastic garden chairs, and these had been delivered earlier in the day. Once they were arranged and matching table clothes were put on the tables no one would realize that underneath, the tables were a mixed match of odd tables that I had stored in the garage, when I had replaced the original garden tables, even the dining table from my house was being used. This was to be the top table so must be elaborately decorated.

Latif came in and out with massive armfuls of bougainvillea; its deep purple leaves making a magnificent contrast to the yellow batik tablecloths that adorned the tables. Each table was decorated, and then we set about placing the colourful array that Latif had amassed for us, in every conceivable place we thought appropriate, we put it around the edge of the pond, draped from the trees and intertwined it around the wrought ironwork of the bar. Karen, Latif and I, stood back and admired our mornings work. We were pleased with our efforts.

Two loud bangs made us all jump. Gunshots, in the near vicinity, my heart was pumping furiously, not today of all days. Karen and I collapsed in a fit of the giggles, which was probably more due to nervous relief than anything else, when we realized that our 'gun shots' were only the balloons popping as the sun moved around and shone on them. We had forgotten that this might happen.

"Seems like your job for this afternoon is replacing them as they pop." I told Karen.

"Thanks a million. I thought my job was over and that I was going to sit back and enjoy the afternoon."

The D.J. arrived. Oliver had arranged this himself. He had been the previous day, luckily arriving just after the judge and the court party had left, to establish what facilities, I could make available to him. I had taken Ousman's advice before agreeing to the D.J. as it was contravening the court injunction that the Peace Haven had taken out against us, prohibiting us from having any live music or entertainment in the garden that could interfere with their guests. Ousman assured me that as long as it was over by 8pm, there would not be a problem. I hoped not.

Surprisingly for Shendi, Oliver and Fatima's wedding had been held, earlier rather than later, than scheduled. I was taken completely by surprise, when their arrival was heralded, in true Shendian style, by loud hooting of horns, banging of drums and much shouting. They made a very striking couple; they were both splendidly attired. Oliver worn an elaborately embroidered white African robe, together with his silver grey hair, and full set of beard and moustache; he made an impressive figure. Fatima was in a traditional white European wedding dress, that I knew an African tailor had made for her from a picture she had given him to copy. This was complemented with a long lacy veil, which was held in place by a flattering drop pearl headdress. She was a very attractive girl, with an outstanding figure, her dark skin showed off her white dress to perfection.

Even before I had a chance to congratulate them Oliver said, "Quick get me a beer Helen, before everyone else arrives, I'm in need of one more than they are."

Jed did this for me, as Fatima went outside, and with eyes wide open with amazement said, "Oh Helen, thank you, this is beautiful, I didn't know you were going to do all this for us. I have never seen The Dominion look so good for a wedding. Oliver said you were going to decorate for us, but I expected it to be the same as you do for birthdays." She was right about one thing; The Dominion had never been so well decorated for a wedding before, possibly because it had never hosted a wedding before.

The guests all arrived together a few minutes later; I was told afterwards that several tourists and a small crowd of Shendians had gathered in the car park to watch their arrival. The guests also made a spectacular sight. Oliver's family that had travelled from the U.K. were all dressed in smart formal wedding attire, the ex-pat ladies were in European style dresses, but these were made by local tailors in bright African coloured fabrics, colours much bolder than most of them would have considered wearing at home. Fatima's family and the couple's African friends wore traditional African dresses and robes, from every colour of the spectrum imaginable. These were many different styles, as Freetonian styles differ immensely from Shendian. The Dominion had not seen such splendour in my time here.

During high season the bar was always busy during the evenings, so I had not considered 75 people all needing to be served drinks a major problem, but never before had we had so many customers all arriving at the same time, and all requiring drinks simultaneously. I was struggling through as best I could, trying to get drinks to everyone as quickly as possible, but Shendians only have one speed, no matter what the occasion. I was overcome with relief when everyone had their first drinks in their hands, this did not bode well; had I over estimated my staffs' capabilities. I hoped not. At least now that everyone had a drink they would be approaching the bar in small groups and not en mass. Most of the guests had waited patiently except for one lady cousin of Oliver's who had come over from the U.K.; this was her first visit to Shendi.

"This is awful keeping us waiting like this at a wedding. Why didn't you engage more staff for the day?" she said to me in a very abrupt tone.

A kept my calm, and gave her a gentle smile as I answered, "Sorry for the inconvenience, we will serve you as soon as we can."

"Oliver would not expect his guests to have to queue like this simply for a drink."

I served her next hoping that she would go out into the sunshine of the garden, thinking that would brighten her mood. I saw no point in trying to explain to her that it takes a long while to train staff here, and that you can't just phone up an agency to hire extra staff for the day.

After this initial hiccup, all went like clockwork. The kitchen did me proud, all my time spent planning things to the last detail, had not been in vain. The food had been served at the requested time, and all to Oliver's specification. It was served buffet style, there was roast meats and poultry, lamb, beef, chicken and turkey, various styles of potatoes, there was roasted, mashed, chips, and a full compliment of vegetables, so the European could have a traditional roast if they wanted. We also supplied a variety of Shendian dishes and curries for the Africans. Ironically most of the Africans chose the roast meats, and their western counterparts ate African style. I looked on proudly as my kitchen staff stood behind the serving tables carving the joints of meat, in their kitchen 'whites'.

All the while the D.J. that Oliver had hired played background music. After they had all eaten, Oliver gave a short speech, then Fatima went up on the stage and amid much cheering from their guests, and a little help from the D.J.'s karaoke machine sang to Oliver, everyone was in very high spirits. Oliver signalled to me that they were ready to cut the cake. I rushed into the kitchen; the cake was still in the fridge. I had checked it earlier in the day; it was confidant that it would be fine. As I hadn't been able to get a cake board large enough, I had covered a tray with tin foil to place it on, and I knew this would be sturdy enough to hold the weight. I hurriedly removed it from the fridge, as it still needed to have the decorations added; Karen followed me into the kitchen to offer her assistance.

I put a deep purple ribbon around it to match the bougainvillea; I held this in place with pins for speed. I was very pleased with the centre decoration, Rick had recently returned from a trip to the U.K. and bought me back a traditional wedding cake decoration, of a bride and a groom beneath an arch, but this decoration had a white groom and a black bride, it couldn't have been more perfect. Once this was in its place of honour, Karen and I added lucky horseshoes to each corner.

"You can still see where the icing is a bit uneven at the bottom." I said to Karen as I put the finishing touches to it.

"Now you can't." She told me, as she placed bougainvillea that we had used to decorate the serving table, onto the tray around the bottom of the cake.

"Brilliant, covers up the imperfections, and camouflages the tinfoil."

"Yeah, but get it out to them quick, look it's starting to melt."

She was right the whole cake had started to glisten; it was already melting in the heat.

I proudly carried the cake out into the garden, to present to Oliver and Fatima, with all my staff following behind eager to catch a glimpse of the proceedings; they had never witnessed a sight like this before. I was relieved as I set the cake down on the top table; I hadn't realized the immense weight of it. Oliver said a few more words, and I kept my fingers crossed behind my back, as the happy couple cut the cake.

Oliver's cousin, who was stood near me said, "Well done, I must congratulate you, this has been a magnificent afternoon. I'm impressed how you have managed to create a U.K. style wedding out here. I really wasn't sure what to expect."

I simply said, "Thanks." But I took her praise as an apology for her curtness earlier in the afternoon.

The D.J. raised the tempo and the dancing began as I took the cake back into the kitchen to slice it into fingers and place on the two large trays, that I had already prepared with paper serviettes, for the waiters to hand out to the guests.

I sliced off the marzipan and icing from one side of the cake, and put it on a separate plate to give to the staff as a little treat, being they couldn't try any of the cake itself, because of its alcohol content. All my staff were Muslims. I tasted a small piece as I sliced it. I was pleased with the result; it was moist, rich and a lovely dark colour. I was satisfied that I hadn't let Oliver down.

As I was replenishing Jed's tray for the second time with fingers of the cake, I said to him,"I've put some marzipan and icing on that plate over there for the staff, don't let them eat any of the cake."

"Why?"

"It has alcohol in it. Brandy."

He was visibly shaken. "No, no, don't say that. This is awful. Why didn't you tell us before? We have given it to the Muslims. They are eating it. What can we do?"

There were arms waving in the air all around me, as the staff worked themselves up into frenzy. Shendians, like most Africans are very excitable. I was unsure what to do to quell the situation, but I did need to calm them down and quickly. We had a garden full of customers to attend to. Besides the wedding party, customers were drifting into the bar, not only my regulars, but tourists were coming in for a drink, wanting to catch a glimpse of the wedding. Fatima, like most Freetonians, was Christian. I had genuinely forgotten that some of the African guests would be Muslim.

"Shh shh" I tried to quieten them. "We will do nothing, it is too late now, and they will have eaten it. If we don't tell them they won't know so it will be O.K."

"It is not O.K." Jed told me."We have to tell them. This is a terrible sin, they must be told what they have done, so that they can beg Allah for forgiveness."

"You will say nothing." I tell them my voice crescendoing to be heard over the increasing shouts of the staff. "How can it be a sin, if they don't know that they are having alcohol, and anyway it is only a very small amount to give the cake extra flavour. It was my mistake to forget to tell you, so how can it be their sin? If you tell them now, it will cause all sorts of problems, it will spoil Fatima's wedding."

"If we don't tell them, the marriage will be cursed." Jed informed me.

"Fatima and Oliver are both Christian. I don't believe that Allah will curse a Christian marriage for having brandy in their wedding cake."

"You don't understand sin." Jed told me.

"Maybe not, but in my eyes it would be a sin to go out there and tell Muslims that there was brandy in the cake. They have eaten it and enjoyed it. I will not allow you to say anything. Is that understood by all of you?"

Most of them had started to calm down; Ebou took Jed aside and was talking to him, in a corner of the kitchen. Ebou, often did understand different situations quicker than most of the staff, he was aware of the consequences of telling the Muslims that they had been given brandy, it would have caused mayhem, and spoilt the day for everyone. I heard him trying to explain to Jed, that if they didn't know that they were having alcohol, that it wasn't their sin. I also heard him mention that it wasn't really my sin either, as I hadn't given it to them deliberately.

After that little incident I went back into the bar a little shaken, to see Kevin coming in from the garden, where he had been enjoying, or so I thought the wedding. He had his shirt off, and his shorts were dripping wet, his trainers were squelching with every step he took.

"What you been doing?" I asked. "Got a bit over heated, and had a dip in the pond?" Kevin and Alana had done just that the previous Christmas; I thought that maybe Kevin was going to make that his party piece.

"So that's all the thanks I'm going to get, for jumping in the pond and saving that bloody kid that has been getting on all your nerves this afternoon. Perhaps I should have left her there to drown; no-one else seemed very bothered."

"What the little 'un that's been running in and out of here."

"Yeah the one that's been causing havoc, I don't even know who she belongs to."

I was told later, that Kevin, who can be a problem himself when he has too much to drink, and there was plenty flowing on this occasion claimed he was taking a photo and accidentally backed into the little girl and she fell into the pond. Others say that she upset him and he pushed her in, then when he realized that he had been seen pushing her, he jumped in and rescued her. I reserved judgement on that one, but had inkling that the latter was closer to the truth.

When Oliver came in the next day for his lunch, and was telling me how pleased he was with their reception and how happy Fatima was with everything, I told him of the near rebellion I had in the kitchen over the cake. He was highly amused, but I don't know if he told Fatima this behind the scenes story of their wedding. She may not have been so amused, as it was her Muslim friends who had eaten the cake.

Chapter Thirteen
A Shotgun Wedding

Oliver's wedding had appeared to have the desired affect. The Dominion was now being patronised by people who had not previously been customers of mine. It appeared that the success of the event had been the talk of many expat circles because many of my new customers had not even been at the wedding but had heard about it. It was either that or they were coming out of curiosity to see this mad island woman running a bar on her own. What their reason for coming I didn't mind as long as they kept on coming. The staff seemed to realise the importance ensuring that this new clientele developed a good crop of regulars and for the next few weeks service improved and I had less trouble with them. Bookings for my Christmas Day lunch came flooding in; even the Deputy British High Commissioner was coming.

I was on good terms with the High Commission as I had recently hosted a party for off duty crew of a visiting naval ship on the first evening of their visit. This visit was something of a landmark in Shendi-UK relations. Prior to a coup in the nineties visits by naval ships had been a regular occurrence. Since then and the subsequent withdrawal of recognition by the UK government all such visits had stopped. With improved relations between the U.K. and Shendi, this was to be the first naval vessel in Shendian waters for eleven years and the High Commission wanted to turn it into a high profile visit which included the party at The Dominion.

I raised money to fund the evening by holding a raffle which the expats willingly joined in. They were looking forward to the break in the routine; new faces were always welcome and a crew load would provide many ears for their old jokes. On the night two coaches of sailors were bought to The Dominion and together with the ex-pats we had a good old knees' up.

Many of our naval guests, who were returning from a long tour of duty in the South Atlantic, were determined to let their hair down and arrived in fancy dress. One dressed as 'Cat Woman', one as 'Tarzan', another sported a mini dress and four inch heels. After a couple of drinks, one stood on a chair, and stripped down to a throng. I stopped him going any farther; Shendi is a Muslim country that would not have gone down well. Custom like this could only be to my advantage, and connections within The High Commission would be useful if my problems with The Peace Haven really did turn against me.

The situation between The Peace Haven and I was still the same but rumours were rife that it was to be sold. This was not new. Shendi was a country where rumours, often unfounded, spread like wildfire and this was a regular one on the rumour circiut. I had no means of knowing if there was any truth in this latest tale, but, as usual, I eagerly listened to all I heard, hoping to gain any shred of truth that I could from the gossip and chitchat of the grapevine.

I did know that the situation over the wall was not a happy one with staff morale at a very low ebb. The hotel staff were all in fear of losing their jobs because the director Mr. Smithers had been out of the country for many months. His absence meant that the running of the hotel now the responsibility of Claus, the hotel manager, who was even more ruthless than Smithers himself. Claus had been known to dismiss staff for trifling reasons and I could often hear him shouting at his staff, when I was in the bar, so the hotel's own guests would have heard this. A takeover would be as warmly welcomed by them, as it would be by me.

Ousman had told me that since Smithers had left Shendi, he had received a letter from government officials advising him that he would not be welcomed back if he was to return. This piece of news made me think. How had he heard about this? Surely it was sensitive government information. Much as I wanted to believe him I was unsure. It led me look again at my relationship with him. Even though Ousman was my lawyer, I did not fully trust him. I sometimes wondered if he wasn't working against me, as much as for me. Keeping my ear to the ground I got on with the business in hand, of running my bar, in what was proving to be a highly successful high season, which was providing me with the income to continue financing the court case, and would enable me, to run the bar during next low season.

Time seemed to pass faster in Shendi than back home. Maybe this was because my life was so busy, or maybe because the year only had two seasons, wet and dry. Christmas in Shendi always panicked me. In mid November, when we were enjoying wall-to-wall sunshine after the rainy season and with my brain stuck in mid-August I would suddenly realise that Christmas was only five weeks away. Unlike the U.K. where Christmas lunches have to be booked weeks or even months in advance, things in Shendi were more relaxed. Most ex-pats would leave it till the last minute; presumably like me their brains were still in summer mode.

Finally in December I would tackle Christmas at the Dominion. One morning in early December I would retire to my office and write my Christmas cards, a much smaller pile of them than I had been accustomed to sending in the UK. Even if my brain had acknowledged the imminence of Christmas before mid November, I would have had to have left card writing until now. Items posted in Shendi for the UK would at best take several weeks to reach the U.K., if they arrived at all. Any post, including my Christmas cards I would give to one of my regular tourists to take back with them, and post in the U.K. for me. Thus the need to wait until the tourist season started.

Receiving mail in Shendi was a difficult business at any time of year. There were only three main post offices in Shendi, and no postmen, so everyone had P.O. boxes at one of these post offices, and mail was collected from there. A delivery service would have been impossible to run. Only major roads had names consequently when asked to give your address it was only possible to give the general area which was accepted by all as sufficient. There were no letter boxes either. The only place to post mail was at one of the three post offices. In theory internal mail should have been a simple process, with all mail being posted at, and delivered to, one of these three buildings. In practice it is not, local mail generally took up to three weeks to arrive at its destination.

The slowness of the post affected the delivery of bills. These were usually delivered by hand for example the meter reader would deliver the electric bill. When he made his monthly visit to read the meter, he also delivered an invoice based on his previous month's reading. During the last week of each month, an employee of the telecoms was supposed to call with the telephone bill. This seldom happened, the onus being on the customer to go to your nearest tele centre, and ask for the bill. Whenever I did this the bill was never there but the staff were able to look up my account on the computer and give me the amount owed. This may not seem very reliable, but the systems worked though how they managed before computers I do not know.

I always tried to provide a traditional Christmas lunch, but sometimes it was a case of 'make do and mend'. Suet for the puddings was never available in the not very adequately stocked supermarkets. Talking this over in the bar one night with one of my regular tourists, they offered to bring some out the next time they came. So at the start of the tourist season, in early November, I would remember that I had no suet, and send off a hasty e-mail asking for some. This worked fine until the year of 'foot and mouth' disease in England and it was forbidden to take any beef or dairy products out of the country. I had to find someone who I knew would be prepared to smuggle my suet out of the U.K. Some of my tourists had had their coffee whitener that they had in their luggage taken away from them so I held out little hope of my suet getting through. However, desperate times, desperate measures and one of my regulars came through with the necessary packets.

As with the wedding cakes, I couldn't always purchase all of the ingredients that I needed, but I knew that once I had the suet, I could improvise, and that the result would be an acceptable Christmas pudding. Mincemeat for the mince pies was often another problem, but again if I couldn't buy this, I knew I could make a substitute, so again there was no cause for concern.

One year the turkeys that had been ordered, and paid for in mid November, failed to arrive in Shendi until the 23rd of December, this caused many of us in the catering trade many sleepless nights. One of the hotels near The Dominion, fed the vultures every morning and many of them would fly in circles over my bar waiting for their morning feed. I, tongue in cheek, asked the lads around the bar if they would be able to catch me a few if the turkeys didn't arrive in time, they said they were prepared to have a go, saying it would make a change from fishing. I crossed out 'turkey' on some of the menus that I had on the bar, and wrote 'vulture', in its place. This caused laughter from some customers and concern from others, who were not quite sure if I was joking or not. After dinner mints were another matter, some of the ex-pats got quite paranoid if they didn't finish the meal with these. I would tour the supermarkets, buying up any confectionery that would be passable to serve at the end of the meal. Another problem was the little extras that make Christmas, such as crackers and party hats, these were always a headache, but eventually we usually managed to find these. As the years went on these things became more readily available. My biggest worry each year was power. Without mains electric, I would have a major problem in the kitchen, my generator could not run all of the microwaves and without these it would be difficult to serve so many lunches all at the same time. Thankfully during the whole of my time in Shendi there was only one Christmas that we were without power.

As most of the hotels provide gala dinners over the Christmas period, most of our festive guests were ex-pats, or a few tourists in self-catering accommodation. Although they wanted to spend Christmas in traditional style, most wanted to eat alfresco, to make it different from the Christmas they would have had at home.

I never decorated The Dominion before December the 23rd, and I always took them down, first thing on January the 2nd. My Christmas music, which Euan had supplied me plenty of, over the years, stayed firmly in the house, and was only played on the evening of Christmas Eve and on the big day itself. There was no way that I was going down the same road as the U.K. and play Christmas music throughout the whole of December.

New Year was always a big celebration. Again, most of my customers were ex-pats as the tourists were enjoying gala meals in their hotels. I would put on a free buffet for customers who had come to The Dominion for their Christmas lunch; this was always well appreciated. At midnight I put on no entertainment as we could watch all of our neighbouring hotels fireworks from the beer garden. My stage, overlooking The Peace Haven was a prefect vantage point; the car park was also a good viewing area. Many tourists would come to wish my regulars, who they regarded as friends, the staff and me a happy new year, once the festivities in the hotels were over, so the night would take on a new lease of life. We would have singing and dancing, some years right through until morning.

One year Nick, and a friend of his, in Shendi for Christmas climbed The Peace Havens tree in the middle of the car park, and took down the giant balloons that were decorating it. They were closely followed by some of my tourists, some of whom were more agile than others. I had to administer first aid to one lady, who had fallen from the tree amidst shouts of protest, from the hotels security staff, which accused us of trespassing. Their protests were ignored and the loot carried back in triumph to The Dominion. The fun that my guests had playing volleyball, with these giant balloons, using my wrought iron rafters as a net, was well worth the aggravation that the hotel's security had given me. I did enjoy the celebrations, but for me, once the last firework had gone out on New Year's morning, it was over.

January bought with it the mammoth annual round of paperwork. This could be a headache for the general ex-pats, with their immigration papers, alien I.D. cards, and driving licenses to be renewed, but for me, all my business papers had to be reapplied for, and renewed, this was very time consuming, and was an added burden in the height of the tourist season. Sidi would spend every morning in Port Albert, calling at the various offices until we had achieved everything to make the business legal for the coming year. Sidi did the leg work, but it was me who sat for hours in the office, form filling, and balancing the books, then waiting anxiously for him to return, dreading that he would tell me they weren't satisfied with something, and that it had to be redone. Every year the government seemed to move the goal posts, the tourist board always required more information from us, and it was guaranteed to cost more. My immigration license would not be granted until all my taxes, both personal and for the business had been paid and the business had met all the requirements for all my licences. This included inspections from the electric company, fire officers and the police. Weights and measures would also call and check the optics to be sure we were supplying the correct measures. The relief that I felt, usually in mid February, when we had achieved this was immense.

A few weeks into the New Year, Jainaba, the Shendian girlfriend of Paul, an ex-pat who generally came in for a drink on a Saturday afternoon following a round of golf, came to see me with a friend of hers.

"Paul and I are getting married next month. I would like to have our reception here at The Dominion." she told me. "We had thought of somewhere else, but because I enjoyed Fatima's wedding so much, I would like you to do it for me."

I was thrilled, Paul was a customer of mine, but his 'local' was one of the other ex-pat bars. I knew he and Jainaba were getting married shortly, but I assumed that the reception would be at Paul's local. Another wedding, as a direct result of the success of Oliver's gave my confidence a boast. A second wedding would be so much easier than the first.

"I would love to." I told Jainaba. "Let's discuss what you would like to have."

Jainaba was a little vague as to what she wanted, in fairness Fatima and Oliver had had a European style wedding, and this would be unfamiliar to Jainaba. She wanted the food similar to Fatima's, so that would make this easier for the kitchen, she asked for the garden to be decorated the same, which would make it easier on Karen and I. She said she didn't want a cake, and for us to expect about 60 guests.

They happy couple were getting married at The Justice of the Peace Office in Port Albert during the morning. This was to be followed by African wedding celebrations at Jainaba's family compound. Early evening at 5 o'clock the European style reception was to be held at The Dominion with food being served at approximately 6 o'clock, and the reception was expected to be over by about 8. Perfect for me. We had most of the day to decorate the garden, and for the kitchen to prepare the food; we all had the experience of Oliver's wedding behind us. This would be simple in comparison, and it would all be over in time for my evening customers.

I made notes of things I wanted to clarify with Paul concerning the arrangements I had made with Jainaba, to make sure that he was aware of her instructions. Paul told me simply to go ahead with anything Jainaba wanted, he said it was her big day, and that for once he was happy to take a back seat. Two weeks later, Jainaba came back to see me again and ordered a cake. She had seen Fatima's photos of her and Oliver cutting the cake, and would like to have the same. This was not a real problem, there was insufficient time for the cake to mature properly, but a little extra brandy added at the end would help to solve that.

Jainaba had been adamant that she didn't want a D.J.; she had told me dance music on a C.D. player would be fine. Then, only two days before the wedding, she had changed her mind over this. I explained to her that it was too late for me to arrange this, but if she could find someone to do it at such short notice, that would be fine. The same evening Paul came in for a drink, and told me. "Jainaba has found a D.J., so that is all sorted. You know what the girls are like, they don't really know what they want and keep changing their minds."

"That's fine. Tell her to get him to pop in tomorrow, so that I can show him where our electric plugs are, and he can familiarise himself with the place." I told him, and then he gave me a much greater problem.

"I don't expect it will make much difference to you, but you know that we have sent out 60 invites, well Jainaba has verbally invited another 25, I don't expect they will all come, so prepare food for 75, that should be fine."

"OK, OK, the food will be fine no problem but if verbal invites have gone out, you can't hold me responsible for the guests."

"What do you mean?"

"At Oliver's wedding, I had arranged security at the entrance, so that nobody came in without an invite. You know what happens here, all and sundry will come when they hear there is free food. If verbal invites have gone out, my security won't know who has been invited and who has not."

"Right, I see what you mean, I hadn't thought of that, but don't worry it will be alright. I don't think there will be any problems."

Paul was more confident than I was. Shendians welcome the opportunity to dress up in their finery, and with the added bonus of free food, this was an occasion of which to take advantage. There would be verbally invited guests, who would eagerly extend their invitations to include their family and friends. A chance to attend a wedding reception at a restaurant in the tourist area would not be missed by many of the locals.

The big day arrived, and I was feeling full of confidence, there was none of the nerves I had felt on Oliver's wedding day. We had all day for the preparations; we had done it all before, we knew what we were doing this time. Karen, who was always a great support to me, once again helped me with the decorations, but again we were basically repeating what we had done a few months earlier, but with more time to do it in, we were all much more relaxed.

Some of Paul's friends came in for a few drinks at lunch time, telling me that they had been to the ceremony in Port Albert, and that the wedding party had all gone back to Jainaba's family compound, for readings from the Koran, and Shendian marriage customs, without which her family would not consider that she was really married. I was satisfied that all the preparations had been thoroughly carried out, and was confident that all would go well as we waited for the guests to start arriving. The D.J. had already arrived and was busy on the stage setting up his equipment. The guests arrival in small groups would be easier for the bar staff to handle than at Oliver's, when all the guests arrived together, directly from the wedding ceremony.

The guests started to filter in. Not only do the Shendians like the chance to show off their brightly coloured ceremonial clothes, the ex-pat ladies also welcome the excuse to dress up, there are not many occasions in Shendi, that require the wearing of your Sunday best. The garden soon became a mass of colour, in every shade imaginable, bright vivid colours, right through the spectrum to subtle pale shades. The styles were just as varied, flowing Africa gowns, to short, straight European dresses. The men's attire was just as varied, colourful African robes, formal suits, and casual slacks with short- sleeved shirts, were all the order of the day.

Paul arrived just after 5. He was dressed in cream coloured Muslim robes, elaborately embroidered in gold silk, he had changed his religion a few weeks ago, so that he could take part in the Muslim wedding ceremony that had been held two days previously in the local mosque at the insistence of Jainaba's family.

"Is everything going O.K.?" he asked me. I strained to hear what he had said. The D.J. who had by now set up his equipment was making his presence felt, or should I say heard. He was blasting out African dance music, a few decibels higher than I considered normal, or necessary. I had already spoken to him about this, while he was doing his sound checks, and he had assured me that he would lower it, but I couldn't tell the difference.

"All is fine, don't worry." I told Paul as I pulled his first pint.

"Jainaba has gone to the hairdressers, you know what the girls are like about their hair, apparently it was blown about too much in the car, on the way back from Port Albert. She will be here at about 5:30, so is 6 still alright with you for the food?"

"Yeah, fine, all is under control in the kitchen."

I did know of the local girls' obsession with their hair and the time that they spent at the hairdressers, but I was curious as to why Jainaba needed to go to hers again, when it had been done before the ceremony in the morning. The car journey can't have dishevelled it too much. I was aware of the length of time this may take and I thought it likely that Jainaba might not have even arrived by 6 o'clock. I went into the kitchen and told Ebou, that the food may be later than we had originally thought.

The guests continued to arrive, and the D.J. continued to blare out his music, which was well appreciated by the locals, many of whom were already dancing, which provided entertainment for the other guests. Five thirty came and went and as I had suspected no sign of Jainaba. This went largely unnoticed by most of her friends, who had flung themselves into the swing of things, and with the help of her over enthusiastic D.J. were enjoying her wedding celebrations. Just before six Paul came and spoke to me.

"Sorry Helen, I really didn't think Jainaba would be this long, I don't know what she can be doing. Will the food be alright if we postpone it for a while, we can hardly start without the bride."

"Don't worry, enjoy yourself. I don't think her friends have missed her yet, they are too busy dancing, so they are unlikely to notice that the food is late being served."

I acted more causally than I felt, we could delay the food, but with a mostly African kitchen, without all the mod cons that an English restaurant would have, this was not an easy task. I was also getting concerned about the number of guests, with many up and dancing, it was impossible to do a head count, but at a glance I would estimate that there were at least a hundred people in my garden, besides the few stragglers that were sat chatting in the bar.

I double-checked that I had 75 plates piled on the serving table, with an equal number of sets of cutlery. If we served extra meals, I needed to know how many. I instructed the kitchen to prepare more potatoes, vegetables and salad, as I thought these would be needed. Luckily I had quoted Paul a price per head, and not quoted for the entire reception and that was before I knew about the verbal invitations. The decibel crazy D.J. was still keeping everyone well entertained, as 6:30 approached many Europeans were also dancing, the celebrations were going well.

The delay in serving the food was mostly unnoticed, but by this time the bride's absence was not. Paul and his best man Jerry, who had been a witness at the wedding, were pacing up and down near the entrance. Every now the then, one or the other of them, would go out into the car park and check if there was any sign of Jainaba yet.

"Sorry, Helen." Paul said to me as he ordered another beer. "I can't understand this. I know what she is like when she goes to the hairdressers, but this is ridiculous, this is the second time she has been to- day, she knew the food was ordered for six. She should have been here."

"Don't worry all is under control." I told him, feeling a bit deflated, but trying hard not to sound it. The meat had been turned down low that would be fine. The vegetables would have to be reheated, and I was afraid that they would spoil, and the roast potatoes would be past their best.

There should be no problem with the African dishes and the curries, but I was hoping that they wouldn't be simmered for too much longer. I was beginning to think that this opportunity for a good piece of P.R. aimed at ex-pats that don't usually visit The Dominion might backfire on me.

At long last, just before seven thirty, we heard the welcome sound of car hooters, loud hailers, drums and shouting, heralding the bride's arrival. Many of the Shendian guests rushed to the gate, to welcome Jainaba, and to catch their first glimpse of her in her wedding dress. After telling Ebou that Jainaba was here, so the meal would soon need to be served, I also joined the crowd at the gateway to welcome the bride.

She did look very stunning. Like Fatima she has also opted for a traditional white European style wedding dress, which looks much better on a coloured bride than it does on most Europeans, who tend to look pale in their long white outfits. She had layers of frilly lace, in her long flowing skirt; a small train was attached to the shoulders of the pearl studded bodice. She didn't have a veil, instead she wore small white rosebuds in her expertly styled hair, these were shown off to perfection by her shinny, jet black hair, very effective; but I did wonder had it really been worth missing part of her reception while she sat in the hairdressers. She also wore long white satin gloves, which she showed off, by elegantly giving a Queen Mum's royal style wave, as she flaunted through the throng, and into the garden. As she did this, I heard Paul, who was stood near me mutter to Jerry, "I just don't believe this." And seeing me near him said, "Sorry Helen, just get the food out as soon as you can now, please."

It was all systems go then. I went into the kitchen, and with me shouting instructions to the staff, we proceeded to take the meats out of the ovens, and put the vegetables and potatoes onto serving dishes. The waiters were taking the tinfoil off of the salads and placing them on the serving table. It would not take us long to be ready to start serving. Jed came running into the kitchen. I was busy, straining water off of the carrots. "Quick, quick Helen, you must come there are soldiers here to see you."

Without looking up from what I was doing, I told him. ""Tell them I'm busy we are having a programme, say they can come back tomorrow, and give them a drink to keep them happy." (In Shendi, any occasion, whether it is a wedding, a funeral, a birthday or any celebration what so ever, it is referred to as a programme.)

"No, no, I think you had better come. There are four of them in the bar, and others went into the garden, I don't know how many. They have guns and are shouting. I want you to come." Jed, who was excitable, was very worked up. He was agitated and spoke quickly, and waved his arms in the air. "Carry on." I instructed Ebou, "I had better go and see what they want."

With a garden full of guests and a wedding feast about to be served that had already been detracted from by the bride's late arrival I did not need a problem with the military. The fact that they had guns was generally not a threat, very often they had no ammunition in them, but you could never be sure. My stress level must have been at an all time high, I often amazed myself at the calm exterior that I managed to portray, when inside my heart would pound against my chest. Sometimes I thought those around me must be able to hear my heart beat.

I followed Jed back into the bar.

"Can I help you gents?" I asked trying desperately not to let my voice quiver.

"What is going on here?" The officer, who I noted was a sergeant, aggressively asked me.

"We are having a programme, a wedding. A taubab man has married a Shendian girl." I replied.

"Not any longer. We want all of these people out of here. To save you embarrassment we will give you half an hour to get them out. If this programme is still in progress in half an hour's time, we will be back with reinforcements to close you down."

"Come on lads, be reasonable, we are just about to serve the food, we will give all of your boys some chop."

He didn't even reply, he just turned and walked out followed by his inferiors. It was unusual for the army or the police to refuse free food when offered as appeasement. This must be a serious threat. Jack the builder, who was sat at his usual table number five, opposite the bar, from where he could observe what was going on and soak up the atmosphere, rather than being in the hub of things, beckoned me over.

"Did I hear that right?" He asked.

"I guess so." I replied, not sure whether to laugh or to cry. "Looks like I have a tricky situation on my hands."

"What are you going to do?"

"I had better get the food served in double quick time! I will phone Sidi; hopefully he will know someone who will pull a few strings for me. If not it seems I'm right up the creek. I bet this is those bastards next door, jealous that I have more people in here than they have in La Parisian."

"Jed." Jack called, "bring me a pint every five minutes for the next half an hour please." Then to me he said, "I'll need plenty of refreshment to enjoy while I'm watching the best entertainment that you've provided in ages."

"Cheers" I said as I went into the house to phone Sidi.

I dialled Sidi's mobile, it rang and rang, with my heart beat increasing every time I heard the tone. Where was he? I asked myself, I expected him to keep his phone on him, so that I can call him if necessary. I seldom did call him, but this time when I really needed him, I was getting no reply. Eventually he did answer just as I was about to give up and replace the receiver.

"Where were you?" I asked him, before he even had a chance to speak. I really was het up by then.

"I left my phone in the car," he explained, "Someone told me they could hear it ringing."

"That's helpful; you know I always tell you to have it on you."

"O.K. O.K. why are you shouting? Have you got a problem, isn't your programme going well?"

"It was, but now there is a very big problem. I was just about to serve the food, and the army came and told me that they will close me down, if I don't get everyone out of here in half an hour."

"Don't be stupid they can't do that."
"I'm telling you that is what they said. They had guns and all, there were four of them in the bar, and others in the garden."

"Just carry on, I'm on my way."

"What do I do if they come back before you get here?"

"Don't worry, I will sort it out, just go back into the bar, and get on with your wedding," he told me sternly.

"Fine, fine, but I do worry, and you know that I'm afraid of guns."

I returned to the bar and instructed the kitchen to serve the food. I went out into the garden to find Paul and Jainaba to tell them that the food was about to be served, and ask them as the hosts, to be the first in line at the buffet table. I was careful not to alert them to any possible problems, but as we made our way inside Paul asked me.

"What was that all about before with the soldiers?"

"Nothing to worry about, just enjoy yourselves," I told him with more confidence than I felt.

The guests filed into the bar, behind Paul and Jainaba. I felt the same pride when I saw the kitchen staff, headed by Ebou, serving the buffet in their kitchen uniforms, as I had at Oliver's wedding. I kept a beady eye on the plates, the piles seemed to be getting low, but the queue of guests hardly seemed any smaller. I looked at the food, there was plenty left and I knew there was still more meat and vegetables in the kitchen, but the queue did seem endless, it still stretched the whole length of the bar and beyond.

The plates ran out, so we must have served the seventy-five meals that I was asked to cater for. I went into the kitchen, where the waiters were already collecting more to bring out.

"Wait a minute", I told them "I must know the exact amount of plates that are going out, that is the only way I can calculate how many meals we have served." They nodded and helped me look for more plates. We managed to find another twenty decent plates, and a few more that was not quite up to our usual standard, but would serve the purpose. Still the queue seemed endless and it wasn't long before Momodou came up to me with a message from the kitchen.

"We are completely out of plates."

"Come with me, we'll have to go out into the garden, and collect the plates from the people that have finished eating and wash them quickly, so that we can use them again."

We soon collected a sizable amount of plates; quite a lot of time had passed since we served the first of the guests and there were plenty of finished plates lying around. No-one questioned our clearing up in the middle of the party. Perhaps they thought I was just a tidy soul. Back in the kitchen the staff and I washed them and took them out to the tables where we were able to carry on serving.

Jerry, Paul's best man came to see me.

"How is the food going Helen? Paul is getting worried."

"O.K. at the moment, but what you can see on the table is the last of it. Where have all these people come from?"

"Paul doesn't know half of them, and I'm not sure that Jainaba does either. You know what Africans are like if they hear of free food."

"Sure. This is what I was afraid when Paul told me that verbal invites had been given out."

"Never mind, this is the end of them now. Paul thought there would be nothing left. You have managed well."

As I watched Jerry go back into the garden, I caught a glimpse of Sidi among the crowd, he gave me a 'thumbs up', and so I assumed that all was well. He was talking to two of the waiters, who then came indoors to collect some chairs. It was after that, that I realised that Sidi had several men with him. I didn't recognise any of them, but they looked important. They were all well dressed, tall and well built, there whole appearance was rather awesome, and the way the waiters approached them I could see that they were being treated with respect.

"Sidi wants us to take these gentlemen some food and drinks, is that alright?" Jed asked me. "And he wants you to go out and meet them."

"Fine, fine, do you know who they are?"

"Not all of them, but the ones I know are military. Important military."

I went into the garden, where Sidi introduced me to his companions. They were indeed high-ranking army officers. "You have a nice place here," one of them told me. "Why do The Peace Haven make you problems, it isn't nice to make problems for people on their wedding day."

I heartily agreed with him, then excused myself and went back into the kitchen. There was still ice cream to be served as a sweet. All African girls seem to have a liking for ice cream, and the cake had still to be decorated cut and served. I got on with the preparations for the dessert, much more relaxed now that the threat of the army arriving to close us appeared to be over. It was also a relief that we had managed to cater for the, larger than expected, wedding party.

Sidi would explain to me later, how he managed to avert the crises with the army .I knew from his behaviour towards the men that were with him, that he didn't know them very well. I was eager to hear what had happened, but more eager at the moment to successfully finish the catering, then at last I would be able to relax.

We had finally served 135 meals, a mammoth task, when we were only expecting 75 guests. I was proud of my kitchen staff; they had done well and they had coped without panicking, as I told them all the next day.

When I finally managed to talk to Sidi alone, he explained that he had spoken to an uncle of his who knew an important army officer. Sidi had gone to the army barracks that were in charge of our section of the tourist area where he talked to his uncle's friend and explained what had happened. It was this man and some of his colleagues who had sat in the garden with Sidi, ready to stop the soldiers who were trying to close me down. Fortunately they did not return. Sidi told me afterwards that whilst he was at the barracks he had found out that no official complaint had been made and that no orders had been issued for the closure of The Dominion. The soldiers that had come to close the bar must have been paid by The Peace Haven to do this and uncharitably I hoped that they wasted a great deal of money.

As Sidi explained to the army officers, we had paid license fees just like The Peace Haven, so surely we were entitled to have music the same as the hotel. The fact that we had a court injunction against us was a civil matter, of no concern to the army. Sitting around a table in my garden, enjoying the wedding festivities, they agreed.

I felt completely stressed out by the time I locked the gates of The Dominion that night. On reflection, on the surface at least, all had gone well. Paul and Jainaba had had a good day, and that had been the main objective. There was one thing I was certain of I would never forget their wedding day. Unfortunately Jack had left the bar at the end of the evening, without seeing the exciting entertainment that he had been anticipating, but the events of the day did bring on a whole new meaning of a 'shotgun wedding'.

The following morning as I had a coffee with the 'breakfast club' lads there was much banter flying around about Paul's wedding.

"You can all laugh." I told them, "At least I carried it off. I've proved I can put on a wedding against all adversity, so which one of you lads is brave enough to book the next one?"

I met with silence.

"Come on lads, I'll give you a good deal, and it will be low season soon. A girl has to earn a living you know."

"How about Terry and Lena?" volunteered Nick.

"Terry isn't here to defend himself, besides he's still married to Sally. How about you Nick?"

"Don't talk daft woman."

"I'm not; you know Maria wants a wedding."

"Yeah, sure she does. She's managed to get her hands on enough of my cash already. My God if she was my wife I would be bankrupt. Anyway, like Terry, I'm still married in the U.K."

"No you're not."

"True, but I tell her I am and don't you forget it. That's the best possible excuse for not getting married."

"You're a coward." I told him.

"Maybe I am, but I'm certainly not stupid."

Danish Dave had kept very quite all through this conversation. Dave had become an ever-increasing regular to the bar, and very often came in for his morning coffee with the lads. Dave had a girlfriend from Sierra Leonne, she was not a Freetonian, but came from a village way up country, where tribal traditions were of the utmost importance. Aysha, Dave's girlfriend had been in Shendi for a long while, and was well known around the tourist area as 'a lady of the night'. Many of the girls who came to Shendi, looking for work, ended up as prostitutes as there was not the employment in Shendi, which they imagined that there would be in a tourist orientated country. Many of the girls eventually manage to find permanent boy friends and settle down, but Aysha showed no signs of this. She was also foul mouthed, and her general behaviour was often an embarrassment to Dave. We were all bewildered by his infatuation with her.

In the early days of Dave's relationship with Aysha, many of us had tried to make him look realistically at his situation. Aysha rarely came into The Dominion with Dave, she would tell him that she didn't like the woman there as she had been in Shendi too long, and had seen and knew too much. She was right there. I had seen many people, male and female, ruined by African partners. I was suspicious of Aysha from the first time that I met her.

Dave softly, almost apologetically said "Sorry, I can't book a Dominion wedding Helen, mine will have to be in the village."

"You are joking I hope." Rick told him.

"No guys, I'm going to make an honest woman of Aysha."

"You got rocks in your head." Nick told him. "It would take more than a wedding to make Aysha an honest woman."

"O.K., O.K., I know, but I love her, I really do, I can't help that."

"When is the wedding going to be?" I asked Dave.

"Probably in the summer. It will be amazing, magical. I have to go to the village, and met the elders, and tell them I want to choose a virgin from their village for my bride."

This caused hoots of laughter.

"We misunderstood; we thought you were going to marry Aysha." Kevin said.

"Of course I'm marrying Aysha. The day after I visit the elders, they will organise a procession of village virgins, all dressed the same, in white shift dresses, with flimsy white veils over their faces. I will be sat in the middle and I have to choose the one that I want, which of course will be Aysha."

"What if you pick the wrong one? If they are all dressed the same, with their faces covered, you may not recognise Aysha." I told him.

"No. No, I would know Aysha anywhere."

"You will know her, if she opens her mouth." Rick informed him.

"Anyway, when I have picked her out, they will arrange the wedding for the following day."

"You're in cloud cuckoo land." Nick told him.

Terry arrived for his breakfast, and the lads turned their wedding banter towards him. I was relieved, as they were likely to all end up arguing with Dave. It was obvious that he was in love with Aysha, and none of us are very good at controlling our actions, when our emotions are in control.

Nigel and Alana joined the group; they had come in for an early lunch, while in our area doing their weekly shopping.

"We're trying to boast Helen's profits, by arranging more Dominion weddings." Kevin told them. "Did you hear about Paul and Jainaba's yesterday, now that one nearly did go with a bang?"

"Yeah, we've heard about this." Nigel told Kevin, and turning to me said. "Is there nothing that you wouldn't stoop to, to make sure everyone remembers your functions?"

"We think she staged it all too." Rick said.

"Anyway being you are all discussing weddings, I take it you haven't heard the news about the borders. We have just bought two extra bottles of gas, in case it goes on for a while."

"What are you talking about?" I asked Nigel.

"It seems that the powers-that-be, have fallen out with our less than friendly next door neighbours, over the rise in the river ferry fares and they have replied by closing the borders."

Shendi was continually having minor disputes with Furnanda, our neighbouring country, Furnanda had once been a Portuguese colony, their people were very proud of their links with Portugal, and still had much stronger ties with it than Shendi had with Britain. Most disputes were short lived, but if the borders had been closed, this did seem serious, and would have more dire consequences for Shendi than for Furnanda, as we imported necessities from them.

"Why have you bought extra gas?" Terry asked Nigel.

"Wake up Terry. The borders are closed. Where do our bottles of gas come from?"

"Oh no. Not only the gas eh?"

"No not only the gas, much of our food supplies, especially rice, that will hit the locals bad, but it is the gas that will affect us most."

"And cement." Nick said. "That will affect me more than gas. How long do you reckon this will last?"

"There's no knowing." Nigel informed us, "but you know what these governments are like, the more one digs their heels in, the more the other one will refuse to budge."

"Well at least you can't accuse me of organizing this lot." I said trying to lighten the general mood around the bar.

"I'm going," said Nick. "I'm off to get as many bags of cement as I can find, before they put the prices up, they are sure to do that if there is a shortage."

As Kevin watched Nick leave he said. "Humm that is all Nick worries about the price of bloody cement."

The situation was discussed be everyone that came into the bar that afternoon. All in all most of us considered the consequences to be serious. With the smooth running of the business being foremost in my mind, gas was indeed my largest concern. If some food were in short supply, hopefully we could find an alternative, but without gas, the kitchen simply could not function. Most Shendians didn't seem to think this would become too serious, but the ex-pat community were not so optimistic.

As goods were imported every day from Furnanda, it was only a few days before the first shortages became apparent. Gas was, as we had suspected the first casualty. As supplies dwindled, the suppliers that still had stock predictably increased their prices considerably. Within the first week prices rose by 150% this was a staggering increase for a small business like The Dominion to absorb. Black marketers were quick to appear.

Fishermen were going out at night, in their small dugout boats, and returning with a cargo of gas, instead of fish. With Shendi, only being a small country, these tiny inadequate vessels, didn't have far up the coast to travel to land on Furnanda's beaches, to purchase gas from their shopkeepers, who were only too eager to sell it to them at exorbitant prices. This made the price in Shendi rocket even farther. Food supplies were not fairing well either, rice was the first commodity to be in short supply, but other essentials like, flour, sugar, potatoes and chickens were all difficult to purchase.

Talking over the problem of gas with Ebou one day, I was pleased when he suggested that we started using charcoal in the kitchen, as there were still ample supplies in the local shops.

"Is it possible to use charcoal for our needs here?" I asked him.

"I don't see why not. We couldn't use it for everything, as you can't control the heat, but for boiling the kettle, and cooking the local dishes, it could be used, also for things like cooking the vegetables, in fact we could use it for a lot of things."

"We would need to buy charcoal burners, how much would that cost?"

"Not too expensive, we can buy locally made ones from Malaville market."

"But what about the fumes? They smell, in your compounds you cook outside."

"We couldn't use it in the kitchen; we will set the burners up in the yard, outside the kitchen door."

"O.K. we will give it a try, it would be much cheaper. I don't know how long I can continue to buy gas at the price it is now."

The following morning, while they were out shopping, Ebou and Sidi bought two large locally made charcoal burners, each large enough to use for either two large, or three smaller pans. These were placed as Ebou had suggested outside the back door of the kitchen. The burners were only about a foot high, so the staff sat on upturned drink crates when they were using them. They were not used to cooking like this at The Dominion, but I was well aware that this was how they prepared their meals at the compounds, so they would have the necessary skills.

The situation went from bad to worse. I initially bought gas from any source I could, Sidi spent much of his day driving around various suppliers but as time went on many of these sources dried up. Fewer fishermen were attempting the nightly gas runs. Not only was the sea in the area treacherous, especially for their small vessels, there was now soldiers patrolling looking out for smugglers. Rumours were always rife in Shendi, and news broadcasts, and the local papers were censored so it was difficult to establish the truth but I heard of at least three smugglers being shot and killed by the river patrols.

About four weeks into this crisis, when Sidi had been unable to buy us any gas that day, but had obtained a promise of two bottles for the following morning, I had a particularly busy evening. I gave a sigh of relief, when I saw the last orders being served; I could then relax with the knowledge that I would have gas before my lunchtime trade the following day. The kitchen staff were busy cleaning the kitchen at the end of their shift, when seven burly tourists, who I hadn't seen before, but I got the impression that they could well be lads on a fishing holiday, came into the bar.

"You still serving food luv?" one of them asked and confirming my opinion continued, "We have been out fishing all day, we were back later than we expected and we are starving." These were lads holidaying in Shendi for the first time. I didn't want to let them down, if they enjoyed fishing here, they could well become regular tourists; these were the sort of customer I needed. Without hesitating I showed them to a table and gave them menus. As I walked away from the table, it suddenly dawned on me that we might not have enough gas to cook meals.

I went into the kitchen, "Ebou, I've got seven fishing guys in the bar, will there be enough gas to cook for them?"

"It isn't finished, but we don't have much, it depends what they order, maybe we can use the charcoal for most of it."

I listened to the lads giving their orders to Momodou, not only did they order main courses, but they ordered starters that also needed cooking. Why couldn't they have ordered shrimp cocktails or melon for starters?

I followed Momdou into the kitchen to ask Ebou if they would be able to cope with the lad's meals.

"We will do our best, some of this can be cooked outside, and I think we will have just about enough gas for the rest."

"I hope the gas lasts out while they cook those meals, it's going to be touch and go." I told the lads around the bar as I made yet another journey into the kitchen to check on how things were progressing. I am sure that Ebou was too polite to tell me to go away; I must have been making him nervous.

"You're practically a Shendian now." Nick told me, "You can make an excuse for anything. Tell them you always serve rare chicken as well as rare steaks; say it's a custom here. They are first timers they will swallow that."

"And when they have a Shendian stomach tomorrow, they will know who to blame." I replied.

"No." Kevin chimed in, "it has to be the warm beer that they were drinking out on the boat."

Just then the waiters came out with the starters. So far all was well. As I put my head around the kitchen door again, Ebou called to me "All is fine, fine, we did the starters outside so we should be alright."

I was relieved to hear that. I stood behind the bar chatting to the ex-pat lads, and Jane who had come out that evening with Adam, which was unusual for her, with my fingers crossed behind my back, situations like this was not good for my blood pressure. It was true that the staff were good at improvising most Africans have had to be since childhood, but I wasn't accustomed to it.

I don't know what the reaction of those seven lads would have been, if they could have seen the kitchen staff preparing their meal. Some of it was prepared as they would expect in the kitchen but some of it being prepared by staff sat on drink crates, in our back yard over a charcoal burner, only about a foot above the ground. Sat nearby was my ever-faithful larger than life African cat, eyeing the pot, and wishing for the staff to spill some of the contents on the ground. I helped the waiters to serve the lads their main courses, hoping that my unsuspecting customers couldn't see the relief in my eyes, as I wished them 'bon appetite'. We had averted yet another crisis, but it was essential that Sidi was out exceptionally early the next morning searching for gas. It was unlikely that we had sufficient for the breakfast customers.

The phone rang as I settled back into the conversation around the bar.

"That's late. Must be more trouble." Terry reassured me.

"Give over, why must it be trouble? More likely to be my secret man, the one that I don't mention to you lot."

"Better not be." Kevin told me. "Nick and I will soon sort him out, if it is."

I rushed into the house to answer it; my curiosity was getting the better of me. Terry was right, the phone ringing at 11:30 pm, did usually spell trouble.

"Good evening The Dominion." I answered it.

"Hi Mum."

"Kevin. Hi love; this is a surprise at this time."

"Just wanted to tell you that you have been a gran for about the last four hours," he told me. "Steph had a little girl just after 7."

"What! Brilliant! Congratulations, that's a surprise. I wasn't expecting to hear that for a few weeks yet." I mumbled as the tears streamed down my face.

"I was surprised as well, or shocked rather, she is three weeks early."

"But is all O.K.?"

"Steph had a bit of a rough time and Karen, that's my daughter's name by the way, has a few small problems, but nothing too much to worry about, apparently that is to be expected with an early baby."

"Fine, I don't know what to say, I wasn't expecting to hear this yet, I'm just so thrilled."

I was overcome with emotion. I was overwhelmed when Kevin had told me Steph was pregnant, but now that baby Karen was here. This was reality. I was a grandmother. This put everything else into insignificance. What did it matter that I had no gas? What did it matter that I had a never-ending court case, like a ball and chain around my ankle? This brought on a whole new meaning to my life.

"Give Karen and Steph a hug for me, I love you all. I'll ring you tomorrow, to see if your girls are alright. I had better go now." I uttered through my tears I sat alone in my lounge for a few moments composing myself before I went back into the bar. I didn't want anyone to see me crying. Probably foolishly, I always tried to put on a tough exterior. Emotions were considered a weakness here. I couldn't afford to appear vulnerable.

The fishing lads had just finished their main courses, and had ordered another round of drinks as I went back into the bar.

"That filled a hole nicely luv. We will be back to see you again, thanks for cooking so late for us."

"No problem, we will be pleased to see you again."

Little did they know the stress their dinners had caused me, but by then I had more important things on my mind. Problems like the shortages that we had experienced over the past few weeks, were all part of 'Life in Shendi.'

"You O.K.?" Jane asked me, as I took up my normal position behind the bar. I had started to consider the bar, to be a barrier between me and the rest of the world. It was my comfort zone. I felt safe behind my bar.

"Yeah, yeah fine Jane. That was my Kevin; Steph has had a little girl." I tried so hard not to show my emotions, but I felt a single tear meander its way down my cheek.

"Oh Helen, that's brilliant. I'm so pleased for you."

"Ssh don't tell the lads please. Tomorrow we will have drinks all around to celebrate. I need to compose myself, men don't understand. This lot will think I'm crazy if I start crying."

"Come on girls stop whispering to yourselves. I have an important issue to raise here." Rick told me.

"What's your problem now Rick?" I asked.

"How are you going to cook my breakfast, when you have used the last of your gas cooking for those tourists?"

"How about charcoaled toast and barbecued eggs?" I asked him.

"Sounds like a fancy word for burnt to me."

"Don't be selfish, you know that a girl has got to earn a living, and I do charge the tourists more than I charge you!"

The lads banter could be relentless at times, but they helped me to see the lighter side of life, and now that I had a real family in the U.K., not only would I fight The Peace Haven until the bitter end, but I would also fight to get back to the U.K. to see my baby granddaughter.

Chapter Fourteen

Water Ways

I was up bright and early next morning, feeling very positive about the day despite the potential problems of running a restaurant without any cooking fuel. Nothing could stop me now, I was a grandmother and I would succeed. Even the sound of Sidi's car rattling to a halt outside failed to annoy me and his grinning face as he walked round the corner simply added to my good mood. I was even more pleased to hear his news.

"Morning Helen, you look happy today. You'll be even happier when I tell you I've bought in two bottles of gas. What's more I can get you more if you want it."

"Brilliant, and just in time for opening, I ran completely out last night. Rick will be pleased he will be able to have his breakfast and of course we want more but you won't find it easy to get any more will you?"

Sidi sat down, leaned back in his chair and smiled. "No problem. There seems to be more around than there has been. I even saw several shops with it in Malaville as I came in."

"Where are they getting it? Are the fishermen going into Furnanda again? No one in the bar last night had heard anything"

"I don't know but I did hear in the village last night that the borders were open again, but you know what village news is, I don't know if that is right."

"If that is right the prices should come down again, but I doubt if they will."

"Maybe they will or maybe not. Anyway it is good to see you smiling again; I didn't think that two bottles of gas could make you so happy."

"It hasn't. Yes I am very pleased about the gas but I've had some great news from home. Steph had a baby girl yesterday and they are going to call her Karen. Perhaps she is the good omen I've been waiting for. We need some good luck around here. Anyway, thanks for the gas and if you can get anymore I would be very pleased."

Ebou, when he came in to start preparing food confirmed that Sidi's village had heard some reliable news, for a change. The borders had been opened again at 6 o'clock the previous evening, and a steady convoy of lorries was filtering through with our much-needed supplies. The dispute over the ferry fares was still continuing, but the Furnadese government had agreed to re-open the borders on the condition that the two presidents meet to discuss the situation. The opening of the borders was welcome news for all of us. I had been driven to distraction trying to cope with cooking over charcoal, which obviously did not conform to the hygiene regime that I preferred. It was not simply a case of easier access to fuel either. Shortages had pushed up the prices of basic necessities such as rice to such a level that it was out of the reach of many of the locals.

"Any suggestions what I can have for breakfast?" Rick asked sarcastically as he came in.

"Whatever you want, I have gas." I told him. "We've heard that the borders are open again."

Rick sat down at his usual place and I took his order for bacon, egg, toast and tea. I was behind the bar making a list of what was needed from the store when Nick walked in and made his way over to Rick.

"At least I won't have you under my feet all day to-day." I told him as I took him a cup of tea.

"Don't bank on that. I wasted enough fuel yesterday searching for cement."

"I think the borders are open, so there should be some to-day."

"You sure?"

"No, but Sidi heard it in the village last night and Ebou told me the same when he came in. Apparently there is no trouble getting gas this morning so there should be other things, like cement, available."

"You two want to get a life." Rick told Nick. "She's only interested in gas, and all you think about is cement."

"Just getting our priorities right." I retorted. "Without gas, you wouldn't be eating that bacon butty."

Rick looked at Nick, who grinned and nodded in agreement. Deciding he was on a losing battle, Rick carried on with his breakfast. I was impressed how quickly supplies reached the shops, within two days most things were readily available again, and the recent crisis soon seemed like just another bad dream to me.

Things were settling down again when Colin, the head of maintenance at The Peace Haven came in one evening, earlier than usual, and made the comment that he would have to limit his drinking because tomorrow was an important day for him.

"You having a big event at the hotel?" I asked him, always anxious to find out what was going on next door.

"No. I'm flying down to Nigeria in the morning. I have a job interview at The Hilton."

"Are you serious? Nigeria? I've heard all sorts of horror stories from there, will you be safe?"

"I'll be O.K. I'm being met at the airport, but I do need to suss out how dangerous it is. People do exaggerate you know. Besides anything has to be better than having Claus breathing down my neck all day; things were bad when Smithers was here, but now it's unbearable, I've had enough."

"Have you heard the rumours that I have, about the hotel being up for sale?"

"Yes, but I don't know if there is any truth in them, and if there is a take- over Claus is likely to stay, and he is why I want out. He's a bastard."

"Don't tell me, I know. It was him that sent the army here to close me down, when I had Paul's wedding."

"That sounds like him. A take over maybe more beneficial to you, than to me, if it means a change in the top management"

"You maybe right. But if you are that fed up, you have to go if you get the chance. I'm not certain about Nigeria though."

"That's how I see it, and Nigeria, well, it will be different, a challenge. I will go down and see what they offer me. Keep it quiet please, I don't want next door to get wind that I'm looking around, I will be back late tomorrow evening, so they won't realize that I've been away."

Colin went to Nigeria, the next day, and surprised us all on his return by announcing that he had accepted an appointment with the flagship of The Hilton group. He would be missed by the ex-pats around the bar, and there was much speculation as to if he had really made the right decision. We had all heard many reports of bandits operating in Nigeria. Colin had told us, that he was to be given an armed guard, whenever he left the hotel compound. He felt this move would be the answer to his problems within The Peace Haven. He had not settled there, and felt no loyalty towards their management.

A small group of us were discussing Colin's decision around the bar, a few evenings later when we heard a commotion near the entrance. As I could hear Jed's raised voice above the noise I thought I had better go out and investigate what trouble my staff were causing now. In the midst of the crowd was one of the locals who I recognised as Mustapha from Reggie Preston's village. When I had agreed to take on the responsibility of Reggie's property until it was sold, I had engaged Mustapha as watchman at the compound. He seemed an ideal choice, as his shop was opposite the house making it the perfect vantage point during the day, and he had agreed to sleep at the compound at night. The agreement had been carried out with Sidi's help as Mustapha spoke no English and Sidi had arranged to visit the house weekly, on his way back to his own village. I was too busy to do this myself and because of Mustapha's lack of English would have had to take Sidi to translate for me anyway. Every month I gave Sidi Mustapha's salary from money that Reggie sent out to me regularly and every month Sidi returned with Mustapha's mark in the book as a receipt. This routine had been going on for some time now as the compound still had not sold, but as far as I was aware Sidi had been paying his weekly visits and delivering Mustapha's wages regularly.

"What's going on?" I asked Jed.

"This is the watchman from your friend's house."

"I know it's Mustapha, but what is the problem?" I could tell that Mustapha was very agitated as not only was his voice raised but he was waving his arms about and gesticulating wildly. "Please, please", I thought, "don't let there be any trouble like a break in or a flood."

Jed spoke to Mustapha and although I could not understand a word I could tell he was angry not scared. The crowd was getting larger and nosier as everyone around was determined to have his or her say. My security were trying to manhandle Mustapha off of the premises, even some of my kitchen staff, having heard the commotion, had left their duties and were gathered at the entrance joining in the argument.

Jed turned to me and said, "He is asking for his wages, he says he should have had them last week."

"Sidi took them to him last Friday, tell him that."

"He says he hasn't seen Sidi for two weeks." Jed went on. "But we are telling him he has been paid. Momodou knows Sidi went to pay him."

Momodou pushed forward, "Yes that's right, I know he has been paid, he is a bad man to say this."

I took a deep breath, "Just get him out of here." I told Jed. "I can't have all this going on with customers in the bar. Give him transport money from the till, and tell him I will sort this out with Sidi."

Jed went into the bar, and took fifty shillings from the till to give Mustapha for his transport back to the compound. I knew that the journey would cost a great deal less than this but the extra would help Mustapha to be satisfied with the outcome of the evenings' events. Mustapha thanked me and left, seemingly happy.

Mustapha might have been happy, but I wasn't: far from it. As far as I could see, either Sidi had stolen the money or Mustapha was trying to trick me into paying him twice. I would have to talk to Sidi, which I was reluctant to do. I was only too well aware that all my staff were untrustworthy, to a greater or lesser extent. Kevin and Nick once told me they had been for a drink in the hotel opposite, and as they left by the back entrance to cross the car park to The Dominion, they saw frozen chickens flying over my wall. I also knew that false receipts were easy to obtain for a few shillings, so I was aware that some of the receipts I was given from the daily shopping were not always correct. I even suspected that when I was off duty between 4pm and 7pm, and during the day shift on Sunday that false bills or no bill went out to customers, but since the episode with Jatou I had not been able to prove it. I had made an example of Jatou when I caught her doing that, but the resulting problems I had from that incident considerably out weighed the money that she had stolen. The staff were aware that any disputes between them and me, were very biased in their favour. I accepted this petty thieving, even in the U.K. the catering industry is considered one of the worst trades for staff pilfering; it tends to be considered a perk of the job. As an employer I monitored this as closely as possible, even to the point of sitting in the garden on a Sunday, with my friend Karen, making a note of all the tables in use, so that I could check if I had invoices for all of them. I did what I could but knowing how most Shendians live, I rather stupidly, turned a blind eye to many of the staff's smaller misdemeanours. All the ex-pats had similar tales to this and we would simply laugh about it. However, with Sidi, my concerns were deepening and I had become increasingly suspicious of him after some of his actions in the last year or two.

Petty thieving seemed almost a part of Shendian culture, at least amongst the locals that I heard about but would Sidi stoop as low as to steal, or "borrow" as the locals always termed it, Mustapha's salary? In Sidi's favour was that fact that Momodou had said that he knew Sidi had paid Mustapha, but I took that with a large pinch of salt. I knew, as did all the ex pats, that whenever there was a problem with staff they would all stick together and back each other up, even if it meant telling lies.

On the other hand there was the possibility that Mustapha was short of money, and had been hoping I would pay him again. He would guess that Sidi would not be at the bar at night, the only Shendians who came down to the tourist area after dark were those who had jobs there, and so Mustapha could gamble on seeing me without seeing Sidi.

The first thing to do was to look at the wages book. I went into the office and took it out. Looking at the last entry I saw, as I expected, a cross, but had Mustapha made it? I had no way of knowing. It was no good; I would have to talk to Sidi, hopefully before my staff told him what had happened. I went into the office and dialled his number. It rang and rang but finally he answered.

"Good evening Sidi"

"Helen, this is unusual, is there a problem?"

"Yes, there is. Mustapha from the house has just been here."

"What! Why would he come to the bar? He has my phone number; he knows he can call me if there is a problem at the house. I always tell him not to worry you, you are too busy. It is my job to sort out his problems. He is a bad man for disturbing you."

"No, no, there is no problem with the house but with him. He says he hasn't been paid this month. I gave you his money last week."

"Ah! So he is a very bad man and trying to create a problem."

"Well, have you paid him or what?"

"Helen, how can you ask that? Haven't I given you the book with his signature for his wages on it?"

"You have bought me back his wages book with a cross on it but it isn't a signature, just a mark"

"So you are trying to say that I have stolen the money. Helen, how could you? You know that I am honest. I would not cheat you or Mustapha."

"I'm just telling you that I have given you the money, and you had better get this sorted out and quick. I'm trying to run a business here, and I really don't need scenes like I've had here this evening, when I have customers in the bar."

"All right, all right. I will go around in the morning and see him before I come in."

"You do that, and early, there is a lot of shopping for the morning, so I need you and Ebou out early."

"Fine, fine, why are you talking so sharply to me?"

"I'm afraid that's how I'm feeling about all this. This is one problem I don't need; you will have to sort it out."

He put the phone down before I could say anymore.

The niggling doubts in my mind about Sidi were definitely increasing. I needed to be able to trust Sidi in some aspects of the business. He had lost my trust, like all of the staff, in many small ways, but if he were going to start being untrustworthy to a greater extent, this would severely add to my problems. When I returned to the bar, after phoning Sidi, I was still upset and bewildered by the situation. I wanted to believe Sidi, but I knew deep down I didn't. The lads around the bar asked what all the commotion had been about.

"Oh, nothing to worry about," I told them, "That was the watchman from Reggie's house causing a bit of trouble."

"You have enough problems of your own. Why do you take on everyone else's?" Terry asked me. "You should have known this would cause you aggro in the end."

I thought that was classic coming from him, whom I had helped out on many occasions.

"That's me Terry I'm stupid eh?"

"Well at least you know it," he told me.

"Thanks a lot for your support, Terry," I thought, but refrained from saying.

The next morning Sidi arrived bright and early. Over a cup of coffee we discussed things that needed to be done, while he was out shopping with Ebou, he made no mention of Mustapha or his wages. I knew it was down to me so, once the shopping was sorted out, I asked him. "Have you been around to Reggie's compound this morning?"

"Yes, I went on my way here."

"Well?"

"Well?"

"Don't just say well. You know what I mean. Tell me what happened, had Mustapha been paid?"

"Of course he had, I told you on the phone last night, you know that you gave me the money last week and I showed you the book"

"I know when I gave you the money, I have it written down. I have the book with the mark but is it his mark? I can't tell, that is why I'm asking if you had paid him."

"Are you accusing me of stealing the money?"

"I'm asking you if you paid him last week when I gave you the money. If you did, why did he come here last night causing a scene? It was embarrassing for me."

"Just drop it, he has had his money, he won't be coming here again."

Of course there was no way I could be sure, but I think that closing remark of Sidi's and his attitude that morning answered my question. I don't think Sidi had paid him the previous week, I believe he went to the compound that morning and gave him his salary. I would keep a watchful eye on Sidi, maybe his intention wasn't to steal the money, but to 'borrow' it for a while, and hadn't thought that Mustapha would come to the bar, but the fact that he had come, suggested to me that this wasn't the first occasion that his salary had been overdue.

Living in Shendi was often like living in a long running soap opera. No sooner was one crisis averted than another loomed, and today was to be no exception. That very lunchtime when I was still upset over Mustapha's wages and the uncertainty of that situation, Ebou came out of the kitchen and told me that there was no mains water.

When I first came to Shendi, water had not been a problem, but over the years it had become increasingly scarce. While water cuts were nowhere near as regular as power cuts, they did create more of a worry. Although the generator was expensive to run, it could be relied on when there were cuts. I had a reserve water tank, which had a high capacity, but when the bar was busy, which it was at the time, we used a large amount of water, and the reserve supply would only last two days at the most. There was one possible ray of hope. If the pressure of the water was lowered, as opposed to a complete shut down, we would have water in some of the outside taps, and possibly the public toilets, as these were closest to our mains connection. I called Latif, and asked him to check all of the taps.

After testing them all, he came into the bar and gave me the bad news. "We have no water anywhere, and shall I turn on the reserve tank?"

"Yes, we need water in the kitchen and the toilets, but stop watering the garden; we need to conserve as much water as we can." I then went into the kitchen and told Ebou that Latif was switching over to the tank, and asked him to reduce their water consumption wherever possible.

"Our water went off just before I came out." Terry told me when I went back into the bar.

"It must be fairly widespread then." I replied.

"Yeah, power we can cope without but water is a different matter; none of us can cope without it."

"At least I have my reserve tank, but if that runs out, I will be in trouble here. I may be able to run the restaurant without gas for a while but without water there is no chance."

The water was still off, when I went off duty for my afternoon break and I took a quicker shower than usual, as my contribution towards eking the water supply out as far as possible.

When I woke up after my afternoon nap, I found Sidi sat at the table in my garden, he went and ordered me a snack and both of us a coffee. It was unusual for him to come back to The Dominion in the evening, he knew if I needed him for anything I would phone him. We sat and chatted, while I ate, during our conversation, I rightly or wrongly kept thinking; he is trying to get back into my good books after falling from grace over Mustapha's wages. I think he knew that I didn't really believe him. Finally he stood up and I went into the bar wondering what was going on.

As I went through the door one of my regular tourists came over from his table near the entrance. He looked as if he had been looking for me, and wondered vaguely what was so important. Please, please I thought let it be good news.

"Helen, do you know that the staff are allowing people to fill up the 20 litre plastic containers from your outside tap?"

"You are joking! We are using the reserve tank."

"I thought you probably didn't know, I've been waiting for you to come in, not sure what to do. I've been sat over there for an hour, and there has been a continual queue ever since I've been here. Some of them have had several containers on a push-push."

"Thanks, I will sort it." I told him.

I went straight out to my entrance and as I had been told, there was a queue of locals stretching down The Peace Haven's car park nearly as far as the arch, many of which did have four or five containers on their push-push. Sidi must have seen this when he arrived. Why had he not told me? I was furious; I stormed back into the bar and called Jed over.

"What's going on out there?" I snapped.

"We're giving them water. It's a form of charity."

"Not any longer, we're not." I fumed. "Go out there and get rid of them."

"You can't deny people water, they have none in their compounds and we do have some. We have to share what we have; it says so in the Koran."

"Doesn't it also say in the Koran, that it is a man's duty to provide for his wife and family? How will you provide for yours if I have to close this place?"

With that I turned and called all the staff into the kitchen.

"I need to talk to you all about the water. Do none of you understand that we, like the people in their compounds, have no water either. We are using our reserve tank and that is all we have."

"We know that." Momodou told me. "But we do have some, these people have none, we have to give it to them."

"Fine, fine. So tell me what will happen tomorrow when our tank has run dry, and I have to close the bar. That will mean you won't have any wages. Is that O.K. for you and your families?"

"We don't understand what you mean."

"Exactly, I thought not. Now listen our tank should last for two days, if we all are careful. But I don't know how long it will last now that you have allowed these people to take so much. We will be lucky if it lasts until tomorrow lunchtime. When it runs out, that is it. We will not be able to cook; many dishes need water to be able to cook them. We won't be able to wash the dishes and glasses, you won't be able to wash your hands, nor will the toilets be able to be flushed. Has anybody any suggestions what we will be able to do, other than to close the business until the water comes back on again?"

"We didn't think." Jed said.

"Obviously, now get out there, and get these people off of my property, and let's get back to running our business and all of you had better hope that the mains water comes back on before we run out." I went to look for Sidi to get him to help Jed, in case the locals who were without water turned angry. He was not in the garden, I walked out the front, and his car had gone. He must have known what was going on and rightly guessing that I would be angry when I found out what was happening, he had wisely decided to leave before I had the chance to turn my anger on him.

Terry was laughing when I went back into the bar. "That was kind of you giving the locals water, Allah will reward you."

"Don't start; I'm not in the best of moods. I feel sorry for them, but the water I have I'm going to need. I can't believe the staff, they don't think."

Kevin came in soon afterwards.

"Somebody must have water down this way. The locals are getting it from somewhere near, there's a steady flow of push-pushes with water containers going up the Strip, I had to have my eyes everywhere driving down, they were weaving in and out of the traffic."

"You're having a laugh aren't you?" I told him.

"No Helen luv, why?"

"They've been getting it here. I'm using my reserve tank, and the silly sods have been giving it away."

"Come off it Helen, when was this, while you were off duty?"

"Yes."

"Wise up. How long have you lived here? If you weren't around they were selling it.
This bought on a few sniggers around the bar.

"Oh no! I hadn't even thought of that! But yeah, I expect you are right, the sods."

It wasn't very pleasant working behind the bar that evening. Jed, who was working with me, sulked all evening, because I had stopped them supplying the locals with water. He was so upset, that I suspected that Kevin had been right and that they had been charging for it. Maybe Sidi was behind that also, which might explain why he disappeared so quickly. I wasn't being as hard on the locals as the staff were trying to make me believe. Many of the villages in our area didn't have water supplied to all of the compounds, but had stand pipes in the streets at regular intervals. Some of these standpipes received their water from the mains supply; these villages would have been without water the same as we were. In other villages where it had not been viable to put mains pipes, the water company had sunk boreholes, to supply the standpipes. These villages still had water. There were a few such villages in the near vicinity. The locals could walk to these villages to fetch water with their push-pushes.

Besides Jed's bad mood, I also had to contend with the wise cracks from my regular lads, about how generous I had been giving my water away, when I didn't have much for myself. I decided to get them to change the subject.

"Terry it's your birthday on March 25th isn't it?"

"That's right, you should know, you've been celebrating it for a few years now. Am I having a party?"

"I usually give you one, don't I? But this year we will make it a double celebration."

"Why are you getting married?"

"Very funny. Colin is leaving for Nigeria on the evening of the 26th; we will have to give him a good send off."

"That's come around quickly." Rick said. "When he first mentioned it, it seemed a long way off."

I had succeeded in getting the lads off the subject of my water, they started chatting about Terry's birthday, they all agreed that we had to have a leaving party for Colin, and started making plans for the joint party.

I woke in the night. Silence. I sat up and listened carefully. There wasn't a sound outside. I cursed to myself. I had been hoping that when I woke, I would hear the sound of water flowing into the water tank, which was situated just outside of my bedroom. If mains water had come on during the night, the noise that it would make, as the tank filled from the pipe at the top of it, is loud, I would have expected it to wake me. I listened again, if it had been filling for a while and the water didn't have so far to fall, it is much quieter. I thought that I may have been mistaken, but I wasn't, we still had no water. I twisted and turned for the rest of the night. What could I do, when the reserve tank ran dry? I could see no alternative but to close the bar until the mains water was restored.

"This can't go on for long." Sidi tried to reassure me over coffee, when he came to collect Ebou for the mornings shopping.

"We will be out of water by this evening. Latif has checked how much is left in the tank. It's a shame that the staff gave so much away yesterday. Did you know anything about that?"

"No, how could I?"

"You must have seen them all waiting outside with their containers when you arrived."

"I didn't take any notice. Anyway that's past, forget about it now, let's think how we are going to manage. Famara has water, we have a borehole. I will get some 20litre containers. In fact you have some here in the store, I will take them with me when I go and bring them down this evening with water for you, if your mains doesn't come on. Just remember I can't bring many at a time, they are too heavy, they will damage the suspension of the car."

"We use loads of water, not only in the kitchen; think how much we need for flushing the toilets."

"I will get a boy from the village to drive back and forth all day, we will be able to get enough that way."

I was sceptical, we did use a large amount of water, and if I had to get my supply in the way that Sidi suggested it would be expensive. The lad's wages wouldn't be too much, but the diesel for the vehicle would be. However, it would be a temporary solution to the water problem and we would be able to stay open. By 3:30 that afternoon, my water tank was empty. Sidi had bought me a couple of trips of water, after he and Ebou had finished the shopping. That should last us the evening. Hopefully by the next morning the mains would be on again.

Before Latif went off duty that afternoon, I asked him to take one of the containers into my bathroom for me; I would need water in there. When I took my afternoon break, I went into the bathroom and looked at this container, and wondered how the locals managed permanently with only water from standpipes. How did they cope with personal hygiene? I was used to showering at that time of the day; I wouldn't feel clean if I only washed. A shower was necessary in this heat. I had been told that the locals poured water over themselves with a plastic cup. I knew that this was what I was going to have to do.

I fetched a plastic cup and a plastic bucket from the kitchen, and returned to my bathroom. The container with its 20 litres of water was heavy. I couldn't lift it properly. I raised it to my knees and gripped it between them. I was then able to tip some of its precious contents into my bucket. I placed the bucket in my bath. I stood in the bath and poured cups of water over myself until I was sufficiently wet to be able to make my shower gel lather. When I had washed myself, I once again poured cups of water over myself to rinse the shower gel off. I did not find this a pleasant experience, and hoped that this situation would not last much longer, but at least I was clean.

The following morning there was still no sign of our mains water being restored. Sidi bought a lad from Famara, who I had never met before, and told me he would be willing to transport water from the village for us, as long as we needed it, for the cost of his diesel and a small wage for himself. I was relieved to know that at least I could keep the business running during this crisis, but on top of the other problems we had experienced recently, I once again watched my profit margin dwindle.

During the days I had Latif, and in the evenings my security lads, to go into the toilets and fill the flush tanks, from the water containers each time the toilets were flushed. I instructed the staff not to mention to the tourists that we had no mains water. I was afraid that they would consider the kitchen unhygienic if they knew this, albeit that all the bars and restaurants were in the same boat. The hotels didn't have this problem as they all have their own boreholes.

This water shortage went on longer than any of us imagined that it would but it only affected those of us on mains water. The fact that the boreholes didn't run dry, meant that water was available, but something was causing the shortage; although no-one knew what. Rumour had it that because the pipes were so old, narrow and badly maintained they simply couldn't cope with the increase in demand for water, from the new buildings that had been constructed. It seemed a reasonable explanation but we never did find out. Occasionally, at night when demand was low, The Dominion had water, but with very low pressure. It was so low that it didn't reach the house or the kitchen, but there was a trickle of water from some of our outside taps, that were closest to our mains connection. When this happened my night security lads could fill some of the containers for us from those outside taps. After the first fortnight of this water shortage, I started to consider the inconveniences caused by it as normal.

Terry and Colin's party, held with the bar still waterless, made a welcome light relief during these problems. Everyone enjoyed themselves. I hoped Colin would leave with some fond memories of Shendi, in spite of the difficulties he had had with The Peace Haven management. By the end of the evening I was the only sober person in the bar, so I didn't expect to be serving breakfast very early the next morning, I thought most of the lads would be having a lie in. Despite that I was in the bar at my normal time, hoping that Colin would find time to pop in and say good-bye before he flew out that evening, but due to the condition he was in, when he left the party, I thought it was doubtful I would ever see him again.

That lunchtime the usual lads were sat around the bar, drinking coffees, teas and soft drinks, having very little conversation. They all denied it, but I suspected that they were all felt slightly hung over.

"Hiya mate." Kevin said as Colin came into the bar. "We didn't expect to see you to-day."

"I had to pop up and see Helen," Colin told him.

I was amazed knowing how much alcohol he had consumed the previous evening that he looked so bright eyed and fresh compared to the rest of the lads around the bar. Under his arm he had a large roll of paper. He put this down on the bar and said to me. "There you are Helen, a going away present from me. Thanks for all the fun whilst I've been here and for last night. This is what I promised you before I left. Take it into the house and put it away until it can be of use to you."

I told Momodou to get Colin a drink, and I took the rolled up paper into the house, eager to see what Colin had given me. I was bewildered.

What had he promised me? As I unrolled the paper and spread it on my table, I let out a gasp of amazement. It was the plans Mr. Smithers had shown Simon and I, when we visited him in his office, when we very first arrived. A long time ago Colin had promised me he would get me a copy of the plans before he left, but his promise had completely slipped my mind. This roll did not contain copies; it contained the original plans just as Simon and I had seen years ago. Quickly I looked at each sheet. There were two options it appeared; one showing 56 bedrooms built where The Dominion now stood and the other showing the same number of apartments, taking in The Dominion property and part of the car park. This was proof that they intended building over The Dominion land. To me it was conclusive evidence that the court case was a farce, they wanted me off my land, plain and simple. I would let Ousman know that I had these plans; surely this would be to our advantage in the court case.

That was in the future, what about now? I had to keep them safe but didn't know how. Hastily but carefully I re-rolled the sheets and re-tied the ribbon around them. Where could I hide them? I went into my bedroom, and rapidly pushed them under my bed, then taking a deep breath I returned to the bar.

I called Colin aside. "Thanks, Colin; I don't know what else to say. That is the original set. How on earth did you get them?"

"I knew exactly where they were, but I didn't want to take them, when they may have missed them while I was still here. Like this I will be in Nigeria, before they realize that they are gone."

"I didn't expect you to take any risks on my behalf."

"It was no problem, Helen, honest. I simply went into the office, where I knew they were kept, took them out of the filing cabinet, and walked out with them under my arm."
"But the security at the arch could see you coming in here with them."

"They wouldn't know what I was carrying; besides being obvious is often the best policy, it doesn't arouse suspicion."

I was sorry to see Colin leave, he had become a good friend, and together with the other lads around the bar, we had shared many laughs. Still if he had not gone, I would not have been given the plans so some good came out of it.

We came back into the bar from seeing Colin into his taxi and Kevin remarked, "Well that is one of us on his travels, the next one of us to go will be Dave. I met him up the Strip earlier and he was telling me that he flies down to Sierra Leone next week for his wedding."

"Already?" I questioned. "He told me it would probably be August or September."

"He's bought it forward. Aysha is eager apparently."

"I bet she is." Nick said. "Can't wait to get her hands on his cash."

"I don't think he has that much, that is why he has started working," remarked Kevin.

"He doesn't have much here, that is why he is working for Kawso, but he has plenty of assets in Denmark. If Aysha got her hands on all that she would be a very wealthy lady by African standards," added Rick.

Dave had recently been employed by Kawso, a Shendian who owned a restaurant near here, to run a new venture for him, an estate agency. Kawso had been educated in Europe and had a keen business sense. Dave was the only one employed in that side of Kawso's business, and together they were making a success of it. Tourists intending to purchase land or a holiday home were more inclined to put their faith in a fellow European.

Conversation that evening centred on the wisdom of the changes in lifestyle being made by both Colin and Dave. General consensus was that, Colin might have better job prospects, but generally he would have more problems in Nigeria than he had in Shendi; and although Sierra Leone was now considered a safe area that maybe Dave's marriage would be a danger zone. We might never find out about Colin but we would find out about Dave. Just as we were deciding that, he came into the bar.

"Hi Dave, a G and T?" I asked.

"Put that on my bill." Terry said, "it might be your last chance to take a drink from me."
"Why's that?" Dave queried.

"Kevin has been telling us you are off virgin hunting."

Dave laughed. "Yeah, that's right, but I will only be gone about ten days."

"Don't talk daft man. It will take a hell of a lot longer than ten days to find a virgin in Sierra Leone, let alone marry one."

"You Mickey taking so and sos. We can all have our imaginations. A virgin, I may not find, but I do know that I want to marry Aysha, I have never been more certain of anything in my life."

"Good luck to you, you will certainly need it." Rick told him.

Joking about weddings and virgins relentlessly continued into the early hours, I felt that maybe Dave regretted coming in to see the lads before he travelled to Freetown, the following week. I was glad he came, this banter made a pleasant respite for me, from the continuous worry of the harsh reality of running the business without the luxury of water.

Vivian, who was a relatively new friend of mine, came in for a coffee the next morning. Viv had had a house built in Shendi, largely encouraged to do so by Dave, whom she had met several years ago when they were both staying at the same Shendian hotel, As a result Viv, together with her long-term partner Greg, had become close friends of Dave. It was Dave who first introduced me to Viv. He bought her to meet me, when she came over to stay in her new house, without Greg. Dave had told me that she didn't have many female friends here, and that he was confident that we would get on well. We did, and Viv and Greg often visited The Dominion, usually during the day, or the early evening.

Over coffee that morning we discussed Dave's forthcoming visit to Sierra Leone. "I'm worried about him." Viv told me. "You know the village is several hours journey up country. Dave says he doesn't see another white man the whole time he is there."

"I don't suppose he does. Most ex-pats here live near the coast, Sierra Leone is probably the same, and with the recent troubles there, I don't suppose there are many ex-pats anyway." I told her.

"I don't think he should go alone, he should be taking someone with him. I would go if he asked me."

"No, Viv he wouldn't ask you, just think, you've said it's several hours journey to the village, even if he can hire a decent vehicle, which is unlikely, it will be a hazardous journey, and when you get there the heat would be very oppressive. Goodness knows what the water situation is like, you would hate it, and Dave knows that."

"The water situation isn't exactly good here at the moment, is it?"

"No, but we are hoping that this is only a temporary set back, there a water shortage is the norm."

"Yeah, I know you're right, but I don't like to think of Dave going alone. He has plenty of friends, someone would go with him. Anyone of your ex-pats here would go, if he asked them."

"Yes, I'm sure they would, they would consider it an adventure, but the lads have been quite relentless in their jokes about weddings and virgins. Dave is a proud man. I don't think he would ask any of them."

"I know. He is a grown man, but I can't help worrying about him."

Viv and I put Dave to the back of our minds and chattered on about general things as we finished our coffees.

The following Thursday was an important evening for me. The Dominion had been chosen to host the monthly dinner for the Port Albert branch of "The Dog House Club." The club is a world wide charity based society with twelve members in each branch. Once a year, each member has his turn to host their monthly meeting and dinner. There are concrete rules laid down as to the form these dinners must take. There has to be at least three courses. At least two different red, and two different white wines must be served and the meal must conclude with cheese and biscuits served with port. If the other members consider anything unsatisfactory, the host, who foots the bill for everything, including all the drinks, before and after the meal, is fined. This fine, along with other fines that are levied during the evening goes into the group's chosen charities. The club does raise a substantial amount of money from these 'fines' at their dinners, and from the several charity events that they arrange during the year. In a country like Shendi, there are ample projects for their money to be channelled towards.

Last year I had hosted Nigel's dinner for him, and he had asked me to arrange his again this year. I enjoyed the challenge of this, and was grateful for the chance to show off my culinary skills. It was not a large dinner party; each of the twelve members could invite a guest if they wished, so at the most there would be twenty-four. The biggest problem was the port; this was not always readily available. Last year I had been lucky enough to find some, surprisingly in a small local shop. This year, I purchased two extra bottles at Christmas, when the wholesalers do stock it, and hid it away in my office, in the hope that Nigel would choose The Dominion for his dinner again when his turn to play host came around.

The members of the club were mostly influential ex-pats, many with connections with The High Commission, so I was determined to make a success of the evening for myself, besides not wanting to let Nigel down. Before the dinner the club members needed somewhere private to hold their monthly meeting. I would cordon off part of the garden to ensure their privacy, and then they would retire into the bar for their meal.

"How about if I make you a punch to serve during your meeting?" I suggested to Nigel when we were discussing the menu. "That will be a bit of a novelty, so may win you a few brownie points, and they will drink that slower than most drinks, so should work out cheaper as well."

"Sounds good to me Helen, anything different goes down well."

"And maybe a sorbet to clear the palette, if we are serving garlic mushrooms for starters."

"That's the way sweetie, let me leave it to you, all was fine last year, so you know what they expect."

I knew Nigel would be satisfied as long as I produced him everything that was within their guidelines. Last year he had paid me in sterling, or as we called it in Shendi, 'Queen's Heads', which was an added bonus as I could put those aside for my eventual return to the U.K. and I was hoping he would do the same this year. He had also given me a healthy tip, so I was determined everything would be done correctly again this year. Nigel had given me plenty of notice of the date of the diner but just a few days before it I received a visit from a warden from the High Commission. It seemed that another naval ship was due in and after last year's party I was on the list of approved bars. However, the first night of the visit coincided with Nigel's diner and although no party was to be laid on, the bar would be busy. This was good for business but I did wonder how I would cope if there was no water.

Sidi phoned me from the village, as I was relaxing with a quick coffee and scrambled egg on toast before facing what promised to be my busiest Thursday evening of the season.

"Abdul, the lad that brings the water is here with me," he explained. "There is a problem with the water; so many people are coming to the village to use our borehole that the water is now so low it is dirty. It should be all right again tomorrow; it will fill again overnight when no one is drawing water from it. I've told Abdul dirty water is no good to you."

"What do you mean by dirty water?"

"Well—er—it's sort of hazy, it's got bits of sand in it."

"Tell him to bring it. It will be no good in the kitchen, but I'm expecting to be busy, we can use it to flush the toilets."

I quickly finished my snack, and went to see how many containers of water we had. There were six, less than I had anticipated, but if used sparingly, it might last the evening, but I was doubtful. I asked the security lads to carry the remaining containers into the kitchen, so that there was no possibility of the clean water getting muddled with the cloudy water that Abdul was bringing to us.

"Abdul will be bringing some more containers of water shortly, but they are cloudy, it is no use in the kitchen. Make sure you keep it out here near the toilets, it can be used to put in the flush tanks." I instructed them as they returned to their post by the gate.

I went back to the kitchen to prepare the punch, ready for Nigel's meeting in the garden, thinking about the water situation. At first it had been a novelty showering with a bucket and plastic cup, and washing and rinsing the dishes in a giant plastic laundry bowls instead of in the sink, but it had been four weeks since I had last had any mains water and the novelty had worn off. The situation was getting desperate, not only for us, but also for the locals. Some were walking for miles with their wheelbarrows in search of a borehole. When they located water, they often faced the wrath of those living near the borehole, who accused them of stealing their water. They seemed to have forgotten the need to share what they had, in the name of charity, as my staff had initially told me the Koran instructed us to do.

The evening progressed well; the punch was a huge success. With their meeting over my V.I.P. guests had started their dinner. They had eaten their starters and were having their lemon sorbets, which I presented to them proudly. I had been unable to buy any, and a chef from one of the hotels had shown me how to make it. Considering it was my first attempt, I was pleased with the results. As I expected, we did have a steady stream of navy lads, together with my regular tourists; the evening was very hectic. I had no time to dwell on the water, or rather its lack.

"Ebou wants you in the kitchen." Jed came and told me as I was dealing with a bill at the bar.

I turned and went into the kitchen to find Ebou, dreading that he was about to tell me of some disaster that had happened with our guest's main course.

"Look at this water Abdul has bought us. It is no good," and he pointed to a container full of muddy looking water.

"You're right. Have you used all the containers that the security bought in here earlier?"

"Yes, that is finished."

"Right, let me think. Do you need anymore for cooking?" I asked remembering that I had about half a container in my bathroom.

"No, cooking is fine but we can't use this for washing the dishes."

"You will just have to leave them; we will have to wash them in the morning, when hopefully we will have some clean water. Most people have finished eating; it is only the dinner party that will have greasy dishes. It's the glasses I'm worried about; let's hope we have enough for the rest of the evening."

Just as I said that, Momodou came into the kitchen with a tray full of the fancy cocktail glasses I had used to serve the sorbets. There was an extremely gooey mess trickling down inside each of the glasses, which we knew that by morning, in this heat would be a haven for germs, and probably food for ants. Ebou just looked at me expectantly; I felt he thought I was going to conjure up some clean water. I sometimes thought the Africans consider that Taubabs could produce anything on command. Shendians definitely had great faith in their jujus; maybe they did think that all white men were magicians.

"Just leave them there." I told Momodou as I pointed to a spare space on top of one of the kitchen units, to Ebou I said. "Come on, let's get on with things, we have a main course to serve to our dinner party."

The evening progressed, and everything was fine except for the constant worry that we would run out of clean glasses. Wherever possible we served repeat drinks in the same glasses. I had also been to the storeroom, and collected the spare glasses stored there but would it be enough? Was it fate that things like this always seemed to happen when we were at our busiest, was it jujus working against me or was I getting paranoid and exaggerating everything in my mind? I was relieved when the early hours arrived. Most of the tourists had retired to their beds, the sailors returned to their ship and Nigel's dinner party started to say their farewells and drift off to their homes. Finally I was left with Nigel and a couple of his guests, plus my usual late night ex-pats around the bar.

"You look stressed," Kevin told me. "The dinner party prove too much for you?"

"That's an understatement, I have had no water, we haven't been able to wash any dishes or glasses, since mid evening and so there is hardly a table top in the kitchen without a dirty glass on it."

"Why? Where is the lad that's been getting your water?" Terry asked.

"He bought some this evening, but it was full of silt, it could only be used to flush the toilets. This water situation is getting ridiculous. They are hoping the borehole will be all right again in the morning."

"If you haven't got any tomorrow, I will go in the pick up and see if I can find you some." Nick told me.

Everyone soon drank up and went home. They undoubtedly saw my fatigue. Relived to be alone at last, I collected the last of the glasses and took them into the kitchen. I glanced around me; there were glasses everywhere, and I didn't realize I had so many. There were several glass dishes with the remains of ice cream and trifle in them, dirty plates from late suppers, pans and bowls from the kitchen and enough cutlery to start a shop with. The sorbet dishes were probably the worst, but there were also liqueur glasses that were sticky, and many beer mugs, with the remains of froth on them; their smell turned my stomach. I felt my eyes sting with tears behind the lids. I must be strong. I would not give in to tears over a few dirty dishes. I had faced worse problems than a pile of washing up. Too late. My eyes smarted as the warm tears spilt down over my cheeks. I felt so utterly helpless.

I wiped the tears away with the back of my hand, and started locking the bar up for the night. I brightened myself up to go and say 'good night' to my security, and to instruct them to keep trying the outside taps over night, and to fill as many containers as possible if we did get any water supply.

When I finally got into bed the tears flowed in earnest. I was so deflated. I had come through a lot, but now I was totally physically and mentally exhausted. I was so tired and drained. I did not know how much longer I could cope with the continual problems that I faced in Shendi. Sometimes in the depths of the night I still imagined I was stuck in some awful nightmare, and would eventually wake-up and find myself, tucked up in my familiar bed, in my cosy little house, back on the island, with Simon by my side.

No, this was not a dream. I woke early the next morning alone, in my now familiar bed at The Dominion in Shendi. I rose well before the day staff were due to arrive. It was as usual a bright sunny morning, even when

I was in low spirits, there was nothing cheered me more than the wall-to-wall sunshine, sometimes I felt that alone made everything worthwhile. I went out to see the night security, felling much happier than I had the previous evening.

"Did we get any water during the night?" I asked expectantly.

"Very small, small we have filled ten containers."

"That's fabulous; at least I will be able to start washing the glasses. When I've unlocked will you carry them into the kitchen for me please."

This they did and I prepared myself for the mammoth task ahead. I fetched two of the brightly coloured plastic laundry bowls, filled one with cold water to rinse the glasses, and set about boiling kettles to fill the other with hot water to wash them. I placed both these bowls on the floor, as I couldn't lift the water containers to fill the bowls, if I had put them any higher. Besides there was nowhere to put the bowls every conceivable space was filled with dirty glasses.

Like my staff, when they were cooking over charcoal, I up turned a drinks crate to sit on, and set about my task. Stupid as it may sound, I enjoyed the solitude sat there, getting on with the job at hand, before the day staff arrived. I really was in much higher spirits than last night; I couldn't always explain my mood changes. Hard work never fazed me, but I was not so good at coping with all the unexpected circumstances, that 'Life in Shendi' seemed to throw at me.

Two weeks later I woke with a start in the middle of the night. I had been woken by a loud noise outside, which startled me. I didn't know what was happening. As I came to, I soon realized it was my water tank filling. The relief I felt was immense. Altogether there had been six weeks that we had been without water in the bar or the house. On reflection, I was amazed how we had survived, and managed to cope so adequately. The staff were very adaptable, as they had been when we had no gas; they could find ways of coping and even making a profit. Europeans like me did not find this as easy as our African counterparts. I jumped out of bed, in spite of the early hour, and rushed to the bathroom to put the tap on. I had water. I stood there with the water seeping through my fingers, watching it swirling around the sink then running down the plughole. It was liquid gold. It was very early. I returned to my bed, knowing I was unlikely to sleep due to my euphoria, but I knew I had a long day ahead of me and had to try and rest.

I was up bright and early, the next day. I momentarily turned on the tap over the bathroom sink, to convince myself that I did have water, and it hadn't all been a dream. I stepped into the bath and turned the shower on, I had had water there also, I stood for ages allowing the cool liquid to run through my hair and down over my body, it felt so good, For the past six weeks, my hair had felt continually sticky, with only cups of water to rinse it, it was impossible to thoroughly remove the shampoo. After shampooing that morning I was able to completely rinse the shampoo away. I stood under the shower with the refreshing water tingling all over my body, taking a long luxurious shower. This was sheer bliss. As I dried myself, I felt so refreshed. I counted my blessings, and knew that I truly understood that it is the simple things in life that mean so much.

I was in high spirits while I polished the bar, waiting for my early morning regulars to arrive. Rick cycled in for his pot of tea with eggs bacon and toast; he was usually the first to arrive. He was closely followed by Nick who always came in for his morning coffee. I had the usual morning teasing from the lads, often rude remarks about how frightening I looked when my hair was hanging wet in 'rats tails' if I had washed it and been unable use my hairdryer when we had no electricity.

"You're full of bubbles to-day, what have you got to be so happy about?" Nick asked.

"I was full of bubbles not so long ago. I have mains water. I've just had a shower, it was gorgeous."

"I thought it smelt sweeter in here to-day." Rick said. "Mine came back on yesterday evening."

"It came on in the middle of the night here. I stood letting it run through my fingers, at about three o'clock this morning, I couldn't believe it was for real."

"I worry about you sometimes." Nick said. "I've heard something else that might cheer you up, do you think you are up to hearing more possibly good news, or shall I ask your shrink if he thinks you can cope with it?"

"Spit it out, good news I can always cope with, it's bad news I'm not so good at."

"I said possibly good news, not definitely. I've heard through one of Maria's high positioned uncles, so I think there is some element of truth in it, that The Peace Haven has been sold."

"Really, do you know who to?"

"Well I'm hearing Hussaini, have you heard of him?"

"Yes, but I don't know much about him."

"He's a Saudi business man, well heeled, a multi-multi millionaire, very close to the President. So this may not mean the end of your problems. Apparently he has a string of hotels, mostly in the Middle East, but he is into other things also, such as farming and construction. They say he wants to build another five star hotel, farther along the coast, maybe The Peace Haven is just a foot hold into the country for him."

"I won't get too excited, a take over could go either way for me. At the moment things are going nowhere, at least I may know where I stand."

"If what I hear is right the President is welcoming him with open arms, which he is bound to do, this is a very wealthy man, willing to invest a small fortune in Shendi. I hear he is going to build roads in exchange for favours, so he is likely to get anything he asks for." Nick explained to me.

"Fine, I get what you are saying, but change is often good. At least I maybe able to start afresh with my negotiations over my entrance."

Nick went off to collect his workers saying he would see me later and Rick went with him to get a lift up to his bank. I was left on my own wondering what difference, if any, a change in ownership would mean to me, if in fact Nick was right about the sale. In his favour was the fact that due to his association with influential Shendians his news could generally be relied on. Also, knowing how much I would welcome the news surely he wouldn't have told me if he wasn't sure? Against it was the fact that rumours were what we lived on in Shendi. There was no way of knowing if it was true and if it was, what would it mean to me? It could mark the beginning of the end or it may have no significance whatsoever. I refused to even think about it. I would simply concentrate on the return of the water which was true and was great news. What would be would be about the sale of Peace Haven.

Chapter Fifteen

Money To Burn

I was still in high spirits when Rick and Nick left after their breakfasts. Nick was generally right with information he gave me, due to his association with influential Shendians. He wouldn't have told me about a possible sale of The Peace Haven, knowing it was news I would welcome, if he weren't confident of the rumour's source. What would this mean to me? It could mark the beginning of the end or it might have no significance whatsoever. Enough I had work to do.

With that decision made, I went on a tour of the gardens with Latif. Generally the garden has a thorough watering every day in dry season but six weeks without water in the dry season, had had serious consequences for the gardens. Latif had been watering with the cleanest of the wastewater from the kitchen but this had been insufficient to keep the garden in prime condition. The fruit trees in my side of the garden faired better than the plants in the main garden. The citrus and mango trees which were never watered in the wild were adapted to the drought with their greatest need for water in the rainy season, when their fruit was swelling and ripening. But the vegetable garden was a complete disaster area. Latif's whole crop had died and we would need to replant everything. Until we could replenish our own garden I would now need to buy all the kitchen and salad vegetables for the next few months. Once again my mind was reassessing my profit margin.

"You will have a lot of work out here, Latif. I want you to concentrate on this garden first." I told him as we strolled through the beer garden.

"Shouldn't I try and sort out the vegetable garden first?" he asked, which was a sensible question given how much we relied on our home grown vegetables.

"No, the tourists like sitting out here, because it is peaceful, and they enjoy looking at the plants, if we lose this garden, we may lose some of our tourists also. Most of the plants we have here, people in the U.K. can only grow in small pots in the heat of their homes, or in glass houses in their gardens. They can't grow outside in English gardens as it is too cold."

"But Ebou needs the vegetables in the kitchen."

"I agree but I'm hoping much of the beer garden will spring back to life in a few days with some thorough watering. Then you can see what can be done in the other garden. The citrus trees and the mango trees are fine. They are not accustomed to being watered but the vegetables are already dead. You will have to pull them all out and dig the garden again. Then we will get some new seeds and plants and start all over, but I want this garden to be your priority."

I knew Latif didn't really understand me. Most of the plants in the beer garden grow along the sandy roadways in the villages in abundance. He couldn't comprehend that the tourists appreciated sitting among these common plants, relaxing in our garden, but I knew he would do as I instructed him, even if he was bewildered by it. Like all locals, Latif felt things were grown to eat otherwise it was a waste of effort. In a way I agreed with Latif. The lack of home grown vegetables would affect my profit margin but tourists did like the garden, it was a strong selling point for The Dominion.

I stood on my stage, and looked over the wall at The Peace Haven, and felt a pang of jealousy as I saw their garden. It was in full bloom and in pristine condition. They had their own borehole and had not been affected by the water shortage. A familiar voice broke into my thoughts.

"What's so interesting over The Peace Haven's wall or are you thinking of making a take over bid? It is up for sale you know." It was Dave back from his wedding in Sierra Leone.

"Hi Dave. How are you? I wasn't expecting you back just yet. How is Aysha? Is she with you?"

"No, I've left her at the village. I will go back for her in a few weeks. It is traditional for the bride to stay with her family for a while after the wedding, so I decided to come back. I was only kicking my heels down there, and Kawso needs me up here, now that the business is getting on its feet, I can't afford to be away for too long. Anyway, how are you and how are things going here?"

"Fine at the moment. The water has been off all the time you were away, but it came back on again during the night, which is such a relief, I just hope it lasts. As for The Peace Haven being for sale, Nick has heard that it has already been sold."

"Kawso told me that the water in the restaurant had been off but was on this morning. I didn't realise it had been off for so long. It must have been hard without it. The Peace Haven sold? Maybe but Kawso hasn't mentioned that, and he is usually in the know. If he had heard that he would he would have told me to tell you."

"Nick heard it from one of Maria's uncles; he seemed to think it was reliable information."

"Does he know who is supposed to have bought it?"

"He says Hussaini."

"Ah, that would make sense, he is close to the President, so the powers that be would still have a hold over the hotel, or even the President may remain a share holder, we will have to wait and see. In the meantime I'll have a coffee and tell you all about the wedding, before the rabble arrive."

Dave and I sat in the garden enjoying a coffee as he enthused about his wedding, and showed me the many photos he had. It was as he had previously described in the bar started with an audience with the village Elders who were all very highly respected men in their village. This audience was held in a shabby little mud hut, stinking of the chickens and goats that had obviously only recently been ejected from it, and furnished only with reed mats. Dave had sat in the centre of the floor surrounded by seven elders sitting on similar mats. The elders asked Dave to explain why he had come to their village in search of a bride. Not knowing how he should answer, and being temporarily distracted by a goat wandering through the circle he hesitated for a moment. What if he said the wrong thing, what if he insulted them? Taking a deep breath and lifting a chicken from his lap he started his speech. He told them he lived in Shendi, and news of the good virtues of the brides from their village had spread as far as there. He explained he wanted a wife that would take care of him and that he had heard girls from their village were groomed from an early age to look after their men folk. He also insisted he marry a virgin.

"Ah, a virgin," one of the elders said to him. "You have come to the right place; we take special care of the girls here, to ensure they are in perfect condition when they are given to their husbands."

It did cross my mind to wonder what had gone wrong in Aysha's case but I said nothing. The elders accepted Dave as a potential husband for one of their maidens; they obviously took their responsibilities towards their girls very seriously. A procession of village virgins was arranged for noon the following day. Dave had not seen Aysha since his arrival in the village, and had started getting nervous about the whole affair. In spite of his bravado in front of the lads in the bar, he had started to get serious doubts about his ability to recognise Aysha. All the girls would be dressed the same, in white to signify their virgin status. They were to wear veils over their faces. A mistake could be made and what would happen then he wondered.

Dave had spent the remainder of the day, after he had been accepted by the elders, wondering around the outskirts of the village, hoping Aysha would find a way of contacting him, and giving him some means of recognising her the following day. He didn't see Aysha, and even though he was the centre of the local's curiosity, especially the children, most of whom would never have seen a white person, nobody spoke to him. He was completely alone and isolated. He had regrets that he hadn't tried harder to persuade Aysha to have a civil ceremony in Shendi. Following his unsettling day, Dave had an extremely restless night.

Dressed in the African robes the village Chief had given him, the following day at noon, Dave was sat on a small wooden chair, which had had a brightly coloured cushion ceremoniously placed on it, in the shade of a large mango tree in the middle of the village. The girls were escorted out from a large mud round house, which was used as the village meeting place, and paraded in front of him. They were all dressed exactly alike, their heads slightly lowered to the ground. There were about twenty girls for him to choose from. He had not expected so many. I could imagine the jibes the lads would make about there being twenty virgins in one small remote village in Sierra Leone if Dave related his story in the bar.

Fear started to grip him, what if he did choose the wrong girl? Would they force him to marry her? Where was Aysha? He knew she was the only one in the village that would help him. A seemingly endless line of girls filed slowly passed him. Dave's stomach turned over and over, he was in turmoil. Suddenly his heart lightened. The girl third from the end, he thought was Aysha, he wasn't quite sure why, he couldn't really see her, he thought it was her walk, he couldn't be sure. He kept his eyes on this girl, hoping she would make some sort of a sign to him. As she strolled past him, she raised her head slightly; all of the others had kept their heads bowed. This had to be Aysha. The veil covering the girl's heads and faces were flimsy, as she raised her head, he was sure he recognised her dark almond shaped eyes that he knew so well.

After filing passed Dave the girls stood in a row, with the full heat of the midday sun blazing down on them. One of the elders approached Dave and told him to make his choice; he could walk up and down the line examining the girls for as long as he wanted. When he had made his choice he had to walk up to the girl and tap her on the shoulder. She would then remove her veil, and her identity would be made known to him. Dave slowly walked up and down the line, a number of times. He was certain by now which one was Aysha, but he was determined, after the stress she had put him through, to reverse the situation, and make her sweat for a while.

He walked up to a couple and looked into their faces, which were recognisable from close up, and walked on again. He could not keep this up for long, the relentless heat of the sun, was getting too much for Dave, who unlike the girls, had no protection on his head.

He walked up to Aysha; hesitated for a while, building the momentum of the occasion and slowly tapped her on the shoulder. She hastily removed her veil. Dave told me, the look in her eyes, and the smile that gradually spread across her face, would always stay in his memory, and was worth all the stress and anxiety he had been through since he had arrived at the village.

Aysha was then whisked away by an elderly lady, before they had even had the chance to speak to each other. It was explained to Dave, that now he had chosen his bride, she would be looked after by the wives of the elders, who would prepare her for the wedding ceremony the next day.

All of the women set about preparing the wedding feast, while the men of the village started celebrating; this partying went on well into the night. Dave who couldn't communicate with many of them, retired early to be bright and fresh for his wedding. The actual ceremony was simple compared to the build up and the celebrations that followed. In fact Dave was hardly aware that the marriage had taken place. I thought he seemed disappointed by this, as he glossed over it quickly, saying little compared to the excitement he had in his voice when he told me about the pageantry of the 'choosing of the bride'. After the ceremony the celebrations started in earnest quietly at first, then becoming much noisier as the day slipped into the evening. The gentle tribal rituals of the afternoon, built into fast and furious tribal dances with cresendoing drumbeats as the night progressed.

Finally, Dave and Aysha were escorted to the hut that contained nothing else but their 'marriage bed', by four burly tribesmen. These tribesmen were clad from head to foot in tribal regalia and brightly coloured masks which hide every part of their bodies. Dave could only see their large ebony almond eyes: these seemed to bear a close resemblance to Aysha's and Dave wondered if they were her brothers. After they entered their hut, the sound of the drums softened, and the beat slowed to a regular tempo, but continued the whole of the night.

The next morning Dave was shocked when Aysha told him, she would be expected to go back to her family compound for another month, before Dave could claim her as his wife. He had not expected this, he had made plans to return to Shendi, he had work to do, Kawso was expecting him back, and he was determined to take his wife with him. After much persuasion from Aysha, he decided to go along with this stipulation. He knew that if he argued against the villagers, being greatly out numbered, he would have no chance of over ruling their tribal traditions. He had done all this as he knew it was Aysha's wishes, so he considered another month wasn't too long to wait for what he really wanted, which was to have Aysha with him as his wife.

As Dave had just finished telling me about his experiences in Sierra Leone, Terry came in for a late breakfast, so the two of us went into the bar to talk to him. Dave related a much shorter version of his wedding ceremony to Terry.

"Well, well, well." Terry exclaimed. "I really didn't think a virgin would be that easy to find in Sierra Leone. I didn't expect to see you again until way after next Christmas."

"You can laugh, I told you I would prove you all wrong, and I will. Just wait till I get Aysha up here. You will see that you were wrong about her. She will be a good wife, I'm completely confident of that."

The lads were all pleased to see Dave back and know that he was safe, many of them had been sceptical, and were concerned about him while he was away but none of them was more relived to see him back than Viv and I.

Over coffee the next morning Viv, Greg and I discussed the wedding.

"Dave is so proud." I told them. "He was here with me yesterday morning, showing me the photos and explaining the proceedings to me in detail."

"You girls." Greg chaffed us. "Dramas, dramas, you have to be dramatical about everything, I don't know what you two thought could possibly have gone wrong. Aysha was there she would have made sure nothing happened to Dave."

"O.K. if you say so, but I'm not convinced she would make sure he was alright. He was miles away from civilization, not a white man in sight; you never know what might happen." Viv told him.

"You were the one saying you would have gone with him. What would you have done if there had been any problems?" Greg asked Viv.

"Alright. Anyway he is back now; I just hope everything will be fine when Aysha arrives. My feminine instincts don't trust her."

Things were settling down well, we only had one water cut in the following week for a few hours. I did panic when this first happened; the thought of another prolonged period without water was unbearable. My relief when the mains came on again, only a few short hours later, was nearly as great as it had been when it returned after six weeks. The high tourist season was drawing to a close, it had been a fairly successful season, but the unrelenting strains that had plagued this year had left my bank balance less healthy than I would like it for the start of low season. I would survive. I always had done, over the past low seasons. I had to; there was really no other option.

Rumours were rife about the sale of The Peace Haven but that was all. Several weeks had past since Nick first mentioned it to me and I had expected to hear something concrete by now if they had been true. Whenever I went out I always spoke to the hotel's security at the arch, and they would often be willing to talk for a brief while. These lads had told me they had heard the rumours and they were also hoping they were true, as Claus often made their lives unbearable. From the outbursts I had heard, I knew this to be true. I knew that they felt no allegiance towards the hotel's management and I looked upon them as allies in the enemy camp.

Hussaini's name had started to be heard in the news bulletins on the radio almost daily, and his popularity soured with the publicity he was receiving. He was pouring money into Shendi in a large way. He was building roads up country, which would be a boast to the farmers, giving them much easier access to the large markets in Malaville and Port Albert. He was obviously intending to impress the President, and by all accounts he was succeeding.

Whether the rumours were true or not, I had a bar to run and towards the end of the season, I found more reason to doubt Sidi. It was the end of a busy Saturday evening, after I had washed the last of the glasses, I went into the office to cash up the last of the evening's takings. As was my practice I had cashed up the bulk of the takings two hours earlier at about 11.30pm just prior to sending the bar staff home. Besides saving time at the end of the evening, this let me check if the takings were correct whilst the staff were still on the premises.

This particular Saturday I cashed up the remainder of the money and unfastened my bunch of keys from inside my pocket. Shaking the safe key loose I tried to put it in the keyhole but it wouldn't go in. Tiredness must be getting to me I thought and tried again. No luck. I tried again. It still didn't seem to fit. I started to panic and my hands started to shake. I pushed and prodded it. It wouldn't budge. I couldn't be this tired. I'd opened the safe hundreds of times; it must be a problem with the safe. But, and this was what worried me, there hadn't been a problem with it just two hours ago, when I had done the main cashing up for the evening.

It was Saturday night. This was my 'cockroach night'. Every Saturday, the kitchen staff completely cleared the kitchen of every dish, plate and cooking utensil, and after I had closed, it was my job to spray every nook and cranny of the kitchen with a strong industrial insect repellent, to ensure that we were cockroach free. This was not a job I enjoyed. I would don an old dress, and a tatty headscarf to protect my hair from the spray, and to prevent dieing cockroaches falling into my hair. Liverpool Kevin had bought me a mask, as he insisted this practice wasn't healthy for me. I'm sure he was probably right, but it was a necessity.

I decided to go into the house, and get changed ready for spraying, then go back into the office and try once again to open the safe. By then I might be calmer and my hands less shaky. The safe was old, it had originally belonged to the Dutch couple, and maybe the lock was getting stiff. I had had a problem with it once before, and Latif had sprayed it with oil. I hadn't had a problem with it from then until now.

I went back into the office, feeling very nervous as I went over to the desk. The safe wasn't very big, and had originally stood on the floor. To make it accessible whilst sitting at the desk, and because Simon and I had thought that a determined man would be able to lift it, we had had it cemented to a base of concrete blocks, bringing it up to a reasonable height. Normally I sat at the desk and turned the key but now I bent down slightly, until I was level with the lock and started to enter the key. Suddenly I stopped. From this new angle I could see bright scratch marks around the rim of the lock and on the top. Metal tarnishes quickly in Shendi so I knew that these marks had to be fresh.

I put the key in, or rather tried to. It went part way in and then stuck and refused to go any farther. I looked again at the new scratches. Someone had clearly tried to get into the safe. My hands shook as the tension flowed over my body, I could feel my heart beating, a lump rose into my throat and I thought I was about to cry. Taking a deep breath I went outside and examined the office door. The lock on the door looked fine, but it was obvious to me that someone had been in the office in the last two hours. I looked again at the door lock. It was a new one that I had had to have fitted six months earlier at the start of the high season, when I had found the office door lock damaged and looking as if someone had tried to force it. I had thought then that it was a failed break in but the night security had tried to convince me that I had forced it myself, as the lock was stiff, and sometimes difficult to open.

At the time, Latif had bought a new lock which he had fitted the same day. He had given me the three new keys that came with it and I had put them away. It was not until I saw that the office door lock hadn't been tampered with, that it crossed my mind, either Latif or Sidi, who had insisted on collecting Latif from the locksmiths, could have had a fourth key cut. It would have been difficult for Sidi to have one cut without Latif's knowledge, but I knew they all worked together against me. One of the keys I had on my key ring that I always kept with me. The other two I had hidden, one in each of the upstairs bedrooms. I doubted it, but knowing how the staff always watched what I was doing, it was possible they realized that I had taken those keys upstairs. The upstairs rooms were always kept locked. There was only one key for those rooms and that was also on my key ring. It was rare that I entered the upstairs now; there was no necessity to do so, as I didn't use these rooms anymore. I decided there and then to check if those two keys were still where I had hidden them.

I slowly walked up the wooden outside staircase that led to these rooms. My trembling hand put the key in the lock, as I told myself to pull myself together, what could there possibly be in these empty rooms to frighten me but I had always had a fear of unused rooms, even back on the island. I gingerly put my hand inside and felt for the light switch and peered in before entering. With my nerves getting the better of me, as they had started to do quite regularly by then, I was very conscious that the only means of exit from those upstairs rooms was via the narrow passage as you entered, there was no way of escaping if someone entered behind me. (I had never liked the design of the house, too many narrow passageways for my liking.)

Just as I went in I saw Pouka, one of the security boys, walk under the stairway and glance up at me, without saying a word. He was starting out on one of his regular patrols which I expected them to carry out every quarter of an hour. I wondered what he was thinking. They knew my routine every night after I closed, did he suspect I knew something was wrong? I quickly checked the two hiding places for the spare keys, they were both still there. If someone had got into the office, without any sign of entry, there had to be another key. I went back to the door and saw that Pouka, by now, was on his mobile phone. He came around the corner from the direction of the generator room, I wondered who he was talking to, and what was so important that he was on the phone while he was patrolling. He finished his conversation as he saw me descending the stairs.

"Has anyone been here this evening?" I asked him.

"I don't know what you mean." Pouka replied.

"Has Sidi maybe been here, and I haven't seen him, or maybe Latif, or any of the staff that are not usually here in the evening."

"No. Why should they come here so late?"

"I don't know, they could have come here to collect something, I just wondered."

"I haven't seen anyone."

"You are my security, you would have seen if someone had been here, wouldn't you?"

"Yes."

"And you have been walking the perimeter every 15 minutes, have you?"

"You know we do. Why is there a problem?"

"No, everything is fine, I will be doing the kitchen in a few moments so I will say good night."

I went back into the office and examined the safe again, I wasn't imagining it; there were scratch marks and there was no way my key was going to go into the lock. What should I do, should I phone Sidi or should I leave it until morning? No, if I was awake, then he could be awake as well. I took out my mobile and dialled Sidi's number. He answered quickly.

"It's late," he said. "Are you alright? Is there a problem?"

"I can't open the safe."

"What do you mean, you can't open the safe?"

"As I say, it was fine when I cashed up just before the staff went home. I put that money in, but now my key won't go in, and it looks as if someone has tried to open the safe."

"Are you saying the office has been broken into?"

"No, there is no sign of a break in."

"Then you are imagining it."

"No, I'm not imagining it, my key will not go into the lock, and there are scratch marks near the top of the door and around the keyhole."

"You don't need to open it tonight do you?"

"I was going to put the last of the takings in it, but that's not much, I can put that in the house for tonight, but I will need to get into the safe in the morning."

"It's very late Helen, and aren't you spraying tonight?"

"Yes, and that takes me best part of an hour but this business of the safe is worrying."

"Yes I agree but just forget about the safe, and go and get on with the spraying or you won't have any sleep tonight. We can't do anything now. I was in bed, you woke me up you know; I will come down early in the morning, we will get it open somehow, don't worry."

Sidi had answered his phone on the second ring. He may have been in bed, but he certainly hadn't been asleep. I wondered if it had been him that Pouka had been talking to on his mobile, maybe he was warning him I was aware that something was wrong, or was my paranoia once again getting the better of me.

I went into the house, and hid the money in my bedroom; when I had done that, I returned to the kitchen and started my spraying. I am afraid that I did not concentrate too well on the spraying; my brain was darting from one thing to another. It must have been after three o'clock, before I finally slipped exhausted into my bed. I was too tired and too worried to sleep and spent my time tossing and turning, until finally I gave up the uneven battle and got up.

Sidi didn't usually work on a Sunday, but he was at The Dominion early the next morning as he said he would be. We went towards the office and as I unlocked the door, he said. "There has been no break in here."

"I know that, but look at these scratch marks on the safe." I said pointing the marks out to him.

"Those, oh Helen, come on, you could have done that anytime while putting the key in the lock."

"What, these up above the door as well." I answered, showing him the scratch marks at the top.

He ignored my comment, held out his hand and said, "Give me the key, let me see if I can open it."

He could no more unlock it that I had been able to the night before. He hesitated then said. "It's no good, it won't open, I will go and get a welder friend of mine; he will be able to cut it open."

"A welder!" I cried "You can't. There is money in there, and not only mine. I also have my passport, and some of the ex-pats passports. I don't want a welder he will set the lot alight."

"Don't be daft. I will make sure he is careful, look he will cut it here." He told me as he pointed to the side of the safe, where the metal rods from the lock were housed. "If he cuts it here, he will be able to take this metal piece out, and then we can push the metal prongs back into the lock, and the safe will open."

It sounded simple, but I was a long way from convinced.

"I will need to buy a new safe won't I?" I asked as usual thinking about the cost of this, money was a commodity I was fast running out of.

"Maybe not. Lets get it open first, and then we will see what we can do."

"I need it open, until it is I can't send the chef out shopping."

Sidi went off to fetch his friend and I went into the bar. My spirits were at a low point when Kevin and Dave came in for their breakfasts. I explained what had happened to them. Neither of them made much of a comment, but I could tell from their faces that they had the same instincts about this as I had.

"Don't worry, Helen." Kevin told me, "We know you have money to burn."

"True, but it's not only my money in there, I have some of Terry's and Rod's, and remember your passport is in there Dave, as well as mine and a couple of others."

"Oh yeah, my passport, I will be needing it again soon, to go and claim Aysha."

"Oh wait a moment I've just had a great thought," Kevin said "I want to be there when you explain to Terry you had a welder brake into your safe and his money accidentally went up in smoke."

They both laughed, their repartee usually cheered me up, but it did not work as a tonic for me on that particular morning. I hoped Sidi and his friend knew what they were talking about, as good as Africans are at improvising, I was not convinced that a welder was the man for the job at hand.

Shortly afterwards I saw Sidi return with his friend. When I saw them walking past the bar with the welding apparatus and the gas bottle, my heart started to beat faster. I followed them, into the office. They spoke between themselves in one of the local languages and I only understood a small portion of their conversation. The welder ran his fingers up the side of the safe, and reached for his welding gun. He put on his goggles, and switched the gas bottle on, then his gun. The noise was deafening in the confined space of my small office, and the heat from the flame was intense.

"Stop!" I shrieked.

The welder switched the flame off. "What's the matter?"

"You can't do that, there is paper in there."

"Go back in the bar Helen." Sidi told me. "I know you are too nervous for this. He knows what he is doing. He is going to cut here; nothing is going to get burnt. He tells me it will take about 20 minutes. O.K."

"Fine, fine, but I know exactly what is in there. Alright?"

Sidi let out a large sigh. "Helen, you are tired and anxious otherwise you would not say that. Do you think we would touch your money? I will call you as soon as it is open."

I did go back into the bar. I couldn't bear to watch, the office was too small for all three of us and the bulky welding equipment. With only the small window high up in the wall for ventilation, the fumes were starting to aggravate my throat. By the time I went back into the bar, Rick was sat eating his breakfast. The noise of the welding could easily be heard and the smell of the smouldering metal was filtering through.

"What on earth are you having done?" Rick asked.

"Don't ask! I couldn't unlock the safe. Sidi has bought a welder to cut it open."

"Sounds like a good idea. I assume you have fireproof money inside it."

"Don't even go there. I'm not happy about it."

Just then Nick walked in. "Don't mention the noise or the strange smell in here, it seems to be a sore point." Rick advised him. "Helen has Sidi and a welder breaking into her safe, but best not to comment on it."

"Ah-well-umm maybe it will be alright! You have to give the welders their due; some of them are good. Sidi wouldn't be that stupid as to let anyone loose with a blowtorch on your safe, if he couldn't do the job. Or would he?"

As Nick was saying this Sidi came to the bar door, and beckoned to me. I followed him back into the office. To my amazement the safe door was open and the contents unharmed.

"Brilliant." I said with relief. "I really didn't think you would be able to do that."

"I told you not to worry, now you empty the safe and go and hide it somewhere for the time being, while we go into Malaville with the lock and see what can be done with it. We may be gone a long while."

"What do you mean? Why are you taking the lock into Malaville, the safe is damaged beyond repair, so why repair the lock?"

"I can fix the safe. If we can either get a locksmith to repair the lock or if we can find a new lock to fit the safe, it will be an easy job. Once I have fitted the lock, I only have to weld the metal up here, where I have damaged it." The welder confidentially told me, as he pointed to the work he had just done.

I was still dubious, but so far he had done what he had said he would do, so I should have had more faith in him. I gave them sufficient money for what they were likely to have to buy for these repairs.

They were gone for some hours, and when they returned they had a third man with them. I was busy with the lunchtime rush in the bar by then. Sidi came in to see me and, asking for the office key, explained they had bought a locksmith with them. He stayed about half and hour and then I could hear the welder using his blowtorch again. By the time he had finished welding the bar was quietening down and I ventured into the office to see how things were progressing. Sidi and the welder were both examining the job, with a sense of pride.

"Have you managed to do it?" I asked optimistically.

"It's done." Sidi smugly told me.

I ran my fingers up the side of the safe, where the welding had been done.

"Here's the key." Sidi said as he handed me a large unfamiliar key. "It is a little bit stiff, I will put some oil in the lock to make it easier, you see if you can open it."

"But this key is totally different, it won't fit."

"It is a new lock, that's why the key is different, you try it."

To my surprise the key did fit, and although, as Sidi had said, it was stiff, it worked, and I could open and lock my safe again. After bartering with the welder over the payment for his work, he was paid, and Sidi drove him back to his welding shop.

I didn't see Sidi again until he arrived for work the following morning; I queried with him why I had a new lock for the safe with only one key.

"It is not a new lock," he told me. "It is a reconditioned one. If you want another key I can take the one you have with me, I can have one cut while I'm out shopping with Ebou."

"I only need one, I was only asking. I just thought it was normal to have three keys."

"You ask about everything. I don't think you trust anyone; that is not good you know."

Sidi was right; at one time I had trusted everyone until they proved otherwise but not now. Perhaps it had all started when Simon left, perhaps it was as a result of being continually let down in Shendi but by now I trusted no-one Shendian or otherwise. I knew it wasn't good to be like this, and it certainly was no good for my nerves, but there it was. I was without a doubt getting paranoid.

After Sidi and Ebou had gone out shopping, I got on with things with a spring in my step. This was a new day, and the anxiety of yesterday, with the tension I had over the safe was gone. Robert was arriving on the afternoon's flight for another short break with my regular fix of family photos from Kevin. Kevin was able to keep me up to date with Karen's progress by posting photos of her to various friends of mine, when they were due to come to Shendi and I knew that Robert would have some. It was two months since I had received my last batch of photos, I knew at her age Karen would have changed considerably since then and I waited impatiently for Robert and my photos.

When I saw Robert enter during the evening, I was quickly out from behind the bar to welcome him. I gave him his usual hug and greeted him with. "Good to see you Robert, you look well, but first things first, have you received my photos from Kevin?"

"Don't fret Helen, here they are." He said as he handed me a large white envelope, my hand was trembling with anticipation as I took it from him.

"Let me go inside and open this, I don't want everyone to see my tears." I told him jokingly, but I knew I would shed a few tears as I first looked at Karen's photos, I always did, but I liked to keep these moments private.

I beat a hasty retreat into my house. As I expected I did have tears in my eyes as I excitedly glanced through the photos. Karen was beautiful but no longer a baby, she was crawling and her hair had grown considerably, she was a little girl now. I had missed out on so much. This was the grandchild that I hadn't dared dream of having, and now I had missed her important early months. This time was irreplaceable. My tears were a mixture of pride and misgivings. I must get out of The Dominion and Shendi. I must get back to the U.K. and see my granddaughter. This was paramount in my mind. I was determined to get out of this situation, and take command of my life again.

The following morning I was returning from, what many of my regulars referred to as my 'meals on flip-flops', which was delivering meals on a tray to some of the shops and offices in the near vicinity, in this case breakfast to a lady working in one of the nearby shops, I was stopped by The Peace Haven's security lads at the arch.

"Good morning Helen, have you heard that the stories of a take over were right?"

"Good morning, no, I haven't."

"We attended a meeting early this morning, and were officially told, as we had heard, the hotel has been bought by Hussaini."

"How are the staff feeling about this?"

"There is lots of talk going on; we don't know how this will affect us yet. Nothing was said about Claus, we would all like to hear that he was going."

"Thanks for telling me. I will also have to wait and see if this will affect me."

I was pleased with this news. Hussaini's popularity was spreading fast. Hopefully I may at least be able to discuss my position with the new management. I would wait awhile and let the dust settle before deciding on my best options.

Nick, Robert and Rick were sat at their usual breakfast table when I returned to the bar. Still carrying the tray of dishes from my delivery, I went over and sat with them.

"Ah up lads that's our peace shattered lads, she's come to put her tuppence worth in." Nick told the others.

"Shut up, I've something important to tell you."

"Important, I don't do important, time I was going." Rick said.

"Just listen to me." I ordered them; "You remember you told me about The Peace Haven being sold to Hussaini, Nick? Well it's true; the staff had a meeting this morning and they were told then. The security at the arch has just told me."

"How long ago did I tell you that?" Nick asked.

"I don't know, a long while now."

"I've told you before to have faith in my contacts. I wouldn't have told you if I didn't think it was right." Nick told me, sitting back in his chair and folding his arms with a smug grin on his face.

"Perhaps I should start listening to you, anyway I welcome this news. It may possibly give me a little chink of light at the end of the tunnel."

"Oh no. Don't get on too much of a high." Rick warned me. "We can't cope when you come back down with a bang."

"Give over!" I told him as I picked up my tray, and took it into the kitchen.

Low season ticked by slowly with no major upsets. Business was quiet; many evenings I only had my regular lads sat around the bar, and a handful of tourists. During low season most of the few tourists that came were either bird watchers or charity workers, who generally went to bed early, so I was able to take things a bit easier and build up my strength for the following high season. There were no visible developments at The Peace Haven. Claus was still the manager, but I had heard mutterings from the staff that the new owners were not happy with his methods of management. Hussaini was known to be a tough, ruthless businessman, but he definitely had a human side to his nature, and looked after the welfare of his workmen. Claus had no consideration whatsoever for his staff, or their feelings. I knew this from the countless times I had heard him yelling and screaming at them, often swearing and humiliating them. The morale among the staff remained very low, on several occasions tourists staying at the hotel had commented to me about the conditions the hotel's staff worked under.

When I hadn't been expecting to hear any news, one of the cleaners from La Parisian called out to me, as I crossed the car park from the supermarket, one morning.

"Helen, we are all very excited, we have just heard Claus is going."

"Are you sure?"

"Oh yes, it is official. Our new manager is arriving this afternoon and Claus leaves next week."

"I bet you are pleased, but don't get too excited, he maybe even worse than Claus." I warned her.

"That's impossible. We have been told the new man is starting now, so he can make changes before high season starts again."

"Do you know anything about him?"

"Not a lot, he is Tunisian, and has been the manger of a big hotel in Oman."

"This seems like good news for you, and maybe for me also, let me know what is happening please."

Things were moving at the hotel at last. I knew someone like Husssaini would not buy a hotel like The Peace Haven and leave things the way they were, he was sure to want to improve it. The cleaner had said the new manager had been a manager of a hotel in Oman, this was more than likely one of Hussaini's hotels, he owned several hotels in the Middle East. Hopefully this was a positive move as far as I was concerned. I would watch the new manager's arrival with bated breath. I would bide my time for a while, then when I thought the time seemed right, I would make an appointment to introduce myself to this Tunisian.

Meanwhile, Dave had been down to Sierra Leone again, to claim Aysha and bring her back to Shendi. All did not seem to be going as well as Dave had anticipated. He came in most evening by himself for a quick drink and often spoke around the bar about arguments between them, and her behaviour when she was with others, whether his friends or business contacts. When they did come in together they did not seem like a newly married couple, more like two people who were finding it difficult to like each other.

One evening there was a particularly bitter row, because Dave had, in the past, told Aysha, he would get a visa for her to go to the U.K. to visit his parents. As yet he had still to collect the necessary forms from the High Commission and Aysha resented this. We knew that Dave had told us he would like to take her to meet his family, but that she wasn't behaving very well, so he wouldn't take her till she learnt to control herself better. He didn't enlighten us on this, but those who knew here well said that she could be very abusive and foul mouthed. A few days after the row it was clear that her behaviour had not improved and that the visit to the UK was no nearer. It was lunchtime and they were sitting at the bar. I heard Dave explain to her that he would take her to the U.K. when she learnt to treat people with more respect. "My father is an old man, like the elders in your village," he told her. "He would be shocked at how you sometimes behave. I have told you we will go and see him when your behaviour is better."

She turned towards him and with a face twisted with contempt, snarled "I know your fucking father is old, you don't need to tell me that. He is in his eighties. That is why I need to go and visit him. He can't live much longer. It is time the old bastard died and left us all his money."

Dave, who had just had a swig of his beer, inadvertently spat it over the bar in horror. I could not believe my ears; I thought I must have misheard. I got a cloth, and wiped the beer off the counter without any comment.

"Sorry Helen, I didn't mean to do that. Come on Aysha, drink up, we're going home and you had better forget about going to England for a long while yet."

After they had gone, Terry who had been sat quietly in the corner of the bar, drinking his lunchtime pot of tea commented "Let Dave enthuse about his virgin bride now, and I will tell him a thing or two."

"Let it be, Terry." I told him. "I think Dave knows himself that he has made a huge mistake, we all knew she would get worse and not better after the marriage, but there is no point in us bringing it all up to him. He must feel bad enough as it is."

"Yeah, you are right. Most of the silly sods here need to get their brains out of their trousers and back in their heads."

This was true, but I thought it was classic coming from Terry, who was totally besotted by Lena and was completely oblivious to her many many faults.

A few days later when Dave was sat with the lads, he suddenly announced. "Aysha flew back down to Freetown this afternoon. Things are not going too well. I don't know when she is coming back, or even if she intends to come back. I know I'm daft, but I miss her already."

"That's a good miss, I assume. Are the drinks on you this evening Dave?" Terry asked him.

I gave him a warning glance over the rim of my glasses. The lads all knew to let things go, when I gave them what they referred to as my 'Ann Robinson' look.

"Maybe some of us have more emotions than you have Terry. I've told you before, I love the girl, I can't do anything about that, stupid as you may think I am, and if she doesn't come back I will go and fetch her in a few weeks."

"Good on you." Nick told him. "Just be careful that you continually watch your back, I think you need to."

"Yeah, I know what I'm about."

I hoped he did. I was fond of Dave, and I was concerned about him. Some of these girls were callous. I had seen so many men devastated by girls like Aysha, and she did have a particularly bad reputation. I saw the lads giving knowing glances to one another. I believed they all thought the same as I did, but considered it wise not to voice their opinions. Dave thought he was in command of the situation, and was unlikely to take kindly to well meaning advice.

That was the way things stood between Dave and Aysha when I caught my first glimpse of The Peace Haven's new manager. I was not certain of his name; the staff called him Mr. Ali or simply Ali. They were quick to inform me that every morning he walked around the entire hotel, visiting every department and speaking with various members of staff from the head of the department to the newest 'boy'. This was a change from the way Claus had behaved; perhaps it boded well for The Dominion and me. However, I would need to see him to decide that. That would be easy, if, as his staff said, he checked around the hotel on a daily basis. I would simply look over the wall every morning until I saw him. On the very first morning of my patrol I was lucky enough to see him walk from the fish restaurant back to the main reception, with Hans the catering manager.

He looked more of a hotel manager than his predecessor ever did. Claus had often worn shorts and a tee shirt, which was comfortable in the

Shendian climate, but I felt very unsuitable for the position he held in a five star hotel. Ali, however, was dressed in smart, dark formal trousers, with a short sleeved, light coloured shirt and a contrasting tie. He chatted with Hans, not shouting at him as Claus would have done, and I heard him say "Good morning," to a gardener who was tending plants outside of the fish restaurant. Claus would not have even noticed the gardener, let alone acknowledge him.

The security at the arch had told me Ali was a mild mannered man and softly spoken. From this, and my observations of him on that first morning, I thought he might be approachable. I decided to give him a few weeks to settle in, and then I would make an appointment to introduce myself. If nothing else was achieved by this meeting, I hoped I would be able to establish the new owners of The Peace Haven's stance on The Dominion, and our right of way through their car park. I listened eagerly to the local gossip about Ali over the next few weeks. According to the staff he was a good boss. He had made no changes, just visited them all every morning, and left them to get on with their jobs. I didn't make any comments but thought underneath, he was probably a ruthless businessman or he wouldn't be in the position he held, within a large empire like Hussaini's. I assumed he was observing them all and accessing the situation, and when the time was right he would act and make the changes he thought appropriate to make his hotel more efficient. Maybe the staff won't be so enthralled by him when this happened.

Meanwhile Dave had only heard from Aysha once since she had returned home and after two weeks with no contact, he decided to go back to the village and insist she return to Shendi with him. He knew the village Elders would look disapprovingly on her return without him, now she was a married woman; she was expected to be with her husband, no matter what the circumstances. "Before I leave tonight Helen, I will need to have my passport; I've booked to go to Freetown tomorrow." Dave told me. "I'm hoping a couple of weeks back in the village, will have made her realize how much better off she is here with me. I also hope she will have learnt how to behave herself while she has been there. I know the Elders will not be happy with her, and you know the respect they have for their Elders. I'm confident she will have changed." Dave, like a few of the ex-pats kept their passports in my safe. It was other people's property, even more than my own that had worried me when the welder was cutting my safe open.

"Will you be gone long?" I asked Dave.

"No, I need to get back for work. Kawso isn't very pleased that I'm going. In fact he was insistent that I stay away from Sierra Leone, he says I should leave things as they are, but there is no way, I'm staying here, and leaving her there. I will probably be back by the end of the week."

Dave flew down to Freetown the following morning. A couple of evenings later when Viv and Greg were sat at the bar having their evening meal, during our conversation Viv asked me. "Have you heard anything from Dave?"

"No, but I don't expect to, he doesn't usually contact me when he's away."

"I haven't heard anything either and I'm worried about him."

"You panic too much. He has only been gone a couple of days. If he is enjoying himself with Aysha, why should he think about us?" Greg told her.

"You know he sends me a text every day, when he is away."

"Well not this time, he's a married man now, it's no big deal."

Viv frowned and shook her head. She was clearly worried about Dave, but Greg was right, if he were enjoying himself with Aysha, he would not even think of any of us. Viv and Greg were going back to the U.K. shortly, she had been undoubtedly hoping to see Dave again before she left, and was maybe starting to think she would have gone before Dave returns.

The next morning Viv came to see me while she was out shopping.

"I've had a text from Dave," she told me.

"That's good, is he alright?"

"No, I mean yes he says everything is fine, but no it is not good or at least I don't think so. I am still worried and Greg is getting annoyed with me; he says I've had a text and should stop worrying. But I can't and Greg told me that I'm only happy, when I have something to worry about. He told me to stop be so silly."

"Why? Is there something wrong?"

"I know you will probably say I'm stupid the same as Greg has, but I don't think Dave sent the text. It is from his phone, but it just doesn't feel right somehow."

"What do you mean doesn't feel right? Is it not written how you would expect Dave to write or what?"

"I can't really explain it. It just doesn't seem right, it's just not how Dave texts. I have read it over and over looking for a cryptic message or something. Look, you read it and see what you think."

She took her mobile phone out of her bag, found Dave's text and gave it to me to read.

"I don't know. I've never had a text from Dave." I told her. "I agree it isn't how I would expect him to text. I really don't know what to say, what does Greg think?"

"When he finally read it he agreed that it wasn't like his usual texts, but he thinks I'm over reacting. I don't care, I am worried, Helen."

"He is a long way away, we can't pop over and see if he is alright, there isn't really anything we can do, and taking the text on face value, he is fine. Maybe you will hear from him again soon."

She agreed and climbed down from her bar stool, picked up her shopping and went out. I didn't know what to think, yes the text hadn't sounded like Dave, but then texts were strange things to read and I had never had a text from Dave so really had no idea how he wrote them. I shrugged my shoulders and got on with my morning's work.

Viv came in with Greg in the evening for their supper, and she was very subdued. She hadn't heard anymore from Dave, and I sensed this was becoming an issue between them. None of us took her concern seriously. Viv had had several problems in Shendi, like most of us, but whereas we generally tried to look on the brighter side of things, Viv did dwell on the dark side, and often saw problems that didn't really exist. However, the next morning it turned out that her worries well founded. Both Viv and Greg came to see me mid morning, with Viv in an agitated state.

"I knew something was wrong." Viv told me. "No one would listen to me, but I knew there was something wrong. Dave has been arrested; he has been taken to a prison, in a town near the village. He wants me to contact The High Commission in Freetown."

She was starting to hyperventilate and I called to Momodou to bring coffee for the three of us, while Greg and I took her into the garden, where it was peaceful to try and calm her down.

"Right, now explain to me what has happened, why has he been arrested?"

"We're not exactly sure." Greg explained to me. "There was a fight, but we don't know who was involved. It may have been with Aysha; she has brothers, it may have been with one of the brothers, we don't know, but it seems Dave has been injured, but we don't know how badly. Anyway he wants The High Commission informed."

"And we don't know how to get hold of them; we don't know how to get the phone number. We don't know what to do. Anything could happen to him in jail in Sierra Leone. I told you all something was wrong." Viv exploded.

"I have the number of The High Commission here, if you phone them and give them all the details I'm sure they will contact The Commission in Freetown, or at least give you their phone number."

"Oh Helen, what a good idea. I didn't even think about our High Commission." Viv said sounding a bit calmer, she looked at Greg and continued. "I would rather go to the High Commission, if we are there, they will probably phone Freetown and let us know what is happening there and then. If we phone them, they may put it off, or not do it at all."

Greg agreed that going to the High Commission would be a good idea and it was a measure of his anxiety that he drank his coffee as quickly as Viv.

As they went they told me they would be back as soon they had been to The High Commission and had any news to let me know what was happening.

It was several hours before they returned. Apparently the Commission in Shendi, had been very sympathetic and helpful, but their counterparts in Freetown had been unconcerned. They had said if Dave had been held in Freetown they would have visited him and made sure he was being treated correctly, but being he was several hours journey away, they could do nothing unless they were certain he was being ill treated. They seemed to take the stance, that if Dave had got himself into trouble it was down to him to sort it out. Greg and I finally convinced Viv that Dave probably wouldn't be held for long. In Shendi ex-pats were arrested on a regular basis, often for trifling reasons, and were released again shortly afterwards, if they were prepared to pay a few shillings as a bribe. We assumed Sierra Leone was probably similar.

Greg and I were proved correct and Viv's fears unfounded when the next day she received a text from Dave telling her he had been released, and was fine. What was even better news was that Dave and Aysha were getting on really well; their relationship had never been better. Fortunately this time she was content that it was him who had sent the text and she was noticeably relieved that evening, and was in a much lighter mood. Dave continued to text her everyday until he returned to Shendi at the end of the week. He came back alone. Aysha would return in a couple of weeks, family commitments were keeping her in the village, and Dave needed to return to his estate agency business. Viv was delighted he had come back as she and Greg were flying to the U.K. for a few weeks the day after Dave's return.

Dave was in high spirits when he came into the bar with Viv and Greg on the evening of his arrival.

"A coke for me, please, Helen, and Viv and Greg's usual."

"Whisky in the coke?" I asked him.

"No, neat coke please. I've a bit of a dickey tummy. I've been a bit off for a couple of days."

"Keep an eye on it." I advised him. "It's not so long since you last had malaria; you should have a test done, if you're not well in a couple of days."

"I agree", said Viv. "If I wasn't going home tomorrow for a fortnight, I'd come with you."

"Are you coming back so soon?" I asked.

"Yes, James is staying here because he is doing some charity work and much as I love my son and trust him, I don't think any 19 year old should be left in Shendi too long. So yes, I will be back in two weeks and Dave, make sure you get to the doctors."

"OK, OK now let me tell you what happened." Dave took a long drink, pulled a face, presumably at the taste of neat coke, and started to tell his tale. He had fallen out with Aysha's brothers, they had had him arrested, and put into a Sierra Leone jail in the back of beyond, but everything was fine now. He and Aysha were getting on really well; she had promised him she would be better behaved when she came back to Shendi. Dave was on cloud nine.

After much deliberation the next morning, I finally plucked up the courage to make an appointment to see Ali. I was nervous about doing this, remembering that a couple of years before, I had made an appointment with one of the hotel's receptionists to see Claus. He had failed to recognise not my surname, and had not realised who the appointment was with. When he arrived for our meeting, and saw me sat in his outer office, he went berserk. He yelled at his receptionist and ordered her to have me removed from the hotel's premises. As I left, through the hotel's main reception area, he followed me, shouting that I had tricked him, was trying to see him under false pretences and I wasn't to return to his hotel under any circumstances. Witnessing the scene were tourists, many of whom were customers of mine sat in the hotel reception. I had left with my face bright red from embarrassment and humiliation. I had not entered The Peace Haven since, not wishing to repeat that degrading experience.

Nevertheless I felt that I should meet Ali and at least find out where I stood. Taking a deep breath, I dialled the hotel's number. On the third ring, much too quickly, it was answered. "Good morning, The Peace Haven, Shendi, how may I help you?"

"Hello, this is Helen Russell from The Dominion, next door." I wanted to make sure there could be no mistaking who was making the appointment this time. "I would like to make an appointment to see Ali please."

"I will put you through to Ali's personal secretary, will you hold please."

When I had been transferred to the secretary, I once again made it clear I was from The Dominion, and would like an appointment to introduce myself to Ali.

The secretary replied, "Ali is out of the office at the moment, he has mentioned he would like to meet you, but he has been very busy since his arrival, and hasn't managed to get around to it yet. May I take your phone number, and I will get back to you when I have spoken to him." I gave her my number and hung up, wondering if she had any intention of getting back to me, or was she just trying to fob me off, without seeming rude, as Ali's predecessor had been.

Dave came into the bar again that evening.

"A coke please, Helen."

"Not drinking yet, you still not well?"

"No, I don't feel great."

"In what way, you are sure it's not malaria, aren't you?"

"I don't think so, I haven't got a fever. I can't even really tell you what is the matter with me; I can't put my finger on it. I'm just not myself, it's strange really, maybe I ate something at the village that disagreed with me."

"Think I'd feel a bit off, if I'd eaten monkey." Rick said.

"I haven't eaten any monkey." Dave said with a grin.

"You sure? Stew it up with a bit of peanut soup and you would never know."

"Oh shut up! I feel rough now. You are making me worse. I feel sick whenever Aysha talks about them eating monkey, she wouldn't dare give me any; besides it is very expensive and treated as a delicacy, she wouldn't waste it on me."

Dave didn't have a fever and he looked well, but like most of the men in Shendi, he was rarely off alcohol, and he hadn't eaten much since he returned from the village, so he clearly wasn't well. Malaria is much more prevalent in the more remote villages in Shendi, I assumed the same applied to Sierra Leone. There are many strains of malaria, which could account for Dave not recognising the symptoms.

Before Dave went home, I said to him. "If you don't feel good tomorrow, please get a malaria test done, just to be on the safe side. If you don't Viv will be cross."

"O.K. Helen, I will, I was thinking of doing that anyway. I know I've got something wrong. It's just I feel a bit of a fool going to see a doctor and not being able to tell him precisely what is wrong. I will go and see Dr. Dawda, I know him socially, he is Kawso's cousin, so I will be at ease with him."

"Good, he will sort you out, I know him, he has been in here a few times, and he has a good reputation."

Dave left earlier than usual. I was concerned about him; he was living on his own, which was not ideal, with him not being well. It was unfortunate that Aysha hadn't come back with him.

Quite early the next morning my phone rang. I was surprised when I answered it, to find I was speaking to Ali's receptionist.

"Ali would like to know if you are free tomorrow evening at six. If you are he would be pleased if you would join him for coffee at the hotel."

I was taken aback. I had been doubtful if she would get back to me, and here she was inviting me for coffee. My heart fluttered, this sounded hopeful, at least Ali was acting friendly towards me; this was a completely different attitude to Claus.

"Just a minute please, while I check my diary." I would have accepted any time for an appointment with Ali, but I thought it was to my advantage not to appear over eager. "Yes, I am able to fit that into my schedule, please tell Ali I look forward to meeting him."

I had a smug smile on my face, as I put down the receiver. Maybe nothing would come of this meeting, but the fact that there was to be a meeting, was a break through. An invitation to coffee, suggested this was to be informal, a complete contrast to when Simon and I visited the same office to introduce ourselves to Mr. Smithers, on our arrival in Shendi, which now seemed an aeon away.

Chapter Sixteen
Death by Misadventure?

The phone was ringing as I stepped out of the shower the following morning. Dripping a trail of water behind me and clutching a towel around my body, I dashed to answer it. It was seldom I had a call that early, and I was anxious to find out who the caller was, perhaps something was wrong in the UK. I snatched the phone up.

"Hello Helen, how are you?" I breathed a sigh of relief. It was only Ousman, my lawyer. My mind rushed ahead wondering what he wanted to speak to me about; it was another three weeks before we were due back in court, so why was he ringing now?

"Morning Ousman, this is a surprise."

"I had meant to phone you yesterday, but I'm afraid I didn't get around to it. I haven't got you out of bed have I?"

"No, I was up." I omitted to mention I was still wrapped in a towel.

"I had a call from Mrs. Sullais yesterday afternoon, The Peace Haven have dropped their court case against you. You understand what I'm saying do you? That is their court injunction against you, preventing your music. This will not affect the right of way case that is your case; it was Simon who took out that court injunction."

"Yes, I understand that. In reality that case didn't really get started did it?"

"Well, no, it didn't, but it was still pending, and would have come to court eventually. We did have two adjournments before anything even happened do you remember?"

"Yes, but does this make any difference to me?"

"It does mean you can play music, even live groups if you want to."

"I doubt if I will, the music from La Parisian is loud enough to entertain my diners, but it is nice to know I can have music if I wish to. Why do you think they have suddenly dropped this case?"

"I'm not sure, it really wasn't of much significance to them, and it was rather tit for tat, because of your injunction against them. I think the new regime at The Peace Haven will possibly be better to deal with than the last. Hussaini is out to make a name for himself in Shendi and for his hotel to have a court case against a small business like yours is something that he wouldn't like. He is more than likely tidying up all the loose ends."

"Thanks Ousman, we will have to wait and see if there are any other developments."

I rested my hand for a few moments on the receiver as I replaced it. I was letting this news sink in, milling it over in my mind. Was it purely coincidence they had dropped this case now, when I was having coffee with Ali the same evening. I hadn't mentioned this meeting to Ousman; I would keep this to myself for now. Was this an olive branch, were they trying to soften me up before my meeting with Ali? This phone call from Ousman made me all the more impatient for my meeting. It was going to be a long day, waiting for the evening to come around.

When Nick came in for his morning coffee, I told him. " I've had a bit of a surprise this morning, my lawyer has phoned to tell me, The Peace Haven have dropped the 'noise and nuisance' case against me, what do you reckon to that?"

"Huussaini doesn't know you yet. When he does he will know how much of a nuisance you are and will slap it back on again. Don't get your knickers in a twist; all will be fine, fine in the end."

It was always hard to get a serious opinion out of any of the lads.

The day dragged on but finally it was time to prepare for my meeting with Ali. Although I was due to be back at work when I returned, I did not want to go in my uniform. I was eager to make a good impression and decided on a simple black dress, with a large red design around the hemline. Smart, but casual, I had always felt good in this dress; it would make me feel at ease and give me confidence. I hadn't mentioned this meeting to anyone, staff or customers. I felt that the less people that knew, the better, especially my staff. When and if they found out about this meeting they would read into it things that didn't exist and my internal problems would probably increase.

I went into the bar; I saw the expression on Jed's face, as he saw me walk in without wearing my uniform.

"I'm going out for a little while Jed, I may be slightly late starting this evening. You will be able to manage without me."

"Fine, fine," he answered, nodding his head in agreement.

I could feel the eyes of all the staff boring into my back as I walked away, they were curious to know where I was going. Terry was sat at the bar, eating his evening meal.

"Have a date, have you?" he asked.

"Maybe I have Terry, but I'm not telling you about it. I don't want to make you jealous."

"I don't care why would I? I have my Lena, but I will have to mention this to Nick and Kevin when they get here, they won't want you running off with any strange men."

I strolled out of The Dominion and followed the same route Simon and I had taken several years before. This time, however, I was on my own and I was suddenly very conscious of this. I gave a quick glance over my shoulder to see if any of the staff were watching where I was going. I couldn't see anyone, but felt certain at least one of them would be peering over the wall.

I was nervous as I entered the main reception area of Peace Haven. I was relieved to see John, a tour rep, who regularly came to The Dominion, sitting behind the reps desk waiting to see any tourists who needed him. It gave me confidence to see a friendly face, even if he wasn't part of the hotel's staff. I went over and spoke to him, which put me at ease. One of the hotel's receptionists must have overheard our conversation and realized who I was, as she came out from behind her desk and spoke to me.

"Good evening. You are Helen from The Dominion?"

"Yes, that's right. I have an appointment to see Ali."

"He is expecting you, when you are ready will you come with me."

I drew my conversation with John to a close, and was ushered into Ali's outer office by the receptionist who introduced me to his secretary.

She greeted me by my first name and added, "Ali has just received a phone call, he will be free shortly, take a seat."

I sat on the plush settee as she continued working on her computer. Glancing around, I recognised the same colourful African paintings that Simon and I had seen years earlier. Some of the furniture looked familiar too although it had been moved around. Not too many changes here yet, no sign of a new broom sweeping clean, I thought. I looked down at my hands, nervously fiddling with my fingernails that were once my pride and joy, but now looked rather the worse for wear. Shendi was taking its toll in more ways than one. Fortunately I didn't have too long to wait before the same man whom I had watched doing his morning rounds appeared at his office door. With his hand outstretched he introduced himself.

"Pleased to meet you Helen, I'm sure you know I'm Ali and I've been the manager of The Peace Haven since Claus' departure. Come through to my office will you?"

Turning to his secretary he said. "Order coffee for us will you please Binta."

I couldn't help but notice the contrast between this and my two previous visits to the manager's office. It all seemed so unreal, as if I was in another world.

After much small talk about the good high season we had both had the previous year and the difficulties this low season was causing us, the coffee, together with cakes and biscuits arrived. Binta served these to us, on a dainty silver tray, with matching coffee pot, cups and saucers. The difference between the bone china decorated with delicate pastel flowers filled with filter coffee and the large chunky coffee mugs of instant I served at The Dominion just served to highlight the dreamlike nature of the meeting. At the back of mind though was the thought that I would have to wake up sometime. I just hoped that it wasn't into a nightmare.

The polite small talk continued a while longer then Ali leant forward and asked. "Has your lawyer contacted you to tell you we have instructed our lawyer to stop the court case the previous owners had started against you?"

"Yes, he phoned me this morning."

"Good, I am glad. Hussaini doesn't like petty squabbles like that going on within his companies. We are a very straightforward people, and like everything to run very smoothly. There is one thing that you can do to help."

Here it comes, I thought, the nightmare awakening.

"In return for our dropping the court case," Ali continued, "we would like you to drop the case your husband started against the hotel. It has been going on for several years now, you must realize, as we do, it is going nowhere. It will never end, so why continue with it? It is costing both of us unnecessary money. Hussaini would like to see everything running smoothly within his businesses in Shendi." He sat back and assumed the business man's pose of folded arms and a patient look.

I thought for a moment. He was right, there was no sign of the court case ending and it would be very advantageous to be on good terms with my powerful neighbour. Even if it did end there was no guarantee that I would win. What should I do? Ali waited patiently for me to answer. Taking the proverbial deep breath and trying to keep my voice level I said, "I agree, the case has been going on for a long time. I do appreciate your dropping of your case, I really do. In return, I will stop the case against The Peace Haven immediately, if you instruct your lawyer to draw up a legal document giving me permanent right of way through your car park."

He looked at me strangely. "I don't understand. I'm not certain how easy it would be to arrange. Why do you want it? We don't cause any problems for your customers who use the car park, or do you think there are problems?"

"No, there are no problems now, but there have been in the past. For over a year my customers were forbidden to use the car park, and when the arch was first built the hotel's security even stopped my customers walking through. You can appreciate that I cannot operate like that. "

"Yes, but as you have said, that was in the past. You have had no trouble since we have owned the hotel, so why do you feel you need this in writing. I am giving you my assurance we will cooperate with you as long as you cooperate with us. Our clientele are different. We both have our own customers, so why would we want to interfere with your business. Are you not prepared to take my word on this? We have already stopped our court case against you, as a good will gesture, we were hoping you would reciprocate."

"These are totally different matters. The case the hotel took out against us, does not really affect you. If I drop the original case, without securing a permanent right of way, it could have great implications for me."

"I don't understand. I have given you my assurance we will continue to allow your customers to use our car park, so why are you reluctant to stop this case? Don't you trust me?"

"It is not that I don't trust you but I have to think ahead. What concerns me is if you resell the hotel, without a right of way agreement the next owners may refuse to allow my customers through the car park, and I would be back to square one. Also supposing I wanted to sell my business, I would have more of a problem selling it without some sort of agreement over this."

He was silent for a moment and then asked, "Are you thinking of selling your business?"

I was absolutely desperate to sell The Dominion, but it was not in my best interest to let Ali know this. I also knew while the court case was in progress, there was little chance of this happening. However, I was not prepared to drop the case, without obtaining my right of way. The Dominion would be a much more saleable proposition if I acquired this. I had started to feel slightly uncomfortable. Ali had behaved in a friendly manner towards me, but I now saw he had an ulterior motive.

"Of course, every property has a price tag on it. If the opportunity arose, to sell at the right price, I would possibly consider selling, but it is certainly not on the market." I was eager for the opportunity to move on with my life, but certainly didn't want Ali to detect this.

"If you did ever consider putting it on the market, be sure to let us know first, there is a chance that we might consider purchasing your property, but at the right price of course."

With a smile I said. "Yes, I'm sure you would, but somehow I doubt if your right price and mine are the same."

Ali laughed. "Probably not."

The small talk carried on for another half an hour after that, with Ali bringing again towards the end of the conversation, that the hotel would welcome an end of the court case, and asked me to consider this once more. I repeated my request for a legal document giving The Dominion a right of way; otherwise the court case would continue.

We parted on outwardly friendly terms, but I knew that Ali however pleasant and informal he had been had had that ulterior motive. I was unsettled; there was no possible way I intended dropping the court case without obtaining a result. I thought I had made the right assumption about Ali. He was a mild mannered, softly spoken gentleman, but underneath was a, fierce and ruthless businessman. He would have to be to survive in a business empire such as Hussaini's. Only time would tell how the situation between The Dominion and The Peace Haven would develop under the new ownership. As I walked back through the bar's entrance, my security, who had not been on duty when I left for my meeting, said "Good evening," and gave me a knowing smile. I was certain the staff had seen where I had gone and would be discussing the reasons I may have gone to the hotel. They could think what they liked; I knew that they would not ask me, but Sidi might drop a few pointed remarks into the conversation over the next few days. It would be interesting to see if he did.

The usual lads sat at the bar, turned and waved as I passed the wrought iron doorway. Terry would have told them I had gone out, which in itself was unusual, I imagined them deliberating on where I had been and with whom. I quickly changed into my uniform and took up my usual position behind the bar, to be greeted by Nick

"O.K. spill the beans. Where have you been, and who is the lucky man?"

"That's for me to know."

"And for us to find out." Terry finished. "And we will."

"Come on tell us, we need to know." Kevin told me.

"A girl has to have a life outside of The Dominion, you know."

"Who put that idea in your head?" Nick asked. "And we do need to know, we don't want you getting yourself into any trouble. Besides I may need to punch him on the nose."

"He was tall dark and handsome." I told them. "So none of you could even think of competing with him."

"Don't worry lads, seems she has been trying her luck up the street, and there is no way she could compete with the local lasses, that is why she's back so early she had no success." Terry told the others, which bought on the laughter he intended it to.

Even the next morning it was made clear the lads were keen to know my whereabouts the previous evening. Nick and Rick arrived at roughly the same time, and I served their coffees bringing a mug out for myself also. I set the three of the coffees down on the boys' usual breakfast table.

"Joining us for coffee are you? We're not sure we want you with us, not now that you have been unfaithful to us." Rick said.

I ignored him and turned the conversation to the news of the drop in the exchange rate, this was sure to distract them. The government had made the decision to drop the rate from 58 Shendian shillings to the pound, down to 40, the rate had slowly risen over the years, but none of us could have possibly predicted such a severe and sudden drop. My diversionary topic worked. Fewer shillings in our pockets affected all of us and discussing the possible outcomes took their minds off my affairs.

"I'll have a beer to-day." Dave said when he came in during the evening. "And a packet of cigarettes please, Helen."

"You are obviously feeling better." I told him.

"Yes, I'm fine, maybe not completely better, but well on the mend. I'll leave the whisky alone for now. I'll have a couple of nights on beer before risking that. I did go and see Dr. Dawda this morning."

"What did he say?"

"It's definitely not malaria, he gave me a test, which was negative, and you know Dawda always retests European blood after two hours if the first test is negative to be sure, my second test was negative also, so I'm fine."

"If it's not malaria, what does he think is the matter with you?"

"Like I told you the other night, I couldn't really explain to him what is wrong with me. He checked my blood pressure, and listened to my chest, you know, all the usual things, and everything was fine. He says I'd probably eaten something, or maybe picked up a bug or something. I'm much better now, so I won't worry about what it was."

Dave was much livelier than he had been since his return from Sierra Leone, and joined in all the fun around the bar. He eat heartily, again he hadn't done this since his return. I had been worried about him, but he was undoubtedly well on the road to recovery. As a result I was not concerned when I didn't see Dave the following day. He came in most days but not every day, and if he was feeling better I thought he was probably catching up on his work. He had let things slip slightly since his return, as he hadn't been able to concentrate properly.

The next day being Sunday, I was up early and opened the bar as usual, but as this was officially my day off, and I didn't work until the evening shift, I was sat in my garden reading when Jed came looking for me.

"Kawso is in the bar, he wants to see you."

"He knows this is my day off, tell him I will be in the bar from seven this evening, he can come back and see me then."

"I have told him that, but he says this is important and you must come."

"O.K. tell him I will come out in a minute." I was annoyed, Kawso was full of his own importance, and how dare he try and dictate to me as I have seen him do to others.

Shortly afterwards I went through into the bar. On Sundays I generally had a larger group of ex-pats and long term tourists that came in for breakfast. They would sit at the large table just inside the door that led into the garden, their usual breakfast table not being large enough for the Sunday group. After breakfast they would sit there, deep in conversation, drinking coffees for most of the morning.

As I entered I saw Kawso sat at a table, in the middle of the room. Determined to make him wait, and also not wanting to ignore my customers, I went over and spoke to them for a few minutes before going over to where Kawso was sat. As I approached the table, he stood and pulled the chair next to him out for me to sit down; I acknowledged his gentlemanly behaviour with a nod and sat next to him. I was aware of the lads watching us

"You have many ex-pats in this morning." Kawso noted.

"Yes, on Sundays I always have a large group of them."

"I don't want any of them alarmed. You will listen to me, keep calm and make no reaction, not while I'm here anyway."

I looked at him quizzically, not quite sure what he meant. He called to Jed, who had gone back behind the bar.

"Get your Boss Lady a drink boy."

Jed came over to ask what I would like.

"Get her a brandy." Kawso told him.

Jed looked shocked; he knew I didn't touch alcohol. "B- b –b- but ….. She doesn't."

"Bring me a coffee please Jed."

"Plenty of sugar then," Kawso interrupted.

"No, I don't take sugar. Bring me a coffee as I usually have it Jed."

Kawso's manner was so domineering. I knew he ruled his staff with a rod of iron and he had tried his high handed ways in the past, when he had been in with Dave and here he was, trying it again. He would have to think again. The way he was acting on this Sunday morning was making me feel quite hostile towards him. It was rumoured he was highly respected by both the Shendian underworld and the S.S.G.; consequently, in spite of my dislike for him, I was careful not to let my resentment show.

"I am capable of ordering my own drink, in my own bar, thank you Kawso."

My hand was on the table; he reached across and gently patted it. "Sorry Helen, I know I sometimes upset you, but I just want you to relax and keep calm."

Pulling my hand away I said. "I'm fine, fine. What is so important it couldn't wait until this evening? You have interrupted my day off; I was relaxing and calm before you arrived."

"I wanted to talk to you before anyone else, even though we don't always hit it off, I do respect you, and I respect your friendship with Dave. Before I go any farther I would like you to go and get me Dave's passport."

I paused for a few seconds before answering; I thought my words through carefully. I was curious to know where this was leading. Out of the corner of my eye I saw the lads glancing in our direction, their curiosity was also getting the better of them.

"Kawso, I don't have Dave's passport, but if I did, I wouldn't give it to you. I would give it to no-one but Dave himself."

"I know you have it, and you have to hand it over. It isn't me that wants it, the police want it, and I have told them you have it in your safe."

"What....the police? Why?" I said louder than I intended.

Jed bought my coffee, and Kawso said no more until he had moved away from the table again.

"Are you going to get me the passport? The police will get angry with you if you don't hand it over."

"I gave it to Dave when he went to Sierra Leone, and he hasn't given it back to me yet, but why do the police want it? Where is Dave?"

"Dave's gone."

"Gone? Gone where? Back to Sierra Leone? Into Furnanda? Why are the police looking for him?"

"No, you are not understanding me. I mean he is gone... passed on, dead."

I didn't fully take this in, my eyes widened, my mouth dropped open.

"Keep calm, slowly sip your coffee, you should have let me get you something stronger. I don't want you drawing attention to us."

I did as he said, allowing this news to sink in before I said anything else.

"What happened?" I slowly asked after a short interval.

"You know he hadn't been well, we found him dead in his apartment at about midnight last night. It appears that he had been dead for about 24 hours."

"So you are saying this happened Friday night?"

"Yes, probably close to midnight."

"He was in here until about 10, and was much better than he had been since his return."

"He came up to my bar for a drink after he left here, and got in a taxi at around 10.30. We think the taxi driver was the last one to see him alive."

"Do you know what the cause of death was?"

"Cerebral malaria."

"No! It can't be. He saw Dr. Dawda on Friday, he did two malaria tests and they were both negative."

"Perhaps Dawda made a mistake. He has signed the death certificate. Dawda was with me when I found Dave."

"Explain to me how you found him. Why was the doctor with you? I'm confused."

"I didn't see Dave yesterday, which was unusual, I phoned his mobile several times, and obviously got no answer. So just before I went home last night, I decided to go around to his apartment. I took Dawda and the police with me as I was afraid something awful had happened, and see I was proved right."

"..But... he was much better on Friday, and you are telling me he died within two hours of leaving here. Besides Dr. Dawda's tests would have shown if he had malaria, and they were negative."

"Cerebral comes on very quickly, you are soon dead."

"I know, but not usually that quick, you usually go into a coma and drift away, it can take a couple of days, not a couple of hours."

"Not always. Anyway I have a lot to do, I must be going, but listen carefully to me Helen, Dave died of cerebral malaria, don't be thinking anything else. You are in Shendi now, not U.K. and we know better how things work here than you do. I'll come back and see you later, there will be arrangements to make, and I don't know what you Europeans do, I may need your help."

Kawso got up to leave; he hesitated, and then suddenly asked me.

"What did Dave tell you about the divorce papers?"

"What divorce papers?"

"He gave Aysha divorce papers. That was what the fight with her brothers was over."

"No, that's wrong. He told me there were arguments when he first got there, he glossed over the fight to me, but told me he and Aysha got on really well afterwards, and things had never been better between them. If he was going to divorce her I'm sure he would have told me, and certainly Viv would know about it."

"O.K. that's fine, fine, forget I mentioned it, he would have told you what happened."

I sat and watched him leave, he seemed to be calm and unconcerned, I couldn't understand this, and what was this about divorce papers? Dave was a friend of his, and worked for him, how could he be so cool about this? I let the news sink in. I couldn't believe this. Dr. Dawda had trained and practised in Europe for many years. He was very aware that Europeans often suffer more when they have malaria than their African counterparts, as our bodies are not accustomed to it, especially the first couple of times we get it; which is why he always did a second test if the first result was negative. This had been done. Dave had told me this himself.

I sat welded to the spot in deep thought trying to absorb the news of Dave's death, but also what Kawso told me somehow didn't ring true. I wanted to delve deeper into this. What did Kawso mean when he said Dave died of malaria and don't be thinking anything else? Why had he taken a doctor and the police with him when he went around to Dave's apartment? I could understand him not wanting to go alone, but why assume a doctor and the police would be needed? The lads, who had been watching Kawso and me, bought me out of my revere.

"OK, OK, come clean. Is Kawso your new man?" Rod called across to me.

I got up and went over to their table.

"Give me a bit of credit please. Kawso came to give me some bad news Dave was found dead in his apartment late last night."

"Dave? Which Dave are you talking about? Not Danish Dave?" I didn't even know which one of them had asked the question.

"Yes." I answered quietly. "I can't believe this, he was so much better Friday night."

"How did he die?" A much more reserved Rick than usual asked.

"Cerebral malaria. I don't think so."

"Cobblers," someone exclaimed. "Where is Aysha?"

"Supposedly Sierra Leone." I told them. "None of this rings true to me, Kawso went around to the apartment late last night, as he hadn't seen him all day, and he hadn't answered his phone. He took Dr. Dawda and the police with him."

"What? Why did he assume he would need a doctor and the police?"

"My sentiments exactly."

"Poor old Dave," Rod said. "When did this happen?"

"Apparently he had been dead about 24 hours when he was found, so approximately midnight on Friday."

"He was in here and much better till about ten." Rick said.

"Exactly."

The lads were very subdued after I had given them the news. I left them reminiscing over Dave and took the rest of my coffee and sat at the table in my garden. I sat staring straight ahead sipping my coffee, as my eyes moistened and the tears slowly dampened my cheeks. I brushed them aside with the back of my hand. Dave had been a good friend to me. I knew Viv would be absolutely devastated. All sorts of thoughts drifted in and out of my head. Had Dave really given Aysha divorce papers? He hadn't told me that, nor had he told Viv, she would have told me. If this were true it would give Aysha a motive for wanting Dave dead.

My most outstanding thought was that Dave had been poisoned, possibly with Aysha giving him a small dosage to make him unwell, to make his death seem feasible, and someone here giving him the lethal dose on Friday evening. It was even possible that Aysha was in Shendi and we didn't know she was. Could all this be possible or was my paranoia once again getting the better of me. I was relieved I didn't have to work until the evening. I could hear the chatter and laughter of my lunchtime customers; I was not in the mood for playing 'mine host'. I had to get a grip of myself before the evening.

The mood around the bar was sombre that night. I was not the only one having difficulty in absorbing the news of Dave's death, nor was I the only one querying the cerebral malaria diagnosis Kawso had given me. James, Viv's son came to see me, he was devastated, and I knew his mother would be also. James had great respect for Dave, and while Viv was away and he was in Shendi alone, he told Viv that Dave would be his surrogate father, and I would be his mother substitute. He was young, this was the first time he had faced death at such close quarters. He had been with Dave on Friday afternoon, he could not comprehend he had died so shortly afterwards. James gave me Viv's UK phone number as I was very keen to speak to her; I expected her to be tearful and subdued, but she was not, she was angry, very angry.

"Helen, what is going on there? You know Dave didn't have malaria, as well as I do. We have to do something; we can't let them get away with this. What do you think we can do?" I could feel her anger and her determination being transmitted down the phone to me.

"Take it easy Viv, I understand you are angry, but we must be careful, you know that. I don't believe he had malaria, but Viv, we can't bring Dave back, whatever happens now."

"I know, I know, but if Aysha has done this we have to find out. You know what a bitch she is."

"Did Dave mention anything to you about divorcing her?"

"What? Why are you asking that?"
"Kawso told me that this morning, but I can't believe it. Dave had said things had never been better between them, Kawso said that was why Dave had gone down to Sierra Leone, and that was why he had fallen out with

her brothers. If Dave had had divorce papers drawn up he would have told you, for sure."

"I'd have thought so, but why would Kawso have told you that?"

"I don't know, but you know my thoughts on Kawso. I've never liked him, the slimy git kept patting my hand when he was here this morning, and I kept pulling it away. Yuk!"

Viv gave a little chuckle. "I'm back on Friday. Dave's father has asked me to go to the apartment and clear Dave's belongings. He has arranged for someone from the High Commission to come with me. I don't want to go alone. It will also be good to have someone in authority to oversee what I'm taking out of the apartment. This is a bad affair altogether."

We said our goodbyes, as I walked back towards the bar, I was amazed that everyone's initial reaction was the same as mine; no-one thought this was malaria, but no-one would be brave enough to officially voice this opinion.

I was bewildered with Sidi's reaction to the news when he arrived for work the next morning.

"SSh don't be saying these things, in fact don't you be talking about this in the bar, careless talk can only bring you problems, I keep telling you, you talk too much to the ex-pats, they fill your head with all sorts of rubbish, and besides Dave wasn't popular with some of the local lads, and you know what can happen when you upset people here. It is best to mind your own business."

"Are you trying to tell me you know what happen to Dave?" "Did I say that? See you imagine all sorts of things, best you just forget about all this."

"Dave was a friend of mine, I will not just forget about this, I would like to know the truth surrounding his death, it all happened so quickly."

"You know people get ill and are dead in no time here."

In spite of Sidi's warning Dave was still the main topic of conversation in the bar that lunchtime. The news had fully sunk in by then, and although we had all come to terms with his death, and were thinking more clearly about the circumstances, we still all felt we could not comprehend it. I was talking quietly with a couple of the lads having their lunch, even before Sidi's warning we had always been careful not to allow my staff to overhear if we were discussing anything controversial and it appeared Dave's death was. Just as one of us was again questioning the official line, the CD player stopped, the lights went out and the generator which had been running since early morning fell silent.

"Gennie has stopped; you've run out of fuel." Terry called.

"No, I'm not out of fuel, I bought some yesterday."

"Well it has stopped," he said stating the obvious.

"I'll go and see what the problem is."

I walked to the generator room which was in a small separate building just large enough to take the gennie, near the garage. Latif and Petreeni, who was Latif's 'apprentice' and was a general help to him around the garden, were looking in the doorway in amazement at the generator and shaking their heads.

"What's happened?" I eagerly asked as I approached them.

"The generator has stopped." Latif told me.

"Yes, I noticed that." I answered trying not to sound too condescending. "Do you know why it has stopped?"

"Petreeni washed it."

"What do you mean?"

"Sidi and I told him to clean the generator room, and he washed the generator with the hose pipe."

"What? Are you telling me the gennie has been hosed down with water, while it was going?"

"Yes, we think it was a mistake."

"I think it was a mistake also, I think you are lucky Petreeni that the gennie stopped before it electrocuted you. Now what are we going to do?"

"I think you should phone Sidi, and get him to collect the generator man and bring him here." Latif told me.

Again not intending to sound condescending I replied. "That seems like a good idea, probably the best one you've had to-day. You go and phone him before I explode, and you had better hope we can get it fixed without costing me too much money."

I was at the end of my tether when I returned to the bar, and by the reaction I got from the lads it was obvious it showed in my face.

"You won't believe what the silly sods have done." I told them. "They have only hosed the gennie down to clean it."

There were hoots of laughter around the bar.

"I'm glad it's amused you lot, you're as daft as they are."

"You have to admit it's funny." Rick told me.

"I hope you find it as funny when you are drinking warm beer this evening."

"Don't be so touchy." Terry told me. "You may have the mains back on by then."

I gave a huge sigh of relief when the mains did come back on, at roughly the same time as Sidi arrived with our generator maintenance man. They both waved to me as they walked around the outside of the bar. The generator man had a huge smile on his face. I wondered if this were a warm greeting to me or a smile of satisfaction as he thought about the unexpected extra income he would be earning this afternoon. I decided to leave them for a little while to allow him time to assess the damage before I went out to get his prognosis.

Latif and Petreeni were stood outside the generator room looking concerned, when I went out to see their progress. As I approached, they both glanced at me, and then looked back towards the generator. Their expressions didn't bode well, I cautiously looked inside the generator room, this seemed ominous to me. Sidi and Babu, the generator man, were leaning over the generator, there were cogs and wheels and pieces of machinery everywhere on the floor.

They stopped and looked up when they saw me.

"We are taking it apart and thoroughly drying and cleaning it." Sidi told me. "Hopefully it will be alright, but Babu thinks this is damaged and will have to be rewound." He picked up a cylinder and showed it to me.

I called him outside and took him out of earshot of the others.

"Will we have this repaired by this evening?"

"Maybe, but you have had no power all day, now it has come back on you should have it all evening."

"I can't rely on that, and how much do you reckon this will cost?"

"Depends if he finds anything else wrong, but a rewind will take a few days to have done and is expensive. That part is old and wearing out anyway, we would be better to buy a new one."

"How much will that be? Remember it is well into low season and money is getting short."

"It will be dear, I don't know how much until we go and look for one, maybe eight or nine thousand."

"You are joking?"

"We could try and get a reconditioned one that would be cheaper. Do you have the money?"

"In the bank, money I need for wages, but we must have the gennie repaired. How the hell did Patreeni manage to hose it? He was lucky he didn't kill himself."

"Latif and I told him to clean the gennie room; it's not his fault he thought he was doing a good job."

"Yeah, he has done a brilliant job."

I went back into the bar and left them to it. I was fast despairing. I would have to go to the bank when I went off duty to withdraw enough money to pay for the repair. This low season my resources were running very low, there was only one month left before the tourists started to arrive, but cash flow would be a real concern until then. Yet again, my staff and their bungles were the source of entertainment for my regulars, and numerous jokes were made about my spotlessly clean generator.

I walked to the bank, which was only about five minutes from the bar, when I went off duty. As I stood in the queue waiting to withdraw the last of my hard earned cash, I selfishly thought all I wanted to do was curl up in my bed and have my afternoon nap, the stress of all this was making me tired and wary, I just wanted to close my eyes to the world for a short while.

Everything in Shendi took so long, no one was ever in a hurry, and the cashier's polite conversation and pleasantries with her customers seemed endless. Why was I the only one in the queue getting irritated by this? I was tense and edgy as I strolled back down the main tourist strip after I finally came out of the bank clutching my money. I was irritated, my eyes were downcast, and I was wishing I was anywhere but here. The sun was shinning, exaggerating the bright Shendian colours of the bars and restaurants, and the gay dresses and robes of the locals. Most people would love to be me, living in a beautiful country like Shendi, being able to enjoy the clement climate, being surrounded by all this colour and endlessly smiling faces. I should not feel as I did.

As I walked under the hotel's arch, Sidi was driving down the car park; Latif, Patreeni and Babu were with him. He pulled over when he saw me.

"I was looking for you. Have you been to get the money?" he asked.

"Yes, are you going to get the parts?"

"We are going to Malaville, we will get the parts, and I will go back and pay for them later."

He drove off, I went into the office, and put the money in the safe, then took a shower and slipped exhausted and frustrated into my bed, for a short rest before my evening duty. I was once again bewildered by the day's events. Was Patreeni really stupid enough to hose down the generator, especially when it was in use? How would I know how much the parts really cost? With my mind spinning, it was no wonder sleep evaded me. Shortly afterwards I heard banging and the clanging of metal. The lads were back, and were working on the generator; I gave up on sleep and got up, eager to know the outcome of their trip to Malaville.

Sidi and Latif were stood outside the generator room, watching Babu and Patreeni working inside. As he heard me approach Sidi came over and said.

"I'll go and order you some coffee. You haven't slept long, sit down in the garden and relax. You look tired and you don't have to be back to work yet."

I let him go and order my coffee; I was in need of one. As I sat down I thought these parts are costing more than I expected, that is why Sidi wants me to be relaxed before discussing it with me.

When he returned I sharply asked. "Well come on, come on, tell me how much this is costing me."

"Why are you always so quick tempered?" he inquired. "We are trying to help you, and you are jumping at us."

"Just tell me how much, and if it hadn't been for Patreeni's stupidity I wouldn't be needing this done anyway."

"Ssh, don't let him hear you say that, he will be upset. We went all over looking for the cheapest and the best. In the end we got one from a friend of Babu's who supplies him with lots of parts, so we have got a very very good price."

"How much?"

"Well there is Babu's workmanship as well, and he will be here another two hours yet."

"How much?"

"See what I mean. You must keep calm, all this anger is no good for you, you will make yourself ill."

"How much?" My voice rose, I was getting angry by then. The fact that he didn't come straight out and say, suggested to me I was being given an exaggerated price.

"Everything, the parts and Babu's time. Twelve thousand."

"What? Twelve thousand! Before you went into Malaville you reckoned eight or nine."

"Well I was wrong. Do you have the money?"

I grunted and banged my hands down on the table, which probably hurt me more than any effect it had on Sidi. I went to the office and got the money. I was sure it shouldn't be that much, but if I asked to see a receipt I knew they could obtain a false one, and I did need my generator in full working order. My hands were tied.

I went back to the outside, with a thunderous expression on my face. I slapped the money down noisily on the table. Without a word Sidi picked it up and started counting it. When he was satisfied it was correct, he stood up, put it in his pocket and went back to the generator room, leaving me alone to drink my coffee. I was furious. I was sure the lads would all be getting a nice little hand out from the twelve thousand shillings, but with no mechanical knowledge whatsoever, I had to rely on the help at hand.

When Nick came in I explained the outcome of the gennie problem to him.

He sniggered then said. "Don't know for sure, I'm a builder not an electrician, but I would agree you've been had. The bastards! Never mind eh? You had to have it sorted, and you are the wealthiest woman in Shendi, so what's the odds?"

While I was chatting to Nick, Viv and James came into the bar, I was surprised to see them, with my generator problem foremost on my mind, it had completely slipped my memory that Viv was coming back on this afternoon's flight. I was pleased to see her. James had been so very upset over Dave; he would start to feel better with his mother's support. Viv hugged me, and we shed a few tears together. "I'm glad to be back." Viv told me. "While I was in England all this seemed surreal, now I'm back I can come to terms with it."

Viv had been angry when I had spoken to her on the phone, she seemed much calmer now as she sat at the bar, chatting over things rationally with the lads. On the phone she had told me she was determined to get to the bottom of this, like most of us, she didn't believe Dave had malaria, cerebral or otherwise. After talking things over calmly face-to-face, she agreed with me that it was better to go with the flow, and not make any unnecessary ripples. Both of Dave's parents were still alive, he was their only child; they were obviously devastated over losing their son. How much worse would they feel if we did unearth any evidence to prove he had been poisoned as we had suspected. As Viv and James were about to leave she told me. "I spoke to The High Commission as soon as I got back, they have arranged for someone to come with me to Dave's apartment tomorrow morning. I'm not at all looking forward to it; that is why I wanted to do it as soon as possible."

"That isn't going to be pleasant. What are you going to do with Dave's things?"

"I have a list of things his Mum and Dad have asked for, other than that they have said I can do what I want with the rest. I don't even know what to expect when I go there. Dave hadn't lived there for long, as well you know. I have never been there, maybe there are some of Aysha's things there, I just don't know."

"It is good someone from The High Commission is going with you, besides having someone else there, they can witness what you take from the apartment; you know what it's like here, best to cover your back."

Viv left telling me she would be in for a coffee as soon as she had finished at the apartment. I did not envy her the task.

I woke during the night to hear the familiar groaning of the generator. The night security were instructed to put the generator on, two hours after a power cut had occurred, during the night, when the bar wasn't open it was not necessary to put it on any sooner. As I came around from my slumber, the events of the previous day dawned on me; the generator was going, so at least it was in full working order, even if my bank balance had suffered considerably.

Early the following morning I went across to the small supermarket, at the bottom of the car park near the hotel's arch. I strolled slowly up the narrow aisles between the over ladened shelves, concentrating on my purchases, and putting then into my wire basket, completely oblivious to the other customers around me.

"Good morning Helen. How are you?" It was Ali's softly spoken voice that greeted me.

"Oh, good morning Ali, sorry I was absorbed in my shopping, I didn't notice you. I'm fine thanks."

After exchanging further pleasantries Ali suddenly said, "When we had coffee, you implied you would sell The Dominion if the price was right. Am I assuming things or would you seriously consider selling?"

"I would sell, but I'm not actively looking for a buyer, but as you say, if the price was right."

"We, or should I say the management team of the hotel, would be more than interested in obtaining your property. You have to be honest Helen, if you look at the plans of The Peace Haven, The Dominion, does appear to be part of the same compound. From our point of view it would certainly tidy things up for us, but as you say the price has to be right, and we do have to persuade Mr. Hussaini of this, he may not be as keen as we are. Would you like me to talk to our accountants, and maybe we could all have a chat before putting this idea to Mr. Hussaini."

"Well....yes if you wish to." I desperately tried to sound only remotely interested; it would not be to my advantage for me to allow my real eagerness to show.

"I have your phone number, I will give you a ring when I have spoken to the powers that be; it may take a few weeks."

"That's no problem, as I said; I'm not desperate to sell."

I smiled sweetly at Ali, as we said our good byes. Could this really be the start of the end? Ali's remark about The Dominion appearing to be part of the same compound as The Peace Haven rang in my ears. Their lawyer had bought this point up in court many times; she maintained our land had once belonged to The Peace Haven, and that The Dominion had been built illegally on their property. I was never completely sure about this; I had heard many stories that appeared to substantiate this. My mind had gone into overdrive. I looked at the items I had in my wire basket. I couldn't even remember if this was all I wanted, my mind was a blank as far as the shopping was concerned. I got in the queue to pay for the items I had collected, if I had forgotten something I would have to come back later for it.

Rick and Nick were breakfasting when I returned to the bar; I made myself a coffee and joined them.

"What's up with you? Why are you so chirpy this morning?" Nick asked. "You should be crying over the cash you lost yesterday on your gennie, not full of the joys of spring."

"What's money to her?" Rick told him. "Easy come, easy go. She rips us off, the staff rip her off. What comes around goes around, that's what keeps Shendi ticking."

"True." I told them. "So I'm not going to cry over spilt milk, or washed generators. All is fine, fine."

Viv didn't look as if everything was fine when she returned from Dave's apartment in the middle of the afternoon. She looked gaunt and pale in spite of her bronzed sun tanned face; her eyes appeared sunken with dark puffy lines circling them.

"Hi Viv, you look in need of a coffee. Was it really awful?" I asked even though I knew it was.

"Helen, I don't know what to say. Can we go and sit out in the garden?"

I asked Momodou to bring us both a coffee, and we went and sat under a shady tree, out of earshot of my staff.

"There was hardly anything there." Viv told me.

"What do you mean? Are Dave's things missing?"

"I think someone has already been there. There were things all over the place, Dave was fussier than that, but as I told you before, this was the first time I had been to the apartment, so I can't say for sure, but he had lots of things at his last place. He may have taken things down to Sierra Leone to Aysha, so how am I to know what should be there? The guy from The High Commission has told me to make a list of what I think is missing, but I don't really know where to start."

"Did you find his lap top?"

"No, and that should have been there, unless Kawso has it in his office. I have asked him and he says he hasn't got it, but I've a feeling he wouldn't give it to me, if he did have it. As you know Dave's Dad has asked for his lap top. What will he think if I say I can't find it? Kawso told me the police had had the apartment cleaned up, so that it was all right for me to go in. I didn't know what he meant, but Helen it was awful. I was retching, all the windows have been closed, and the smell of stale blood was unbearable."

"Blood?"

"Yes, they had left the rags they had mopped it up with, on the floor. It hadn't been washed properly, it looked as if they had wiped it up with dry rags, and there were smears of it all over the tiles. A police guy that was with us saw me looking at the rags and kicked them into a corner of the room."

"Where was the blood from? Was he injured when he fell?"

"No, I was told it was from the back passage, and there was loads of it."

I sniggered. "Yeah…sure…that always happens with cerebral malaria! I didn't know about this blood. That can be a sign of poisoning, it thins the blood."

"Oh, right. I thought it was strange with malaria, but I hadn't thought about thinning of the blood. There was also a glass stood on the floor, and the police guy casually told me Dave had been getting himself a drink."

"Wasn't the glass broken?"

"No, and it was stood up, that is strange also."

"Yeah…A glass dropped unto tiles does tend to smash, and like I've mentioned before cerebral malaria can take you quickly, but not as quick as Dave died, it is general to go into a coma and drift away. It isn't normal to drop down dead when getting a drink, especially while being careful not to break the glass."

This remark made Viv give a slight smile. "We both think the same, but what can we do?"

"Not a lot, as we have already said, what can we achieve except bringing more problems unto ourselves? The police are involved, so whom else could we turn to, and The High Commission tend to keep a low profile. Look at Reg Preston's case, that trial isn't over yet and that is an open and shut case. It is best for us to turn a blind eye: also we can't help Dave and can only cause his family heartache."

"You are right. This darn country, it's a law unto itself. It is funny though that Aysha hasn't turned up, isn't it?"

"Yes, but I'm sure she will in time."

I brightened Viv up by telling her the story of my washed generator; she was highly amused by this. We had a second cup of coffee and both giggled over our various experiences since we had arrived here, and we decided we must all be a bit eccentric or just plain crazy to stay. Life was undoubtedly different to the lives we had all left behind.

Dave's parents had arranged to have his body flown home. After a discussion with Kawso, we agreed The Dominion would be the venue for our 'memorial' in Shendi. Kawso seemed eager for me to host this; I had expected him to want to hold it at his own restaurant. We decided this would take place at the same time as the funeral in Dave's hometown in England. I wrote a small speech to open the ceremony, talking about how I first met Dave and recalling some of my favourite and lighthearted memories of him. I would then invite anyone else present who wished to share their memories of Dave with us to speak, I knew Viv wanted to say a few words, and several of the lads had tales they wished to relate. After this a buffet would start our celebration of Dave's life, we knew he wouldn't have wanted it to be a sad occasion, and we were willing to remember the good times and not to dwell on the suspicious circumstances surrounding his untimely death.

The result of the post mortem took longer than we had expected, but there was nothing unexpected when the coroner finally gave his verdict at the inquest. Cerebral malaria. When we heard this we felt cheated, even though this was the result we expected. Due to the lengthy delay of the inquest, it was nearly three weeks before Dave's body was released to The High Commission and flown home to his family for burial.

By pure coincidence Peter and Frank from the U.K. police arrived again, for the never ending murder trial of Datu and Kebba, on the same plane that Dave's body was being flown home on.

"Nice to see you lads. I didn't think it was going to be necessary for you to come out again." I said as I greeted them.

"We were hoping not to return after our last visit, but yet again there are a couple of points they want us to clear up." Peter explained to me.

"Like my case over my right of way, they go on for ever."

"Yes, we have to really push for a verdict this time; we can't keep on coming out like this. How are you? Is everything alright?"

"I'm fine, still in court of course, and not getting any farther ahead with that. You will find the lads a bit subdued this evening. Do you remember Dave? He died recently and his body was flown home this afternoon on the flight you came out on."

"Sorry to hear that. What happened to him?"

"Well, according to the inquest it was cerebral malaria."

"You don't sound very convinced."

"I'm not, but maybe I'm paranoid, I'm probably speaking out of turn, and should keep my mouth shut."

"Spit it out. What do you think and why?"

I explained to Peter and Frank that Dave had had two malaria tests the same day that he had died and they were both negative. I went on to tell them how the body was found and the circumstances. I said my imagination was probably running wild, but I suspected he had been poisoned.

Peter and Frank gave each other a knowing glance.

"There will be an inquest back in the U.K." Peter told me. "But three weeks is a long time for them to have kept the body, before releasing it to the family." Maybe my imagination again, but I thought Peter was trying to tell me; it was too long to detect some poisons in the body, especially in the Shendian heat.

Chapter Seventeen

Light at the End of The Tunnel?

Kawso came to see me the morning of Dave's funeral.

"Have you written down what you are going to say this morning, Helen?" he asked.

"I've made notes to prompt me, yes," I replied, curious to know why he was interested.

He held out his hand and said, "Let's see them. "I need to know what you are going to say."

I looked at him astonished that he would make the demand and think that I was going to agree. "Pardon, why would you want to see them? You need to know what I am going to say. Why? What do you think I'm going to say? I'm going to talk about the first time I met Dave, a story I know will amuse some of my regulars, and then just generally talk about him. Is there a problem with that? Anyway, I haven't got them here; they are in the office".

"That's fine, fine, but Helen, please be careful. I am only trying to help. I do have respect for you, and I don't want you getting yourself into trouble, there maybe some Shendians that may not like some things you might say."

"What's that meant to mean? What could I possibly say that might offend anyone? As I said, I am just going to talk about Dave and how we met."

I was getting cross by now. What right did Kawso have to talk to me like that? I wasn't a member of his staff and I did not have to take it. However, I kept my thoughts to myself and just smiled at him.

"You do know what I mean, so don't make out that you don't. I will want to say a few words also."

"That's fine. I'll see you later." I said dismissively, hoping he would take the hint, and leave me in peace to get on with the preparations for the buffet. He stood there for a moment and then with a shrug of his immaculately clad shoulders and a shake of his coiffured head, he walked out of the bar.

We had expected this memorial to be long over by now. Dave's body had been flown back home two weeks ago, so it was now five weeks since he had died. As Peter had told me there would be, there was an inquest held in the U.K. The coroner in England had requested a more detailed death certificate, and a comprehensive report of the Shendian inquest. The death certificate that travelled with Dave simply gave the cause of death as natural causes. When a more detailed report was sent it gave the cause of death as cerebral malaria, as we knew it would. After having read the details of the Shendian inquest the U.K. coroner gave a verdict that mirrored this and gave leave for burial. There was no mention of poisons or anything untoward. If Dave had been poisoned as Viv and I suspected, there would have been no trace of them by the time the UK inquest was held.

As the guests started arriving for the memorial, I fully understood my conversation with Kawso earlier that morning. Four burly Shendians, who I didn't recognise, came in and stood at the back of the bar leaning against the wrought ironwork, near to the doorway. I glanced across at them. Unless I was mistaken, they were S.S.G. officers, dressed in their uniform of dark shirt, pastel coloured shirt and contrasting ties. Why were they here? One of them raised his hand in a friendly gesture, as he saw me look in their direction. I would be very careful what I said; there was no point in deliberately aggravating the authorities. The memory of my experiences with them after Jatou left my employment was still very fresh, I had no intention of leaving myself open to a repeat of that.

We started our memorial at exactly the same time as the funeral was due to start in the U.K. Greg, who had not returned to Shendi with Viv the previous week, was attending the U.K. funeral, representing all of Dave's friends in Shendi. He had told the family we would all be with them in spirit. We started by having a minute's silence, as a sign of respect, and to allow everyone a few moments alone with his or her thoughts. I then opened the proceedings, I knew Dave would not have wanted this to be a sad occasion, and being it was so long after his death the initial shock had worn off. I spoke of a few amusing events that bought laughter to the proceedings, and put everyone in a lighter mood. After I had finished, several others including Viv and Kawso gave their tributes and as we were finishing, the four Shendian gentlemen started filing out. Determined to make them aware I had noted their departure and their presence, I called a toast. "Would you please raise your glasses?"

"To Dave," someone interrupted.

"No," I said as I raised my glass in the direction of the obligatory picture of The President, hanging on the wall opposite the entrance. "Please raise your glasses to our President, and also to Dave."

The last of the S.S.G. men, who was stood in the doorway, turned and nodded in my direction. My small gesture hadn't gone unnoticed, they were now aware that I had known who they were and had been careful not to say anything controversial. Another half an hour passed before everyone who wanted to say a few words about Dave or share with us all an amusing story the likes of which we knew would keep Dave alive for us for many, many years.

The kitchen staff then served the buffet and the celebrations started. Everyone present signed the condolence book and added some memories of Dave, Viv and Greg were going to take this book, which had been on the bar for a few weeks now, to Dave's parents. We hoped that along side the messages of sympathy which would be a comfort to the family, this book would also give them an insight into Dave's life in Shendi.

It had been a busier than usual day shift with many regulars still in the bar when I went off duty at four. I was just nodding off when the phone went. I was surprised to hear Binta, Ali's secretary greet me when I answered." "Hello Binta, how can I help you?"

"Would it be possible for Ali to come and look over your property with three of our senior staff?"

"I don't see why not. When would they like to come?"

"Is mid-morning next Wednesday convenient?"

"That's fine; tell Ali I look forward to meeting him again."

Ali had obviously been serious when he spoke to me in the supermarket. I wondered who the others were, possibly the accountants he had mentioned to me. With the previous owners being well accustomed to The Dominion, it had slipped my memory that Ali had never visited the property, but had only seen plans of The Peace Haven, showing The Dominion as a blank shaded area. This boded well for my campaign of leaving. There was however, one huge drawback to their visit. My staff, who no doubt knew exactly where I was and who I had seen the other day, would now have confirmation of The Peace Haven's interest in The Dominion. This would need careful handling if it was not to add to my staffing problems.

Returning to the bar for my evening shift, I was amazed to find the bar was still bustling. Dave's memorial now had a party atmosphere, I smiled to myself, some might think this disrespectful, but I knew Dave would have approved. Carole an ex-pat girl, who was inclined to be vocal after a few drinks, was stood on a chair singing, unfortunately she was giving us her rendering of a different song to the one bellowing out from the C.D. player, non the less everyone seemed to be enjoying themselves. I had a pleasant surprise when I cashed the days takings, the memorial had gone on much longer than I had expected, and not only had I re-cooped the money I had spent on the buffet but I had made a nice profit, which was more than needed.

It was now only one week away from the staff's payday. After having withdrawn from the bank the last of the profits from the preceding high season, to pay for the repair on the generator, I had a shortfall on the staff's wages of about ten thousand shillings. Being low season the chance of accumulating that amount of income in a week was slim. Many of the bars and restaurants on the main tourist strip near to The Dominion closed either for all or part of low season. However, closure for me was not an option. Our court injunction with The Peace Haven over our right of way was in force for as long as we were trading. The Dominion was one of the few bars that remained open in the tourist areas, as I was afraid that if I closed even for a short while, the hotel might again attempt to build a wall across the entrance as they tried to do when Simon was around. If I had been able to shut for a while in low season The Dominion would have been a much better business proposition because I would have had no overheads or staff wages to find. As it was profits amassed during the high season soon diminished once the majority of tourists had gone home and we were left relying on expats and a few hardened visitors. In addition to the financial benefits, I was sure my mental and physical health would have improved. Working for many years without any break had landed me in a continual state of despair; total fatigue and depression were definitely setting in.

"Is there a problem?" Sidi asked me a couple of days later when I was having a coffee with him in the garden, discussing plans for the day.

"No, all is fine, fine. Why?"

"You seem very jumpy, and I've been told you were nigglely with the staff yesterday."

"What is it to do with you? Yes I was complaining at them, I do get annoyed when I'm working in the bar and I go into the kitchen and they are all sat down chatting when there are things they should be doing. Why do the staff tell you things like that, you are not their boss?"

"No, I am not but they do talk to me. You have been here a long time now; you know you must not judge locals like you judge Europeans."

"That may be but I expect my staff to work when I'm working, whether I'm in Africa or Europe."

"It is much hotter here, so you can't work so hard."

"I have to, so why not the staff?"

"See you always complain, you didn't used to be like this."

"I didn't used to have all the worries that I have at the moment. You know after the problems there had been lately, money is short, and it is pay day in a few days."

"Don't you have enough to pay them?"

"I've some towards it, but not sufficient."

"Don't worry about that, you know some of the hotels don't pay their staff in low season, the staff live off their tips. It's not a problem; pay them when you have the money."

I was astonished by his attitude. One minute he was telling me I was too sharp with the staff, the next he was suggesting that I delay paying them, which in my mind was a much more serious issue than a few complaining words from their boss. "I can't be like that; they have always been paid on time."

"I've told you not to worry, no other employers seem to care, and even the military and police don't always get paid on time."

"I know, that is why at the end of the month if they are short of money, everyone gets stopped at check points, they are hoping to collect bribes."

" Helen, you shouldn't say that! I must go now or we will be late back from shopping, just stop worrying."

Shendians seldom worry themselves over much, but I was amazed how lightly Sidi could dismiss that present cash crisis, he knew the staff would be up in arms if I failed to pay them.

I waited with trepidation for Wednesday and Ali's visit to come around. I wasn't exactly sure what they wanted to see. They might only want to walk around and familiarize themselves with the layout of the property, or they might want a tour of the house. I was trying hard not to raise my expectations too much, not wanting my high hopes dashed. I found it hard to concentrate on the running of the business, when foremost on my mind was Ali's visit, and my deepening financial problems. There was no way I would be able to hide Ali's tour from the staff on duty, they would be sure to draw their own conclusions from it. I knew there would be much speculation.

Ali arrived with four companions somewhat earlier than I had expected. I was glad that the usual breakfast crew had gone and, an extra bonus, Sidi and the chef had departed for a mornings' shopping, making two less pairs of eyes to follow us.

I was cleaning the counter of the bar when I first saw Ali waving to me as he and the four others came through the gateway. They were all smartly dressed in shirt and ties, emphasizing that this was a formal visit as opposed to a causal visit. None of them came into the bar and so I left my cloth on the counter, and went out to greet them. I shook Ali's out stretched hand,

and he introduced me to his companions, who were all Saudi businessmen, employed by Hussaini. I was told two of them were the hotel's accountants. Ali didn't explain who the other two men were; he only introduced them by name.

Latif was watering the beer garden, he watched my guests arrive with a surprised expression on his face. His eyes met mine; he looked away, turned his back towards us, and started watering the flower bed behind us. He acted as if he wasn't interested in what was happening around him, but I knew he would be eagerly watching us, to be able to report back to the other staff. I looked back towards the bar as I followed Ali and his comrades over the small wooden bridge that led to the main garden. As I suspected Momodou, who was the waiter on duty that morning, was cleaning the wrought ironwork gates, a perfect vantage point to watch the garden. This was the first time any of the staff had cleaned the ironwork without me asking them to.

Ali stopped in the middle of the garden, in the shade of the 'chandelier' tree.

"This is absolutely charming. I never imagined you had such lovely gardens here," he told me.

"We did a lot of work on the gardens, when my husband and I first arrived. The tourists appreciate the tranquillity here. Most lunchtimes in season, every table out here is occupied and we have only a few customers inside."

"I can understand that, I am pleasantly surprised."

There were nods of agreement from his companions. One of them followed by the others went over to the stage. They stood, as I had done many times, looking down at their hotel. Wishing them to feel free to look around unhindered, I stood back and left them to their own devices. After they had spent several minutes chatting among themselves, they turned their attention towards my house, and I watched them point at various things. Ali came back to join me.

"I assume that is your house over the wall?"

"Yes, and I have a garden there also, do you want to come and see that side of the property?"

"Please, while we are here we would like to see everything."

"May I order you all drinks for when we get back to the garden here?"

"Thanks, but no. The temptation to sit in your garden could become too much, and we may not return to the hotel. We all have a meeting in half an hour, and must not stay here too long."

We all went into my garden. This time I led the way, after the splendid colourful, floral display in the beer garden, the vegetable patch, fruit trees, and the plastic table with three wonky chairs that had seen better days, provided a stark contrast.

"This garden is larger than the other one, isn't it?" asked one of the accountants.

"Yes, but not very much." I told him.

"I'm impressed to see you growing your own produce," said Ali.

"We aren't able to grow sufficient for the restaurant, but what we are able to grow certainly helps, and if the garden wasn't put to good use it would only be wasted. I don't get much time to relax in it."

They didn't ask to see inside the house, but stayed awhile in the garden, strolling around the out buildings, nodding to each other, but saying very little.

"Would you like to come inside the house?" I asked.

"No," said Ali. "We have no interest in the building; we basically wanted to see the size of your property. It's all very well looking at plans, but you need to be able to see a site to appreciate the full concept." Two of them walked back through the small gateway leading to the beer garden, the rest of us followed; they had obviously seen all they had wanted to see. They stopped and all shook my hand, as we stood outside the main bar entrance, Momodou who was still enthusiastically washing the ironwork, smiled and nodded to my guests.

After they left, I went back to cleaning the bar; Momdou's cleaning seemed to come to an abrupt end. As he walked past me with his bucket in his hand, he asked me. "Wasn't that the Arab men from The Peace Haven?"

"Yes, they came to introduce themselves; they seem friendlier than our last neighbours. Have you finished cleaning the ironwork already?"

"Most of it, but best to stop now, the lunchtime people will soon be here."

I couldn't suppress the smile that came involuntary to my lips; sometimes I thought the staff considered me stupid. Momdou was soon followed into the kitchen by Latif, who had apparently finished watering the garden. "Watering finished?" I asked as he walked passed the bar.

"Nearly, I have come in for a drink of water."

I heard the voices coming from the kitchen, I could only understand part of the conversation, but I knew they were discussing Ali and his companions' visit and were making assumptions for the reason for it.

Latif had returned to his watering by the time Sidi and Ebou had returned from shopping, Momdou hurried out to help them unload the car. Latif called to Sidi, who instead of helping to carry the provisions into the kitchen, as he usually did, went into the garden to speak to Latif. I watched them from the bar. Shendians are very animated, when they speak, especially if they are excited or agitated. I was too far away to be able to overhear any of their conversation, but there was much arm waving and exaggerated hand movements, from both of them. The visit had undoubtedly disturbed the staff, which was only to be expected.

The first of my lunchtime customers arrived while Sidi and Latif were still talking, so Sidi was unable to quiz me about the visit, as I knew he would be eager to. Generally he left The Dominion as soon as he had returned from shopping to get back to his own shop in Famara, but that morning he went and got a coffee and sat in the garden drinking it. I'm sure he was hoping I would go out and speak to him. He was unlucky. I had no intention of discussing Ali's visit with him, or anyone for that matter. By the time he had finished his coffee several of my regulars were sitting around the bar. He took his cup back into the kitchen, and as he walked past the bar, said, "I will come back and see you when you are off duty this evening."

It was unusual for him to return in the evening, his curiosity was definitely getting the better of him.

True to his work, Sidi came back shortly after I had got up from my afternoon nap. "Are you rested now?" he asked.

"I'm fine. Will you go and order me a coffee, I need to be back in the bar soon."

"Go and sit in the garden and relax, I will have a coffee with you."

I went and sat in the garden, under the shade of the large mango tree that was producing a huge crop which, I noted, would be ready in a few weeks time. I prepared myself for the bombardment of questions I was expecting from Sidi. In a few short minutes he returned with the coffee, and pulled out a chair sat opposite me and lit a cigarette.

"Why were the Arabs here?" he asked.

Obviously he was concerned, there was to be no beating around the bush today.

"Arabs? What Arabs?" I asked innocently.

"You know what I'm talking about, the Arabs that were here this morning."

"Oh you mean Ali? He came to introduce some of his staff to me, but what business is that of yours?"

"Who is this Ali? And of course it is my business; you know I have to know what is going on. You know as well as I do you need a Shendian to help you with everything you do here."

"Sidi stop being awkward, you know Ali is the new manager next door, and if he is friendly towards me, I will be friendly towards him. You may help me with some of my business matters, but I do not need to tell you everything that I do."

"I know you went to the hotel a few weeks ago, you didn't tell me that either."

"No I didn't. There is no need for you to know if I meet someone for coffee."

Sidi didn't answer; in fact he drank the rest of his coffee in silence. I was comfortable with this silence. I didn't intend discussing any dialogue I had with The Peace Haven with him. Our conversation made me fully aware, as I had suspected that my staff did watch my every movement, and report what I did to Sidi. I had little doubt he was in complete control of the staff, but was confused how he had this power over them; they must hope to gain from this situation sometime in the future. I was met with hostility from the staff all that evening. I knew Sidi had gone into the kitchen and spoken to them before he returned to his village. I found their silence and hostile behaviour more threatening than Sidi's silence. I eagerly immersed myself in the friendly banter from my regulars around the bar. I only ever confided small portions of my problems to the lads, so they were generally unaware of the tower of strength they had become to me, albeit unknown to them.

I woke with a start that night after hearing a loud thud. It was still pitch black outside: it had to be the middle of the night. Squinting at my alarm clock I could see it was 3.40am so why could I hear voices.

This was not the first time I had been woken by noises at this time of night but it was not always easy to distinguish exactly where noises were coming from. The sandy, dirt track that ran behind The Dominion and led merely to The Peace Haven's tradesman's entrance, was only a few yards from my bedroom. I had thought in the past the sounds were coming from that road but on this occasion I wasn't so sure. The scuffles sounded closer, something heavy was being dragged, and the voices were getting nearer.

I managed to pick out a voice I knew. It was Pouka's voice – one of my security staff. He had worked for me for a long while, and most of the staff treated him with respect. In fact they tended to look to him for guidance and leadership when Sidi was not around. Pouka and Sidi were from the same village; and had grown up together, they were close friends, I was fully aware they both controlled the staff as much as I did, this was a situation, although I didn't like it, I reluctantly accepted, and tried to use to my advantage. I was tempted to get up and find out what was going on, but on reflection decided against this. I knew from the hushed voices there were at least two others besides my own security. Again my imagination started running wild, if I went out there, I could be overpowered from behind, and my security would claim no knowledge of what had happened. I was staying firmly in my bed any investigation could wait until morning. I didn't even put my light on, not wanting to draw their attention to the fact I was awake. I thought I had heard something heavy bought over the wall from the roadway and taken around to my main entrance, at the front of my property. No-one had left so, maybe the other voices I had heard were outside and not on my property at all, I couldn't be sure.

About an hour later a vehicle drove into the car park and pulled up outside my entrance. There was the sound of sliding metal like the sliding side door, of a local gilly-gilly. I listened carefully until amidst the scuffles and other unidentifiable noises I heard Pouka's voice again but I could not make out what he was saying. There were a couple of loud groans, they were definitely handling something heavy, and putting it into the van. Shortly after the van drove off. I lay in my bed bewildered. If this was something that had come over the wall and later been picked up from here, it was probably wisest of me to simply turn a blind eye to the events I had heard that night. Perhaps I would say nothing in the morning.

This was not the first time I had heard this vehicle, or a similar one in the car park during the night. I had thought it was someone joining the security lads for a glass or two of attaya, (green tea). I knew my security lads often sat in the middle of the car park and drank attaya with the security of The Peace Haven, and of The Mango Tree Hotel, whose back entrance was also in the car park. This was a practice I encouraged, hoping that if there was ever a problem during the night, they would join forces and help each other sort it out. I now wondered about this vehicle, I couldn't think of anything heavy from The Dominion that was being loaded, but I would start doing more thorough searches in the evenings before I went to bed. The kitchen was locked at night, and I had the only key, but maybe it was possible the kitchen staff were hiding provisions outside for collection during the night. I rarely went into the yard behind kitchen after closing. I knew, like everyone in the catering trade worldwide, I was losing stock from my kitchen. This was maybe how it was being done, but I knew what I had heard being moved that night was much too heavy to be a few provisions from my kitchen.

First thing in the morning, I went around the back of the garage; there was a small garden here, it was about six feet from the perimeter wall to the garage. We sometimes planted seed beds here but during the rains, which were now drawing to a close, this little garden tended to get overgrown with grasses and weeds. To clear this and to prepare it for seedbeds was one of Latif's first jobs after the rains had finished. I walked around the garden, where I seldom went this time of the year. I had no difficulty finding proof of last nights events. I expected to see downtrodden grass, instead of this; right in the corner, where the wall of the car park met the sandy lane, was a small patch of ground where nothing had grown, not a sign of any grass or even a weed. This small area of soil was solid packed hard ground; this had been trodden on many, many times during the rains.

I was in a quandary, should I mention it to Sidi which was tantamount to taking out a full page advertisement in the local paper, or should I keep quiet. I decided to show him the evidence. When Sidi arrived to take Ebou shopping, I said to him. "Before you go I want to show you something. Come and look at this, I want to know what you think."

I led the way around the back of the house, and showed him the patch of ground I had found.

"I don't understand. What are you showing me this for?"

"Look at this patch, there is no grass on it."

"Well."

"There is no grass here because it has had people walking on it repeatedly during the rains."

"You are crazy what are you trying to say? Nobody walks around here, they have no need to."

"I heard someone talking out here last night." I didn't intend telling him anything else I had heard.

"Maybe you heard the security speaking the hotel's security over the wall while they were patrolling."

"Yeah, maybe. That could be but I have told you many times I've heard a van in the car park at night. That van was here again last night."

"Oh please don't start all that again. I've told you that van is in the lane, not in the car park. You hear things at night and imagine all sorts."

"I heard Pouka talk to the driver."

"O.K. so maybe Pouka knows the driver. Come on Helen, sound travels a long way at night. You are just making things up. "

It was obvious Sidi had no interest, or at least was intent on dismissing this incident, which implied to me, that he probably knew more than he was letting on.

Pay day minus two, and I was still several thousand shillings short of my target, in spite of Sidi's insistence, that I simply tell the staff they would receive their salaries late this month, this weighed heavy on my mind. The worry of this distracted my thoughts from the events of the previous night. I always paid the staff on the 28th of the month, which was a few days before it was due, they should be paid on the last day of each month. I decided to broach the subject with Jed, when I came into the bar for my evening shift.

"There has been a few problems this month Jed, and you know we have been very quiet this low season, I'm afraid I won't be able to pay the staff on the 28th this month, you will have your money in a few days." I explained to him.

I saw by his expression, that he wasn't very happy about this, but he said, as he looked at me with blank eyes that gave away no emotion. "Fine, fine I will tell the others, but they won't be pleased about this."

"I know they won't like it Jed. Do you think I like to be in this position? But the staff should also appreciate that they all have jobs all year round. You know most of the restaurants in the tourist area close for a few months during low season, and those that do stay open put their staff on short time. Besides many of the bars and even some of the hotels keep their staff on, but don't pay them."
"Of course we know this, but we are used to being paid on time each month."

"Fine, fine, but as I have already said, you should remember I keep you all on, when you know I don't need you all, maybe next year I should put some of the staff down during low season, so the rest of you are paid on time, and as a point of fact your wages are due on the last day of the month not the 28th, I hope to pay you by the last day."

He reluctantly accepted this, and disappeared into the kitchen where I knew he was passing our conversation on to the rest of the staff. I was once again grateful to the regular customers around the bar, who unknowingly raised my spirits. None of the staff spoke to me after Jed had told them their wages would be paid later than usual this month. Their silence would have made the evening seem very long, had it not been for the friendly banter I had from the regulars.

The first of them to speak to me was Pouka, when, after I had locked up for the evening, I went to the small security hut, situated near the main entrance, to give the security lads the key to the main gate.

"Do you ever hear a vehicle stopping out here during the night?" he asked me.

As I had heard this many times, and Pouka was asking me this now, I assumed Sidi had spoken to him.

"Yes, I do actually, in fact I heard it last night, and it sounds a bit like a gilly-gilly to me."

"That's right, that's what it is a gilly-gilly. It is my brother, he finishes work at about 2 o'clock, and his last trip is to Malaville. He sometimes comes to drink attiya with us before going home to Famara."

"Your brother?" I asked. "Same mother, same father?"

In Shendi 'brother' can be anyone from an actual brother, to someone bought up in the same village. I always liked to clarify this, and I knew Pouka had sisters, but as far as I knew he had no brothers.

"No, not same mother, same father. A cousin brother, his father is my father now that my father is dead, so he is my brother." Relationships in Shendi are more complicated than in the west, the staff always seemed bewildered when I questioned the actual relationship of anyone introduced to me as a brother or sister.

"I only asked if you ever hear my brother coming, as I don't want you to worry about this."

"That's fine, fine, I will know who it is now."

Rather than allay my concern, this heightened it. Pouka and Sidi had obviously discussed this or why had Pouka suddenly told me this, the evening that I had mentioned it to Sidi. I had heard the vehicle many times, but Pouka hadn't found it necessary to mention it to me before. I decided the next time I heard it I would get up and walk around to the little garden behind my bedroom. If I stood on something I would be able to see over the wall. I must place an empty drinks crate in the garden; I thought that would be high enough to allow me to watch over the wall, as long as I had built up the courage to leave my bed at night.

A few more tourists were starting to arrive. All the flights of high season were due to start the following week, during this last week prior to season, the flights gradually increased, but the tourists that were here now were insufficient for me to be able to make up the short fall in my wage bill, in the next couple of days before the end of the month, when I had told the staff I would pay them.

"Don't fret." Sidi told me every time I mentioned this all-consuming worry to him. "I've told you it will be alright. If you don't have the money I will bring you enough to pay them, and you can give it back to me next month when the tourists are here."

This both consoled and concerned me. It was good to know he could loan the money to me. I knew I would have no problem paying it back next month, but where was he getting the money? He was always short of money, or at least he appeared to be. My mind flashed back over all that had happened that low season. As I suspected many times in the past, he was possibly gaining financially from many of my mishaps, this was all part of 'Life in Shendi'. Now I was suspecting he knew more, or was possibly behind the nocturnal events at The Dominion.

As I stood behind the bar drinking a coffee with my friend Karen the following morning, discussing my financial problems with her, and asking her opinion of what I had heard a couple of nights previously, (I confided much more in Karen, than I did in any of the lads) I was surprised to see Binta, Ali's secretary come into the bar. I watched her eyes flit around, I could see by her expression, she was more impressed by my premises that she had expected to be.

"Morning Binta, nice to see you."

"Hello Helen, I hope you are well. Ali has asked me to ask you if you would come to his office to have a chat with him and two of his companions from the other morning. He probably meant me to phone you, but I thought I would stroll up and visit The Dominion."

"Would you like a drink while you are here?"

"No, I don't have time. I shouldn't really have left the office. Are you able to come over next Tuesday evening at 6.30?"

"Yes Binta, that will be fine, I'll see you then."

Karen turned and watched her quizzically as she walked out of the bar.

"That was Binta, Ali from the Peace Haven's secretary." I told her. "Could this possibly be the end of my problems and release from my life sentence?"

She grinned. "Maybe parole not release. She seemed nice and friendly though."

"Yeah, she is, so is Ali. I have no hassle with the new regime at the hotel, but where these meetings will lead, if they lead anywhere at all, I have no idea."

"Any glimmer of hope has to be a morale boaster for you at the moment; but back to your immediate problems, if Sidi says he can lend you the money, let him. You know none of them ever have any money, but they can all find it when they have to. He will probably get it from someone in his family; you know some of his relatives have money. The unfortunate thing is he will feel you are in his debt, even long after you have repaid him."

"Yeah, I know what he is doing, I'm not stupid, but I'm in a hopeless mess. I have plenty of time to think over things, I know I get paranoid and tend to imagine things, but just think over some of the things that have happened here, I think he is partly to blame for the mess I'm in. I know he has gained from some things that have happened, look at the generator for example, now he will save the day with cash he has had from here, and try and get more control over me. My hands are tied, you know I need him to sort things for me, the authorities eat taubab women like me alive."

Karen giggled at this, but she knew what I meant.

"I desperately need the glimmer of hope, that maybe Ali can give me."

"How about the lads?" Karen suggested. "Would you consider asking any of them for the cash, it isn't that much, and you know you can repay it in a few weeks."

"We all know Terry has plenty of cash, or at least he keeps telling us he has, but I really wouldn't ask him, and I'm not sure he would lend it anyway."

"Nick?"

"He would help I know he would, but I have my pride also, I don't want to ask him, I will think about it though."

Terry arrived for his late breakfast, so Karen and I quickly changed our conversation to a much lighter topic, in spite of her suggestion Karen knew I didn't want any of the lads knowing the position I was in. This was not the first time she had advised me to confide in Nick, I knew as well as she did that he would help me if he could, but independence has always been a failing of mine, as long as I felt able to resolve the situation I would do it on my own.

Monday arrived, the last day of the month, this is the day I should pay the staff, and I was still seven thousand shillings short of the wage bill. I was deeply distressed by this, none of the staff raised the subject until I went off duty for my afternoon break; and then Momoudu broached it with me.

"It is the last day of the month, are we going to have our pay this evening?"

"Not to-day I'm afraid. You will get it in a few days, sorry." I said this in a whisper. None of them could possibly know the emotional pain this gave me; I walked out of the bar, my mind in turmoil. I went into the office to cash the lunchtime takings, and broke down. I was a quivering mess, I sobbed and sobbed. I knew Sidi was right when he told me I shouldn't worry about this, many people don't get paid at all in low season, but this didn't make it right. I knew the staff weren't completely without cash, they had had their share of the tip money each Saturday, to which I added considerably, as I knew most of them were not good at handling money, and were inclined to spend all their wages at once, so I did this to help them eke out their pay. I also knew they were stealing from the kitchen, so none of them or their families would go hungry.

The staff themselves had two meals a day, while they were at work, and I allowed them to take left overs home to their families, besides the stock that went unaccounted for, so I really shouldn't feel too bad; but I had never been in a position like this before, and on my own I found it a very heavy burden to carry. Sidi arrived soon after I had gone into the house.

"Just look at you." He said. "You have been crying your face is all red and puffy. You will have to pull yourself together before you go into the bar this evening. Why do you carry on like this? I will never understand taubabs; this is nothing."

I didn't answer him; I couldn't be bothered with anything at that moment. A book lay on the coffee table beside me; I picked it up and made out to read. My eyes scanned the page, but I knew I couldn't concentrate, and if I attempted to read the words, my mind wouldn't absorb them, but I hoped Sidi would leave me alone, when he realised I wasn't in the mood for conversation. He sat opposite me for a while, then thankfully took the hint, and said. "Fine, if you are not going to speak to me I will go and have a coffee in the kitchen with the lads. I will get them to send you in something to eat, then when you have had that, you must try and do something with your face, it will soon be time for you to return to work, and your eyes are still red."

I didn't bother to answer, but thought, 'aye, aye boss,' which made me realise my sense of humour wasn't completely lost. I hoped the lads would be in good humour during the evening; this was more the tonic I needed than the food Sidi had ordered for me.

The following day, I eagerly waited for the evening to arrive, curious to know what Ali and his companions wanted to discuss with me. Sidi had come to take the chef shopping as usual, he hadn't mentioned anything about the staff's wages and neither had any of them. I had expected some mention of their pay, but as nothing was said, I thought Sidi had possibly discussed this with them the previous evening.

I dressed conservatively in a calf length dark skirt, with a neat formal contrasting blouse, my aim was to look business like, but glancing in the mirror before I left I hoped I wasn't dressed too formal for the occasion. All the staff's eyes turned towards me, as I walked into the bar, they were unaccustomed to seeing me wear anything other than my uniform that matched their own.

"I should be back before I'm due on duty." I told Jed as I strolled through the bar.

I saw the staff glancing at each other, their curiosity getting the better of them. As last time I went to see Ali, I knew they would be watching where I was going. I was relieved none of the ex-pat lads had arrived for the evening yet, or their curiosities would be heightened also.

My nerves started to get the better of me as I slowly walked past La Parisian and one of their bar staff called out to me, "Evening Helen, you taking a stroll?"

"Yes, just relaxing before I start work again."

I could feel their eyes on me as I entered the hotel's main entrance. I knew what my staff didn't see for themselves, they would tell them.

I hoped Ali would be waiting for me to arrive, the thought of sitting in his outer office waiting for him may prove too much for me. My heart beat faster and faster the closer I got to the hotel's reception. I gave a small sigh of relief as I saw Ali stood near the reception desk talking to one of the hotel's guests. When he saw me enter the reception area, he broke off his conversation, and turning towards me said.

"Good evening Helen." and indicated the door that led through to his office, which I was familiar with by then. "Go through, Binta is in her office, ask her to order coffee for all of us please, I will be with you very soon." He followed after me almost immediately and before I knew it I was in his office and feeling much more at my ease.

"The others will be here very shortly; Binta has let them know you are here." He told me, and continued to make small talk with me in his usual pleasant manner until Binta came into the office, to serve us coffee and fancy cakes, and we were joined by one of Ali's companions that had been with him at The Dominion, and another Arab gentleman I didn't recognise as having been there.

"Do you remember Tascali, our head accountant? And this is Abdul, he is also an accountant."

I stood and shook hands with both of them. "Pleased to meet you." I said to Abdul.

We all sat at the elegant round oak table, near the window, which was open to its full extent making the room nice and airy. Tascali and Abdul sat near each other, with Ali only a short distance away from them. I was opposite them, feeling somewhat out numbered and alone.

"Shall I pour the coffee?" Tascali asked Ali. It had been served to us in the same impressive coffee pot as on my last visit to this office. Ali told him to, as he offered me a cake.

"We were impressed with your property." Tascali told me, as he poured my coffee "Ali would very much like to extend our hotel into it, and we can both see the advantages of that, a few extra bedrooms would certainly be an asset if this coming season is as busy as the last."

"That's a fact." Abdul interrupted him. "Last season, especially over the Christmas period we had to refuse bookings."

"But before we can seriously discuss this, we have to sell the idea to Hussaini. " Tascali told me. "He has already invested heavily into Shendi, and I'm sure you know he is now going ahead with plans to build another five star hotel, farther along the coast. We need to present him with a good business package, if we want him to come around to our way of thinking."

This conversation was not going in quite the direction I had dared to hope it might. It was becoming plain to me Tascali was building up to offering me a ridiculously low price. They were fully aware of the position of The Dominion, and the never-ending court case, it was very unlikely anyone other than themselves would have any interest in purchasing my property.

"Do you wish us to make some serious calculations, and put together a case to present to Mr. Hussaini?" Abdul asked me.

"If you are serious about purchasing The Dominion, I think you should start talking cash to me, before assuming I will sell."

"Not many people with a good business head would be keen to take on The Dominion where it is situated. We are offering you a chance to sell a property, which you know as well as we do, is basically unsaleable."

I definitely didn't like the course this conversation was taking.

"To a degree you are right, but as I said start talking hard cash."

"Without careful calculations, we cannot say for sure, but as a rough estimate I would say we could possibly offer you something in the region of $50,000."

At the time the exchange rate was approximately two dollars to the pound.

"What!" I exclaimed, I was by then expecting a low offer, but I considered this a sheer insult. "My husband and I paid £125,000 for The Dominion over seven years ago; I have documentation to substantiate this. During the first year we were here we spent several thousand pounds more renovating it. $50,000 I wouldn't even consider."

"You must remember we are looking at this venture in two different ways." Tascali pointed out to me. "You are thinking you are selling your business, but we have no interest in your business whatsoever. We are purely interested in the land to enable us to extend our hotel. We would knock down your bar, and extend the hotel on the site."

"I hope you are aware that is also my home, there is a three bedroom spacious house on the property besides the bar."

"Yes, yes, but as I am trying to explain to you that doesn't come into it. We are businessmen; we look on every new project we undertake as a five-year investment. In the first five years we expect to recoup the original investment. In this case the original investment would be the money spent on purchasing your property, plus all the expenses incurred in our constructions, we have to off lay those expenses against the profit we anticipate making from the new extensions. We have made a rough estimate and feel $50,000 is the fairest offer we could make you."

"As you have said I am looking at this from a different angle to you, and that figure is way below what I would need to re-house myself, possibly back in the U.K. to start a new life, let alone compensate us for our initial outlay, when we purchased The Dominion."

"Oh, come now." Abdul, who had allowed Tascali to do most of the talking, interrupted abruptly. "When you purchased The Dominion, you must have realized the position it was in, and that there were no long term business prospects there. Surely you bought it with the intention of enjoying a good income from it for a few years, and moving on, I consider we are offering you, your best option to move on with your life. You must have known the possibility of regaining your original outlay didn't exist."

"Well no, I didn't actually, and I don't accept that."

"Then you can't have researched the background of your property very well, but never-the-less, we will be fair to you. Working on the five year business plan, that most investors work on, if you can produce your books showing your annual profit from the business is one fifth of your purchasing price, we may re-think and come up with an offer that is more to your liking."

He knew as well as I did the profits from a business like The Dominion in Shendi, would not measure up to the figures he commanded, which is probably why he said this to appear that they were being reasonable.

"It is you that initiated these talks. I am happy to sit on my property until such a time that I decide to sell, or I get a good offer for it." I told him determined to make a stand, and desperately hoping I was keeping my voice on an even keel, and not giving away my bitter disappointment.

"So you are showing yourself to be the difficult women we have heard about, destined to become a thorn in our sides, are you?" asked Abdul.

"That's unkind." Ali told him. "Helen is bound to see things in a different light to us. Let her think things over for a while."

"Yeah, anyway we have business to attend to. Nice meeting you Helen." Abdul told me, although I doubted the truth of this. Both he and Tascali stood up and shook my hand before they left the room, having spoken a few words in Arabic, to Ali, which I considered rather rude.

"Would you like another coffee?" Ali asked me as the others shut the door behind them, and we were alone again.

"No, I really must get back, I am due on duty." I told him.

"We are serious about your property Helen; it has a lot of potential for us. Think carefully about the position you are in, as you know the reality of finding another purchaser is slim. Bide your time they will possibly come up with a better offer in due course. I will instruct them to get a package together, for us to present to Hussaini; he is a decent man. If he visualizes this extension in the same way that we do, he may even up the offer himself."

"Yes Ali, I do understand what you are saying, and I don't consider I am an unreasonable person, but I will fight for my rights, and I won't go away for a pittance."

Ali and I parted on friendly, albeit on somewhat strained terms, and I walked the short distance back to The Dominion downhearted, in fact practically in tears. I had had high hopes of this meeting, but instead I saw the light at the end of the tunnel flicker and diminish to a mere partial darkness.

I gave a quick wave to the few customers sat at the bar as I walked past, I told myself I must quickly raise my spirits to go into the bar and not let my emotions show. I saw one lone figure sat at a table, at the far side of the beer garden, as I slowly strolled around the outside of the bar, to go into the house, to change into my uniform in readiness for my evening shift. On seeing me the figure stood and walked towards me, as he got closer I realized it was Sidi. I fleetingly wondered what he was doing here at this time of day, it did cross my mind the staff may have informed him I had gone to the hotel again and he had come to investigate.

"Where have you been?" he asked aggressively as he came near to me.

"I've been out to have a coffee with some friends. Why do you ask?"

"You are usually here. The lads told me you had gone into The Peace Haven."

"I did, they serve coffee there, you know."

"Why have you been out, have you seen someone to try and raise the money to pay the staff?"

"What business is that of yours?"

"I don't understand why you speak to me like that, I always try and help and you speak rough to me. I told you I would sort the money and I have, look here is enough to pay the wages." He held out a plastic carrier bag to me.

"Oh." I said surprised, I had been caught off my guard; I didn't know what to say.

"Put it in the safe, and when you go out into the bar, tell them you will pay them tomorrow. You can sort their envelopes out before you get busy in the morning, and pay them as soon as possible."

"Where did you get the money?" I asked suspiciously.

"Now that's not your business, but I will need it back as soon as you have it."

"That's not a problem; I will have it in a couple of weeks. All the flights start coming this week-end."

I watched Sidi walk out, clutching the bag of money in my hand. I went into the office and put it in the safe. As I placed each bundle on the small inner shelf, I wondered where the money had come from. Sidi may have borrowed it from some of his family, but with the growing mistrust of him I had had for several years, which had been heightened over the last few months, I convinced myself that this was actually my own money that he was loaning me. I didn't like feeling like this, I liked to trust people, which had been one of my downfalls since arriving in Shendi. I quickly dismissed this thought; he wouldn't do that surely?

I was in a lighter mood when I returned to the bar. My meeting at The Peace Haven hadn't gone at all as I had hoped it would, but I now had the money in the safe to pay the staff, and soon with the coming high season to look forward to, my finances would be greatly improved.

Viv looked angry as she came into the bar with Greg for their evening meal.

"Evening, what's up?" I asked as she sat herself on her usual bar stool.

"I've had a bit of a set to with Kawso."

"That's easily done, what over?"

"Still the on going saga of Dave's laptop. Greg and I fly home again in four days and I promised to take it back for his dad."

"Are you sure Kawso has it?"

"At first he said he didn't, and then he said he did, and then he had misplaced it. Now he says he never had it in the first place. These people irritate me; I will punch one of them one day."

"Ssh." Greg told her. "Remember Helen's staff can hear."

"That is certainly strange, but then again a lot of what Kawso does is strange." I told her.

"Yeah, I know. It's not that I'm really bothered about the laptop myself, if Dave's dad hadn't asked for it I wouldn't be concerned where it was, but I will feel awful visiting the family if we haven't got it."

"It is a tricky situation, but why would Kawso want it? There has to be something he is trying to find on it. I wonder if he knows Dave's password."

"Surely he doesn't? Anyway there is nothing else we can do, but I won't let it rest. I will go and see Kawso everyday until we go home."

About an hour after Viv and Greg arrived, in which time several topics of conversation had been raised and Dave's laptop had slipped to the back of Viv's mind, her mobile rang. Viv went into the garden to answer her phone, the reception wasn't very good in the bar, due to so much steel and wrought iron in the building, and obviously the bar was generally noisy. When Viv came back she was shaking her head. "I can't believe this. That was Kawso, he was adamant, when we spoke to him this evening that he didn't have the laptop. He has just told me that if we go and see him in the morning he will give it to us."

"Don't be worrying yourself as to what he may or may not be up to. " Greg told her. "We will go and collect it in the morning, and that will be the end of all this."

"Yes, I'm just relieved we will have it, but you must admit it is all very strange."

"As we have said, lots of things are strange here, but let's let everything be. We can't do anything about them, and Dave's family will be happy they have his laptop."

Greg was as ever the calming force behind Viv.

Chapter Eighteen

Things That Go Bang in the Night

Three days later Viv and Greg were sat on the U.K. bound flight content they had Dave's laptop in their luggage, together with our condolence book and a few of his possessions that the family had asked for. I was stood in my usual position behind the bar, as I heard the plane pass overhead. I was also content. I had paid the staff with the money Sidi had loaned me; the tourists had started to arrive, so I would soon be able to repay him as the arrival of the tourists spelt the end of my financial problems, or at least a respite from them until next low season.

The start of high season was only six weeks before Christmas. I resolved to focus my mind on this. Christmas bought with it the potential of high financial gain, and this was something I desperately needed. Coming so close to the start of the season, it tended to creep up unnoticed and suddenly spring itself upon me. Thinking of Christmas put Kevin, Steph and little Karen foremost in my mind. Karen was now a bonny little girl, far removed from the baby in the first photos I had of her, she had recently had her second birthday, and I was no nearer to being able to travel to the U.K. to see her. Kevin had mentioned bringing her to Shendi, but I quickly quashed this idea. I would never forgive myself if they bought her to visit me and she was unfortunate enough to contract malaria. I obviously missed Kevin and Steph, but I felt I was missing so much by not being able to be a part of Karen's life.

Many of my regular tourists bought me photos to show off their new grandchildren, and give me news of their families. I looked enviously at their photos, pleased they wanted to share them with me, and knowing they were oblivious to the emotional pain their photos caused me. Sometimes in my darkest moods, which seemed to be occurring more and more frequently, it was only the knowledge I would see Karen when I finally could return to the U.K. that kept me sane. I needed something positive to cling unto, and seeing Karen was proving to be the goal I was aiming towards.

"Is the season starting O.K.?" Sidi asked when he came to collect the chef for shopping the next morning.

"Going quite well. Why? Are you worried about your money?"

"No, not worried about it, I know you will give it to me when you have it, but if you have any cash to spare I could do with some of it now."

"If you wait a couple of weeks I will give you it all."

"I'm thinking of extending my business in the village, into the property next door to the shop. I was intending to get a few tables and chairs and making it into a small non-alcoholic bar for the Muslims. Do you think that is a good idea?"

"Yeah, that may work well in the village. It certainly wouldn't go down well around here. How much do you want?"

"As much as you can afford. I need two thousand up front for the rent, so I would like that. If you can spare more I can start buying the tables and chairs."

"I will see what I can spare while you are out shopping, and we will talk about it when you come back, but if you are having it a bit at a time, I want you to sign for it as I give it to you, so I know exactly where I am."

"Fine, fine, I can see you don't trust me."

I didn't answer that last comment, but he was right, the trust I once had in him was much diminished now.

As soon as Sidi and Ebou went out shopping I went into the office to reassess my finances, I decided to give Sidi 4,000 shillings. I actually could have repaid him most of the loan, but considered it unwise to let him know how well the season was going. When they returned from shopping I offered him the 4,000 and luckily he was satisfied with this.

"There's something else I've been thinking about." Sidi said to me as I handed him the money.

"Yeah, what's that?" I asked with trepidation wondering what money making scheme he was about to suggest to me.

"I've been thinking about Reggie's compound?"

"What about Reggie's compound?"

"There is a long time now we have been looking after it, and the watchman is a problem at times, you remember the problem he caused when he came here? At first a few people looked at it, and it didn't sell. People knew how he died; I think that is why it didn't sell. Tourists and new ex-pats that want to buy compounds now probably have never heard of Reg. It should be easier now".

"Yes, that is true, maybe we should be trying harder to sell it again. I must admit I used to mention it to everyone that was looking to buy a property a few years back, but with so many things on my mind now, I tend to forget about it. If it were sold, it would be one less worry."

"Did you see me sitting with four guys in suits in the garden, a few days ago?"

"Yes, I saw you chatting to some men, but I was busy and didn't take much notice."

"They sell houses, they tell me they are very successful at it, and are looking for more properties to sell."

"You mean they are estate agents?"

"Not like the taubab estate agents with offices up the tourist strip, but they always wear suits and are very smart, so they manage to sell to tourists, they are not at all like the lads that go looking for property to sell on bikes, these are professionals. Is it alright to take them to look at the compound and see what they think about it?"

"Well, as I said it would be a relief to have the house sold and off our hands, when I agreed to look after it, I never imagined it would still be unsold a few years later. Yes, take these men but keep me informed what is going on."

"Don't I always? You confuse me sometimes; you act as if you don't trust me anymore."

Once again I didn't answer his comment. As I walked back into the bar, I thought that maybe my luck was turning. The season was progressing well, and the possibility of Reggie's house being sold would be another load off my mind. In spite of my recent meeting with Ali and his colleagues, I still clung to the hope of an eventual positive result with The Peace Haven, and I definitely wanted Reggie's compound sold before I left Shendi, or goodness knows what would happen to it.

Late in the afternoon, Nick came in for a couple of drinks before going home for his afternoon nap.

"Do you remember a few weeks ago, Kevin and I telling you when we walked across the car park from The Mango Tree, we saw some lads hanging around outside your wall at the back of your kitchen. Some of your staff were talking to them over the wall, and ducked down when they saw us. We said we thought they were up to no good."

"I remember that."

Grinning from ear to ear, Nick went on. "I've just had a drink in The Mango Tree with Jimmy the new manager. You know him don't you?

"I do, but not very well. He's Shendian isn't he, recently come from spending a few years in the UK?"

"That's him; well, he told me he regularly sees frozen chickens flying over your wall. Never mind eh?" Nick appeared to find this very amusing.

"Oh no." I obviously knew from my stock checks, I was losing chickens, and I did wonder if they were going over the wall. "The buggers! What makes it worse is I laughed a few months ago when Rod told me he had seen this happening to Brian." Brian ran a well established ex-pat bar farther along the coast, and was my main competitor.

"That will teach you not to laugh at others misfortunes." Nick told me sternly. "Now we know what they are doing, I will help you keep an eye on them. I will causally stroll outside and see who is hanging around whenever I go out for a pee."

"Thanks, but if you keep going outside the gate every time you go to the toilet, my security will soon realize what you are doing, and tip the kitchen off."

"Yeah, I suppose, but at least it will act as a deterrent we'll get the other lads to keep an eye open as they come and go. Something else Jimmy told me."

"Oh no, there's not more is there?"

"Don't panic, it's not you that's losing out this time. Jimmy lives in one of the top rooms opposite here, if he can't sleep, he sits outside on the balcony, so he sees what goes on here at night."

"Really, this I do want to hear. I've been woken by strange noises, but am a bit scared to investigate."

"Right well this should please you. You know The Peace Haven has those two large tanks in the back lane to store their diesel."

"Yes, you can't exactly miss them."

"Well apparently some lads leisurely stroll down the lane and siphon diesel out of these tanks into barrels that just happen to be left there earlier, Jimmy doesn't know who puts them there yet."

"But the hotel's security on the back gate must see this."

"Yeah--well I think they even help sometimes. These barrels then come over your back wall behind the garage."

"I can show you the exact spot. No grass has grown there this rainy season."

"The barrels are moved around to just inside your gate."

I interrupted Nick. "Where they are collected about an hour later by a van with sliding doors, maybe a gilly-gilly."

"Oh, so you already know." Nick answered, surprised by my knowledge of this.

"I told you I had been woken by strange noises, I hadn't figured out what they were doing, but I knew something heavy was coming over the back wall, being dragged around to the front, and collected by a van. I'm pleased now I know what they are doing, but what do I do about it?"

"It's not your problem. That has got to be a nice little earner for your security lads; they must be the wealthiest security in Shendi."

"I had wondered what was going on and Sidi told me I was imagining things. Thank Jimmy for enlightening me about this."

"Yeah, I have asked him to keep an eye on things for you. Remember his room is much higher than here, he can see all that goes on here from his balcony he knows all about your problems with The Peace Haven and he reckons you are getting a raw deal, without being ripped off by your own staff, so he will help you if he can."

"What does he say about the diesel?"

"Like I said, let it be, in fact he was quite amused by it also, he doesn't like The Peace Haven anymore than you do. They should realize they are losing diesel, if they don't it is their problem, not yours."

"Yeah, but if my security are involved, it is my problem also."

"Don't talk daft, if they are nicking from next door, they're leaving your things alone. Let it go."

On reflection I realized Nick was right, I wasn't losing anything personally, and if I interfered in this little scheme of theirs, it would bring repercussions for me.

The next couple of weeks drifted by without incident, no more disturbed nights and my stock of frozen chickens seemed to last longer. The tour reps were telling me Shendi's tourists were down on the previous year, if this was correct, I was more than content with the amount of custom that came through the gates of The Dominion. I had repaid Sidi in full for the loan to pay the staff's October salary. I was saving every shilling I could to pay the taxes and licences that fell due every January. I was also saving as much sterling as possible. This would be transferred to Kevin's bank account in the UK for him to buy birthday and Christmas presents for his family. I was late sending it this year, Steph and Karen's birthdays had been and gone, but the perilous state of my finances had meant the usual transfer of funds had had to be delayed.. All was going well now and I had enough sterling to transfer. The plan was to give the sterling to Oliver, my bank manager, when he came in for his lunch in a few days, for him to send to them. Much as I would have preferred to go shopping for them myself, whilst there was an array of locally made merchandise for tourists to take home as gifts, there was nothing else. Shendi was definitely not a shopaholic's paradise.

As the evening quietened down towards the end of yet another successful day, and the usual dozen or so diehards were propping up the bar, I went into the office to cash the evening's takings, which I hoped would be good. Automatically, I put the key in the office door and turned it only to find it was unlocked. I stood there, I was dumbfounded, locking the door was automatic, there was no way I would ever leave it open, so had I simply forgotten to lock it? No, I couldn't have but I must have left it open. I thought back over my actions since cashing up the lunchtime takings. I had gone to the office at four as I went off duty, had I been since? No, so the door had been open all that while. Wait a moment, I had gone back for some change at about 8pm so had I left it open then? Surely not, but the proof was there, the door was unlocked. I was obviously getting more and more absent minded. What on earth had I been thinking of – or rather not thinking of? I looked around the office; everything seemed to be in order. There was the usual clutter of cases of wine, next to bottles of spirit and various fruit juices on the floor, stacks of boxes containing invoices and paperwork going back years which I would need for any inspection and crammed in the corner the safe and my desk which I had inherited from the previous owners' eight year old daughter. I looked around again; nothing seemed to have been moved. I was simply getting absent minded.

I sat at my tiny desk and the unlocked door was soon forgotten as I calculated the evening's bills and counted the money. The takings were good; the evening had been as profitable as I had hoped. Sat in the office, counting the takings, always gave me deep satisfaction, and convinced me this life style was worthwhile. Reaching into my pocket, I took out the safe key to deposit the takings. The small safe was always fairly full, besides the petty cash and unbanked money, used for the day to day running of the business, there were several passports, my own and some of the ex-pats who didn't have their own safes, and several envelopes, some containing money I was saving for various things, one of which had my sterling in for Kevin and the family, other envelopes were sealed and contained money I was looking after for other people.

I kept my takings in a bundled together in piles of a thousand shillings ready either to bank or to use to pay for supplies the next day. As I picked this 'ready money' off the shelf. I immediately realized this it was a lot lighter than it should have been. I never knew exactly what was in that pile, but I did know how many thousand shilling bundles should be there, and I knew three of these bundles were missing. I stared at the pile in disbelief. I knew there should be five, one thousand bundles; there was only two. I continued to stare at it, as if by doing so, it would suddenly materialise again, before my eyes. I knelt down in front of the safe and peered in. My hands started to tremble as I took envelopes out of the safe to check them.

I could see at a glance that all the ex-pat's envelopes were still sealed and that they had not been tampered with. Then I checked my envelopes. I knew exactly what should be them as I always wrote it on the outside and it was with great relief that I counted the first two and found they were correct. However the third was two thousand shillings short, and another was a thousand short, so altogether there was six thousand missing. Then I picked up my sterling envelope which should contain £250. I always kept this at the bottom of the pile as it was the one I used the least. It felt and looked too thin. Fearing the worst I closed my eyes and opened it up. I could feel nothing inside it; shaking like a leaf I opened my eyes and looked. It was empty.

I stood staring at the envelopes and money on the desk. For a moment I stood still, forgetting even to breathe. I carefully recounted everything again, every now and then checking the sterling envelope, still in some unexplainable way expecting to see it had been there all the time, and I had woken from an awful nightmare. Of course it wasn't, this was reality, I wasn't dreaming. I watched my hands as they picked up each envelope and bundle of money as if in slow motion, they were acting involuntary; I was not consciously doing this. I must pull myself together. The missing sterling hurt me more than anything. The shillings were incidental. I would need them in January to pay my licenses, but they could be replaced. It was the sterling. There was absolutely no chance of saving enough sterling to send to the family in time for Christmas. I placed everything back in the safe, and relocked it. My mind was clicking back into action. The office door had been unlocked, but I remembered unlocking the safe. I inspected the lock. There were scratch marks around the keyhole, but I couldn't be sure if these were new ones, or were these from when the safe was tampered with before?

Numb and slightly unsteady on my feet, I locked the office door, and went and sat in my lounge. Why was I so stunned? This wasn't a unique occurrence; hardly a week went by, that I didn't hear about an ex-pat having a break-in. Why should I assume it wouldn't happen to me? I was fortunate to have lived here so long without a break-in. I was not special; I was not immune to theft. In most cases if a culprit was ever found, it proved to be an inside job, the maid, gardener or watchman. This was what I was suspecting now.

I sat pondering. The security lads walked the perimeter of the compound every ten minutes. I had seen them patrolling that evening. It would take longer than ten minutes for some one to break into the safe. The office door had been unlocked. I was usually very careful about doing this, of course I doubted myself now, but I still thought it unlikely the door had been left unlocked. I considered the possibility as before that some one had a key. I thought about the stupidity of the perpetrator, if he or she had only taken from the envelopes, it might have been several days before I realized anything was missing. I had only checked the envelopes when it was obvious to me money was missing from my bundle of 'ready money'.

Sidi was my main suspect, the missing money was probably sufficient for him to open the local bar he was planning to run in his village; but he couldn't have done this alone; even if he had copies of the keys. This was a possibility, my mind leapt forward. Maybe the previous attempted break-in had been staged so that the lock of the safe would have to be changed. I remembered querying the number of keys I had for the new lock. The security team would have seen him in the office, and he would also have needed a lookout, to warn him if I left the bar. Some evenings, I went into the office several times, to get change for the till, as I had done that evening; or to get wines or spirits we had run out of in the bar.

I was aware all the staff often acted together against me. I sat there feeling very alone and vulnerable. I was conscious of someone walking past the door. I quickly got up and walked the short distance to the sliding glass door that led into my garden, When I looked out I saw Pouka, patrolling around the out buildings. I called to him. "Is everything alright this evening, Pouka?" I asked.

"Yes, why do you have a problem?"

"I just wondered if anything unusual had happened."

"No, like what?"

"Has anyone been in my private areas this evening?"

"No."

"Anyone at all. Has Sidi been back this evening, or any of the waiters or kitchen staff been around the back here, any of the customers anyone?"

"No. Are you all right? Is there anything bothering you?"

"Umm—I'm fine." I said, as I thought, he knows exactly what's bothering me.

I went back indoors and still trembling, I picked up the phone, and stood looking at it before I dialled Sidi's number. I wasn't sure it was him that I wanted, but whom else could I call? I was tempted to call the police, but I knew deep down they wouldn't really be interested, this was a very common occurrence, and as the office door was open they would say I hadn't been broken into, I knew they wouldn't treat this matter seriously.

"Where are you?" I asked as soon as he answered.

"At the top of the strip." He was only two minutes drive away at the top of the tourist strip! What was he doing in this area at this time of night? My suspicions were heightened; but on the other hand, why tell me he is this close? If he told he was at home in Famara, I wouldn't have known any different.

"What are you doing down here?"

"I gave two lads from the village a lift. I'm going home now."

"Come down here."

"Why, has something happened?"

"Just get here. NOW."

I slammed the phone down. Not only was my heart beating rapidly, I was physically shaking. I resolved to calm myself in the short while before Sidi arrived. Fear was setting in. I couldn't really afford to lose the money, but knew I would eventually be able to replace it. The fear was what might happen next. It was clear to me; the problems I had had recently were more than mere coincidence.

"What's wrong? What has happened?" Sidi asked, as he came into the house and found me pacing the lounge.

"There is money missing from the safe."

"What?"

"About six thousand shillings and all my sterling have been taken from the safe."

"Sit down and explain this to me slowly. Has the office been broken into?"

"No, the door was unlocked."

"Why? You know you should always keep it locked. Why did you leave it open?"

"I don't think I left it unlocked, in fact I know I didn't."

"Of course you did. If it wasn't locked it had to be you that left it open. Was the safe damaged?"

"Not really, there are a few scratches. I'm not even sure if they are fresh ones, or from the last time."

"Was it locked when you went into the office?"

"Yes."

"Well, then it is obvious there has been no break-in. No thief is going to lock the safe after him again. You must have put the money somewhere else."

"NO. I have NOT put the money somewhere else!"

"Maybe you have, and you have forgotten."

"I would know if I had. I'm not stupid."

"You do forget things sometimes. Look at how worked up you are now, when you get like this you don't know what you are doing."

"Of course I'm worked up. I have just lost a lot of money. The sterling was for Kevin and the family for Christmas."

"Maybe you are mistaken. Maybe the money wasn't there in the first place."

"What? If you are trying to convince me I'm going crazy, forget it. I want something done about this, let's call the police." I knew this would be pointless, but I wanted to see Sidi's reaction to this.

"Now you are being silly. You know they won't do anything, but they will charge you and you will lose more money. They will want transport money before they even come, then they will want you to pay their wages while they carry out their investigation."

"What do you suggest then?"

"If the money is missing."

"IF……" I interrupted.

"It must be one of the staff, we will keep a close eye on them and see who starts spending lots of money, and it will be simple to know who the thief is."

I gave a small chuckle at this. "So you are suggesting we do nothing, are you?"

Sidi smiled when he saw me chuckle. "That's better, you take everything too seriously. We will watch the staff carefully and you see we will soon sort this out."

With Shendian and European emotional and behavioural differences, Sidi seemed unaware my chuckle was a sign of my annoyance and frustration, not bought on by a lightening attitude to my losses.

"I want all the staff in here, one at a time, I want to question them."

"Why?"

"It is impossible for anyone to have been in the office and no-one else to see them."

"I don't think that's a good idea, then they will all know what as happened. I keep telling you taubabs talk too much; you must keep things to yourself."

"Why do you not want me to talk to the staff? Are you afraid of what they might say?"

"What? Are you accusing me of being the thief?"

"You said that not me. Now go and get one of the waiters, and we will speak to all of the staff on duty, one at a time, like I said before, and we will see if anyone saw anything unusual."

Sidi reluctantly did as I asked. As I suspected this would be, it was a complete waste of time. They all claimed they hadn't seen anything. Every one of them expressed shock at the suggestion of a break-in; this shock in every instance was too exaggerated to be natural. After questioning the staff, and having a further fruitless conversation with Sidi, I returned frustrated, and I'm sure with my anxiety showing on my face, to the bar. I was grateful that most of my regulars, both ex-pats, and tourists had left. I couldn't cope with discussing this with too many people.

Carolyn and David, who had both been ex-pats but were now living in the UK and coming over for holidays, were still in the bar. "What's happened?" Carolyn asked me. It most have been obvious how long I had been out of the bar, and with me taking the staff into the house, one at a time that something had happened.

"I've lost money out of the safe."

"Oh shit," expressed David. "A break-in?"

"That's debatable." I said.

"Listen Helen, remember we come and go a lot, and see and know lots of things from when we lived here. You must have known this was inevitable, next door are squeezing you, and the staff are out to get you. You know it can only get worse. It is time you did some serious thinking." David told me.

"Yeah, I do know."

"I know, you know, but there is no point in hanging on until they completely break you. It is time for you to get out, and you know that as well as I do. Euan told us this trip, that he is concerned about your safety, I'm sure he will help you if you need help to get home, he has been good to us, and I'm sure he would be good to you also."

"I will start thinking about what to do, but I have hung in here so long, I can't just give up now. I have to see some sort of an outcome to all this."

"Just don't leave it too long, believe you me, time is running out for you."

When Carolyn and David left it was time to send the staff home. I poured myself a drink and went to sit with the two remaining customers Jack and his girlfriend.

"There has been a lot of comings and goings here this evening Helen." Jack said. "What's happened, a break-in?"

"Yes, how did you know that?" It was a silly question really. Jack always sat at his regular table rather than at the bar, he liked to be an observer rather than be in the hub of things, but he had a good view not only of the bar, but what was going on outside. He usually knew what was happening.

"Just watching, as I always do. I guessed it was something like that. Lost much?"

I told him, and was angry with myself as a lone tear trickled down my cheek, as I mentioned the sterling I was saving for Kevin."

"Oh look," said Sanibu, Jack's local girlfriend. "Helen is crying, they shouldn't do things that make her cry."

"Sorry, it's O.K. Sanibu, I didn't mean to cry, I am just so angry, and upset about the money I had for my family." Shendians don't understand taubab emotions, and are confused by white women's tears.

"You are good to your staff, not like a lot of taubabs; they shouldn't do this to you."

"I don't know for sure it was the staff."

"Come on Helen, you are just like me when I've had similar things happen. You do know really, but you don't want to admit it not even to yourself." Jack told me.

"Yeah O.K. we are the daft ones eh?"

"Not daft, soft maybe."

We changed the subject and Jack told me a few more amusing stories of mishaps he had had over the many years he had lived in Shendi. He succeeded in raising my spirits and together we laughed at our own misfortunes.

I slumped into bed shortly afterwards, and in spite of feeling exhausted, I tossed and turned most of the night, going over the evening and taking in things both David and Jack had told me. I knew they were right. I did need to get away from her. If not permanently, I at least needed a respite from the life I was leading. The next morning when I served Jack and Saibu with their usual morning pot of tea and eggs on toast for their breakfast, Jack pushed a clench fist across the table in my direction.

"What's that?" I asked.

"Just take it and send it to your son," he told me.

It was a bundle of sterling. "Oh, no Jack, I can't take that, you are both going home for Christmas next week, and there is no way I can repay you before then."

"Don't worry about it, I can afford it or I wouldn't give it to you. I have told you many times I would help you out if I could. You have enough on your plate without upsetting yourself because you have no money for the kids at Christmas.

"I don't like doing this, but I will because as you say I want to send money to Kevin, and there is no way I will let him know the mess I'm in here. It will be awhile before I have this much to be able to repay you. How about if I give it to you as credit behind the bar, like that you will still be in credit for a good while after you return from the U.K."

"That will be brilliant, drink all night and no bill at the end of the evening. Heaven"

"I don't know how to thank you Jack, the theft of sterling has really hurt me. I feel I've let Kevin down by not being able to be part of little Karen's life, let alone not being able to send them anything for Christmas."

I was extremely grateful to Jack. I had some good friends among the ex-pats, but didn't want to burden them with my problems, I knew if I did a few of them would help me if they could, but I was determined to sort things out for myself. I have always been independent, but I was starting to realize that other than being the virtue I considered it to be, it was fast becoming my downfall. Terry and Nick came in at lunchtime; they had left the previous evening while I was still in the house, questioning the staff. I didn't mention the break-in to either of them; they were my customers they came into the bar to relax and enjoy their selves, and not to be burdened with my problems

As I was cleaning the bar after the lunchtime rush, the phone rang. I went into the house to answer it. Although the phone in the bar rang, it could not be used; a couple of years previous to this, the power points had been affected by an electrical storm. The bar phone could probably be fixed, but I hadn't bothered to have it repaired. It was an extension of the house phone, and several times when I had been on the phone in the house, I could hear music and sounds from the bar, so it was obvious the staff were listening to my calls. Sometimes it was an inconvenience to have to go into the house to answer it if I was busy; but it gave me confidence knowing my calls were confidential.

"Good afternoon, Helen, I hope you are well." It was Ali; I was slightly taken aback, Binta usually phoned on his behalf, and with other things to think about, my meeting at The Peace Haven had completely gone out of my mind.

"Hello Ali, I'm fine thanks."

"I have good news for you. We have put an extension package together to put to Hussaini and we have had the go ahead from our head office in Saudi to purchase The Dominion." My heart skipped a beat. Had I really heard him correctly? "In fact they are very eager to go ahead with our suggested plans. Will you be able to attend a meeting at our head office in Poutapi this Thursday afternoon at three o'clock? Your appointment is with our West African director; his name is Mustapha. Just go into the reception and tell them you have an appointment with Mr. Mustapha. Do you know where our office is?"

"No, but I will go in a taxi, the driver will be sure to know."

"As you go down the main street in Poutapi it is on the right between the electrical board and the little local market. They are serious about this purchase Helen, I am aware what The Dominion means to you, but please remember Mustapha is an important man in our organisation. He is in charge of all of our projects in West Africa, but he is not used to doing business with a woman. He is used to a woman being submissive."

"Unfortunately European women are not submissive Ali."

Ali gave a little laugh. "Yes I know this."

I sat down in my lounge digesting my conversation with Ali, before returning to the bar. I was thrilled they now had official permission to purchase The Dominion, but The Peace Haven's accountants had suggested a very low price to me, would this Mustapha make a better offer? They held a reputation of being fair but ruthless businessmen, I doubted if my interpretation of fair and theirs were the same. I knew deep down the time had come for me to sell if I could. I was by then more than eager to return to the U.K. to see my family again, and especially to get to know my precious little granddaughter. It was also time I moved on, and started a new life for myself.

Simon and I had been separated for over five years now, and he had moved on and made a new life for himself with a new partner. Possibly more than the burden The Dominion was to me, I felt trapped there. Due to my mixed up emotions at the time, I possibly exaggerated things in my mind, but I felt Simon had put me in the situation I was in. He had moved on, and I was unable to, so although I hadn't even had any contact at all with him for about two years, I felt he was still manipulating me. I very much resented this.

That same evening Randi, a local taxi driver I knew well, was in the bar having a drink with some Dutch friends of his. I arranged for him to collect me at 2.30 the following Thursday to drive me to my appointment with Mr. Mustapha. Poutapi is only about 20 minutes drive away. I considered this the best time to leave, I didn't want to be late, but neither did I want to arrive too early and appear too eager.

The next morning Sidi was later than usual arriving to take Ebou out for the supplies.

"I'm late because I've been talking to the taxi driver Randi up the strip."

My heart sank, it had slipped my mind that Sidi was once a taxi driver, and knew most of the ones operating in this area.

"Yeah, fine, fine but you must get out shopping now, or Ebou will be late back for lunchtime."

"O.K. but just tell me why you have asked Randi to take you out on Thursday, you know I will take you anywhere you want to go."

I could hardly tell him I didn't want him to know where I was going. "I didn't want to keep you away from the shop in the afternoon, and it is a little bit of extra money for Randi."

"That's no problem, I will ask my brother to look after the shop, and I will take you."

With that he went into the kitchen to tell Ebou he was ready to take him out shopping. This was not going according to plan. I had wanted neither Sidi nor any of my staff to hear of my meeting at Hussani's head office. I should have realized whichever taxi driver I chose to take me would either tell Sidi or one of my staff, who would consider it their right to know what I was doing, especially if it had any bearing on the future of The Dominion. The staff felt they owned The Dominion as much as I;

they referred to it as our place. Sidi hadn't asked where I was going, so I assumed Randi had already told him this. I was soon to know I had assumed correctly. When they returned from shopping, Sidi asked me. "Why are you going to see these people?"

"What people Sidi?" I innocently asked.

"You know what people I mean. These Arab people. You know we don't trust Arabs here, they always cause problems. No good will come of this. Why do you want to be involved with them?"

"Ali has arranged for me to meet them. They are my neighbours and very influential people; I would rather be friendly with them than otherwise."

"I hope you know what you are doing, the staff won't want you mixing with these people."

"You don't have to worry about what I do; neither does the rest of the staff."

With that I returned to the bar, as some of my lunchtime customers were starting to arrive. As Sidi walked past the entrance, he gave me a disapproving look.

Nick, who was sat at the bar asked. "Been upsetting Sidi again, he gave you a filthy look?"

"No more than usual, he is easy to upset sometimes...... Remember you were going to take this place apart and ship it out to Pucket. Well what do you reckon; shall we give it a try?"

"The shipping will cost an arm and a leg; otherwise the idea has plenty of potential. A sun lounger on a Thai beach, with an ice cold beer in my hand, supplied from The Dominion, yeah that is appealing, especially after the shitty morning I've just had."

"So you reckon we could get this place down O.K."

"You serious or what?"

"I'm serious; I've had enough of running a bar in Shendi, what's wrong with Thailand?"

"You got rocks in your head woman," he told me as he got off his bar stool and assessed the possibility. As he sat down again he said. "Of course it could be done, but how much could be salvaged is debatable. Please tell me you aren't serious."

"Just wanted to know if it could be taken apart, a girl must weigh up her options. If I can't sell the bloody place I may take it apart and sell it a piece at a time."

"That confirms it; you have definitely lost the plot."

Terry came in and sat next to Nick. "Careful what you say to her to-day, she's finally losing it big time."

"I could have told you that a long time ago, but as long as she keeps serving me breakfast at lunchtime, and my supper and beers in the evening, I will be careful not to upset her, and you will be wise to do the same."

I knew taking The Dominion down wasn't a realistic option, but I wanted to know all the possibilities before my meeting with Mustapha. I was determined not to go there feeling deflated before we had even started any dialogue.

A few months previous I had asked Oliver if he could find out the actual value of my property for me. The finance company Oliver was employed by had a property division, he spoke to his counterpart in that division, who investigated the possibilities and in his opinion The Dominion had no commercial value except to The Peace Haven, who because of their standing with the government were the only ones who would be given planning permission on the site. He also established that due to the position of The Dominion, The Peace Haven could block any sale as a going concern, if they wished to. At that time the current value of a plot of land the size of mine in the tourist area was the equivalent of £40,000. When Oliver gave me that news I was absolutely shattered by it, but now I was trying to think positively even though I realized the odds were stacked heavily against me.

Sidi had gone to the fishing village to get our supplies of fish and shrimps when he left looking annoyed with me, so I was surprised when he returned looking cheerful, he smiled as he came through the bar and said. "If you have a few minutes, I would like to speak to you."

"O.k. when you have bought all the supplies in."

He seemed light hearted, maybe he had been thinking about my meeting while he was out, and decided to take a different stance. When we started our conversation, I soon discovered it was a different matter entirely.

"Remember I told you about those boys, who will try and sell Reggie's house for us? I've just met them up them up the road, they have two tourists that want to see the place this afternoon and a Nigerian man and his Swedish wife that want to see it tomorrow. At first I told them the watchman could show them around, but I think I will go too, if that is alright."

"Sure, if you want to, but if they are used to selling houses, leave it to them to do the talking, you just go along."

"Yeah, yeah I know what to do."

This was good news, if the house was getting viewings; there was a chance it may sell. Initially people might have been put off purchasing the property because of the nature of Reg's death. Now that the dust had settled there might be more chance of a sale. It would be a relief not to have the responsibility of the compound, especially if my fortunes changed and I did leave Shendi. I would feel I had let Sharon and Reggie down if the house was still on the market when I left. Besides my hopes of the prospects of a sale for the house had seemed to take Sidi's mind off my meeting with Mustapha for the time being.

Thursday came around quicker than I thought it would. Sidi didn't mention the meeting to me before he went out for the shopping in the morning. I even wondered if he had forgotten about it, but before he left The Dominion after they had returned from shopping he said to me. "I will be back for you just after two. O.K.?"

"Yeah, fine, fine."

True to his word he returned about 2.15 and waved to me as he passed the bar, and went and sat in the garden. When I saw him arrive I went into the house to change. This didn't take long, I had already decided what I would wear, and had laid it out on the bed, so that it wouldn't take long to slip into. I had chosen an ankle length aqua green, wrap around skirt, not wishing to offend Mustapha's Muslim faith; in fact I was always careful how I dressed, if I was going out of the tourist areas. While I didn't completely cover my arms, I choose a contrasting yellow and gold floral print blouse with sleeves that finished just above the elbow.

"Do you know where we are going?" I asked Sidi as we got into the car.

"I know exactly where we are going," he informed me. "I drove over to Poutapi yesterday afternoon to check where Hussani's office is, I didn't know before that."

That was the last Sidi and I spoke during the short drive to Poutapi, I know he was eager to know the real reason for my visit, but he was as determined not to ask again, as I was determined not to tell him. The unanswered question hung like a cloud over us during the drive. When we came to a halt in the small car park outside the compound, I opened the door and as I started to alight from the car I said to Sidi. "Just wait here for me; I probably won't be very long."

"I'm coming in with you," he said as he opened his door.

"No, I don't need you with me." I told him.

"I think you do. You know with these people it is best to have a man with you, they won't even want to talk business with a woman."

"I've told you I don't need you with me, I am going for an introduction, not to discuss any business, but thanks anyway."

He got out of the car, and leant on the open door, I was conscious of him watching me as I walked the short distance to the compound gate. By his remark, I was aware he realized I wasn't merely going for an introduction. As I approached the gate, the security guard stepped out of his hut, and asked me if I had business in these offices.

"I have an appointment with Mr. Mustapha." I told him.

Pointing to an elaborate wrought iron doorway, which was open he said. "Go through that door and speak to the receptionist at the desk."

I walked across the small, immaculately kept garden and up the few tiled steps to the door the security had pointed out to me. I found myself in a medium sized reception area, with a cream coloured leather settee and two matching armchairs. An oval glass topped coffee table with a figurine of an eastern dancer as its centre- piece, was in front of these. The receptionist was sat at the other end of the room, behind a large leather topped desk. The floor and staircase, which was adjacent to the receptionists desk was a delicate rose pink marble. This reception, although not very large, was fitting for a five star hotel, and seemed far too grand for the exterior of the building.

"May I help you?" The receptionist asked, as I neared her desk.

I once again explained I had an appointment with Mr. Mustapha, and she directed me up the stairway to his secretary's office. I was so busy taking in my surroundings, and looking at the intricate patterns on the banisters that the nerves I had felt in the car, had all but disappeared.

There were three oak finished doors on the large first floor landing, I looked at each in turn; the middle one was ajar and had a small brass sign on it simply saying 'secretary'. I knocked on this door, and pushed it open.

I was more than surprised as the secretary, who was stood looking through a drawer of the filing cabinet, turned and faced me. It was Jenny, an ex-pat lady, who had lived in Shendi for many years. I had only met Jenny on a few occasions, when she had attended functions at The Dominion. She and her husband occasionally came in for a meal, the last time had been only a few weeks previous, this had been the first time I had seen them in a long while, generally speaking they were a couple who kept themselves to themselves.

"Hi, Helen, how are you?"

"I'm fine thanks Jenny, but surprised to see you here I thought you worked at The High Commission."

"I did, but was offered this job with the Hussani group, it's fewer hours, and much more money. You know Joe and I like a quiet life, and this fits in with our life style better."

"Pleased to hear it, a good life style is all any of us want."

"Yes, Joe had come to pick me up from a meeting at The Peace Haven, when we came into The Dominion the other week. That is why I asked you how things were going with them. I know why you are here Helen, I know they are going to make you an offer, but don't give in too easily. They are ruthless; they would get blood out of a stone if they could. Don't let them bully you. I'm here for the money; I feel no allegiance what so ever towards them. I know what this means to you, but unfortunately they know they hold all the trump cards."

"I would be grateful, if you kept this to yourself, I obviously don't want my staff to get to hear about this, in fact at this stage I don't want anyone to know."

"Oh sure, I understand that, I don't speak about anything I hear here, I doubt if I would keep my job if I did. I hope it all works out well for you. I know you have been through a lot since you came to Shendi, and want to get away, but if The Dominion goes, I know a lot of people will be sad about it, and that's tourists as well as ex-pats."

"I desperately need to get away, but if this makes any sense Jenny, I have very mixed feelings about it. I will be sad, even feel guilty about it, if I close The Dominion."

At that moment Jenny's intercom buzzed and a loud precise, eastern voice asked her to show me through. The calmness I felt as I ascended the stairs and chatted to Jenny reverted back to the sheer panic I had felt in the car on the short journey here. Jenny showed me into the room to the right of her office. There was a gigantic panoramic window at the far end of this large room, with an imposing view over the coast with its grand expanse of white sand and palm trees, and the intense blue of the sky where it met the rolling white horses of the Atlantic Ocean. I took in the view, and momentarily thought, are you really sure you want to leave Shendi? There was a bookcase along the whole length of one wall containing leather bound volumes. The other two walls had units blending with the bookcase, adorned with tasteful figurines and ornaments. An impressive oak table with matching intricately carved chairs were the focal point of the room. There were about a dozen chairs around this table.

Mustapha introduced himself, and then introduced me to the other man with him as Esa, telling me that Esa was the groups head accountant in Shendi, he then indicated to a chair for me to sit down and asked Jenny to order coffee for us. I was sat on the first chair at the near end of the table, with my back to the window, with Esa opposite me, Mustapha sat at the head, leaving the rest of the table seeming very empty. I suddenly felt very lonely in this larger than life boardroom with these two Arab gentlemen I had never met before. Had this meeting been in a small cosy office, I would have been much more at ease. In spite of the adequate air conditioning, I was very hot and sticky; I could feel my face flush which caused me embarrassment, which made me feel even more uncomfortable.

"Sorry to have kept you waiting." Mustapha started. "I'm afraid something has cropped up that has delayed us. Unfortunately I now have to fly to Ghana this afternoon, and I have to leave for the airport in half an hour, so we will have to make this brief, but we all know why we are here, so let's get to the point of this meeting."

There was a small knock on the door, and a Shendian lady wearing a neat full length black dress and a white apron entered with a tray of coffee served in a similar coffee pot and matching cups and saucers as I was served at The Peace Haven. She placed the silver tray on the table, and Esa started pouring us all coffee. The lady gave a courteous nod in Mustapha's direction and left the room.

"Back to business." Mustapha continued. "You have been told Hussaini has given the go ahead for us to purchase The Dominion from you, so that we can commence the next stage of the development of our hotel. I believe Tascali has even opened negotiations with you."

"Mr. Tascali hasn't exactly opened negotiations with me. He did mention a sum to me, which was laughable. I will only sell The Dominion at a realistic price."

"Fair enough, what was it Tascali offered you? $50,000 I believe?"

"Yes that is what he mentioned, but it wasn't exactly an offer, and I dismissed it immediately."

"O.K. maybe you think he was having a laugh at your expense. What do you call realistic?"

"As I told Tascali, my husband and I paid £125,000 for it, and spent several more thousands renovating it during our first year."

"You are the one having a laugh now. Let's be honest about this, the offer Tascali made is fact what the land is worth, but we are reasonable people, we don't want you to lose out on this deal. We will come to a compromise. I will make you a serious offer of $75,000."

I looked at him in amazement. "I thought you said a serious offer I wouldn't even consider that."

Esa, who had not spoken, other than when we were introduced, now spoke to me in a very sharp tone. "Madame, I think you should seriously consider your position. As Mustapha had said we are reasonable people, we do not wish you any harm; we have allowed you to continue with your business unhindered. Your customers walk through our property to get to your premises. Any time we wish we could we could close your business simply by refusing to allow your customers on our property. If we did that your business would become worthless, we are offering you $75,000, I think that is more than generous and yet you say you will not even consider it."

Mustapha patted Esa's hand that was resting on the table, I took this as him telling Esa to hold back, and he then spoke to me in a much softer tone. "As I said Helen, I have to leave for the airport. We have made you what we think under the circumstances is a fair offer. I am not unsympathetic, I do understand your feelings on this, but I'm afraid what you paid for the property, whether it was the value of the property when you bought it or not, is not for me to comment, but I assure you $75,000 is above the market value of your land to-day."

I took a deep breath and closed my eyes to calm myself; opening them again I looked Mustapha straight in the eyes and said. "I am not selling my land only. I am selling my business and my home, to me that is worth much more than $75,000."

"Many of us tend to think our assets are worth more than they are in reality we are interested in purchasing your land. We have no interest what-so-ever in your buildings. It will be Christmas in a few days, which I know is very important to you Christians." As he collected his papers together, that were on the table in front of him, and put them in his briefcase that had been on the floor beside him, he continued. "You go back to your bar, and enjoy your celebrations. I will be back in Shendi during the first few weeks of the New Year. I will arrange for us to meet again then, perhaps by then, you will have had time to fully understand your position, and we can do some serious business."

By the time he had finished talking he had pushed his chair back and stood up. It was plain fully obvious from his actions; our meeting was over. I rose also, they both shook hands with me. "Enjoy your Christmas." Esa said to me as he opened the door for me to leave.

I forced myself to smile at them and said. "I look forward to meeting you again in the New Year." This was a white lie, but seemed appropriate at the time.

I placed my hand on the banister as I slowly walked down the impressive stairway. My feet were unsteady. My ego was crushed, maybe I should have taken a man with me, I knew women had very little standing in their community. I had had high hopes of this meeting; I had really thought they were going to be beneficial. What I had considered may have been one of my best Christmas presents ever, had just been snatched from me.

I returned the receptionist's smile as I left the building and was met by the gorgeous heat of the Shendian sunshine, which I found welcoming. The security guard opened the compound gate as he saw me leave the building, and said a polite. "Good afternoon, have a happy Christmas." I smiled at him, but was too choked to speak.

Sidi was sat on a wooden bench in the car park talking to a taxi driver whose taxi was parked next to his car. He stood when he saw me coming and asked if I was ready to go home. Still choked, and not wanting to speak, I nodded and got on the car. As Sidi started up the engine of the car he said. "Well how did you get on with these people? You don't seem very happy."

"Fine, fine, but Sidi I'm tired, I don't want conversation, just take me home."

We headed towards The Dominion in total silence. I stared out of the window, but on that journey home, I was completely oblivious to the palm trees, that I loved so much as they slowly drifted passed, my mind was otherwise occupied.

Chapter Nineteen
January Sales?

My head was reeling when we got back to The Dominion. It was my break time and Sidi offered to sit and have a coffee with me before I went into the house for my shower and rest. I declined with a weak smile, and told him to get back to his shop, telling him I had taken up too much of his time already.

"You seem upset, Helen, I don't like leaving you like this. Are you sure you wouldn't like some company?"

"I'm fine, fine, I'll see you tomorrow." I said dismissively, realizing Sidi probably had some idea of what had happened at Mustapha's office. Several times on the drive home I had seen him glance in my direction. I had always found in hard to hide my feelings, and I knew my disappointment was etched on my face.

I lay on my bed with Mustapha and Esa's words going around and around in my head. To be honest, sat there in that unfamiliar boardroom, with those two imposing Arabs, instead of focusing on what they were saying, my mind had gone blank. I realised that neither side had mentioned the court case. As long as the case was in progress my court injunction prevented them from being able to close my business, or so I understood it. They seemed sure of their stance, I knew they had the backing of the government, maybe they could have the injunction over ruled, this I didn't know. I tossed and turned, sleep was impossible. All I could think of was their paltry offer for years of my life. Finally I realised that any sort of rest was unattainable and time was ticking by. I would soon have to be getting ready for my evening shift. I rose and ordering a coffee from the bar, sat in my lounge composing myself in readiness to face the evening ahead of me.

When I went back into the bar on duty I saw Nick. I went over, said "Come and have a chat in the garden," picked up his beer and walked out. I knew he would follow his beer, if not me. I went to the table near the water feature. The sound of the steady, gentle flow of water always had a calming effect on me and I could see the entrance to the bar, so I knew who was coming or going. When we were both seated I looked over at the bar and said. "Right Nick, a serious conversation please, would you be interested in taking this place down."

Nick stoked his moustache, as he also looked across at the bar, and then turning to me he said. "What, you do actually mean you want it taken down?"

"Yeah, that is what I said. I know if The Peace Haven did ever have any interest in The Dominion they would want the land only, and that is all they would be prepared to pay for."

"If I really thought it could be done, and reconstructed again, I would buy it off you and rebuild it at my place, but no luv, too much of it would be damaged taking it apart. It is a tempting idea, The New Dominion, but sorry I don't think it really would be viable."

The evening customers were starting to arrive, as they came through into the garden, Jed put the outside lights on; it was only then that I spotted Sidi sat at the far end of the garden. Realizing we had seen him, he came towards us and Nick mouthed to me to stop our conversation, as Sidi pulled out a chair and sat down.

"What are you still doing here?" I asked sharply.

"I was worried about you. You seemed upset earlier."

"I told you I was fine, and besides you don't have to worry about me." "Yeah, and she has plenty of friends to help her if she needs help." Nick told him.

I wondered if he had heard my conversation with Nick, although he was sat a fair distance away from us, with the garden being quiet he might have done. I didn't have to ponder on this for long, after a short awkward pause in the conversation Sidi said. "You don't think we could take The Dominion down Nick?"

Nick glanced at me then told Sidi. "Well, I wouldn't be interested in it, I didn't say it couldn't be done, but I wouldn't think much could be salvaged other than the steel and the corrugate."

"I see. Anyway if all is O.K. here I had better get going," and with that he got up and left. Nick and I sat there, looking at each other.

"What was all that about? Does he know what I am assuming is going on?"

"I haven't told him anything, but you know he is about a lot, and the staff report everything to him, they know my business better than I do, or at least they think they do. They all know the Arabs have been here and looked around."

"Well be careful luv, you know what I mean, and give a shout if you need a hand."

"Thanks Nick, I know you are there for me, but you know that I'm independent."

We both went back into the bar, Nick to relax with a few beers, and me to get back to the business at hand.

"Oh, I see," said Terry, who had arrived for the evening while we were outside. "Cosy little chats in the garden now, is it? I'm keeping an eye on you two."

"You do that." Nick told him. "Tell me if anything happens, I don't want to miss it."

In the midst of all this was the looming prospect of Christmas. In spite of the resolutions I had made at the start of high season, I did not feel as prepared as I would have liked to have been. This could be The Dominion's last Christmas and I wanted it to be the best yet. Giving myself a good talking-to, I ran over what was done and what had to be done. All the advance cooking had been finished, with the puddings, which were always a major concern, made in early November. This year I was pleased with the result, they smelt fine and were a good dark colour. We had been fortunate enough to be able to buy mincemeat unlike some previous years when we had had to improvise. I had purchased the small table gifts, but these still had to be wrapped, I would do that tomorrow during my afternoon break, rather than take a nap. The turkeys were ordered and paid for, but were not due in Shendi until a few days before Christmas, which suited me fine as we would not have room for them in the freezers. Decorations would go up on December 23rd and not a day before, so all in all it seemed that I was more prepared for the big day than I had thought.

I had decided to do things differently this year. This year there would be one sitting at 2pm instead of meals from midday to 8pm and it would be buffet style. This meant we could provide a wider choice of food and because everything was cooked at once we would not be reliant on the generator. A power cut last year had taken the microwaves out of use for most of the day, so by having one sitting that removed that worry and buffet style took the pressure off the waiters and it meant I could relax once the meal had been served. During the evening we would serve meals from our normal menu, plus turkey if there were any left overs as I suspected there would be. Time passed by quickly with so much to focus my mind on, and before I knew it December had slipped by and the big day had arrived.

The Dominion was looking its best, the tables were rearranged and decorated, I had put extra effort into the decorations and Latif and Petreeni decorated the garden with me early Christmas morning. I had decorated a table under the awning near the entrance, where I would greet and serve a choice of alcoholic or non-alcoholic Dominion cocktails to my guests on their arrival. Looking around I felt very pleased and proud of our efforts and I was quietly confident all would go well. We had hosted several weddings now, so the kitchen was much more used to the big occasions than they once had been, so I was content to supervise and let Ebou and his team do the work.

Once the cocktails, which proved a great ice- breaker with everyone, had been served, ex-pats and tourists alike mixed together in groups chatting and laughing, I stood behind the serving table helping the kitchen staff. By the time the main course had been served I was completely relieved and relaxed, as it had been my main concern. Now that was over the sweets that had been prepared earlier would cause no problems. Besides traditional Christmas pudding we offered a large selection of sweets, including sherry trifle, apricots soaked in apricot brandy crumble, various cheesecakes and fruit pies, all these were served with cream, ice-cream or custard. I placed several bottles of liquors at the end of the table, in case anyone fancied ice cream with a liquor sauce.

I was amazed; maybe I shouldn't have been, by the amount of alcohol that was poured over the sweets. One ex-pat lady who had her 80-year-old mother in their party asked me. "What have you put in the apricot crumble?"

"Only apricots and apricot brandy."

She burst out laughing and told me. "Mum has had a large portion with ice-cream and we put some apricot brandy on top of it, thinking it would do her good, and now she is as giggly as could be."

My problems were the last thing on my mind as the afternoon progressed and I enjoyed the company of my guests who were full of praise for our festive spread, many said it was the best ever Dominion Christmas they had had, which was exactly as I intended the day to be. I was so proud of my staff, the kitchen had coped well, and the waiters were rushing to and fro to the garden expertly balancing trays of drinks. Was it possible these same staff were stealing from me, and causing many of the problems in the running of my business? On occasions like this I found it hard to believe. Our Christmas definitely won the approval of my regulars, possibly due as much to the cocktails and alcoholic sweets as anything else but for whatever reasons our festivities were spoken about around the bar for a long time afterwards.

I was also in very high spirits as I slumped exhausted, but very happy into my bed at the end of a very tiring day. I lay there wondering if this would be the last Christmas I would celebrate at The Dominion. My thoughts drifted back to our first Christmas here. Simon was still here then, Kevin had come to spend the holiday with us, he came by himself as it was before he was with Steph; it seemed decades ago, so much had happened since then. The Dominion's festive celebrations had been very low key then, compared to the event we had staged today, there was no comparison. I had wanted today to be a Christmas to be remembered in case it was The Dominion's last, and I was grateful with the staff's cooperation I had managed to achieve that. The business had grown since my arrival. That first Christmas, we had only a few regular ex-pats and not many regular tourists, now the business was booming, the customers had proved that to me to-day with their appreciation. When I was depressed and down cast, I thought I had made a complete mess of everything around me since I had come to Shendi, in reality this was not so. I must be assertive, I knew that during the next few weeks I was going to have to be confident, I would be facing Mustapha once again; I must do this believing in my capabilities and myself.

I was still tired when I woke the following morning. It was Boxing Day, but I was not doing any thing special to celebrate this, besides changing my 'special's board' to include cold turkey, salad and chips, and Christmas pudding with brandy butter at cut down prices. One of my main faults was I tended to over cater. Sidi came to take Ebou shopping, and I told him there was no need to as we only wanted a few things, and I would go to the local supermarket, at the far end of The Peace Haven car park for these.

"Fine, fine, that is what I was hoping. I will go and have a coffee in the kitchen with the lads, and then go, as I've arranged to meet those estate agent boys at Reggie's house."

"Is someone going to see it?"

"Yeah, that Nigerian boy I told you about. He and his wife are going back, and I want to be there, I want to know what is going on."

"Fine, fine keep me informed." I was in very high spirits as I laughed and joked with the customers around the bar, everyone was still gripped by Christmas fever, the ex-pats were enjoying the festive season, and many that only came in during the evenings were partying at lunchtime. The tourists were in holiday mode, as well as celebrating the season; in short everyone was enjoying themselves, including me. Maybe my life was turning around again, with the prospects of a sale for Reggie's house, and a sale for The Dominion possibly on the horizon; I looked forward to the New Year optimistically.

January, although a good month for the business with tourists flocking in for a break in the sun during the long cold U.K. winter and in the aftermath of Christmas, always bought the pressures of sorting the business papers for The Dominion for the coming year. Even though the government gave us until the end of March to get all our papers in order, I liked to get everything completed as soon as possible so I could forget about them until the next year. Generally I had everything done by mid-February. When everything for the business had been paid, and the licenses granted, they had to be presented at the immigration offices, along with the fee for my ex-pat license. I would then be granted my immigration papers, I always gave a sigh of relief, when this was all completed and I knew the business and I were completely legal for the coming year at least.

As the income tax, and my foreign workers permit which also had to be paid at the income tax office, were the most expensive, I paid these first, so that they were out of the way. I always filled out the forms, and gave these and the money to Sidi to go into Port Albert to pay them for me. All these fees were paid in cash; cheques were unacceptable. I set about sorting my papers as soon as the New Year celebrations were over.

"No shopping to-day, I'll send Ebou out in a taxi to get the supplies." I told Sidi when he arrived one morning in early January. "I want you to go into the income tax office, and pay the taxes and my foreign worker's permit for me."

"O.K. if you want me to, but the offices will be very busy, everyone is paying their taxes now, and there will be a long queue."

"Yeah, you say that every year. But it has to be done, there will be long queues tomorrow and the next day, so you might as well go to-day."

Sidi was never very keen to do this and so I thought no more about it as he sighed and reluctantly agreed to go. He left The Dominion just before 10 o'clock, when I went off duty at 4, he still hadn't returned, thinking he had been queuing all this time, I felt a pang of guilt for insisting he went, when he hadn't really wanted to. When I went into the house I thought I had better show some sympathy and so I dialled his mobile number.

"Hello, Are you alright?" he asked sounding more cheerful than anyone who had been queuing for hours in a hot, steamy office had any right to sound.

"Yeah, fine. I thought you would still be queuing. Are you on your way back?"

"No, I'm in Famara, where do you think I am? Do you need me?"

"No, it's just I was expecting you to come back here, with the receipts like you usually do. You drive passed the top of the road on your way to Famara, so it wouldn't have taken you long to bring them to me."

"It was getting late by the time I had finished at the income tax office. You don't need the receipts to-day; I will bring them to you tomorrow."

"O.K. fine, fine, but don't forget to bring them, I know what your memory is like."

"They are in the car, so I can't forget them."

"Fine, fine, I'll see you in the morning."

I slowly put the phone down and my hand hesitated momentarily on the receiver. This was not usual. Sidi had been paying my taxes and licenses, both the annual and monthly ones, ever since I had been Shendi. He always bought the receipts to me on his way back to his village. Many times he had told me he was afraid of losing them, which was why he bought them straight to me. Why had he not done so today and why did I have this mistrust of him now?

The following morning I was sat in the garden, having a coffee with Viv when Sidi arrived.

"Do I need to go into Port Albert again to-day?" he asked.

"Not Port Albert, but I want you to go to the Tourist Board's office on Kudo and pay the operational license and the money for the renewal of the staff's ID badges." I left Sidi chatting to Viv while I went into the office to collect the money and the application forms for him to be able to sort these. When I returned I asked. "Have you bought me the receipts from the income tax office?"

Sidi made an exaggerated gesture with his arms and said. "Damn it, I've left them in the car."

"Well go and get them and then I can file them away."

"Sorry, sorry, I don't have my own car this morning, it is in the garage and I'm using my brother's."

As Sidi walked off, Viv and I exchanged glances.

"A problem?" she asked.

"I hope not, or at least there had better not be." I answered feeling very unsure of myself.

"Be careful."

I simply nodded in reply to Viv.

Shortly afterwards, two suited gentlemen came in who I recognised as the men that were trying to sell Reggie's house. They nodded to me as they sat at a table near to where Viv and I were.

After Momodou had taken their order, one of them called over to me. "Is Sidi here?"

"No." I told them. "He will probably be back in about an hour."

"If he doesn't come back while we are here, will you ask him to phone us, he has our number?"

I told them I would, wondering if they had any news on a possible sale for Reggie's house, although my curiosity was getting the better of me, I didn't ask them, knowing they would rather deal with Sidi than with a woman.

I went back into the bar after Viv and I had finished our coffees, the estate agents sat in the garden for a while afterwards, but left before Sidi returned. As they walked passed the bar; one of them called out to me, "We are going now. Don't forget to get Sidi to phone us."

By the time Sidi came back I was busy with lunchtime customers, and could only speak to him briefly while I was serving. I told him the estate agents had been here looking for him, and wanted him to phone them.

"O.K. I will do that, I will see you later."

"Hang on, how did you get on? Were the papers in order?"

"Fine, I have to go back next week to collect the staff's badges."

"O.K. put the receipts in the house; I will sort them out later."

"I've only got the receipt for the badges, I will get the other one next week when I go back for the badges."

"Why didn't you get it to-day? Now we have no proof that we have paid."

"That cashier had finished her receipt book, and didn't have a new one, you see a different cashier for the badges that is why I have that one. Helen you worry too much, I know the boy who is the cashier, he is from my village, and I will get it next week."

As he left I reminded him again to phone the estate agents, and I resumed serving, my mind not fully on my work. I knew that bureaucracy in Shendi ran to different standards to European bureaucracy. Receipts were hand written, and it was not unknown for stationery to run out. I recalled one year recently, when many ex-pats had no immigration papers until June, as there were insufficient forms in the country to obtain them. Still I was worried. This was another lot of receipts missing. Those for my income tax and now my operational license but was I worrying unduly? If Sidi had given me the income tax receipts I would probably have accepted his explanation without hesitation. At least I did have the receipt for the staff's badges, without paying for the license; we would not be eligible to have the badges.

January was slipping by quickly, every time the phone rang, I was half expecting it to be either Ali or Jenny, to make an appointment for me to see Mustapha, but it never was. Ever since my brush with the S.S.G. after Jatou had left my employment, I was always fastidious about everything being legal as soon as possible after the New Year. By the middle of the month, there were still no sign of my income tax receipts and I was beginning to feel physically sick with worry. Without those receipts I was unable to continue with the paper work I needed to make the business legal for the year and to work towards my immigration papers.

"Good morning. Got my receipts?" became my increasing curt and hostile greeting to Sidi when he arrived in the mornings.

One morning he obviously decided to bite back. "Why can't you just relax and put those receipts out of your mind, I am fed up with you keeping on about them. Why are they so important to you anyway, you know it has been paid that should be enough."

"What? I can't believe you said that, you know until I have all my licences and receipts for my taxes, I can't get my immigration papers. Until everything is in order, I am living here illegally."

"Helen, Helen, you always worry too much, I keep telling you this. Anyway I have lent my car to Musa for a week, and I am using his car. I forgot to take the receipts out before I let him take it, so you will have to wait another week for them, but that isn't a problem, I will get all your papers sorted then, O.K.?"

Musa had been a close friend of Sidi's since childhood and was a motorbike out rider for the President. I knew him well; he would often come to The Dominion if he was on duty when the President was attending a function at The Peace Haven. I generally gave him a drink or a snack and he would sit in the garden until the President was ready to leave again.

"That's OK then; ask Musa to bring them back to you, or bring them to me if he is in this area."

"He has gone to visit is family up country that is why I have given him my car, it is a better one than his."

"He has gone up country with my receipts in the car. I don't believe this." I shouted at him, I was exasperated.

"Calm yourself Helen, I keep telling you all this stress isn't good for you. I can't do anything about these receipts now, but as soon as Musa is back all will be sorted, you really mustn't fuss so much. Some businesses won't even have started doing their papers yet. Our's will soon be in order I promise, so please let's just not mention this again till we can have the receipts back."

I could not believe how softly and emotionless he answered my angry outbursts. I watched in amazement as he calmly strolled into the kitchen, to see if Ebou was ready to go out shopping. I felt my eyes welling up with tears, there were no customers in the bar and I decided to go into the house as I suddenly didn't feel like being sociable. Momodou was on duty; I knew he could cope with any customers that came in.

I slumped down in my armchair, and with my head in my hands the tears started to flow. I cried tears of frustration, tears of temper; these were not tears bought on by sadness, but the tears of a desperate woman. I was devastated. I didn't believe Sidi, but what could I do? If he had taken the money, as I suspected, he may have known he would have the money to pay the taxes the following week, and that is why he was delaying things. Alternatively was he purely playing for time, giving himself a bit of breathing space, until I knew the truth. I was at a complete loss as to what I should do. I couldn't prove I had given him the money, it would purely be my word against his, and so it would be pointless to call in the police or the military.

I could not even risk an all out confrontation with Sidi as this could prove disastrous. I knew he had friends and family in positions that could make running the business very awkward for me. After careful consideration, when my tears had abated, and I was thinking more clearly, I decided much against my better judgement to leave things alone for the time being. A small part of me was still hoping I was misjudging Sidi and next week, when Musa returned he would bring me my receipts and restore my faith in human nature; but I didn't really expect this to happen.

At last the phone call I was pinning all my hopes on arrived. Ali called to tell me Mustapha was back in Shendi and I agreed to another meeting at their offices in Poutapi. This time I knew where I was going and would not be fazed by the opulent surroundings, nor would I be unprepared for the meeting as I was on the previous occasion. The odds may have been stacked against me, and they may hold the trump cards, but I was determined to stand my ground. I may eventually be defeated, but I would fight them every inch of the way.

The meeting was arranged for 10.30 the following morning, which suited me fine, it didn't give me too long to dwell on things. Ali had explained to me that he wasn't expecting Mustapha to be in Shendi for long, and he thought he was eager to finalize things while he was here. I decided to go in my uniform, as I should have been working at the time and didn't want to draw too much of the staff's attention to my absence. I would tell them I was going to a tourist association meeting. I phoned Sidi and told him we needed a lot of supplies, so I wanted him to come early to take Ebou shopping. By doing this I could go in a taxi to Poutapi and on my return hopefully no one would know where I had been.

I waited for Sidi and Ebou to leave, then went into the bar and told Momodou "I'm going to a tourist association meeting, I will be back before the lunchtime rush."

He looked surprised I generally told them early in the morning if I was going anywhere that day. "Oh, alright, you didn't say you were going out. Sidi could have given you a lift."

I knew Sidi could have given me a lift, but I was getting as devious as they were, I didn't want any of the staff to know where I was going. I strolled across the hotel's car park full of confidence. "Going out Mrs. Dominion?" asked the hotel's security as I walked under their arch.

"I won't be very long." I told him, and noted the disappointment in his face that I hadn't enlightened him more.

I walked up the tourist strip to the taxi rank, pleased with myself that I had managed to leave The Dominion without raising the staff's suspicions. I felt a strange sense of freedom. The taxi rank was only a few hundred yards up the strip; but this simple stroll felt like a walk in the park. Most of the taxis were empty, with the drivers sat on rickety wooden benches under large trees taking advantage of the shade, and drinking attiya or eating breakfast from a small local restaurant situated in a corrugated shack in the corner of the site. As I walked into the taxi rank I was immediately surrounded by a group of taxi drivers who had been sat under the nearest tree, all offering their services; I was being pushed and pulled in all directions, and understood why many tourists felt intimidated. I pushed my way passed these and approached a taxi in the corner with the driver sat inside. I asked him how much to go to Poutapi, to wait for me and bring me back.

"Four hundred," he replied.

"Come off it. I'm not a tourist; I could get a bush taxi and pay ten. I don't want to go by bush taxi, but I won't pay tourist rates. I will give you a hundred, take it or I will get someone else."

"O.K. O.K. I know you are Taubab Shendian I will take you for one hundred."

I got in and we set off. The taxi driver didn't talk to me until we were roughly half way there, which suited me fine, but I was taken aback when he suddenly said. "Where is Sidi this morning? I thought I saw him arriving earlier." So the driver did know me.

"He has gone shopping with my chef."

"He should be with you. You know you shouldn't go to offices like this without someone with you."

"I haven't told you where in Poutapi we are going."

"You are going to Mr. Hussaini's office."

"Really who told you that?"

"No one, but you went there once before, so I just thought you were going again."

Shendi is a small country and everyone does know everyone else's business, I had not told anyone about this meeting. I knew this driver didn't know for sure where he was taking me, but this conversation bought home to me that everything I did was common knowledge. I also realized Sidi and the rest of my staff would soon hear where I had been, probably before I returned.

We pulled into the Hussaini office's car park, where two of their workman's pick-up trucks were parked with their unmistakable registration plates proceeded by HUSSAINI. When Hussaini himself was in the country he drove HUSSAINI 1, Mustapha drove HUSSAINI 2. These two pick-up trucks were obviously well down the pecking order as they were HUSSAINI 36 and 42.

The gate was opened by the security as I approached, and I was greeted with. "Good morning Mrs. Dominion, did you have a nice Christmas?"

"Yes thanks, I hope you are well." I replied.

"You remember the way in?"

"Yes, I'm fine, thanks."

I proceeded as I had before up the few steps into the reception area, where I was greeted by the same receptionist as on my first visit, who told me I was expected and to go straight up and tell Jenny I was here. I went up the stairs to Jenny's office, this time I was not as overwhelmed by my surroundings as I had been on the previous occasion. Jenny's office door was open; I knocked and entered.

"Hi Helen. I hope you are O.K. I've heard some good reports of your Christmas lunch this year, as I told you before a lot of folks will miss The Dominion when it goes."

"Yeah, things ran very smoothly this year; I pulled out all the stops. If I do leave this year, I'm determined to go out with a bang; I want to be remembered."

Jenny grinned at this. "Don't worry about that, you will be remembered. They are waiting for you. I hope it works out well, I have my fingers crossed for you."

Jenny walked passed me out of her office, and knocked on the boardroom door. When she opened the door, Mustapha and Esa, who were sat in the same places at the huge boardroom table as last time, rose and shook hands with me.

"Pleased to see you again Helen, sit down will you?" said Mustapha as he indicated to the chair where I was sat at our last meeting and turning to Jenny he said, "Order coffee for us please, Jenny."

Before I had even sat down Esa said "We have heard from the hotel you had a successful Christmas, so we are hoping you are prepared to start proper negotiations with us now."

As I sat I looked at Esa, and showing more confidence than I was feeling I said. "I have always been prepared to start realistic negotiations, but I thought I had made it plain I'm not prepared to leave my business and my home for a pittance."

"A pittance!" intervened Mustapha. "We have offered you $75,000; most people would welcome a sum like that."

"Most people don't own a plot of land next door to a five star hotel, onto which the hotel wants to expand."

"I'm sure you know we are building another hotel farther along the coast, which will be even grander than The Peace Haven."

"Yes, I know that."

"We didn't pay anything for the land that is being built on; it was given to us by the government, as it will be beneficial to the country's tourist trade."

"I hope you are not suggesting I should donate you my property."

Mustapha sniggered. "Certainly not, but as I told you on your last visit here, I think you have over estimated the value of your land. Do you know land behind The Paradise Lodge Hotel is selling for $30 a square metre, which is what we are offering you for your property."

The Paradise Lodge was a very exclusive small hotel situated slightly farther along the main highway from the tourist areas, it had no beach access, and so land there would not have the same commercial value as my land.

"That land is not in the main tourist area so cannot be compared to my land."

"It is next to a very exclusive hotel, so is very sort after land."

"Fine, but you can hardly build the extra bedrooms you want on that land, if you want to extend you need to purchase my land."

Mustapha was growing inpatient with me and it showed in his voice. "Helen, we are trying to be fair to you, but you seem unwilling to cooperate. I told you on your last visit, we don't really want to, but we will stop your customers crossing our car park and then you will have no business to bother yourself about."

"Do you intend to stop The Mango Tree guests from crossing the car park?"

"No."

"Then what issue do you have with my customers?"

"That doesn't come into it."

"No, but only because you don't want The Mango Tree land at a rock bottom

price. Also I hope you are remembering the court injunction I have against you, allowing my customers right of way across the car park until there is a conclusion in our court case."

Mustapha banged his fist on the boardroom table, and said in a raised voice. "We care nothing about your court case, it is a pointless case, and we have no interest in it."

I surprised even myself with the inner strength I found to stand my ground with Mustapha and Esa, in spite of the extreme nerves that were making my heart pound against my chest, and caused the awful shaking inside my body. I said in a much harsher tone than I intended. "You may dismiss the court case as nothing, but if you contravene my injunction I assure you, you will soon find out that The Shendian High Court, has more authority than you or your hotel." Inadvertently mirroring Mustapha's behaviour, I slapped my right hand on the table in anger, and immediately wished I hadn't. I quickly moved my hands onto my lap under the table, and out of their view gently rubbed it on my thigh to relieve the stinging, which was really quite painful.

I was met by silence, possibly for only a few seconds but it seemed much longer. I was looking down at the table, without moving my head, I raised my eyes to look at Mustapha, he was gazing blankly at the wall opposite him, and he then glanced towards Esa.

I was unsure what to expect to happen next, but was surprised when Mustapha spoke to me in a soft, gentle, controlled voice. "Fine Helen, we are trying to see your point of view, but you are really not making this easy for any of us. I will be reasonable to you, I will raise our offer to $100,000, and I would like you when you have calmed down, to think very carefully about this. We will meet here again, at the same time, same day next week, then I want to hear your final decision."

In a concerted effort to control my emotions I quickly and quietly said, "Thank you." and without another word I rose to leave.

The taxi driver was still waiting for me when I left the office compound. Luckily he didn't attempt to make conversation on the journey home; I was not in the mood for making small talk. $100,000 was double the figure Tascali had originally mentioned but was still a long way short of our original investment. I told the taxi driver to drop me off at the taxi rank, I would walk the short distance back to The Dominion from there, I didn't want him to take me right home, hoping no-one would learn where I had been, although being the taxi driver had mentioned he knew Sidi, I knew he would eventually get to know where I had been.

On the short stroll home after I left the taxi rank, I managed to calm myself, in readiness to face my lunchtime customers. I always tried very hard to hide my feelings, but in spite of my efforts, I sometimes failed dismally to do this. As I entered the main gateway I saw Sidi sat at the first table on the other side of the small bridge, chatting to the estate agent lads, he beckoned to me. I took a few deep breaths as I crossed the tiny wooden bridge, determined to face them in a cool and calm frame of mind.

"Good news." Sidi told me. "The Nigerian boy and his wife have made an offer for Reggie's compound."

"That's great, but is it a reasonable offer?"

"We think so." Ismaila, who was usually the spokesman for the estate agent lads, told me. "They have offered a million shillings, I don't think you will get a better offer than that, will you accept it?"

"I will phone Reggie this evening and see if he will accept that. I think he will be agreeable, but it isn't up to me. If you will all excuse me, I have to get back to work."

Sidi's phone rang as I walked away from the table, I only heard the start of his conversation, and he was speaking in his local language, but by what I understood, I think he was speaking to my taxi driver. I went into the house for a few minutes to brush my hair and freshen up before going back to work. When I came out of my sliding glass doors, Sidi was leaning causally against the wall of the house, waiting for me.

"Why didn't you agree to the offer?" he asked me.

"It isn't up to me, I will phone Reggie later, he will be at work now."

"Last time Sharon was here she would have accepted 800,000, so you know they will agree."

"Sharon would have taken 800,000, when John was interested and Reggie would have had all the money after the capital gains tax had been paid, but now there are the estate agents to pay, and they have been paying the security and the water bills for several years now, all that has to taken into consideration."

"Yes, I understand. The boys will want 10%."

"I know, that makes me angry, in the U.K. it is usually 1.5% – 2%, and the estate agents there have large over heads, rents, wage bills, adverts, many costs. These lads don't even have an office, their only over heads are taxis and phones."

"You complain about everything here. Let's forget that for now, why have you been back to the Arabs again? You didn't tell me you were going, how can I help you with the smooth running of things if you don't tell me what is going on."

"Nothing is going on."

"The staff next door speak with us you know. Ebou was telling me while we were out this morning the hotel is planning to build more bedrooms here."

"Really, how can they do that if I own this land and not them?"

I expected Sidi, who was already annoyed that I hadn't readily accepted the offer on Reggie's compound, to get even more worked up, but instead he put his hand on my arm and said in a gentle tone, "Helen, please be careful, these are not Shendians you are dealing with, they are Arabs, they are dangerous people, I know you want to leave, but I do worry about you, you can't trust these men."

I carried on walking towards the bar, as I told him. "I am always suspicious of people I don't know, you know that."

"Yeah, but I really am getting worried about you; you don't listen to me. I will be back this evening to hear what Reggie said."

"Fine, fine, I'll see you later. As he started walking away I added. "If you are coming back; remember to bring my receipts with you."

He turned around to face me. "What?"

I calmly told him. "What I said, bring the receipts with you; I noticed your car parked out the front so Musa must have returned with my receipts."

Without another word Sidi walked away shaking his head. Had he really thought I had forgotten about them?

I phoned Reggie early in the evening. He eagerly agreed to the sale but we both knew he needed a Shendian lawyer to arrange the legal side of the sale for him. I told him Ousman was representing me, in my court case and was the only lawyer I had had dealings with, so was the only one I could recommend. Reggie had a list of reputable lawyers from the High Commission and Ousman's name was on the list, so Reggie agreed he should act for him. I ended by telling him I would phone him the following evening, after I had spoken to Ousman, and discussed the sale with him, then I could explain to Reggie what was required for the sale to be completed. Ousman would also be able to tell me how long the sale was likely to take to go through all the required procedures. I was also interested in this; I was still hoping to come to some agreement with The Peace Haven over The Dominion.

Sidi arrived soon after I had spoken to Reggie; he tapped quietly on the open sliding glass door, which led into my lounge. I was sat in my armchair, with my back to him, as he walked in I put my hand out and said. "Receipts!"

"Good evening, that wasn't a very nice greeting."

"Ok. Good evening. Receipts!

"I will bring your bloody receipts tomorrow, stop keeping on about them. Anyone would think you didn't believe I had them. We have more important things at the moment like the sale of Reggie's compound. Have you spoken to him?"

"Yes, I have spoken to Reggie, and he has agreed to the sale. Back to the receipts. I am beginning to doubt if you have them."

"So you are accusing me of stealing again. I will bring your bloody receipts, and then you will be sorry you have been so bad to me. If you keep behaving like this I will go, but if I do, you know the staff will support me and between us we will ruin your business."

That was the problem, I did know this, and I had seen it done to so many others. A taubab woman alone up against her staff had the odds stacked against her, and with my negotiations with Husaini's men in progress, I needed the business to be running smoothly. At least now the threat was out in the open.

"Let's get on with the business at hand." Sidi continued in a much calmer voice now that he had delivered his threat. "We need to find a lawyer for Reggie; I will sort this with the estate agent boys in the morning."

"No need. I've spoken to Reggie and I will phone Ousman in the morning and arrange for him to do what is needed."

"Why Ousman?"

"Why not? I know Ousman and am used to dealing with him."

"I know that, but you have too much to do without bothering yourself with this sale. I will sort it all for you or don't you trust me to do this either?"

"It is not that. I'm the one with the power of attorney over the compound, so I have to be involved, and it will be easier with Ousman."

"O.K. O.K. sort it yourself." Sidi obviously wasn't pleased with this. I wondered if he had made some arrangements with the estate agents. They possibly knew a lawyer that would do the job at a discounted price, and they would then charge Reggie the full amount for his services and share out the proceeds between them. I knew if I used Ousman, he would give a legal receipt, itemising all the costs that I could send to Reggie. Besides I didn't want to risk any more receipts going astray.

By then it was nearly time for me to return to work, Sidi was leaving, but when he reached the door, almost as if it was an after thought, he turned, and once again in a much gentler tone than he had been using said. "I almost forgot to ask, you didn't really answer me this morning, why did you go back to see the Arabs?"

I answered him just as calmly. "Sidi, when there is something to tell you, I will let you know, but there is nothing to tell. You also have plenty to do at the moment, you haven't finished sorting the business papers for the year, and now there is the sale of Reggie's compound, I have a lot of running around for you to do. You concentrate on these at the moment, if we don't get the papers sorted soon, the government will be closing us down."

He gave me a curious look that I was unable to interpret, and said softly. "Please remember Helen, if you are thinking of selling, there will be problems with the staff, they will be very angry, they will not have jobs. Think of them and how they will react. You will need my help to sort things with the staff. Think very carefully about everything."

There it was again, a subtle threat. "I will, don't you worry, but I don't know where you get these ideas from. I must go back into the bar now, I will see you in the morning." I walked passed him, to go back to work. I had thought about the staff, at length, there was no need for Sidi to remind me, they would all be out of work, if I closed the business. I did feel some guilt but against that I balanced some of the things that had happened to me over the last my eight years. As a result I had decided I owed no loyalty whatsoever to my staff. I would provide generous redundancy packages but that was all for the future. As far as I was concerned my negotiations with The Peace Haven still had a very long way to go.

Sidi's remark rang through my ears several times, as I served behind the bar that evening. How much did the staff know? Had any of The Peace Haven staff heard rumours and passed them on to my staff? I certainly hadn't even hinted to anyone of a possible sale, but Sidi probably wasn't the only one that was drawing their own conclusions about my visits to the Hussaini offices.

"You O.K.? You seem to be miles away tonight," asked Nick late that evening, after the staff had gone home, when only he and Terry were left drinking at the bar.

"Yeah, I'm fine,"

"Come on spit it out, staff giving you problems? Sidi throwing a wobbly? If we don't know we can't help."

"I'm fine, honest. I do have one bit of good news Reggie's compound is being sold."

"About time that's been years hasn't it?" Terry asked.

"Yes, about five years, a Nigerian guy and his Swedish wife are buying it."

"That's one less problem for you, I remember the night when the watchman came here kicking up a fuss." Terry replied.

"All I need now is to sell this place."

"Don't talk daft; I keep telling you, you've got rocks in your head. Who in their right mind would buy The Dominion with all its problems? Have you forgotten about your court case, and your access problem?" Nick pointed out, the obvious that was constantly foremost in my mind.

"He's right." Terry backed him up. "You will still be here when we are all coming in using our Zimmer frames."

"Talk for yourself, she may serve on her Zimmer, but I'll still be coming in on my own two feet."

"I'll get mine motorized so I can zoom out to the garden with my tray at lunchtime, and that would be good for chasing you lot around the bar."

"Now that does sound like fun." Nick said, and Terry once again agreed with him.

I contacted Ousman the following morning, and he agreed to take on the sale of Reggie's compound, he asked me to get Reggie to fax him the paperwork he had for the property, so he could verify it was all in order, and told me to get either the estate agents or the purchasing couple to make an appointment to see him, to arrange payment for the sale. Although Sidi simply said he would pass that on to the estate agents, he was visibly annoyed by this: I assumed he was still hoping I would relent and allow them to use their own lawyer. Late that afternoon Ousman phoned me. "Helen, I have just received the paperwork from Mr. Preston, there is a small problem with the deeds. Datu's name was originally on them as well as Mr. Preston and his father's. You know many non-Shendian's have a Shendian's name on their deeds to enable them to have the property freehold as opposed to leasehold."

"Oh, will that be a problem?"

"Not a major one, but it will hold the sale up for a while. Mr. Preston says his father objected while they were in the land office, apparently Datu had told the clerk in local language to add his name on the deeds, the others didn't realise what was happening until it was too late. The clerk in the land office crossed Datu's name off, but that isn't good enough. I will have to arrange to have it done legally. I have no reason to disbelieve Mr. Preston, but Datu's family could claim he crossed the name off himself. That would cause problems."

"Will you get on with that as soon as possible please, the family are eager to complete this and put a closure on things."

"Yes, I will go to the land office in the morning."

"Good, once you have sorted that out, how long should the sale take to go through?"

"It will take a few weeks, possibly six."

I looked favourably on the sale of the house, I was eager to have it sold before I left Shendi, but besides that I considered it a good omen. Reggie's compound first, next The Dominion.

Although the bar always seemed to be busy, my takings were down on the previous year. The tourists were here, but there were signs the credit crunch, in the U.K. was starting to take a hold in Shendi. With no jet lag and only six hours from the UK Shendi usually benefited from people taking a break in the sun to recharge their batteries after Christmas. These tourists were in smaller numbers than usual, many of them saving their money for their main holidays later in the year. Those that came did not spend as freely as in the past. Many customers were sitting down to snack style meals, in the evenings, and beers were replacing sales of wine. Still at least I had some custom. The blight of maintenance problems I had the previous low season continued. The forces seemed to be against me; or were my staff being opportunists and benefiting from The Dominion whilst they were still able. I was fairly certain they had heard rumours and were taking advantage of the situation. Whatever the cause, my bank balance wasn't as healthy as I would have anticipated for that stage of the season, and the worry of the forthcoming low season, started to weigh heavy on my mind.

Late in the evening, two burly Shendians, with briefcases came into the bar and asked me to step outside to speak to them. I recognised one of these as a gentleman from the Tourist Board Offices, although I couldn't recall his name. When we were out in the garden they both showed me their I.D. cards.

"It is early March, Madam," one of then told me sternly. "Your operational licence is now overdue, and we have come to collect your payment. If you don't pay us, we will return at eight o'clock tomorrow morning to put a closure notice on your gate."

"One of my lads came and paid this a few weeks ago."

"Good, then you will have a receipt to show us."

"Um, no, he told me your cashier was out of receipts." I knew as I said this, the license hadn't been paid, and I was making a fool of myself.

"Our records show that on January 22nd one of your employees came into our office and paid for your staff's I.D. badges, but not your operational license. You must know he should not have been able to get the badges without paying for the licence, but he saw a friend of his that works in our office, and that boy arranged the badges for him."

"I had given him the money for both, and thought he had paid both, being that he bought me the badges."

"That is not our concern. We have no record of your payment, you have no receipt, so you have to pay us now or we will close your business until you do."

I closed my eyes and uttered an audible sigh. "O.K."

I went into the office, the cost of the license nearly emptied my safe, but I was grateful the cash was there to pay them, no way could I have the business closed down; besides my lose of earnings, it could jeopardise my bargaining power with The Peace Haven.

"More grief?" asked Nick, who was the only one in the bar when I returned.

"No more than is normal for Shendi." I told him, I was momentarily tempted to share with Nick what had happened, but quickly reconsidered. Nick had his own problems and it wasn't fair to burden him with mine.

The next morning, I was sat in the office, engrossed in my paperwork, when I heard Sidi talking in the bar with Momoudu, and then heard his footsteps heading towards the house.

"I'm in here." I called out as he passed the office. He tapped on the door and came in.

"Good morning, are you alright to-day." he asked.

"Fine". I said trying extremely hard to control my temper, and then gave him instructions for a couple of errands I wanted him to do while he was out shopping with Ebou. After a few more pleasantries, I calmly pointed to the receipt on the desk that the Tourist Board staff had given me the previous evening. "Before you go, I have the receipt for the operational license. Now I have that, I only need the income tax receipt and then I will have everything I need to be able to apply for my immigration papers. I watched Sidi's eyes glance towards the receipt on the desk; he was astounded. The muscles in his face twitched, his mouth quivered, he was dumbstruck. After a slight pause he stuttered slightly as he said. "Oh --- oh—who bought it around?"

"Two guys from the Tourist Board came here late last night."

"Really? I – I told you they had run out of receipts didn't I?"

"Yes you did." I was feeling agitated, but amazed myself how steady and calm my voice was sounding. "They threatened to close the business at eight o'clock this morning, if I didn't pay them."

"What? You paid them. Why?"

"It hadn't been paid. You know that, as well as I do. You must think I'm stupid. Did you really think they wouldn't eventually come around to collect their money? Whatever have you done with so much?"

After a long pause that seem never ending he quietly said. "There was a family problem, I needed it."

"So did I; to pay my licence! Do you think I can afford to lose that amount, you know the long hours I have to work to get my money. What about the income tax money, have you had that also?"

"What do you mean?"

"What I say. The mysterious income tax receipts that have been to the garage then up country, and since then just haven't been mentioned."

"This operational licence has nothing to do with the income tax."

"I know that but you were sent to pay them all. Now I want the truth, have the income tax and my foreign worker's permit been paid?"

"Well -- um – I've explained. I needed the money, I am paying it back, don't worry, it isn't a problem."

"It is a problem to me." Despite my best intentions my voice rose uncontrollably. "Sidi, you must know that I'm here illegally until my immigration papers are sorted. I have enough problems without having to worry about the Immigration Authorities coming to arrest me as they will eventually do, if my papers aren't in order."

"Calm down, I will soon have the money; I will sort everything out very soon."

"You had better; I don't have the money to pay it again. Just get out of here and do what I've asked for a change." I collapsed on my desk in floods of tears as Sidi left. I was devastated. I knew I was in an impossible situation. I just about had enough in the bank to pay the income tax, but I certainly wouldn't let Sidi know that. This money I had I would need in low season to meet my wage bill, if nothing came of my talks with The Peace Haven. After a few more sobs, I pulled myself together and I went into the house to make myself presentable before I went back into the bar to prepare for my lunchtime trade. I was in no state to make decisions at that moment, when I had calmed down I would be more able to see things in a better perspective.

Chapter Twenty

Deal or No Deal

As Sidi came into the bar carrying supplies with Ebou, about two hours after our encounter in the office, I was still very agitated. Simply seeing him made me shudder but I could not let him or any one else know how I felt. I really had to calm myself, to put it to one side. Tomorrow I was due to meet Mustapha and Esa again and it was vital that I was in the right frame of mind for that meeting. In a way what had been stolen was irrelevant; the only thing that mattered was the result of that meeting. I had to get away from Shendi and that meeting held my one hope. I was tired of coping on my own, tired of having no one to share problems with, tired of feeling depressed and only seeing the worst in any situation. How I longed to be able to simply talk over the events of the day with someone who understood, someone who wasn't out to make a fast shilling, someone who could run the bar and give me a break. For over eight years, apart from stays in hospital, I had not spent a night away from The Dominion, and for almost every day of those eight years I had worked morning and evening behind the bar. I had had enough and knowing that I could no longer trust Sidi over money matters was the final straw. I needed to be in the bar as much as possible, but with my trust in Sidi now completely gone, I had no-one I could rely on to go and pay all the bills and taxes. I would have to go myself. In addition business was slowing down and it was going to be difficult, possibly even impossible to run the business during the low season. A deal with The Peace Haven seemed to be my only salvation now. I tried to put Sidi out of my mind, and concentrate on the more important business of selling The Dominion. I would deal with Sidi and the missing money later when I had had time to consider the matter rationally. I knew I had to be careful. Even without his recent threats I was well aware that he and his family could ruin me. I knew I had to think about every move I intended to make, very carefully before acting.

I was awoken from my reverie by Kevin ordering another pint, and Sidi saying. "Bye, I'll see you in the morning" simultaneously.

"O.K. I'd like you early in the morning; I'm going out and want to get the shopping sorted before I go." I called to Sidi as I pulled Kevin his pint. I noted Sidi hadn't wasted any time leaving that morning. Generally he would have had something to eat with the kitchen lads before he left, but today he was eager to get away, presumably expecting some form of repercussions from our confrontation earlier. I was glad he had gone; I didn't even want to see him around the place at the moment.

"What's up luv? You seem miles away." Kevin asked.

"Sorry Kev, I'm fine, you have my full attention now." With Sidi gone, I did feel a weight lifted from me and I returned to giving my customers the attention they deserved; I would have plenty of time when I went off duty to dwell on the difficulty I faced over my taxes.

The next morning when Sidi arrived he didn't seem very happy. "What's the matter with you now?" I asked rather sharply, still in an unforgiving mood.

"The Nigerian boy and his wife have been to see Ousman about the house sale," he told me, "and Ousman is trying to delay things, I'm not pleased about this. Why couldn't you leave this to me, the estate agent boys had a lawyer who would have sorted everything out quickly."

"What do you mean, how is he trying to delay things?"

"He is telling them the deeds need to be sorted or something, I don't know. I didn't really understand what the boys were saying."

"If you don't understand, stop complaining, and I will explain." I told him. I tried to make it clear that if the sale went ahead with Datu's name simply crossed off the deeds, there could be repercussions from Datu's family if they came to hear the property had been sold. The fact that Datu was in police custody or might end up imprisoned as a result of the trial did not prevent him from owning property.

"O.K. I understand that, but if his name is crossed off that is fine."

"Legally it's not. I want this done properly; I don't want Reggie or Sharon getting any further problems in Shendi when all this is completed."

"Taubabs, Taubabs!!!!! Always problems of some sort, if there is no problem, you will make one."

"Coming from you who is my biggest problem, that is classic. I suggest you go and wait for me out in the car, and leave me to get ready to leave."

I was sure, between Sidi and the estate agents, they could have found a lawyer to push the sale through quicker than Ousman was doing, but I wanted to make sure no more farther scams would be tried on the Preston family. This sale would go through to my satisfaction. I had decided to get Sidi to drive to my meeting with Mustapha and Esa; it was now obvious to me that he would be informed of my meeting before too long, so I might as well save the taxi fare.

"What are you seeing these men about this morning?" he asked soon after we started the short journey to Poutapi.

"Sidi please, I have told you before, this is none of your business, and I would rather you just leave me in peace, don't work me up I want to be calm when I arrive at their offices."

"Fine, fine, have it your own way, but remember as I have told you before, you will need my help if you are doing what I think you are doing."

I stared out the car window, and watched the landscape drift passed me, the palm trees never failed to calm me, and the views of the golden sandy beaches peeping through the swaying palms at regular intervals couldn't fail to raise me from even my darkest moments. I didn't bother to answer Sidi's last remark; I didn't feel it was necessary to. As we pulled to a halt in the office car park, I opened the car door, and noted Sidi had done the same, I got out and started to walk the short distance to the compound gate. Sidi was quickly by my side. "Where are you going?" I asked knowing full well what his intention was.

"I am coming with you."

"You definitely are not. I have told you this is none of your business."

"But Helen," he replied, "you asked me to come with you, and you know you need me."

"I asked you to drive me so I wouldn't need a taxi, I didn't mention you coming into the office with me, and sorry I do not need you."

He caught hold of my arm, "Helen, I think you do need me, I can speak to these men, you don't know how to handle them, they are Muslims like I am, they will respect that and things will go nice and smooth, you will see."

I stopped, looked down at his hand on my arm and said nothing. He shrugged, reluctantly moved his hand and I carried on walking simply telling him to wait in the car as I did not expect the meeting to be a long one. As I reached the compound gate, I looked back over my shoulder, and was pleased to see him making his way to the car.

He was looking at the ground, his shoulders slightly hunched, clearly his whole body language expressed complete dissatisfaction with my rebuff; but after recent events, surely he didn't expect me to take him into my confidence. There was a different security guard on the gate that morning. "Good morning, I have an appointment with Mr. Mustapha." I told him.

"Fine, fine, come in, do you know your way to his office?"

I told him I did and made my way, into the reception area, where I was once again welcomed by the receptionist who had grown accustomed to my visits. She told me Mustapha and Esa were free and expecting me, so I could make my way straight up to the boardroom. This I did, when I reached the top of the stairs, I looked into Jenny's office, before going to the boardroom. Although the door was ajar Jenny was absent. I missed her smiling face, seeing her had made me feel I had an ally in these offices, and had given me confidence. As I stepped out of her office, I saw her coming down the elaborate stairway leading up to the next story, she simply said "Good morning Helen, Mr. Mustapha is expecting you," but held both her hands up in front of her with her fingers crossed. This small gesture helped put me at my ease.

I knocked on the large highly decorative wooden door of the boardroom, and entered when I was instructed to by Mustapha, in his distinctive loud voice. Esa stood and greeted me, Mustapha remained seated, and in a rather off hand way asked me to be seated also. In the same breath he said, "We've wasted enough time on dialogue already let's get straight to the point. You have made it clear you are not really happy with our offers, I will offer you $125,000, take it or leave it."

I was still dithering over this amount, I was tempted to take it, it was an extra $25,000 on top of last week's offer, but still far short of our original investment, and the figure I would have liked to hear him offer. "Still no response, come on you must realise we are not going to keep on upping our offer, I will give you one last offer of $150,000. That is our absolute final offer, and I want a definite answer from you right now."

Mustapha's abrupt manner shook me. In my more confident moments in the security of my own home, I had decided I would sell The Dominion, and return to the U.K. before mentioning anything to Simon. I had had no contact with him for over two years now; in fact the last time he had spoken to me was shortly after Kevin had told us Steph was expecting Karen, and she had passed her second birthday. I fully intended sending him his half of the proceeds, but I would have felt some satisfaction, to draw this to a conclusion myself. It was him who had distanced himself to all our affairs here, he had made a new life for himself, and I would have liked to prove to him that I was capable of doing likewise, but definitely not at such a loss, that would not be fair.

"Sorry I am not prepared to accept this much of a loss on my own, this is also my husband's business, and I must discuss this with him."

"Surely he knows you are having talks with us?" asked Esa, now speaking equally as abruptly as Mustapha.

"Of course," I lied, "but I'm not prepared to make a final decision without consulting him."

Mustapha pushed his mobile phone across the table towards me. "Phone him now," he demanded.

"He will be at work now, and he isn't allowed to have his mobile on him at work, I won't be able to speak to him until this evening."

"Right, do you understand this is our final offer, there is no way delaying things any longer will result in us changing that offer. It is already well above the value of your land. We will give you till tomorrow morning to sort this out with your husband. We will all meet here at the same time tomorrow morning for our last meeting on this matter; I have no more time to waste on this."

Mustapha rose and walked out of the room, leaving the door open, for Esa and myself to leave. Esa stood and limply shook my hand. "Take things easy Helen, Mustapha is not a man that likes being messed around, in fact I am very, very surprised he made you that final offer, before you came into the office he told me $125,000 was the highest he was prepared to go to for your land, he has been more than fair with you. It is up to you now to be fair with us and accept this generous offer."

I had mixed feelings as I walked down the stairs and out of the building, I knew deep down we had to accept this offer. I understood what Esa was telling me, I knew Mustapha's patience with me was wearing thin; I had to make a decision. $150,000 was less than I had been hoping for, and approximately half the amount we paid for The Dominion eight years previously, but it was also much higher than £40,000, which was the amount the estate agent director of Oliver's bank had estimated for my land a few months before.

"You don't look very happy," Sidi told me, as I got back into the car, "I said I should have come in with you, I could have helped you."

"Shut up Sidi, I don't need you patronising me at the moment, just take me home."

I was surprised that he made no attempt to make further conversation as we drove back to The Dominion. I sat watching, but this time not really seeing, the palm trees and the miles of golden sand, while I wondered if this would be one of the last times I would have the opportunity to gaze at this outstanding view.

"Do you need me for anything else?" Sidi asked as we pulled up outside, the brightly painted main gates of The Dominion.

I shook my head and said, "No, you go back to your shop, I will see you in the morning, come early I want you to take me out again tomorrow."

I got out of the car and as I walked around to his side of the car, Sidi put his head out of the window, and asked, "Where are we going tomorrow, back to the offices again?"

"Yes." I abruptly said as I started to walk away.

"Helen," he called after me, and as I turned said, "I will stay with you if you want someone to talk to."

"I've told you I'm fine, if I had needed you I would have asked."

I went into the bar, and although my heart wasn't really in what I was doing, I started to serve the few early lunch time customers. I went through the motions, smiling at everyone, serving them and joining in their light chatter, but not really registering what I was actually doing, my mind was several thousand miles away. I was daydreaming about the new life I hoped would shortly be mine. I wondered where I would eventually settle, I didn't really want to go back to the island, I had left; the prospect of going back again wasn't very appealing. I would need employment as soon as possible; my share of the proceeds of the sale would soon diminish, if I wasn't working.

"Any chance of a drink, Helen darling?" Kevin asked.

"Sorry Kev, I was miles away." I answered him as I pulled his pint. This was truer than he realized, I was physically stood behind the bar, but I was mentally back in the U.K. I must concentrate on what I was doing, if Simon did not agree to accept the price The Peace Haven were offering us, I would need the business I had now, I must make sure I kept up The Dominion's standards. Kevin was chatting away and I still wasn't fully listening to him until I heard him mention the excessive amount of check points he had just been through to get from his compound down to The Dominion.

"What do you think is going on?" I asked, "I've been out this morning but I went in the other direction, everything was fine where I've been."

"Really don't know luv, maybe just a visiting President, all will probably be O.K. later."

As the lunch time regulars came into the bar Kevin asked all of them about checkpoints but no-one had seen any. At least it was a topic of conversation that interested everyone and it gave me a chance to think about something far removed from my own problems. By the time I went for my break I felt calmer and once in the house I picked up the phone intending to speak to Simon immediately. I realized he was probably still at work, and I needed his full attention, It would not be fair to speak to him while he had his mind on other things. I put the receiver back down again and decided to ring him after I had had my shower and short nap. I lay on my bed, sleep eluding me, and my thoughts drifting in overdrive. I wasn't sure how Simon would feel about me starting negotiations over the sale without consulting him. I weighed up many different aspects of the sale, and with my mind going around in circles, I decided to get up again; I realized I wasn't going to get much rest that afternoon.

I ordered a coffee and sat sipping it staring into space and drifting away again, I pictured myself visiting Kevin and Steph, and seeing little Karen for the first time ever. I was determined I was going to get back to the U.K. I doubted Simon would have any opposition to the sale, he would probably welcome his share of the money, but if he did have any objection I would fight him all the way, the time had definitely come for me to leave Shendi. Finally I decided I could not cope with any sort of confrontation with Simon. I would text him. I picked up my mobile and sent him a simple text that said 'The Peace Haven have offered to buy for £75,000 do I accept?' I sat there with my mobile in my hand expecting a quick reply.

I sat and waited, the reply didn't come. I was still sat there half an hour later waiting eagerly for the reply that didn't arrive; it was time for me to go back to work. I returned to the bar with my mobile in my hand, and placed it on the shelf behind the bar. This was out of character for me, I only ever took my mobile into the bar if I was expecting a call, very few people had my mobile number, and certainly none of my regulars had it. If any of them asked for my number I told them they didn't need it as they had my landline number and I was nearly always on the premises.

"I see you are expecting your boyfriend to phone." Terry, who rarely missed anything, observed as I put the phone down.

"Hardly." I truthfully answered him.

I picked up the phone at regular intervals during the evening, to check if a text had come through, while I was busy. The text I desperately wanted didn't arrive. Several times during that shift I had joking remarks from the lads watching me around the bar.

"Seems he doesn't love her as much as she thinks he does." Rick told the others.

"She certainly is keen, how often she is checking her phone." Nick observed.

"What man would take her on, when she spends all her evenings here with us?" was Terry's contribution to their banter.

"I can't understand why she's bothering, she has all of us at her disposal, but she still wants more. Some women don't know when they are well of," offered Nick

"You lads must think I'm hard up, if you think I would be interested in any of you."

"One day the Iron Maiden will melt, that's when she will need us." Kevin joined in.

I vowed not to check my phone so often, maybe Simon was out, and hadn't read my text yet, why was I panicking; he was bound to answer before the evening was over.

I was very wrong. When everyone had gone, I stood in the kitchen washing up the last of the evening's glasses and wondering why there had been no reply. I realised that we had not been in contact with each other for over two years and I knew that he had made a new life for himself, so possibly didn't want any contact with me now. But surely he knew he had to respond to my text. The sale of The Dominion was of importance to him as well as to me. He would be financially better off once everything was resolved, we both would be, so why his hesitation now. He must be aware that until things were sorted I could not move on and make the new life for myself that I now desperately craved. I guessed that he was probably disappointed in the money we had been offered, as I myself was and that he would be unaware how hard I had fought to get the offer as high as it was. Maybe that was why he hadn't replied; even so I could understand why my text hadn't prompted some sort of reaction from him, whether by text or phone. I was completely confused by his lack of reaction.

I climbed into bed somewhat bewildered, and aware that once again sleep was likely to elude me. My mind was in confusion, I had to go to the final meeting in the morning, if we turned this offer down; it could well be my last chance of freeing me from my present life for the foreseeable future. The scale of the loss was so large, I did not feel it right to make that decision without contacting Simon. I was up early the next morning, the first thing I did was to check my phone, to see if he had replied over night but as I picked up the phone, I knew deep down this wouldn't be the case. I had spent a very broken night; I doubted if I had been in a deep sleep at any time. As I had more or less expected, there was no text and no missed call. I went into the bathroom to have my shower; with Simon foremost in my mind. I cleaned my teeth, and then in frustration throw my toothbrush into the sink. Simon had to answer this, I would text again and if he hadn't responded by the time I had showered I would phone him. It wasn't ridiculously early, if I was up worrying about this why shouldn't he be?

'Have a meet's with Peace Haven @ 10. Must give answer on £75,000 offer. Yes or no?' I sent.

I took the phone back into the bathroom with me; I showered while I eagerly listened for the sound of a text coming through to my phone. 'Come on Simon, get a move on', I said to myself as I started to towel myself dry. With him ignoring my texts I felt less inclined to phone him than before but knew I would have to. Just as I had finished drying myself, the sound of a text arriving on my phone, echoed like music to my ears. I grabbed the phone from the small bathroom shelf I had put it on, glancing at it I could see, almost unbelieving as I had nearly given up hope; I had received a text from Simon.

My hands shook with impatience as I waited for the text to open. The text very simply said 'Yes.'

I clasped the phone to my chest, and whirled around in a circle as if dancing with my phone, I was excited; I had half expected Simon to say he wouldn't accept their offer, because it was too low. I dressed quickly and went out into the bar kitchen to make my morning coffee. I took my mug and went to sit in the beer garden which was much nicer than the vegetable garden I had next door. I always enjoyed sitting in it especially in the early morning; when I shared it only with the many African brightly coloured birds, and the lizards, the males of whom were starting to change from their greyish brown to the delicate yellow and violet they adorned themselves in for the mating season. I knew I was too late to see the monkeys that sunny morning; they were up before me and had already made their way to the neighbouring hotels for their breakfasts, I had heard them going over my roof as I had read Simon's text.

"Good morning." I said to Pouka, as he came out of the night watchman's hut, near the main entrance to the bar. I suspected he had just woken up, as he hadn't come out of the hut when he first heard me around. The security were not meant to sleep at night, although I had caught them asleep on several occasions. However, on this glorious sunny morning, when I was confident at long, long last my life was going to change for the better, I couldn't have cared less if he had slept all night, or if he had spent most of the night selling The Peace Haven's diesel. I was on cloud nine, this was the beginning of the rest of my life, and I was determined to enjoy the last few weeks of my life in Shendi.

"You are up early this morning." Pouka remarked.

"I'm always up early Pouka, I just don't always come outside, but this morning I have decided to take advantage of the early morning sunshine in this side of the garden before the breakfast customers start arriving."

"As long as all is fine, fine. I thought maybe something was wrong."

"No. All is fine, in fact being I'm going to sit out here till the day staff start arriving, you can go home."

After Pouka had left I was completely alone at The Dominion, a very rare occurrence, this gave me an unexplainable feeling of freedom, there were times when I felt I was living in a gold fish bowl, there was always members of staff around; and possibly it was my imagination, but I often felt I was continually being watched. As I was finishing my second cup of coffee I watched a troop of soldier ants, busying themselves manoeuvring the remains of one of my last evening's diner's supper into one of the many entrances to their warren underneath my garden slabs. I still marvelled at the wild life that there was to observe in my own garden; it was a large contrast to the odd neighbour's cat back in my island home. My solitude didn't last for long; I was sharply bought back to reality by the clanging of the main gate opening. It was Sidi.

"What are you doing here?" I asked somewhat more sharply than I intended, I was annoyed at him for intruding on my much welcome peace, and interrupting the elation I was feeling.

"Why are you so jumpy? I came down because I saw Pouka in the village; he told me you sent him home early. I wondered why, I thought something was wrong."

"If something was wrong, would I send him home early? I don't think so."

"Don't be so sharp with me; I keep telling you, you are going to need my help. Is it alright for me to make myself some coffee, I came straight away when I saw Pouka, and I haven't had any breakfast."

"That's fine, there is bread in the kitchen if you want to make some breakfast. I don't mean to be short tempered with you, but don't you understand I sometimes like to be on my own, I like to have some peace, the people here don't seem to understand that."

"You are right we don't understand Taubabs wanting to be alone, you must realise we have many people living in our compounds with us, and we are never alone, and we don't like it when we are."

Sidi went to make himself some breakfast; I dwelt on what he had just told me. He was right. Shendians are never alone, they are accustomed to living in compounds, usually consisting of several small buildings as sleeping areas, and communal buildings where the women cook and they all eat, due to the climate sometimes these areas are in the open air at the centre of the compound; this is a vast difference to the single dwellings we are accustomed to. If you have lived like that all your life, I could imagine it would be daunting to be alone. Over the last few years when I have seldom had any privacy, I had valued my solitude more than ever. I was annoyed with Sidi for interrupting my tranquillity on that particular morning, but on reflection realised he maybe thought he was being of assistance to me. Deep down although I was reluctant to admit it even to myself, I knew was going to need Sidi's help to ease the situation with my staff before I left Shendi.

Sidi returned soon afterwards with an omelette sandwich, which was most Shendians favourite breakfast, and a mug of coffee on a tray. "I think it is time we talked about what is going on don't you?" he said as he pulled out the garden chair opposite me.

"I don't really want to, but yes, I suppose you are right."

"I think you should have taken me into your confidence a long time ago. Everyone is talking; everyone knows what is happening, the staff don't want to believe it, and you are going to need my help, I told you yesterday you should have taken me into those offices with you. I could have helped, if Simon was here he would have had to see them not you, a man is who should be dealing with these Arabs, and I am the only one you have to help you."

"I see what you mean." I replied, but because of recent events I knew I would never trust Sidi again, certainly as far as money was concerned. Looking back now, and being honest about matters, I have to say that, even though I was never sure of his true allegiance, he had always stood by me, both with problems with the staff and with any brushes I had had with the authorities. There were many things I would need assistance with before I finally flew home, and Sidi would be invaluable to me here. I momentarily dithered, and then decided I must tell Sidi my intentions. I knew only too well how he had let me down, but if he suspected The Dominion, which was his main source of income, was shortly to close, and he wasn't sure of his future, then maybe that was why he had taken the money. Again, Shendians, because of the uncertainty of their lives, tend to live by different standards to those in the West. Most Africans, not only Shendians, milk situations, without much thought of the outcome, or the long term effects to them. They live for today, not for tomorrow.

"I have to go back to their offices this morning and give them my decision on the offer they have made me."

"Is it a good offer?"

"No, in fact roughly half of what we originally paid, so we will be losing a lot of money."

"Then why accept?"

"Who else will buy it? The Dominion has too many problems. The court case is unlikely to ever finish, and if it does there isn't much chance of it being in our favour, you know that as well as I do."

"What about Simon, does he think you should sell?"

"Yes, he is in agreement with me." I had had Simon approval in a single word text, so wasn't really aware how much he was in agreement, but I certainly wasn't going to let Sidi know this, it was probably to my advantage to let him assume I was in full contact with Simon; but deep down although I wasn't prepared to sell at such a great loss without contacting Simon, I considered he had forfeited his right to have much of a say in my decision as he had had no involvement in the business for the past seven years.

"Are you going to take me into the offices this morning, now that I know what is going on?"

"No, this is something I must do on my own, but when we come back here we will sit and discuss, what we must do next." I knew it was then I would need to rely on Sidi, I would need his advice on how to smooth things over with my staff. The following few weeks were not going to be easy. I knew I would have more turmoil in my life before I was free of this nightmare.

Sidi wasn't happy I had said I didn't want him to come into the offices with me, but seemed more content now that he knew that was happening. We sat and chatted in the peace of the garden waiting for the day staff to arrive and for me to open the bar.

"At the moment, no-one is to know about this, I will need to speak through a few details with them this morning. It is quite possible in could be a couple of months before this is completed, please don't mention this to the rest of the staff, or I will lose even more from the kitchen, if they all know things are going to end. I don't want any of the customers knowing either, or word will soon get around the staff will be even more annoyed if they hear from any other source."

"Fine, fine, you know you can trust me, we will sort all this out between the two of us." Strangely enough, even though I was well aware I couldn't trust Sidi with money, I did believe he wouldn't let me down over this. I was now pleased that I had confided in him, he seemed genuinely happy for me, he knew I was desperate to get back to the U.K. and see my Karen. I also felt great relief that I now had someone; I could talk to about the sale, it made me feel less isolated

At the appointed time, we both set off to pay what I hoped would be my final visit to the offices at Poutapi. I was by then accustomed to the lush surroundings there, but I never felt at ease in them, I would have had more confidence to fight my case with those two intimidating men, had I been on my own territory. We arrived a few minutes early, but I went straight in nevertheless, wanting to get this meeting behind me as soon as possible. I was as usual greeted by the security guard and the receptionist and by Jenny as she showed me into the boardroom, they were by then all used to my visits that had become a regular occurrence. Both Mustapha and Esa were sat in their usual chairs waiting for me to arrive even though I was early. Maybe they were as eager as I was to finally put an end to our negotiations.

They both stood and shook my hand, as Mustapha indicated for me to sit down. "Well Helen, no more discussions now, we want to know your decision, have you spoken to your husband?" Mustapha asked.

"Yes," I told a slight white lie, "he is in agreement, like me he is disappointed with the price, but we both agree."

"Good, I understand your disappointment, but as we have told you we are actually offering you considerably more for your land than the currant market value. You did pay way too much for the property when you bought in you must realise that now."

"Yes, I do, but can I please clarify with you that you are buying my land."

"Well yes, of course, what do you think we are purchasing?" Mustapha asked, seemingly slightly confused.

"My land has buildings on it; I want it written into the conditions of sale that you are only buying my land."

"Fine, but Helen what are you getting at, I don't understand what you are trying to say", he replied glancing at Esa as he did so.

"I want it in writing you are only paying me for my land, because if this is so, that is what you will get."

"What do you mean by that? You know we have no interest in your buildings we made that plain at the start."

"If you are not paying for the buildings, you won't get them." I was fully aware the buildings of The Dominion, would have no place within such a high class establishment as The Peace Haven, but I was also aware that once they owned the property they would demolish it and be able to recycle a substantial amount of it, if not in the buildings they intended putting on the site, maybe in staff accommodation or they could sell it.

"They are on the land." Mustapha reminded me.

"Yes, but I will knock them down."

Their laughter that followed my answer had the same effect as holding a red rag at a bull. I was angry; I knew they considered me as insignificant because I was a mere woman. I could have coped with a snigger from the two of them, but this was uncontrollable laughter, I was not amused. I slammed my fist down on the table, and in an angry outburst told them "No-one laughs at me like that, if you pay me for the buildings you can have them if not I will knock them down and sell it piece by piece, just as you will if you have them." I stood in preparation to leave the office.

"Helen, Helen, we are sorry you are so upset by all this, but be serious you know you can't do that you are only a woman." Esa tried to calm me, but his last remark incensed me even more.

"Sorry I don't get laughed at. If I say I will knock it down, that is what I will do. You instruct your lawyer to start the sale, and I will speak to mine this afternoon, you know where to find me, if you want me." I walked out the office, without shaking hands with them or even a good bye. I felt annoyed with myself for my angry outburst as I walked down the elaborate stairway for the very last time. The receptionist said a polite "Salaam Malaikum" as I reached the bottom of the stairs, knowing how exceptionally rude, in fact an insult to her Islamic religion, if I didn't respond I said "Malaikum Salaam" as I passed her desk. This simple civility softened my anger, and I felt ashamed of my behaviour in the boardroom.

Sidi was sat on the wooden bench in the car park, which I assume was there as a seat for drivers, who were waiting for anyone in the offices, it is very hot sitting in a parked car in the fierce African sun; he was talking to a taxi driver. On seeing me leave the compound Sidi got up and started walking towards the car.

I got in without speaking to Sidi. "Are you alright?" he asked.

"Yes, fine, fine." I answered, "Let's get home quickly."

We drove in silence at first then I opened the conversation with, "We are going to knock it down."

"Sorry knock what down?"

"The Dominion, they will only pay for the land that is all they are going to get."

"But you have spoken to Nick about this and he said it can't be done."

"No, he did not. He said he wasn't interested in doing it, not that it couldn't be done, and besides they laughed at me."

"Who laughed at you?" Sidi's expression gave away his thoughts, he was obviously not pleased.

"Who do you think laughed at me? Mustapha and Esa, I told them if they didn't pay for the buildings, I would knock them down, they laughed at me. Fine, fine, I will show them what this insignificant woman can do."

"Oh, Helen, no. You haven't caused trouble with these Arabs have you? I told you I should have come in with you; everything would have been easy, easy if I was there."

"Don't you patronise me or I shall get angry again, and you know you don't like it when I get angry. Just drive me home, I don't want to talk about this now, when we get back, I will go back to work, and I want you to go home. By the time you come down in the morning I will have had time to think this through, and I will have phoned Ousman to tell him about the sale. Then we will talk through how we are going to do this."

"Helen, I think you should think very carefully about this."

"And I think you should drive me home as I have asked you to, and leave me to get my head together."

I didn't need to phone Ousman, in the afternoon the phone rang shortly before I went off duty for my afternoon break, which had been when I had intended to call him.

"Hi Helen, are you well?" I was surprised to hear Ousman's voice when I answered.

"I'm fine, funnily enough I was going to phone you this afternoon."

"Well, then I've saved you a call, I've finally got everything sorted for the sale of Mr. Preston's house, you are fully aware of your duties as power of attorney aren't you? You will have to sign on Mr. Preston's behalf for the sale to go ahead, then I will pay you the proceeds after all the taxes and my fee has been paid, then it is your responsibility to send the money to him."

"Yes, that's fine, and the sooner it's all over the better."

"May I bring the papers to The Dominion on my way home this evening for you to sign?"

"That's fine; I also have something I wish to talk to you about. If you are coming here will you have time to discuss a different matter with me?"

"Of course, I will be there about six o'clock."

This suited me well, I had always preferred to discuss things face to face rather than on the phone, and I needed Ousman's advise before I actually signed the papers for my own sale. Ousman, even though he was a lawyer, that had been educated at Cambridge, still had some Shendian tendencies, punctuality, or the lack off; being one of them. He still hadn't arrived at seven o'clock and it was time for me return to work. I glanced towards the wrought ironwork doorway several times during the first hour I was behind the bar, to no avail; there was no sign of him.

"Who are you expecting?" Terry, who was sat alone as none of the other lads had arrived yet, asked.

"Sorry? What do you mean?"

"You are looking at the door every few minutes; you must be waiting for someone."

"Just wondering who may have come in on this afternoon's flight." I answered him, then seeing Ousman, and knowing, because of his Muslim faith he didn't like coming into the bar, I said to Terry. "Excuse me the lads will look after you for a while, I'm going to see someone in the garden."

I felt Terry's eyes follow me as I walked towards the entrance to greet Ousman I knew his curiosity would be getting the better of him. He didn't know Ousman was my lawyer, so was sure to be anxious to know who I was meeting. My staff knew Ousman, no doubt Terry would quiz Jed, and when he knew who I was with, would possibly be even more eager to know the reason for his visit; but it would be quite awhile yet before I would tell any of them. There was a very bright light at the end of my tunnel now, but I was well aware the road ahead would be a long uphill struggle before I was finally free of the shackles that held me here.

Ousman and I sat out in the beer garden and I put my signature to the relevant papers to enable Ousman to complete the sale of Reggie's house. "How do you want me to pay you the money?" Ousman asked, "I can either pay it into your bank account or give it to you in cash."

"Pay it into my bank. Oh hang on, in second thought how will I stand, if the government find out I have this money, I wouldn't have to pay any taxes on it, would I?"

"Well no, you shouldn't have to pay tax on it, but, with you having a business it may be wisest to have it in cash."

"Right, bring me the cash; I will get it sent straight to Reggie's U.K. account. While you are here, I want to speak to you about The Dominion. The Peace Haven is going to buy it, so I now need you to complete my sale for me."

"Are they paying you a decent price?" He asked.

"Not as much as I would have liked $150,000"

"Ummm, yes I do imagine you would have liked more, and this place is worth more than that to them, but I know you have been aware for a long while that you were never going to get your money back on your investment. How does Simon feel about it?"

"Oh, he's in full agreement." For the second time, I told a white lie on this subject. Simon had agreed in his text, but what his feelings were about the sale, I had no idea.

"That's good then, I know you want to get back to U.K. When is this going to go through? At the end of the season?"

"Their lawyer will be getting in touch with you; I would like it to go through as soon as possible, but with the season being well advanced now the end of season would seem realistic."

Ousman finished the coffee I had ordered for him, while we chatted generally and he told me how pleased he was that I was going to be able to return home, he knew I was eager to leave. This time I suspected it was Ousman that was telling a white lie, he was a businessman and would not be happy to be losing the income my never ending court case was generating for him.

Back in the bar, it soon became obvious that my meeting with Ousman in the garden had been the main topic of conversation. The lads were eager to know what was going on.

"Come on spill the beans." Kevin said, "What are you up to?"

"Why do you lot always think I'm keeping you in the dark, if you don't know what I'm doing every minute of the day. All I was doing was signing the papers for the sale of Reggie's house. I have power of attorney over it remember?"

"See," said Terry, "I told you it was best not to ask, I said it was none of our business."

"You creeping out git." Nick told him. "It was you who was dying to know. We said, so what if she is selling our local from under our feet without telling us, we will soon find another one."

"Thanks a million." I said, as I wondered what they really would think when they knew I was leaving them without a local.

Over coffee with Sidi the following morning I discussed Ousman's visit the previous evening. I told him I had signed the papers for the sale of Reggie's compound to be completed. His only response was, "How long will it be until we get the money?" which completely unnerved me.

"I don't know, but I don't think it will be very long, now everything has been completed, Ousman only has to pay the taxes, then he will let me have the rest of the money; but I have given all this serious thought, and I have decided I'm not paying the estate agents the 10%, they are expecting, they haven't done enough to warrant that high a fee. I will give them 8%, which I still think is too high, but I don't want to upset them too much." I was absolutely amazed by Sidi's reaction to this I had expected yet another confrontation, but instead, to my great surprise he answered.

"That seems fair to me, but you know they won't be happy with this, but I can sort them out." The estate agents seemed rather unsavoury to me, I deliberately hadn't got myself too involved with them, they were always dressed very smartly, but I didn't like their general attitude; I would not relish getting on the wrong side of them, I had been more than pleased to let Sidi deal with them. He always seemed somewhat ill at ease with them himself, so I was bemused, in fact slightly unnerved, by him readily agreeing to my suggestion of a reduced fee for them.

"What did Ousman have to say about the sale of The Dominion?" Sidi asked changing the subject away from the estate agents' fee.

"He will sort it out for me, but I told him not to do anything until their lawyer contacts him."

"What was his opinion of you wanting to knock it down?"

"Well, I didn't actually mention that part of things to him."

"As I've told you before, you have to be careful Helen, these Arabs are not good people, and you have to be sure of what you are doing."

"Yes, I will be, but at the moment, if you have finished your coffee, I suggest you take the chef out shopping or I won't have enough supplies for the rest of the day, and for the time being at least I have a business to run."

I sat in the garden after Sidi had gone out shopping, I was still pondering on his reaction to a reduced fee for the estate agents. This was very uncharacteristic of him, he didn't even make the slightest resistance to my suggestion, and I found this bewildering especially as he had seemed very interested to know when the money would come through.

The sale of Reggie's compound was closer to completion than I realised. That very day, as I was preparing to settle down for my afternoon nap, Ousman phoned to say he had paid all the taxes, and had just collected the remains of the money from the bank, which he would bring to me later that evening. "I don't want to give you that amount of money, in front of your customers, so can you please keep a look out for me, and take me somewhere private where we can sort everything out, I shall be at the bar at about 10 o'clock." he told me.

"Oh yes, I don't want anyone to know I have that much money on the premises." I agreed with him.

I was pleased that I would at long last be able to bring my duties of power of attorney over Reggie's property to a close. Ever since the evening the watchman came to the bar and complained he hadn't been paid, I had felt it was another weight on my shoulders, I could well do without; but on the other hand, I had been hoping Ousman was going to bring me the money during office hours, as I had intended taking it straight to Oliver at his bank, for him to transfer to Reggie's account in the U.K. I had mentioned this to Oliver a few days previously, while he was having his lunch. I didn't relish having that amount in my possession over night.

Even though Ousman was a notoriously bad time keeper, all that evening while I was working, I kept one eye on the entrance watching for Ousman to appear. I had a long time to wait, true to form he finally arrived at 10.45pm. As I spotted him, he gave me a quick wave and carried on walking, so I knew he had no intention of coming into the bar. I made my way towards the ornate wrought iron doorway that led into the garden; this was the closest exit from the bar to my house. Ousman and I reached this door from the two different directions at the same time. I greeted him and led the way into my lounge. Slung over Ousman's right shoulder was a large sports bag, I assumed he had been to the gym, but thought this was a strange thing for him to do, with so much money in his possession. He had been into my house several times before, so felt at ease there, he immediately sat down in one of my arm chairs, and opening his huge holdall and asked "Have you got something to put the money in?"

I stared in amazement, "Is that full of money?" I asked rather stupidly.

"Yes, didn't you realise it would be so bulky? It is all in the sealed bundles as I collected it from the bank; so it won't take long to count."

I had realised the money wouldn't fit in my small safe, but wasn't expecting it to be so bulky. The only thing I could find large enough to put it all in was an empty crisp box. As Ousman took each bundle from his bag, I counted it and gingerly placed it in my crisp box, wishing I could take it directly to the bank. Ousman had no idea that I had lost money from in my office in the past. After the money had been counted, and carefully placed and sealed in my inadequate cardboard box, and all the relevant paperwork had been signed, Ousman prepared to leave.

"When will you bank the money?" Ousman asked.

"First thing in the morning, I want this off the premises as soon as possible."

"Best thing, that is too much to have lying around, you never know who may realise I have bought this to you this evening."

We made our way to the office, where I put the crisp box in among the boxes of invoices, I had there. The thought of this amount of cash on the premises all night was making me nervous. Ousman was right, you never knew who might realise I had the cash. I had told no-one Ousman was bringing the money to me that evening, but if no-one else had noticed, my night security would have seen him arrive with his sports bag full, I hoped they wouldn't realise his bag wasn't so full when he left.

I went back into the bar, concentrating more on the box of money in my office that the job at hand. On a couple of occasions when I saw the security lads setting out on their patrol of the compound's perimeter, I went to the doorway and watched until they had walked past the office door. I was probably over reacting, but I would not be happy until the money was safely deposited into the bank. My behaviour was, of course, noticed and commented on.

"What's up?" Nick asked when everyone had left except himself and Terry.

"Nothing all is fine, fine."

"You are pretty jumpy tonight; you are watching the security boys like a hawk."

"Is it that obvious? I was trying not to show it. Everything is fine, just keeping an eye on things."

Nick was always quick to pick up on things at The Dominion, and as my friend Karen had told me many times, I probably should have confided in him some of my problems long ago, but my independent self, wouldn't allow me to do this. After the staff went home, I quickly washed up the last of the glasses, and hastened into the office where the first thing I did was to check on the money. It was still safe where I had put it. I cashed up the end of evening takings, and glanced again at the crisp box. I couldn't leave it here all night. I needed to take it into my bedroom with me.

I went to the security hut, and gave the security the key to main gate, and went back to the office to collect the crisp box. I looked out of the door to see if I could see the security boys, they were nowhere in sight, so I assumed they were in their hut. Clutching the box tightly, I went into the house. I securely locked the glass sliding door, and went around to the other door at the side of the house and locked that also. In the bedroom I placed the precious box on the far side of the bed, where I could see it whenever I woke up. I felt uneasy as I undressed and prepared for bed. I went back into the lounge to check the door. No-one could get in without a key, I hadn't changed the locks on the house since my arrival, and I doubted if anyone could possibly have a key, but could I be certain? My paranoia was surfacing again. Before I realised what I was doing, I had fetched one of the dining room chairs and leaned it at an angle, wedging it under the handle of the door. If anyone did have a key, which I still doubted, this would not have prevented them entering, but at least it would make a noise that would wake me. I took another chair, and did the same to the other outer door. I took a third chair and repeated this with my bedroom door. This was an occasion when I wished I could have locked myself in my bedroom; but with my chairs firmly in position, if anyone had tried to break in that night, I would be awake and waiting for them. I got into bed, and spend a restless night, with one eye on the money, in its innocent looking box. I had several boxes of books on my bedroom floor; this box didn't look out of place among the others.

I rose early the next morning, and leaving the outer doors locked and with their booby trapped doors still in place I showered. Next came my morning cup of coffee. Usually I sat in the garden but today had to be different. Locking the house door behind me I went into the bar to make my morning coffee, and returned to the house to drink it. I was clock watching, anxiously waiting for the hands to move around to nine o'clock, Oliver should be in his office then, and I would be able to deposit the money into his bank. My eagerness got the better of me, at ten to nine I dialled Oliver's mobile number.

"Hi Oliver, I have the money for Reggie's compound, I am bringing it to you very shortly. Can you please arrange for me to come straight through to your office with it, I don't want to wait in a queue and get it out at the counter."

"Yeah fine, fine is it in old notes?"

"Yeah, but it is all in sealed bundles as it came out of the bank, so it is easy to count."

"That's good, would you rather I came and collected it from you?"

"Thanks, but I can get a taxi, see you shortly."

Once again my independence was getting the better of me, it would have been much easier for me to allow Oliver to come and collect it, but on the other hand the sooner it was off the premises the better. I asked Latif who was working in the vegetable garden outside my house to go to the taxi rank up the strip and get a taxi to come and collect me from the main entrance. I went into the office, carefully carrying my precious crisp box in front of me, I took out four bundles, which was 80,000 shillings, approximately £1,600 with the exchange rate at the time, which was a vast fortune in Shendi, and put it in my safe. That was the 8% of the sale I had agreed with Sidi to pay as the fee to the estate agents.

"I have the taxi for you, Helen." I heard Latif call as I was locking the safe.

"Tell him I'll there in a minute." I answered.

Rick was in the bar, drinking his coffee and waiting for his breakfast to arrive as I walked through.

"Going out gallivanting again, this early in the morning?" he asked.

"I won't be gone long; I'm only going to see Oliver."

"What with a crisp box full of money, I knew this place was a gold mine, but......"

"Shh" I interrupted him quickly, "that is truer than you know, I have the money from the sale of Reggie's compound, and I want rid of it as soon as possible, see you soon."

"Morning, where's my coffee?" Nick asked as he came in to join Rick.

"Don't hold the lady up she's on a mission." Rick told him.

"You going out? There's a taxi blocking your entrance."

I left the boys and went out to my awaiting taxi. Seeing my large box, the taxi driver, who was stood outside his taxi talking to Latif, quickly went around to the rear of his cab and opened the boot.

"No, this is fine thanks; I will take the box inside with me." I told him.

He then opened the back door, and said. "Put it on the back seat."

"No, it isn't heavy; I will put it on my knee."

I got in the front of the car, clutching the box on my lap. The taxi driver gave me a strange look as he got in beside me. Most Shendians tended to think 'taubab' women were crazy; the look he gave me seemed to reaffirm this fact to him. I wasn't leaving this box out of my sight for a single moment, not even on the back seat. There was the possibility of us being stopped at a military or police check point, I wouldn't want them to see the money, that would make the temptation to ask for a substantial bribe too much for them, my box was staying securely on my lap.

Fortunately we arrived at Oliver's bank approximately ten minutes later, having passed two checkpoints without being stopped, I instructed the taxi driver to wait for me, and went into the office, the small bank was crowded, there was only two cashiers who both had long queues, fortunately one of them looked up and saw me enter the office.

"Mr. Oliver is expecting you Mrs. Dominion, come through," he instructed me as he raised the counter flap for me to enter. I went through into the outer office, where the three employees that were sat at their desks all glanced up and greeted me, one of them told me Oliver had said I was to go up to his office and give the money I was depositing to him. I felt slightly anxious about this, but handed over the box and made my way up the stairs and through the maze of small corridors that eventually led to Oliver's office. I spent a few minutes chatting to Oliver, and gave him Reggie's bank details, he told me the money would be in Reggie's account within five working days. As I was about to leave Oliver said to me, "I will see you out, I can't believe they didn't show you up, I know you have been here before, but these corridors are not easy to navigate, especially when you get to the outside area." He was right, it wasn't easy to find his office; I had only been a couple of times before and I seemed to take a different route through the labyrinth every time.

When we reached the inner office my crisp box was there as I had left it on the floor in the corner. "I thought they were going to count it while I was with you." I remarked to Oliver, somewhat confused.

"Don't bother about that, you said it is all in sealed bundles, didn't you?"

"Yes, it won't take long to count."

"Fine, fine, I will see you at lunchtime." Oliver said as he showed me out. I can't explain the feeling I had as I returned to my waiting taxi, the sheer relief of getting the money paid into the bank without a hitch, put me in exceptionally high spirits, I chatted happily to the taxi driver on the return journey to The Dominion. This was a complete contrast to the drive there when I didn't speak to him at all. This possibly would have reinforced his knowledge of all taubab women being slightly unbalanced.

Rick and Nick were both still sat at their usual breakfast table when I returned. "Oh, Mrs. Moneypenny, Shendi's only millionaire bar owner is back," remarked Rick is his normal sarcastic manner, "will the drinks be on you tonight?"

"They would be if the money was mine." I replied as I walked through to the house to get ready for work. It wasn't until much later in the day, that I that realised in my rush to relieve myself of the money, I hadn't waited for a receipt. Another problem with receipts, not to worry though I thought, Oliver comes to the bar everyday for his lunch, I'll ask him for one tomorrow.

Chapter Twenty-One

Powers of Attorney

Not long after I returned from Oliver's bank, Sidi arrived to take the chef out shopping. I was still in the bar chatting with Rick and Nick. "Morning Sidi, order us both a coffee and come in the house," I told him. I went into the office, collected the 80,000 shillings from the safe and walked into the lounge where I put it on a small table between the armchairs. "What's that?" asked Sidi as he entered the lounge carrying the coffees.

"What do you think it is? It's the estate agent's fee for you to pay them. Now sit down and drink your coffee. You don't know how relieved I am to put a closure on that matter."

Sidi reluctantly sat down and shook his head. "I don't understand. Where did you get it? If that is the money for the fees where is the rest of the money?"

"Where did I get it? Where do you think I got it? Ousman bought it around last night, and the rest of the money has been paid into Reggie's account."

"What? I don't believe this." He was still shaking his head, and had started raising his voice. "Helen, Helen, You should not have paid it into the bank, before we have made sure there is no more to pay, and anyway how have you paid it into the bank?"

"Calm down, what are you shouting about? Ousman has paid all the taxes, and taken out his fee, there is the money I agreed to pay the estate agents, so what else could there be to pay?"

Sidi picked the money up, and stuffed each bundle into separate pockets of his cargo trousers. "You can't possibly know there will be no more expenses, and as I said where is the rest of the money? Have you put it in your bank account?"

"Calm down. I don't understand Sidi. Why are you getting so angry over this? Where do you think it is? It certainly isn't here. I have taken the money to Oliver to pay directly into Reggie's account in the U.K. It is all sorted; there will be nothing else to pay once you have paid the estate agents, which I want a receipt for, by the way.

"What? How did you get to Oliver's bank?"

"In a taxi. I had just got back before you arrived."

He gave a large sigh and said, "Um it's O.K. you think I get angry over things, but I just worry about you, and you think I'm annoyed about other things, when all I do is think of what is best for you, and I'm not happy that you went all the way to Oliver's in a taxi with all that money. Anything could have happened to you. If you had phoned me I would have taken you"

"I know you would have done but it's been done now. As I said the money is safely on its way to the U.K. so there is no need for you to worry now."

Sidi gave another large sigh and left the room, giving me a look, which I was not sure how to interpret. He hadn't even finished his coffee, which was unusual for him. I picked up my cup and went to sit in my garden. Before returning to the bar I wanted some peace and quiet to finish my coffee after my hectic start to the day. Sitting there calmly, I mulled over my conversation with Sidi. Why had he been annoyed that I hadn't told him Ousman had brought me the money? I hadn't even told him that I was expecting Ousman to bring the money, let alone that I had it in the house. He had certainly been agitated and when he realised that I had already paid it into the bank, his annoyance was clear in his body language let alone his words. Was he simply irritated because he had been kept in the dark about the whole process or was it something more? Whatever it was, it was disturbing and added to my relief that the sale was now completed with the money on its way to Reggie where it belonged. No matter which angle I looked at it from, I came to the same conclusion. He had an ulterior motive to this but what was it?

I was still sitting there with a cold cup of coffee when the phone rang. It was Ousman, "Morning Helen, how are you, and have you managed to bank Mr. Preston's money yet?"

"I'm fine, and yes the money was banked first thing this morning, I didn't want it here longer than need be."

"Good. I have just had Mrs. Sullais on the phone, have The Peace Haven given you anything in writing?"

"Not yet, we have verbally agreed to the sale, they were going to instruct her to draw up the conditions of sale."

"That's what I'd gathered. I have to warn you to be careful, you know only too well by seeing her in court, she is a very good lawyer and a very ruthless women, and she is annoyed with them for negotiating with you without consulting her."

"Fine, fine, but what can she do about the sale?"

"I'm not sure, but you know she has maintained all along that The Dominion was built on Peace Haven land. She maintains that even though the bar was built first it was built on land that had been allocated for the hotel. She has advised them not to buy, but to bide their time with the court case, as she is hoping they can obtain your land without paying for it."

"That isn't likely is it?" I asked as I fought an overwhelming desire to burst into tears. Surely I hadn't come this close to a finish only to have it snatched away from me.

"As I have told you many times, your case is complicated. The original owner of your bar also had a court case with the hotel, while they were still building it. He was paid compensation by the government to leave the property."

"I know, and I have never understood how he managed to sell it on afterwards."

"Neither have I, but I think you sometimes forget you are not in the U.K. now. There are ways and means here. I didn't have any involvement with either property then, so I honestly can't answer that. All I'm trying to say to you is be careful until we have things in writing and signed, these Arabs are ruthless people, doing business with them isn't easy at the best of times; nothing ever seems to be to be straight forward with them. I will look very carefully at Mrs. Sullais' conditions of sale before I let you sign."

"Thanks Ousman, I will bear in mind all you have said. I was looking favourably on this now I fell quite deflated."

"Sorry, but I do want you to be fully aware of the situation. I maybe over reacting to Mrs. Sullais' phone call, but I felt I had to warn you."

I did agree it was part of Ousman's job as my lawyer to keep me fully informed, but his news had deflated me. After my hard bargaining with Mustapha and Esa, surely they wouldn't renege on our deal. Ali was desperate to be able to start his expansion plans, if the hotel was as eager to build more bedrooms, as they had led me to believe, my land was their only possible option. Mrs. Sullais was a ruthless woman, but I couldn't imagine her thwarting their plans, simply because they hadn't involved her from the onset.

I returned to the bar and threw myself with vigour into cleaning the counter tops, and polishing the bottles, it was incredible the amount of dust that found its way indoors in this sandy environment, especially with the open wrought ironwork of the bar. I had always found physical work or exercise a good pick-me-up in times of stress, and at that moment I was feeling practically stressed. There was many years since I had taken 'St. John's Wort' I made a mental note to see if it was available at the local pharmacy , I somehow doubted it, but it may be worth a try, my stress levels were definitely rising.

The following day the estate agents came in for their breakfast. "Is Sidi around?" one of them asked me as they ordered their food.

"No, he is out with the chef," I told them, "Can I help you at all?"

"We wanted to speak to him; you must be pleased the sale is going through so well." Not wishing any long conversation with them I simply replied, "Yes," and went to give the kitchen the order for their breakfasts feeling confused. They must know the sale had already been completed; Sidi had paid them the previous day. I assumed this was once again a language problem, Shendians can speak English, it is the official language of the country, but their comprehension is not always as clear as they, or we, think which often leads to misunderstandings. From the short conversation I had with the estate agents, I thought they were going to question Sidi about the fee I had paid them. That was his problem; he could deal with them, not me. They had their breakfasts and left before Sidi returned. I was relieved by this. If there was going to be any form of confrontation over this I would rather Sidi sorted it out elsewhere, than where my customers could overhear.

When Sidi came back, I told him the estate agents had been looking for him. He didn't seem overly concerned, yet there was something about his expression when I told him, that set off alarm bells in my head. "You have paid them?" I instinctively asked.

"Of course I've paid them, don't start this money thing again."

"Have you got me the receipt I asked you for?"

"Receipts, receipts, receipts. Sometimes I think that is all you care about. Boys like these two are not like U.K. businessmen you know, they don't have receipt books."

"Fine but I told you I need a receipt to send to Reggie. I know, come into the office with me where I have a receipt book. I will give you one for them to sign."

Together we went into the office, and I made out a receipt to myself, from the handwritten receipt book for Sidi to get signed. "They want to see you, so make an appointment to meet them, and while they are sorting out, whatever they want with you, you can get them to sign that." I told him. He once again gave me a strange look, and left saying he would bring the receipt back signed the following morning when he came to take the chef shopping.

I was inexplicably surprised, but also very relieved when Sidi bought me the signed receipt the following morning. I had fully expected yet another excuse, or impossible explanation as to why it was missing. I carefully put it in the safe, with Ousman's receipt and the other paperwork connected to the sale of Reggie's property. I would put this all together in an envelope before the next U.K. flight and give it to one of my regular tourists to post on their return home. I always gave my post to tourists I could trust to post them, as the post in Shendi was so unreliable and at its best exceptionally slow.

The next couple of weeks dragged by at an unbearable pace, my impatience to hear some positive news from Ousman concerning my sale to The Peace Haven, made the days seem endless. Every time the phone rang, I rushed to answer it, feeling sure it was at last the call I had been waiting so eagerly for, only to have my hopes dashed when it was only the employees from one of the nearby shops or offices wanting to place an order for their lunch. Not that I wasn't eager for these orders. I needed all the business I could muster to have the finances to run the bar, if I was to remain open during the coming low season, which was approaching far quicker than I would have liked. At long last, after two weeks of not hearing anything, the phone call I had been expecting came, but not from Ousman from Mustapha. "Helen?" he enquired in an abrupt tone, which gave me a feeling of impending doom, before our conversation had even started.

"Speaking," I answered nervously, "I wasn't expecting to hear from you Mustapha. I expected our lawyers to conduct our business affairs for us."

"That is what I had been hoping Helen, but I felt I had to speak to you concerning a few points Mrs. Sullais has bought to our attention. Firstly, she is convinced the land that you are intending to sell to us, actually already belongs to us."

"I am aware she has made claims to that effect in court, but you have always maintained you were not interested in the court case."

"That was before she had made this point plain to us, it appears the man that originally built your property built it on our land."

"I believe this is so, but though the land had been allocated to the hotel, I don't believe the hotel had ever bought the land."

"Maybe, but he was paid compensation by the government, and should have left the property."

"By rights possibly, but all this was long before we purchased the business, and I do have all the correct paperwork for the compound."

Mustapha was starting to get angry. I had been told he was a ruthless businessman, but I believe he was also used to getting his own way. However, I was a fighter, and I wasn't only fighting for my rights now, I was fighting for my future, and for the new start I was so desperate to have. I was determined my chance to get back to the U.K. and to see my precious little Karen, was not going to be snatched away from me.

"Mrs. Sullais will be looking at that paperwork, very very closely, but before we even get that far," at this point his voice rose several decibels, "how you had the audacity to come to my office and attempt to sell us property that doesn't even belong to you I will never know."

Trying to keep my calm, and not lower myself to the level he had slipped to, I answered on the most even tone I could manage. "I'm sure when Mrs. Sullais has gone through all the paperwork she will find that we bought the property legally from the Dutch couple that owned the premises prior to us."

"That's as maybe," he replied just as agitated as he was previously. "But the property doesn't belong to you, it was bought by your husband, your name is nowhere on the deeds at all. The land, the business none of it is anything whatsoever to do with you, yet you think you are such an important business woman you can come to me and dictate, the condition you want for this sale."

"Just calm down a minute, Mustapha." I quietly said while shaking from head to foot, in temper and humiliation, "My name may not be on the deeds, but my husband bought the property for both of us, and I do have power of attorney over it, so I am entitled to sell it."

"No you are not, you do have a form of power of attorney, but it is insufficient for you to sell it, your husband is the only one that has that right."

I was dumbfounded, Simon had had Ousman draw up a power of attorney when he had last come out to Shendi in 2001. As far as I knew it gave me complete power, the same as the one I had over Reggie's property. "Has your lawyer told you this?" I asked, as I sat down on the stool near the phone to steady myself.

"Where else would I have got this information?" Mustapha replied in a voice that to my relief was much calmer than he had been using.

"As far as I know, I do have the rights to sell, but I will speak to my lawyer about this. If there is a problem, we will get it sorted out."

With that Mustapha bade me a curt goodbye and put down the phone. I was badly shaken by his revelation. In my conversations with Ousman about the sale, no mention of problems with the power of attorney had been mentioned. He had drawn it up and should know whether or not I could sell The Dominion. I sat on the stool there trembling with both anger and embarrassment. There was nothing else I could do but speak to him. I picked up the phone again and dialled Ousman's number.

"Ah Helen," he said when he realised I was on the other end of the line, "I was just about to call you, we have hit a small problem over your sale."

"So I believe I have just had Mustapha on the phone." I told him.

"Really, he should have left this to me and their lawyer to sort out; he was probably only trying to humiliate you."

"Well he succeed there alright, I feel a right idiot. Is this correct that I can't sell the property?

"Well, I've gone through the power of attorney with a fine tooth comb, and don't see a problem. It is giving you power to carry out everything concerning the business and the property, as far as I'm concerned that includes the sale, but Mrs. Sullais is saying that the words 'including the sale of the property' is not on the document so she won't accept your signature. I will speak with her again now that I've been through the papers, and see if I can get her to change her mind. As I told you before she is not happy about this deal and is trying to delay things."

"Fine, but what happens if she still insists my signature is insufficient?"

"Let me talk to her first, hopefully I can make her see reason, but if not either Simon will have to come out and conclude the sale, or we will have to have a new power of attorney drawn up for Simon to sign."

"I don't know if Simon would be able to come out, if he can't how can we get him to sign the new papers?"

"It would be far easier if he came, but if not he will have to get a lawyer on the island, and I would have to send the papers to the lawyer for him to witness Simon's signature, or alternatively he could get a lawyer to draw it up and sent it out to us."

"I will speak to Simon, but please see how you can best sort this out, lawyers in the U.K. are expensive, I'm sure you realise this, and I really don't think Simon will want to come here."

I sat on the stool. With my head buried in my hands, I felt sick in the pit of my stomach. I was still shaken from my verbal confrontation with Mustapha, and Ousman's reading of the situation had been another body blow. It was Ousman who had drawn up the original power of attorney; surely he should have made sure it gave me complete power over the property. To have a new one drawn up, although cheaper than it would cost for Simon to get a lawyer at home to do it, would still be expensive. I was relieved that I had asked for Simon's approval of the sale, whatever would he have thought if he was to find out about it in this way. I would wait for Ousman to get back to me, and then I would have to phone Simon and tell him what is happening. I was aware of my increasing paranoia, but

I couldn't help wondering, if Ousman and Mrs. Sullais were milking the situation. They had both earned a handsome sum from the never ending court case; neither of them would relish this source of income drying up. I sat there with all sorts of thoughts drifting in and out of my mind. I knew these final days were not going to be easy, but whatever direction I looked I saw problems looming on the horizon. Were these problems really there or were they all in my imagination?

After a few minutes contemplating over my thoughts then deciding that was unproductive, I pulled myself together and returned to the bar. As I was walking through the beer garden, I saw the estate agents sat in the garden, having their lunch, I glanced at them, thinking that was another problem I could do without. As far as I was concerned, I had no unfinished business with them, but for some reason their presence always made me feel uneasy. I gave them a welcoming wave, even though that was not how I felt.

"Can you spare us a few minutes Madam," their usual spokesman called out to me.

I walked towards their table, still feeling heavy hearted from my phone calls; I really didn't want to be bothered with them. I just wanted to go into the bar, and go through the motions of running the business, until it was time for my afternoon break; then I would bury myself into the depths of my bedclothes, and hopefully drift off into a peaceful sleep, where I could forget all that was around me, for a precious short while.

"Where is Sidi? We need to talk to him," they asked me.

"He is not here, I expect he is at his shop in Famara, if you want to see him go and see him there, but you have his phone number, give him a ring."

"We have just come from the shop, he is not there, and neither is he answering his phone to us."

"If he isn't at the shop I don't know where he is. I will tell him you are looking for him."

"He knows why we want to talk to him. Just tell him he can't avoid us forever."

"Fine, fine." I said as I walked away from their table, I assumed Sidi had handed over their fee to them without telling them it was lower than they had expected, but I really didn't want to be involved with this. Sidi had said he would sort this business out for me, and I was determined he would. I didn't have the mental resources to concern myself with what I saw as his problem. My mind was stretched to its limits coping with my own problems.

When I next saw Sidi I raised the subject of the estate agents looking for him. He simply said, "They know where to find me, if they want to speak to me they will have to come to me, I'm not chasing about after them." He spoke as if it was a simple matter, as if he was unconcerned about their search for him, but his body language perturbed me. He had seemed ruffled as soon as I had mentioned the agents. I hoped he had finalized everything with them. I had always been cautious of them; in spite of them always being dressed very smartly in suits, complete with collar and ties, they definitely had rough edges, and I did not want to tangle with them. They gave me the impression they may have walked straight off the set of an American gangster movie!

Ousman phoned me again early the following morning. "I've had a long and difficult discussion with Mrs. Sullais," he told me. "There is no way she is going to accept your power of attorney for the sale, but I have managed to make her relent a little; she has agreed to allow me to draw up another document, similar to the original with the words, 'including the sale of the property' added to it."

"Fine, but we have to get Simon to sign it, how will that be done?"

"You will be pleased that this is where she has relented most. She has agreed to accept his signature on a fax, so all we have to do is fax it to him for him to sign and then he can fax it back to me. That won't be as expensive as Simon getting one drawn up in the U.K. or take as long as posting it to him. She could have been much more difficult over this had she wanted."

"Good, you go ahead and draw it up for us, and I will speak to Simon; but when you have completed it can you please give it to Mrs. Sullais for her approval. I don't want to get Simon to sign it only to have her raise some other objection to it."

"I don't think that is necessary," he replied.

"I do, I was under the impression the first one was sufficient for me to sell, and you agreed it was, but she still managed to raise an objection. I don't want any more messing about. I want this sale to go through as quickly as possible now."

Ousman agreed to do this, but I could tell by his tone, he was not too pleased on my insistence that Mrs. Sullais gave her approval of the new document before we had it signed by Simon. I was still under the impression that the two lawyers were somehow working together over this and causing delays. Delays which may have been to their advantage, were most certainly were not advantageous to me.

I knew the evening was probably the best time to phone Simon, I decided I would speak to him as soon as I had had my afternoon nap. This phone call preoccupied my thoughts most of that day. Simon and I had not spoken for about two years and the thought of phoning him made me unexplainably nervous. I had stood up to the S.S.G. police and the military at different times and under different circumstances during the past few years. More recently I had stood my ground with Mustapha and Esa, so why did I find the thought of speaking to my estranged husband on the phone so daunting? What was I so perturbed about, it wasn't my fault the power of attorney needed amending, and I had acted in both our interests over this sale, but would Simon see things in the same light.

My fingers trembled as I dialled Simon's number, the ringing tone seemed endless as I waited for him to reply, and I had considered replacing the receiver, when I suddenly heard his still familiar voice answer.

"Hi, its Helen," I greeted him in a shaky voice, "How are you?"

"Alright," he answered, without enquiring about me or without any other form of greeting. This unnerved me more, and his tone suggested he would rather not be speaking to me. It was he that had decided to return home, it was also he that had stopped contacting me, after so many years of marriage, so I supposed I was being unrealistic to have expected him to show more interest in me.

"We have a problem with the power of attorney you gave me when you last came over." I explained to him.

"What sort of a problem, Ousman drew it up, if there is a problem with it that is down to him not me."

"Yes I agree, but apparently their lawyer won't accept it, she says it doesn't give me the power to sell, you know what Mrs. Sullais is like, she is probably just being awkward; but whatever the case, we have to have a new one drawn up actually using the words 'including the rights to sell'."

"Shit. How much will that cost?"

"At first Ousman thought you may have to get a lawyer on the island to do it, but she has now agreed to let Ousman prepare it, and she will accept your faxed signature. Ousman will fax it to you, you just have to sign it and fax it back."

"I don't have a fax machine."

"Surely you know someone who has, where it could be sent."

"There is one at work, but I will have to ask if I can receive it there, but I want to know when it is coming, I don't want it being read and everyone knowing my business."

"O.k. that's fine but can you get back to me as soon as possible, I want all this sorted as quickly as it can be."

"Do you think I don't?"

I stood perfectly still near the phone, when I put the phone down. I was visibly shaken by that conversation. Without the mounting problems that I felt were starting to engulf me, I couldn't understand why I was allowing Simon's unconcern for me to upset me so much. I had convinced myself I had no feelings left for him, but in reality maybe this wasn't true;

or maybe I was hurt by his lack of feeling towards me. More to the truth, I was probably over reacting due to my circumstances at the time. Whatever the real cause of my melancholy I had to pull myself together and return to the bar, and get on with running the business. The end of the season was fast approaching, at the rate the sale was progressing; I might still have to survive the coming low season, so for the time being I needed to get all the money I could in my till. Under no circumstances must I let the business slip.

Simon contacted me the next day, purely to say he had arranged to use the fax number at his work, he gave me that number, which I passed on to Ousman immediately after I got off the phone from Simon. I was eager to get this matter sorted as soon as possible, I saw this problem over the power of attorney as simply another delaying tactic, but I wasn't sure if it was the lawyers or Mustapha who was deliberately delaying the proceedings. Every time the phone rang, I ran to it anxiously, always expecting to hear some positive news about the sale, but I was generally disappointed to find the caller once again giving me an order for my 'meals on flip-flops' service that I provided for several of the shops and offices in our area; but at last my patience was rewarded and the call I was hoping for arrived.

"Hi Helen, good news at last, Simon has faxed me back the new power of attorney, I took it personally over to Mrs. Sullais' office for her approval. She has read it and is now content to go through with the sale with you as the signatory. She has assured me she will start drawing up the conditions of sale first thing in the morning."

"Brilliant, so at least I know for sure now things are going ahead."

"Yes, there will definitely be a sale, but let me warn you I will not let you sign anything until I am fully satisfied with the contents of the document."

"What could possibly be wrong with them?"

"They will probably be fine, but I will check and recheck the wording before I let you sign, I have told you before I don't trust these people."

I was glad Ousman was being cautious on my behalf, but was he being over cautious? What could possibly go wrong now? Mustapha, although he had raised the price considerably from the original offer, must nevertheless be well satisfied with the price they were paying for the property. I would have liked a much higher return for our outlay, but was by then resigned to the fact that I had finally agreed to the best offer I was likely to get for our land. I would wait and see what happened next, but I wanted no part of any tit for tat disagreements between the lawyers, I simply wanted an end to all this and some peace of mind.

The clock was ticking faster and faster towards the end of season, I had still received no news from Ousman since the problem over the conditions of sale. I had to make a decision on The Dominion. Should I close at the end of the season; that was now only two weeks away or should I continue trading? If I remained open during low season, I would be using funds I had saved in high season to run the business. If I closed I would not be earning anything, but I would not be paying out wages and running costs, over and above the income I was generating. During my afternoon break one day, instead of my usual afternoon nap, I sat in my garden, under the shade of the mango tree. I looked around the garden and then, on a piece of paper I jotted down all the pros and cons of keeping the business open once the last flights had departed for the U.K. Studying all the notes I had made, I came to the overwhelming decision to close the doors of The Dominion for the last time on April 30th, a few days after the end of season, but at the end of the month, which would make calculating the final salaries of the staff easier. With that momentous decision made, I returned to the bar for my evening shift in very good spirits. The relief I felt was immense, the following morning I would sit in the office and work out the best way of doing this, with the least possible inconvenience to everyone concerned; but for that evening I felt as if a heavy load had been lifted off my shoulders. The business had become an ever increasing burden, which I was finding too much for me carry on my own.

I was sat in the office the next day when Sidi arrived to take the chef out shopping. "I'm a bit early today; do you want to have a coffee with me before I go out with Ebou?"

I told him to go and order the coffees and to take it out into the garden. I had seen him look over my shoulder as he was speaking. I got him out of the office as soon as I could, but I wasn't sure how much of my notes he had seen, or even if he realized what the notes were concerning. We sat in my favourite spot in the shade of the mango tree, at first we sat in silence, and then Sidi asked, "What were you doing in the office?"

"Just jotting down a few notes, working a few things out."

"Seemed to me you were working out wages for the staff, large wages. What were you doing, working out redundancy plans?"

So he had realized what I was doing, without thinking I replied. "Yes, I've decided to close at the end of the month." As the words came out, I could have bitten my tongue; I hadn't intended telling him, anymore than I intended telling anyone else, but it was too late then, I had said it.

"Have you signed the papers with those Arabs?"

"No, not yet but I soon will."

"But they may change their minds; you can't close until they sign."

"I've thought it all through and I've decided I have to close. If I remain open for the start of low season I will be losing money that can be used for paying the staff's redundancy pay."

"I don't understand what you mean?"

"You know in low season I have to take money out of the bank that I have saved in high to pay the wages because the business doesn't make enough in low season. If I close at the start of the off season, I will still have that money. I know they are going to sign soon. It will all work out fine."

"O.K. I understand now what you mean, but if they change their minds you will be in trouble."

"It is going to go through I'm confident of that, but Sidi this is important, please do not tell anyone, I don't want the staff to know until it happens."

"No if they find out they will be taking everything they can, but we must sort all this out so there is no problems. We will sit down together and work out the best way to do this, I will help you to make this go smoothly; but you must tell no-one either, none of the ex-pats, they may talk and the staff will get to hear."

I knew he was right there, I didn't intend telling anyone. I had regretted telling Sidi as soon as the words escaped from my mouth, but on the other hand it gave me someone to confide in; and although I had long ago ceased to trust him as far as money was concerned, he had always been my ally as far as dealing with the staff. Maybe it was best that I had told him; he would be able to advise me on the best way to deal with this situation.

I was relieved when I returned to the bar, and enjoyed the banter with the tourists and the ex-pats more than I had in a long while. Much as I had loathed the work I was doing of late, I knew deep down I really enjoyed being behind the bar, and advising the tourists with some of the small problems they encountered. In many ways I had found my work rewarding. If it hadn't been for the continual uphill battle I had fought with The Peace Haven, I would have enjoyed the life style I had in Shendi. Now I knew this battle was at long, long last coming to an end, I felt as if a heavy load was being lifted from me. I felt as I had done long ago, I was full of enthusiasm, what an awful shame I hadn't been able to keep this momentum going all the while I had been here, but never the less I was determined to enjoy the short while I had left in The Dominion.

"What's going on?" Nick asked me late at night, when everyone else had left.

"What do you mean? Everything is fine."

"I can see everything is fine, that's exactly what I meant, you seem your old self, that's not normal, you are usually a miserable bitch these days, today you seem fine."

"It's nearly the end of season, soon I will be able to take things a bit easier, and I am looking forward to that. Other than that, everything goes on the same."

The following morning I sat in the office continuing to work out the redundancy payments for the staff, some of them had been at The Dominion much longer than I had, in fact a few of them had been there since the first owner. I wanted to be as fair as I could with them, especially these long serving staff. I was thankful now that I had enlisted them all with the social security. Many of them had not been on the social security books when I first arrived, but at least now I knew that everything was in order. Not only would I have no problems with what they called "the social" when I closed; but also none of the staff would have any problems claiming benefits that they were entitled to. I had checked with social security and all the staff would be able to start claiming benefits once they had been unemployed for a month. The amount they were entitled to, depended on their length of service, the longest standing members of staff, would get half of their leaving salary.

The staff that had been at The Dominion, when Simon and I took over, I decided to pay a year's basic wages, the others would be paid on a sliding scale depending on their length of service. I considered this to be reasonable, coupled with the social security benefits they would receive. I was concerned that Shendians, in general, are not good at handling money, and that most of them might spend their redundancy pay in a very short while, but on reflection I decided I had enough problems of my own, and as long as I paid them generously my responsibilities towards them ended there.

Looking back on that period between my decision to close and the actual closure is like looking into a deep fog. I do know that I switched off completely to the chatter and banter from the other side of the bar. This is what had kept me going during many troubled times in the past, and now it became insignificant. It is amazing how in different points of your life different things help you to survive. I do remember being permanently fixated on the closure and the reaction of the staff. Eventually the last day of April arrived, my final day of trading. Other than Sidi the only person that knew I was closing was Adam who over the years had printed out any work such as menus and flyers that I had needed. Retiring early to Shendi, he found that such work kept him occupied, and as he refused payment, I gave him cigarettes and beers in return for his services which suited both of us. I had asked Adam to print and laminate two signs for me; one for the main gate and one for the back entrance, although this was seldom used. I stressed to Adam the importance of no-one else knowing of the closure. He understood my reasoning, and agreed with me, it was the best way to do this; Jane and Adam were two people I knew I could trust, they had been loyal friends to me over the years.

The signs simply said:-

IT IS WITH REGRET THAT AS FROM TODAY, MAY 1ST 2007, THE DOMINION, BAR AND RESTAURANT WILL BE CLOSED. THE PREMISES WILL SHORTLY BE INCORPORATED WITHIN THE PEACE HAVEN HOTEL. I WOULD LIKE TO THANK ALL MY FRIENDS AND CUSTOMERS FOR THEIR CUSTOM ANDVALUED SUPPORT OVER THE YEARS.

HELEN

Underneath that notice there would be a smaller one, giving a date two weeks later, when I would hold a sale on the premises to sell all the equipment from the business. I was hoping to gain enough from this sale and a further one I would hold shortly afterwards for the sale of my personal possessions to pay the redundancy money to the staff. When Simon and I had arrived, we had shipped a twenty foot container out to Shendi, with the contents of our house on the island, plus many boxes of charity goods that had been given to us to. On my return home, I would have only my suitcase.

The last evening of my trading came around quicker than I imagined it would. I was confident the sale to Peace Haven would go through as planned, but I still had nothing in writing but even so I was going ahead with the closure. Earlier in the day, taking advice from Sidi, I had posted a notice in the kitchen telling them there was to be a staff meeting at 9o'clock the next morning. As soon as I put the notice up the kitchen staff read it, and although I couldn't understand all they were saying in their local languages; I knew they were speculating about the meeting. Everything for the next day was planned in my mind. I was dreading the staff meeting, but that was the only part. After the meeting, which would not be easy for either the staff or me, I intended to spend the remainder of the day, sorting out the paperwork in the office, and having a bonfire to burn all the papers I would no longer need. I was afraid that as soon as the authorities learnt of the closure; I would have visits from many officials all trying to milk the last they could out of the business, so I considered burning everything would be my best policy.

That last evening which was in the first week of the low season was a quiet one. Most of my customers were now the regular expats. It felt very strange, I wanted a party atmosphere but the needs of secrecy precluded that. I also just wanted to get the whole evening over with and never have to serve behind a bar again. I am afraid I was very absent minded and had to be asked several times to serve beers and spirits. Fortunately no-one asked me what the matter was otherwise I might have told them. Finally only Nick and Terry were left along with the staff. I decided that I would send the staff home and then tell my two remaining regulars that The Dominion would not be opening for business ever again. However, fate intervened for as I was about to tell the staff they could go, Nick finished his beer and said, "That's me for tonight, I have to make an early start in the morning, see you tomorrow."

I felt sad as I watched Nick leave the bar for the last time, I wish I had confided in him, I knew he would be upset when he came down for his morning coffee and he found the gates padlocked with Adam's notice on them. I would not tell Terry now that Nick had left, it would not be fair. Nick had looked after my interests for me many times. He would bring some army friends in for drinks when he knew I had the possibility of problems with customers and he kept me well informed about what was happening outside my small world of The Dominion. This was essential as I rarely left the premises and was not always well informed as to what was going on in the country. Nick would be hurt, and not without reason, if I confided my closure in Terry and not in him.

I didn't have long to battle with my conscience over whether to tell Terry what was by then the only thing on my mind, as he finished his drink shortly after Nick had left he said, "That will be me too, low season is with us, I expect we will have some early nights now, with Nick gone, I will let you get to your bed."

"That's up to you Terry." I replied. "Adam will probably come in yet, you know he always comes out late, I will wait until he comes in, so if you want another one, you are welcome."

"No, I will go home early tonight, that will surprise Lena."

No sooner had I heard Terry drive off than Adam came in. "Well I had expected to see the lads still here. Nick and Terry at least."

"Nick has an early start in the morning so he wanted an early night, and Terry left shortly after he went, you have only just missed Terry. It's a bit of a shame, in one way I would have liked to have had a party atmosphere for the last night, but I couldn't without the staff knowing."

"The place would have been packed if everyone had have known, the regulars would have wanted to give you a good send off."

"I do feel this evening has been an anticlimax, I built myself up for this for so long, and feel a bit let down. On the other hand some of my customers will feel let down when they arrive tomorrow, Rick is always here at nine, when I open for his breakfast, and Nick joins him, very shortly afterwards, I feel a bit guilty now, that I haven't told them, but I don't see how I could have done this any other way."

"No, you are doing this the best you could, they will all get over it they will have to, you have been thinking about your customers for long enough, now is a bit of you time. You have to put yourself first for once. How long do you think it will be before you leave?"

"That's an unknown quantity at the moment but I won't be here any longer than I have to be. I am pretty eager to get away."

As Adam carried on talking about different things that had happened at The Dominion since I had been here, my mind drifted a little. I hoped to be back in the U.K. within a month of closing, but I did have a few major problems to overcome yet, the largest of all was probably the fact that I still didn't have my residential papers. This important matter had slipped to the back of my mind with so many other things to occupy my thoughts at that time. I vowed to talk this out with Sidi again as soon as I had a chance. Another major obstacle was that The Peace Haven and I had still not signed any conditions of sale. I was confident the papers would be signed before too long, but until they were, I supposed I was taking a bit of a gamble, Ousman had pointed this out to me, but once I had made the decision to close I was not going to let anything deter me.

When Adam left, and I went into the kitchen to wash up the glasses for the very last time, I did feel disappointed the evening had not gone as I would have liked, I wished I had been able to tell Nick, after how he had helped me over the years, I felt I had let him down. It would have been nice even though I was unable to have the closing party I may have liked, to have had a last drink with Nick, Terry and Adam; but this wasn't how the evening had panned out and I must now put my mind to the events ahead. After locking up the gates for the last time, I walked slowly, feeling down hearted into the house, and slipped disappointed and mentally exhausted into my bed. Once again I was denied the slumber I so desperately needed to face the day that was ahead of me.

I was up early the next morning, preparing myself for the staff meeting at nine o'clock. Sidi arrived earlier than I expected, and was very encouraging and supportive. He told me he would be sat next to me at the meeting and would take over from me, if any of the staff became aggressive, which I felt was a real concern. I had put together a much better redundancy package than most employers here did, but I knew they would not take this lightly. Sidi and I went out into the garden, and put several of the plastic garden tables together, so that everyone could sit around a large table and hopefully discuss this rationally. We put this table on the far side of the beer garden, closest to the house, so that we couldn't be seen from the main entrance; I didn't want any of the early customers calling out to us, and interrupting our meeting. I put out a selection of soft drinks on the table, hoping to put everyone at their ease. I had convinced myself the staff would understand that it was inevitable The Dominion would have to close, but deep down I knew they wouldn't see the situation in the same light as I did. I could understand how they would feel; I knew that I would see things differently if I was in their position.

The staff all seemed in reasonable spirits as they arrived, even though I thought some of them suspected the reason for the meeting. When they were all gathered together and chatting in small groups in the bar, I indicated to Sidi to put the notices on the main gate, and asked the staff to make their way into the garden to the table we had prepared for the meeting. I had left it until now to have the notices displayed as I did not want any one – customer or staff – reading them before the meeting.

I was nervous, I was not physically shaking, but I felt as though I was. I felt guilty about letting the staff down. I have no idea why I felt like this but I did. I owed my staff nothing; every one of them had let me down on different occasions and would continue to do so if I carried on running the business to the bitter end. However, in spite of the generous redundancy package I had put together for them, I felt I was letting them down. The bitterness I had felt towards them at certain times over the years quickly dissolved, as I saw them taking their seats around the table. I wished no hurt to any of them, and hated myself for what I was about to do. I knew who were the most militant among them, and glanced around the table to see where these were sat. I had seated myself nearest the gateway leading to my garden and house. I was hoping to be able to discuss this in an orderly manner, but if necessary I knew I could take the coward's way out and retreat into the privacy of my house.

I waited until Sidi had put the notices on the gate and was sat by me before I called order and started the meeting.

"I really don't know how to tell you this," I started in a weak and feeble voice, "In fact there is only one way to say it. As from today The Dominion is closed." No one said anything but there were audible gasps from many of them. "You all know I have been in court with The Peace Haven since soon after Simon and I arrived."

"That is all long over, why does that mean we have to close now?" Momodou was angry and it showed in his voice.

"No, that is not over, the court case has never finished. I am aware that several of our regular tourists have been told by some of the waiters that the case is over and we have won it. I have no idea where you got that information from, Momodou, you know I have been attending the court regularly, if you think the case is over, why do you think I go to court, do you think I have another case?"

"We don't know, but what has that to do with you closing the bar now, and why are we closing, has the business been sold?" Pouka asked. They were all muttering among themselves now; these mutterings were growing louder and louder, my nervous were getting more and more frayed with each raising decibel.

"Yes, the land has been sold to The Peace Haven." I told them.

"What!" shouted Ebou, who was normally quiet and not very outspoken. "You have no right to sell our business without conferring with us."

Even though I knew that Shendians genuinely considered any where they worked as being their business, this annoyed me and I answered perhaps more abruptly than was politic. "Sorry, this business belongs to Simon and me and we have the rights to sell it at any time without consulting anyone."

"Are we going to be working for The Peace Haven, or are we losing our jobs?" this came from a voice at the far end of the table.

"I'm afraid they are buying the land only, not the business, so I have to make you all redundant."

"That isn't normal!" an even angrier Ebou protested. "If you sell your business to another establishment they have to employ your staff. That is always part of the deal. How do you think we are all going to live, we all have families."

"Believe me; I do know how you feel. This is not how I wanted this all to end. I have had long and heated discussions with the owners of The Peace Haven. I have asked them to consider employing you, but to no avail. You are not the only ones losing out. Simon and I have lost a fortune in this sale, but if we try and continue with the court case, eventually we may lose everything, and you would be no better off."

"You are not allowed to just close like this you have to give us notice." That was Momodou again still very aggressive.

"I know this, and I am giving you all two weeks' notice, which is the length I have to give you to-day."

"We need this in writing." Ebou forcefully informed me.

"I have been through this. Now let me speak, so that I can explain everything to you" I answered just as forcefully. I tapped a pile of envelopes in front of me. "I have letters here for each of you. These letters give you your two weeks' notice also in there is a date and time in two weeks, when we will all meet here again, and you will receive your final pay envelopes. I paid you your monthly salary a few days ago, that was all your wages until yesterday. Your final envelopes will contain two weeks' pay for your notice period, which I'm not asking you to work, all the holiday pay you are entitled to for this year and your redundancy pay. I have spoken with the Social Security and you will be entitled to claim from them in a month's time if you haven't found alternative employment by then. I am as sorry for this as all of you are; but there really is no point in discussing this any farther."

"Are you going back to the U.K?" I'm not sure who asked this question.

"Eventually, when everything has been finalised here." I answered. "I do have employment for a short while for some of you if you are prepared to stay on and help me." I told the maintenance and security teams, the cleaner and washer ladies that I wanted to talk to them, and asked the others to leave in their own time reminding them to meet up again in two weeks when I would give them their final envelopes. I was taken aback, when after the aggression I had felt, and understood, they all left the table quietly and one by one came up to me and shook my hand. This made me feel quite humble.

Once alone with the staff I was going to keep employed on a temporary basis, I explained to them their rate of pay would be the same as it always had been. Like the others they would receive their envelopes in a fortnight's times which would enable them to receive their social security benefits in a month's time. In the meantime I would pay them cash in hand. I told the security boys I would possibly be here for a further two months, so I would need them for that time and their duties would remain exactly the same, I then told them they could go, and to report for their duties that evening the same as usual. I next spoke to the two ladies, and told them I wasn't sure how much longer I would need their services, but that it would be for at least a month. I explained that I would need washing and cleaning done, also meals prepared for the staff that were still here. "You go home now, and take the rest of the day off and we will start afresh tomorrow." After the ladies had left, only Latif and Petreeni remained, besides Sidi whom I noted had been silent throughout all the proceedings. I had been hoping for his support, but I didn't get it.

"Right lads, we have a big job ahead of us." I started telling Latif and Petreeni, "As I told you in the meeting The Peace Haven is buying this land and the land only, we are going to knock the buildings down."

"Knock it down?" Latif asked. "We can't do that."

"We will! You don't understand how much I'm losing over this and I am determined they are not going to get the better of me. Sidi has spoken to some steel boys who are going to come and look at the possibility of taking the steel down for us, I'm sure you can get most of the rest down."

"Yes, yes if we get help with the steel, we can do this, if it means getting even with The Peace Haven we will help you."

"Good, we will all work hard together, if we don't knock it down they will and they will either sell it, as I hope to, or they may use the materials in other buildings of theirs. Now you go home also and come back tomorrow, we will start then."

"No, we will stay now, where do you want us to start?"

"First of all before we start knocking down, we have to get everything that can be sold ready for the sale next week, I need to try and sell as much as possible from the kitchen, to try and get a bit more of my money back."

Latif was uneducated and could not read or write but was more intelligent than many of my staff who could read usually understood when things were explained to him and had also proved himself to be loyal to me on several occasions. When I had finished discussing the situation with him, he realised I needed to salvage everything I could from this sale. He and Petreeni, stayed together with Sidi, and started gathering the drink stock from the bar. Knowing this would be easy to sell, it would be my starting point.

The relief I felt as the meeting was over, was completely overwhelming; as I strolled back into the house I was slightly dizzy, due to relief, I slumped into the closest armchair and let out an audible sigh. I sat there for a few moments, going over the meeting in my head; it had gone better than I had dared to hope. Sidi came in to see what I was doing.

"You O.K.?" he asked.

"Yes, just gathering my thoughts. That went better than I expected it to."

"I told you it would be alright, you have looked after them well for many years now, they know that, and now you are treating them fairly. Some European employers close their business and leave Shendi without even telling their staff, usually owing them wages. You are paying them good redundancy; they are even being paid for the next two weeks when they aren't working. There is nothing they can complain about."

"Yeah, I suppose but I'm still feeling bad over this. Leave me alone for a while, and then I'm going over to the internet cafe, and sent an e-mail to all the tourists that I have e-mail addresses for, so that everyone knows as soon as possible. When I come back I will spend the rest of the day in the office, sorting out the paperwork. Please ask Latif to get the barrel he uses for burning things ready for me to use, I'm going to burn a lot of the papers."

"What are you going to burn?"

"The invoices for starters. As soon as the authorities hear we are closed they will probably be calling on us, they will want to milk all they can from me, once they know I am leaving."

"Well yes, but you have nothing to worry about, once a business is closed here, all debts from the business are wiped out, you owe nothing."

"That is not exactly true. What about the taxes, you didn't pay?"

"Don't start that again. I've just told you, now the business is closed; there are no debts from it."

"It's not as simple as that. Remember I don't have my immigration papers."

"You are going back to U.K. you don't need them now."

"Of course I do, I can't leave the country without my papers."

I shuddered as I saw the smirk on Sidi's face. "I hadn't thought of that, but that is nothing I will sort it out, don't worry," he smugly said, as he turned and walked out the house.

I was feeling uneasy again; Sidi knew every non-Shendian had to have their papers in order, or their passports stamped with a holiday visa, when they passed through the airport, until I had my papers I couldn't leave the country. I must not let this matter rest, I vowed to pester him about it until I had my papers, I was going to leave as soon as I had demolished the buildings, hopefully in about six weeks time.

I went across to the internet cafe that was on the other side of the car park. I cannot fully explain my feelings as I strolled across and the staff from La Parisian called out to me, "Good morning Helen, you not open today?" Obviously my staff had spoken to them on their way out, and if they hadn't heard anything concrete they would have heard rumours, that their hotel was buying The Dominion. I was not feeling as happy as I had expected to feel, the high I was on after the meeting had once again given way to melancholy, now that at long last I was free of my obligations; I was mourning the passing of The Dominion.

After having gone over many times in my mind, what I was going to say on this e-mail to my customers, who I classed as my friends, I sat staring at the computer not knowing what to type. I had let them all down. They would come to Shendi on their next holiday and their 'Shendian local' wouldn't be there for them. It was the end of an era. I knew Paul and Di, who had been close friends of mine when they lived in Shendi, where coming out on holiday during the next few weeks, they would be staying at The Mango Tree opposite The Dominion, normally they would spend every evening in the bar. I eventually wrote my e-mail, but possibly it didn't say all I had intended it to, and by the time I clicked on 'send' I could feel the tears dampening my cheeks; this was not how I had visualised this day.

I went back to the bar, and without speaking to anyone went into the office and immersed myself into sorting out the many boxes of paperwork I had accumulated over the years; this was a seemingly endless task. As I sorted each box, I took the unwanted papers into the garden and burned them in our makeshift, metal barrel incinerator. Amazingly I found this therapeutic and by the time the Latif, Petreeni and Sidi went home, late in the afternoon I felt more at my ease.

After they left I decided to I would also finish work, I could take life a bit easier now, it was only 4 o'clock, normally I would be finishing my day shift, and taking my shower and afternoon nap, before returning to the bar for my evening shift. A sense of freedom overcame me; the lads had gone home, and until the security, which I had cut down to only one each evening now that the bar was closed, arrived at about 7.30; I was on my own. This was a luxury I hadn't had over the past eight years; there had always been some members of staff on the premises. I smelt strongly of smoke from the bonfire, so I decided to take a much needed shower, and instead of dressing in my uniform as I was accustomed to doing, I put on a loose African dress, ideal for relaxing in. Glancing at my mobile I saw I had received a text while I was in the shower; not many people had my mobile number, I assumed it was Viv, she was the only person in Shendi who I could remember giving my number to, if not it had to be Simon; he knew I was closing the business that morning. On opening it, I was surprised to see it was from Nick; it simply said, 'U O.K?'

I phoned Nick, "Thanks for the text, I didn't know you had my number. Did you come down for your coffee this morning?"

"No, Viv and Greg waved me down as I was coming. It was Viv that gave me your number, but don't worry, she isn't giving it to just anybody. They were with Rick having a coffee up the strip, don't worry about us, we can get our breakfasts elsewhere you know."

"I know. I knew you wouldn't miss me for long."

"I was going to come down when they told me, but Viv said they could see you had the staff with you, and Sidi's car was outside so she said I should keep away."

"I didn't really want anyone there at that time, I did want to tell you last night after the staff had gone, but you left early."

"Terry is wild you didn't tell us."

"Yeah, I can imagine, I'm sure you understand why I had to keep it quiet."

"Yeah I know, but now is it O.K. to come down, or don't you want to see anyone?"

"I don't want everyone coming down, I don't mind you, and some of the others, in fact I will welcome visits from my friends."

"Fine I will be down for my coffee as usual in the morning. How long will you be here?"

"A while yet. I'm going to knock it down."

"Oh no! Tell me you're not serious! It was a joke, you and me shipping it off to Thailand and drifting into the sunset."

"It may not get shipped to Thailand, but it will come down. I'm on a mission."

"You've lost the plot honey, but looking on the bright side, if you are going to be here until it has been knocked down, I needn't be fretting about where to go for my morning coffee for ages yet. I'll be down in the morning. Take it easy, easy till then."

I was cheered by my conversation with Nick, I would take his advice and take it easy, I had a lot of work ahead of me, but the lads start work early and finish at four, after that I could relax. I picked up my crossword book and a pencil and retired to the peace and solitude of the beer garden.

It was seldom I sat in this side of the garden, now I was free to sit where I wished, knowing I wouldn't be disturbed. I glanced around me with new eyes, and for the first time really appreciated the beauty of the garden, the African flora was so much more varied than the European, and the colours in my garden covered the whole spectrum, from pale pastels to vivid purples and deep oranges. The trickling of the water down over the small rocks of the water feature in the pool was relaxing. A frog sat on the wooden bridge over the pool that led from the entrance to the garden, croaked loudly trying to attract a partner, I was always amazed at the sound that came from such a small creature; it would soon be their mating season, the noise they made then after dark was deafening. A lizard darted out from under the bushes and climbed over my bamboo fence into The Peace Haven, it was a male, sporting his bright yellow head, which contrasted well with his purple body. He had already shed his dull grey skin; he had during the winter months, in readiness for his mating season. There was always something to watch in a Shendian garden, I now understood why my tourists enjoyed lunching in my garden; this was paradise. Why had everything gone so wrong?

Chapter Twenty-Two

Demolition

As I was sitting there, concentrating on my crossword, I heard the phone inside the bar. It had been ringing periodically throughout the day and I had ignored it each time. I assumed that it was someone ringing to check on the local gossip, that The Dominion was closed. Not feeling ready to deal with such enquiries I simply let it ring. When I felt able to I would speak to everyone and answer their questions. My mobile was sat on the table beside me, if anyone didn't have my mobile number, I didn't want to talk to them. The constant ringing was disturbing my peace, and had started getting on my nerves. I went into the house and unplugged the landline. I didn't realise it then; but The Dominion phone had rung for the very last time. My peace was now complete.

I sat in the garden, content for the first time in a long while. I was sat in beautiful surroundings, the heat of the sun engulfing my body with a sense of well being, with not a responsibility or care in the world, besides the answer to four down; Geek mythology had never been a strong point of mine. I wanted this moment to last forever; I knew I had much more stress to endure before this period of my life was over, and I was finally sat on a U.K. bound flight and at long, long last seeing my precious little granddaughter Karen. I stayed in the garden until the sun disappeared behind the roofs of The Peace Haven, in the evening shade, even in Shendi, once you are acclimatised it does become chilly, I decided to make a coffee and take it in the house while I was waiting for the night security to arrive. Sidi phoned to see if I was alright, and asked if I wanted him to come down and keep me company, he didn't seem to appreciate I was more than content to be on my own. Once Pouka had arrived I went to bed and watched a DVD all the way through, something I had never had the time to do before and settled down for my first night free from the burdens of running a bar.

After a good night's sleep, I sent Pouka home as soon as I was up once again revelling in my solitude. It felt so good; I knew this wasn't going to last long, Latif and Petreeni and the cleaners would arrive soon, but for the time being I wandered around, enjoying the peace. The Dominion seemed vast, and after so much activity, it seemed very empty.

The staff arrived and I set them to work, they were washing the ovens and fridges, and sorting out cupboards. I was washing plates, glasses and dishes, preparing everything for my sale. Nick arrived for his coffee as he said he would, I sat in the garden with him. "I can't believe this, we all knew your closing was on the cards, but never really thought it would happen."

"I'm still taking everything in; I'm in a bit of a daze. You know I've wanted this for ages, but it is so final now, but I meant what I told you yesterday, those bastards are going to find out I'm not the push over they think I am, I'm determined to get the bloody place down."

Nick shook his head, "It's not going to be easy, how do you think you are going to get all that steel down. I've told you I don't think too much can be salvaged from it."

"Sidi is bringing some steel lads here later this morning, they haven't seen it yet, but seem to think they can get the steel down, they can use it as scrap if nothing else. Just look around, there is a lot here that can be sold, the garden slabs for a start, Simon and I spent a small fortune on this garden when we first arrived, and there is loads and loads of sand under the slabs, the garden was so uneven they needed several lorry trips to lay them, when the slabs are up we will be able to do something with that. The entire house is tiled, both the floors and most of the walls, they can all be sold."

"But you won't get them up whole."

"I know that, but there is a big demand for broken tiles among the locals, and some of the ex-pats, they can be used for verandas and patios; we will sell them by the sack full."

Nick grinned. "I see you have it all worked out, it's not going to be easy, but good on you if you get the better of those bastards, they have taken the piss out of you for long enough."

Viv and Greg started rattling on the chain on the main gate as I was walking towards it to let Nick out. "It's great here now." Nick told them. "Morning coffee, same standard, same service but no crowds and no bills. Shame she didn't close down ages ago."

"It seems a hive of activity here." Viv noted as Nick left. "Are you alright?"

"Yeah, I'm fine. I must admit I'm swinging from relief to sheer panic, but it will all be alright in the end." I went on to explain to them that I didn't actually have anything in writing yet, but I was confident the sale would soon go through. They didn't offer much of an opinion, but I could tell by their reactions they had the same reservations as Nick did about me knocking the buildings down. My stubborn streak once again came to the fore. I had made up my mind this was what I was going to do, and no opposition from my friends would change that, in fact it had the reverse effect; it made me more determined.

Sidi arrived mid-morning, with a large group of lads, only one of whom I recognised. "Do you remember Babu?" Sidi asked. "He has been to The Dominion a few times, he knows you. All these lads work for him, they want to have a good look around, and work out how much they think it would be worth for them to take it down." The steel lads spent about half an hour walking around the buildings with Sidi, they were taking this very seriously, they all went out into the garden and sat talking for a farther half an hour before Sidi came to speak to me.

"They tell me it will be a harder job than they thought it would be; this is a very well built place."

"I know that, I've told you before it was a steel man from the U.K. that built it, this is probably one of the sturdiest buildings in Shendi."

"Yeah, but that is going to make it harder to get down, they are saying they will pay you 30,000 shillings to knock it down and take the steel away. What do you think?"

"I was hoping for more, much more in fact, but on the other hand there is no way, Latif and Petreeni can take this steel down."

"If we could get the steel down we could sell it for a lot of money, but you must think Babu, has the equipment to get it down, he also has to pay wages to all these boys while they are working here, so by the time he sells it, his profit will not be that great."

I gave a slight sigh, I had hoped for more, I knew none of this was going to be easy, and if we did manage to get the steel down, I would then have to sell it, which would also be difficult, and there was no guarantee how much I would be able to sell it for. Also to find anyone else with the equipment to do the job would be an arduous task. I reluctantly agreed. "O.K. give them the job, tell them I want them to start a week next Monday, after the sale, and I want half the money up front." Amazingly when Sidi arrived the next morning, he handed me 15,000 shillings, the fifty per cent of the amount I had agreed with Babu for the steel. I had been initially disappointed with the 30,000 we had agreed on, but when I was alone, relaxing once again in the garden the evening, we had come to the agreement; I decided I was satisfied with this. Babu was going to have a major demolition job on his hands, and once the steel was down, Latif and Petreeni would be able to complete the job.

Those first few days passed very quickly, callers were coming to the gate offering to buy various items from the bar and kitchen. Both Oliver and Nick had shown interest in the bar furniture. Oliver was thinking of taking over a small restaurant, and Nick intended storing it until his hotel was completed. Oliver was known to be more than careful with his money, so I thought Nick would be easier to do business with; I was proved right. I told them both what I was hoping for, and Oliver offered me a far less amount, Nick agreed on my price as long as I threw in a few plates and glasses into the bargain; so there was no contest, and I was thrilled to have sold a large portion of the business assets without too much effort on my part, I was certain I would recoup the staff's redundancy pay.

With so much going on I had forgotten to pester Sidi about my immigration papers as I had intended to. One afternoon I decided that I would not let him go home without asking him about it. Sidi had been taking Petreeni home with him as he lived in the same village; Latif lived farther away and came on his push bike. This was not an easy journey as much of it was on deep sand roads. As the lads were ready to go home Sidi said to Latif, "Put your bike on the roof rack of my car I will take you home."

I knew Latif would be grateful for this as we had all had a strenuous day. "Before you go, I want to talk to you." I told Sidi.

"Is there a problem?" He asked as he followed me into the house.

"I want to know what you are doing about my immigration papers."

"For goodness sake, you have bought me in here just to ask me that, when the lads are waiting for me to take them home. Don't you know they are tired?"

"So am I tired, but I am also fed up with having to keep on at you about this."

"Then don't. I have told you I will sort it out and I will. I am busy making sure everything runs smoothly here and all you care about is these bloody papers. You aren't leaving yet, so you don't need them now, when you need them you will have them."

As he left the house I sat down in my armchair, closed my eyes and gave a loud sigh. I had no choice but to trust I would have my papers before I left, but I couldn't help the unease that ran through me.

The next few days flew by without a hitch. I was too busy to dwell on too many things; we were sorting and cleaning everything for the sale, and arranging the next steps towards the demolition. The day after the sale Latif and Petreeni were going to remove the corrugate from the bar; they seemed to think this would be easy as it was in large sheets. Between them they had gone up on the roof of the house and replaced a couple of sheets for me a few years ago when I had had a leak, but the bar was much higher than the house. I didn't share their confidence and I was starting to wonder if I had taken on too much. However, both Latif and Petreeni understood the reason I had undertaken this, and were both being very supportive. They were convinced all would be fine, so I simply had to trust in them. There was something else that was bothering me and that was the relationship between Latif and Sidi. They tolerated each other but had fallen out many times over the years. Since I had closed the bar I had seen them talking together on several occasions, they often seemed to be disagreeing, I had asked each of them individually about this, but both denied there was a problem between them. I must keep an eye on the situation.

The steel lads were booked to start work the day after the corrugate was taken down from the roof; everything was going as smoothly as I could expect it to. I had got myself into a routine that I enjoyed after so long running the business, single handed. I was up at the same time as before, but instead of my usual work, I was planning and helping with the demolition. I was doing jobs like chipping off the tiles from the walls in the house and bagging them in sacks ready for sale; as I had expected these broken tiles were in great demand, Petreeni was selling them for me to locals who were actually queuing at our rear entrance waiting for the next batch to be ready for sale. The cost of the staff redundancies no longer caused me any concern, money from the demolition would cover it.

The lads always went home about four o'clock as they did when I was running the business. After they had all gone, as on the first day, I would shower, dress casually and relax in the garden with either a puzzle book or a novel; I found this most rewarding. Every evening the monkeys that often woke me in the morning as they made their way to the neighbouring hotels; meandered back through the garden making their way home to the sanctuary of 'the monkey forest' where they would spend the night, they sometimes stopped and snacked on the fruit of my cashew trees, that were in season. I enjoyed watching them as the adults showed their offspring which fruit to choose, and childlike they were often disinterested and preferred to play, generally swinging from my wrought ironwork. They never failed to fascinate me, they were like little humans, they squeezed the fruit, to ensure it was ripe before picking it, and sat on the dividing wall between my two gardens, to eat their snack, with their legs crossed, dangling over the edge. They watched me with the same fascination as I had in them.

The monkeys going home, was a sign evening was fast approaching, dusk falls very quickly in Shendi as it is not so very far from the equator.

After they left and the sun started its fast decent beyond the horizon, I would go indoors to wait for the night security to arrive, when they were here, I enjoyed the luxury of an early night either with the company of my book, or a DVD, on my small player. I was getting used to that life style, I was a shame I knew it wouldn't last for too long. As eager as I was to get back to the U.K. and see my family, I was also apprehensive, I hadn't even fully decided where I would eventually settle; I had to find employment, I knew this wouldn't be an easy task, and I had nowhere to live. It was important that I relaxed as much as I could to prepare myself for the difficult time I had ahead of me, before I eventually had the new life I so desperately craved.

One lunch time I was chatting to Latif, Petreeni and Sidi in my side of the garden, waiting for Tina, to bring out our lunch. Tina was a young girl who had only worked for me for a few months, but I had decided to keep her on to help with the washing and to cook for us. I wished I had found her earlier as she was a hard worker with a pleasant disposition. After cooking breakfast for the boys, and making coffees for my friends when they visited, she cooked lunch. On this particular day we were all sitting around one of the remaining plastic tables ready to dip into the large enamel bowl with either fingers (the staff) or with a spoon (me) and chatting about the demolition when we heard shouting from the car park.

"Whatever is going on?" I asked.

"I'll go and check." Sidi said.

The shouting got louder and louder, the crowd were getting closer, then there was the sound of metal being shaken. I realised it was the padlock on the entrance gate being banged aggressively. There were so many voices yelling all at the same time, it was impossible to hear anything that was being shouted. Sidi came back and said. "It is the staff with two men from labour and welfare; shall I let them in or what?"

"Tell them I will not speak to them while they are carrying on like this, they sound as if they are after my blood. Tell them to behave in a reasonable manner, and I will gladly speak to them."

Sidi turned to Latif and said. "They sound very angry, you go and talk to them, tell them they can come in and speak with Helen, if they stop this shouting with discuss this properly. I will stay here with the boss lady; she should not see them alone. Take them into the bar and get them all to sit down, when they are sat and you think there will be no trouble from them, we will come and speak with them."

Latif went to do this, and I said to Sidi. "Hark at them I'm scared, they sound like a pack of wild animals! What can they do?"

"Nothing you have done this properly, they will calm down, you see."

I could pick out many familiar voices among the throng, as I waited out of sight on the other side of the wall, trying to calm myself. I did not want any of them to see the terror in my eyes. Latif's voice was audible above the others. "Sit down, and be quiet," he was telling them. "Helen will come and talk to you when you settle down, this is no way to behave."

I then heard an unfamiliar voice, which I took to be one of the men from the labour office. "This woman will come and speak to us now, you tell her staff this is no way to behave, and after how she has behaved to them they can behave as they wish towards her."

"Helen has been reasonable with us, you know that." Latif addressed the staff."She has only done what she had to, and she is looking after all of us well."

"She may be looking after you," The labour representative told Latif, "but she has done nothing for these people, they have no job, no redundancy pay, nothing." This was greeted with raised voices and cheering from the staff.

"They will get their pay when we have the staff meeting next week, she is paying them all well, they know this, and she gave them all letters telling them this." This bought on a deluge of shouting.

I picked out Pouka's voice shouting at Latif. "How do you know what the letters said you can't even read, she is going back to the U.K. before that meeting, we are getting nothing."

"He is right," the labour man said to Latif, "you are a very stupid boy, if you think this women is going to pay you, go and get her, we know she is here."

I looked at Sidi in horror. My face gave away my sheer terror, this was an uncontrolled mob. I was happy to discuss this in a reasonable manner with them, but I knew I wasn't going to be given that opportunity. Latif returned looking solemn, and shrugged his shoulders. "They are going crazy" he said, "they will not go away without seeing you Helen, come on Sidi we will all go out there together, if there is any problems there is us two and Petreeni to support Helen."

"He is right," Sidi told me, "now they are here, they will not go without seeing you, but they are very wrong, they should not have bought these labour men here. Latif is right we will all go in there together and sort this out."

I let the lads lead the way, when we reached the bar; I sat near the entrance, as at the original staff meeting, I wanted the security of knowing I could leave anytime.

As I entered the shouting became unbearable, it was difficult to decipher what anyone was yelling. I looked around me, very disturbed, taking notice who was being the most vocal; I was deeply upset by this.

Pouka, who I was employing until I left as one of my night security was shouting more than anyone, and was stirring up unrest among the others. They were yelling abuse at me, also at Sidi, Latif and Petreeni for sitting with me. Latif, taking offence at this stood up and started shouting back at them, "You are all crazy, she has done nothing to you, why cause trouble, why have you bought these men here?"

Pouka and Momodou also stood up, and started waving their arms about, I was afraid Latif was going to come to blows with them. This was a despicable spectacle. I understood how they must be feeling about their redundancies, but I had been fair with them, I was totally bewildered by their involving the Labour and Welfare. I had had a couple of unpleasant experiences with them in the past, one when I had sacked a member of the kitchen staff, who had been caught stealing red handed and he had claimed unfair dismissal. And on the other occasion I had given a girl that worked in the kitchen six weeks paid leave during low season, to sort her health problems out, she had had reoccurring unspecified illnesses over a long period of time. I had even taken her to a Cuban doctor that I knew well, who was doing tests to try and establish her problem. This was a doctor; she could not have afforded to visit otherwise. This girl had gone to the labour offices and claimed I was looking for an excuse to sack her. Both of these experiences with the Labour and Welfare office had been extremely unpleasant. I recognised one of these men from the labour office as being the man who I had had dealings with over the kitchen theft, this recognition drained my last shred of confidence from me. I wished the ground would open up and swallow me.

The Labour man I didn't recognise stood and shouted at the staff to sit down and let him speak, he turned towards them and said. "We have come here today, to speak to this woman, and make her put right the wrongs she has done to you." He turned to me and said. "Madam this staff have worked for you for many years, they have built your business up to be very successful." This bought on cheering and mutterings of "Yes, yes we have done this."

"Let me continue," the man went on, "Without these people you would be nothing and not be the wealthy woman you are today, yet you think you are going to the airport at the weekend and get on a plane to the U.K. and leave these people with nothing."

"Whoever says I'm leaving at the weekend?" I asked.

"It is no business of yours who told us this, it is enough that we know." If I had been leaving I could understand their anger, the meeting I had arranged when I was going to give them their redundancy pay was scheduled for next Tuesday.

"I have no intention of leaving yet." I told them, "I still have unfinished business....."

Before I could finish what I was saying the Labour man interrupted. "You will be going nowhere Madam. Until we say you can leave, we have put a stop on you at the airport. You are unable to leave Shendi."

"Why would that worry her?" Sidi who was also getting angry and started waving his arms and raising his voice asked the Labour representative. "She has told you she still has unfinished business here, how could she leave. These people will be paid next Tuesday as she has told them." I detected a quavering in his voice; this made me feel uneasy he was obviously not as confident as he liked to portray himself. The temperature in the bar seemed to soar. I was hot and clammy; I shut my eyes, in an attempt to distance myself from the proceedings.

"She has an air ticket." Pouka's voice could be heard over the muffled shouting of the others.

"That's rubbish." I angrily retorted.

"This is not rubbish Madam, we know this too; that is why we have taken the step to have a stop put on you at the airport."

Latif stood up again; I was sat by him and pulled gently on his arm, in an attempt to make him sit down again. He looked at me and said quietly. "It's O.K. they can't treat you like this."

As he addressed the room he spoke loudly and in a tone far removed from the way he had just spoken to me. "We have all worked for Helen for a long while we know her well. When has she ever not done what she has promised? Haven't we been treated better than many employees in the tourist areas? Why have you turned on her like this? Wait until Tuesday, if she doesn't pay us then, that is the time to call in the Labour."

"She owes us money and we want it now, our families are suffering. We need it before she goes." Pouka shouted back at him, there were shouts of agreement from the others at this.

I was angered by this, losing any composure I had left I also started shouting. "I owe you nothing yet! Didn't I pay you as usual on the 28th of last month? If the business was still running you would not be paid until the end of this month, so how can your families be suffering?"

A voice at the back intervened. "Taubabs have no idea what it is like to suffer." It was painfully obvious I was not going to get a fair hearing, I was fast losing control of myself, I was afraid I was likely to say or do something I may regret later. I got up and walked out of the bar. I went into my garden and sat on one of the few chairs that remained; I rested my head on my hands, and broke down in tears of frustration.

Sidi followed after me a few minutes later. "You can't do this, I know they shouldn't have bought these men here, but now that they have, you have to face them. The labour man has sent me to make you come back."

"He will have a long wait then." I replied, through my tears.

"Helen, you can't behave like this, you must speak to them."

I wiped my tears away with the back of my hand. "What point is there, you know I have no chance of even speaking with everyone shouting, and they won't listen to me anyway? Go back and tell the labour men I will speak to them only, if they come in here and speak to me in a proper way, I will answer all their questions; but no way am I going back in there while they are all carrying on like that."

"He won't like it if I go back in there without you."

"Then he won't like it, because I'm NOT going in there. Now you go back and tell him what I said."

"Well---O.K. but they won't be happy. The man with the limp, the one that hasn't been here before he is the director at The Labour office, he will not like you behaving like this, he is a very important man."

"An important man in a high position should not be shouting and stirring up a near riot like he is. I don't consider that is behaving properly towards me, especially on my property."

"Alright, I will go and tell them what you have said, but if they come and sit with you, you behave correctly with them or there will be big problems, I'm warning you."

I watched Sidi going back towards the entrance of the bar and heard the staff start shouting, "Where is she?" as he entered. They were again acting like an enraged mob.

Latif had followed Sidi when he had come into the garden to try and get me to go back, he had remained silent, but now spoke to me. "You are right; they should not be doing this to you. They will not let you speak, so why stay there. Go inside and wash your face, it is better when they come and speak with you, that they don't know that you are upset."

I knew Latif was right and went into the house, and wiped my face, hoping to wash away, the stains from my tears. I took a few deep breaths to calm myself and returned to the garden. As I came out the house, the two labour men and Sidi were sitting down around the plastic table, Latif was returning from the beer garden with another chair so that I had somewhere to sit. I thanked him and joined the others at the table.

"Well Madam, this boy here says you will speak to us alone, but not to your own staff. Why is that, are you ashamed to talk to them?"

"No, let's get this straight first. I will gladly speak with the staff, if they would speak to me. How can I possibly even be heard while they are all shouting? They are not interested in speaking to me. I had a meeting with them last week, and explained everything to them then. We have a meeting scheduled for next Tuesday, on that day I am paying them all their redundancy pay and any other payments, such as holiday pay for this year."

"You shut this business without telling these people, you can't do that." He reached into his briefcase and took out a copy of labour and welfare guide lines. "I will show you in here, where it tells you if you are closing a business you have to give your staff two weeks' notice of this." He hurriedly turned pages looking for the appropriate paragraph.

"Do you remember coming here when I had a problem with a kitchen lad who was caught stealing from my kitchen, then went to your office claiming unfair dismissal?"

"I remember this very well Madam, I also remember that was handled most incorrectly."

"You are right, I hadn't been here very long then, and was unaware how you did things in Shendi, that is why I sent this man," I indicated to Sidi, "to go to your office and collect me a copy of your guide lines. Since then I have always looked in that booklet before taking any action towards my staff as I did in this instance."

The Labour man smiled at me and said. "Good that is very good, I didn't know you had our booklet, but if you had read it properly, why did you not give them the two weeks' notice they have to have."

"I gave them all letters last week, explaining everything to them. I am paying them full pay for this fortnight, which is why we are having the second meeting next week that is when they are officially ceasing to be employed. They are not working but are on full pay, I thought they would be pleased about this."

"I know nothing about this or any letters. I only have your word for this Madam."

"I have a copy of the letter they were all given in my office. I will go and fetch it. I also have my salary book showing all the redundancy pay, and the other payments they are due that they will receive next Tuesday, I will show this to you, and I feel sure you will agree I am being fair with my staff. Would you like to have a drink?" I saw the mature man with the limp who Sidi had told me was the director of The Labour office, give a small smile. The offer of a soft drink was always welcome to the locals, who could rarely afford them; I was hoping to win them over, and be more sympathetic towards me. The men, having accepted my offer, I asked Latif to go and get drinks for them and to get Tina to make me a coffee; I needed to increase my caffeine intake. While he was doing this I went into the office to collect the copy of the staff letters and also my calculations of their redundancy money.

When I returned the men were chatting cheerfully to Sidi and Latif and all enjoying their drinks, this indicated to me that they might be willing to listen. The director took the letter from me, and slowly read it, nodding his head a couple of times, but I was unable to determine if this was a good sign or not. He handed the letter to the other man, whom I remembered was named Jatto Roma. I had seen Jatto glance at my copy of their guide lines, which I had placed on the table in front of me. I doubted if I would need this pamphlet, but thought it may be in my favour for them to see I did have a copy, and was not simply telling them I had referred to it.

"Explain again, why you have not given them any notice."

"As I told you before and it does state in that letter, I gave them notice on the day of the first meeting I had with them on May 1st. That is why I'm not paying them until the next meeting on May 14th, two weeks' later. That is their notice period, they are on full pay, but they do not have to work. I will also give them their redundancies then." As I said that my mobile rang, I glanced at it, it was Reggie Preston; I quickly answered it and told Reggie I was in a meeting and would phone him during the evening.

"That is irregular Madam." The director said, "But if they are on full pay, yet not working, I didn't see how they can complain, I did not understand this from your staff."

"Let me see your calculations for these redundancies." Mr. Roma asked. I pushed my salary book across the table to him.

To my amazement, after only a short while of scanning the papers with swift eye movements, he glanced up and said, "Madam how did you come by this figure?"

He was pointing to Ebou's name. "This man has worked for me since I have been here, that is one year's salary as redundancy pay, and this figure is his four weeks' holiday pay, as he hasn't had any leave yet this year. In fact none of them have. I make them take their leave in low season." My finger followed my calculations across the page, "and this is his two weeks' pay in lieu of notice."

Mr Roma handed the list to his superior and still pointing at Ebou's calculations spoke in local language to him, my knowledge of the language was insufficient for me to follow the lengthy conversation that followed. I looked at Sidi and Latif hoping one of them would give me some indication how the negotiations were going. Neither looked at me they both looked from one to the other of the labour representatives as they spoke; they seemed mesmerised. Mr. Roma placed the salary book on the table in front of all of us. "Fine Madam, these are your proposed redundancies from your staff, but these figures do not answer the question we all want to know. When are you leaving the country?"

"I don't know so I can't tell you."

"—But you are going Madam."

"Yes, I am going as soon as all my business here is concluded. I can't say when that will be for certain, but I will be here for at least another month, maybe longer."

"Unfortunately, being we couldn't trace a ticket for you we have to take your word for that."

"You won't be able to trace my ticket if I haven't bought one yet."

"Fine." He once again looked at my calculations, "we don't agree with these sums." My heart sank, I considered I had been generous towards the staff and would find myself in financial difficulties if they raised the amount considerably. "These people will be able to claim social security before too long, in some cases you are paying them too much." I could not believe my ears, I had been looking at the book on the table, and I didn't look up. I was afraid to let them see the amazement on my face. "A year's salary is not necessary, nine months is more than sufficient." He crossed out my figure by Ebou's name that was the first on my list, with a bright red pen and replaced it with a lesser amount. "We don't feel it is necessary to give holiday pay for this year either, they have worked less than six months this year, so are not entitled to it. Recalculate your figures using the guide we have put there for you. I will go into the bar and tell your staff we have sorted out their redundancies for them, and tell them to come back next week as you told them in their letters. I will come back here tomorrow to approve your new calculations; as long as I am content with them we will both be back next week when you pay your staff. All of them will sign for their money as they have each month in your salary book, then you will sign at the bottom and both of us will also sign. Then and only then will everything be legal, your staff will have no come back on you, and we will lift the stop we have put on you at the airport."

With great relief I thanked them. I sat listening to the shuffling of chairs and chattering as they all left, I was riveted to the spot I could not believe my luck, was this really happening. The staff had bought the Labour and Welfare into this, and they had eventually supported me; it seemed unbelievable. Before they left, Mr. Roma leaned around the corner leading into the garden where I was still sat, and said, "We will be back at about two tomorrow afternoon, have your calculations ready for us by then." Shaking his head he added, "I cannot believe your staff bought us here without mentioning the letters you had given them." I was so grateful I was in the habit of keeping copies of everything; I knew it was the letter that had swayed the labour men in my direction. I needed a clear head to recalculate all my figures, if they weren't coming back until the afternoon I would do these the next morning.

When everyone left I told Sidi, Latif and Petreeni we would do no more that afternoon, and I sent them home, I felt I wanted some peace and solitude to recover from the ordeal I had just been through. Before they left I told Sidi that after Pouka being so vocal and abusive to me, and from comments make by Mr. Roma, it was obvious he was one of the ones that had been to the Labour office to represent the staff I did not want him here as my security. It was his night to be working; all my security lads lived in Sidi's village so I told him to arrange for one of the others to work that evening.

"Pouka will not accept me telling him he services are no longer needed. I have no authority to do that."

"I'm not asking you to, I am asking you to arrange for one of the others to come this evening, and I will talk to Pouka when he gets here."

After they had all gone, I turned my mind to Reggie and wondered what he wanted to talk to me about, all the business with his compound had now been successfully concluded. I made myself another coffee and sat in the garden, which had become my favourite pastime when I was alone, I dialled Reggie's number.

"Hi Helen, how are you? Are things going well for you now you have closed the bar?"

"Yes, everything is going fine." I answered him. Slightly tongue in cheek, the day had had a successful finish, but I was not convinced everything was going in my favour. "Are you well, and Sharon and her family?"

"Yes we are all O.K. but there is a bit of a problem, the money isn't in my bank account yet. It is three weeks since you paid it into the bank in Shendi, and you told me five working days. I am getting worried about this."

I also found this concerning, Oliver had definitely told me five working days, why would this take so long? My heart sank, rumours were rife here that Oliver's bank was in trouble, but I had used his bank to transfer money for me in the past without any hitches; this was a problem I could well do without. "I will chase it up this end, other than that there isn't much I can say. You should have received it long ago."

"I have spoken to my bank about it, and they told me to take it up with the transferring bank's U.K. office in London, and I have done this."

"What did they say?"

"They said they know nothing about it."

"I will phone Oliver, the bank manager, I know him well. Don't worry it has to be there soon."

"I know but three weeks is a long time isn't it?"

I was on a mental roller coaster, one minute up, the next spiralling down. So much had been happening at the time, I had paid the money to Oliver, and it had completely slipped my memory I hadn't had a receipt for it, I had meant to bring this up to Oliver but I had forgotten about it. I got straight on the phone to him. "Do you remember me paying the money for Reggie Preston's compound to you a few weeks ago?"

"Of course I do Helen," he gave a slight laugh, "how could I possibly forget, it isn't every day someone comes into the office with a crisp box full of money."

"I have just been speaking to Reggie, he hasn't received the money yet, that is a long time isn't it?"

"Well-um-yeah, I will follow it up, it was transferred from this office the same afternoon you bought it in. How are things going with you?"

"Fine everything is fine, I will be touch shortly, I will need to come and get some cash to pay the staff's redundancies."

"When you know what you want, let me know I will bring it down to you, I don't want you turning up again with your crisp box," he gave another small laugh as he put down the phone.

I sipped me coffee, once again deep in thought, I hoped the rumours about the bank were untrue; I had money in it that I would need before I left Shendi. Reggie had suffered enough in this country, the trail of his father's murderers was still ongoing, I could not understand why. The last thing I wanted now that we had at last managed to sell the compound was a problem with the transfer of the money. Why was there a hold up over this? I just wanted to finally put an end to all the business over the compound, my own problems were more than sufficient for me to be handling at the moment, my nerves couldn't cope with much more.

The previous evening, when I had been waiting for my night security to arrive, the estate agents had come to the gate. Thinking it was my staff arriving I went to let them in. When I saw who it was, I stayed in the shade of my bushes. It was dark. I was sure they hadn't seen me, but they were very persistent. They rattled the gate, they called out. "We know you are there Madam, you can't hide forever." They eventually went away, leaving me with a raised heart beat and jaded nerves. I had meant to mention this to Sidi, but with so much going on with the staff and the men from the Labour Office, I hadn't got around to it. All this had to be sorted out. Closure on this was way over due. I must remember to raise this with Sidi again.

I sat in the bar waiting for my night security to arrive, wondering which one of the lads Sidi had got to work instead of Pouka. I was hoping Pouka had heard I didn't want him here anymore, but I thought he would come for work as if nothing had happened. I was right I didn't have to wait long for him to arrive. He called out to me to come and open the gate for him. I went out, but did not unlock the large padlock that held the gate secure. "Sorry Pouka, but after how you behaved this afternoon, there is no way I want you working here anymore. After things that you said, how do you think I will feel safe with you being my security?"

"You can't do this. You told me I could work here until you leave the country."

"That was before you treated me like you did today."

"We have to stick up for our rights, you have treated us unfairly. Now unlock the gate and let me in." He was raising his voice and shaking the gate.

"You will get nowhere shouting at me like that." I said as gently as I could under the circumstances. "I no longer feel safe with you here, you were without a doubt one of the ring leaders' to-day, and I am terminating your employment."

"Just you wait till I tell Jatto Roma you have done this, this is going to make things very bad for you," he yelled.

"Being I have given you a letter stating I have already terminated your employment, a letter that Mr. Roma has seen a copy of, I think you will find there is nothing you can do, this extra work I was giving you was unofficial, remember? And for your information, by behaving as you have, you have now lost about three months pay you would have had if you were still here. Mr. Roma considered I was paying you all too much redundancy pay, and unless I am very much mistaken, the labour office has charged you all for coming here today, I think if you work it all out, you are well out of pocket."

Pouka's face was like thunder. He had a bag over his shoulder, I was grateful I had not unlocked the gate; I thought he was going to hit me with it. He hurled it over his head and smashed it down on the ground, I heard something inside the bag break as it came in contact with the paving slabs Simon and I had had lain outside the gate, soon after our arrival. The poor bag was then powerfully kicked across the car park. Pouka looked me in the face, scowled, and muttered under his breath then turned and walked away, picking up his bag as he left.

The next morning I was up bright and early, sat in the office recalculating my figures in readiness for Mr. Roma and his boss to arrive in the afternoon, when I heard Sidi calling me. I answered him and told him to get Tina to make some coffee for us; I would speak to him about the estate agents while we were drinking it. But, by the time the coffee was ready, the other lads had arrived and were starting work, and Nick had popped in for his usual morning coffee. I sat and chatted with Nick, and Sidi joined the lads so any chance of a private conversation was gone. I made a mental note to speak to him before he left in the afternoon. I recounted the Labour and Welfare guys visit the day before to Nick.

"That will teach them. Most of them have been bastards to you and now you have turned the tables on them."

"Yeah, I was trying to be fair to them, but now they have come off worse; but I was petrified when they all arrived here, they were like an uncontrolled mob."

Nick laughed at this, "I can imagine, wish I had been here, but I am amazed the labour guy voted in your favour in the end."

"So am I, but at least I've got the last laugh. You should have seen Pouka last night when I told him I no longer required his services. He threw his bag on the ground and was kicking it. What did he expect, he was the ring leader there was no doubt about that, yet he comes here the same evening as if nothing had happened."

"I've had similar things with my lads, as soon as something is over with, it is over and forgotten, they don't seem to realise that damage has been done. Maybe that is the best way to be, perhaps we are wrong."

"Maybe, but no way would I feel safe with him as my security now."

"Definitely not, you must have people you have faith in around you now, all this isn't over yet, you must realise that. There are several hurdles to cross yet before you will be going home. You do have my number in your mobile don't you? You can ring me any time day or night you know that."

"Yeah, thanks, but I will try not to call you, but it is good to know there is someone beyond these gates I can depend on." I went into the office as soon as Nick left to ensure I had the new calculations ready for Mr. Roma and his boss when they came back in the afternoon. As I sat down and got my papers out, I thought about what Nick had said. I did have a few hurdles to cross yet, in fact more than Nick knew about. There was still no written agreement between myself and The Peace Haven. If they backed out now I would have a serious problems on my hands. I had closed the business, sold much of the equipment and had started dismantling the building. Then there was the problem of Reggie's money. The fact that he had yet to receive it was very worrying and on top of that was the visit from the estate agents. I again reminded myself not to let Sidi go without mentioning this to him. However, the largest problem of all was my immigration papers; I must also ask Sidi about these. So much seemed to be happening all at once I was dealing with things one at a time as they were happening, I must focus myself on the whole picture and get to the bottom of everything. I took the salary book out of my desk and got on with the matter on hand.

Mr. Roma arrived by himself in the afternoon, and was with me for a surprisingly short time. He looked over my figures and agreed they were to their specifications. He repeated to me his regret this had been necessary, and said he thought my staff had acted unreasonably, and had not told them all the facts when they went to their office. He told me if I ever came back to Shendi to open another business to contact his office and they would help me set up the staff's contracts, ensuring next time there would be no misunderstandings. I informed him this was highly unlikely. He finished his business and drank the drink I had given him, asked me for the obligatory transport money, and left the premises, saying he would see me the following Tuesday. I was relieved that was one more thing sorted.

Sidi prepared to leave at the same time as the other lads, I called to him. "Stay and have a coffee with me I want a chat." I said to him.

"I'm giving the lads a lift home; I will come back later if you want me to."

"No, I want to speak to you now; I will give the boys transport money."

I put the kettle on and went to get some money for the lads. It was obvious Sidi had been trying to avoid being alone with me, while I had him here I was not intending to let him escape, without having my questions answered. He reluctantly went and sat in the garden waiting for me to bring the coffees.

"I had told the lads I was taking them home, why did you insist I stay? It will take them longer to get home than if I had taken them."

"I have given them transport money, it is early yet, so they won't be late home, and I wanted to talk to you. You have been trying to avoid me."

"Trying to avoid you? What do you mean? Have I not been here every day? How can I be trying to avoid you?"

"You make sure you are never alone with me, so I can't ask you things I want to."

"Like what? What do you want to ask me?" He was getting fidgety, his nerves were showing, he had always portrayed himself as being very confident; this confidence had been seeping away over the last few weeks.

"Let's start with the estate agents."

Sidi gave a long exaggerated sigh, and took a sip of his coffee. "What about the estate agents? You have never liked them, all that is over; why are you bringing this up now?"

"They were here two evenings ago, if it is all over, why were they here?" He looked very perturbed when I said they had been here. "They were here? What did they want?"

"I don't know, I didn't speak to them, they were rattling the padlock on the gate, I thought it was the security arriving, when I saw who it was I didn't answer, I didn't want to speak to them."

"If you didn't speak to them, you don't know what they wanted. They probably only wanted to thank you for signing the papers, so they could finish their business. Or maybe they didn't know you had closed, they may have been coming for food." He was stumbling over his words; I knew he was hiding something.

"They seemed pretty angry to me, I don't think they wanted to thank me. Now tell me what is going on? Have you paid these lads?"

"Don't start all that again." He voice was rising considerably, he was getting very agitated. "It is obvious you don't trust me. If you don't want me here just say so, but remember I am sorting the steel boys for you and there is other things I have to sort for you before you go."

It was me that was losing my cool then, this conversation was starting to get out of hand. "Yes there are other things you need to sort for me; I was going to get around to my immigration papers after we had discussed the estate agents."

Sidi got up knocking the garden chair he was sat on over. "You keep on and on about everything, I'm fed up with trying to help you and all you do is complain."

"I have plenty of reason to complain, it is obvious you have not sorted things with the estate agents, and we both know my immigration papers are no nearer to being sorted than they were in January, and I can't leave the country until they are in order. Of course I keep complaining about this, it is entirely your fault I don't have them. If you had paid my taxes instead of spending the money, I would have those papers now. Now stop threatening to withdraw your help." I yelled at him. "Feel free to do that, but if you do I shall go straight to the police and get them to sort all this mess out for me."

Sidi slowly walked over to the stage, and slumped down on the steps leading up to the platform with his head in his hands. "Alright, alright," he softly said, "I haven't paid the estate agents."

"OH BRILLIANT!!!!" I exclaimed, "Now what do we do? What the hell have you done with the money; that was a fortune?"

"I have the money, it is at my compound," he said still speaking very quietly.

"Then why haven't you paid them?"

"I will, but I have a problem with them, look you don't understand how things work here. You never trusted them, and I know now you were right. I will sort things with them, you are not to worry yourself about this, and I promise you don't have to worry about them, just send them up to the village to me if they come here again."

As I was about to ask Sidi about my immigration papers again, there was a rattling on the padlock, we both looked towards the gate; it was Ousman. "I will go and let Ousman in and leave you talk to him alone," Sidi said with a look of sheer relief on his face, "I will see you in the morning."

I watched him walk over the wooden bridge to the main gate, although I was pleased to see Ousman and hoped he had some positive news for me; I did not welcome his arrival at the very moment when I had wanted to take my conversation with Sidi much further. There were still many questions I wanted the answers to, but now they would have to wait for the next day.

"My goodness, what is going on here?" Ousman asked as he looked around and saw the corrugate from the bar lying in the far side of the garden.

"I am starting to knock the buildings down; I told you I was going to do that."

"Good on you, but are you maybe a little bit premature, the papers aren't signed yet I hope you aren't forgetting that?"

"I know, but it will go through alright in the end."

"I certainly hope so, now that you have started doing this, I know you told me you were going to demolish the place; but I didn't really think you would do it, I thought it was just talk."

"Ousman you know me better than that, if I say I am going to do anything, I will do it."

"As I said good on you, not many folk would do that, and after all they have put you through, and they aren't paying you for the buildings, so if you can make anything on it, I admire you."

"I'm not going to make much on it, but it will pay the redundancies, and it has become a matter of principle for me."

"Yes, you are right, but I'm afraid it is the conditions of sale I have come to see you about. I'm not happy with some of the wording, and more so now I see what you are doing here." He pointed a few things out to me. Without him I would possibly have gone ahead and signed them, but under his advice I decided to let him argue all the finer points out with Mrs. Sullais. We said our good- byes after I had asked Ousman to sort this out as soon as possible I was getting a bit concerned over the time it was all taking.

Once I was alone again, my mind started racing round, and round in circles, I could not get things straight in my head; I was back in my on-going nightmare again. When would I eventually get the sale papers signed? When would Sidi sort out my immigration papers? What was Sidi playing at with the estate agents, why hadn't he paid them? How come Reggie's money still wasn't in his account? I could not think straight my head was in turmoil. Another rattling at the gate, bought me out of my thoughts, I looked up, and my heart sank as I saw a girl dressed in an immigration officer's uniform. She has seen me sat in the garden, so I couldn't ignore her efforts to open the gate. I walked slowly towards her.

"Can I help you?" I asked without opening the gate.

"You look busy here, are you going to build a new bar?"

"No, the bar is closed now; we are just knocking it down." This girl made me nervous, it was possibly my frame of mind as much as anything she did or said.

"Where is Sidi? Is he here?" She asked.

"No, he has gone home. Can I help you?"

"No, it's alright, I just came to say hello to him, and to see if you are well."

"I'm fine, if you don't want anything else, I must go I'm busy." I rather rudely said as I walked away from her without asking her in, I didn't know this girl and I was in no mood for small talk.

I tried to settle down and relax as usual at that time of day, but I just couldn't. I wasted my time trying to do a crossword puzzle; I could not concentrate, every so often I got up and walked around the garden, I went up on the stage and looked over the wall to The Peace Haven. There were no changes there, business went on as usual, and it looked just as it did on the numerous occasions I had looked over the wall in the past. I sat down again and picked up my paperback, this was also to no avail. I read several pages over and over again, and still made no sense of what I was reading. I put the book down again, my hand rested on it, as I shut my eyes, in an effort to block everything out.

I must have been sat there a long while, it was dark when I had been bought out of my reverie by voices shouting through the gate at me. I looked about me in amazement; I was temporarily unaware of where I was. I looked towards the gate, two of the estate agents were there, and their voices were getting louder and more aggressive. I stood up and shakily walked over the bridge, with the intention of telling them to go to Famara and speak to Sidi. I did not agree with him withholding their money, and if I was honest I was not convinced he had this money at his compound, but as far as I was concerned this was nothing what-so-ever to do with me.

"We have to give you this Madam" one of them said angrily as he thrust a piece of paper through the bars of the gate.

"Your business is with Sidi not me; I want nothing to do with it. You go to Famara and give that paper to him."

"No, this is for BOTH of you," he yelled as he threw the paper through the gate and they turned and walked away. I stared after them and gingerly stooped to retrieve the paper that had been thrown at me. I read and reread the paper. I could not take this in, I had to be misunderstanding the words just as I had been when I had tried to read my paperback. I went into the house and put the light on to ensure I was seeing it clearly, that had to be the problem, it was dark outside I had tried to read it in the dim light that was shining through the trees from The Peace Haven.

I sat in my armchair and stared and stared in disbelief at the crumpled paper. It was a summons to appear before a military hearing at 10 o'clock the following day at the main military camp at Timpara to answer a complaint made by the estate agents for non payment of their fee. I was completely horrified. I screamed with anguish and was so grateful for my solitude, anyone hearing me would believe I was completely out of control, which I 'm ashamed to admit I was. I reached into my pocket for my mobile, it wasn't there. It was several moments before I came to my senses enough to realize I must have left in on the table where I had been sitting in the garden. I walked unsteadily back to the table, my mobile was there, I hadn't lost all sense of reasoning. I dialled Sidi's number with difficulty, my hands were trembling uncontrollably. It rang and rang, he didn't answer. I slumped down on the same chair that I had been sat on earlier, my hands clasped in front of me, as if in prayer, staring into space, the music from La Parisian going around and around in my head. I lost all track of time.

I was bought back to reality by my mobile ringing. I quickly grabbed it off the table, it slipped from my grip onto the ground, I eagerly scooped it up; this had to be Sidi. I was alarmed when I looked at the screen and saw it was Reggie Preston. I gently placed the phone back on the table, it may have been Reggie wanting to tell me his money had now arrived, but I didn't feel like talking to anyone, and especially Reggie, if he still hadn't had his money; with the problem I was having here over the sale, that would be the very last thing I wanted to hear. I was so distraught, I would probably be incoherent, and I didn't want Reggie or anyone else to know my current circumstances.

When the phone stopped ringing, I picked it up again and dialled Sidi's number. Again in rang and rang; where was he? Did he know we had to report to the military base, and had decided to avoid speaking to me? I started pacing up and down the garden, I felt so isolated, and thoughts were flashing in and out of my mind, all negative thoughts. I was so overcome by an all consuming tiredness; I wanted to curl up on my bed and sleep, a deep deep sleep and wake up far away from Shendi; laying on a sun lounger on a deserted beach, with palm leaves swaying in the sea breeze, providing me with shade from the direct heat of the sun in the Utopia I had once believed to be Shendi.

A phone started ringing in the distance, disturbing the peace on my paradise beach. It continued to ring bringing me back to consciousness. It was my mobile, I darted back to the table and picked up the phone; this time it was Sidi. I answered and shouted at him. "Where have you been? I have been trying to phone you?"

"Take it easy, stop shouting, I left my phone in the car. Someone has just come in the shop and told me it has been ringing. It is late, what is the matter."

"Come here." I screamed at him.

"Now?"

"Right now." I put my finger on the receiver and placed the phone back on the table, it rang again, I picked it up and seeing it was Sidi, I didn't answer. I had no intention of talking this over with him on the phone. There was a rattling at the gate; I walked around the side of the building, so that I could see who it was without being seen. I was relieved when I heard the familiar voice of Fatah, my night security lad call my name. I let him in and went inside the house. I knew he would let Sidi in when he arrived. Much as I didn't really want to see Sidi because I was absolutely disgusted with him, I hoped he was going to come. I did need to try and get to the bottom of this, and now wondered if he would come here, being I had put the phone down on him and not answered when he returned the call.

In fairness to him, he must have left the village straight after he phoned me. I was sat on my bed with tears streaming down my face as I heard his car screech to a halt on the gravel outside the main gate. He must have driven like a maniac to have got here so quickly. He seemed calm and relaxed as I heard him joking with my Fatah, maybe he was oblivious to what was happening. I went into the lounge to wait for him to come through to the house. I was sat in my armchair with as much composure as I could muster, when he entered.

"What on earth is going on?" he shouted at me, "I was in the shop; I've had to close it to come here."

"Have you seen the estate agents?" I asked desperately trying to keep my voice on an even keel.

"Oh No! I haven't come running down here, over those darn boys have I? I've told you many times, tell them to come and see me; this is nothing to do with you."

I didn't answer, I simply pointed at the paper that was laid on the foot stool near my armchair. Sidi picked it up and looked at it, the smug expression on his face soon disappeared as he read, he stood looking at it, for much longer than it would have taken him to digest the words. He then put it back on the stool where it was.

"Well?" I asked. "What now?"

"Well nothing. I have told you this is nothing to do with you just ignore it, I will sort it."

"No this is something to do with me. My name is on that paper as well as yours." I could no longer conceal my anger, and I started shouting uncontrollably. "You have got me into this bloody mess and you are right, you are going to sort this out, and this evening. I have never been so humiliated in my life."

"They should not have done this." In spite of his face showing signs stress, he sounded extremely calm.

"Where is the money?" I asked, even though I had asked the same question earlier in the day.

"I've already told you once, and as I said this is not your business." His voice was now less composed than a minute ago.

"I want you to go and fetch the money and take it to these boys tonight."

"No, that is not the way to go about this," he told me, and I thought especially if you don't have the money, which I strongly suspected he didn't. "Just forget about all this, I will think about it over night and see what can be done in the morning."

"We have to go to the army camp in the morning, and I want you to bring the money with you; we will give them the cash and that will be this finished with."

"No, no, no, you forget about that, you will stay here, and I will go and everything will be alright, this is not your problem."

"You are right this should not be my problem, I have given you the money, it is all down to you; but now it seems it is my problem, through no fault of my own. You say you will go to the army camp and I needn't, but if you have read that paper properly, it says if we are not there at 10 o'clock in the morning they will arrest us. I have no intention of being arrested because of you."

"No, no. Listen to me, you don't understand; as soon as we go there they will arrest us anyway. You stay here, and if they do come for you just tell them you gave me the money, I don't want you being drawn into this."

"Too late, it seems I am already involved, and I am coming with you, I am humiliated enough without having the army coming here to arrest me."

"You never listen to me, I keep telling you, I know better than you how to sort things here; but if you must have your own head, we will go together, all you have to is tell them it is me that has the money, and they will let you go, it isn't anything for you be worrying yourself about. Look at the state you are in, just calm down and take things easy, easy."

"Maybe you are used to things like this; I assure you I'm not. I am absolutely devastated; and another thing there was an immigration girl here this afternoon."

"What immigration girl? And what did she want?"

"I don't know who she was, she was asking for you."

"She wanted me? What did she look like?"

"Young, slim and black." I sarcastically answered.

"There is no need to be like that, see it's your attitude that upsets people, why get so uptight if an immigration girl comes here."

"Being I'm still waiting for you to sort my papers out, I think I have every reason to get uptight over a visit from immigration, it may be nothing to you, but I'm petrified by all of this."

"It was probably a girl called Mariana, she is an immigration officer from the village and a friend of my sister's, she was possibly on duty near here and popped in to see me, did you offer her a drink?"

"No, I got rid of her as soon as I could."

"See, like I said you upset people, you have to be sociable to folk, what would it have hurt to give her a drink. Nick comes here every morning to see you and he always gets offered a coffee, why not this girl?"

"Go away and leave me in peace, Nick is my friend, I don't even know this girl why should I offer her a drink?"

"Yeah, I will leave you in peace. I will be back just after nine in the morning, and I will tell you what we are going to do."

"Right but you be here in plenty of time, or I will go by myself."

"For goodness sake, I will see you tomorrow." Sidi was trying to convey a calm exterior, but he didn't fool me, I could see his anxiety etched in his face, his emotions may have shown in different way to mine, but I could see his desperation, and this unnerved me farther. This was entirely his doing, but I had no proof of that. I was petrified of what may happen the next day, but one thing I was certain of; there was no way in the world I was going to lie to cover up what he had done, and no way was I prepared to take any part of the blame for his actions either.

Chapter Twenty-Three
Military Camp

Not surprisingly the night seemed to be endless and I found sleep elusive. Eventually there came a time that seemed not too early to get up and face the day. What should I wear to face the army? I had no idea but picked out clothes that were not too smart or too casual. I dressed slowly and then made myself a cup of coffee and went out into the garden to wait for Sidi. What was going to happen? What could I do? It was all Sidi's fault that I was in this mess. Suddenly a voice woke me from my reverie. "Morning, Boss Lady". It was Latif ready to carry on with the demolition work. I was surprised to see him and looked at my watch – 9.15 – it was late. I had been so deep in thought that time had gone by and my coffee had gone stone cold. Where was Sidi, he should have been here by now. I had better go and get ready and stepping over the rubble that was starting to clutter the pathway, I took my coffee cup back inside and went to run a comb through my hair.

Sidi still hadn't arrived when I went back into the garden, I gave an audible sigh and paced the garden, where was he? I glanced at my watch again, 9.25. It was a twenty minute drive to the army camp. I took out my mobile and dialled his number. No reply. I was not going to sit here and wait for the military to come and get me. I was scared stiff by the situation I was in, but not near as scared as I would be if the army was to come here and arrest me. I found Latif making his breakfast and said, "If Sidi comes here tell him I have gone on without him, I maybe gone for a long time, you know what you have to do today don't you."

"Yes, we know what to do, will Sidi know where you have gone?"

"Yes, just tell I couldn't wait any longer for him."

I walked out of my gate across the hotel car park and into the main tourist strip. Even at that early hour there were many tourists going up and down to the supermarkets to buy their water and postcards and those that I knew greeted me warmly. Not being in the mood for small talk, I took a deep breath and chatted happily but briefly with them. One of my customers for "meals on flip-flops" saw me as she was outside her shop feeding a pack of wild dogs as she did every morning. She waved and called to ask how I was. Just as with my tourist ex customers I was determined not to show signs of stress but I simply did not have the time or inclination to go and chat to her as I would have done on a normal day. Sheila would probably have been the best person to confide in; she had lived in Shendi for many years, and like the majority of ex-pats had a vast expanse of experiences behind her, she could possibly have given me some sound advice. I had to answer her and without being rude. Waving cheerfully, I carried on walking and shouted back, "I have an appointment, sorry can't stop and chat, will come up and see you shortly."

I reached the top of the strip and hailed a taxi, as I did so my mobile started ringing, I took it out of my bag. It was Sidi, I was not surprised – should I answer it or would I maybe better to do this on my own, hoping to wash my hands of all of this. I decided I had better answer.

"Where the hell are you?" he angrily asked.

"No, where are you? You should have been at The Dominion half an hour ago."

"I'm there now, but you are not."

"I'm at the top of the strip, about to get in a taxi."

"Don't. I will be with you any minute. What do you think you are doing, you know you mustn't go to places like this by yourself."

I waited, looking towards the Strip to see Sidi's car arrive, every now and again glancing at my watch, panicking as the minutes ticked by. Another taxi pulled up beside me, I was about to wave it on when I saw Sidi sat in the front of it chatting to the driver.

"Get in quick," was the only greeting he gave me, "we are late." This was not exactly news to me and I was concerned that we were not presenting the best of impressions to the army. The driver sped off dangerously fast as soon as I was in the car. "Where is your car?" I asked Sidi.

"I left it in the village, my brother may need it later, this driver is a friend of ours, and he will wait and bring us back, when we have sorted this thing out."

"You have the money with you?" I asked my anxiety showing in my voice.

"No, I've told you to leave this to me."

"And I told you to bring the money. You say you have good reasons for not paying them, but surely it is better to have the money with you, and if the army decide you have to pay, you have it on you."

"I'm not in the mood for chatter, you are making me angry, and I need to be calm to deal with this."

He needed to be calm! Well so did I but I took the hint, and sat in the back of the car, without saying another word. All I wanted to do was be on my way back to The Dominion, and have all this behind me. I fumed and worried until we reached the camp. The driver pulled on to an area of waste land opposite the entrance, stopped and turned to Sidi. I could not understand all their conversation but it was obvious by their body language and the few words that I did understand that they were disagreeing about some matter. This did not help my stress level.

Sidi and I got out the car and negotiated our way between the traffic on the busy main road outside of the army camp. There were army vehicles darting in and out of the camp's main entrance at high speed, many of these had groups of military sat in the back holding their AK47's in full view. The sight of guns, even after years of living in Shendi, still made me nervous. There were armed guards at the main entrance that asked our names and our business at the camp. Sidi spoke to them at length. I was confused and not sure what he had told them or what their reply was, however, they shook hands and we were let through into the camp. I had heard horror stories about this army camp which did nothing for my confidence despite being unsure of the substance of these tales. My fear must have shown because Sidi gently touched my arm as we slowly walked down the pathway deeper into the interior of the camp and asked "Are you alright?"

Surprised by his concern but unwilling to show any weaknesses, I snapped back. "What do you think? I told you last night I have never been so humiliated in all my life. No, I'm not alright."

"Shh, be calm, I have told you this is nothing, we will be out of here soon, you see."

We continued our slow walk past narrow concrete paths leading to huts which I took to be the barracks as off duty soldiers were lazing around in the sun and drinking attya. One of them called out to Sidi who left me and walked over to the hut where they shook hands. They chatted away, seemingly cheerfully for quite sometime leaving me standing on the main path becoming more and more agitated. Finally I had had enough, it was five past ten, and our appointment was for 10 o'clock. Timekeeping was considered unimportant in Shendi, but I was anxious about the time and now was not the time to be late.

"Come on Sidi, we are late." I reprimanded him.

"Don't worry Boss Lady," the soldier told me, "they won't be ready for you yet, but you had better go Sidi, we don't want the lady getting upset."

We went on deeper into the camp. "Do you know where we are going?" I asked Sidi.

He smiled at me, "Of course I know where we are going, did you think I was just walking aimlessly?"

"It's just that all the buildings look the same to me, we could be walking around in circles for all I know."

"We will soon be there," he told me. I wondered how he knew his way around the army camp so well. Had he been here before and if so, why?

We reached a small clump of different block built buildings, in the heart of the camp; we could hear the yelling of a sergeant major drilling his troops presumably not too successfully as his shouting was getting louder and louder. Our path took us between two of the buildings on the outskirts of the drill area and I could see a group of about thirty soldiers being put through their paces. Compared to the 'trooping of the colour' which was my only other experience of drill, this was a motley crew, most of their uniforms looked as if they were third or fourth hand, and the boots were certainly not polished to the shine, expected of UK troops. However considering the economic climate of the country they were no doubt the best Shendi could provide. In spite of their dishevelled appearance, the sight of them marching back and forth with their guns at the ready terrorised me. This whole episode frightened me, but these soldiers definitely heightened my fear.

"We are almost there," Sidi told me as we passed the soldiers, "that is the building we are going in." He pointed to a large construction stood by itself with a high wire fence around it. "Let me do all the talking, I wish you hadn't come with me. If they say anything to you just tell them I was dealing with these boys, not you. Okay?"

"Okay." I quietly said, and followed him towards the building.

There was a soldier at the gateway into the enclosed area. Sidi told them who we were and we were admitted. We went across the small sand enclosure to the shabby block building, which had at one time a coat of deep yellow paint; this was now only evident in small random patches. The corrugated metal door at the side led us into a small outer office. There was a cluttered old wooden desk near the back wall, a large fierce looking sergeant sat behind this desk, fiddling with the pens in front of him. Sidi gave him our names and showed him the paper the estate agents had thrown at me the previous evening, the sergeant called to two of the soldiers who were out in the enclosure, they came into the office, as they did the sergeant looked from one to the other of us, and said, "I am arresting you both for the theft of 100,000 shillings from the estate agents that sold your house for you."

Before we had a chance to answer we were physically pushed into an inner office by the two soldiers who had entered only moments before. I was devastated, Sidi still seemed fairly unconcerned. I was totally bewildered by his attitude. We found ourselves in a small office, with several rows of wooden benches, there were other people sat on these benches, I don't even know how many there were, I was too concerned about my own situation to bother myself with anyone else who was in the room. We sat down at the back of the room, on a bench by ourselves. The only ventilation in the room was a small window, with no glass, high on the opposite wall. It was extremely hot and stuffy, my hands were clammy, and I was starting to perspire; this was as much due to my nerves as the heat in the room. "Well, what is going to happen now?" I asked Sidi, trying to keep calm, but aware that my anger and fear were apparent in my voice.

"Don't panic," he told me, "the estate agents will arrive soon, then we will tell them our side of the story, they will give their side and we will be allowed to leave."

"It doesn't seem that simple to me. When they arrive they will say we owe them the money, and being they sold the compound, and they haven't been paid their fee, I would have thought they were in the right."

"Give over, I told you not to come here, now that you are here, you must keep quiet and let me do all the talking. All right?"

"Not all right. This is your doing, not mine. I have given you the money, you are the one who hasn't paid them, and if you think I'm going to sit here and take the blame for this lot, you are joking." I sternly told him as I waved my finger at him.

After what was possibly only about a quarter of an hour, but what had seemed an endlessly long while to me as I sat there in a daze, getting hotter and hotter and silently cursing Sidi for involving me in this deception, the sergeant, who when he was stood up, was even larger than I had initially thought came into the room and settled himself on the seat behind the desk that was in the corner. He started speaking in one of local languages. I understood some of what was being said, but not everything. People stood as their names were called; the proceedings resembled a small scale court hearing. After each case was heard, the offenders were taken from the room, until only Sidi and I were left. Two of the estate agents came into the office, followed by a third who I recognised as their boss. Sidi stood and caught hold of the sleeve of one of the lad's jackets and had an angry exchange with him. One of the soldiers approached and aggressively pushed Sidi down onto the wooden bench again. I felt physically sick.

Our names were called and we stood. The sergeant, still speaking in his own language opened our case. One of the estate agents started talking, Sidi shouted over him, and complete mayhem broke out. I stood there looking on in horror. I did not understand, what was being said, Sidi once again was squaring up to one of the lads, and the soldiers intervened and separated them. The sergeant banged on the desk in front of him with a wooden mallet, this startled everyone into silence. I surprised myself by daring to speak. "Can we please speak English? I haven't a clue what is going on."

One of the soldiers came over to me, and gently holding my forearm led me out of the room. He took me right outside and sat me under a tree in the enclosure outside of the offices. I was grateful for this; I was feeling quite ill, the stuffiness in the small inner office and my bewilderment with all the shouting had driven my stress levels up to somewhere unimaginable. I was dizzy and shaking.

"Would you like some water?" The soldier asked me, I eagerly accepted his offer. He went over to a large plastic bottle, which was on a rickety table behind the tree and poured me a cup of water.

When he gave it to me he said, "You sit there, the sergeant will come and speak to you shortly." I sipped the tepid water from the chipped and grimy cup the soldier had given me, if I hadn't been feeling so awful, I doubt if I would have drunk it, as it was it did make me feel a bit calmer, if nothing else. In due course the sergeant came out to me. "Right Madam, I want you to answer some questions, I want to determine your involvement in this. I want you to tell me about your house these boys sold for you."

"It was not actually my house," I explained to him, "the house belonged to a friend of mine in the U.K. this friend didn't want to come back to Shendi, for his own reasons so he gave me power of attorney to sell it for him."

"Fine, but these boys they sold the house?"

"Yes, but I haven't really had anything to do with this. Sidi has been dealing with it for me."

"What is your relationship to this Sidi?"

"He works for me and that is all."

"How much was the house sold for?"

"A million shillings."

"Do you know the estate agents have to be paid 100,000 shillings as commission for the sale?"

"I know the going rate is 10% on a property sale, but I told Sidi I was not prepared to pay that much. The agents did not do much work in respect of this sale, and their overheads were very small. I told Sidi I considered 80,000 shillings was more than fair for the work they had done for us."

"That was not your decision to make, Madam. If you did not think the work was worth the fee, you should have consulted a legal adviser. Having made your decision, why did you then not pay the lower fee to them."

"I gave the money to Sidi the day after I received it."

"Where is the rest of this money now?" The sergeant was speaking to me in a soft voice, without much expression. I was relieved by this, I felt much more at ease than I would have done, if he was still acting as aggressively as he had in the office. I explained to him I had paid the remainder of the money into the bank, to be transferred to Reggie's bank account in the U.K.

"So I understand you correctly do I? You have paid Sidi 80,000 for the estate agent's fee, and the rest of the money has gone to the U.K. so you have none of the money"

"That's right."

He got up from the seat beside me where he had been sat, and said, "I will need a statement from you to this effect." Without waiting for any response from me, he turned and went back into the building. The estate agents came out shortly afterwards and sat down on the other wooden bench in the enclosure, under a tree opposite where I was sat. They appeared to be very serious, they were in deep discussion presumably about what had happened in the office. They appeared to be arguing, but as they were speaking in local language, and Shendians are very animated when they speak, it was not easy for me to establish what was going on. I listen earnestly hoping to understand some of the conversation. I was curious to know what had happened after I had left the office.

I looked at the ground I did not want to make eye contact with any of them. The sergeant came out again and called one of them back inside, this left me sat there with the other one. Even though I didn't look in his direction, I felt his eyes boring into me. Still looking at the ground I saw a shadow approaching and heard the soft sound of footsteps on sand. I looked up. It was the agent, who had stayed outside, who after all this time had never spoken to me before, and whose name I didn't even know. He sat by me and said. "You mustn't upset yourself Madam Dominion, we didn't really think this was your fault, this is Sidi he is bad you know."

"Then why did you have me bought here?"

"Our boss said we had to, but don't worry it will all be alright. We couldn't be sure which one of you had the money. Give them your statement and they will let you go."

The other two men came out of the office and sat back on the seat opposite me. They gave their colleague a dirty look; it was obvious that they were angry with him for speaking to me. Quickly he returned to his colleagues where they started to talk again but this time they spoke in English, "Why are you speaking with her. You know Taubab women are no good, she is in this with him, they are trying to steal our money and you are being friendly to her. They will have agreed to say she doesn't have the money, he is her friend he will take the blame, but she is bad they all are."

I gave a deep sigh and sat there fuming. I knew this was being said solely for the purpose of demoralising me and it was working. I felt degraded and totally humiliated. Continuing to stare at the ground, I started drawing patterns in the sand with my flip flops. Never in my life had I been in such a situation as this. My feet went back and forth drawing meaningless lines and curves as I continued my designs on the sand. My mind flicked back and forth, how had I got myself into such a position? What could I do? As first one foot moved and then the other, I began to realise the basic cause of all my problems was fear. Fear of the staff and of Sidi, of how they could ruin me, that they would ruin me if it was to their advantage, of what lengths they might go to if I didn't turn a blind eye to many of their escapades, fear of the situation that I was in now, fear of the unknown, what would happen to me in the next few weeks, in fact fear of almost everything and everyone. It was all my own doing, I should have been stronger. I should never have allowed my fears to let me be drawn into the situation I now found myself in.

I stood up, and paced the enclosure, I let out several audible sighs as I paced. I looked from the sky to the ground. The intense heat of the sun was unbearable, it was close to midday. Why were they keeping me here? If they wanted a statement, why didn't they come and take one? The estate agents were watching me, I sat down again. Band music started playing from the parade area, the brass band was practicing, and this was so surreal. When I was back in my cosy little life on the island, I could never in my wildest dreams imagine myself in such a position as this. When I was first in Shendi, there were times when I thought I had walked onto a film set; this was definitely another of those occasions.

An important looking military gentleman came and spoke to the estate agents, they had a short conversation and all three stood up ready to leave. One of them came towards me, and without speaking put out his hand, without a thought I shook it, afterwards, I both wondered why he had done that, and why I so eagerly shook it without even considering we were here on different sides of this argument. I watched as they walked away, chatting cheerfully as they went, they were patting each other on the back, I even heard a hoot of laughter as they went out of sight beyond the camp huts.

They were obviously pleased with the outcome of the hearing; I wished it was me walking away, my nerves were completely shattered, I would have loved to be safely back at The Dominion curled up on my bed, shutting out the world for awhile.

Soon after the lads left, an army officer, I hadn't seen before came towards me. "Madam we need you to write a statement." He told me, he explained exactly how they wanted it set out, and reminded me to put everything in the statement including what I had done with the remainder of the money after I had paid Sidi the estate agents fee.

"Where is Sidi?" I asked him.

"That is not your concern Madam, just write what you know, and you will be free to leave."

I took the paper and pen from the officer and sat there on the wooden bench under the tree, I wrote my statement, I knew it would condemn Sidi, but this did not deter me, it was about time he took responsibility for his actions; through fear of the outcome I had allowed him to get away with much too much. My shaking hand momentarily hovered over the paper, and then I gathered my thoughts together and started to write. I found this difficult at first, but soon after I started the words flowed easily across the page. The officer appeared again as I was reading through my statement.

"Have you finished Madam?" he asked.

"Yes, I'm just checking through what I've written."

He took the paper from me and said. "Wait here while I show this to my superior, if he is content with it, you can leave."

I cannot describe my relief at his words. I remained on the bench, drawing patterns once again in the sand with my flip flops. I was pleased with myself, I knew there would be repercussions from my actions, Sidi had told me to tell them the truth and say I had given the money to him; which I had, it was not my fault he had not passed in on to its rightful owners. The officer was soon back, he told me I could leave and nodded to the military personnel at the gate of the enclosure, presumably that was his way of telling them I could go. I once again asked where Sidi was.

"We are keeping him here for awhile." he answered.

I slowly stood up and strolled towards the gate, not wishing my eagerness to leave their premises to be evident in my actions, one of the soldiers on the gate said good-bye to me, I simply nodded to him as I was unable to speak. I glanced around me as I left the enclosure, all the buildings looked similar, I was deep inside the camp, and unsure of my way out. I went in the same direction I had seen the estate agents leave. Soon I came to parade ground which was now deserted. At least I was on the right track. I carried on down a path that looked familiar. There were the same lads that had called out to Sidi, still sat outside their hut. These soldiers had obviously had a more enjoyable day than we had. The one that had seemed most friendly had a glass in his hand and his feet up on a cardboard box. He called out to me, "Ah there you are Boss Lady, is everything alright? Where is Sidi?"

"Sidi will be coming soon." I answered him although I doubted Sidi would be released for quite awhile yet. I knew I was going in the right direction now, in fact I could see the main entrance to the camp, and I started walking faster. There were soldiers sat outside many of the barrack huts, I could feel them all watching me, I felt most uncomfortable. I looked straight ahead of me and walked with my head held high, my eyes fixed on the exit of the army camp. I had to report to the office again so they could sign me off the premises.

To my astonishment as I walked out the main gate, a taxi pulled off the waste land opposite and stopped by me, it was the taxi driver who had bought us here, I thought he would have long gone. "Where is Sidi?" he asked.

"They have kept him there; take me back to The Dominion." I told him.

"Get in, but we can't go yet, we have to wait for Sidi."

"No, you take me home or I will get another taxi. If you want to come back and wait for him that is up to you, but I am not."

He drove me to the Dominion, and on the way there he asked me what he should do, Sidi had told him he had to wait for both of us. He wanted to know what had happened. I didn't tell him much but advised him to go to the village and get Sidi's brothers. I thought he probably needed them to get him released. The driver didn't seem very pleased with this, but to my amazement when we got to The Dominion and I asked him how much I owed him, he told me he was a friend of Sidi and his brothers so I didn't have to pay him. I had barely got out the car when with a crashing of his gears he sped away and was out of the car park, I glanced after him but only saw the dust settling. Still nervous and legs quivering like jelly, I entered my gate.

The place was a hive of demolition: Latif was working near the entrance and a group of men were busy dismantling the steel framework of the bar. "Hello, did Sidi find you? He came here looking for you."

"Yes, I've seen him." I told him as I walked passed and stepping over the rubble I went inside the house. "He will be here shortly." I answered as I disappeared into my own comfort zone.

I lay on my bed, exhausted; milling everything over in my mind. Where would all this end? Would they keep Sidi there? At first that didn't worry me, in fact I was fairly satisfied by this; it would serve him right for what he had done to me, besides this money he should have paid the estate agents. Then reality sank in. If they kept Sidi there, how would I ever get my immigration papers sorted out, and without my papers, I couldn't leave Shendi. My satisfaction turned to panic. My mobile rang; I looked at the screen as I always did before answering. It was Sidi. I was tempted to put it down again, but reconsidered and answered.

"Where are you?" he abruptly asked.

"At The Dominion, where did you think I would be?"

"You have to come back and pay these people 10,000 shillings, before I can leave."

"What? Why do I have to pay anyone anything?"

"They showed me the statement you wrote, it is your fault I am here, and now you have to pay for me to leave."

"It is your fault you are there. I gave you the money as I said in my statement, so why is it my fault. Besides did you not tell me to tell them that?"

"Yes I did, but I didn't think you would put it in a statement, they are talking about taking me to court if I don't pay this 10,000 today."

"As I said that is your problem not mine."

"Okay, okay, but we can talk about this later, just bring the money." His voice sounded desperate; maybe I had the upper hand at last.

"What if I don't have 10,000?" I asked causally, trying to sound as if I wasn't concerned.

"--- But, but you do have the money, you have the money that Babu gave you for the steel."

"I need that for my airfare."

"Don't worry about your airfare there will be more money before you go, do this for me now and we will sort all your things out for you, don't worry. PLEASE." He was trying to appear calm but his voice was almost pleading now. I did not want to part with any more money but I knew as well as he did that I did need him to sort my papers out for me, and if I didn't help him now, I could find myself in a very difficult position.

"I will have to check if I have the money," I told him, knowing full well I did have, but not wishing him to know I had money on the premises.

"Don't be too long." Sidi said as he put the receiver down.

I went into the office to check if I would be left short of cash if I did pay. I knew I still had a fair amount to sell before I left Shendi, but that was beside the point. As I unlocked the safe, I suddenly realised I would soon have to decide what I was going to do next. Never mind sorting out Sidi, I had to sort out my living accommodation. The house wasn't very safe now, with the demolition work progressing. Tina had asked to move out of the kitchen to do the cooking as she no longer felt safe in the kitchen. Latif had moved our one remaining gas hob into an outhouse at the bottom of the garden; this building had no roof, so I was hoping all this would be over before the fast approaching rainy season arrived. The office was situated next to the bar, I had to step over rubble to get in the door, and I would soon have to move everything out of there. More important yet, I would soon need to move out of the house, Latif and Petreeni had already taken the corrugate off the lounge side of the house, my bedroom and the bathroom was the only roofed area of the building that remained.

My thoughts were disturbed by the steel lads shouting greetings to someone at the main gate; I then heard the clattering of the gate opening. I went out to see who had arrived. It was two of Sidi's brothers and his cousin, who was one of my night security; there were two others with them, whom I didn't recognise. I realised they had been sent by Sidi to collect the money to secure his release.

"Hi," Ebi, one of Sidi's brothers cheerfully greeted me, as he took hold of my elbow and led me into the garden area away from the others. "Sidi has sent me to get money for the soldiers."

"Yes, he phoned and said he needed money," I answered him, "Why does Sidi assume I will give you this money?" I knew I would have to but I wondered how much Ebi knew.

"Helen, you know you must pay this, if you don't they will keep Sidi at the army camp until someone pays it, and you know the family doesn't have that sort of money."

"Where is the money if the family doesn't have it?" I asked him.

"What money? I don't know what you are talking about," his tone of voice was changing and I could detect his growing urgency.

"Don't play the innocent with me; you know exactly what all this is about and what money I am talking about. You can pay his release out of the money I paid him for the sale of Reggie's compound."

"We don't have the money, and you are able to pay it so you must. It is your fault he is there; they are keeping him because of the statement you wrote; so it is up to you to get him out."

"Excuse me, whose fault is it that he is there?" I asked, once again feeling my temper about to erupt.

"If you hadn't given them that paper, he would have been released when you were."

"I really don't know what makes you think that. Sidi is always trying to convince me I am crazy, it is all of you that are crazy. Why will none of you ever take responsibility for your own actions, why do you always blame others for your misfortunes? Sidi is there because he kept the money he should have paid the estate agents. That is his doing not mine."

"None of that is anything to do with me, I don't know if you gave him the money or not, but I do know we now need the money to get Sidi released, which is what we all want. You need him to help you here, and the family need him at home, if our mother hears about this she will be so very upset, have you thought about that? She is an old lady, she doesn't deserve this worry, and it is you getting Sidi to sort your business for you that has caused all these problems for him, it is you that has to help him; you are the only one that can."

I didn't bother to answer him. I was boiling inside, and decided it was best to say nothing than to say something I might regret later. I went into the office to collect the money I had already taken out of the safe and placed on the desk in readiness to pay Sidi's release. I reflected on the fact that whatever you did here there was always someone who was prepared to blame you for their problems. I knew Ebi was right, I did need Sidi to help me, if with nothing else I needed him to sort my immigration papers for me, in fact there may be other times I would rely on him before my departure. I was also soft at heart, this had always been a failing of mine, and in spite of all Sidi had done to me, he had also helped me on many occasions. Even recently, he had been of great assistance to me, when the staff had involved the Labour and Welfare office with their redundancies. I could not bear to think of him, being kept at the army camp; I had heard many horror stories of experiences at the hands of the military, I didn't know how many of these were true, but none the less my conscience wouldn't allow me to leave Sidi at the camp.

I took the money to Ebi who, much to my annoyance had made himself at home in my garden. I considered it best to say nothing, and simply held the money out, to his hand that was outstretched in anticipation long before I reached where he was sat.

"We will bring him here when we have him," Ebi told me.

"As you want, but I really don't care less where you take him," I answered, trying to sound unconcerned.

I sat and watched them all leave. The other lads had been laughing and joking with the steel lads while Ebi had been with them, none of them seemed to be taking this too seriously. I sat there for quite awhile after they had gone pondering on the day's events. I realised I was probably stupid to pay the bail money, but felt in many ways my hands were tied. I must have been deep in thought as before I knew it, they had returned and had Sidi with them. He walked in looking very pleased with himself, shouting out to the steel boys the waving his arms in the air to them, giving them a victory sign. I just stared at them; I was sickened.

Sidi's high spirits melted away as he saw me sat in the garden, he glared at me, and I could see his anger etched on his face. "What have you done?"

he yelled at me, "Why did you write that paper for them? You have doomed me, those boys are now going to try and take me to court over this."

I stared straight in front of me, not even glancing in his direction I replied, "That is your problem not mine, rather than blame me, why don't you blame yourself, it is you that has bought all this on you; not me."

"I can't believe you have done that, it will ruin me."

"It was easy actually, I just wrote the truth, and besides don't you remember telling me to do that."

"No, I told you to tell them, not to write it down for everyone to see, and to have it used against me."

"I don't see what difference that makes, and I always intended to tell them the truth. I told you I have never been so humiliated in my life; there was no way I was going to take the blame for your actions. Anyway why are you shouting at me? Why don't you think who paid the bail money for you to get out. I've had an awful day."

"Not near as bad as my day. Why did you not tell the soldiers boys they were holding me? They would have got me out" he retorted in loud angry tones.

"What soldiers are you talking about?" I answered as roughly as he had spoken to me.

"You know which soldier boys I mean, the ones that were sat outside their house, they told he they asked you where I was when you left. If you had told them they would have got me out without paying any money."

I doubted that, but had no intention of arguing that point out with Sidi. My energy was completely spent. "Be quiet. I don't even want to speak to you at the moment. Go home with your brothers, looking at them over there with Babu; it seems they all want to celebrate. I want the whole lot of you out of here."

Sidi didn't even answer me, he went back towards where the lads were working, as he did so, I could visibly see his mood changing again. He once again raised his arms in a victorious manner, and beckoning to the steel lads joyfully shouted, "Come on lads, pack up for the day we are going back to the village, meet at my compound when you get there."

Petreeni, who also lived in Famara prepared to leave with them, and Latif, who had obviously been told by the others where we had gone in the morning, looked on in bewilderment. After the others had left Latif came to me, where I was still sat in the garden, and asked if I would like him to make me a coffee. "No thanks, I will make one myself later. You go home as well; there is no point in you being here if everyone else has gone." I was left in no doubt who was controlling things here. Sidi appeared to have the steel lads at his beck and call; Latif seemed to be the only one he hadn't mastered. I had realised for a long while Sidi didn't have the command over Latif that he would have liked. I noted this, as it may well be to my advantage in the not too distant future.

After Latif had left I made my way into the house to shower, I felt dirty and degraded after the events of the day, and wanted to wash all those feelings as well as the grime of the day away. I was surprised when I entered the bathroom, to see that Latif and Petreeni had taken the roofing corrugate off of the bathroom, all the walls were still standing but only the iron rafters remained above my head. No buildings overlooked that part of the house, so there was no danger of anyone being able to see me in the bathroom, but I still felt self conscious undressing, with the open sky above me. I spent longer than usual in the shower, in an attempt to wash the day away, which of course was futile; but I did feel slightly better by the time I had put on some body lotion and body spray. I felt more human again.

I returned to the garden with my paperback, and even surprised myself at how quickly I managed to immerse myself in its pages and put the day behind me. I was bought back to the present and away from the enthralling thriller I was reading, by my mobile ringing. I picked it up; if it was Sidi I had no intention of answering. I was delighted to see it was Nick; he was usually able to cheer me up.

"Hi, you okay?" I asked.

"Yeah, I'm fine, I've just finished work, and am about to go into The Mango Tree to have a couple of beers and see what film they have on this afternoon. I came down this morning for my coffee and was surprised you were out. You know you are not to do that without permission." This made me smile to myself.

"Sorry about that I had to pop out. The lads didn't tell me you had been down," I had no intention of telling Nick where I had been.

"Don't worry about not thinking of your regulars, I was looked after they made me a coffee and I sat in the garden being waited on like the lord of the manor. I just wanted to check all is alright."

"Yeah, I'm fine; I'm just relaxing in the garden."

"Righto, as long as you are alright I will go, I can't waste good drinking time talking to you. I will see you in the morning."

It was good to know Nick was out there, I had long realised he was the only friend I could really rely on if it ever became necessary. The experience at the military camp had unnerved me, but once I had been disturbed from my book, my mind started to contemplate my situation. First of all there was Peace Haven and the sale. I still had nothing in writing but strangely enough this didn't perturb me, although I'm sure it probably should. Then there was the problem of my immigration papers. I did feel uneasy about this but especially after having bailed Sidi out today surely he would get them sorted for me soon. Finally looming large both in a physical and theoretical sense was The Dominion and its demolition. What I was going to do next? It was clear I couldn't remain in the house much longer. The only areas that were roofed were my bedroom and the office.

I went into the office, it was small, but I could put the single mattress from the small bedroom on the floor and sleep in there. The room only had a small window which was high up; this wouldn't be very practicable, rainy season was fast approaching it would be too hot and humid. It would soon become unbearable. Besides that, it wouldn't be long before they would want to remove the steel from the roof there. So I needed somewhere else. I went out into the garden and looked back at the house. There was nowhere that would be safe.

Turning round I saw the little round outhouse, that Simon had been building when he left and it was the only one of his various ideas that I had had finished. At one time I had intended making it into a library for my customers, but that had never happened. Although it was two eight-foot round houses joined together and therefore very small, it should do. I stood in the first section and looked around; I could put one of the plastic garden tables in a corner of it, which would give a bit of space for a chair and a stool. I put my head through to the inner section. It was easy to see that my bed would not fit, it was too big and we would never get it through the outer part of the house but my mattress could go on the floor. Even that would be a tight fit, but I could manage, I would manage. I didn't intend staying longer than was necessary. The floor was just packed dirt so I would need to buy two large local mats at the market that would keep things cleaner but the windows presented a bigger problem. They had been made with decorative building blocks, the sort used for building decorative walls on verandas. The designs in them were sufficient to let in light, but would also let in the rain, when the fast approaching wet season arrived in a few weeks. Hopefully I would be gone by then. There was no electricity but I could get around that by getting a rechargeable lamp. Power in the main house was getting quite unsafe; in fact I was very cautious whenever I switched the lights on. Once I moved into the small house I would have it disconnected, we would still have a supply in the night security men's hut; I would be able to recharge the lamp and my phone there. I glanced around me, this building certainly was not ideal, but I could cope here for my remaining few weeks in Shendi. One security issue which occurred to me as I left the building was the lack of a lock on the door. Despite this I decided to move in the next day; it would be Latif and Petreeni's first job tomorrow to help me. I would also insist they did no more demolishing on the bathroom; I had no water in my new home. My shower was vital to me, my living standards may be deteriorating but my personal standards certainly would not.

As soon as Latif arrived the next day I told him of my plan, and voiced my concern to him that the door to my new abode didn't have a lock. "If you are moving everything out of the office, it will be easier and quicker to take the door off, and replace it with your office door, they are the same size," he told me.

"Fine, fine make that you first job, if you want me I shall be in the house, getting my things ready to move, it won't take long I haven't got much in there now." This was right; I had looked around what remained of my house the previous evening as I was putting my plans together in my head. I didn't have many of my personal possessions left, I had sold some things when I was selling off things from the business, and I had given other things away, this move wouldn't take long.

Soon after I had gone into the house I heard Nick talking to Latif in the garden, and went out to have a coffee with him. "Tell me Latif is having me on, you are not seriously moving into the round house?" he asked.

"Yeah, why not, the house isn't safe now; they have even taken the roof off of the bathroom. I have to sleep somewhere."

"You're duff girl," duff is a local expression for crazy,"you've been near it before, but you have well and truly lost the plot this time. There is only a bare concrete floor, the walls aren't even painted. The rains aren't far off, you will get soaked with those lattice work windows, come on start thinking seriously."

"Have you any better ideas?" I asked.

Nick sighed and shook his head and sat down at the only table that was left in the garden. The garden slabs had all been taken up; in fact Nick had bought most of them for the hotel he was building. The sand was deep, as the garden had been very uneven when we first arrived and had be levelled out with sand before the slabs could be laid. It was an art that we had all had to master managing to sit on the garden chairs without the back chair legs sinking into the sand, and you tipping over the back of the chair; it had happened to me on several occasions when the slabs had first been lifted.

I sat with Nick and waited for Tina to bring us coffee from the makeshift kitchen we had made her in another of the outbuildings.

"What do you think of your boss lady living in the round house?" he asked her when she bought us our coffees.

Tina looked at Nick and gave him a cheeky, nervous grin; I could tell she was unsure how she should answer him. "You could move out all together," Nick advised.

"Oh yeah, and where would I go? Sidi suggested a few days ago I could move up Famara to his compound. I don't think so eh?"

Nick laughed, "That sounds like a good idea! You could move into my compound."

"Maria would love that."

"You know there is nothing between me and Maria now, and I pay all the bills, so if I say you are moving in; you are moving in, simple."

"I think I had better stay here. I know the round house isn't much but you must admit the house isn't really safe now. And it won't be for long."

"If you say so, but I'm really not happy with you living in there. I keep saying you only have to ask, and I will sort you out."

"I know Nick, but I'm fine, this will soon be over and I will be out of here."

"What about my morning coffee then?"

"Blow your morning coffee."

I walked to the main gate with Nick when he was ready to leave. There was no sign of Sidi he was usually here before now. Perhaps he had decided to keep out of the way for awhile. I would be grateful for a bit of respite from him. I stepped outside the gate and watched Nick drive off, just after he drove under the hotel's arch, a large four wheel drive vehicle came into the car park, I saw it but didn't think anything of it as I turned and went back into my garden, intending to go back into the house and continue with my move; I assumed it was some officials visiting the hotel. I had only taken a few steps inside my gate when I heard the vehicle pull up in my entrance and heard the slamming of car doors. I turned, my heart started pounding as it usually did when I sensed danger. I was faced by three Shendian men in immigration uniforms. "May we come in Madam?" one of them asked. Only a few short moments ago I was grateful Sidi hadn't arrived yet this morning, but now I wish he was here, I knew I was about to need his support. They filed in and followed me out into the garden, without being asked, they sat down at the only remaining garden table. "We have reason to believe you don't have your immigration papers Madam," their spokesman informed me, "will you show them to us please."

"I have my alien card, "I told them; "I will go and fetch it for you."

"Are you sure you have an alien card? We have reason to suspect you haven't."

"I will fetch it." I hastily said as I headed off in the direction of my office.

"You okay?" Latif asked as I opened the office door, he was at the entrance of my garden, keeping an eye on the situation.

"Yes it'll be alright." I answered much more confidently than I felt.

Once inside the office, I took my mobile out of my pocket and dialled Sidi's number. It rang and rang to no avail; he didn't answer. "Damn him."

I cursed out loud. Maybe he didn't have his mobile on him, or more likely he had seen it was me and decided to let me sweat; he had no way of knowing the immigration officers were with me. I took my alien card out of my purse and made my way back out into the garden and without speaking placed my card on the table. One of the immigration men picked it up and inspected it. He studied my photo on it, and then eyed me; he then turned it over and carefully read all my details on the reverse side. When he was satisfied it was genuine he passed it on to one of the others for them to examine.

"Fine, fine you have an alien card Madam, but where is your immigration papers."

"I have had many problems this year and still haven't been able to get all my papers in order for this year." There seemed no point in telling them otherwise, if I pretended to look for them, it would only delay things and cause myself further problems.

"Really Madam that is what we believed. It is now the end of May; we give you until the end of February to sort all your affairs. What about last year; did you have your papers then?"

"Oh yes," I nervously replied, "I have always had my papers until this year, when I have had many problems."

"We all have many problems; most of ours are caused by ex-pats like you that think they can behave as they wish in our country. Bring me all of your papers since you first arrived."

I returned to the office, and noted Latif was still watching the proceedings, but I was aware he would be unlikely to help me. Once again I dialled Sidi's number again to no avail; he still didn't answer. I collected my papers together for all the years since my arrival. I picked up the phone and dialled Sidi yet again; surely he will answer if I am persistent. I literally jumped as there was a loud banging on the office door. It was a very small room, and was nearly empty by then; the sound reverberated around the walls. It was one of the officers; I hadn't heard his footsteps approaching, the loud banging frightened me.

"Come out with all your papers Madam; or I will come in."

I stood absolutely still, my legs were welded to the spot, in a very shaky voice, I replied, "I'm on my way." I cursed Sidi once again under my breath, he got me into this mess, and he should be here, helping me. I returned to the garden, and once again without speaking, and without looking at any of them I placed all my papers for the last eight years on the table. I sat down near them, and watched as each of them picked up one of the papers and they proceeded to read them. This careful examination of my papers, which was obviously intended to increase my uneasiness, seemed to last forever. Although I tried to hide my feelings, I was aware my horror of the whole situation must be apparent to them. They knew before their visit I didn't have my papers for this year, and knew what course of action they would take.

The most superior of my guests finally put down my papers and looked at me. There was a long pause before he said, "Madam, it is very obvious to us you have not even applied for your correct papers this year. We have no choice but to take you into custody."

"Where are you going to take me?" I asked in a shaky whisper.

"Initially to the immigration offices."

They all stood up, I sat welded to my chair. The junior of the trio caught hold of my arm and pulled me to my feet. Just then the main gate clanged. The thought of more trouble flashed through my mind. I looked up. It was Sidi. My relief at seeing him was immense. After the previous day I hadn't wanted to see him again, now here I was so grateful and relieved. How things had changed in a few short hours. Sidi must have seen the officers as soon as he came into the garden, but he strolled causally towards where we had been sat. This caused the immigration officers to stop in their tracks. Sidi came over and they all shook hands sat down at the table and started talking. There was no chair for me and I stood there like a spare part not understanding what was going on and feeling ignored. Sidi stopped talking and called out to Latif, "Go and fetch something for Helen to sit on."

I sat down and watched as Sidi carried on. He was pointing at intervals to various papers that were on the table. They were still speaking at great speed and I could not understand much of what was being said. I thought I heard Sidi explaining I had had a particularly bad season and at the end of last low season he even had to sell his car to help me pay the staff. I saw red when I heard this but thought it best to say nothing. This conversation seemed to me to be endless, I simply sat there, slightly bewildered, remaining silent throughout.

At length Sidi turned to me and said, "We have talked this though and have sorted things out to suit all of us, but you must give these men something for their troubles."

I had known that if we sorted this out at all it would cost me; most situations could be resolved in Shendi if money changed hands. "How much?" I asked with a mixture of relief that this problem was being resolved and annoyance that I had to pay for the privilege.

"Five hundred shillings." Sidi replied without looking at me. I did not reply, I stood up and went into the office to fetch the money, considering I had got away quite lightly, I had expected to be asked for much more.

Once the money had changed hands, the officers wasted no time in leaving, in fact they seemed eager to go. As they went towards the gate Sidi walked with them, still shaking hands with each of them in turn. I followed on behind. Sidi turned to me and said, "I will see our guests out." I was being dismissed; he obviously wanted to have farther dialogue with the officers and didn't want to risk me understanding the conversation.

I returned to the table and sat down again, watching what was going on in the gateway, the conversation seemed light, they were all jovial and there was still hand shaking and back slapping. Sidi stayed by the entrance as they got back in their car and drove off. He stood waving until they had driven under the arch and out of sight.

When he came back to the table, I asked, "Did you know those men?"

He didn't answer me straight away, he called out to Latif, and asked him to ask Tina to make us some coffee, he then spoke to me and said, "I didn't know all of them, but one of them I know quite well, that is why I could explain all our problems to them and get things sorted out." I was well aware my paranoia took control at times, but deep down I was suspicious of this. I remembered the immigration girl who had come looking for Sidi not long ago. I had no idea what connections he had; this had made me uneasy, any of my staff could have reported that I didn't have my papers, but they wouldn't know this, Sidi was probably the only person that knew this. Coming so soon after the previous day's events at the army camp, if it was designed to take my mind off Sidi's part in that, it had. Life was closing in on me.

Before I knew it Tina was serving us our coffee. Once she had left us I asked Sidi, "Fine, they have gone and I have paid them five hundred shillings not to take me in, but what now."

"What do you mean?"

"What I say, they have gone away, but I am still in the same situation, I still don't have any papers, so I'm still illegal, and I still can't leave the country."

"I told you I will sort it, and I will."

"No, I want to know more than that, how are you going to sort it, and when? I have told you before, it is you that has got me in this position, and you are going to sort this out and soon." My anger was starting to show again.

"Look at you getting worked up again; keep calm. Now I have spoken with them they are not going to come back again, so you don't need to worry about them. They have said being the business is now closed you can get non- working ex-pat papers. You know those papers are cheaper than working papers, and as long as you have them before you go to the airport, all will be fine. Helen I keep telling you stop worrying about that, and let's get on with the business at hand of getting these buildings down and selling what we can, all is going to be fine, fine."

This news was a consideration and went someway to calming my nerves. Non-working papers would be much easier to obtain and at much less cost. Relieved though I had been to see Sidi my paranoia was still there and I couldn't be bothered to hold much of a conversation with him. I simply let him get on sorting things with the steel lads and was more than grateful when he told me he had to go as he had business to sort out in his shop. After Latif had helped me move the rest of what was left of my belongings into the small round house I had made my new home, I spent the rest of the day chipping cement away from the back of some of the garden slabs to make them saleable. The ones we had laid in the beer garden were sat on sand and only cemented together were easy to make as good as new. Some of the slabs in our private garden had been laid before our time and were set in cement. There was a lot of hard work involved in cleaning these up for sale, and although it absolutely ruined my hands, I found this work therapeutic. As I chipped away at stubborn cement I imagined each piece was someone I had dealt with recently such as the estate agents or the immigration people. By the end of the day I had reduced them all to rubble.

The day passed quickly and I needed a shower. I had given instructions that the bathroom was the last to go but access to it was difficult. I had to negotiate a huge pile of rubble and walk over huge chunks of masonry that had been left to lie as they had fallen. Latif had suggested to me his first job in the morning would be to knock a hole from the old kitchen into the passage way outside the bathroom so I could get to it that way to save me climbing across the rubble to take my shower. This would be fine for tomorrow but I need a shower now. I stepped gingerly from stone to stone, testing each slab with my toes before I trod on it to see if it moved. I was so grateful I didn't get many visitors I would hate too many folk to see how I was living. When I finally reached the bathroom, I took a long luxurious shower hoping once again to wash the memories of the day away.

Afterwards I made my way back over the rubble to my new little house. This was actually quite cosy, Viv had loaned me a mosquito net that fitted securely over my mattress, I could make myself comfortable in here, I now had some cheap but brightly coloured local mats on the floor, which made the place look cheerful, and I had a rechargeable lamp so I would have light at night. I collected a crossword book and a paperback and went and sat at the lone table in the middle of the sandpit that had once been my garden and settled down to relax.

Chapter Twenty-Four

I was deeply involved in 13 down – someone who isn't what they seem (4 letters) - and was trying to fit SIDI when my mobile went. If it was him, I would not answer but it wasn't, it was my lawyer. What now, I wondered.

"Hello Ousman."

"Hi Helen, how are things going with you?"

I had no intention of telling Ousman the truth of all the problems I had encountered over the past few days. "Everything is fine, I have steel boys taking down the main buildings, and my lads and I are backing them up. I'm pleased with how things are going. I have moved into the little house in the garden today as the house is best part down now."

"Oh Helen, I hope you haven't been a bit premature with your demolition work."

"Why? Is there a problem?" Not another one please was my whispered prayer.

"Well... actually yes! Maybe I'm being a bit over cautious, but please listen carefully to what I have to tell you, I don't want to worry you, but you have to know what is happening."

"This is sounding rather ominous." The moment someone says "Don't worry" it becomes the first thing you do, so what was the matter?

"Mrs. Sullais is very angry that they have agreed a sale with you without consulting her. She has told them that they have agreed to buy land that already belongs to The Peace Haven."

"It belongs to us, not the Peace Haven!" I retorted as worry got the better of me.

"Listen Helen please. I have heard from good authority from one of her clerks that she is encouraging them to try and take over your property."

"All this will be more delaying tactics you know. I have legal papers for the property. First she wanted a new power of attorney drawn up, now this. Why is she causing all these problems?"

"I think this has become very personal for her, she was confident in winning the court case and she isn't happy how things are panning out. She probably feels you have won and she isn't happy about it; but nonetheless she is determined to win the day. Now please take this seriously, I don't want you to leave the premises, you must be there at all times."

"Ousman, it is just gossip. Why should I stay in?" My brave words about gossip were, I knew, just me clutching at straws in the wind. Gossip was how Shendian society ran and I knew how proud Mrs Sullais was. She would not like being defeated.

"I think if you are not there they will enter the property and claim it, remember, possession is nine tenths of the law."

"You are joking?"

"I'm afraid I'm deadly serious. You are not to leave the premises or allow anyone from the hotel to enter. Something else to be very watchful of, do not allow anything from the hotel or to do with the hotel on your property. If you do, they can say it must be their lands if they have things there, so whatever you do, don't allow anyone to deliver anything to you for them or anything like that."

"I'm finding this hard to comprehend."

"I did think I would have a problem getting you to understand; please do as I say Helen, this is very very important. If they take hold of your land, we will have a hard task trying to reclaim it."

"Ousman, Ok, I will do as you say, but I can't really take this in. I don't really go out now, only as far as the supermarket at the bottom of the car park, and sometimes friends come to visit and I go to The Peace Haven coffee shop the other side of the car park, and to the internet cafe next door to the coffee shop. Must I stop that now? Am I to be a prisoner in my own grounds?"

"What you are doing is alright, that isn't really leaving the premises as it is part of their property; but no farther than the supermarket. When you do go don't be gone long and make sure someone is always there. I will pop down and see you in a few days and will be in touch if anything else happens."

I put the receiver down and slowly replaced my phone on the table in front of me; I remained staring at it as if it was likely to start talking to me again. I had trouble comprehending all that was happening to me. When I had closed the bar I had thought it was the beginning of the end. But it wasn't. So much had happened in the short space of the few weeks since then, I really didn't know what to expect next. My thoughts went round and round in ever decreasing circles. Surely The Peace Haven couldn't really take possession of my property. It all seemed farcical, things like this happened in books not in reality. I would soon be back in the U.K. and look back on this as some sort of awful dream. I sat with my book open in my hands, but not reading, my mind darting from one thing to another until I could no longer think straight. I wished I had someone to talk to, to confide in, to trust and who maybe could offer me some advice. There was no-one. Karen, who was my usual source of help, was back in the U.K and there was no-one else I felt I could burden with my problems.

I must have been sat there for a couple of hours because the next thing I was conscious of was the monkeys in the garden on their short journey home for the night, from the neighbouring hotels. I went inside the little building that was to be my home for the foreseeable future, and waited for my night security to arrive. Once they were here I would settle down for the night. I had only the light of my rechargeable lamp, but it was sufficient to read by. I sat on a stool at the plastic table I had moved into my house and tried to carry on with the puzzle to pass the time. To my surprise my brain was functioning enough to do this so maybe my mind was in better condition than I thought. At least I managed to solve 13 down – fraud.

My mobile rang; I was relieved to see it was Nick. "Hi Nick." I said as I answered it.

"Hi Luv, you okay? Where are you, are you in your little house?"

"Yeah, where did you think I would be?"

"I don't like you living in there, I'm just up in the King's having a drink before I go home, do you want to join me? It would do you good to come out and enjoy yourself for a while. Or would you like me to come down for a while?"

I thought for a moment, what should I say? I really did need to tell someone and here was the perfect chance. However, I could tell from Nick's voice he had had a few drinks, so it probably wasn't the best time to try and talk to him. "I'm fine honest except that I can't come out. My lawyer phoned me this afternoon and asked me to stay in"

"Stay in? What do you mean? I don't understand."

"Don't worry, it is complicated. I will explain when you come for your coffee in the morning. I'm fine; get yourself off home, but thanks anyway."

"If you are sure, I will come down if you want."

"No, I'm not good company at the moment, I will see you tomorrow."

I clasped my hand over my mouth and nose and took a few deep breaths, in an attempt to calm myself. How easy it would have been to have asked Nick to come down, but it wouldn't have been wise. If my security reported to Sidi, which they would, that Nick had been here during the evening, Sidi would assume any grip he had over me was slipping away and he might resort to desperate means. In addition there was the question of Nick and his relationship with Maria. He was still living with Maria, even though I knew it was a very long time since they shared a bedroom, and the relationship, or what was left of it was a convenience to both of them; but any assistance I received from Nick, could and probably, would be misconstrued by her, and may cause me more problems. I was aware I was in a very precarious position and didn't need any more hassles.

As usual Nick arrived soon after nine the following morning for his coffee, while he was doing his water run. As we sat down together, to relax for a while in the garden he asked me to explain again what I'd told him on the phone the previous evening. "My lawyer rang me late yesterday afternoon to say he had heard through a clerk in next door lawyer's office, that they may try to take over this place without paying for it." I was hoping that he would dismiss it as gossip to be ignored but, wise in the ways of Shendian society, he didn't. Instead, he looked as bewildered as I felt as I explained what Ousman had told me. "Like the court case, all this is very complicated; the land had been originally allocated to them, so they think they still have a claim on it. Most of the problems here are down to the first owner, but regardless of where the problems originate, it seems that their lawyer is put out that they have come to an agreement with me over the sale without asking for her advice. She is a forceful lady and is determined to stir things up."

"I still don't understand how they can claim your land; you have all the right papers for the place don't you?" He took out a cigarette and lit it.

"Yes everything is in order. I'm not sure I fully understand it either, but my lawyer is taking this very seriously. He has told me I can go as far as the supermarket, but no farther, and to make sure nothing belonging to the hotel is on my property. It seems that if that happens they could then claim the land as theirs because their property is on it.

Nick looked only slightly less bewildered and then his practical side appeared. "Well look on the bright side you haven't really been anywhere for the last eight years, so you won't be missing out, if you have to stay put now."

"You're right there, but the thought that I can't go out makes me feel like a prisoner. I stupidly thought when I closed the business that I would go out and about and have a bit of a holiday before I returned to the U.K."

Nick grinned, "I don't know where you get your ideas from, you live in cloud cuckoo land, but I hope for your sake this soon gets sorted, if they pull out of the sale now you are in Shit Street."

"Don't go there; my nerves are rather jaded already."

I went to the gate and watched Nick as he drove off under the arch; my heart sank as he left, because I knew he was the only one I could really rely on. I knew I was in an extremely volatile situation, in an equally volatile country. There was no way of predicting the final outcome, or come to that predicting what the next move might be. My previous confidence in my demolition work was starting to evaporate; possibly Ousman was right, maybe I had been a bit premature with it, but at the same time if I hadn't started it when I did, there would not have been the time to complete it. I was so disturbed, and my odd glances in a mirror told me I was physically, as well as mentally, starting to suffer with the stress I was under.

After Nick left I went back into my little house and sat on my mattress for awhile deep in thought, I was bought back to the present by a knock on the door. It was Sidi, I went outside and he told me he had asked Tina to make us a coffee, so I sat down once again at the small garden table in what we had all started to call my 'beach', as all that was left of it was the sand from under the slabs. "I have just had a coffee with Nick, I can't sit here too long I haven't done anything yet this morning and I have plenty of the slabs I should be working on."

"You shouldn't be doing that anyway, Helen, let the lads do it, that is hard work," he berated me.

"What do you expect me to do, sit here and do nothing all day."

"Tell me what is happening here?"

"What do you mean, nothing is happening."

"That is not what I hear, I thought Ousman had told you not to go anywhere, is the right?" He lent back in his chair and folded his arms.

I was bewildered. How Sidi could possibly have known this? Ousman had phoned after everyone had gone home the previous afternoon, so there was no-one who could have overheard that conversation. I decided he must have been told on his arrival by someone that heard me speaking to Nick, the steel lads had been walking back and forth and both Latif and Petreeni could have been in ear shot. It didn't matter that he was aware of this, what did concern me was that everything that happened was being reported to him, and I must be more watchful of who is around when I'm speaking.

"Ousman has told me I'm not to leave the premises as there is a possibility of The Peace Haven trying to claim the property if I'm not here."

"I don't see how they can do that."

"Neither do I really, but I will stay here anyway, as Nick said when I told him I don't go out anyway, so it won't make much difference."

"Ah Nick. You talk too much to Nick, I don't trust him."

"Maybe you don't, but I do, he has always been supportive of me."

Sidi had finished his coffee by then and got up to leave, "I have to go and pick up some supplies for the shop, I will be back later to check on things. Think what I said about Nick, you are easily taken in."

I grinned to myself as I watched him walk away. Yes I was easily taken in especially when I was in a vulnerable situation, which was how I originally stared trusting Sidi, but I knew now I could rely on Nick a thousand times more than I could rely on him.

Shortly after Sidi left and I had set about my day's work, chipping away at the garden slabs, my mobile rang. My instinctive reactions was "Now what" and "Should I answer?" When I saw it was Reggie Preston I felt a huge pang of guilt. I was ashamed to say with so much going I had more or less forgotten that the last time I had spoken to him, about a week ago, he was still waiting for the money. On top of my guilt for forgetting about his problem was a new concern. After the events at the army camp if it became known Reggie hadn't had his money either, it would put me in an extremely bad light.

"Hi Reggie, how are you?" I asked when in fact what I really meant was has the money been paid into your bank account yet.

"I'm fine Helen, and how are you, and is everything going well with your sale."

"Yes, everything is fine." I told a white lie, but there was no point in burdening Reggie with my problems, and I was eager to hear about the money. "How is things your end has the money come through yet?"

"That's what I was phoning about; the money was paid into my account yesterday." I gave an audible sigh of relief.

"That's brilliant Reggie, I tried not to convey my anxiety to you, but I was worried about the money, rumours are rife here that the bank is in problems."

"I felt the same, six weeks is an awful long time for a transfer to go through, even from a different country." Reggie and I went on to have a general chat about Sharon and her family, having a conversation with someone that had no idea of my present situation, boosted my morale immensely.

The next few days passed fairly uneventfully, Nick continued to visit each morning and usually rang or sent a text in the evenings to check on me. Viv and Greg who were due to go back to the U.K. the following week for the summer, came down as before and took me over to the coffee shop to get me away for awhile; and Adam and Jane took me for coffee on Tuesdays when they came up this way to do their weekly shopping. Although things seemed more settled my nerves were getting stretched to breaking point; every little thing seemed to get me down and each day as I heard nothing of the sale seemed an eternity. These outings were a terrific mural booster for me, much more so than the others realized.

Two of my regular tourists, Jill and Peter, who were also friends of Viv and Greg, were staying at The Peace Haven for a fortnight's holiday. We had all arranged to meet at the coffee shop, for a sweet, high calorie fix, of cappuccinos and homemade biscuits. We spent a pleasant hour and a half, chatting away and laughing as each of us, retold amusing memories of The Dominion. It was the chance to reflect, on occasions like this that I realised in spite of my all my desperation and misgivings, over the years I had also had many good times. Hearing my friends relating their tales, and remembering folks, some of whom had passed away and some of whom simply didn't holiday in Shendi anymore, I felt nostalgic. It was such a shame things had turned as sour as they had, but I was grateful the others' memories all seemed to be of happy times we had shared; if I hadn't always been happy I could comfort myself knowing I had spread a bit of happiness among my guests.

I returned to The Dominion after my get together with my friends in high spirits. As I entered the gate, I saw Sidi, who had been working with Latif when I left, sat at my table with three strangers who looked very official drinking coffee. My heart sank; years of dealing with officialdom in Shendi had made me instinctively suspicious of all official looking people especially those I did not know. I pasted a smile onto my face and greeted them all.

"These gents are from the water company." Sidi told me as he introduced them individually.

"Pleased to meet you," I said, even though I had a strange feeling by the end of our meeting I would not actually be pleased to have met them. "What can I do for you?"

"Nothing, I've done it all. I've sorted things for them," Sidi informed me. "Two of their colleagues are looking at our septic tank."

"Why?" I asked, my paranoia rising to the surface once again.

The senior member of the group replied "We are shortly to do extensive improvements to this area and just want to see the layout of your property Madam. This gentleman has been very helpful"

"I'm sure he has but my septic tank has nothing to do with the water company. We have it privately emptied, and in fact I didn't even know you did any sewage work."

"We don't at the moment, but you will soon have a much improved service. We are going to connect your septic tank to The Peace Haven's system, and then we will empty the two premises from one communal tank, so you won't need anyone coming to your property to do this. In fact you won't even be aware that the work has been done."

"Can't you see my business is closed, and we are demolishing the buildings, I won't be requiring your services, thank-you. Your company should know that I am closed. Who sent you? I am assuming you are from the water board, but do you have your I.D. with you?" Sidi shot me an angry glance, but he said nothing.

"Our company Madam, who do you think has sent us? We are a government run company as you know"

That was may be but none of them made an attempt to produce their I.D. cards and the speaker continued, "Madam, you don't have a choice, this is the service we are giving in your area. When the work is completed the government will not allow any septic tank lorries in the tourist area, that is why we are carrying out this work at great expense so the tourists won't have to see these unsightly lorries in this area."

"This sounds like a very good system to me." Sidi causally added shooting another glance towards me, this seemed to be designed to me keep quiet.

It took more than disapproving looks from Sidi to silence, "I agree it is a good system, but you can see what is going on here, without any buildings, there won't be any waste water. If you connect my premises to The Peace Haven's you may be wasting your company's money, and we don't want you doing that do we?"

"It is not for you to decide what is wasting my company's money, Madam. We have been sent to view your property and draw up the plans for our work and that is what we are going to do." He was starting to lose control and his tone of voice was becoming quite threatening; but after Ousman's advise there was no way I was going to allow this continue.

"I'm afraid you are not. I want you and all your colleagues to leave my property now." Sidi shook his head as I said this, stood up and walked away.

"Your property Madam? Are you sure of that? We were informed this is Peace Haven property."

"This land may eventually belong to The Peace Haven, but for the time being it belongs to me; and I am requesting you and all your party to leave my property NOW." I was getting agitated and it showed in my raised voice which due to my anger also quivered.

"We were warned you are a difficult woman. We will report this matter to our director; he will not be pleased you are holding up this work that is very important to our government." He called his men and prepared to leave. I sat down with a sigh, and watched them gather their equipment together. I saw Sidi go over and speak to them.

After they had left, Sidi came back to me. "What have you done now, they are very cross with you, they are going to go back and tell their director this, why do I always have to apologise for things you do and say, sometimes you behave very badly."

"Go away and leave me in peace. You make me so angry, what did I tell you Ousman said? We are not to allow anything of The Peace Haven's on this land. I leave the place for a short while and when I come back you are here allowing these men to make plans to join our waste water to the hotel. Do you never think?"

"I don't see any problem with that, and you have no rights to prevent those men doing their jobs; besides you were very rude, that is unforgivable."

"You make me laugh, fine I was very rude." I chuckled to myself, "you leave me now I've had enough, my poor brain needs some peace and you are doing my head in. I don't suppose I should bother I will be long gone, by the time this work is done."

"Don't be too sure of that, remembering you don't have your papers yet."

"True and whose fault is that? You had better get a move on with them, it won't be that long before I need them now."

"I think there is plenty of time to worry about them, you haven't sold this place yet."

I saw the smirk on Sidi's face as he walked away; he appeared unexplainably pleased with himself. He was right I still hadn't sold the place, but equally unexplainably this was not concerning me, my all consuming worry was my immigration papers. I had let this matter slip for too long. I would again bring this up to Sidi every time I saw him, until he sorted this out; but for the time being I was extremely angry with him, and trying to explain situations to him that he either didn't understand or had no intention of understanding, was very infuriating. I was content to see him say his farewells to the lads and leave. I had calmed down by the time the lads went home, and was relaxing in the late afternoon sun under the shade of the mango tree, when I heard my name being called. It was Ousman, he couldn't get in because, as usual when I was on my own, I had locked the gate I went to the gate and let him in.

"Hi Ousman, can I offer you a coffee?" I greeted him.

"No, Helen, that is kind of you, but I have only popped by on my way home to check if everything is all right here."

"Everything is fine except there was one incident this morning," and I went on to relate the events with the employees of the water company. Like me, Ousman found this suspicious.

"You did right not to allow them to do anything here. I haven't heard of any work going on, and if you didn't see their I.D. I somehow doubt if they were who they said they were. This is the sort of thing I was warning you about. You can always ring me if you are in doubt about anything. Did everything get finalised okay with the sale of Mr. Preston's compound?"

I was taken aback by Ousman's question, it was he who had bought the money for the sale to me; this made me wonder if he knew more of the events that followed the sale than he was admitting. "Oh yes, that is all sorted now thanks, it took longer than I expected to get the money transferred to Reggie though; but all is fine now. He has rung me to say the money is deposited in his U.K. account."

"That's good there is all sorts of rumours going around about the bank you used to transfer the money to him. Don't worry unduly about this place. I'm sure your sale will soon go through, Mrs. Sullais is being dogmatic, she will realise they are going to do as they want in the end, then hopefully she will start cooperating more, and it will all be resolved."

"I hope so; this is starting to get on top of me."

"Don't buckle; you have been strong up until now. Look what you have done here, they called your bluff and you have shown them you are not to be messed with. I admire you for that. We will get this sorted out soon Helen, and then you can get back home and see your family."

"Yes that is what I want, I have a granddaughter, who is two and a half and I haven't even seen her yet."

After reassuring me a bit more, Ousman left and I returned to the crossword puzzle I had started before his visit; on reflexion he was right, I had shown them I was not the meek woman they originally thought I was. However, if Ousman knew the uphill struggle I was having was getting my immigration papers sorted, he might not be so sympathetic. Sitting there in the garden I almost convinced myself that one day I would look back on this and see the amusing side of things. In all probability I was getting things out of proportion in my mind. Sidi had assured me he could sort my papers easily; it was simply unfortunate that I had lost faith in him. I was not stupid, I realised he was benefiting from the cash we were generating from the sale of our demolition work as well as I, but as long as he wasn't being too greedy I was prepared to accept that. The other lads were doing alright as well; but I had made enough from the sale to pay the staff's redundancies and pay my airfare home, which was my original intention. I knew the lads would be losing their income when I left so if they were making a bit on the side now, I wasn't really bothered, most people in the same situation would do the same thing.

The following morning Ousman phoned me. "Hi I didn't expect to hear from you so soon after your visit yesterday." I said as I answered hoping I wasn't about to hear some more bad news.

"What did I say to you yesterday, things will soon be sorted, if only Mrs. Sullais would get of her high horse and allow things to take their course?"

"Are you telling me the sale is going through?"

"Not exactly not yet anyway, but I thought you should know that the head accountant for the Hussaini group is arriving in Shendi tomorrow and will be sure to want to get this sale sorted out while he is here. I can't tell you anymore for now, but be prepared to hear officially very shortly."

"That's great, Ousman, I will get on with getting this place down with more vigour, we still have quite a bit of work to do."

Nick arrived as usual for his morning coffee shortly after my conversation with Ousman, I told him my news as we drank our coffee. "I can't tell you how relieved I am to hear that," I was surprised to hear him say, I hadn't realised he was so concerned, "there has been times when I thought you had messed up on this one, and they were going to pull the rug from under your feet. What will you do now, go back home?"

"I don't want to go back to the island; but back to the U.K. I will go to the island if I can't find work on the mainland, I need a job, and am confident I would get work there, I'm probably still remembered."

"I'll bet you are still remembered, I think you've made sure no-one here will forget you in a hurry." As we were talking the gate clanged loudly as it always did when anyone came in, we both looked in that direction; it was Sidi. "Watch that little bugger," Nick warned me, "he is likely to try and stitch you up when he knows you are getting away."

I knew this only too well, much better than Nick knew; but unfortunately deep down I realised his warning had come too late. Nick left shortly after Sidi arrived; I had noted Sidi had given him a look of disdain as he prepared to leave. "Nick spends an awful lot of time here," he remarked.

"Not near as much as when the bar was open." I replied in a sarcastic tone.

"Well why does he come here? He could get his coffee at lots of places, and he usually comes with his boys when they are collecting the things he is buying from you, why not just send the boys? I don't trust him."

"The feeling in mutual," I muttered under my breath.

"What did you say?"

"I said he comes here for his coffee because he is a Yorkshire man and they don't like spending their money." He gave me a strange look, not understanding what I meant.

"Let's get on there is lots of work to be done here, and I want you to go into Port Albert to-day." I said as I picked up the coffee cups to take to our makeshift roofless kitchen. While I was doing this I though, it was just as well the sale was about to be sorted. We still had one power point in the old kitchen for the fridge, which we needed for cold drinks in the increasing heat of summer. I knew that the power situation was a long way below safety standards and would be impossible to operate in the rains but for the moment it sufficed; but we couldn't carry on much longer like this.

"Port Albert? Why do you want me to go into Port Albert to-day?" Sidi asked, "I don't have the car with me, my brother is using it, he dropped me off."

"That's okay, I will give you transport money to go by bush taxi."

"What's so important it can't wait till I have the car?"

"I want you to go the immigration offices and get my papers sorted, I will need them soon."

I saw the anger flash across Sidi's eyes. "I'm sick to death of hearing about your bloody immigration papers. Half the ex-pats don't have their papers in order, and you don't hear them going on like you, you keep on and on. I have told you I will get them for you before you need them. What more do you want?" he shouted..

I knew I should keep calm but his arrogant attitude annoyed me and I shouted back "I want to have them so I know I can leave any time I want to, without them I'm stuck here." I saw Latif from the corner of my eye watching us, when he heard the raised voices.

"How can you leave you haven't even sold this place yet. So why are your darn papers so important to you, and besides I don't have to go into Port Albert to get them, you remember Mariama the immigration girl that came here looking for me a few weeks ago, she is going to sort them out for us, I was only speaking to her last night in the village about them. Stop panicking you will have your papers long before it is time for you to leave."

Ignoring Sidi, I went to help Latif take up the remaining tiles from my old bedroom floor. We were selling sacks of these broken tiles quicker than we could take them up. I hadn't realised that there would be such a high demand for them until we started selling them. I had always considered physical exertion therapeutic in times of stress, and I was definitely on an emotional roller coaster, I looked ahead to my unknown future through rose tinted glasses as I laboured away.

Sidi who has been working with the steel boys, since I had gone into the house to join Latif, came to me in the early afternoon and told me his brother had come back to fetch him, and he had to go to relieve his sister who was running the shop for him. "Okay I will see you tomorrow," I said and waited until he reached the doorway, then called after him, "don't forget to see Mariama this evening about my papers will you?"

He didn't answer me, but I saw the expression on Latif's face as I said this. He had been here when the immigration officers had come about my papers; he was aware what was happening. "Don't worry too much about those papers Helen; Sidi will sort them for you. You have been good to us; none of us will let you down."

I didn't answer; I just gave him a wry smile. Unfortunately I was not as confident of this as he was.

I had forgotten that the next day was Sunday when everyone took the day off, including Nick so I would not have his reassuring presence over an early morning cup of coffee. Nevertheless, I got up early and relieved the night security of his duties, then having made sure the place was securely locked again, I decided to go back to bed for a while. There was nothing for me to do that couldn't wait until the next day, I was going to make the most of my solitude and relax as much as my over active mind would allow.

But sleep eluded me, so I got up again and made my way via the old kitchen to the bathroom. The new entrance to the house which Latif had made did make life easier for me, but it still involved climbing over rubble. Shower over; I settled down in the garden to relax with coffee, puzzle book and paperback. I was all prepared for a lazy, solitary day with only my ever faithful cats for company. I still had the black cat which we had inherited along with the property. Local myth – or that version believed by the expats - had it that when the black cat died so would The Dominion. She was old and arthritic, but undoubtedly was in a much healthier state than The Dominion. My faithful larger than life grey and black tiger striped tabby, was the dominant tom in the area, but in spite of this was always willing to sit on my lap and listen without judgement to all my problems. His sister was always around, but she was not so eager to be fussed, and was happy as long as she was fed regularly. My cats were the only company I craved that day.

By lunchtime I was feeling completely relaxed, so relaxed in fact that I decided I would benefit from an afternoon nap in the fresh air. To that end I fetched a small blanket from my little home to spread on the sand under my favourite mango tree which looked set to supply me with a bumper crop in the not too distant future. Despite my troubles, which were never too far from my mind, at that moment I felt I was in paradise. Quickly I dropped off into a peaceful undisturbed sleep, for probably a couple of hours and woke feeling groggy and disorientated from my unaccustomed daytime sleep. I was extremely thirsty; I hadn't had anything to drink since my morning coffee.

I stood up and made my way unsteadily towards the old kitchen to get a drink of cold water from the fridge. My feeling of contentment began to disappear. As I made my way through the foundations and rubble of what had once been the bar, I started to feel uneasy, as if someone was watching me. I twisted my head over my shoulder, there was no-one. A few careful steps later I heard a slight noise, stopped and turned round again. There was no-one there. Slowly I continued navigating the rubble and tried to tell myself it was all a result of my imagination. That would teach me to sleep in the middle of the day. The place was securely locked, so I knew nobody could get in. I was being stupid. Any noises were the cats plotting a safe course through the maze of stone and steel that had been their home.

Once in the kitchen I stopped again. I still felt as if someone was watching me. Should I call out? No, that was being ridiculous. I made my way to the fridge, took out a plastic bottle of water and raised it to my mouth to drink. Just as I was about to take a sip of the very welcome cold water I gasped and let out a whispered scream. There was a large figure standing on the rubble that had once been my office watching me. The sun was in my eyes, I couldn't see properly. All I could make out was a dark shape between me and the garden. "Who's there?" I called but there was no reply. I shuddered and in my fear dropped the plastic bottle. Brittle from overuse, it shattered as it hit the ground, spraying water over the debris that cluttered the area. "Who are you?" My voice shook; I was feeling totally vulnerable both mentally and physically. There was still no reply and the figure moved over the rubble towards me whilst my shuddering transformed itself into violent shaking. I cupped my hands around my eyes in an effort to improve my vision. It was Sidi.

"Sidi! What the hell are you doing here? How did you get in? The gate is locked." I yelled as adrenaline rushed through my body.

"Easy, easy," he shouted back, his decibel level easily equalling mine, "look at all the mess you are making. What is the matter with you?"

Still shaking uncontrollably, I stuttered, "What is the matter with ME? It is you that has something the matter with them. How did you get in? You frightened me to death, look at me shaking. I thought I was alone and you come climbing over the rubble, I couldn't see you properly."

"You are crazy. Who did you think it was?"

"I had no idea who it was. What are you doing here, and how did you get in? Have you a key to the gates?"

"Hey, calm down. You know you haven't given me a key. I climbed over the wall. Why are you carrying on like this? I only came to see if you are okay."

"Well you can see I'm fine, so you can go now." I snapped at him, still badly shaken.

"Helen, before I go, answer one question. Have you eaten today?"

"Not yet." In truth food hadn't even crossed my mind; it very seldom had since I had closed the business. Viv had remarked to me over coffee the previous day that I was looking too thin. I was only eating one meal a day, I was having lunch with my demolition crew, except when I had biscuits at the coffee shop, so I suppose it was inevitable I would lose weight, without scales or a full length mirror, I hadn't noticed.

"That's as I thought, I've bought you some food from the compound, you need to eat, and it is no wonder you are getting so thin. You have to keep your strength up. It was then I noticed that he was carrying a bowl wrapped in a checked cloth.

I climbed back over the rubble, still feeling very tense, and sat down at the table beside Sidi who made a production of unwrapping the brightly pattered enamel bowl containing some local delicacy. Any hunger I may have had evaporated as I glanced at the contents of the bowl.

"Leave it here, I will eat it later." I told him.

He started eating and encouraged me to join him. I was still extremely upset and could not have faced any food, let alone the food he had bought me. I was becoming very confused after all that had happened in the recent weeks. Sidi had arrived here in a way he knew would probably frighten me, but had bought me food because he is concerned about me. None of this was making sense to me.

"Why didn't you rattle the gate, you know I would come and let you in."

"I tell you, you are crazy; I thought you would be sleeping, I didn't want to disturb you. Why do you over react at everything? I came to bring you food and you are like this to me, what is the matter with you?"

"If you want to help me, you sort my papers for me. That is all I want from you." Sidi noisily banged the spoon he was eating with down on the table. He stood up, and started walking away. Keeping his back to me he angrily said, "I'm going I'm not staying here listening to you going on and on about your fucking papers. I keep telling you they are not important now until you are ready to leave, and that isn't yet." His voice trailed off, as he walked farther away, I'm not even sure what he was saying as he reached the gate, but I soon heard him as he turned and yelled at me, "How do you think I can get out if you don't come and unlock this bloody gate for me, you know you are the only one with a key."

I got up to unlock to the gate for him, as I walked towards the entrance I wondered how he had got in. Did he have a key and was ensuring I didn't realise this, or had he really climbed over the wall. The wall had broken glass on top, and except in a couple of places it was too high to scale without assistance; but if he had got in without a key, so could anyone else get in.

"If you climbed over the wall to get in, why don't you leave the same way?" I snapped as I put the key in the padlock.

"Huh, I've always been told taubab women are crazy, but you must be the worst of them, you are completely mad."

He left without another word, and I clicked the padlock securely again. I walked slowly around the perimeter wall. If he had come over the wall I couldn't see where he had got in, even at its lowest point it had sharp jagged glass on top making it no easy feat. This whole episode had done nothing to improve my ever increasing nervous disposition. The fright I had got when I first saw Sidi had shaken me rigid, as he was well aware. He knew what effect creeping up on me would have. This bought on real fears that I was very vulnerable. If it was possible to get over the wall, or alternatively if he had a key to get in the main gate; he or anyone he gave the key to could have access to the property at any time. Still shaking I sat back down in the garden feeling very insecure.

Later that night, lying on my makeshift bed I still felt uneasy. The arrival of my night security had done nothing to calm my fears; in fact it had made it worse as the one on duty tonight was Sidi's cousin. I tried reading but could not concentrate, the book could have been written in Chinese for all the sense that it made and the loud African drums from La Parisian over the wall simply served to emphasise my loneliness and the thousands of miles between Shendi and the UK. I turned off the light and tried to sleep. I turned one way, then another and back again. I pulled a pillow over my head to drown out the noise of the drums but it was no good. I turned on the light and tried reading again but the words swam in front of my eyes. Putting the book down, I turned off the light and something splashed onto my hand. Tears were streaming down my face and I had not realised. I lay there with only my tears for company until long after the music next door had finished; I don't recall drifting off to sleep, but the next thing I knew, the birds were singing and the early morning sunshine was creeping in through the gaps in the cloth I had draped over the windows as curtains. Perhaps the episode with Sidi had done me good in a strange way. Like the proverbial straw on the camel's back it had been one thing too much. The night time tears had served as some kind of release - I hoped. Life would seem better in the light of day.

Nick recognised I was suffering with my nerves, when he came for his morning coffee and asked if anything had happened to make me jumpy. I was still reluctant to say too much to Nick, it wasn't fair to burden him with my problems, when I was fully aware he had more than enough of his own. "No, all is fine," I lied to him, "this sale is being dragged out much too long, and with all the demolition work, and living in the little house, it is all starting to get me down."

"I've told you, you can come and stay at my place, but you won't."

"Don't forget Ousman has told me not to leave the compound."

"Okay I had forgotten that, but something has got to happen soon, you can't go on living like this. I can see it is getting you down now; you have stood your ground and shown them you are no push over, but there is a limit to how far you can go, and if I have noticed things are getting you down, it must be quite bad."

I grinned, "I agree if you notice it must blatantly obvious, hopefully this will all be over soon."

I tried to make light of things to Nick, but as usual my heart sank as he left. I knew I may not see or speak to another taubab for the rest of the day. Sidi was right I was gradually going insane, the pressures I was under were proving too much for me; never in my life had I endured such stress as I was under now. I went about my day fairly calmly, pottering about helping Latif and Petreeni wherever I could. Tina had cooked us all lunch as usual and I was pleasantly surprised by how much I ate. The depth of my depression of the previous evening, had frightened me, and I realised that I needed to have the determination to see this through to the bitter end. I was a fighter. I would leave this country with my head held high; I would not allow anybody or anything to get the better of me. With a nod of agreement to my internal self, I reached for some more lunch.

Sidi had phoned quite early in the day to tell me he was expecting a big delivery at his shop, so may not come down at all if he did it would be late. This actually added to my calmer mood, it was he after all that had caused my distress the day before. I was in a fairly relaxed state, when my staff and the remaining few steel boys went home. Their work was nearly finished by now and only three of them were coming in each day. At the start of the demolition when there had been so many of them their continual shouting and whistling coupled with the noise of demolition had made me feel as if I was living in a chaotic spin dryer. Now it was quieter and the reduction in people and noise helped my calmer mood on that Monday. I felt I had turned a corner, I was regaining my composure. I sat in the garden as had become my habit after everyone had left, every now and then I looked around, half expecting Sidi to come climbing over the rubble again, but if he did, I grinned, he would not catch me off guard this time.

My mobile rang, I assumed it was possibly Sidi as he hadn't come down; I looked at the screen and saw it was Ousman. Hoping this was good news and not a further set back. My composure was still fragile and I answered with trepidation.

"Hi Helen, I have some news you will be relieved to hear." My heart skipped a beat; I had been so sure he was going to tell me something that would reverse the positive thoughts I had had all day. "You remember I told you the head accountant from The Hussaini Group would be here for a short time only. Well, good news, he has decided your sale has to be concluded while he is here. He is only here from two more days and wants everything to be completed tomorrow; but he wants a meeting with us at the hotel this evening, is that okay with you?"

"That is absolutely brilliant," I yelled into the phone in my excitement, "I wasn't doing anything this evening," I said almost sarcastically, "but it is also an impossibility to conclude the sale so quickly, there is so much paperwork to do, and so many offices to visit to sort it all out."

Ousman interrupted me there. "You are right it generally takes a few weeks to sort everything, but that is not going to be the case with this time. Forget about all the offices to visit, just remember who we are dealing with. I assure you, if this is what they want, all the doors in these offices will be opened, there will be no problem concluding this in a day. But after the meeting make sure you get an early night, this time tomorrow you will be exhausted. Do you know where the Lands Office is?"

"Yes, on the outskirts of Port Albert, near the hospital."

"Good that is where we will need to start so I will meet you there, but in the meantime I will see you at seven this evening for this meeting they want. Then I will need to know how you want the money paid, they are asking do you want it in Shendian shillings or U.S. dollars? As the property is in Simon's name, by law it should be paid into his bank account, I hope you have sorted out your financial affairs with him, or do you want me to try and make any other arrangements?"

"In dollars, if not we could be losing money having it exchanged twice, and it is pointless having it in shillings; but what arrangements are we going to make about your fee, I don't have enough cash here to pay you."

"That's fine, I will arrange for them to pay me my fee, and all the taxes that will be due from the sale, so I can finalise everything, and the remainder will be sent to Simon, is that okay with you?"

"Yeah, fine, I don't have Simon's bank account number, I will text him straight away to get it, but I don't understand what this meeting is about this evening, I'm confused by it."

"I feel the same, everything has been agreed, but I wouldn't be surprised if Mrs. Sullais has something up her sleeve again."

"We will soon find out, I will see you this evening."

I cradled my mobile to my chest when I finished the call; I was elated. The light at the end of the tunnel had come back into view. A vision of my Kevin and Steph and Little Karen flashed in front of me, I was going to see them, and I couldn't believe all my dreams would soon become a reality. I got up and still cradling my mobile I danced around in a circle, I had not felt this good in a long, long time while. I sat down again, telling myself off. Was I really feeling better from the deep depression of yesterday or was this terrific mood swing just another symptom, I must calm myself down.

I stared at my mobile as if it was a foreign object and even had to give it my full attention to remember how to text, I wasn't as well as I thought I was. Carefully and with many false starts I sent a text to Simon to ask for his bank details to arrange for the money to be sent to him. As I cleared the screen and started for the fourth or fifth time I realised that if I wasn't functioning too well at least I knew I wasn't. Finally the text was done and sent and I retired to my little house to rest until it was time to get ready to go to my meeting next door.

Chapter Twenty-Five

Meetings Galore

I rose again in plenty of time to prepare for the evening, I was slightly confused about this meeting what was it all about? If the sale was to go ahead the following day, why were we all gathering at the hotel this evening? With these thoughts swimming around in my head I took my only remaining smart dress out of my suitcase. I had packed the clothes I hadn't expected to wear again while I was in Shendi when I moved into the small house. There was nowhere in my new home to hang anything, so my case seemed the most logical place to store my belongings; in fact all my possessions were either in my case or, securely packed in a large sturdy cardboard box, which I would send as freight to the U.K. This was a vast difference to the twenty foot container, Simon and I had bought out to Shendi eight years earlier.

In spite of only having a small hand held mirror, so I could only see if my face and hair looked alright, I felt good when I was dressed for the meeting. I was wearing the same navy blue shift dress with a deep swirling red pattern around the bottom that I had worn for my first meeting with Ali, which seemed an eon away now. The general feeling of well being this dress gave me, filled me with confidence. When I was satisfied I was looking my best, I left the building clutching the small torch I needed to light my way across the sand pit that was once the beer garden, and negotiate my way over the small precarious plank of wood Nick had placed over the pond. The once proud bridge had been sold to a couple who had had their wedding reception at The Dominion and wanted it to put in the garden of the house they were building. Nick hadn't minded me selling the bridge but objected when he saw me jumping over the pond – hence the plank of wood. Once over the pond, the torch was no longer needed as light from La Parisian and the car park supplied light to that part of my premises.

"Are you going out?" my security asked as I approached their hut.

"Yes but I don't expect I will be very long." I had no intention of telling him where I was going or what I was doing, so to avoid further conversation, I went outside the gate to wait for Ousman in the car park.

I walked slowly down the car park towards the arch and away from my gate so that I would see Ousman as soon as he arrived. I jumped slightly as my mobile started to ring; I fumbled in my handbag searching for my phone feeling the usual flutter of nerves which was common now whenever it rang. I assumed this was going to be Ousman, to either tell me he had been delayed or was unable to come at all. I had always found Ousman's blatant disregard of time unacceptable and it had been an annoyance to me over the years. I knew that Shendians in general were bad time keepers but Ousman was a lawyer of high standing and should know better. If he was going to be late, I was going to tell him how I felt. However, just as I was working myself up to give Ousman my opinion, I looked at the number. It was not Ousman, but Sidi.

"Where are you going?" he demanded without any form of greeting, not even a simple "Hi"

"What?" I retorted using much more aggression than he had. I was angry. The only possible way he could have known that I was going anywhere was if my security had phoned him to report my movements. To say I was annoyed that my every move was being relayed to him was an understatement. I had long suspected this, but to have my suspicions confirmed not only angered me, but added to my general uneasiness. In addition there was the speed of his reaction. It could not have been longer than five minutes since I had left The Dominion and here he was ringing me to find out what I was doing. Were my few remaining staff, working for me or for Sidi? And to what ends? Suddenly I felt a sharp pain in my chest, like an iron bar was being clamped around me. Was this pain real or once again my nerves were getting the better of me?

"I said where are you going? Don't get angry with me, I'm only trying to take care of you. You know Ousman has told you not to go out. What do you think you are doing, and why are you dressed up?" His voice was more controlled than before, but his anger was still apparent.

"Don't fret I will be fine, I'm going with Ousman so there is no problem." So he knew I was dressed up. There was no doubt the staff were keeping their eyes on me.

"But where are you going?"

At that moment Ousman pulled under the arch in his very smart, gleaming black 4x4 estate car. "I must go now, Ousman is here." I said as I ended the conversation without giving Sidi the opportunity to answer and turned off my phone.

Ousman pulled up near to where I was standing and got out. I was slightly aghast to see what he was wearing. He had expressed the importance of this evening, and I had dressed as I considered fitting for a meeting in a five star hotel, yet here was he in jeans and a tee shirt and most amazing of all rubber flip-flops.

"Looking very smart this evening Helen," he said as he came towards me with his hand outstretched.

I shook his hand and said, "Yes, I thought it best to make an effort," this remark appeared to go over his head, or maybe he simply choose to ignore it. We strolled together down the slight slope of the car park and past La Parisian to the entrance of the hotel. All the while I was conscious of my security watching closely to check on our movements. Out of the corner of my eye I could see that one of them was on his phone. It was a sure bet that Sidi was on the other end. Inside the night club the group were busy warming up for the evening's entertainment and some of their waiters called out to me. They, too, seemed to be watching us closely. I knew many of their staff were watching my demolition work with interest and I suppose that Ousman and I entering the hotel was simply looked on as an extension of this. Sidi could not have every local on his "Watch Mrs Dominion payroll" or could he? The closer we got to the main reception area, the more crowded the driveway became, it was early evening and the hotel guests were on their way to their evening meals.

We entered the reception, I knew some of the tourists in there but I didn't really feel like engaging in conversation with them. Nevertheless, I put on a brave smile and forced myself. My problems were not their fault and they were on their holidays. I was glad that I did so, for as I stood talking to a group of them I spotted Ali and Abdul out of the corner of my eye, emerging from the office area behind the reception. At least I was doing something, not simply hanging around waiting for them. They were greeted by another man I didn't think I had seen before. Ousman stood a slight distance from me, watching both me and Ali's party. It became obvious Ali was looking for me, and Ousman signalled to me, that I was needed. I took my leave of my friends and ex-customers, and made my way over to Ousman's side.

Ali and his colleagues joined us, and he offered us refreshment, I asked for a coffee and Ousman said he would like a fruit juice. Once Ali had ordered these and drinks for the three of them from one of their receptionists, he ushered us over to a seating area in the vast reception. This was in a far corner and the probability of our conversation being over heard was possibly fairly remote. All the same I didn't really feel very comfortable discussing my private business in a public area; to my mind the meeting should have been in an office as all the early discussions had been. We all sat down and it seemed to me to a prearranged formula. Ali came and sat next to me on a generously sized, leather two seater settee; I had expected Ousman, as my ally, to sit with me for support. Ousman found himself alone on another two seater settee, fortunately at right angles to us, so he was close enough for me to feel his support. Abdul and the other man sat on a larger settee opposite to Ali and myself, there was also a leather armchair that was so far unoccupied. Ali introduced his companion as Mr. Janni Giano, a lawyer and accountant for the Hussaini group who was visiting Shendi. I was wondering who the empty chair was for, if anyone, when Ali told us they wanted to wait for a Shendian gentleman to arrive before commencing our business. Just then the waitress appeared and served us our drinks and placed a small platter of nibbles on the central large oval glass table.

"Is Mrs. Sullais not coming?" I asked turning to Ali.

"No, we don't need her here, we are just having a small social gathering to iron out a few small problems we seem to be having." Then he added for my ears only, "You and I should have been left to sort this matter out, we were handling things better than the lawyers seem to be."

I nodded in agreement although I wasn't really sure what he was alluding to. I looked from one to the other of The Peace Haven's representatives. When the other member of their party arrived we would be out numbered two to one, they were all dressed in smart trousers, expensive looking shirts probably silk, with contrasting ties and shiny black shoes. I was dressed in the best I could muster, but my lawyer was looking as if he had just come from a day on the beach. I almost wished I had come alone, Ousman was adding to my discomfort, and then I winced in horror. I had glanced over to Ousman hoping to receive a reassuring look from him, but instead I was absolutely horrified to see him with one of his flip-flopped feet dangling over the arm of the leather settee, and to add insult to injury he was picking at one of his toe nails with his fingers. We made eye contact, and I just looked away. I was completely humiliated, this was my lawyer, how dare he behave like this. This all seemed surreal; once again I had that old feeling of being on a film set.

An elderly Shendian gentleman came into the reception, on seeing him, Ali rose and walked towards him, I saw them greet each other with genuine warmth and make their way to where we were all sat. Abdul and Janni both stood up to greet their guest, I glanced back towards Ousman, I could see the recognition on his face as he saw this distinguished looking gentleman, and he also stood. This man, whom I also seemed to recognise, certainly commanded respect. He was immaculately dressed in lime green satin African Muslim robes, with extensive darker green embroidery around the neck and down the front, his outfit was complemented by a matching lime green, also highly embroidered Muslim hat, he made a complete contrast to Ousman. I almost felt embarrassed for Ousman but then I decided it was his fault if he was out dressed and no concern of mine.

When Ali and the Shendian gentleman reached where we were sat, he hugged Abdul and Janni like old friends and shook hands with Ousman. He explained to Ali that Ousman knew him so there was no need for introductions. Seeing the respect this gentleman was receiving from everyone, I stood as I was introduced to him. He took my out stretched hand in both of his, and shook it warmly; my previous discomfort seemed to evaporate by his genuine show affection as he said to me. "We have been introduced before, Madam Helen. I have been to The Dominion with friends, a considerable time ago now, but I have kept a close eye on things from a distance. I know you have had many problems here, and mostly they have not been your fault. We must sit down here this evening and get this sale sorted, I hope you agree. Do you remember me?"

"As soon as I saw you I knew I had met you before, but I'm sorry I can't put a name to you."

Ousman came to my rescue, "Helen, this is Mr. Fattie, and he is a very well respected lawyer. I have known him for a long while but I didn't know that he had been to The Dominion and that he would recognise you."

Mr Fattie was obviously royalty as far as everyone was concerned for we were still standing. Only when he sat in the empty chair did we all sit down. As we settled ourselves, Mr Fattie leant over and spoke to me, "Well I'm a retired lawyer now, but I do have a very keen interest in the law courts, and keep abreast of what is happening in my country. These men," he said as he glanced from Ali to his companions that were sat on the other side of him, "are very dear friends of mine, and they have asked me here this evening help sort any differences you have with them. I know you to be a fair woman Helen, so let's iron out these things once and for all."

"I have no differences with them, I'm eager to complete this sale, in fact possibly even more so than they are." I told him.

We all seemed to settle back in our seats. Ali gently touched my arm and said quietly to me, "Let the lawyers talk, if you are not happy with anything they say, we will speak about it afterwards. Didn't you and I cope fine with the negotiations when we were on our own?" He was repeating what he had stated earlier, I was starting to feel more comfortable, but was this new found comfort justified or was Ali trying, albeit successfully; to give me a false sense of security. I admit I was bewildered, but I was hopeful, that at long last we were getting nearer to the completion of the sale; and this was all I cared about

at that time. Janni Giano started the meeting by addressing Ousman in a fairly argumentative manner, "I am only in Shendi for a few more days, I need to know once and for all if this sale is going to be finalised. I don't get the impression you and your client are very serious about this and I can't afford to waste any more time on this matter."

I was dumbfounded, what was he talking about? I gave Ousman no chance to answer. I was incensed by this remark, "How can you say this? I have closed my business and am demolishing the buildings that you have no intention of purchasing, how can you possibly say I'm not serious about the sale?"

Ali again spoke to me gently, "Let the lawyers thrash this out Helen, there is obviously some confusion."

Speaking just to Ali, I replied, "I don't understand what this is about. You came to The Dominion last week; you must know I'm serious about this sale. Why would I knock it down otherwise?"

"Yes, I know, but I think there is some conflict of interest between our two lawyers."

"Where is Mrs. Sullais?" I asked, "shouldn't she be here also, if we are to solve the problem." The picture was becoming clearer to me now. Had I been mistaken when I had considered the possibility of Ousman and Mrs. Sullais being in league together, and possibly both working against me? Or was I being misled again, and Mr. Fattie had been asked here to intimidate Ousman to maybe determine the truth of the matter.

While I was speaking to Ali, a slight argument had begun between Janni Giano and Ousman. Not hearing the start of the conversation, I was not sure what it was about, but Ousman was telling him he was only here to fight for my interests and to make sure I was not losing out on the finer details of the sale. They were both beginning to get loud and Abdul intervened, "This is getting us no-where, we are not here to point score over the past. We simply want to know what the next move is going to be. Mr. Giano is a very busy man and has more business to deal with while he is here than just this sale." He turned to me and he spoke in much softer tone, "Helen, we need to know, right now, do you intend to proceed with the sale or not."

"Definitely, you knew that was my intention from the start."

Looking towards Ousman, Abdul continued, "Can we assume then that there will be no more hold ups, no more petty arguing over wording of agreements, just a straight forward sale as was originally agreed with Helen." I looked daggers at Ousman, I knew it was he that had contested the wording of the conditions of sale, but surely it was Mrs. Sullais that had caused the bulk of the delays over the past few weeks. This whole meeting was confusing me. Ousman simply nodded. Abdul turned to me again, "Have you considered the payment of the proceeds Helen?"

"What are the options?" I asked, feeling slightly foolish. This was something I should have established earlier, but I had received little advice from Ousman – another point against him.

"As you know we are dealing in U.S. dollars, we can have it paid directly from our bank account in Saudi to your husband's account in the U.K. which would probably be the easiest for all concerned. If you wish to be paid in Shendian Shillings that can be arranged, but I wouldn't advise that if you are planning to leave the country. It would mean two money exchanges and you would probably be losing money on each exchange."

I looked straight at Ousman, and said quietly, "I don't have enough cash in Shendi to pay the capital gains tax, and there is your fee to pay. However, I think it is best the bulk of the money is paid out of the country, which is basically what you and I spoke about earlier."

Ousman didn't answer me, he spoke directly to Abdul and said, "Most of the money should be paid into Simon, Helen's husband's, account in the U.K. but some of the proceeds will be needed here, there will be taxes to be paid." Mr. Fattie, who had not spoken since the introductions maintained his silence, simply nodded. Mr. Giano acknowledged our agreement to proceed with the sale and outlined the schedule for the next day, when they hoped to complete the sale. I once again expressed my doubt that it could be completed in one day. "That is where I come in," Mr. Fattie said, "I will also come along tomorrow, to ensure you don't encounter any problems to hinder your business."

We all shook hands and agreed to meet up the following day at The Lands Office. After what had seemed an endless uphill battle it seemed we were finally starting the sale of The Dominion. I left the hotel with Ousman in silence, I was still bewildered as to where his allegiance actually lay, and deep down I still had very mixed feelings over The Dominion. An unexplainable guilt over its demise still hung over me but I was also feeling elated; now at least I was moving forward. I knew tomorrow would be very tedious and frustrating, but by tomorrow evening hopefully a huge step towards securing my future would have been taken. I bid Ousman good night when we reached his car and reaffirmed the arrangements for the next morning. As he got in, he turned and said, "Remember to bring me Simon's bank details, so I can make the arrangements for the transfer of the cash. There will be a lot of travelling around in Port Albert, and I will have to go to court for a short while in the morning, so can you bring your own transport?"

"Yes, I will do that." Ousman was aware Sidi usually drove me to court, and if Ousman had to leave me for awhile I would need a bit of moral support and didn't really have anyone else I could ask to accompany me. However, I would not allow Sidi into any of the offices with me; I did not want him to know how much money was changing hands.

As I approached my main gate I could see my security sat in the shadows of some of the few remaining bushes near to the old bar. It was dark and I couldn't see them clearly but there seemed to be three of them, sat on the old drink crates which were they often used as low stools. My security habitually shared attya with the security from the Mango Tree, a practice I had encouraged while the bar was open so I was unconcerned when I saw he had company. "Good evening lads." I said as I walked passed without even bothering to look any closer, to establish who his companions were. They all waved me a greeting and without stopping to engage in conversation, I made my way over the very rickety makeshift bridge to retire into my little house for the night, hoping for a good sleep to give me the energy I would need for the busy day ahead.

I had only taken a few steps onto the sand, when I heard the unmistakable creaking of the wooden plank, a few paces behind me. I swung around in fright, with only my small torch for light; I shone this into the intruder's face. It was Sidi.

"Take that darn thing out of my eyes. Are you trying to blind me?" he yelled "Don't creep up on me like that, how do you expect me to know who it is? After Sunday you know I don't like being surprised. Why did you not speak to me? I didn't expect to see you here at this time, but you have saved me a phone call. I need you to take me into Port Albert tomorrow."

"Forget tomorrow, what about tonight? Why have you been to the hotel, with Ousman? I keep telling you don't trust these people, and that includes Ousman, they are all trying to double cross you."

"Leave it out Sidi, I have enough to cope with at the moment, I don't need you playing your mind games with me, just leave me alone now, and come back in the morning. Early, I want you here before eight."

"Sit down a minute," he told me insistently, as he pulled out one of the chairs by the garden table and pointed to it. He then pulled out a seat opposite and sat down, looking up at me. I could feel my temper rising inside, I didn't need this on top of the confusion I still felt after the meeting I had just had at The Peace Haven. "I need to know what is going on, how can I help you if I don't even know what is happening?"

"Nothing is going on, you don't know about." I spoke to him as calmly as I could, but even I could detect the slight tremor in my voice, "I have had a final meeting with the hotel's people, tomorrow we are all going to the offices in Port Albert to finalise everything."

"You know that can't all be done in one day."

"They are going to sort it all, you know they have a lot of influence, everything will be done tomorrow."

Speaking in much gentler tones than he had spoken to me for a long while he said "It is good you are taking me, as I said they will try and double cross you. You will need advice, when they see a Shendian with you they will be more careful what they are doing. Is Ousman going to be with us?"

"Of course he will." I had no intention of either telling him Ousman would be going off to court, or that I was using him as a driver only, tomorrow was quite soon enough for him to realise this.

"Will you get the money tomorrow?" I knew this was the question Sidi was more than eager to have answered.

"Payment will go ahead on completion, yes."

"Do you mean you will have the money tomorrow or not?"

"On completion it will be transferred from their bank in Saudi, it will take a few days to arrive." I found it unnecessary to tell Sidi the money was being transferred to Simon's account not mine.

"Fine, fine, I will be here early."

"Make sure of that or I will get a taxi, no problem. Now I want to go to bed."

"Don't go in a taxi, you know what these taxi boys are like, I don't trust them."

I gave a little grin to myself, Sidi didn't trust anyone, yet he was possibly the least trustworthy of all; that is probably where his distrust of everyone else stemmed from. I retired to my little house, but sleep once again eluded me. I tossed and turned eager to have peace of mind and get sufficient rest to face the day that was to follow. I knew Sidi was still hoping to get a good pay out, and my mind drifted from unease to sheer panic as my immigration papers came to mind again. Tomorrow was going to be a big step forward, but there was still a long way to go before I eventually left Shendi to start my new life. I wondered at what point Sidi would realise the money wasn't even coming to Shendi. All these thoughts drifted around and around in my mind. I was reaching a stage that I hated the thought of night time, everything seemed exaggerated in darkness, and I felt so very alone.

I was up early the next morning, and, as I knew it would, everything seemed much better in the light of day. This was going to be a tough day, but it was also going to be the first day of the rest of my life, and I had a spring in my step as I got ready for the trip to Port Albert. I even found myself singing in the shower, I hadn't sung for many years; it was a sure sign I was in good spirits. Sidi arrived early as promised; I had known that he wouldn't miss this for the world. We even had time to sit and have a coffee before it was time to leave. Our conversation was light, he was also in a good mood; I wondered if he would be at the end of the day. However, I was not going to worry about it now. I had more than enough on my mind; Sidi's possible reaction to the deal would be dealt with later.

When we went outside to leave, I was bewildered to see an extremely old, battered twelve seater van, which had once been white, but with so much paint stripped from it over the years, and what looked like several years of dust and grime on it, parked on the slabs at the entrance, with a driver sat in it. Sidi gestured to him with his hands as we neared the vehicle. The driver jumped out and opened the back door for me to get in. "What's this?" I said to Sidi feeling peeved when I saw my transport, "where is your car?"

"I'm having work done on it, this is my brother, he is driving us to-day," then remembering I always liked to have relationships explained to me, so I knew exactly who everyone was he added, "my cousin brother, also a compound brother, you can trust him." Yes, I thought, I'm told all Sidi's family I can trust but no-one else.

"This isn't a family outing, we have important business to-day," I retorted.

"Just get in." Sidi's tone was no longer the calm one from the garden but the much more vehement one of our recent exchanges. I realised that he too had a great deal riding on this deal and that both of us were on edge. I would have to remember this in my dealings with him today. I climbed in and said nothing on the journey in spite of Sidi attempting to involve me in their conversation. I still had a bit of pride left and didn't want the Peace Haven delegates to see me arriving in this vehicle. I felt as let down by this as I had by Ousman's appearance and behaviour the previous evening at the hotel.

When we reached The Lands Office, I saw Mr. Tascali, and Abdul in a plush, gleaming red vehicle with the hotel's emblem on the side and the unmistakable Hussaini number plates. In the back sat Janni and Mr. Fattie. I felt inferior as I saw their eyes following our vehicle as we pulled into the car park. My eyes scanned the car park; there was no sign of Ousman. If he let me down on this occasion, we would be having a serious discussion before I paid his fee for this transaction; I needed his support more than ever that day.

My fears were unfounded, when, within a couple of minutes of our arrival, Ousman's gleaming 4x4 came speeding into the car park. On seeing him, Abdul, who had been driving the hotel's vehicle alighted from their car, and followed by the others, went over to greet Ousman. Janni helped Mr. Fattie out of the car, he was quite old, I couldn't be sure of his age, but he was getting feeble. I opened the door of the mini bus, and due to the height of the vehicle, literally jumped out. I started to make my way towards where the others were stood and heard Sidi get out and start to follow me.

"I'm okay," I told him quite sternly,"Ousman is with me, I will be fine."

"But I thought you wanted me with you."

"I asked you be come into Port Albert with me; I didn't mention you accompanying me into the offices. You know I'm fine with Ousman. He is my lawyer."

Sidi gave a loud audible sigh, I saw Ousman look our way, and I think he heard this, "I have warned you about these people, you be very careful."

Without turning back towards him, I said, "Fine, fine, you have mentioned that before." I knew Sidi had got back into the mini bus, as I heard the door slam. Ousman remarked to me, "He knows things are coming to an end, be careful he will try and get all he can from you." I simply nodded, what could I say, but I was quite amused how everyone was full of good advice as to whom I should or should not trust, it seemed to me it was no-one.

We went from office to office signing papers, and spending what seemed like endless hours waiting to be seen in each office. Every room we went in seemed to be hotter than the previous one. Ousman went off to court, mid-morning as he had told me he would have to; before he left me he asked, "Shall I get Sidi to come in with you or are you alright?"

"I'm fine, fine." I reassured him.

Abdul had overheard this conversation and told Ousman, "Don't worry, I won't let anything happen to Helen, and Mr. Fattie is looking after her interests as well as ours." In spite of everyone's advice on the trust worthy front, and Abdul being a member of the opposition, I think I probably trusted him as much as anyone at that moment in time. Besides Ousman had no need to have worried, when he returned from court we were still sat there, in the same seats in the same outer office as he had left us, two hours before.

By five in the evening we had only one office left to visit, and had been told on our arrival that we had two choices. Either to wait for an hour or come back the next morning and so we adjourned to the courtyard outside where we had parked the vehicles to wait. It was much cooler there, we were all showing signs of fatigue, it had been a long tiring day and the intense Port Albert heat was taking its toll. Mr. Fattie's assistance had been invaluable, without him we would have waited even longer to be seen and our business definitely would have taken several days to complete. Even though I was exhausted I was grateful to see the sale completed at such speed after all the worry of the possibility of it not going ahead, and Ousman's concern of them trying to take possession illegally. Relief was undoubtedly mixed with my exhaustion, but this did nothing to relieve my tiredness.

Seeing us all gathered outside, a seat having been provided for Mr. Fattie, the rest of sat on a low wall, near the vehicles, Sidi got out of the mini bus, and sat himself next to me. He said nothing. I assumed he had come to listen to what was being said. In the midst of some general light conversation Ousman came over to me and asked," You have bought me Simon's bank details haven't you?"

Opening my handbag and taking out the paper I had written the details on for Ousman, I said, "Yes, here they are." I would have rather he hadn't asked me for this in front of Sidi especially after his warning earlier in the day, but once said it was too late, so I didn't see any harm in continuing the conversation, "When will the transfer be made?"

"It will be too late by the time we are finished here, for them to do it today, but I would assume it will be done first thing in the morning. I will be very disappointed after all their insistence of this all happening so quickly if they delay with the payment. I will find all this out before we leave here today."

I saw Ousman go over and speak to Abdul, and soon afterwards Abdul came over to me, "Don't concern yourself about the money Helen, I will be putting the transfer through myself, I will do it first thing in the morning. I have your mobile number. I will text you as soon as I have done it and I will give you the transfer reference number so you can forward it on to your husband, is that okay with you."

"Yes, that's fine" and almost forgetting Sidi was there I asked, "now the papers have all been signed and once the money has been transferred, The Dominion will legally belong to you, but I still have to sort a few things out. I still have personal possessions on the property, and I have to get a flight, when do I have to leave the property?"

"After everything we have been through together, we don't want to be unreasonable, but at the same time, we want to be getting on with our expansion plans. It is the 13th today if we say we want you off the property by the end of the month, would you say that is reasonable?"

"Yes, that is fine." I replied, aware again of Sidi's presence as I saw him glare at me. Abdul stayed and chatted to me for awhile longer trying to bring Sidi into the conversation. Sidi in turn made it very obvious he had no intention in engaging in small talk with Abdul. I assumed having heard our conversation he had other things on his mind. I felt for once I had the upper hand. We were called into the last office to receive the President's approval to the sale and the final piece of paper was signed. After all the delays and discussions, suddenly with one simple signature, The Dominion was no longer mine. It wasn't until I was walking out of the door that I realised that one episode of my life had really come to an end. Strictly speaking, I was homeless in a far-off country but somehow I couldn't worry about that, I was simply pleased that it was over.

Now that the final papers were signed our business for the day was concluded and we went back outside. We all shook hands in the car park, and headed off in our various directions for some much needed refreshment and rest after a very long tedious day. We had a half an hour drive back to The Dominion and although I was hoping to close my eyes and relax, I knew I would not be allowed that luxury.

Sidi turned to me and almost snarling asked. "What was that all about, with Ousman and Abdul?"

I opened my eyes again and irritably answered with a question of my own, "What are you talking about?"

"The money, what is happening to the money?" He was trying to sound calm, but was failing miserably, his voice was almost pleading.

Looking towards the driver to indicate I had no intention of speaking in front of him, even if he was a cousin brother, and as calmly as I could muster I replied, "This is my business and I have no intention of discussing it now or with you."

"Don't try and be too clever, I will tell you what they are doing to you when we get back home." I didn't answer him, but simply closed my eyes as I had intended doing originally.

When we pulled up at the entrançe to The Dominion, I opened my door as quickly as possible wishing to get inside and find myself some solitude; the day had taken a physical and mental toll on me. I jumped down carefully from the mini bus; trying hard as I had done each time I got out of it, not to dirty my dress on the paintwork. I was startled as I did so by my mobile ringing; I took in out of my handbag and glanced at it. It was Ousman, my heart sank; surely there weren't any problems with the paper work. "Hello," I said to him as walked quickly away from the vehicle into the garden not wanting our conversation to be over heard.

"Helen, I'm sorry to bother you after the tiring day we have all had, but I'm afraid there is another set of papers that you need to sign; and they would like them in Mrs. Sullais' office by nine in the morning."

"Surely not, is it possible for you to bring them here on your way home this evening."

"Sorry, they have to be witnessed. My receptionist is able to sign as the witness, could you come into my office at eight thirty tomorrow."

"Okay." I reluctantly said I had little choice in the matter; I just wanted this whole business finished with. I walked across the bridge into the garden.

Sidi was following close on my heels, "Is there a problem?" he asked as I put my mobile back in my handbag.

"No, not really but I have to go into Port Albert again early in the morning to sign some more papers in Ousman's office."

"That's alright I will take you, I should have my car back by tomorrow; but I want to talk about the money now. Why have you had it sent to Simon, some of that is yours, you can't trust him, he will double cross you and you will get nothing. You should have it all here and sort it out yourself."

"No, I don't need it here, and if I receive it here it will be exchanged from dollars to shillings, then into sterling, with each exchange I will lose money."

"....But you have to pay Ousman, how will you do that, you don't have enough money left for that."

"That's taken care of, they are going to pay Ousman enough in shillings to pay the capital gains tax and his fee, then remainder will be paid to Simon."

"I didn't know that could be done. I am not certain that I believe them. You had better arrange for some more to be paid to you here, and then you will know you have plenty to tide you over, and what about your airfare? Don't forget you will have to buy your ticket and one-way tickets are expensive at this time of year."

I could see where this was leading and I knew that I definitely didn't need any more than was necessary here. "No, I will have sufficient for what I need when you bring me the rest of the money Babu owes me for the remainder of the steel. When will you get that by the way, because I will have to be booking my flight. I don't want to leave it till the last minute. In fact you are going to be busy during the next few days, remember you will have to get my immigration papers sorted now."

".....But what about me?"

"What about you? What do you mean?"

"All the rest of the staff had their redundancy pay; I always assumed you would look after me before you went. Where will you get the money to pay me?" His anger was very apparent in his voice.

I was determined to stay calm and answered trying desperately to hide my emotions, "Have you had nothing from me? Over the years I have paid you well for everything you have done for me. You repaid me by stealing my tax money at the start of the year"

"Stole, stole." I had made him furious by that remark, and he made no effort to hide the fact. "I borrowed it."

Still trying to remain calm I continued, "Steal. Borrow. Whatever you want to call it, you took it and didn't give it back to me. I had to pay it again. Then there was the estate agents' fee. You took that and I paid to get you out of custody. Have you paid me back? No. Not to mention all that we have been selling during the demolition, I'm not as stupid as you think; I know you have had as much from that as I have; so let's not talk about what I should pay you. Let's instead talk about when you are getting my papers sorted, and then we will see where we go from there."

I saw intense hate in Sidi's eyes: he screwed up his face as if in pain. He slammed his clenched fist down on the table and without a word walked out. I knew this wasn't the end of the matter, and thought it might be wise to barricade the door when I went to bed as well as locking it as I sometimes had done in the past. The fact that my night security was a cousin brother of Sidi's did not fill me with confidence either but at this late stage there was nothing I could do about it. Without looking back towards me, as he neared the gate Sidi shouted at me, "I will be here in the morning to take you to Port Albert."

I rose early the following morning, and in spite of my exhaustion the previous day, I was amazed to feel so bright. I wondered if Sidi would come to take me to Ousman's office, not really concerned if he did or not. I could easily get a taxi. When he hadn't arrived by five to eight, I decided that was what I would do; in fact I was almost relieved he hadn't come. I strolled up the strip to the taxi rank and after a fair amount of haggling gave my custom to the first driver that agreed for the 400 shillings I knew was the correct price to take me, wait for me and bring me back. I had seen the driver before, he had been in the bar, but I didn't actually know him although it was obvious from remarks he made, that he knew me.

We hadn't gone very far when my mobile rang, even before I took it out of my handbag I guessed it was probably Sidi, it was unlikely anyone else would ring me so early in the morning. "Morning, are you alright?" he asked, his anger from yesterday seemed to have subsided over night, "Where are you? I phoned Petreeni and he said you had gone out."

"I told you I had to go to Ousman's office early this morning, you were going to take me remember?" I spoke to him as calmly as he had spoken to me.

"Yes, I know, I'm sorry I didn't come in time, but I still don't have my car, I will have it back shortly. Where are you now, I can hear you are in a car, who are you with?" he was unable to hide the anxiety in his voice.

"Who do you think I'm with? I'm in a taxi, I couldn't wait any longer."

"Yes, that's fine, fine, I'm sorry I wasn't there for you." Was this really the same person that left The Dominion in such a huff, just a few hours ago? "Let me speak to the driver will you?"

"Why? Everything is fine."

"I want to make sure he knows where he is taking you; sometimes you get confused in the little back streets in Port Albert." The side streets in Port Albert did all look alike to me, but I was confidant I knew my way into Ousman's office. However I had no intention of arguing with Sidi in front of the driver, and I was eager to keep him in his present frame of mind, so I handed over my phone. It was not against the law to use a mobile in Shendi while driving, but I had never considered this safe practice, especially as many of the drivers were reckless at the best of times. I could not follow the conversation but I was concerned by the length of time they were speaking. How long does it take to give directions, in a city that is well known to both parties? I gestured to the driver to give my phone back to me, "Just wait a minute, Sidi is explaining things to me."

"Fine, but I want to speak to him again."

When the phone was handed back to me, I asked Sidi what had taken him so long to explain to the driver, "I wanted to make sure you are alright, you know I get concerned for your safety when you are out alone, but you will be fine with this boy, I know him." There was nothing unusual in this, Sidi used to be a taxi driver, and he still knew most of the drivers.

"I know Sidi well, he is a friend of mine, and he worries about you that is all," my driver told me as I put my phone back in my bag. Not wishing to engage in too much conversation, I simply nodded at him, and thought to myself, if that is supposed to inspire me with confidence it has had the complete opposite effect. When we reached Port Albert, I didn't need to give my driver any directions, he had been well informed where he was taking me.

We pulled up in a small gap by the kerb, not far from Ousman's office. I got out telling my driver I shouldn't be very long.

"It doesn't matter how long it takes, I'm coming in with you."

I looked at him in amazement. "You certainly are not. I have private business with my lawyer, you wait here for me."

"No, Sidi said I was to come in with you and make sure you are alright," and he climbed out of the car

"I repeat. You most certainly are not. You are being paid to drive me not to accompany me. What is more, if Sidi was with me he wouldn't be coming in either."

"Sidi will be angry if I don't do as he has instructed me," he pleaded.

"I'm paying you, not Sidi and you will wait for me where I tell you, or you won't get paid at all."

The driver reluctantly got back into the car, so that was why he was on the phone so long to Sidi; he wasn't only being given directions but instructions. What did Sidi imagine he would gain by the driver coming in with me? I gave a small sigh to myself as I ascended the stairs to the office. It was several years since I had first come to these offices with Simon, and so much had happened since then. I had very mixed feelings about the whole situation I was in; I would have loved to fall asleep and wake up in six months time to a brand new life and a brand new future, without or the worries and uncertainties I had now.

Ousman was there to greet me as I entered the outer office. I looked about me trying to hide my surprise at my surroundings; it was a vast contrast to the office I had visited previously. Ousman must have seen my eyes flitting around me, as when he escorted me into his office, which was a different room to the one we were in years before, he said, "We have been having refurbishments done, do you like it?"

"Oh yes, this is very smart Ousman, I'm impressed." This office was about three times the size of his old office; it would not have been out of place in one of the tourist hotels, never mind a lawyer's office. There were two large windows on one wall, these windows; which overlooked the bustle of the busy Port Albert streets below, had heavy rich deep green velvet curtains, these must have been imported from Europe. I could not imagine that they were available in Shendi. The walls were papered with an expensive embossed paper, which was the fashion a few years ago in the U.K. but looked very impressive in this large room. I continued to glance round as Ousman showed me to the large oak table in the centre of the room, around which several leather chairs stood. He pulled out a chair for me, and called to his receptionist, who was to witness my signature. Ousman explained to me what I was signing, and told me I was required to sign at the bottom of each sheet of paper. I set about the task I had come to perform, wondering to myself, why my lawyer, who had obviously come up in the world during the years I had been here, had come to the hotel a couple of evenings ago, so shabbily dressed. I still cringed at the thought of him picking his toe nails in the hotel's reception.

With all papers duly signed I bid Ousman good bye and gave a sigh of relief this time, as I descended the stairs and went back out into the street where my taxi driver was waiting for me as I had instructed him. We drove back to The Dominion without speaking; I had no wish to engage him in conversation, now that I knew anything I said would be reported back to Sidi. I also sensed he was annoyed with me that I hadn't allowed him to do as he had been asked. I had long been aware Sidi controlled my staff and they kept him informed of my movements but this was getting ridiculous, I now also had that threat hanging over me if I went out. I should have realised the situation, Shendians stick together against Taubabs, all hoping, because of their own personal circumstances to gain from others' situations. Having seen how many live, I didn't blame them for this, but when I was the taubab in question, I tended to see things in a different light.

I was pleased when I returned home to see Nick was sat in the garden with Sidi having his morning coffee. On seeing me, Sidi got up and said, "I will go and ask Tina to make you a coffee."

When he was out of earshot Nick asked, "Has the sale gone through alright now? Sidi told me, he had helped you sort things all day yesterday and then your lawyer called you back to Port Albert again this morning."

"Yes, well Sidi was with me yesterday, but I didn't let him come in any of the offices with me, Ousman did everything."

Nick smiled, "You know what they are like, and he was pleased to tell me he had sorted everything for you, are you alright?"

"Yeah, but I will be much happier when I'm on a U.K. bound flight." I had no intention of telling Nick exactly how relieved I would be when I was on that plane. When Sidi came back I learnt he still didn't have his car, but had had a friend drop him off so he would know I was alright after my trip to Port Albert. That explained why I hadn't seen his car in the car park when I returned. We were still sat chatting and enjoying a second cup of coffee when my mobile rang, it was a number I didn't have in my phone book. "Ah Helen, this is Abdul, where are you?"

"At The Dominion." I answered surprised at his question.

"You are meant to be at Mrs. Sullais' office. Did your lawyer not tell you?"

"No, he certainly didn't. Is this really necessary, can Ousman not represent me? I have only just returned from Port Albert, I thought everything had been done now, I signed the final papers in his office this morning, and his receptionist witnessed my signature."

"Sorry there is only one more paper to sign before we can transfer the money, we are going to have to ask you to come back to Port Albert. Do you have transport?"

"No, I haven't. I had a taxi this morning."

"Wait where you are, I will arrange for one of the hotel drivers to collect you and bring you here."

"What was that about?" Sidi anxiously asked as I put my phone down with a heavy sigh.

"I can't believe this I have to go into Mrs. Sullais' office to sign another paper."

"When?"

"Now, they are going to send one of the hotel drivers to collect me."

"I'll come with you, this is getting too much, I don't trust these people, and I want to know all is as it should be." Sidi gave a sidewards glance at Nick. I was grateful Nick was with us, I knew Sidi wouldn't be too forceful with him there, he was always careful to create a good impression on Nick.

"There is no need for you to come, they are going to collect me and bring me back."

They were obviously very eager to get me swiftly into Mrs. Sullais' office, as before we had finished discussing this, Ali was walking into my garden.

"Sorry Helen, there seems to have been a misunderstanding between our two lawyers. Are you ready to go?"

I left The Dominion with Ali, who explained to me, he was unable to give me one of the hotel's vehicles as there wouldn't be one available for another half an hour; and they were all sat in Mrs. Sullais' office waiting for me. He came with me to the taxi rank and arranged with one of the drivers to take me anywhere he was instructed and to go to the hotel for the fare when we returned. Ironically, the driver he had picked was a lad named Kita, who I knew was a friend of Sidi's.

Kita also knew me and chatted away to me as we set off. I was being very careful what I told him, as it had soon become apparent to me that he was pumping me for information. Early on in our journey he pulled out his mobile and made a call. From the small understanding of local language I had I realised he was phoning Sidi, to tell him he had me in his taxi. While Kita was on the phone, my mobile rang, I was aghast to find I was speaking to an angry Janni Giano, wanting to know exactly where I was. I was annoyed and becoming anxious. They knew Ali had provided me transport and I was on the way, so why phone me? I was aware as I answered him sharply that my patience wearing thin. When I received a second call from Janni only five minutes later, to confirm my present whereabouts, I had to fight the temptation not to shout at him, they were well aware how far the tourist area was from Port Albert. "They are very eager to get you there," Kita noted, "you are obviously a very important lady going to a very important meeting."

I just smiled at him and said. "Sorry Kita, I really don't feel like too much conversation this morning, just get me into Port Albert as quickly as you can." Shut up Kita, you are getting on my nerves is what I would have liked to have said but this would have been rather rude especially as none of this, tiring as it was, had anything whatsoever to do with him.

Ousman was on the steps outside Mrs. Sullais' office when we pulled into her court yard. "Thank goodness you are here, Helen they are getting very impatient."

"You didn't tell me I had to be here, I wouldn't have gone back to The Dominion had I known I was needed back here so soon."

"Yes, yes, I'm sorry, I didn't realise. I thought I could conclude things after you signed the papers this morning." I knew by this remark that it was Ousman who was to blame. I could see the tiredness in Janni's eyes when I entered the small but well decorated room, the previous day had taken its toll on all of us; that probably accounted for his ill humour on that hot and humid Shendian morning. The meeting was swiftly over, everyone seemed as eager as I was to put a closure on this sale. I signed what was required of me, including, what interested me most now, a paper giving them permission to transfer the processed from the sale to Simon's U.K. bank account. Now The Dominion truly was no longer mine.

As I got back into Kita's taxi, I instructed him to get me back to The Dominion as soon as possible, I lay my head on the headrest and closed my eyes, I considered this hint enough that I didn't want to make small talk with him on the return journey. Within half an hour of reaching home I received a phone call from Abdul telling me the money had been transferred to Simon's account and he should receive it in the next few days. He gave me the reference number of the transfer, which I immediately sent to Simon and asked him to let me know as soon as he received it.

All now completed I went into my little house, which I had started to think of as home and flopped out on my mattress and closed my eyes. Shortly afterwards Sidi knocked on the door and asked if he could come in.

"No, I'm resting, I'm exhausted and want peace and quiet." To my surprise I heard his footsteps as he left, without saying a word. I lay there with my eyes closed trying to relax, going over everything I needed to do before I left Shendi and push the ever increasing worry of my immigration papers to the back of my over active mind.

Chapter Twenty-Six

The Truth Comes Out

After finally completing the sale of The Dominion I had felt entitled to a good night's sleep but it was yet another fretful time of tossing and turning. Giving up I rose as soon as it was light and took the opportunity to walk around what was no longer my garden. The quiet and solitude let some nostalgic feelings rise to the surface of my mind. How hard we had worked to improve the garden and how proud we had felt when it was done. I remembered that first morning after Simon had left and I how had been determined to stay and run the bar and make it success. And I had. I thought about all the celebrations the garden had seen, the Christmas meals, the St. Patrick Day parties when everything was green – even the drinks. Then there were all the wedding parties. How nervous I had been before the first one but it had been a success. Eight years ago, coming out as Simon's wife, intending to do very little but play "mine host" I would never have thought myself capable of running a bar, organising celebrations or of standing up to the machinations of Sidi and his friends. Well perhaps the last hadn't been such a success but he hadn't got away with everything. Now all I needed was my papers.

With that thought in mind I went to open the gate. I did not want any member of staff seeing me wandering idly around the garden. With the gate unlocked I walked to the stage and looked over the wall towards The Peace Haven. There I could see Ali doing his morning rounds of the various departments. The memory came flooding back of when Ali had first arrived, and I stood on that same spot for several mornings hoping to get a glimpse of the man I was going to have to deal with. I took a step back. Suddenly I felt shy; I didn't want Ali to see me. I wondered what he would think, if he saw me. Would he think I was regretting the sale? Would he think I wanted to speak to him? I didn't regret it, not for a moment and I didn't want to speak to him. I didn't even really want to see him. I simply wanted to remember the last few years in The Dominion on my own. I saw Ali look up in my direction and I was glad I had moved back out of view. Yesterday's sale obviously was of less significance to him than to me, but the look on his face as he surveyed The Dominion on that bright sunny June morning gave me some satisfaction. Ali's expression suggested he was as eager to take possession of my property and start his extension plans, as I was to return to the U.K. and start my new life.

My solitary musings were broken as I heard my heavy wrought iron gate opening and turned to see who else was about this early. Surely not the staff already. Fortunately it was Nick, about the only person I could tolerate. "Morning Helen," he greeted me, "did everything finally get sorted yesterday?"

"Yes, it's all over now, as soon as the money is safely in the U.K. the Dominion, or what is left of it will become part of The Peace Haven." I told him as I went to go and make us both a coffee.

"I hope you weren't looking over that wall with misgivings," he had seen me gazing down at the hotel and was concerned that I was regretting the sale.

"No, I was just remembering when Ali first came."

"Now the sale has gone through when will you be leaving?" he asked seeming concerned, as we settled down for our usual morning coffee. I knew when I left I would miss Nick's morning visits. I was sure he wasn't aware how he had managed to lift my spirits when I was down, and the strength he had been to me, when I needed to be strong.

"I have to be out by the end of the month so I will arrange a flight as soon as Simon has the money."

We chatted away cheerfully for at least an hour, I realised Nick would also miss our morning chats over endless cups of coffee. Several times during the conversation I was tempted to tell Nick that I couldn't leave until I had my immigration papers in order. I knew if I told him this, he would confront Sidi and that could turn out to be very pleasant for everyone. I wasn't particularly worried about offending Sidi but there was a limit to how much I could disturb him and a confrontation with Nick crossed that line. I knew I was going to be in Shendi for another ten days or so and I was scared of repercussions if I upset Sidi or any of the other lads too much. I was also concerned about the consequences for Nick for after all he was staying in the country so I decided not to say anything at all. I would have a talk with Sidi, which would no doubt quickly escalate into a war of words, sometime today. Before Nick left we arranged that he would come back later with some of his workers and take many of the remaining plants.

Very soon after Nick's departure Sidi arrived. I did wonder if he had been watching for Nick's leaving, but dismissed that at latent paranoia. He was earlier than I expected, and, much to my concern gave the impression of feeling very smug. However, he said nothing as we discussed what course we would take over the demolition, now we knew time was of the essence. "I've proved a point," I told him, "all we really have left now is a pile of rubble, I would have liked to completely clear the land, but if we don't have time they will have to clear the rubble themselves, in fact that might be better. It will certainly make my point." We both smiled at the thought of the mess that could be left. I decided not to mention my papers until he was on the point of leaving. He was too smug; I wanted things to go peacefully, and I couldn't cope with Sidi getting in a rage, and causing me too much upset this early in the day. Besides which Nick was coming back and I didn't not need any trouble between the two of them. "Nick is coming sometime today with his lads and they are going to take many of the plants out of the garden. That will shock next door, they know we are taking the buildings down, but they will not expect to find the garden devoid of plants."

"I hope he is paying you for them," was the only comment Sidi made. I think money was the foremost thing on his mind at that time.

"I haven't even discussed that, after all Nick has bought from me, I couldn't care less if he pays me or not, I'm more interested to remove as much from here as I can."

Sidi looked at me puzzled and said, "I will never understand taubabs and money. You don't like paying when people help you, you don't like paying transport money but you give away your things. Of course you need money for them, he will plant these things in the garden of his hotel and they should not be free." I simply grinned to myself and got on with helping Latif sort the piles of black rubbish sacks, we were expecting the donkey man to come and collect the rubbish later that day.

Nick arrived shortly afterwards and I was glad that I had not mentioned my papers to Sidi. He reversed his pick-up truck into the entrance so it could be easily loaded with the larger plants that he was going to take alongside the bedding plants. His lads piled out of the truck and together with Latif, Petreeni and Sidi, they started digging up my garden. Nick had bought plenty of big plastic containers with him, so the plants could be up rooted with the soil around them and put in the containers until he was ready to replant them. Nick and I stood at the edge of the garden, giving our instructions to the lads.

"Dig deep around that one with the red leaves Katta." Nick called then turning to me and speaking quietly he said, "When I come home next summer, how would you fancy us taking a little trip to Thailand? It is too late for this Dominion now, but I could still build you a little bar on the beach at Phuket if the fancy took you"

Speaking just as quietly because although this was just banter I did not want any of the lads to overhear, I answered, "I was thinking more along the lines of burning my passport when I finally get back to U.K. That maybe my safest bet."

Nick smiled and said,"Yeah, that's true, what about Morecambe, that safe enough?"

"Try telling that to the families of the Chinese cockle gathers."

"Okay, but you don't have to gather cockles and it is in Lancashire. Thinking about it there is always Scarborough. You can't possibly find any fault with Scarborough; for one thing it is in Yorkshire." Turning slightly, he called," You need to dig deeper yet Katta; we want all the roots for it to grow strong."

"No, no, no Nick you're forgetting we don't get on with the people in Scarborough, so running a bar there is a definite no go."

Looking at me quizzically Nick asks, "What's wrong with folks in Scarborough, which one of them has upset you?"

"Bill the fisherman; imagine running a bar full of Bills."

"Is he from Scarborough? I didn't know that, makes me ashamed to be a Yorkshireman, we will forget that one. Doesn't seem we have too many options left, does it?"

We both laughed, which made all the lads look in our direction, Sidi staring at Nick with hate in his eyes. There was no doubt at all that he was getting nervous of Nick's presence; a situation that I hoped to use to my advantage.

Nick left soon afterwards with his pickup loaded to overflowing with plants and also sacks of soil. Three of his lads sat on the top preventing the load from spilling over out onto the road. Sidi and Latif came to the gate with me to see them all off and as they went under the arch I saw the curious looks the hotel's security gave them. That was nothing to the curious look Sidi gave m as we turned to go back into the garden. "What were you and Nick laughing about?"

We were joking about Yorkshire people. It is an English thing. Anyway, if Nick and I are sharing a joke, what is it to you?" I was annoyed. After all my time in Shendi, I should not have been surprised at Sidi's interest but I was. It was an intrusion into my private life and I went immediately on the offensive.

"I have told and told you, do not trust Nick; you don't see all what I see."

"Give over," Latif intervened, "Nick is the only one you see coming here every day to visit Helen, he is her friend and you know that."

"Some friend." Sidi muttered, I grinned to myself as I walked back into the garden, Sidi was certainly getting my friendship with Nick out of proportion, but that could do no harm to my situation.

It was soon lunchtime so the lads just set about tiding the garden until Tina had the lunch ready, Sidi made another snide remark about Nick which angered me. His interest in what I considered my private life was intolerable. It was like being in prison and I had been imprisoned here for too long. My mobile was on the garden table; I snatched it up angrily and stumped out of the main gate. I knew I was acting like a spoilt child but could not stop the tears that for some inexplicable reason were streaming down my cheeks. I'm not really sure if it was what Sidi had said that had made me snap or a combination of the ever increasing impossible situation I was in, but the relief I felt at having broken free for a short time was immense. I might have been unstable but at that moment I did not care. I marched across the car park and did not slow down until I had gone under the hotel's arch. Calming down slightly I felt able to wave at a small group of local lads who sometimes had bought tourist friends of theirs into the bar, "Are you alright Helen?" one of them called.

"Yeah, I'm good thanks," I cheerfully called back, as I glanced over my shoulder to see if Sidi was following or if he had got one of the others to. To my relief I saw none of them. Wiping my cheeks, I smiled to myself; I was free for a while.

I walked down the small sand path that ran past the side of one of the neighbouring hotels. This path, which was getting more and more precarious with each passing rainy season as more of the sand was washed away each year, held many memories for me. In happier times I had picked up a kitten crying at the bottom of a ditch. She had lost her mother and the rest of the litter and I had been unable to resist her plaintive cries. I had taken her back to The Dominion and had fed her from a baby's bottle as she was too young to even lap her milk. Later on she had given me my faithful cat Buster. But when I had found her Simon had still been here. It was a long, long time ago now.

I glanced down at the ground by the staff entrance at the rear of the hotel. Many years previously I had seen my first snake coiled up by that very gate when I was walking our inherited dog. That poor old dog was long dead now but walking him had given me some much needed freedom in the past. As I strolled on I heard a sound that still thrilled me after all these years in Shendi, the sound of drums coming from a local bar. This was built just where the path met a larger sand road leading down to the beach. There was a small group of locals sat outside the bar; two of them were drumming on a locally made tom-tom drum. I recognised one of the lads so I waved to them, they all returned my gesture and I started to feel good. I turned to glance back along the track I had just come down, it was deserted, I was surprised that Sidi hadn't followed me, but was so pleased he hadn't, I was happy reminiscing and needed no reminders of the present.

I walked on feeling the full heat of the sun on me. The closer I got to the beach the gritty sand of the roads gradually turned into the finer sand of the shore. I took off my flip flops and wriggled my toes in the sand, the feeling excited me; this was truly the Shendi I had first known, in all its glory. I stood and watched the sea from the vantage point near the beach bar at the top of the sand. There were many tourists swimming, and playing in the huge waves of the unrelenting Atlantic Ocean. I would have loved to plunge into the sea with them. I walked down towards the water, it looked so inviting.

Still looking over my shoulder every now and then and seeing nothing, I walked into the sea, and strolled along the beach, kicking my feet in the swell. I stood and stared towards the horizon, watching the sun's rays sprinkle down in sparkling shades of silver and gold, dancing on the waves that were bobbing up and down as far as the eye could see. In spite of my outing making me feel more relaxed, I fleetingly wondered how easy it would be to drown yourself if you were a competent swimmer. I was still contemplating this when I was bought out of my reverie by a young beach seller wanting to sell me a silver bracelet. Even with the very mixed bag of emotions I was feeling, I was amused that when I refused his bracelet he asked if I would like to have sex with him, apparently it would only cost me a packet of cigarettes. I had forgotten some of the seedier side of life in a third world country. I shook my head and smiled to myself, feeling sorry for the lad who was obviously very desperate. I walked on and as I splashed my way along the shore I had to lift my skirt which was starting to get wet from the unpredictable waves. As far as I could see in either direction there was golden sand bordered by palm trees softly waving in the breeze. Further down the coast there was a small herd of cattle, hungrily devouring what was left of the dried grass on the headland. They would welcome the rains that were only a few weeks away. There would have no shortage of food then, but I wouldn't be here to see it – I hoped. I turned around and looked back again, I had walked past all the hotels now, so this part of the beach was fairly deserted, there was no sign of anyone following me, had I really escaped, could I just carry on walking forever? Tempting as that prospect was to my disturbed and desperate mind, even I knew that was impractical.

I came out of the sea and made my way up the beach, to take the small uneven tarmac road that passed the monkey forest, where the troops that passed through The Dominion garden every morning and every evening spent the night. The heat became intense as I left the shore and the sea breeze behind me and headed farther in land. The road had quite a short but sharp incline, but I was struggling to climb it. As I got hotter and hotter, my forehead was wet with perspiration, I heard footsteps behind me. Before I had time to turn around I felt a tap on my shoulder. I gasped as I turned to look behind me.

"Where on earth do you think you are going?" Sidi sharply asked me.

"You startled me, how dare you? There is no need for you to follow me. I can go out for a walk if I want to. You should not question me like this. You have no right. " I angrily retorted. So he had been following me all the time, yet I had looked for him several times and hadn't seen him. Had he followed me all the way or come out looking for me and struck lucky? Then I had proof that he followed me at least since I had reached the beach, when he asked, "Who was that boy you were talking to on the beach? You know I always tell you not to get involved with these boys."

"Sidi, leave off. He was no-one just a beach boy. Actually he wanted to have sex with me." I laughed.

"See, I keep telling you, it isn't safe for you to be out by yourself, we must get you back to The Dominion."

How had he known where I was, had the drummers rung him to tell him? Surely not; but how had I not seen him? I was angry that he had followed me, and was relishing in his annoyance that I had gone out but I was also nervous. Why did he need to know where I was? Determined to strike back I said, "Haven't you noticed there isn't a Dominion anymore, we have knocked it down." I gave a satisfied grin.

"You must behave different; don't you know you are frightening the staff, why do you always upset people?"

I laughed aloud then. Was I really frightening the staff? Maybe I was going crazy, but I didn't really think so, I was just reacting to the stress I was under. My solitary walk was over. Without speaking any farther, we went down the small back lane that led to The Peace Haven's tradesman's entrance and entered by our back gate, which had been used more over the past few weeks than in the whole eight years I had been there. I understood enough of Sidi's conversation with Petreeni to know he had told him; that he had found me on the beach and bought me back safe. Did I need bringing back? Why wasn't I safe? Was I really going crazy; I didn't think so?

Back at The Dominion I didn't speak to anyone. I simply walked past the table where they were having lunch. Once in my little house I shut the door and lay on my bed, feeling completely frustrated and furious. How dare Sidi come looking for me and how had he found me? If, as I suspected, one of the drummers had phoned him, why had they phoned him? I knew from my experiences of the last two days that he had all the taxi drivers monitoring my comings and goings; I knew my security phoned him whenever I went out – but beach bums? Surely not? What was indisputable was that he had known where to find me and even who I had spoken to. This was intolerable but what could I do? I closed my eyes and I became aware I was trembling. I had to pull myself together. I had to be strong. I could hear them all outside eating their lunch and chattering about me. They were talking too quickly for me hear all their conversation, but I was certain that Sidi was convincing them I was crazy. I wasn't sure what his intention was, I couldn't see what he would gain by this, but he must have had an ulterior motive. I lay there pondering all afternoon, with intermittent tears rolling down my cheeks.

I stayed in my house even as I heard them preparing to leave. I heard Sidi say something along the lines of she has never cared what happens to any of us, all she cares about is her cats. I don't know why, but like his earlier remark about Nick that one made me loose my hard earned calm. I got up and with tears pouring down my cheeks – which in retrospect were not a good idea as it probably helped convince them of my unstable state - stormed out of my house and yelled at him. "If you want to talk about me, be man enough to do it to my face and in English, so I know all that you are saying." From the corner of my eye I saw him raise his hand. "He's going to hit me," I thought. Simon had turned violent towards the end of our marriage and the thought of becoming someone else's punch bag horrified me. Instinctively I did something I had never done with Simon, I lashed out. I raised my foot and kicked him hard in the groin where I hoped I would do the most damage. Unfortunately, as I did so, I slipped on the sand and fell backwards hitting my head on the leg of the table. Sidi, never being one to worry about an opponent being down, stamped on my face. Things began to blur and Latif pulled me away as Sidi tried to kick me again. I got up as quickly as I could and retreated into my house. Once in there, with the door firmly shut I paced up and down, stroking my aching jaw. Things went quiet shortly afterwards, and looking out of my little window I saw everyone had left. I lay back on my bed and didn't move again until the next morning, not even getting up to shut the gate or speak to the security. I simply lay there pondering all that had happened. Sidi had hit me, in front of witnesses, not that I held out much hope of their support and I had kicked him first. Were there any limits on his behaviour or did he think he could treat me as he liked and no-one would stop him? My position was looking increasingly precarious.

The following day, no-one mentioned the events of the previous day, I didn't expect Sidi to show but he did, and also without mentioning anything he set about working with the others. Over the years I had learnt that what happens one day in Shendi is forgotten the next. I often found this hard to understand, but maybe it is better than bearing grudges like we sometimes tend to do. After we had finished our tasks for the day, Latif, Petreeni and Tina went home but Sidi hung around. It was obvious he had no intention of leaving with them. Once we were alone, he asked, "I didn't see Nick this morning, did he come before I arrived?"

"No, I haven't seen him today, but with this bruise I have on my chin, I think for your sake that is just as well."

"I wish he had seen you like that, and then he would know you are not what he thinks, and that you need to be kept in your place."

I did not feel like asking what he felt my place was, or who he thought he was to comment on it but simply replied, "I have a feeling he would see it different to that."

Without anymore comment he completely changed the subject "Has Simon had the money yet?"

"No, I don't expect him to have it for a few days yet. Why what has it to do with you?"

"I was just wondering," he said as he fiddled nervously with the cigarette he had just removed from his packet. "So you hope to be leaving soon?"

"I will be gone as soon as the money is through, and besides I have to be out of here by the end of the month. In fact they have been reasonable about that, they could have insisted I leave as soon as the money came through. Which gets me back to my papers; have you seen Mariama about them yet?"

"Not again, will you stop carrying on about your bloody papers, you will have them. If you aren't ready to leave by the end of the month you will have to come and live at my compound, until it is time for you to go."

"Don't worry I will be leaving as soon as the money is through, that is why I'm keeping on about my papers, there isn't much time to spare now." Sidi sniggered, but didn't answer me in fact he didn't even say goodbye as he left. Any previous anxiety I had had about my immigration papers were dwarfed by the sheer panic I was beginning to feel now. There was only 15 days until I had to leave the premises.

The next morning as I carried the tray of coffee to the garden table where Nick was sat, I was aware of him looking me up and down. As I sat opposite him, I wondered if he had noticed my bruise. I had put make up on it to try and disguise it but instead he simply asked "How tall are you?"

Bewildered by his question I replied, "Five four, maybe five, why?"

"I don't want to upset you or anything, but you know the big tree in the middle of Famara where I pick up some of my lads in the morning."

"Yes, I know where you mean."

"There were a group of boys there this morning digging a bloody big hole, it was five foot six or so, I asked them what they were doing, and was told, this isn't taubab business." We both laughed, but I didn't really see the funny side. I'm not sure if Nick was serious or if it was his way of telling me he knew more than he was letting on. Either way I must admit this made me uneasy. When the staff came I puttered around all day, helping Latif and Petreeni where I could, but determined not to overwork myself; I had done enough work at The Dominion for a lifetime. There wasn't much left of the building now, basically it was only a large pile of rubble. I was satisfied, I had proved an important point, or at least it was important in my mind. They had laughed at me, and I felt I had had the last laugh on them. In my mind I had had my small piece of revenge, and it was sweet. Now I would simply take the next few days at a leisurely pace. Sidi failed to put in appearance all day. I still rather stupidly hoped this meant he was busy sorting my papers for me.

Early in the evening when I was on my own, my mobile rang, I looked at the screen wishing against all odds for it to be Sidi phoning to say everything was now in order; I was surprised to see it was Simon. "Hello." I said quietly as I started pacing the garden with my phone clutched to me ear. After all these years and thousands of miles apart Simon still had the ability to make me feel nervous.

"Good news," he told me, "the money is in my bank account, even if it is less than we had hoped for, apparently the exchange rate has dropped since we first agreed the sale, but at least you did manage to get some cash in the end, which did seem doubtful at one time."

It had seemed much more doubtful to me than Simon had any idea about, but I had no intention of telling him that little piece of news. "Great, I thought it was going to take longer than that to be transferred."

"Are you coming home now, or are you taking a holiday there before you travel?"

"I will be away as soon as I can arrange a flight."

"Good that's what I wanted to hear, I think you should be out of there as soon as you can."

Just like you did, I thought but didn't say. Neither did I tell him that I needed to leave quickly: I intended keeping that to myself. After our goodbyes, which were rather stilted, I slumped down into my garden chair, clasped the phone to my chest and just sat there thinking. I hadn't expected to hear that news for a few days yet; now I really was free, but was I? I still couldn't leave until my papers were sorted. I stared at my phone, should I phone Sidi? The sale was over now I had to get away. The longer I sat there thinking the worse my position seemed. All sorts of thoughts drifted in and out of my mind. Reg Preston had died for his compound, and his murderers were still standing trial several years down the line, in what should have been an open and shut case. Dave had died in very strange circumstances, not many ex-pats even mentioned him anymore. Was Nick just making friendly banter about the hole in Famara, or was that his way of pointing out the precarious position I was in.

I paced the garden first one way and then another. I went into my little house. I came out again. I could not settle. Walking over to the stage I went up and looked over the wall. A small group of tourists were carrying beach bags and towels making their way back to their hotel rooms after a day on the beach. I could fully understand why they all enjoyed holidaying in Shendi, and why we had so many repeat tourists. From the holiday maker's point of view the country had everything that was needed to fulfil the criteria for a fantastic relaxing holiday. Endless sandy beaches, edged by palm trees waving in the prevailing wind from the deep blue sea, wall to wall sunshine, good food, good wine, a very acceptable locally brewed larger. To the tourist this was indeed the Utopia I had once considered it to be, why had it turned into this hell? I could ponder over this forever and I doubt if I would ever come up with an acceptable answer. Whatever the conclusions of my rambling thoughts I had to pull myself back to the present and get on with planning my journey home.

I sat there nervously fiddling with my mobile, wondering if I should phone Sidi. I could not plan to leave without that slip of paper, such a small thing with such a big significance. I didn't have to dwell for long on what was my best course of action, as I soon heard the clanging of the main gate. Looking up I saw it was Sidi.

"Hi, I've had a busy day, any chance of a cup of coffee?" he asked light heartedly. I had just been considering a coffee myself to clear my head, so leaving him sat at the garden table I made my way to the makeshift kitchen, thinking Sidi seemed in high spirits, I hoped that I wasn't misinterpreting his mood and that this meant he had sorted things for me. When I returned with the coffees I soon learnt this wasn't the case. He said, "Right I think it is time we spoke seriously about money. Has Simon had the money yet?"

"No," I lied, "but what is that to you anyway?"

"It is everything to me, I don't understand why you had it all sent to Simon. He hasn't been here all these years, it is you and I and all the staff that have earned that money, not him; and you send it all to him. I don't understand."

"What are you on about? You and the staff have been paid well for the work you have done here. The money we have had from the sale is nothing to do with the running of the business. Simon and I bought this place out of joint money and we both will share the proceeds of the sale; but none of this is any of your business."

"That's what you think. It is my business. I have done plenty here and I want paying for it."

"Have you not been paid well for all you have done? And besides your pay, have you not had the tax money from the start of the year, which you know as well as I do is the reason I don't have my immigration papers in order, which incidentally I want very soon now or you will be in big shit. Understand?" My increasing anger was starting to become apparent.

"I think it is you that needs to understand; until you give me a share of the money you don't get your papers."

There, he had said it, the very words that I had been dreading. I knew many ex-pats that had experienced similar demands as they prepared to leave, why had I considered I would be immune to this. In spite of the anger that I could feel racing through my body, I knew I had to look and sound unruffled. It took a huge effort and all my energy to say calmly, "I tell you again. The Dominion belonged to Simon and me. We bought with money we had saved up over many years. Now it has been sold the money is ours. You worked for us and have been paid for working for us." My voice rose slightly as I began to get into my stride, "After all the humiliation you have put me through during the past few weeks, when I should have been relaxing as much as possible before I returned to the U.K. to start my new life, and all the things you have done to me; you imagine I will pay you for the privilege. You are crazy, and I'm not as stupid as you think. I know you and the others have had your share of all we have been selling from here, but I have turned a blind eye to that, knowing it may be a while before you get new jobs, but under no circumstances will I give you any more money."

As I said all this I watched Sidi's face, he was getting angrier and angrier. "You are the one that is crazy," he retorted as he made no effort to hide his rage. Good, he had cracked first. He slammed his fist down on the table, "You had better start listening to me. I will have no work when you go, nor will the others and we need money to live; and there is no way you are going to leave this country without providing an income for me so I can support my family."

I still tried to remain placid, but my pent up emotions were making this increasingly difficult. "Sidi it is not my job to support your family. I have a family as well. As I have already said besides your pay, without counting what you have taken over previous years this year you have had the tax money, not to mention the estate agents money, and cash from the demolition here. You should be able to support your family for years from that alone. You also have your shop that is doing quite well, that alone should feed your family."

His frustration showed itself in the tone of his raised voice as he stood up and standing over me yelled, "Damn your family. You know nothing. You are rich. What do you know about having to survive? You have always been privileged, you will go back and live in luxury and not care at all what happens to me and my family here."

"You know Simon and I have lost a lot of money over this sale, and the money that is left has to be shared between Simon and me. The point of it is, Sidi, I assure you I will not be living in luxury when I leave here. I will need to find a job quickly and I have to find somewhere to live and buy furniture, I have to start all over again, that is not cheap. Just supposing I did give you money, which I have no intention of doing, how would I manage myself."

This caused Sidi to laugh, whether it was a nervous laugh or if he was genuinely amused I have no idea. "You Taubabs are funny, how will you afford to live? You have plenty of money, you just don't like parting with it; but you will learn to, because until you do you will not be leaving." He turned his back on me and putting his hands in his pockets he walked away from me, and went and stood on the stage, looking over the wall towards The Peace Haven, as I had done many times myself in the past.

I thought it best to ignore him, and I picked up the coffee cups, and after getting water from the outside tap, went into our little make shift kitchen to wash them. I was amazed that he had the gall to say I didn't like parting with money after I had helped him and his family and many members of my staff or their families when they had been in difficulties, besides charity events I had hosted at The Dominion. I considered I had done my share of giving over the years I had been here. Perhaps having to struggle to find a living made the past seem irrelevant and I suppose compared to Sidi's living conditions, I would be going back to luxury. Whatever the reason for his inability to see my point of view, he was not getting any money. When I returned he was still sat on the steps of the stage, his head in his hands. Paying no attention to him, I returned to the table and, picked up my paperback, and sat there making out to read, although a riveting thriller was the last thing on my mind at that moment. After what seemed like ages, but in reality was probably only a few minutes he came back and joined me.

"Is that a good book?" he asked as if our previous conversation hadn't taken place.

"Yes, I'm enjoying it." I replied as casually as I could manage.

I could hardly believe the light conversation that was passing between us, in view of the situation. As we were talking the Friday U.K. bound flight flew over head. I stared up at it with envy.

"That's the Gatwick flight." I said more or less oblivious to what I was saying.

"I know there is one every Friday."

"I will be on next week's flight."

"I have told you I want money before I allow you to leave; otherwise you have no chance of being on that flight."

"If I'm not on next week's flight I will consider I'm being keep here against my will."

This remark bought on more laughter from Sidi, " Consider it what you like, but I don't think you understand the position you are in," he sniggered as he went on in a more belligerent manner, "I want you to pay me £10,000, if you don't do that you will not be going anywhere."

At that point I lost my attempts to stay calm. Now was my turn to shout, previously, he had only mentioned money, not an amount. £10,000 was a ridiculously high sum in Shendi, and he could keep himself his family and possibly the whole of his village for many years on that. "£10,000, you have gone completely crazy," I told him, "just supposing I did want to pay you, where on earth do you think I could get hold of money like that."

"Simon will be able to pay it when he has the money from the sale."

"Whatever makes you think Simon will pay for me to be able to leave, Simon and I am not together anymore, it is nothing to him if I am here or in the U.K. so you can forget about that." I said half smiling half shouting. In fact I was in such a state I didn't know whether to laugh or cry. Did he really mean this or was he just trying to frighten me, and see my reaction. It was my turn to get up and pace the garden, I walked away from him to enable myself to take a few deep breaths without him noticing. I needed to calm myself down to be able to think clearly. When I felt relaxed enough to continue the conversation, and when I had worked out in my head what I was going to say, I made my way back towards where Sidi was sat. I was astonished when I neared the table and before I could even start on my speech, he got up and said quite calmly, "I'm going, when I come tomorrow maybe you will be more reasonable."

"Me be more reasonable?" I yelled to no avail as he was half way to the gate by then and had no intention of discussing anything more with me.

I slumped back into my chair, both physically and mentally exhausted. My mind went blank. What to do? Had Sidi really meant what he said, and was he working by himself or was he merely the spokesperson for all of my staff? I considered my options, or at least tried to consider my options, what was more to the point did I have any options? I had no intention of handing over any money. Had none of this occurred I had intended giving a parting gift to the few staff that was still with me at the end, but not now.

The next day when Nick came for coffee I thought about telling him but decided against it. It was my problem and I would solve it one way or another. He didn't stay long; I can't have been a good conversationalist. When the lads came, as had happened in the past, no reference was made by Sidi to our previous day's conversation. Like all the others he was friendly towards me, and we all continued with the demolition. I did detect an increased urgency to complete our work, this pleased me. I was content that most of the building was completely demolished and I would have been satisfied to leave things as they were, but on the other hand the more we removed the more of a point I had made. This physical work was keeping my mind busy and I found it therapeutic as I had known I would. During the day Sidi give me a few sideways glances; he was obviously expecting me to broach the subject of the money with him. He would have to wait a good while longer for that, I had no intention of mentioning until the next Friday flight had taken off, a whole six days away, and then I would once again tell him I considered I was being kept here against my will. Hopefully before that he would have changed his mind about this and I would be on the flight; on the other hand if the worst happened and he was still adamant, I would have had more time to decided what course of action to take.

That evening Simon phoned and asked if I had booked my flight, when I told him no, he became angry with me, "Helen what is the matter with you? You have been saying you want to get away, now that you can leave you are doing nothing about it. Now the sale is through I want you to leave, I'm worried about you." This was the first sign of any sort of affection I had had from Simon for many years, and in a way I was touched by his concern, but there was no way I was going to explain to him the real reason I hadn't booked a flight.

"I will book it soon," I told him, "don't worry all is okay here."

"You do have the money for your fare, don't you?"

"Yes, I will let you know when I am leaving; it will be within the next week."

I closed my eyes, clasping my mobile between the palms of both my hands after we had finished speaking. I simply stood there welded to the spot, my legs weighed down with all my aguish, I simply couldn't move. I took deep spasmodic breaths. I don't know how long I stood there. Over the past few days I had seemed to completely lose touch of time, but I was still in the same position when my mobile rang again. I shook my head as if to bring myself back to the present. It was Nick.

I knew instinctively by his tone of voice he had been drinking, and I could hear the sounds of a bar in the background, "Are you all right Helen? You didn't seem yourself this morning."

"I'm fine, don't worry about me, I just have a lot of things on my plate at the moment preparing to leave."

"As long as you are alright honey." I was touched by Nick's concern for me; I had always been able to rely on him, but there was no way, especially as I knew he had been drinking that I would confide in him. I pulled myself together after Nick's call and actually started to read my book. I needed to recap over what I had already read as my mind had become notorious at going blank, I was on auto pilot and was not always fully aware of what I was doing. I was surprised after my initial recapping how quickly I got involved with my book. It was a thriller, maybe not the best type of book for me to be reading at that time, but it did seem to relax me for a while. I could relate to things that were happening to the heroine in my book, I prayed for her to have a happy ending, I would consider that a good omen.

The next day was Sunday and I spent it like the three wise monkeys. I saw and spoke to no-one, not even Nick and did nothing. I spent the whole day unable to settle to anything, pottering around the plot, tidying up a few things, reading, doing puzzles, watching the wild life and all the while resolutely trying not to think about the situation I was in. It may have been a day of rest but my mind would not settle and keep trying to think the forbidden "What if…"

The following days were also uneventful, Sidi only made fleeting references to the money, asking every couple days if Simon had received it yet. He did remark he couldn't understand why it was taking so long to come through. I spun him a tale of it having to be transferred from Saudi to the U.K. and then on to the island, so it wasn't a straight forward transaction. "It can take a long time to transfer money between countries – like from here to the UK when the names are the same so imagine how long it can take when the money is transferred between accounts," I said at one point. He seemed to believe this, and didn't pursue the matter any farther. Ousman phoned me and asked if the money had arrived. When I told him it had, his reaction was the same as Simon's; he seemed bewildered that I was still here. Ousman may have been the one I should have confided in, but somehow I didn't feel able to discuss it with anyone. In fact I think I was actually denying to myself the severity of my situation.

Inevitably Friday arrived, and I was in the garden with the remaining staff when the U.K. flight with its unmistakable bright yellow and green tail flew over head. "Um there goes the U.K. flight," I said, but no-one took much notice of this remark. Shortly afterwards Sidi came over to where I was stood.

"What did you mean before, there goes the U.K. flight?" He knew very well what I was referring to, that was why he was asking.

"Nothing, I've often commented on the flights, you know that," I replied, as I started watering the few remaining plants in the garden. I knew the others were preparing to leave but Sidi didn't appear to be getting ready to go. After the others had left, I would have this out once and for all with him. I wasn't looking forward to it but I knew it was something that I had to do. Continuing to water the garden I tried my utmost to seem unconcerned. The moment we were alone I said, "You know very well, what I meant when I saw the plane go overhead. I told you last Friday if I wasn't on that flight I would consider I was being kept here against my will. I am not on that flight therefore I am being held here against my will."

"And if you remember I told you at the time, I don't care if you consider you are being kept against your will. That means nothing to me; you are going to be here until Simon pays the money for you."

"You know I have to be out of here by the end of the month. That is Tuesday week."

"So what? If Simon hasn't paid by then, I will take you to the village. I have told you that before. This is all very simple, stop trying to make things difficult, both for you and for me. All you have to do is get me the money."

I was amazed at how calmly I took this, he was obviously determined, and my best policy was not to enrage him too much. I was well aware of his temper. I said nothing and he left. The clang of the gate shutting behind him brought me to my senses. Suddenly the reality of my situation became apparent. This was real, it was my life. This was not a story; I could not turn to the back and see the happy ending. I would not wake up and find it was a dream. I had stupidly thought Sidi would reconsider and appear one day with my papers in his hand saying he was only trying to frighten me. But that wasn't going to happen, it was Friday and I was still here. After all the years I had been here, and all I had been through I was obviously still naive. Why do we always think we are immune to the evils that befall others?

I went in my house and lay on my mattress deep in thought. I had to act and fast, but I didn't know what to do. I could see no solution. I had just over a week before I had to leave the premises. I had to be out of the country before then, otherwise I would end up in the compound in Famara and that was something I had to avoid. I was still laid there when it became dark and I was no clearer in my mind what I should do. The only person I could rely on to help me was Nick, but what could he do about this? I started to dial his number and then reconsidered, he wasn't able to help and I would be putting an unfair burden on him by confiding in him. Half an hour later I once again started to dial Nick's number. There was no-one else who had been as supportive of me over the years, and looking at things from another perspective, was I being fair on him to allow something awful to happen to me without even giving him the opportunity to help. This time I let his phone ring.

He answered on the third ring, I instinctively knew I should have waited until the morning, it was Friday night and before I even heard him speak I knew he would be intoxicated. I even knew which bar he was in by the background music. "Hi honey, you okay?" From those first few words I knew my instincts were correct, there was no point in talking to Nick until the morning. "I'm in the Talisman, the lads are all here and Leanne and Wendy, do you want to come up?"

"No, but I do need to talk to you Nick."

"It would do you good to get out, we are having a good laugh, and I'll come down and fetch you."

"No, sorry, I'm not the best of company at the moment."

"Alright honey, but you should let your hair down a bit. I've told you before I will take you out, but if you want to speak to me I can be with you in about ten minutes."

"No, Nick I need you completely sober, I have something very serious to tell you."

"Shit, that doesn't sound good; I'll see you as usual in the morning."

"Can you come earlier, about 8 o'clock? I want to speak to you while there are no staff here."

"Fine love, try and lighten up, you sound very stressed, nothing is that bad, you now have your freedom." I smiled to myself as I put the receiver down; I wondered if Nick would still think the same when I had spoken to him the next day. He did have a knack of making light of situations and had been here long enough not to take life too seriously. I settled down for the night, feeling better simply for having phoned Nick, perhaps I was putting too much hope in him, but I knew he would do all he could to help me. As they say a problem shared is a problem halved, and someone else knowing my plight and someone I could discuss things with would help lighten my load. I had been alone too long; we all need someone to confide in.

Chapter Twenty-Seven

Papers at Last

Much to my surprise I slept well but was awake early. I felt much better knowing that soon I would be able to share my problems. Why hadn't I done it before? Pride I supposed and not wanting to burden a friend. I went out into the garden and sent the night security home early. It was quite common for me to do this so he wasn't surprised, but he would have been if he had been here when Nick arrived. I didn't want him to report to Sidi that Nick had been here so early in the morning, he would find that suspicious. After he had left, I boiled the kettle on the only form of cooking we had left the single gas hob. It took a long time to boil and I didn't want to waste time making the coffee when Nick was here, I wanted him gone again before the day staff arrived. I also needed something to occupy myself while I waited for him.

Once again I paced the garden, there was compacted sand stretching diagonally across where I had paced so many times in the few weeks since we had taken up the garden slabs. I tried making new patterns in the sand but it only occupied me for a short time. I checked my watch every few minutes, it was ten past eight, where was Nick? I was confident he wouldn't let me down, but I also knew he had been fairly drunk when I had spoken to him the previous evening. Maybe he was still asleep, or maybe he had no recollection of our conversation. I checked my watch again, eight fifteen. I was getting desperate; Latif would be here in about three quarters of an hour, I didn't want him to find Nick here. I dialled Nick's mobile.

"Morning Honey," he answered cheerfully.

"Hi Nick, have you remembered I wanted you to come down this morning?"

"Don't get your knickers in a twist, I'm on the way, a few of us went back to Leanne's last night and after a few more drinks there, well quite a few actually I decided to take a taxi home, so I'm walking around there to collect the pick-up, then I will be with you okay?"

"Okay see you soon." I went back into the kitchen to reboil the kettle so it wouldn't take me long to make when Nick arrived. In an effort to save more time I got out the coffee and powered milk. Dispassionately I noticed that my hands weren't shaking as I spooned them into the mugs. That was a bonus. Soon after I heard Nick's pick-up grind to a halt outside my gate. I quickly made the coffee, and by the time Nick was walking over the makeshift rickety plank bridge I was heading back towards the garden table with our coffees in my hands. "What service! This is just what I need, I'm not used to having to walk so early in the morning and especially not on a Saturday," Nick remarked as he pulled out a chair to sit down. "Right now tell me what's happened."

"It's a long story," I started, really still dreading to tell him the mess I was in, "in short at the start of the year Sidi didn't pay my taxes, which meant I couldn't get my residential papers and I still haven't got them. Until I have them I can't leave the country, and now he is demanding £10,000 to get them for me."

"Shit........the bastard..." Nick stood up pushing his chair away, which being plastic fell backwards onto the sand. He strode to the stage, clenching his fists as if he wanted to hit someone. He pounded the top of the wall and stood for a moment looking into the Peace Haven grounds. I had never seen him so angry. He marched back, and slammed his fist down on the table, spilling much of our coffee, "This is fucking blackmail; we can't let him get away with this." He picked the chair up and sat down. I had known Nick would be angry but the physical expression of his rage surprised me. Thank goodness I hadn't told him when any of the staff were around. He was, however, generally speaking a calm person and I knew he would have some constructive ideas when his anger subsided. He was right this was blackmail, I hadn't really thought of it as such, but in short that was what was happening. Much calmer now Nick said, "Right Honey, there isn't much I can do by myself. I could ask Maria to help, you know she has uncles that can open doors in most offices, do you mind if I tell her."

"That's not a problem."

"Many times you have asked why I stay with her now we are not really together, that is why, it is best to keep her happy; her connections can be very useful at times."

"Yeah, I know, but will they be willing to help and what do you think they can do."

"I don't know Helen, but I don't know where to go to get help with this, let me go and speak to her and I will get back to you. In the meantime, just be friendly to Sidi if he comes down, don't risk upsetting him, hopefully we will sort this out soon." Nick hadn't drunk much of his coffee, but after he had gone, although I still was no nearer to solving my problem, I was more relaxed. I sat there and finished what hadn't been spilt of mine, watching the small wild life that was waking up in my garden. The ants were very industrious, searching for their breakfasts in the sand, life had been much easier for them when the bar was open; the crumbs that dropped on the slabs were easy pickings for them and the birds.

Suddenly realising I didn't want any of the staff to arrive and see I had two cups on the table I went and washed them up. It had only seemed a few minutes since Nick had left so I was surprised when my mobile rang and I saw it was him. "Hi." I answered him, "I didn't expect to hear from you for ages yet."

"If I say I will do something don't I do it? Listen carefully, are any of your lads there yet?"

"No."

"Good, Maria phoned one of her uncles. He has made an appointment for me to see the head of immigration at two this afternoon. I will need your passport and your last year's papers. Get those ready to give me, in case anyone is there by the time I get back to you, but I will be with you in a few minutes."

True to his word Nick was back before the staff arrived. He didn't stay just took my passport and I gave him all my papers since I had arrived so that he had proof that I had always sorted my papers quickly in the past, which may or may not help the situation. Nick told me to try not to worry and he would phone me as soon as he had any news.

Latif arrived soon after Nick had left, quickly followed by Petreeni and Sidi, I was grateful none of them had seen him here; I didn't want to raise their suspicions in anyway. We passed an uneventful morning, all of us finishing jobs that needed doing before I left. The very nature of our work made the morning seem endless but I was time watching as well. Every half hour I would unobtrusively check the time only to find that five minutes had passed. I wondered what sort of reception Nick would receive at the immigration authorities; there was no way of predicting the outcome of this meeting. But I was sure of one thing, it couldn't make things worse.

Two o'clock finally came as we sat down for our lunch, the lads and Tina ate enthusiastically, but I only picked at my food, eating was the last thing on my mind. We were still all sat together talking over coffee when my mobile rang. I nearly dropped it in my eagerness to answer when I saw it was Nick. I got up and walked to the far end of the garden, not wanting my conversation overheard. Sidi looked up and watched as I walked away, his curiosity was getting the better of him. I saw him look as if he was going to get up and follow me, but I saw a warning glance from Latif, and he sat down again.

"Is anyone with you?" Nick asked.

"Yes they are all here, but I have come to the far end of the garden by the rubbish heap no-one can overhear."

"Right listen carefully, "he began, "I told the immigration your story, they insisted on calling the police in and they want to come and arrest Sidi, you okay with that?"

I hesitated; yes this was what I wanted but not now, not while I was still in the country. Before I answered Nick continued, "What's the matter, don't you want that?"

"Well, not really, not while I'm here. Nick you have seen some of his family, he may not be very big but some of his cousins are big buggers, you know what is likely to happen to me, that is why I wouldn't say anything before. I'm scared stiff. I will gladly give a statement and what they do when I'm out of here I couldn't care less."

"Yeah, okay, I see where you are coming from. Look don't move away from the phone I will ring back shortly, I'm sat in the office with the immigration and the police now, I don't think they will be very happy about this but I will explain how you feel."

I was shaking when I came off the phone. I spent the next few minutes sorting out the black sacks, a job that none of us liked but which had to be done. The others seemed content to sit and chat, I saw Sidi glance in my direction every so often, but he or none of the others made any effort to come and help me. As it was Saturday when they traditionally finished work early, I was expecting them to prepare to leave shortly. To my relief Nick phoned back quicker than I had expected. "Right Helen all sorted," he told me, "it cost though. I had to give them £100."

"That's nothing I was being charged £10,000. Do I have to come and see them to get the papers?" I couldn't believe it was sorted out so soon.

"No, I have your passport in my hand, fully stamped, all you have to do is go to the airport, and the £100 also gives us safe passage through the airport, but we have to get you to the airport ourselves, when do you want to go?"

I started to babble on without really thinking, "There's a flight to Brussels this evening, and I would like to be on it." I told him excitedly, I was shaking, whether it was from relief or euphoria I don't know.

"Calm down Honey, think practically," Nick was being more sensible that I was, "we have to arrange your ticket, and there may not even be any seats on that flight, but I think you maybe right about flying to Brussels, their flight times are at a better time for getting you out of The Dominion without drawing attention to ourselves."

A bit less agitated and thinking more clearly I replied, "Yes, you are right, my first reaction was just to get away, but you are right, this is going to have to be planned carefully."

"Yeah, there is a flight next Thursday, we will try and get you on that, do you think you can keep him sweet till then."

"No problem I've been doing that for years."

"That's a girl, you can do this. Now keep calm act naturally, and think how it is best to arrange all this, do you have the cash for your fare?"

"Yeah, but it's in the bank; I will have to get it. Let me think this through. I will talk to you later. They are all at lunch and I need time on my own to think. Nick, I will never be able to thank you enough for this."

"No probs, you know we are all family." That was true; many ex-pats said we were one big family, as none of us had our own families around us. "Can they hear you?"

"I'm still over by the rubbish; they can't possibly hear me. They should be going soon as well."

"Right you go back to them, I will ring you later, I won't come down again today; I don't want any of them to think I'm there too often, talk later." I took a few deep breaths to clear my head, I could hardly believe Nick had managed to sort my papers, I looked over towards the staff, Tina had picked up the food bowl and was heading towards the kitchen to wash it, Latif and Petreeni were starting to collect their belongings together, they would soon be leaving. Sidi was still sat at the table; it was obvious he had no intention of going yet.

I strolled back to where he was sat hoping to appear more composed than I felt. Sidi said nothing as I sat next to him; he simply looked in my direction and glanced away again. He was eager to know who I had been speaking to but would not ask while the others were there. It wasn't long before the lads left, shortly followed by Tina, the next day was Sunday, and they would not be coming back until Monday. "Who was that on the phone?" Sidi asked before Tina had even reached the gate, he was obviously concerned. "And why do you always walk away when you are on the phone."

"Simon," I told him a convenient white lie. He eyed my phone as if he didn't believe me and I could see him thinking about taking it away from me to check. "I walked away because it was a private conversation and you know that I don't to like my private conversations overheard." I must remember to delete my call list I thought, in case he ever checks my phone. Not that I left it about, but I wouldn't put it past him to try.

"Ah Simon, did you talk to him about my money?"

"Yes, I did as it happens he will send it; don't worry. So are you going to sort my papers out now?"

"It won't take long to sort your papers; I will do it as soon as the money is in my bank account."

"So you won't take my word that the money is coming." That was wishful thinking on my part.

"I will do it as soon as I have the money. When will that be?"

I quickly thought up a delaying tactic, Sidi had no idea of European banking procedures, "Simon can't touch the money until it has been in his account for a week. The cheque has to clear and that will be next Thursday. Then he has to transfer it to you, but that could take a few days and with the weekend, I would say it will be Tuesday week at the earliest. You must write your bank account number down for me so I can pass it on to Simon."

"Oh yes, I will do that," he said absentmindedly as if he hadn't thought of that. Once he heard this good news Sidi didn't stay around for long, he left saying he would come down the following evening and go and get a pizza takeaway for us.

"If you want," I told him, "if not I will get myself something to eat." With that he got up and left without saying anything more.

I was elated, I knew I would be going home soon; I sat in the garden deep in thought deciding the best way to arrange my departure. I was much calmer now, thank goodness Nick had persuaded me not to try and leave on this evening's flight, everything had to be planned carefully, to the smallest detail, and I could not risk my plans being discovered. I needed to go to Oliver's bank to withdraw my money, then to the airline offices to purchase my ticket. I sat pondering as the monkeys disturbed me on their way home to the 'monkey reserve' where they went for the night. I had often wondered how many monkeys the tourists actually saw when they visited the reserve during the day, as I was under the impression most of them where in the neighbouring hotels returning to the reserve in the evening. They stopped long enough in my garden to help themselves to my new season's cashew fruits. They sat in the trees, crossing their legs in the same way we do and enjoyed their snack before they continued their short journey home. There were many things I would miss about Shendi.

It started getting dark, the time span between light, dusk and darkness is very short here, I made my way into my little house, where I would read until the night security arrived and I could settle down for the evening and try and sleep I was going to need all the strength I could get. Nick phoned to check I was alright, I was so grateful for his support, I no longer felt I was alone, which in itself gave me courage.

The next day, being Sunday I spent alone but in a much better mood than the previous Sunday. Now I had admitted to myself how serious my problems were and now I shared them with someone, I could truly rest. I did not have to fight against forbidden thoughts. I relaxed in the garden, reading and doing crosswords, I felt a new person, my confidence had certainly had a large boost, every now and then I got up and walked around the garden and as so often in the past stood on the stage watching the comings and goings at the hotel. I had to admit I had had many good times here, and now I had this new confidence busting inside me, and I knew I was free to leave, the good memories were starting to return. I was a new person with a new future ahead of me. I had plenty to look back on and plenty to look forward to; Kevin, Steph and little Karen were never far from my thoughts.

As he had said the day before, Sidi came down early in the evening and I sent him to get us a take away pizza from the local Italian restaurant. I had eaten only a mango and a banana, both grown in my own garden all day; so would enjoy the pizza. Sidi seemed as relaxed as I was over our supper, he didn't mention the money, and I had no reason to broach the subject with him, but just before he was about to leave, I said to him, "Do you want to take the things you are going to need to get my papers, when you get the money I want everything sorted as soon as possible." Being Nick had already sorted everything for me, this wasn't a serious question I just wanted to see his reaction.

"Stop fretting, I thought you would give your moaning a rest now you know how we will sort things." Sidi hadn't said much, but it was obvious I had embarrassed him, and seeing his discomfort gave me pleasure, I was gloating knowing I would soon have the better of him.

Soon after Sidi had left I phoned Nick. "Sorry to ask you for more help, but can I ask a favour from you in the morning."

"Yes, sure I was going to come down early before your boys arrived to discuss how we were going to arrange your departure."

"Before we arrange the escape, I need my ticket, and I don't want to risk going to get it alone, it would only take one of Sidi's cronies to see me going into the airlines office and our plans could be foiled. I would like you to take me to Oliver's bank to withdraw my money and then to buy my ticket. If you come in both the offices with me, if we are seen I can tell him, you were going to the bank and I was with you, likewise at the airlines, you go home for a while most rainy seasons so he wouldn't think that strange."

"He would think it strange that I pick you up and take you to the bank and the airlines."

"I've thought of that, we will tell him you wanted me to go and see your hotel site before I left, after all you have been asking me to go and see it for ages."

"Okay, that's fine I will collect you at about the same time as I usually come down not to raise suspicion."

I felt smug, I was confident with Nick's help all was going to work out fine, and with the idea in my head that at last, I had the upper hand over Sidi; gave me a sense of pride. I slept well that night for the first time in ages.

Latif, Petreeni and Tina had all arrived the next morning and started their work. As soon as it was 9 o'clock I went to the top of the garden, out of earshot of the staff, to phone Oliver to let him know I would be coming to close my account and collect all my money. I felt this was necessary as the rumours about the bank being in trouble were still rife, and there had been occasions when people had gone to the bank to make withdrawals and found the bank didn't have sufficient funds at the branch and been given only a small amount of their withdrawal. Shortly after I heard the gate clang and I looked up to see Nick come in. I was slightly perturbed to see he had bought Alou, a local lad Nick had known for years with him. Alou had been a chef at The Mango Tree when Nick was a tourist and stayed there, he now worked at one of the other hotels. The plan was that when Nick eventually opened his bar Alou would become one of his chefs. I wondered why Nick had bought Alou with him; I did not really want to take him with us. Even though I had also known Alou for a long time through Nick my distrust at that point of all locals was huge. It may have clouded my judgement but I would rather Nick and I went about my business alone.

Nick, Alou and myself had a coffee, and I sat there still bewildered and a little annoyed that Nick had bought Alou with him, until Nick said, "Being you are going soon Helen, I would like you to come and see my hotel, I have been asking you to come for ages, and I don't want you to go without seeing it. Are you busy this morning?"

Latif had just walked past us, so I was pleased Nick asked me to go with him while we could be overheard, there was a strong possibility Sidi would arrive while we were out.

"No, I've got plenty of time to spare now, and I do want to see it before I leave."

Turning to Alou, Nick then said, "You stay here, we won't be so very long, you may be able to give Helen's lads a hand until we get back, then I will drop you to your family home at Pedou." Turning back to me he said, "Come on, Helen, I have things to do even if you don't."

I went into my little home to collect my handbag, earlier in the day I had already put all I would need to withdraw my money and arrange my ticket. As we prepared to leave Nick said to Alou, "Keep your fingers crossed I may be able to persuade her to stay and run the bar, when she has seen the place."

Alou grinned and watched us leave, I told Latif I was going with Nick to his hotel and I may be gone for awhile. As I got into Nick's pick-up I said to him, "I was confused when I saw you arrive with Alou, I thought you were going to bring him with us."

"No, he rang me last night and asked if I could take him to see his family, and I thought this was a good opportunity to make use of him. Sidi will probably arrive while we are gone, and I can tactfully ask Alou later what happened when he found you weren't there. Don't worry, I'm not stupid you know, I'm hardly likely to bring someone we're not sure we can trust with us, but I don't think Alou, would say anything, but best to be safe than sorry."

Nick drove me directly to the bank, where Oliver had told his staff to expect me. As we entered the small outer office, in spite of the queue, the counter hatch was opened and Nick and I were shown through. "Oliver is expecting you, Madam Dominion," the lad sat behind one of the small cramped office desks told me, "Do you know your way up to his office."

"Yes, I've been before." I answered remembering my visit to Oliver's office to deposit the money from the sale of Reggie's compound. I knew the once I had gone up the stairs there was a labyrinth of passage ways before I would finally reach Oliver's office; but I was confident I could find my way.

Nick waited in the inner office, while I made my way up the rickety staircase and looked somewhat bewildered at the passageways ahead of me, at that point I wasn't as confident as a short while ago that I remembered the way. The office lad had obviously phoned up to Oliver to tell him I was on my way up as he was standing at the door ready to greet me. Oliver seemed pleased to see me, "I take it if you are closing your account you are finally leaving us. Are you going out on tomorrow's flight?"

"I'm going soon, but not on tomorrow's flight, I'm hoping to go by the end of the week, but that is confidential information, if you don't mind."

"Don't worry about me; I won't tell anyone, I always knew you would have to beat a hasty retreat when the time came. Are you by yourself, or have you got help?"

"My beloved is downstairs." I tongue in cheek told him, Oliver had often referred to Nick as 'my beloved', I wasn't quite sure why, Nick had always been a very good friend to me, but I think several people mistakenly thought it was more than just a friendship.

"Good, you may need help before you finally escape." Little did Oliver know how true those words were. While I was there I gave Oliver my favourite cookbook, which had once belonged to my mother. Oliver's wife often entertained for him, and at one time he had contemplated opening a small restaurant for her. He thanked me for this and I took my leave. The passage ways seemed different each time I navigated them, but I soon found my way back to inner office where Nick had waited for me where we collected, and together we counted my money. Knowing the money would be bulky I had bought a large bag with me, after we had contented ourselves the money was correct, I bundled it into my bag, and we left the bank, the first part of our mission over. Now for the second part; we still had to book my ticket.

"We are more than halfway to my place, do you want to come and see it?" Nick asked as we got back into the pick-up.

"I would like to see it Nick, really I would, I have heard so much about it, but I'm afraid my air ticket is all that is on my mind at the moment."

"Yeah, sure Honey. Are you absolutely sure you want to go via Brussels?"

"I think I have to. I don't see how I could get out of The Dominion to catch the direct flight; it is too early in the afternoon. The Brussels' flight is in the evening, I can leave when there is no one about. Come on take me to the Brussels' airways office and we can ask what options I have." We drove back towards the main tourist area where the airline offices were situated, I watched with renewed enthusiasm the scenery as it slipped by, there were many more buildings than when I first arrived, in fact the road we were driving on hadn't existed back then, neither had the bank offices we had just visited. There had been so many changes during my short stay in Shendi, but none of it detracted from views of the vast bush land which still dominated the country, with its swaying palms, and roaming cattle.

"Did you tell Oliver you were going?" Nick pulled me out of my reverie.

"Yes, but I didn't tell him when, he was bound to deduce I was going with me closing my account, he won't tell anyone; I told him you were with me, he was pleased to hear I had someone helping me." Nick smiled on hearing this.

Before long we pulled into the car park of the building complex, which housed the airline offices among several other shops and offices with flats above. This was always a bustling area, with many people coming and going from the various premises, there was usually a few taxis parked in the car park hoping to attract some custom. This bothered me knowing Sidi's links with them. There was also a local 'fast food' seller providing breakfasts and lunches for people working in the complex as well as passerbys. Nick pulled into one of the few available spaces, and we got out and made our way into the office. I was glancing all around me, hoping not to recognise any faces in the crowd. Nick obviously noticed this as he said to me, "Relax Helen, it doesn't matter who is around, if Sidi gets told you were here, you can do as you said and tell him I was booking a flight home, as far as he is concerned you can't go until you get your papers."

"I know, but you know how jumpy and paranoid I am," again Nick grinned and gave me a sideways glance.

I was surprised how busy the office was, but it was low season, which is when most people travel, there were ex-pats, many other Europeans than British, going home for the summer, and locals travelling to visit European friends while business was slow. There were no available assistance, Nick and I went over to an advertising board and read it.

"Are you sure you want to go back to the U.K.?" Nick asked, "Look at all the places we could go to from here."

I looked at the adverts almost enviously, it was a big wide world, with many, many places I still hadn't visited, but I knew I had to get back to the U.K. and get my life sorted out. "It's tempting, but no Nick I need to get back and get somewhere to live and a job, and exciting things like that before I think about anymore travelling."

"Don't forget the bar in Thailand."

It was my turn to smile now, "Oh yes, the bar in Thailand I had almost forgotten that."

There was soon a sales assistant free, and we both sat down opposite him, and before I knew it we had booked my flight home. I was flying to Dakar in Senegal, then on to Brussels, where I had a five hour wait before my flight to Heathrow. Nick had queried if I would be alright waiting for my onward flight in Brussels, but I was so relieved to be getting away, this didn't concern me in the least. At last it seemed the gods were starting to smile on me, when we paid for the flight, the company dealt only in American Dollars and the exchange rate had changed that morning making my ticket 1,500 shillings cheaper than it would have been the previous day. I looked on this as a good omen. It was Monday morning; I was flying out on Thursday evening. In only three days I would be away and free to start a new life.

Pleased we had sorted everything out, and in a reasonably short time we made our way back to The Dominion. The colourful bars, restaurants and shops, and the splendid African dresses on the tourist strip suddenly took on a new brighter appearance to me; I think I had been viewing everything from a blighted perspective for a long while. As we pulled under the arch, I could see Sidi's car parked near out entrance. "Damn it,"

I muttered as much to myself as to Nick, "I was hoping to get back before he arrived."

"Don't panic. We have been down to my site, no problem." Nick said as he parked alongside Sidi's car. "Right, you don't want to risk him finding your ticket or your money, give it all to me before we go in. I will go home and put it all in my safe before I go to work."

"Good point. It is their pay day on Thursday, which works out well, I will be able to pay them before I go without raising any suspicion." I did a quick calculation in my head and took out sufficient to pay the staff and to have a bit of cash in my pocket to last me until I left. I opened the glove compartment of the pick-up and put the remainder of the money, which was in Shendian Shillings and my flight ticket in there.

"I need some money exchanged so I will change that into Queen's heads for you, shillings don't go too far back home." Nick said.

I smiled at this I had nearly forgotten I would need my money changed; my brain obviously wasn't working to full power. Together Nick and I walked towards the gate of The Dominion. "Act naturally, don't do anything to make them disbelieve where we say we have been."

"Sure, I'm glad you are with me, I need a bit of moral support."

"You will be fine, just keep them all sweet, you only have a few days now to keep this up, but I need to come down when we can talk in peace, we have to plan how we are going to get you out of here."

I didn't answer Nick as we were crossing the small plank of wood across the pond by then, and all eyes were on us. Latif and Petreeni were clearing some of the rubble from the old bar area, Sidi and Alou were sat at the table, Tina was nowhere in sight, she, I assumed was in the kitchen preparing our lunch. We made our way towards Sidi and Alou.

"Hi," Sidi cheerfully said, putting on an act in front of Nick and Alou, "I was surprised to see you had gone out."

"Nick has taken me down to see his hotel." I replied equally as cheerful.

"What do you think of it?" Alou was keen to know.

"I was impressed it is bigger than I expected." I answered hoping he wasn't going to ask too many more questions.

"Yes, it is going to be good when it is finished, what did you think of the kitchen?" he asked, as I felt myself getting flustered.

Nick came to my rescue, "Alou keeps complaining I haven't made the kitchen big enough."

"Well he may have a point," I replied trying to sound knowledgeable, "but on the other hand Alou, it is better for you if it is compact, you will have everything close at hand."

"I know that," Alou told me, "but it is much smaller than your Dominion kitchen was."

"Yes, but I always considered that one was too big."

"We will discuss the merits of a bigger kitchen later; it is not too late to enlarge it yet." Nick informed him.

"Has Nick tempted you to come and work for him Helen?" Alou asked, I wondered if this was what Nick had given him as his reason for taking me to the hotel. I smiled at the thought. Several times Nick had told me if I could keep The Dominion alive while he finished building I would always have a job there.

"Oh, I don't know about that." I said smiling at Nick.

Tina must have heard us return as she came around the corner of my house from the direction of the kitchen carrying a tray of coffee cups. I was grateful for this an increased caffeine intake would possibly help me think clearer; the conversation was becoming a little too difficult for my tired brain to cope with. I had noted Sidi looking from one to the other of us during this short discussion and not contributing to it. He suddenly looked at Nick and said, "I would like to see your place, can I come and see it sometime."

"Why not, "Nick replied, "if you had been here earlier this morning you could have come with us." It crossed my mind that maybe Sidi intended asking Nick for a job, I could only imagine what Nick's response to that would be.

After they had finished their coffees Nick and Alou left us, I again felt very alone and vulnerable. Sidi became more vocal once the others left, which I had thought would happen.

"How big is Nick's place?" he asked.

"It is a fair size." I vaguely answered.

"If it isn't very big, you were a long time looking at it, you were gone for ages, and if I had known you wanted to go and see it, I could have taken you."

"Do you know where it is?"

"Not exactly, but I could have asked Nick to direct me; but that doesn't get away from the point that you have been a long time. Poor Alou has been here waiting for Nick to take him to visit his family. That is another problem with Taubabs you only think of yourselves." It was obvious he was anxious about my outing, and it gave me pleasure to see Sidi in this agitated state, he had always been nervous of my friendship with Nick.

"We went to the bank on the way back for Nick to collect money for his boys wages, there was a long queue, and as for Alou, he didn't have to wait he could have gone by bush taxi, if he would rather Nick take him for free that is fine, but he has to wait until Nick is able to take him, simple." I told him, imagining Nick quizzing Alou on the journey to his family about Sidi's reaction when he found I had dared to go out without telling him. Sidi's body language, as much as he tried to hide his feelings, made no secret of the fact he was anxious to know exactly where we had been. I can't put my exhilaration into words at seeing Sidi squirm like this; at long, long last I had the upper hand over him. I must keep extremely calm and not do or say anything that could possibly give our plans away.

In my determination to act as normally as possible I went into my house and changed into my old clothes and to set about helping Latif and Petreeni. When I came out of the house again, Sidi was still sat at the table, with one foot up on the chair he was sat on, fiddling with his toes; a gesture which reminded me of Ousman in The Peace Haven's reception, possibly this was a nervous reaction. "Come on Sidi," I called out to him, "if you are staying, there is work to be done." Reluctantly he came and joined us, and in silence for most of the rest of the day we all worked alongside each other. I was satisfied with the demolition work, I would have liked to have cleared all the rubble, but otherwise I was content we had raised the buildings to the ground.

The lads, including Sidi all left soon after they had eaten, but before he went Sidi slipped a small scrap of paper to me, and said "That is my bank details for Simon."

"Okay" was all I replied as I took the paper from him, he looked at me askance, I think he was expecting me to make a bit of a scene, but with the excitement I was feeling why should I bother to react, I thought afterwards maybe I should have made some sort of response not to arouse his suspicions. I helped Tina wash up so that she could also go home, I was so grateful to have my solitude. There wasn't long to go now until I would be home, but I was finding this pretence I had to keep up all day so very difficult.

Simon phoned during the evening, "Is everything alright?" he asked.

"Yes, I'm fine." I lied to him; I saw no point in telling him the truth.

"Then why are you still there. Don't you have the money to pay your fare?"

Without thinking, and regretting it as the words came out of my mouth, I told him what was happening, "I haven't been able to come, Sidi wants you to send him £10,000 before he will sort out my papers for me to be able to leave."

"Oh shit, I had a feeling you had been holding something back, that will make a big hole in the money, aren't you able to sort this out yourself?" I was immediately annoyed with Simon for thinking about the money before my safety.

"Don't worry about me, I have someone helping me now, and he has got my papers for me, and we have been and got my ticket this morning, I will be in the U.K. before the week-end."

"Do I know who is helping you?"

"Possibly not, he does remember you, but he only came out once while you were here, but he has lived here for a few years now."

"Can you trust him?"

"Yes, he has my passport my money and my ticket. I wouldn't give him that if I couldn't trust him." Simon cut our conversation short after I had told him the position I was in, which again rather annoyed me, as I thought he wasn't concerned about my plight; but on reflection he possibly felt guilty that he wasn't here to help me himself. I was on edge after my conversation with Simon, I shouldn't have told him the predicament I was in, it wasn't his problem, and I had no right to give him that worry. Nick was helping me and I was confident all was going to be fine, but as I once again paced my little house that evening; I not only worried myself with concern over how I was finally going to leave The Dominion, but I was so very angry with myself for telling Simon. As I had done so many times in the past I blamed myself for everything, which looking back now was wrong but at the time there was no-one to tell me so. I suddenly remembered I had to phone Euan in the UK. When he had been out recently he had told me he would collect me from the airport when I flew home. He answered promptly and I said, "Hi Euan, are you and Pamela okay?"

"Yes we're both fine, Helen how are things going with you?"

"Well, it's a very long story, things are not too good; I will tell you when I get there. Now please don't tell anyone this, it is important nobody knows I'm leaving. Are you still willing to pick me up from the airport?" Euan had many friends in Shendi both locals and ex-pats, and I knew he was in regular contact with many long term tourists therefore I wanted to be extra sure there was no chance of anyone getting to hear I was leaving. News travelled quickly in Shendi, and I could not to risk Sidi hearing about my plans. There was every likelihood that he would as Euan had friends living in Sidi's village.

"I would obviously want to tell Pamela."

"Oh yes, I didn't expect you not to tell Pamela, but it is very important no one here knows I'm leaving."

"It's like that is it?"

"Yes, I will explain when I see you. I will be flying into Heathrow, terminal four at 10 o'clock Friday morning." I gabbled out excitedly.

"There aren't any flights into Heathrow. Don't you mean Gatwick at 10 in the evening?"

"There are plenty of flights into Heathrow and I will be on one."

"Not from Shendi there's not," he argued with me.

"Maybe not, but I'm flying in from Brussels on a British Airways flight."

"Fine, that does sounds like you do have problems, talk when I see you, I will be there don't worry." I thanked Euan and cut the conversation short there; my paranoia was telling me not to be on the phone too long. I knew my landline had been tapped in the past and didn't want to risk my conversation being intercepted. I knew my mind was overactive but this was becoming reminiscent of scenes on the pages of many thriller novels I had read. I could hardly believe this was happening to me.

I eventually settled down to rest on my mattress, and tried against all odds to sleep. The lively African tribal music was blearing out from restaurant at The Peace Haven, I do enjoy the drumming, but not at that particular time the loud, relentless, repetitive banging was more than I could cope with, I put my pillow over my head, and tossed and turned endlessly. No matter how I tried I couldn't relax; I was so close to leaving, but so much could still go wrong with our plans. I had to get the lads to go home a bit earlier than usual on Thursday so I could get to the airport on time, without arousing their suspicions. I had to think this out carefully, I was shaking, there was no way I was going to get any sleep. I got up and paced again, my eyes were picking with tiredness, my mind was going over and over all that happened to me over the last few years, but this was no good, all the reflecting in the world, would not change the position I was in, I had to find some inner strength I was going to need all my wits about me during the next few days.

I did eventually return to my bed, and against all odds I slept until I was woken by the monkeys playing in my garden. I knelt up on my mattress and looked out of the tiny window that was only large enough to let in a small amount of daylight. I stayed there for several moments watching them with pleasure, my cats were cowered in the far corner of the garden under a shrub, they were always afraid of the monkeys. There were many things I would miss about Shendi.

Nick came as usual for his coffee on the Tuesday morning. In between talking about the ever raising costs of a bag of cement and the difficulties he was having doing manual work in increasing heat and humidity as the rains were fast approaching, when we thought all of my lads were out of earshot he asked quietly, "Are you okay, you look tired."

"I didn't sleep very well, but I'm fine."

"Are you getting yourself sorted, what about your packing, you must be careful they don't realise what you are doing."

"That's not a problem, I packed my case before I moved into the little house as there wasn't anywhere to hang any clothes, and I have a large, heavy box I want sent freight. That was also packed a few weeks ago. Adam and Jane will be coming down this morning to take me over for a coffee, I can trust them I will ask them to send that on for me, that will save you a job."

"I'll send it if you want, but they may be pleased you have asked them to help, they have been friends of yours for ages, and I think you should tell them you are going. I'm going to collect 200 bags of cement this afternoon, so if the prices keep rising, I will have some to keep me going for awhile."

I looked around and saw Latif and Sidi nearing us on their way to the back entrance with two large sacks, and I realised why Nick had changed the subject so quickly.

"I wonder where those are going and what is in them," I said as we both watched the lads, "and, you know what? I don't even care."

We both smiled at the thought of what was possibly left that the lads considered was saleable, "I would love to see their faces when they realise you are gone." Nick grinned.

Adam and Jane came down later in the morning, and as I had told Nick we would, we went over to The Peace Haven's coffee shop. Sat there sipping coffee and watching the entrance to The Dominion. I told them what was happening to me, of Nick's involvement and how I was hoping to get away on Thursday's flight. Jane was slightly amazed, but I don't think Adam was really surprised. They readily agreed to send my box home, as I was sure they would. After our coffee and biscuits, which gave me a much welcome caffeine and sugar boost, they walked back to The Dominion with me, where we said our farewells in our normal manner. I stood by the gate and watched their car disappear under the hotel's arch and wondered if I would ever see them again.

The rest of the day passed without event, the Tuesday U.K. flight flew overhead as we were sat having a late lunch just before the lads were ready to go home. I looked up at it, and noticed Sidi give me a sideways glance, but he said nothing at the time. A little later as Latif and Petreeni were preparing to leave he said, "I saw you watching the plane, I know you want to go, if the money arrives you will be leaving soon."

"Yeah, maybe I will be on next Tuesday's flight."

He looked at me quizzically, "I doubt it. You said the money won't come until Tuesday, by the time I have been to the bank to check it is here, and get your papers from Mariama, it will be too late to get a ticket in time for the flight."

I gave a loud audible sigh and said, "Then I suggest you see Mariama and start sorting my papers, do you want me to give you my passport so you can do that." I regretted saying that as soon as it was out, if he said yes, I didn't even have my passport, Nick had it, and at that stage I wouldn't have trusted Sidi with my passport in any case.

I had no need to worry, Sidi just gave me a dirty look that I couldn't really interpret and walked away. I smiled to myself, if only he knew. Even though I was still scared, the delight I had in the knowledge I was going to get the better of him, gave me a thrill. I had very mixed emotions, but I was feeling a deep inner satisfaction that I don't ever remember feeling in my life before.

Soon after this they all left and I was once again on my own, this solitude was most welcome. I didn't have to pretend and be watchful of everything I said. My black cat came and sat on my knee, she was my greatest concern, the other two had got onto the habit of going over the wall to The Peace Haven every morning as soon as the lads arrived and started making too much noise with the demolition to allow them the peace they wanted after a night on the prowl. They never seemed hungry when they returned, so I assumed they were being feed. The Peace Haven had many cats of their own which the tourist fed so I think mine were just two more. I wasn't worried about them after I left. I would leave them out sufficient dried cat food to last them for a couple of days; by that time I hoped they would realise I was no longer around and fend for themselves. The black cat was a different proposition, she was old, and was reliant on me. Latif had had two of my kittens and he was the only one I could rely on to look after her. He had even mentioned taking her home a couple of weeks ago. My decision was made I would ask Latif to take black cat home with him on Thursday. I continued to stroke her tenderly and she looked up at me, with almost pleading eyes, did she understand what was happening more than I realised?

I turned in for the night as soon as my security arrived, I didn't want too much conversation with him, and I was tired after my restlessness of the previous night. I was starting to doze off when I was bought to, by my mobile buzzing I had received a text; I saw it was from Nick.

'How about I come down for some jigi-jigi before I go home?' I read. I grinned to myself. That was typical of him; he often suggested tongue in cheek, when I had the bar open, that he could stay the night if I wanted him to. I thought for a few moments wanting my reply to be witty.

'Not a good idea you must remember I've been a born again virgin for six years.'

It wasn't long before I received his reply, 'It is you that should remember I have your passport, your ticket and your money.'

My reply to that came easily, 'You can give over, I have enough problems with one bugger blackmailing me.'

His reply simply said, 'I better go home then. Goodnight.'

It had been banter similar to this that had often been my life line when things had seemed really bad in the past; I knew I could rely on Nick to keep my spirits high, as well as being a pillar of strength. The calming effect this text had on me was amazing, I knew beyond the cheeky message his words really meant I'm out here for you, if I'm needed. I gave a broad smile, and cradled my mobile to my chest before I put it back at the side of the bed again. I realized that in spite of my many problems or perhaps because of them, I had leant many things about life and relationships during my stay in Shendi. I knew no matter what happened in the future Nick would always be my 'African brother'.

I snuggled under my thin sheet, even with the intense heat which preceded the rains; I liked the security of something over me. The drumming from the restaurant next door didn't have the same effect on me as it had the previous night, in fact I found it quite soothing; it is astounding how a different frame of mind can change how you feel so much. It wasn't long before I slipped into a deep restful sleep.

Nick arrived early the next morning for his coffee, he greeted me with a very broad grin, "You were a miserable bitch last night," he said cheerfully as he crossed our rickety plank of wood into the garden, where we waited for Tina to bring us our coffee. "You look better this morning though, you didn't have anyone else here I hope," he asked tongue in cheek.

"You must be joking, but I slept much better, and this is my last full day here."

"Don't say that too loudly and don't appear too calm. It wouldn't do to let then think you are too relaxed, you are meant to be getting anxious."

I knew this was good advice, Sidi had known he was getting me worried, it wouldn't do for him to realise things had changed; but not very long after my conversation with Nick I knew it was already too late. I had never been very good at hiding my feelings and Sidi had already concluded I was more relaxed than I was the previous week. "What is going on?" he asked in a manner I wasn't sure if it he was showing concern for me or anxiety himself.

"What do you mean, what on earth can possibly be going on?"

"Well I don't know you seem different. Last week you were awful, everyone was afraid to speak to you, you were shouting at everyone for no reason. Now you seem, I don't know, just different somehow." Sidi was possibly right, no doubt I was acting differently, and I would have to be very careful, a slip up now could be crucial to our plans.

"I know now there is nothing I can do about things, and Simon is sending the money, so you will get my papers and I can go, so there is no point in getting worked up about things I can't change."

"It's a shame you hadn't thought like that all the time then things wouldn't have got so nasty. It is your fault you have had so many problems, you will fight things all the time, you Taubabs do have funny ideas you know. Some things can't be changed so you have to go with them." This incensed me, but I was determined not to let it show.

"Anyway forget all that. I would still like to be on Tuesday's flight." "I've already told you to forget that, there won't be enough time, we will get you on Friday's flight."

"Whatever, whatever, we will see. I have been thinking about the work here. There isn't much more we can do and Saturday is the last day if the month. I think I will pay everyone off then or you will all be asking for another months pay. Then I can spent the rest of my time here relaxing, I can make out I'm a tourist."

That was agreed with all of them, my plans were all falling into place nicely, I was outwardly calm, but most of the day I was trembling inside. My emotions were so mixed, I was excited at the thought of going home, but whenever I thought of how I was going to get out of the country, I went into a sheer panic. The day seemed to drag on forever, I was anxious for everyone to leave so I could finish preparing for my departure.

At long last I was on my own and hurried into my house, I had already sealed the box I wanted freighted to the U.K. Nick was going to take it when I left and give it to Adam and Jane to send on for me. I wrote my brother's address down for them, I thought it unwise to label it yet. My case had been packed for a while but there was a few last minute things that needed to go in it. Every so often I looked over my shoulder, half expecting to see either Sidi or my night security stood there, although it was much too early for him to arrive yet. I thought my nerves had improved but on reflection looking at how I was behaving, going in and out of my house to check if anyone was around, standing and listening for any strange noises, I concluded my nerves were as bad as ever.

I sat down on the small wooden stool I had placed by the plastic garden table I had put inside the house. I rarely used these; I had sat outside most of the time, but it made the little house seem more like home. I took out one of the last headed sheets of headed Dominion paper I had and set about writing to Ali. I was due to leave The Dominion by the end of the month, which was only days away. I didn't want to go down and speak to Ali, it might have raised speculation that I maybe about to go. I explained to Ali, in the letter, I was leaving a few days earlier than I had intended as I had a family crisis in the U.K. I thanked him for his support during his management of The Peace Haven and told him the keys to both the main gate and the back gate were enclosed. I placed my letter in an unsealed envelope and put in carefully in my handbag. When we locked the gate as I was leaving I would put the keys in the envelope and give it to Nick to take to Ali the morning after I had left. Ali had met Nick when we had attended a wedding at the hotel together, I had introduced them, and so Ali wouldn't think it strange that Nick was delivering this letter for me.

After writing the letter I went for my last night time walk around the garden. Where would my next bed be I wondered as I settled down for my final night's sleep in Shendi.

Chapter Twenty-Eight

The Longest Day

Before I knew it I was woken by the enormous African crows making their normal early morning racket. It took me a couple of minutes for me to fully wake and realise that this was the last time I would hear them making their way across the corrugate. My last day in Shendi had arrived. Where would I be at this time tomorrow? Would it be in Europe, would it still be here at The Dominion or even worse, somewhere else in Shendi? I started to shake inside; I would have to be so careful, it was crucial I didn't make any slip ups. If Sidi even suspected I was going there was no telling what might happen. Along side the nerves was excitement. I was finally leaving; at times I had thought this day would never come. Even the roundabout flight did not bother me. I had always enjoyed travelling and I was looking forward to the flight. It was eight years since I had flown, years since I had gone further than 50 miles, years since I had travelled by anything other than a car, so the mere thought of flying was excitement enough.

I flung on my every day work clothes, and as soon as I knew the small supermarket at the bottom of the car park would be open, I went down and bought several packets of dried cat food. This would keep my faithful friends fed for a few days until they settled themselves into a new routine. Latif was the first to arrive and I spoke to him about taking the black cat home with him. He was only too happy to do so and I was satisfied this was the best option I had for her. I was sat inside the house once again, putting the staff's wages in their pay envelopes when Sidi and Petreeni arrived. Sidi knocked at the door, "Can I come in?" and without waiting for an answer opened the door and walked in. "What are you doing with that money?"

"What does it look like? I'm doing the wages, it's payday."

"You said you would finish things on Saturday."

"Yes, I know and I will finish on Saturday but today is the 28th, which is pay day; they will be expecting to be paid today." Sidi wasn't satisfied with this. He told me if I paid them they wouldn't come for the next two days.

"Whatever," I answered trying to appear unconcerned, "they aren't doing much now anyway. I don't mind. One thing you need to know because it affects you. Latif is going to take the black cat home with him this evening."

"Why? You mentioned him having her, but why today, you will be here for another week yet, you like your cats you will miss her if he takes her now, he can take her when you go. And anyway how does it affect me?"

"Right, first of all, I want her gone now, cats don't always like new homes, and try and find their way back to where they lived before, I don't want her to come back and find no one here."

"Don't be stupid," he interrupted me, "Latif lives a long way from here, you know where he lives, this cat can't come back here." I told him the story of the owner of one of the bars on the main tourist strip whose cat had started to be a nuisance to the customers. It had been driven to and left at one of the fishing villages a long way down the coast, where the thinking was that the cat could feed itself well on fish and be happy there. Three days later the cat walked into the bar looking very bedraggled and tired, but it had found its way home. Sidi had heard the story but had looked upon it as a taubab legend. Seeing that I was not going to change my mind, he obviously decided it wasn't worth arguing about. "OK. But how does it affect me?"

"I want you to drive Latif and the black cat home today."

That started off all the objections again. "What? Why? It doesn't have to go today"

"Yes it does, I have told you. I will feel a lot happier if it does. I want it to have time to settle in before I go."

"Well why do I have to drive it there? Latif has his bike, we can put her in a box and he can tie it on the back of his bike. I don't understand why you want me to take him."

"Come on, I know pure black cats are used to make jujus, if Latif takes her on the back of his bike, someone will try and take her from him, he will get a lot of problems."

"Yeah, I didn't think of that, but I need to get back to my village for the shop, I have to take over from my sister, I will be late if I take him home, and he will need his bike, I will take him up to the main road and then he can ride."

"That's an idea but wait a minute. I will let you all leave early; we don't have much to do. You can tie Latif's bike on your roof rack and take him right home, and still be back to your village in time for your sister to leave." Sidi didn't seem very pleased with this, but did reluctantly agree, and of course this suited me fine, I had arranged for them all to leave early without their suspicions being aroused.

Soon after this exchange Nick arrived for his coffee and in the true tradition of cloak and dagger books we waited until no one was near us to make our plans. I was to text him as soon as the coast was clear. He whispered that he would be sat outside King's a bar in the strip from about 3 o'clock so he could see my staff leaving. I had to be to the airport by 5 o'clock so a rendezvous at about four allowed plenty of time. Frightened that the hotel security at the arch would phone Sidi to report I was going out with Nick, we decided I would lay down in the back of the pickup covered by a blanket. A simple but hopefully effective plan, we hoped. I waved goodbye to Nick, with my usual "See you tomorrow" and went back to join the lads in the garden.

Surprisingly the morning passed quickly after Nick left, I had thought that it would drag, but it didn't. We were all pottering about; with none of us doing anything of importance. I asked Tina to prepare lunch early so that the lads could leave early, everything was coming together nicely and it all seemed too easy. However, my excitement and nerves were rising and something must have shown for as we sat down to lunch, Sidi asked, "Are you okay?"

I cursed to myself, what had I done to make him ask this, "I'm fine, why?"

"It is very hot and you are cold, look you have little bumps all over your arms."

I looked at my arms he was right, I had goose flesh, it must be my nerves coming out, I had to act naturally, but what reason could I give? As I was thinking how to answer him a plane flew directly over head, "Where is that plane going?" I asked partly to distract Sidi's attention away from my goose flesh, and partly to establish if he knew when flights were leaving.

"I'm not sure, it's not a very big plane; I don't think it's going to Europe, maybe somewhere like Morocco, why? Are you thinking of your flight next week? Don't worry as soon as the money is in my account, you can book your ticket to the UK."

"I know that, I just wondered where that plane was going; I didn't think there are any European flights today." I answered. As an ex-taxi driver I had thought it was feasible he would have known about flight times but I was relieved to find out that he was not up-to-date. Had I asked about flights to the UK, he probably could quote them chapter and verse, but on flights to other locations he seemed to be vague. This gave me hope for my flight to Brussels now only a few hours away. With that thought I glanced at my watch, it was 2.15 already. I decided to hurry them along, with Shendians tendency to have a disregard for time; life ingeneral is lived at a leisurely pace; but time was of an essence for me, I had a plane to catch. I stood up and said, "Come on lads, there is no point in doing anything else today. Latif, Sidi wants to take you home early so he can get back to Famara in time to relieve his sister at the shop. Start clearing up."

Tina collected the dishes together, and I went into the little kitchen with her to help her wash them so that she would also be ready to leave. The lads started gathering the tools up and putting them back into Simon's tool box. I went into the garden, trying to act casually even though I was trembling inside. I could hear their voices as they showered at the outside tap aided by a plastic cup. This was part of their leaving routine every afternoon but today it seemed to take for ever. As I sat there, hearing their laughter my little black cat came and wound itself round my ankles. She had followed me round for most of the day and I bent down, picked her up and put on my knee. As I fondled her, she looked up at me every now and then, was I imagining it or was there really pleading in her eyes? Did she really understand what was happening? I kissed her lovingly on the top of her head, and quietly told her, I was doing the best I could for her. My other cats were nowhere to be seen. Did they also know what was happening and were showing their disapproval by their absence?

Finally the lads came back chatting cheerfully. I paid them all and told Latif to go and secure his bike on Sidi's roof rack. Petreeni offered his assistance and followed him out of the main gate wheeling his bike for him. I glanced at my watch again, 3.10. I hoped this wouldn't take them too long, Nick was coming for me at 4, and I wanted to take a shower before travelling, time was creeping on. Sidi came and sat by me, I was still fondling the black cat.

"You are going to miss her, are you sure you don't want to keep her until you leave."

"No, I explained to you this morning she may try and come back, it would be awful if she came all this way and there was no one here. Besides Latif will be able to tell me how she is settling in with his other cats and I will feel happier about her."

To my relief Latif and Petreeni were back quicker than I expected. I kissed the black cat again on her forehead, and gave her to Latif, being they were going in the car there was no need to put her in the box, as he would have had to do if he was going on his bike, this was more convenient for all of us; except Sidi, who I knew was still annoyed I had asked him to take Latif home. I followed them outside and spoke to the cat, when they had her in the car, she was old, and looked so bewildered, my heart went out to her. I had tears in my eyes as I said good-bye , she had been a faithful friend; we had been through so much together. I watched them drive under the arch; 3.25. I had to get a move on.

Gone was the goose flesh of earlier, it had been replaced by warm, clammy skin and I was starting to tremble. I had to pull myself together; I didn't have any time to spare. I rushed back into the garden and put through a hurried text to Nick. 'All the lads gone c u @ 4.' I picked up my towel and started to climb over the remaining rubble. I had insisted they left the wall of my bathroom up, so that I could still shower knowing I couldn't be overlooked, the water did more than drip, in fact it poured out of the dilapidated water pipes in several places. The plan, as understood by Sidi and the workforce, was to knock this down on the day I left. However, as things had turned out would be the only wall left standing. Despite the wall I had seldom used the bathroom during my last days in Shendi, preferring to strip and hose myself down in the garden under shadow of darkness. This was a special occasion, and of course it wasn't yet dark. I showered as quickly as I could and then treading warily to avoid falling on the rubble, I clutched my towel around me and made for my small room. Dropping the towel onto the mattress I put on clothes I hadn't worn for a very long while, probably not since arriving. From the start when working in The Dominion I had worn a skirt and top matching the staff's uniform and when off duty I had relaxed in loose, long African dresses. My beige jeans, which I thought ideal for travelling, were too loose. I knew I had lost weight over the last few years, but I really hadn't expected my jeans to be so excessively big, they were slipping down to my hips. Too late I had nothing else to wear and without a mirror I couldn't be sure what I looked like, but vanity wasn't my greatest concern at the time. I put on a navy and white spotted blouse which was also loose, but surely that was the fashion, and would hide the fact that my jeans were too big. I looked down, and was satisfied I looked fine. I had a sun hat with a wide brim; I would wear this until we got to the airport to hide my face if we saw anyone that might recognise me.

I checked my watch as I got back inside the house: 3.40. I pulled my already locked case outside the house, dragged it to the entrance and carefully hid it around a corner, out of sight to anyone that came to the gate. I pulled the bedclothes and damp towel off the bed, folded them roughly and placed them in a box. Next I took up the brightly coloured mats, which had been bought especially for my last little home; I put these in the box with the bedclothes and once again made the short trip to the entrance with it. Finally I took the rechargeable light that had been invaluable to me during these last few weeks and took that to the entrance.

On the way back I looked inside the tool box. Simon would have gone crazy if he had seen it. Once the box had been filled to overflowing; now there were only a few things left, and those weren't in very good condition. He had always been so particular with his tools, and the sight of the almost empty box made me feel inexplicably guilty, I should have looked after his things better. Over the years people had helped themselves to tools as they were needed, and I didn't even know what should be in the tool box. I closed and fastened the sturdy box and added it to the pile of my belongings at the entrance; Nick would be able to use the tools that were left.

I heard my text go as I was returning to the house; I rushed inside and picked up my phone. It was from Nick. I had not expected to hear from him; what had gone wrong, surely his pickup hadn't broken down, not today of all days. This would be more than I could handle. With shaking hands I gingerly opened the text. It didn't make sense; 'Tubby Robinson from Zulu's died 10 mins ago x.'

What? I stared at the small screen; I read and reread the text. This had to be a cryptic message, what did it mean? I kept staring at it. What was Nick trying to tell me, had he seen the lads 10 minutes ago, but why mention Tubby? Tubby Robinson was an ex-pat who ran a notorious night club called Zulus. As his nick name suggested he was fat, in fact I have never seen anyone as large or such a strange shape as Tubby, his fat hung like a skirt over his hips, he was obviously unfit, and it was possibly health problems that caused his gross size. Added to this he had a drink problem, and recently his immense weight had broken the chair he was sat on in a local bar. It had taken six men to get pick him up and man handle him into a taxi, not helped by the fact that he was drunk at the time. Alongside his health problems, Tubby also had financial problems and owed me quite a large bar bill. Several bar owners at one time banded together and had taken him to court to try and get payment for their bills. They had asked me to join forces with them but I had decided against this. I had had enough of court cases with my never ending case over my entrance, besides which he didn't owe me as much as the others and the court costs could possibly outweigh the amount I was owed. I still stared at my phone, what was Nick trying to tell me, and why had he mentioned Tubby? I told myself I was being dramatic, allowing my over active mind to run riot again, and knowing Tubby had health problems it was indeed possible he had died. I decided this was the case and sent a text back simply saying, 'Shit he owes me money x.' I thought this would cause Nick to send another text if I had misunderstood the under lying reason for his first text.

Again I check the time, 3.55, Nick was due to arrive in five minutes, and he hadn't responded to me text, so I assumed poor Tubby was in fact dead. Everything was out of the house, except the mattress, the plastic table and the wooden stool. I locked the door, and threw the key forcefully into the undergrowth. I did not care where it landed and I had thrown it with enough force for it to travel some distance. If anyone went looking for it, it would take them a very long time to find it, if at all. With a contented smile on my face I imagined Sidi breaking into the house to see if I had left anything inside that was worth having. I made my way towards the gate; I could hear Nick's pickup slowing near the entrance, I hurried over the plank of wood across the pond and opened the gate wide from him to reverse in to allow us to load the pickup. He reversed right inside the property, and as he got out of the vehicle he greeted me with, "What makes you think you are so special, Tubby owes us all money." I laughed at this, yes I knew this, but this whole situation seemed so surreal.

"My god," Nick exclaimed are we taking all this?"

"Yeah, that is my case, the tools are for you, and I thought you would take the rest of the things from my house, Maria will make use of them or if she doesn't want them she can give them to someone. There is also a large box that I couldn't move, it is outside the house, I want you to give it to Adam and Jane, and they are going to freight it home for me."

Together we went over to the house to collect the box; Nick lifted it, "What on earth is in here? Not Sidi's body I hope." We both laughed.

"I hadn't even thought of that, why didn't you suggest it before? We could have saved ourselves all of this bother."

Nick let out an audible sigh of relief when we got back to the pickup, "That is heavy" he said as he loaded it into the back of the truck. "Never in my life have I done anything like this before, I've smuggled girls into hotel rooms, but to smuggle a girl out of her own property? This is definitely a first. Fine that's the back and the back seat full, now what about you, I thought I was going to put you in the back, with a blanket over you."

"That was the plan, but I knew we couldn't do that, when I saw how much stuff I wanted you to take."

"I don't think it wise for you to sit up front by me, the arch boys will be sure to ring Sidi."

"Yeah I know, I thought I would walk out through The Mango Tree and you can pick me up around the corner."

"Fine, but the security will see you crossing the car park." Nick seemed quite concerned about this tactic.

"There are several cars, if you pull out slowly I will walk along side you, then I can duck down and dodge between the cars." I was confident I could do this, fortunately for me there was a conference in The Peace Haven so there were many more cars than usual in the car park. "When you get to the arch stop and chat to the security, that will distract them, while I'm going across the car park, they have seen you many times with the pickup loaded up since I closed, so they won't think it odd you have the back piled high. Once I'm inside The Mango Tree I will be fine, I don't think I will even be recognised dressed like this, I will pull the brim of my hat over my face."

"As long as you are happy to do that, you stay here till you see me distracting the security, but cross that car park as quickly as you can. I will watch in my mirrors to see you go into The Mango."

Nick got into the cab of his pickup, and slowly pulled out of the gate; he stopped while I snapped shut the padlock of the gate, and put the key inside the envelope I would give to Nick to take to Ali in the morning. This was it, I had burnt my bridges. Without even glancing back at my home for the last eight years I turned and took a deep breath as Nick asked, "You ready to go?"

"I'm ready."

He started the engine and very slowly pulled away, so I could walk behind the truck, while he turned it to head down the car park towards the arch. As he headed down the car park, I was heading directly across it. Using the parked cars as a screen, I bent down to avoid being seen from the arch. I peeped out from each car, to check that Nick was still distracting the security before I dashed to the next car. The car park was probably only a little over hundred yards wide, but it seemed an endless journey, my feet were moving but it didn't feel I was going anywhere. I was getting very hot and clammy and my heart was missing beats, I was petrified and it was starting to show. At long, long last I reached the back entrance to The Mango Tree. As I stepped inside I glanced down towards the arch, Nick was just pulling away, he must have seen I had reached the hotel safely.

I went through the back door, and past the pool bar where I saw the owner sat at the bar. I walked straight on hoping he hadn't recognised me and continued around the pool. My stomach was churning over, my legs were trembling and I felt faint. It wasn't a very large hotel and it didn't take long to walk through the grounds and into the reception area, but it seemed an endless journey. There was a few tourists sat in the reception area, one or two I recognised. I kept my head down to allow the brim of my hat to hide my face and carried on regardless out of the hotel's main door, into the blazing afternoon sun. Now where was Nick? There he was driving past. All I had to do was side step the fruit girls lying in wait for tourist customers and walk a few yards round the corner, climb into his van and go.

"Hello Madam Dominion." I only half heard the voice. I was still concentrating on making my way to Nick. "Hello Madam", it said again and I became aware of someone sitting on the tiles. I looked down at the figure who had spoken. I was horrified to see it was a boy from Famara. Had Sidi planted him there, in case I went out that way? I was confident Sidi had no idea I was going to the airport, but he would want to know if I went out. I was being paranoid again. He stood up. "Madam Dominion you remember me, I have been to the Dominion, I live in Famara, and you have friends from my village."

"Yes, I know you." I answered him without stopping, by this time he was walking along side me, and I was wishing him thousands of miles away.

"You want me to get you a taxi?"

"No, I'm fine thanks."

"Then I will walk with you." He was being insistent. Perhaps my thoughts about him being a spy for Sidi were not too far fetched. I needed to get rid of him. I saw Nick pull in outside a restaurant a little farther along the road, not where we had arranged. I suspected he had seen me with this lad.

"I told you I'm fine." I said firmly, "I'm just going out for a walk."

"It's not safe for you to be out alone, I must come with you." Not even a local with a new tourist would be this persistent. He had to go.

I laughed weakly, "Not safe, I've lived here a long time. Now give over and leave me alone, go back to your comfortable seat outside the hotel. You may be missing some tourists who want a guide. I don't." With that I left him and started walking towards the pickup. It was probably only another hundred yards away, but each step I took seemed like a mile, my legs were getting heavy, I even doubted I could walk as far as the truck, I was feeling so weak. When I did eventually get to the vehicle, Nick opened the door and I nearly fell into the passenger seat. He patted me on the knee, "Good girl, you are safe now, calm down, we will soon have you away from here."

"I'm fine; did you see that boy talking to me?"

"You are not fine, look at you, you are shaking. I want you to settle down before we drive off. Do you know the lad?" Nick was right I was physically shaking, my legs were trembling, and my hands just wouldn't keep still.

"Just give a minute, I will be okay, the boy is from Famara I can't believe he recognised me." I was still shaken, and I knew it showed in my voice.

"What did he want?"

"He wanted to walk with me, told me I wasn't safe."

"He's probably one of Sidi's cronies, in fact look he is on his mobile now. He will be reporting you have just got into the pickup with me, time we were on the move."

Instead of turning and taking the main tourist strip we went along the back road to avoid too many folk seeing us, eventually pulling out onto the main coastal highway and heading towards the airport. As we drove Nick gave me my instructions. I was to keep my hat on and if we got stopped in a check point to look down and not to speak. He pointed to the space between the two front seats and said, "There is your ticket and your passport and the cash in sterling, I have put a few extra quid there for the things I've taken during the last few days."

"Don't be daft," I told him, "you've paid me well for everything you've had. After all this do you think I would take more money from you?"

"You take all that is there. I know that is all you have till Simon sends you your share of the sale, he may keep you waiting, and anyway it will help tide you over for a while."

We drove in silence for a time; I looked at the new buildings that had gone up since I arrived. In fact this road we were travelling on hadn't been built when I was first here, time doesn't stand still; not even in Shendi.

I saw Nick glance towards me, "You alright now?"

"Yeah, I told you I was fine, but shaken not stirred."

After a few more minutes of silence, Nick said, "I must be some sort of idiot."

"Listen, at this particular moment you are my hero, certainly not an idiot."

"I've spent the last five years trying to get inside your knickers to no avail, then I help you out the country, I gotta be crazy." We both laughed; if nothing else his remark lightened the situation. Unfortunately deep down I knew Nick might eventually go on my list of my biggest regrets, but it was too late to ponder on such matters. My confidence increased with every mile we put between ourselves and The Dominion, but I still looked around me every so often checking we were not being tailed. "I can see in my mirrors you know," Nick told me when he caught sight of me looking behind us, "All's fine now the chances of us being followed are next to nought."

"I know but the Famara lad was on his mobile he may have been phoning Sidi."

"If he was Sidi is probably screeching around every corner between Famara and my compound. Remember he doesn't know you have your papers so the airport is the last place he will be looking; you worry so much woman."

I knew Nick was right, and my mood lightened accordingly, in fact I was fairly relaxed, all the rest of the way to the airport we exchanged light hearted banter; I knew Nick was ensuring I would be calm when reached the airport. The journey was over surprisingly quickly and we soon pulled into the airport car park to the sounds of the Muslims being called to five o'clock prayers at the airport Mosque. It dawned on me that maybe this was the last time I would ever hear this, I had cursed this at five in the morning many times but I was pleased to hear it for one last time. Nick parked the pickup and we got out, I glanced around me, I was seeing everything through new eyes, it was as if that was the first time I had been here, everything seemed exaggerated, my head was in a spin, there was a deep sadness amongst my elation of finally leaving Shendi. Nick took my case out of the back of the truck and we made our way to the very distinctive terminal building. "Don't panic," he instructed me, "but I can't see Ebrima, the airport security guy that is meant to meet us at the entrance."

We entered the building, there was no sign of Ebrima, no one who wasn't travelling is allowed into the check-in area, so Nick confidently told me, "You go through and check yourself in, that is the easy part, I will ring Musa, and find out where Ebrima is. I will be waiting here for you."

The newfound confidence Nick had installed into me on the short drive here, was fast dispersing. Once on my own in the queue at the check-in desk I felt ill at ease. I was aware I was fumbling too much with my ticket and fiddling with my necklace, I hoped anyone seeing me would assume I was a nervous traveller though the opposite was true. I had always liked air travel and I was looking forward to my journey as much as arriving back on home soil. Eventually I booked in and was relieved to be given my boarding card for my onwards journey from Brussels. I was also reassured to be told I would not see my luggage again until I arrived at Heathrow. This relieved any stress of being on my own in Brussels for five hours. I made my way back to the public area where there was a small sunken bar in the middle of the airport concourse. Nick was sat there alone with a bottle of beer in front of him, and a coke beside the empty chair next to his waiting for me.

"No sign of Ebrima yet?" I asked quietly not wishing anyone in the crowded airport to overhear our conversation.

"No, I can't believe this. He has gone to the mosque praying, he arranged to meet us at 5, he knew it was prayer time, why didn't he say come up at 5.30.Oh well. Don't worry about him, I have phoned Musa, he is higher up than Ebrima anyway. He is going to come himself he will be here in a few minutes." Musa was in charge of security at the airport, he had been to The Dominion on several occasions, I didn't know him well, but knew him enough to have confidence in him.

"I'm creating a bit of a problem for you eh?"

"I've told you, just relax now, we have got you here, nothing is going to go wrong at this late stage."

It wasn't very long before Musa arrived, he looked surprised when he saw me, "You didn't tell me it was Lady Dominion that was leaving?" he said addressing Nick.

"There wasn't much time to explain on the phone," Nick answered him, "Helen has a new passport, so she doesn't have all her stamps in this one and we are a bit anxious about her going through security. Ebrima was meant to be seeing her through, and he had agreed to let me go through to departures with her, you will do this for us?" It was obvious Nick had no intention of relating my story to Musa, and in fact it wasn't necessary to do so, we just wanted to get me safely on the plane. Nick and I were aware Sidi had friends working for the S.S.G. at the airport, it was possible one of these maybe in the departure lounge, which is why Nick wanted to come through with me, to ensure I actually got on the plane safely. Nick offered Musa a beer; he was a Muslim but was known to take the occasional alcoholic drink. He refused, suggesting instead that we get on through into the departure lounge and have a drink there. The three of us made our way to the security but as we were in the queue an announcement came over the airport intercom system, 'Could Mrs. Russell travelling to Brussels please make her way to the luggage identification point to identify her luggage or it will not be put on the plane.'

I looked at Nick with terror in my eyes, "Shit what now." I muttered under my breath.

"That's you?" Musa asked. I simply nodded in response, "Fine I will come with you, this is not a problem."

I obediently followed him, as we were on our way to the small office where the cases were scanned Musa said to me, "What do you have in your case Helen?"

"Nothing," I replied bewildered, and the only thought going through my head was that I was being set up, and going to be kept there until the flight had taken off.

"Not even cigarettes?" Musa asked again, looking at me very firmly. Cigarettes are very cheap in Shendi and some tourists take back suit cases of them for sale in the U.K. to subsides their holidays. It is not illegal to take them out of Shendi, it becomes illegal when you enter the U.K. with them. If they are picked up on the scan in Shendi the authorities ask for a bribe from the perpetrator, if this is not paid they mark the case, and the U.K. customs stop them on arrival.

"Musa, I'm eager to get home, there is no way I would have anything in my case, cigarettes or otherwise to hamper this."

Musa could see I was on edge, "It's okay Helen; we will soon sort this out."

Nervously I went into the small office with Musa. It was crowded with other travellers that were there paying their bribes to get their contraband on the flight, there was a narrow conveyor belt where the cases were being passed slowly through a scan and a group of security and customs officers stood behind the belt. My case was on the floor near the conveyor belt. The look of surprise on the officers' faces as they saw Musa with me increased my confidence, as in all countries these officers are usually larger than life, and very officious; had I been alone I would have been petrified.

"This lady is with me, just put her case through." Musa told them firmly. The officer that was nearest my case spoke to Musa. I didn't catch much of what he was saying, but his tone of voice alone seemed rather threatening. Without replying to him, Musa gently took my arm and guided me over to the corner of the room out of earshot of everyone. In a low voice he said to me, "He says there is a gun in your case."

"What?" I exclaimed much louder than I meant to. "How stupid do they think I am? Do you really think I would try and travel with a gun, come on Musa you know this is bullshit."

"Fine, fine Helen, keep calm, we will sort this, but they are saying they have seen a gun in your case. Think what have you have got in there that could be mistaken for a gun, if not they will have to open the case."

"Then let them do that." I said abruptly as I shrugged my shoulders. I could not believe this was happening to me I would never get away. I fumbled in my bag for the key of my case, forcing my poor haggled brain to think what I had that could possibly be mistaken for a gun. Then it suddenly dawned on me, "Musa, I have a hairdryer that is a similar shape to a gun, surely that's not what they have seen?" I said as I handed him my case keys with trembling hands.

We made our way back to the officer that was keeping an eye on my offending case and again Musa conducted a lengthy conversation with him. They once again put my case on the conveyor belt and Musa together with three other security officers looked at the scanning machine, they were all pointing at the screen in turn, I had given the keys of the case to Musa, it would have been quicker to have opened the case. Musa then came back over my side of the conveyor belt and gently let me out of the small office, handing my keys back to me. "Safe journey Madam," one of the officers called after me, I turned and half smiled at him, but didn't answer, I was in no mood for small talk.

"Sorted?" Nick asked as we got back to where we had left him by the queue to the departure lounge.

"They thought I had a gun in my case." I told him with a sarcastic grin.

"You're having a laugh." he replied as he sniggered over this.

I snapped, "I don't think I'm seeing the funny side of things too well today. Surely many women travel with hairdryers, mine cannot have been the first one to go through. In reality I suppose a hairdryer could look a bit like a gun, and I wouldn't be too happy to think passengers were travelling with me having a gun in their luggage albeit in the hold of the plane. Do they stop everyone?" I realised how pathetic I sounded and grinned. "Haven't I always told you this woman is trouble, it's a good job she is going." Nick said, tongue in cheek to Musa, and they laughed with each other. I was feeling in a much lighter mood by the time we got to the front of the security queue. Musa went through and waited a few yards away for us, Nick stayed with me.

On reaching the front of the queue I gave my passport to the immigration officer at the desk, he duly checked and stamped it, and asked if I had enjoyed my stay in Shendi.

"It has been unforgettable." I told him, which bought on another snigger from Nick, he at least was in high spirits.

The immigration officer then put his hand out to take Nick's passport, "I'm not travelling, I'm with the lady." Nick explained.

"You cannot go through here without a passport and a ticket." Nick was told.

Seeing the lighter side of things easier by then, I answered, "We are poor English, we can only afford one ticket; I will sit on his lap during the flight."

Not understanding we were only jesting, the officer seemed totally confused and said, "No madam, no you can't do that, they don't allow it." He looked about him, not sure who he should confer with over this matter. Musa stepped forward and spoke to him. I didn't catch all he was saying but I got the gist that he was explaining I am scared of flying so he had given permission for the man to stay with me until I got on the plane. Nick would be coming back through security with him, when they had seen me safely off. The officer saluted Musa and we made our way through.

As we were going through an inner door into the main departure lounge there was shouting and what sounded like a scuffle near the security desk; I turned to look back, Nick took me by the shoulders and steered me on through into the departure area.

"You're on your way now, no looking back." he told me, all signs of the light hearted banter we had been having only a few seconds ago gone.

"What was going on?" I asked him.

"I don't know, but it doesn't concern us, let's go outside and have a drink till you have to board."

We made our way outside where there was a bar, a nice relaxing place to spend the final moments of your holiday, or your absolute final moments in Shendi. Nick, Musa and I sat at a table at the far end where we could see what was going on, the men had their beers and I had a coffee. I looked around me taking in my last hour in Shendi. Then I saw, stood on the steps leading back inside the building, a S.S.G. officer, who I knew lived in Famara, in fact he lived only two compounds away from Sidi. Had Nick and Musa not been with me I have would have panicked. I watched as he took out his mobile. Grabbing Nick's arm I drew their attention to him. Musa who was his superior simply nodded his head towards him, and he put his phone back in his pocket.

We told Musa how I had knocked The Dominion down. He was amazed he hadn't been down for a while and hadn't even realised I had closed the business. It turned out that he would have bought some of the building materials from me had he known as he was building a new home. He said he needed windows and doors.

"There is one window only left in the bathroom wall that we left standing, and one door, if you want them go and take them before Nick gives the keys to The Peace Haven tomorrow." I said, pleased to be able to help him and to leave less for The Peace Haven and for Sidi.

Musa looked at Nick, "That's no problem," Nick told him, "but you will need to go early in the morning, I want to go to the hotel about 9. I want to go there with Helen's letter

before they hear from anyone else she has left."

It was arranged that Musa was to go to The Dominion very early to take anything he wanted from the little that was still there. Nick handed the keys to Musa and agreed to meet him at about 8.30 to collect the keys and take them together with my letter to Ali. I saw Nick hand Musa a small bundle of notes along with the keys that was his fee for helping us when Ebrima had let us down.

With only ten minutes to go before my flight was called, the waiter came back to see if we wanted everything else, Nick ordered a coffee and turning to me said, "Musa wants me to drop him back home, and I want to get back to the strip before you fly over, I want to tell all the lads you are going. We will all be outside Kings waving at you; will you be alright if we go? They will call your flight any time now, by the time you have finished your coffee it will be time for you to board."

"I'm fine fine; I owe you big time for this lot." I could hardly speak for the tears that wanted to flow and I did my utmost not to let Nick see these.

I stood up and shook Musa's hand, that very familiar Shendian courtesy that had seemed so strange when we first arrived. Nick and I hugged and kissed each other on the cheek, and now the tears did flow uncontrollably. Nick wiped my tears away and said, "None of that please or you may start me off and you don't want to see that, it's not a pleasant sight a man blubbering. You have been really brave, don't crack now."

"I'm fine fine, but I am a bit concerned about him." I said through my tears, indicating the S.S.G. officer with a nod of my head.

"Don't be, now text as soon as you have a U.K. number, I don't want to lose touch with you." With that they were gone, I saw Nick speak to Musa as they walked the short distance to the steps leading back inside, the S.S.G. officer was still there. He had watched us the entire time we had been outdoors. I saw Musa go and speak to him; Nick had obviously conveyed my worries to Musa. Nick turned and waved as the two of them disappeared out of sight. I drank the coffee Nick had ordered for me, keeping a constant eye on the guy standing on the steps, who in turn watched me constantly. I knew Musa had spoken to him and he wouldn't dare go against his superior's orders, but I knew he would be on the phone to Sidi as soon as I was on the plane.

I finished my coffee and went inside where although the flight hadn't yet been called a long queue was forming at the embarkation gate. I decided to join the queue I was eager to board. After meandering slowly around the small departure lounge, I was at last at the front of the queue, and went through the gate to the plane waiting on the tarmac. I boarded and found my seat which was towards the back, I hadn't travelled for eight years, and that was on charter flights. This was a scheduled flight and I was absolutely amazed by the room I had. Leaving Shendi as I was, I would have been content to sit on a wooden bench for the whole trip, but this was complete luxury. I was settling myself down for the journey, putting my paperback and my crossword book into the compartment at the back of the seat in front of me, when I was taken by surprise by my phone ringing. I sifted through the contents of my bag with trembling fingers, hurriedly looking for my phone, which had slipped to the bottom of my bag; I hadn't expected to use it again until I reached the U.K.

I was thrilled to find it was Nick phoning from King's to check I was on the plane alright. He had Liverpool Kevin and several of The Dominion crowd with him, his phone was passed from one to the other of them. I was pleased to be talking to them all as I had felt bad that I hadn't been able to say my good-byes. They were all laughing when I was telling them how thrilled I was with my seat, for some reason they found this very amusing. I stayed on the phone to them until the stewardess came around and asked me to switch my phone off. I once again felt the tears welling as I placed my phone back in my bag. It was dusk, and with the speed that night takes a hold in Shendi I knew it would be dark by the time I took off. The lads had told me they would be outside Kings waving at the plane as it went overhead. Shendi doesn't have many street lights so I thought it may be possible to recognise places as I flew over.

I watched the comings and goings on the steps up to the aircraft, we must be nearing take off or I wouldn't have been asked to switch my phone off. My nervous state albeit much more relaxed than an hour or two ago, was eager for the steps to be removed from the plane. On two occasions the ground staff had appeared to be about to take them away and at the last minute had left them and someone else had boarded. I was conscious now that I had my phone switched off and had no means of communication. The S.S.G. officer in the departure lounge still weighed heavily on my mind. Folks have been taken off planes before, but deep down I knew this was my paranoia again, and I should just lay back and enjoy my journey.

My fears were proved to be completely unfounded as simultaneously the steps were taken away from the plane, the door at the rear was slammed shut, and within a very short while we were hurling down the runway for takeoff. As the plane lifted into the air, I thought of Nick with regret as I knew I would, but also thought of the new life I was about to embark on. I looked out the window, the darkness, if anything made it easier to get my bearings from the air. I could clearly make out the coastal highway, as part of this was now light, and the airport road. The plane flew over Famara and I grinned to myself, wondering how Sidi would react when he knew I had escaped his clutches. We were directly above the main tourist strip and although I couldn't make out Kings, I did spare a thought for the lads, and imagined the banter that would be going on around the bar. Yes, I did have regrets, but too late to dwell on them now, I was free and had a whole new life waiting for me when I reached U.K. Job hunting and finding somewhere to live, would keep me more than occupied for the foreseeable future, and of course most important of all I would soon be heading for Manchester and seeing Kevin, Steph and meeting my little Karen for the first time. I leaned back and rested against my head rest, and closed my eyes, taking deep breaths and realised in spite of my misgivings and regrets I was looking forward to a much rosier future.

I was not even aware how long it took for us to reach Dakar, I think I had possibly dosed off for a short while. I suddenly realised we were descending and watched as the lights of the runway got ever closer and then we landed. As I sat there watching the hustling and bustling on the runway at Dakar I glanced at my watch. It was 8.45, I smiled to myself as I thought this was about the time the night security would be arriving at The Dominion, when he saw I wasn't there he would be straight on the phone to Sidi, I cannot explain the deep satisfaction this thought gave me. I didn't have to change flights at Dakar, but we were on the ground there for approximately two hours; with so much to watch at the airport the time passed quicker than I imagined it would. We were soon hurling down the runway again and onward for the long flight to Brussels. I have always enjoyed flying and this flight was no different. I read a while, tried to do a crossword but found my concentration lacking, so dosed on and off most of the night, glancing out of the window every so often trying to work out where we were.

We started the descent into Brussels, I have never been there and enjoyed watching the picturesque villages gliding by; these were in stark contrast to the flimsy African villages I had left behind. Leaving the plane to make my way to the terminal and my flight to Heathrow, I felt nervous. I had not had to cope with travelling for a long while and was unaccustomed to the new airport procedures. I was very much surprised when having reached the transit lounge an African gentleman, who had been a fellow passenger and now looked completely lost, asked for my assistance. I read his ticket and pointed to direction he needed to go. On seeing this several other African travellers who were not used to travelling asked for my help, this I gladly gave, wondering what they would think if they realised I was also unaccustomed to my surroundings and was also totally bewildered, but I was pleased I managed to keep calm and look carefully at the signs and help these lost souls. When I finished helping these travellers I looked for my own signs to find my onward flight to Heathrow, I knew I had plenty of time to spare so there was no need to rush.

I found my way to the security for my next flight and was horrified when they took away from me a bottle of vodka I had bought in Shendi for Kevin. The last time I had travelled you were allowed to take liquids on the flight, and as Musa was seeing me through security at Shendi airport, no-one had mentioned this, or tried to prevent me from getting on the plane in Shendi with a litre bottle of vodka in my hand luggage. I protested not being up to date with all the changes in travelling since 9/11, but in reality the events of the previous day completely dwarfed losing a bottle of spirits, I could easily purchase another bottle in the duty free, I had plenty of time.

I found a nice little corner in a coffee shop, where I sat on a comfortable leather settee watching the early morning flights pulling away from their stands. Looking at my watch, I realised that just 24 hours ago I had been waking up in my little hut. I sat in the same spot until my own flight time was drawing near. I made my way to the ladies to ensure I was ready to leave when my flight was called. Coming out of the cubical I walked towards the wash hand basins and caught sight of myself in the mirror, from a little way away I had nearly a full length view of myself. I stopped and stared in amazement, I hadn't seen myself in a full length mirror since I had arrived in Shendi. I had thought I looked smart in my beige jeans and navy and white spotted top; on the contrary I resembled 'Orphan Annie'. I was horrified. I washed my hands and stepped away from the mirror again, to take a second look, was this really my drawn anxious features staring back at me? My jeans appeared to be several sizes too large, they were suspended on my hips, and even my blouse was hanging limply from my shoulders. Someone else came into the ladies and taking a last swift look in the mirror, I left vowing to buy some new clothes as soon as I was repatriated, and settled into my new life.

I looked at the departure screen as I made my way back to the seating area, and saw my gate number was showing, so I made my way down to the waiting area, feeling proud of myself for managing to negotiate Brussels airport, with all the new pitfalls of modern air travel. After a short wait at the gate I boarded the much smaller aircraft for the short final leg of my journey home, I would soon be arriving at Heathrow where I knew Euan would be waiting for me. The flight was so short that we had barely undone our seat belts before it was time to fasten them for landing. I promised myself that I would not cry but the sight of the familiar London landmarks of the Thames and Tower Bridge which signalled the end of my African adventure and the longest day of my life did cause the tears to flow. I was home.

Epilogue

Although Nick and I exchanged texts and the very occasional phone call after my return to the U.K. it wasn't until several months later when Nick himself came home for a few months, and visited me in the flat I had made my home, that I learnt the full story of the aftermath of my departure.

The commotion I had heard at the airport as we were disappearing into the departure lounge was indeed Sidi; presumably he had been phoned by the lad who had spoken to me outside The Mango Tree – or – as seems more likely, one of his friends at the airport had spotted me and phoned him. Apparently he made quite a fuss because the airport security wouldn't let him through into the departure lounge to speak to me. Sidi had to leave the airport without speaking to me or hindering my departure in any way.

That same evening Sidi saw Nick's pickup outside Kings. This must have come as a surprise to him. He had seen Nick go through to departures with me and assumed that he was travelling also. Feeling frustrated and annoyed for not only had I escaped from his clutches but Nick had tricked him. He collected a group of friends from Famara, burst into the bar and confronted Nick, demanding to know where I was. Nick told him he hadn't seen me since that morning. Sidi informed him that he was lying as he had seen the two of us at the airport. Nick replied that he did not like being called a liar and Sidi must have been mistaken. Anyway he had added, he was under the impression that Sidi had my immigration papers, so I couldn't possibly be boarding a flight. Disgruntled once again Sidi left Nick to finish his pint in peace.

The following morning Musa as we had agreed at the airport, went to The Dominion to see if there was anything left there that was of any use to him. About an hour later Nick received a phone call from him telling him he had better come to the site as a group of boys from Famara had arrived and they were taking the gates off the property. When Nick arrived, less than half an hour later he found Sidi, Petreeni and Latif together with some others some of whom he recognised as ex Dominion staff busy dismantling not only the gates but the bar toilets which had been left standing as they were obviously needed. After much shouting on all sides Nick put Sidi in the picture. I had been at the airport yesterday and had flown out in the early evening. Sidi grew even angrier than he had been initially. He shouted and swore. Last night Nick had accused Sidi of lying but who really had been the liar? Taubabs sticking together as always! Where was the money I was meant to be having sent out for him? Nick should know. He wanted that money. By now Sidi had worked himself up into a huge rage. Nick apparently resisted the temptation to tell him a few home truths, just looked at him and told him he could forget about any money. Now I was gone he wouldn't be getting anything more from The Dominion.

Leaving Sidi and his friends to do what they liked, Nick went to The Peace Haven and gave Ali my letter together with the keys of the property. He did tell him he wouldn't actually need the keys as the boys had just driven off with the gates on the back of a lorry. Ali apparently found this very amusing.

Having dealt with my affairs, Nick then went to Kings for his morning cup of coffee. As he was sat at the bar, three S.S.G. officers came and took him in for questioning at their headquarters. Sidi had put in a complaint, through his numerous friends in the S.S.G. that Nick had helped me out of the country. As I had fled owing him £30,000, and being as Nick was responsible for me leaving, he was demanding this £30,000 from him. Nick asked them how the ransom could possibly go up from £10,000 to £30,000, when their hostage had escaped. It seems no-one had an answer to that. After lengthy questioning, and it all getting rather tiresome, Nick asked if he could make a phone call to get a friend to attend this interview. They allowed him to do this probably assuming he intended phoning an ex-pat. They obviously did not know Nick. Instead he phoned an uncle of Maria's - a high ranking police officer who knew me very well. This gentleman arrived and told the S.S.G. officers Nick and I were good friends. If he had taken me to the airport it was no-one's business but ours and that they were to release Nick.

All this happened before I had even shed a few emotional tears over Tower Bridge and landed at Heathrow airport.